The World's Classics

✔ KU-314-655

CCXXXIV
WAR AND PEACE
VOL. II

OXFORD
UNIVERSITY PRESS
AMEN HOUSE, E.C. 4
London Edinburgh Glasgow New York
Toronto Melbourne Capetown Bombay
Calcutta Madras
HUMPHREY MILFORD
PUBLISHER TO THE
UNIVERSITY

WAR AND PEACE

A NOVEL BY
LEO TOLSTÓY

TRANSLATED BY
LOUISE AND AYLMER MAUDE

WITH AN INTRODUCTION
BY AYLMER MAUDE

IN THREE VOLUMES
VOL. II

HUMPHREY MILFORD
OXFORD UNIVERSITY PRESS
LONDON NEW YORK TORONTO

LEO TOLSTÓY

Born, Yasnaya Polyana, Tula
      August 28 (old style) = September 9, n.s., 1828.
Died, Astapovo, Riazan
      November 7 (old style) = November 20, n.s., 1910.

A part of 'War and Peace' was first published under the title of 'The Year 1805' in a Moscow magazine, the 'Russian Messenger'. The whole work appeared first in Moscow as a six-volume novel under the title of 'War and Peace', the first four volumes in 1868 and the last two in 1869. In 'The World's Classics' L. and A. Maude's translation was first published in 1922–3, and reprinted in 1928. The new revised translation was first published in 'The World's Classics' in 1933 and reprinted in 1939, 1941, and 1942.

PRINTED IN GREAT BRITAIN

CONTENTS

DATES OF EVENTS MENTIONED
1812

17th May   o.s. Napoleon leaves Dresden.
12th June   „ Napoleon crosses the Niemen and enters Russia.
14th June   „ Alexander sends Baláshev to Napoleon.
13th July   „ The Pávlograd hussars in action at Ostróvna.
4th August „ Alpátych at Smolénsk hears distant firing.
5th August „ Bombardment of Smolénsk.
7th August „ Prince Nicholas Bolkónski leaves Bald Hills for Boguchárovo.
8th August „ Kutúzov appointed Commander-in-Chief.
10th August „ Prince Andrew's column abreast of Bald Hills.
17th August „ Kutúzov reaches Tsárevo-Zaymíshche and takes command of the army.
„   „ Nicholas Rostóv rides to Boguchárovo.
24th August „ Battle of the Shevárdino Redoubt.
26th August „ Battle of Borodinó.

(To adjust nineteenth-century old-style dates to our western calendar twelve days have to be added in each case.)

CHAPTER CONTENTS

BOOK VI

BOOK VII

BOOK VIII

BOOK X

BOOK VI

THE CHIEF FAMILIES IN THE NOVEL
AND A FEW OTHER CHARACTERS
The names chiefly used are in CAPITALS

THE BEZÚKHOVS

COUNT Cyril BEZÚKHOV.

PIERRE, his son, legitimized after his father's death, becomes Count Peter BEZÚKHOV.

Princess CATICHE, Pierre's cousin.

THE ROSTÓVS

COUNT Ilyá ROSTÓV.

COUNTESS Nataly ROSTÓVA, his wife.

Count NICHOLAS Rostóv (Nikólenka), their elder son.

Count Peter Rostóv (PÉTYA), their second son.

Countess VÉRA Rostóva, their elder daughter.

Countess Nataly Rostóva (NATÁSHA), their younger daughter.

SÓNYA, a poor member of the Rostóv family circle.

BERG, Alphonse Kárlich, an officer of German extraction who marries Véra.

THE BOLKÓNSKIS

PRINCE Nicholas BOLKÓNSKI, a retired General-in-Chief.

PRINCE ANDREW Bolkónski, his son.

PRINCESS MARY (Másha) Bolkónskaya, his daughter.

Princess Elizabeth Bolkónskaya (LISE), Andrew's wife.

TÍKHON, Prince N. Bolkónski's attendant.

ALPÁTYCH, his steward.

THE KURÁGINS

PRINCE VASÍLI Kurágin.

Prince HIPPOLYTE Kurágin, his elder son.

Prince ANATOLE Kurágin, his younger son.

Princess HÉLÈNE Kurágina (Lëlya), his daughter, who marries Pierre.

———

Princess ANNA MIKHÁYLOVNA Drubetskáya.

Prince BORÍS Drubetskóy (Bóry), her son.

JULIE Karágina, an heiress who marries Borís.

MÁRYA DMÍTRIEVNA Akhrosímova (*le terrible dragon*).

BILÍBIN, a diplomatist.

DENÍSOV, Vasíli Dmítrich (Váska), an hussar officer.

Lavrúshka, his batman.

DÓLOKHOV (Fédya), an officer and desperado.

Count Rostopchín, Governor of Moscow.

ANNA PÁVLOVNA Scherer (Annette), Maid of Honour to the ex-Empress Márya Fëdorovna.

Shinshín, a relation of Countess Rostóva's.

Timókhin, an infantry officer.

Túshin, an artillery officer.

Platon KARATÁEV, a peasant.

BOOK VI

CHAPTER I

PRINCE ANDREW had spent two years continuously in the country.

All the plans Pierre had attempted on his estates—and constantly changing from one thing to another had never accomplished—were carried out by Prince Andrew without display and without perceptible difficulty.

He had in the highest degree a practical tenacity which Pierre lacked, and without fuss or strain on his part this set things going.

On one of his estates the three hundred serfs were liberated and became free agricultural labourers—this being one of the first examples of the kind in Russia. On other estates the serfs' compulsory labour was commuted for a quit-rent. A trained midwife was engaged for Boguchárovo at his expense, and a priest was paid to teach reading and writing to the children of the peasants and household serfs.

Prince Andrew spent half his time at Bald Hills with his father and his son, who was still in the care of nurses. The other half he spent in 'Boguchárovo Cloister', as his father called Prince Andrew's estate. Despite the indifference to the affairs of the world he had expressed to Pierre, he diligently followed all that went on, received many books, and to his surprise noticed that when he or his father had visitors from Petersburg, the very vortex of life, these people lagged behind himself—who never left the country—in knowledge of what was happening in home and foreign affairs.

Besides being occupied with his estates, and reading a great variety of books, Prince Andrew was at this time busy with a critical survey of our last two unfortunate campaigns, and with drawing up a proposal for a reform of the army rules and regulations.

In the spring of 1809 he went to visit the Ryazán estates which his son, whose guardian he was, had inherited.

Warmed by the spring sunshine he sat in the calèche looking at the new grass, the first leaves on the birches and the first puffs of white spring clouds floating across the clear blue sky. He was not thinking of anything, but looked absent-mindedly and cheerfully from side to side.

They crossed the ferry where he had talked with Pierre the year before. They went through the muddy village, past threshing-floors and green fields of winter rye, downhill where snow still lodged near the bridge, uphill where the clay had been liquefied by the rain, past strips of stubble land and bushes touched with green here and there, and into a birch forest growing on both sides of the road. In the forest it was almost hot, no wind could be felt. The birches with their sticky green leaves were motionless, and lilac-coloured flowers and the first blades of green grass were pushing up and lifting last year's leaves. The coarse evergreen colour of the small fir-trees scattered here and there among the birches was an unpleasant reminder of winter. On entering the forest the horses began to snort, and sweated visibly.

Peter the footman made some remark to the coachman; the latter assented. But apparently the coachman's sympathy was not enough for Peter, and he turned on the box towards his master.

'How pleasant it is, your Excellency!' he said with a respectful smile.

'What?'

'It's pleasant, your Excellency!'

'What is he talking about?' thought Prince Andrew. 'Oh, the spring, I suppose,' he thought as he turned round. 'Yes, really everything is green already . . . How early! The birches and cherry and alders too are coming out . . . But the oaks show no sign yet. Ah, here is one oak!'

At the edge of the road stood an oak. Probably ten times the age of the birches that formed the forest, it was ten times as thick and twice as tall as they. It was an enormous tree, its girth twice as great as a man could embrace, and evidently long ago some of its branches had been broken off and its bark scarred. With its huge ungainly limbs sprawling unsymmetrically, and its gnarled hands and fingers, it stood an aged, stern, and scornful monster among the smiling birch-trees. Only the dead-looking evergreen firs dotted about in the forest, and this oak, refused to yield to the charm of spring, or notice either the spring or the sunshine.

'Spring, love, happiness!' this oak seemed to say. 'Are you not weary of that stupid, meaningless, constantly repeated fraud? Always the same and always a fraud! There is no spring, no sun, no happiness! Look at those cramped dead firs, ever the same, and at me too, sticking out my broken and barked fingers just where they have grown, whether from my back or my sides: as they have grown so I stand, and I do not believe in your hopes and your lies.'

As he passed through the forest Prince Andrew turned several times to look at that oak, as if expecting something from it. Under the oak, too, were flowers and grass, but it stood among them scowling, rigid, misshapen, and grim as ever.

'Yes, the oak is right, a thousand times right,' thought Prince Andrew. 'Let others—the young—yield afresh to that fraud, but we know life, our life is finished!'

A whole sequence of new thoughts, hopeless but mournfully pleasant, rose in his soul in connexion with that tree. During this journey he, as it were, considered his life afresh and arrived at his old conclusion, restful in its hopelessness: that it was not for him to begin anything anew—but that he must live out his life, content to do no harm, and not disturbing himself or desiring anything.

CHAPTER II

PRINCE ANDREW had to see the Marshal of the Nobility for the district in connexion with the affairs of the Ryazán estate of which he was trustee. This Marshal was Count Ilyá Rostóv, and in the middle of May Prince Andrew went to visit him.

It was now hot spring weather. The whole forest was already clothed in green. It was dusty, and so hot that on passing near water one longed to bathe.

Prince Andrew, depressed, and preoccupied with the business about which he had to speak to the Marshal, was driving up the avenue in the grounds of the Rostóvs' house at Otrádnoe. He heard merry girlish cries behind some trees on the right, and saw a group of girls running to cross the path of his calèche. Ahead of the rest and nearer to him ran a dark-haired, remarkably slim, pretty girl in a yellow chintz dress, with a white handkerchief on her head from under which loose locks of hair escaped. The girl was shouting something, but seeing that he was a stranger, ran back laughing without looking at him.

Suddenly, he did not know why, he felt a pang. The day was so beautiful, the sun so bright, everything around so gay, but that slim pretty girl did not know, or wish to know, of his existence and was contented and cheerful in her own separate—probably foolish—but bright and happy life. 'What is she so glad about? What is she thinking of? Not of the military regulations or of the arrangement of the Ryazán serfs' quit-rents. Of what is she thinking? Why is she so happy?' Prince Andrew asked himself with instinctive curiosity.

In 1809 Count Ilyá Rostóv was living at Otrádnoe just as he had done in former years, that is, entertaining almost the whole province with hunts, theatricals, dinners, and music. He was glad to see Prince Andrew, as he was to see any new visitor, and insisted on his staying the night.

During the dull day, in the course of which he was entertained by his elderly hosts and by the more important of the visitors (the old count's house was crowded on account of an approaching name-day), Prince Andrew repeatedly glanced at Natásha, gay and laughing among the younger members of the company, and asked himself each time, 'What is she thinking about? Why is she so glad?'

That night, alone in new surroundings, he was long unable to sleep. He read awhile and then put out his candle, but relit it. It was hot in the room, the inside shutters of which were closed. He was cross with the stupid old man (as he called Rostóv), who had made him stay by assuring him that some necessary documents had not yet arrived from town, and he was vexed with himself for having stayed.

He got up and went to the window to open it. As soon as he opened the shutters the moonlight, as if it had long been watching for this, burst into the room. He opened the casement. The night was fresh, bright, and very still. Just before the window was a row of pollard-trees, looking black on one side and with a silvery light on the other. Beneath the trees grew some kind of lush, wet, bushy vegetation with silver-lit leaves and stems here and there. Farther back beyond the dark trees a roof glittered with dew, to the right was a leafy tree with brilliantly white trunk and branches, and above it shone the moon, nearly at its full, in a pale, almost starless, spring sky. Prince Andrew leaned his elbows on the window-ledge and his eyes rested on that sky.

His room was on the first floor. Those in the rooms above were also awake. He heard female voices overhead.

'Just once more,' said a girlish voice above him which Prince Andrew recognized at once.

'But when are you coming to bed?' replied another voice.

'I won't, I can't sleep, what's the use? Come now for the last time.

Two girlish voices sang a musical passage—the end of some song.

'Oh, how lovely! Now go to sleep, and there's an end of it.'

'You go to sleep, but I can't,' said the first voice, coming nearer to the window. She was evidently leaning right out, for the rustle of her dress and even her breathing could be heard. Everything was stone-still, like the moon and its light and the shadows. Prince Andrew, too, dared not stir, for fear of betraying his unintentional presence.

'Sónya! Sónya!' he again heard the first speaker. 'Oh, how can you sleep? Only look how glorious it is! Ah, how glorious! Do wake up, Sónya!' she said almost with tears in her voice. 'There never, never was such a lovely night before!'

Sónya made some reluctant reply.

'Do just come and see what a moon! . . . Oh, how lovely! Come here . . . Darling, sweetheart, come here! There, you see? I feel like sitting down on my heels, putting my arms round my knees like this, straining tight, as tight as possible, and flying away! Like this . . .'

'Take care, you'll fall out.'

He heard the sound of a scuffle and Sónya's disapproving voice: 'It's past one o'clock.'

'Oh, you only spoil things for me. All right, go, go!'

Again all was silent, but Prince Andrew knew she was still sitting there. From time to time he heard a soft rustle, and at times a sigh.

'O God, O God! What does it mean?' she suddenly exclaimed. 'To bed then, if it must be!' and she slammed the casement.

'For her I might as well not exist!' thought Prince Andrew while he listened to her voice, for some reason expecting yet fearing that she might say something about him. 'There she is again! As if it were on purpose,' thought he.

In his soul there suddenly arose such an unexpected turmoil of youthful thoughts and hopes, contrary to the whole tenor of his life, that unable to explain his condition to himself he lay down and fell asleep at once.

CHAPTER III

NEXT morning, having taken leave of no one but the count, and not waiting for the ladies to appear, Prince Andrew set off for home.

It was already the beginning of June when on his return journey he drove into the birch forest where the gnarled old oak had made so strange and memorable an impression on him. In the forest the harness-bells sounded yet more muffled than they had done six weeks before, for now all was thick, shady and dense, and the young firs dotted about in the forest did not jar on the general beauty but, lending themselves to the mood around, were delicately green with fluffy young shoots.

The whole day had been hot. Somewhere a storm was gathering, but only a small cloud had scattered some rain-drops lightly, sprinkling the road and the sappy leaves. The left side of the forest was dark in the shade, the right side glittered in the sunlight, wet and shiny and scarcely swayed by the breeze. Everything was in blossom, the nightingales trilled, and their voices reverberated now near now far away.

'Yes, here in this forest was that oak with which I agreed,' thought Prince Andrew. 'But where is it?' he again wondered, gazing at the left side of the road, and without recognizing it he looked with admiration at the very oak he sought. The old oak, quite transfigured, spreading out a canopy of sappy dark-green foliage, stood rapt and slightly trembling in the rays of the evening sun. Neither gnarled fingers nor old scars nor old doubts and sorrows were any of them in evidence now. Through the hard century-old bark, even where there were no twigs, leaves had sprouted such as one could hardly believe the old veteran could have produced.

'Yes, it is the same oak,' thought Prince Andrew, and all at once he was seized by an unreasoning spring-time feeling of joy and renewal. All the best moments of his life suddenly rose to his memory. Austerlitz with the lofty heavens, his wife's dead reproachful face, Pierre at the ferry, that girl thrilled by the beauty of the night, and that night itself and the moon, and ... all this rushed suddenly to his mind.

'No, life is not over at thirty-one!' Prince Andrew suddenly decided finally and decisively. 'It is not enough for me to know what I have in me—every one must know it: Pierre, and that young girl who wanted to fly away into the sky, every one must know me, so that my life may not be lived for myself alone while others live so apart from it, but so that it may be reflected in them all, and they and I may live in harmony.'

On reaching home Prince Andrew decided to go to Petersburg that autumn and found all sorts of reasons for this decision. A whole series of sensible and logical considerations showing it to be essential for him to go

to Petersburg, and even to re-enter the service, kept
springing up in his mind. He could not now understand
how he could ever even have doubted the necessity of
taking an active share in life, just as a month before he
had not understood how the idea of leaving the quiet
country could ever enter his head. It now seemed clear
to him that all his experience of life must be senselessly
wasted unless he applied it to some kind of work and
again played an active part in life. He did not even
remember how formerly, on the strength of similar
wretched logical arguments, it had seemed obvious that
he would be degrading himself if he now, after the lessons
he had had in life, allowed himself to believe in the
possibility of being useful and in the possibility of happiness or love. Now reason suggested quite the opposite.
After that journey to Ryazán he found the country dull;
his former pursuits no longer interested him, and often
when sitting alone in his study he got up, went to the
mirror and gazed a long time at his own face. Then he
would turn away to the portrait of his dead Lise, who
with hair curled *à la grecque* looked tenderly and gaily at
him out of the gilt frame. She did not now say those
former terrible words to him, but looked simply, merrily,
and inquisitively at him. And Prince Andrew crossing
his arms behind him, long paced the room, now frowning
now smiling, as he reflected on those irrational, inex-
pressible thoughts, secret as a crime, which altered his
whole life and were connected with Pierre, with fame,
with the girl at the window, the oak, and woman's
beauty and love. And if any one came into his room at
such moments he was particularly cold, stern, and above
all unpleasantly logical.

'My dear,' Princess Mary entering at such a moment
would say, 'little Nicholas can't go out to-day, it's very
cold.'

'If it were hot,' Prince Andrew would reply at such
times very drily to his sister, 'he could go out in his
smock, but as it is cold he must wear warm clothes, which
were designed for that purpose. That is what follows
from the fact that it is cold; and not that a child who
needs fresh air should remain at home,' he would add

with extreme logic, as if punishing some one for those secret illogical emotions that stirred within him.

At such moments Princess Mary would think how intellectual work dries men up.

CHAPTER IV

PRINCE ANDREW arrived in Petersburg in August 1809. It was the time when the youthful Speránski was at the zenith of his fame and his reforms were being pushed forward with the greatest energy. That same August the Emperor was thrown from his calèche, injured his leg, and remained three weeks at Peterhof, receiving Speránski every day and no one else. At that time the two famous decrees were being prepared that so agitated society— abolishing court ranks and introducing examinations to qualify for the grades of Collegiate Assessor and State Councillor[1]—and not merely these but a whole State constitution, intended to change the existing order of government in Russia: legal, administrative, and financial, from the Council of State down to the district tribunals. Now those vague liberal dreams with which the Emperor Alexander had ascended the throne, and which he had tried to put into effect with the aid of his associates, Czartoryski, Novosíltsev, Kochubéy, and Stróganov—whom he himself in jest had called his *Comité de salut public*—were taking shape and being realized.

Now all these men were replaced by Speránski on the civil side and Arakchéev on the military. Soon after his arrival Prince Andrew, as a gentleman of the chamber, presented himself at court and at a levée. The Emperor, though he met him twice, did not favour him with a single word. It had always seemed to Prince Andrew before that he was antipathetic to the Emperor and that the latter disliked his face and personality generally, and in the cold, repellent glance the Emperor gave him, he now

[1] These were the sixth and fifth grades of the fourteen *chins* in the Civil Service, and were equivalent to the ranks of lieutenant-colonel and colonel in the army.

found further confirmation of this surmise. The courtiers explained the Emperor's neglect of him by his Majesty's displeasure at Bolkónski's not having served since 1805.

'I know myself that one cannot help one's sympathies and antipathies,' thought Prince Andrew, 'so it will not do to present my proposal for the reform of the army regulations to the Emperor personally, but the project will speak for itself.'

He mentioned what he had written to an old field-marshal, a friend of his father's. The field-marshal made an appointment to see him, received him graciously, and promised to inform the Emperor. A few days later Prince Andrew received notice that he was to go to see the Minister of War, Count Arakchéev.

On the appointed day Prince Andrew entered Count Arakchéev's waiting-room at nine in the morning.

He did not know Arakchéev personally, had never seen him, and all he had heard of him inspired him with but little respect for the man.

'He is Minister of War, a man trusted by the Emperor, and I need not concern myself about his personal qualities: he has been commissioned to consider my project, so he alone can get it adopted,' thought Prince Andrew as he waited among a number of important and unimportant people in Count Arakchéev's waiting-room.

During his service, chiefly as an adjutant, Prince Andrew had seen the ante-rooms of many important men, and the different types of such rooms were well known to him. Count Arakchéev's ante-room had quite a special character. The faces of the unimportant people awaiting their turn for an audience showed embarrassment and servility; the faces of those of higher rank expressed a common feeling of awkwardness, covered by a mask of unconcern and ridicule of themselves, their situation, and the person for whom they were waiting. Some walked thoughtfully up and down, others whispered and laughed. Prince Andrew heard the nick-name 'Síla Andréevich'[1] and the words, '*Uncle* will give it us hot,' in

[1] His real name was Alexéy Andréevich Arakchéev. In Russian many shades of feeling may be expressed by various

reference to Count Arakchéev. One general (an important personage) evidently feeling offended at having to wait so long, sat crossing and uncrossing his legs and smiling contemptuously to himself.

But the moment the door opened one feeling alone appeared on all faces—that of fear. Prince Andrew for the second time asked the adjutant on duty to take in his name, but received an ironical look and was told that his turn would come in due course. After some others had been shown in and out of the minister's room by the adjutant on duty, an officer who struck Prince Andrew by his humiliated and frightened air was admitted at that terrible door. This officer's audience lasted a long time. Then suddenly the grating sound of a harsh voice was heard from the other side of the door, and the officer—with pale face and trembling lips—came out and passed through the waiting-room clutching his head.

After this Prince Andrew was conducted to the door and the officer on duty said in a whisper, 'To the right, at the window.'

Prince Andrew entered a plain tidy room, and saw at the table a man of forty with a long waist, a long closely cropped head, deep wrinkles, scowling brows above dull greenish-hazel eyes, and an overhanging red nose. Arakchéev turned his head towards him without looking at him.

'What is your petition?' asked Arakchéev.

'I am not petitioning, your Excellency,' returned Prince Andrew quietly.

Arakchéev's eyes turned towards him.

'Sit down,' said he. 'Prince Bolkónski?'

'I am not petitioning about anything. His Majesty the Emperor has deigned to send your Excellency a project submitted by me . . .'

'You see, my dear sir, I have read your project,' interrupted Arakchéev, uttering only the first words amiably and then—again without looking at Prince Andrew—relapsing gradually into a tone of grumbling contempt.

uses of a man's Christian name, surname, and patronymic. The substitution of 'Síla' (force) for Alexéy indicated the speaker's conception of Arakchéev's leading characteristic.

'You are proposing new military laws? There are many laws but no one to carry out the old ones. Nowadays everybody designs laws, it is easier writing than doing.'

'I came at his Majesty the Emperor's wish to learn from your Excellency how you propose to deal with the memorandum I have presented,' said Prince Andrew politely.

'I have endorsed a resolution on your memorandum and sent it to the Committee. I do *not* approve of it,' said Arakchéev rising and taking a paper from his writing-table. 'Here!' and he handed it to Prince Andrew.

Across the paper was scrawled in pencil, without capital letters, misspelt, and without punctuation: 'Unsoundly constructed because resembles an imitation of the French military code and from the Articles of War needlessly deviating.'

'To what Committee has the memorandum been referred?' inquired Prince Andrew.

'To the Committee on Army Regulations, and I have recommended that your honour should be appointed a member, but without a salary.'

Prince Andrew smiled.

'I don't want one.'

'A member without salary,' repeated Arakchéev. 'I have the honour . . . Eh! Call the next one! Who else is there?' he shouted, bowing to Prince Andrew.

CHAPTER V

WHILE waiting for the announcement of his appointment to the Committee, Prince Andrew looked up his former acquaintances, particularly those he knew to be in power and whose aid he might need. In Petersburg he now experienced the same feeling he had had on the eve of a battle, when troubled by anxious curiosity and irresistibly attracted to the ruling circles where the future, on which the fate of millions depended, was being shaped. From the irritation of the older men, the curiosity of the uninitiated, the reserve of the initiated, the hurry and preoccupation of every one, and the innumerable committees and commissions of whose existence he learnt every day, he felt that now, in 1809, here in Petersburg a vast civil conflict was in preparation, the commander-in-chief of which was a mysterious person he did not know, but who was supposed to be a man of genius—Speránski. And this movement of reconstruction of which Prince Andrew had a vague idea, and Speránski its chief promoter, began to interest him so keenly that the question of the army regulations quickly receded to a secondary place in his consciousness.

Prince Andrew was most favourably placed to secure a good reception in the highest and most diverse Petersburg circles of the day. The reforming party cordially welcomed and courted him, in the first place because he was reputed to be clever and very well-read, and secondly because by liberating his serfs he had obtained the reputation of being a liberal. The party of the old and dissatisfied, who censured the innovations, turned to him expecting his sympathy in their disapproval of the reforms, simply because he was the son of his father. The feminine society world welcomed him gladly, because he was rich, distinguished, a good match, and almost a newcomer, with a halo of romance on account of his supposed death and the tragic loss of his wife. Besides this the general opinion of all who had known him previously was that he had greatly improved during these last five years, having softened and grown more manly, lost his former affectation, pride and contemptuous irony, and acquired the serenity that comes with years. People talked about him, were interested in him, and wanted to meet him.

The day after his interview with Count Arakchéev, Prince Andrew spent the evening at Count Kochubéy's. He told the count of his interview with *Síla Andréevich* (Kochubéy spoke of Arakchéev by that nickname with the same vague irony Prince Andrew had noticed in the Minister of War's ante-room).

'*Mon cher*, even in this case you can't do without Michael Mikháylovich Speránski. He manages everything. I'll speak to him. He has promised to come this evening.'

'What has Speránski to do with the army regulations?' asked Prince Andrew.

Kochubéy shook his head smilingly, as if surprised at Bolkónski's simplicity.

'We were talking to him about you a few days ago,' Kochubéy continued, 'and about your free ploughmen.'

'Oh, is it you, Prince, who have freed your serfs?' said an old man of Catherine's day, turning contemptuously towards Bolkónski.

'It was a small estate that brought in no profit,' replied Prince Andrew, trying to extenuate his action so as not to irritate the old man uselessly.

'Afraid of being late . . .' said the old man, looking at Kochubéy.

'There's one thing I don't understand,' he continued. 'Who will plough the land if they are set free? It is easy to write laws, but difficult to rule . . . Just the same as now—I ask you, Count—who will be heads of the departments when everybody has to pass examinations?'

'Those who pass the examinations, I suppose,' replied Kochubéy crossing his legs and glancing round.

'Well, I have Pryánichnikov serving under me, a splendid man, a priceless man, but he's sixty. Is he to go up for examination?'

'Yes, that's a difficulty, as education is not at all general, but . . .'

Count Kochubéy did not finish. He rose, took Prince Andrew by the arm, and went to meet a tall, bald, fair man of about forty with a large open forehead and a long face of unusual and peculiar whiteness, who was just entering. The new-comer wore a blue swallow-tail coat with a cross suspended from his neck and a star on his left breast. It was Speránski. Prince Andrew recognized him at once, and felt a throb within him, as happens at critical moments of life. Whether it was from respect, envy, or anticipation, he did not know. Speránski's whole figure was of a peculiar type that made him easily recognizable. In the society in which Prince Andrew lived he had never seen any one who together with awkward and clumsy gestures possessed such calmness and self-assurance; he had never seen so resolute yet gentle an expression as that in those half-closed, rather humid eyes, or so firm a smile that expressed nothing; nor had he heard such a refined, smooth, soft voice; above all he had never seen such delicate whiteness of face or hands—hands which were broad, but very plump, soft, and white. Such whiteness and softness Prince Andrew had only seen on the faces of soldiers who had been long in hospital. This was Speránski, Secretary of State, reporter to the Emperor and his companion at Erfurt, where he had more than once met and talked with Napoleon.

Speránski did not shift his eyes from one face to another as people involuntarily do on entering a large company, and was in no hurry to speak. He spoke slowly, with assurance that he would be listened to, and he looked only at the person with whom he was conversing.

Prince Andrew followed Speránski's every word and movement with particular attention. As happens to some people, especially to men who judge those near to them severely, he always on meeting any one new—especially any one whom, like Speránski, he knew by reputation—expected to discover in him the perfection of human qualities.

Speránski told Kochubéy he was sorry he had been unable to come sooner, as he had been detained at the palace. He did not say that the Emperor had kept him, and Prince Andrew noticed this affectation of modesty. When Kochubéy introduced Prince Andrew, Speránski slowly turned his eyes to Bolkónski with his customary smile, and looked at him in silence.

'I am very glad to make your acquaintance. I had heard of you, as every one has,' he said after a pause.

Kochubéy said a few words about the reception Arakchéev had given Bolkónski. Speránski smiled more markedly.

'The chairman of the Committee on Army Regulations is my good friend Monsieur Magnítski,' he said, fully articulating every word and syllable, 'and if you like I can put you in touch with him.' He paused at the full stop. 'I hope you will find him sympathetic, and ready to co-operate in promoting all that is reasonable.'

A circle soon formed round Speránski, and the old man who had talked about his subordinate Pryánichnikov addressed a question to him.

Prince Andrew without joining in the conversation watched every movement of Speránski's: this man, not long since an insignificant divinity student, who now, Bolkónski thought, held in his hands—those plump white hands—the fate of Russia. Prince Andrew was struck by the extraordinarily disdainful composure with which Speránski answered the old man. He appeared to address condescending words to him from an immeasurable height. When the old man began to speak too loud, Speránski smiled and said he could not judge of the advantage or disadvantage of what pleased the sovereign.

Having talked for a little while in the general circle, Speránski rose and coming up to Prince Andrew took him along to the other end of the room. It was clear that he thought it necessary to interest himself in Bolkónski.

'I had no chance to talk with you, Prince, during the animated conversation in which that venerable gentleman involved me,' he said with a mildly contemptuous smile, as if intimating by that smile that he and Prince Andrew understood the insignificance of the people with whom he had just been talking. This flattered Prince Andrew. 'I have known of you for a long time: first from your action with regard to your serfs, a first example, of which it is very desirable that there should be more imitators; and secondly because you are one of those gentlemen of the chamber who have not considered themselves offended by the new decree concerning the ranks allotted to courtiers, which is causing so much gossip and tittle-tattle.'

'No,' said Prince Andrew, 'my father did not wish me to take advantage of the privilege. I began the service from the lower grade.'

'Your father, a man of the last century, evidently stands above our contemporaries who so condemn this measure which merely re-establishes natural justice.'

'I think, however, that these condemnations have some ground,' returned Prince Andrew, trying to resist Speránski's influence, of which he began to be conscious. He did not like to agree with him in everything and felt a wish to contradict. Though he usually spoke easily and well, he felt a difficulty in expressing himself now while talking with Speránski. He was too much absorbed in observing the famous man's personality.

'Grounds of personal ambition maybe,' Speránski put in quietly.

'And of state-interest to some extent,' said Prince Andrew.

'What do you mean?' asked Speránski quietly, lowering his eyes.

'I am an admirer of Montesquieu,' replied Prince Andrew, 'and his idea that *le principe des monarchies est l'honneur, me paraît incontestable. Certains droits et privilèges de la noblesse me paraissent être des moyens de soutenir ce sentiment.*'[1]

The smile vanished from Speránski's white face, which was much improved by the change. Probably Prince Andrew's thought interested him.

'*Si vous envisagez la question sous ce point de vue,*'[2] he began, pronouncing French with evident difficulty, and speaking even slower than in Russian but quite calmly.

Speránski went on to say that honour, *l'honneur,* cannot be upheld by privileges harmful to the service; that honour, *l'honneur,* is either a negative concept of not doing what is blameworthy, or it is a source of emulation in pursuit of commendation and rewards, which recognize it. His arguments were concise, simple, and clear.

'An institution upholding honour, the source of emulation, is one similar to the *Légion d'honneur* of the great Emperor Napoleon, not harmful but helpful to the success of the service, but not a class or court privilege.'

'I do not dispute that, but it cannot be denied that court privileges have attained the same end,' returned Prince Andrew. 'Every courtier considers himself bound to maintain his position worthily.'

'Yet you do not care to avail yourself of the privilege, Prince,' said Speránski, indicating by a smile that he wished

---

[1] 'That the principle of monarchies is honour, seems to me incontestable. Certain rights and privileges for the aristocracy appear to me a means of maintaining that sentiment.'

[2] 'If you regard the question from that point of view.'

to finish amiably an argument which was embarrassing for his companion. 'If you will do me the honour of calling on me on Wednesday,' he added, 'I will, after talking with Magnítski, let you know what may interest you, and shall also have the pleasure of a more detailed chat with you.'

Closing his eyes, he bowed *à la française*, without taking leave, and trying to attract as little attention as possible, he left the room.

CHAPTER VI

DURING the first weeks of his stay in Petersburg Prince Andrew felt the whole trend of thought he had formed during his life of seclusion quite overshadowed by the trifling cares that engrossed him in that city.

On returning home in the evening he would jot down in his note-book four or five necessary calls or appointments for certain hours. The mechanism of life, the arrangement of the day so as to be in time everywhere, absorbed the greater part of his vital energy. He did nothing, did not even think or find time to think, but only talked, and talked successfully, of what he had thought while in the country.

He sometimes noticed with dissatisfaction that he repeated the same remark on the same day in different circles. But he was so busy for whole days together that he had no time to notice that he was thinking of nothing.

As he had done on their first meeting at Kochubéy's, Speránski produced a strong impression on Prince Andrew on the Wednesday, when he received him *tête-à-tête* at his own house and talked to him long and confidentially.

To Bolkónski so many people appeared contemptible and insignificant creatures, and he so longed to find in some one the living ideal of that perfection towards which he strove, that he readily believed that in Speránski he had found this ideal of a perfectly rational and virtuous man. Had Speránski sprung from the same class as himself and possessed the same breeding and traditions, Bolkónski would soon have discovered his weak, human, unheroic sides; but as it was, Speránski's strange and logical turn of mind inspired him with respect all the more because he did not quite understand him. Moreover Speránski, either because he appreciated the other's capacity or because he considered it necessary to win him to his side, showed off his dispassionate calm reasonableness before Prince Andrew and flattered him with that subtle flattery which goes hand in hand with self-assurance, and consists in a tacit assumption that one's companion is the only man besides oneself capable of understanding the folly of the rest of mankind, and the reasonableness and profundity of one's own ideas.

During their long conversation on Wednesday evening, Speránski more than once remarked: '*We* regard everything that is above the common level of rooted custom' . . .; or, with a smile: 'But *we* want the wolves to be fed and the sheep to be safe . . .' or: '*They* cannot understand this . . .' and all in a way that seemed to say: '*We*, you and I, understand what *they* are and who *we* are.'

This first long conversation with Speránski only strengthened in Prince Andrew the feeling he had experienced towards him at their first meeting. He saw in him a remarkable, clear-thinking man of vast intellect who by his energy and persistence had attained power, which he was using solely for the welfare of Russia. In Prince Andrew's eyes Speránski was the man he would himself have wished to be—one who explained all the facts of life reasonably, considered important only what was rational, and was capable of applying the standard of reason to everything. Everything seemed so simple and clear in Speránski's exposition that Prince Andrew involuntarily agreed with him about everything. If he replied and argued, it was only because he wished to maintain his independence and not submit to Speránski's opinions entirely. Everything was right and everything was as it should be: only one thing disconcerted Prince Andrew. This was Speránski's cold, mirror-like look, which did not allow one to penetrate to his soul, and his delicate white hands, which Prince Andrew involuntarily watched as one does watch the hands of those who possess power. This mirror-like gaze and those

delicate hands irritated Prince Andrew, he knew not why.
He was unpleasantly struck, too, by the excessive contempt for others that he observed in Speránski, and by
the diversity of lines of argument he used to support his
opinions. He made use of every kind of mental device,
except analogy, and passed too boldly, it seemed to Prince
Andrew, from one to another. Now he would take up
the position of a practical man and condemn dreamers;
now that of a satirist, and laugh ironically at his
opponents; now grow severely logical, or suddenly rise
to the realm of metaphysics. (This last resource was one
he very frequently employed.) He would transfer a
question to metaphysical heights, pass on to definitions
of space, time, and thought, and having deduced the
refutation he needed, would again descend to the level
of the original discussion.

In general the trait of Speránski's mentality which
struck Prince Andrew most was his absolute and un-
shakable belief in the power and authority of reason.
It was evident that the thought could never occur to
him which to Prince Andrew seemed so natural, namely,
that it is after all impossible to express all one thinks; and
that he had never felt the doubt, 'Is not all I think
and believe nonsense?' And it was just this peculiarity
of Speránski's mind that particularly attracted Prince
Andrew.

During the first period of their acquaintance Bolkónski
felt a passionate admiration for him similar to that which
he had once felt for Bonaparte. The fact that Speránski
was the son of a village priest, and that stupid people
might meanly despise him on account of his humble
origin (as in fact many did), caused Prince Andrew to
cherish his sentiment for him the more, and unconsciously
to strengthen it.

On that first evening Bolkónski spent with him, having
mentioned the Commission for the Revision of the Code
of Laws, Speránski told him sarcastically that the Commission had existed for a hundred and fifty years, had
cost millions, and had done nothing except that Rosen-
kampf had stuck labels on the corresponding paragraphs
of the different codes.

'And that is all the State has for the millions it has spent,' said he. 'We want to give the Senate new juridical powers, but we have no laws. That is why it is a sin for men like you, Prince, not to serve in these times!'

Prince Andrew said that for that work an education in jurisprudence was needed which he did not possess.

'But nobody possesses it, so what would you have? It is a vicious circle from which we must break a way out.'

A week later Prince Andrew was a member of the Committee on Army Regulations, and—what he had not at all expected—was chairman of a section of the Committee for the revision of the laws. At Speránski's request he took the first part of the Civil Code that was being drawn up, and with the aid of the *Code Napoléon* and the Institutes of Justinian he worked at formulating the section on Personal Rights.

CHAPTER VII

NEARLY two years before this, in 1808, Pierre on returning to Petersburg after visiting his estates had involuntarily found himself in a leading position among the Petersburg Freemasons. He arranged dining and funeral Lodge meetings, enrolled new members, and busied himself uniting various Lodges and acquiring authentic charters. He gave money for the erection of temples, and supplemented as far as he could the collection of alms, in regard to which the majority of members were stingy and irregular. He supported almost single-handed a poorhouse the Order had founded in Petersburg.

His life meanwhile continued as before, with the same infatuations and dissipations. He liked to dine and drink well, and though he considered it immoral and humiliating could not resist the temptations of the bachelor circles in which he moved.

Amid the turmoil of his activities and distractions, however, Pierre at the end of a year began to feel that the more firmly he tried to rest upon it, the more the Masonic ground on which he stood gave way under him.

At the same time he felt that the deeper the ground sank under him the closer bound he involuntarily became to the Order. When he had joined the Freemasons he had experienced the feeling of one who confidently steps onto the smooth surface of a bog. When he put his foot down it sank in. To make quite sure of the firmness of the ground, he put his other foot down and sank deeper still, became stuck in it, and involuntarily waded knee-deep in the bog.

Joseph Alexéevich was not in Petersburg—he had of late stood aside from the affairs of the Petersburg Lodges and lived almost entirely in Moscow. All the members of the Lodges were men Pierre knew in ordinary life, and it was difficult for him to regard them merely as Brothers in Freemasonry and not as Prince B. or Iván Vasílevich D., whom he knew in society mostly as weak and insignificant men. Under the Masonic aprons and insignia he saw the uniforms and decorations at which they aimed in ordinary life. Often after collecting alms, and reckoning up twenty to thirty rubles received for the most part in promises from a dozen members, of whom half were as well able to pay as himself, Pierre remembered the Masonic vow in which each Brother promised to devote all his belongings to his neighbour, and doubts on which he tried not to dwell, arose in his soul.

He divided the Brothers he knew into four categories. In the first he put those who did not take an active part in the affairs of the Lodges or in human affairs, but were exclusively occupied with the mystical science of the Order: with questions of the threefold designation of God, the three primordial elements—sulphur, mercury, and salt—or the meaning of the square and all the various figures of the temple of Solomon. Pierre respected this class of Brothers, to which the elder ones chiefly belonged, including, Pierre thought, Joseph Alexéevich himself, but he did not share their interests. His heart was not in the mystical aspect of Freemasonry.

In the second category Pierre reckoned himself and others like him, seeking and vacillating, who had not yet found in Freemasonry a straight and comprehensible path, but hoped to do so.

In the third category he included those Brothers (the majority) who saw nothing in Freemasonry but the external forms and ceremonies, and prized the strict performance of these forms without troubling about their purport or significance. Such were Wilarski and even the Grand Master of the principal Lodge.

Finally, to the fourth category also a great many Brothers belonged, particularly those who had lately joined. These according to Pierre's observation were men who had no belief in anything, nor desire for anything, but joined the Freemasons merely to associate with the wealthy young Brothers who were influential through their connexions or rank, and of whom there were very many in the Lodge.

Pierre began to feel dissatisfied with what he was doing. Freemasonry, at any rate as he saw it here, sometimes seemed to him based merely on externals. He did not think of doubting Freemasonry itself, but suspected that Russian Masonry had taken a wrong path and deviated from its original principles. And so towards the end of the year he went abroad to be initiated into the higher secrets of the Order.

In the summer of 1809 Pierre returned to Petersburg. Our Freemasons knew from correspondence with those abroad that Bezúkhov had obtained the confidence of many highly placed persons, had been initiated into many mysteries, had been raised to a higher grade, and was bringing back with him much that might conduce to the advantage of the Masonic cause in Russia. The Petersburg Freemasons all came to see him, tried to ingratiate themselves with him, and it seemed to them all that he was preparing something for them and concealing it.

A solemn meeting of the Lodge of the second degree was convened, at which Pierre promised to communicate to the Petersburg Brothers what he had to deliver to them from the highest leaders of their Order. The meeting was a full one. After the usual ceremonies Pierre rose and began his address.

'Dear Brothers,' he began, blushing and stammering,

with a written speech in his hand, 'it is not sufficient to observe our mysteries in the seclusion of our Lodge—we must act—act! We are drowsing, but we must act.' Pierre raised his note-book and began to read.

'For the dissemination of pure truth and to secure the triumph of virtue,' he read, 'we must cleanse men from prejudice, diffuse principles in harmony with the spirit of the times, undertake the education of the young, unite ourselves in indissoluble bonds with the wisest men, boldly yet prudently overcome superstitions, infidelity, and folly, and form of those devoted to us a body linked together by unity of purpose and possessed of authority and power.

'To attain this end we must secure a preponderance of virtue over vice, and must endeavour to secure that the honest man may, even in this world, receive a lasting reward for his virtue. But in these great endeavours we are gravely hampered by the political institutions of to-day. What is to be done in these circumstances? To favour revolutions, overthrow everything, repel force by force? . . . No! We are very far from that. Every violent reform deserves censure, for it quite fails to remedy evil while men remain what they are, and also because wisdom needs no violence.

'The whole plan of our Order should be based on the idea of preparing men of firmness and virtue bound together by unity of conviction—aiming at the punishment of vice and folly, and patronizing talent and virtue: raising worthy men from the dust and attaching them to our Brotherhood. Only then will our Order have the power unobtrusively to bind the hands of the protectors of disorder and to control them without their being aware of it. In a word, we must found a form of government holding universal sway, which should be diffused over the whole world without destroying the bonds of citizenship, and beside which all other governments can continue in their customary course and do everything except what impedes the great aim of our Order, which is to obtain for virtue the victory over vice. This aim was that of Christianity itself. It taught men to be wise and good, and for their own benefit to follow the example and instruction of the best and wisest men.

'At that time, when everything was plunged in darkness, preaching alone was of course sufficient. The novelty of Truth endowed her with special strength, but now we need much more powerful methods. It is now necessary that man governed by his senses should find in virtue a charm palpable to those senses. It is impossible to eradicate the passions; but we must strive to direct them to a noble aim, and it is therefore necessary that every one should be able to satisfy his passions within the limits of virtue. Our Order should provide means to that end.

'As soon as we have a certain number of worthy men in every State, each of them again training two others and all being closely united, everything will be possible for our Order, which has already in secret accomplished much for the welfare of mankind.'

This speech not only made a strong impression, but created excitement in the Lodge. The majority of the Brothers, seeing in it dangerous designs of Illuminism, met it with a coldness that surprised Pierre. The Grand Master began answering him, and Pierre began developing his views with more and more warmth. It was long since there had been so stormy a meeting. Parties were formed, some accusing Pierre of Illuminism, others supporting him. At that meeting he was struck for the first time by the endless variety of men's minds, which prevents a truth from ever presenting itself identically to two persons. Even those members who seemed to be on his side understood him in their own way, with limitations and alterations he could not agree to, as what he always wanted most was to convey his thought to others just as he himself understood it.

At the end of the meeting the Grand Master reproved Bezúkhov with irony and ill will for his vehemence, and said it was not love of virtue alone, but also a love of strife that had moved him in the dispute. Pierre did not answer him, and asked briefly whether his proposal would be accepted. He was told that it would not, and without waiting for the usual formalities he left the Lodge and went home.

CHAPTER VIII

AGAIN Pierre was overtaken by the depression he so dreaded. For three days after the delivery of his speech at the Lodge he lay on a sofa at home receiving no one and going nowhere.

It was just then that he received a letter from his wife, who implored him to see her, telling him how grieved she was about him and how she wished to devote her whole life to him.

At the end of the letter she informed him that in a few days she would return to Petersburg from abroad.

Following this letter one of the Masonic Brothers whom Pierre respected less than the others forced his way in to see him and turning the conversation upon Pierre's matrimonial affairs, by way of fraternal advice expressed the opinion that his severity to his wife was wrong, and that he was neglecting one of the first rules of Freemasonry by not forgiving the penitent.

At the same time his mother-in-law, Prince Vasíli's wife, sent to him imploring him to come if only for a few minutes to discuss a most important matter. Pierre saw that there was a conspiracy against him and that they wanted to reunite him with his wife, and in the mood he then was, this was not even unpleasant to him. Nothing mattered to him. Nothing in life seemed to him of much importance, and under the influence of the depression that possessed him he valued neither his liberty nor his resolution to punish his wife.

'No one is right and no one is to blame; so she too is not to blame,' he thought.

If he did not at once give his consent to a reunion with his wife, it was only because in his state of depression he did not feel able to take any step. Had his wife come to him, he would not have turned her away. Compared to what preoccupied him, was it not a matter of indifference whether he lived with his wife or not?

Without replying either to his wife or his mother-in-law, Pierre late one night prepared for a journey and started for Moscow to see Joseph Alexéevich. This is what he noted in his diary:

'Moscow, 17th November.

'I have just returned from my benefactor, and hasten to write down what I have experienced. Joseph Alexéevich is living poorly and has for three years been suffering from a painful disease of the bladder. No one has ever heard him utter a groan or a word of complaint. From morning till late at night, except when he eats his very plain food, he is working at science. He received me graciously and made me sit down on the bed on which he lay. I made the sign of the Knights of the East and of Jerusalem, and he responded in the same manner, asking me with a mild smile what I had learned and gained in the Prussian and Scottish Lodges. I told him everything as best I could, and told him what I had proposed to our Petersburg Lodge, of the bad reception I had encountered, and of my rupture with the brothers. Joseph Alexéevich, having remained silent and thoughtful for a good while, told me his view of the matter, which at once lit up for me my whole past, and the future path I should follow. He surprised me by asking whether I remembered the threefold aim of the Order: (1) The preservation and study of the mystery. (2) The purification and reformation of oneself for its reception, and (3) The improvement of the human race by striving for such purification. Which is the principal *aim* of these three? Certainly self-reformation and self-purification. Only to this aim can we always strive independently of circumstances. But at the same time, just this aim demands the greatest efforts of us; and so, led astray by pride, losing sight of this aim, we occupy ourselves either with the mystery which in our impurity we are unworthy to receive, or seek the reformation of the human race while ourselves setting an example of baseness and profligacy. Illuminism is not a pure doctrine just because it is attracted by social activity and puffed up by pride. On this ground Joseph Alexéevich condemned my speech and my whole activity, and in the depth of my soul I agreed with him. Talking of my family affairs he said to me, "the chief duty of a true Mason, as I have told you, lies in perfecting himself. We often think that by removing all the difficulties of our life we shall more quickly reach our aim, but on the contrary, my dear sir, it is only in the midst of worldly cares that we can attain our three chief aims: (1) Self-knowledge—for man can only know himself by comparison. (2) Self-perfecting, which can only be attained by conflict, and (3) The attainment of the chief virtue—love of death. Only the vicissitudes of life can show us its vanity, and develop our innate love of death or of rebirth to a new life." These words are all the more remarkable because, in spite of his great physical sufferings, Joseph Alexéevich is never weary of life though he loves death, for which—in spite of the purity and loftiness of his inner man—he does not yet feel himself sufficiently prepared. My benefactor then explained to me fully the meaning of the Great Square of creation, and pointed out to me that the numbers three and seven are the basis of everything. He advised me not to avoid intercourse with the Petersburg Brothers, but to take up only second-grade posts in the Lodge, to try, while diverting the Brothers from pride, to turn them towards the true path of self-knowledge and self-perfecting. Besides this he advised me for myself personally above all to keep a watch over myself, and to that end he gave me a note-book, the one I am now writing in, and in which I will in future note down all my actions.'

'*Petersburg, 23rd November.*

'I am again living with my wife. My mother-in-law came to me in tears and said that Hélène was here and that she implored me to hear her; that she was innocent and unhappy at my desertion, and much more. I knew that if I once let myself see her I should not have strength to go on refusing what she wanted. In my perplexity I did not know whose aid and advice to seek. Had my benefactor been here he would have told me what to do. I went to my room and re-read Joseph Alexéevich's letters and recalled my conversations with him, and deduced from it all that I ought not to refuse a suppliant, and ought to reach a helping hand to every one—especially to one so closely bound to me—and that I must bear my cross. But if I forgive her for the sake of doing right, then let union with her have only a spiritual aim. That is what I decided, and what I wrote to Joseph Alexéevich. I told my wife that I begged her to forget the past, to forgive me whatever wrong I may have done her, and that I had nothing to forgive. It gave me joy to tell her this. She need not know how hard it was for me to see her again. I have settled on the upper floor of this big house, and am experiencing a happy feeling of regeneration.'

CHAPTER IX

AT that time, as always happens, the highest society that met at Court and at the grand balls was divided into several circles, each with its own particular tone. The largest of these was the French circle of the Napoleonic alliance, the circle of Count Rumyántsev and Caulaincourt. In this group Hélène, as soon as she had settled in Petersburg with her husband, took a very prominent place. She was visited by the members of the French embassy and by many belonging to that circle and noted for their intellect and polished manners.

Hélène had been at Erfurt during the famous meeting of the Emperors, and had brought from there these connexions with the Napoleonic notabilities. At Erfurt her success had been brilliant. Napoleon himself had noticed her in the theatre, and said of her: '*C'est un superbe animal.*'[1] Her success as a beautiful and elegant woman did not surprise Pierre, for she had become even handsomer than before. What did surprise him was that during these last two years his wife had succeeded in gaining the reputation '*d'une femme charmante, aussi spirituelle que belle*'.[2] The distinguished Prince de Ligne wrote her eight-page letters. Bilíbin saved up his epigrams to produce them in Countess Bezúkhova's presence. To be received in the Countess Bezúkhova's salon was regarded as a diploma of intellect. Young men read books before attending Hélène's evenings, to have something to say in her salon, and secretaries of the embassy, and even

[1] 'That's a superb animal.'
[2] 'Of a charming woman, as intelligent as she is lovely.'

ambassadors, confided diplomatic secrets to her, so that
in a way Hélène was a power. Pierre, who knew she was
very stupid, sometimes attended, with a strange feeling
of perplexity and fear, her evenings and dinner parties,
where politics, poetry, and philosophy were discussed.
At these parties his feelings were like those of a conjuror
who always expects his trick to be found out at any
moment. But whether because stupidity was just what
was needed to run such a salon, or because those who
were deceived found pleasure in the deception, at any
rate it remained unexposed and Hélène Bezúkhova's
reputation as a lovely and clever woman became so
firmly established that she could say the emptiest and
stupidest things and yet everybody would go into raptures
over every word of hers, and look for a profound meaning
in it of which she herself had no conception.

Pierre was just the husband needed for a brilliant
society woman. He was that absent-minded crank, a
grand seigneur husband who was in no one's way, and far
from spoiling the high tone and general impression of the
drawing-room, he served, by the contrast he presented to
her, as an advantageous background to his elegant and
tactful wife. Pierre during the last two years, as a result
of his continual absorption in abstract interests and his
sincere contempt for all else, had acquired in his wife's
circle, which did not interest him, that air of unconcern,
indifference, and benevolence towards all, which cannot
be acquired artificially, and therefore inspires involuntary
respect. He entered his wife's drawing-room as one
enters a theatre, was acquainted with everybody, equally
pleased to see every one and equally indifferent to them
all. Sometimes he joined in a conversation which
interested him and, regardless of whether any 'gentlemen
of the embassy' were present or not, lispingly expressed
his views, which were sometimes not at all in accord with
the accepted tone of the moment. But the general opinion
concerning the queer husband of 'the most distinguished
woman in Petersburg' was so well established that no
one took his freaks seriously.

Among the many young men who frequented her
house every day, Borís Drubetskóy, who had already

achieved great success in the service, was the most
intimate friend of the Bezúkhov household since Hélène's
return from Erfurt. Hélène spoke of him as '*mon page*',
and treated him like a child. Her smile for him was the
same as for everybody, but sometimes that smile made
Pierre uncomfortable. Towards him, Borís behaved with
a particularly dignified and sad deference. This shade
of deference also disturbed Pierre. He had suffered so
painfully three years before from the mortification to
which his wife had subjected him, that he now protected
himself from the danger of its repetition, first by not being
a husband to his wife, and secondly by not allowing himself to suspect.

'No, now that she has become a blue-stocking she has
finally renounced her former infatuations,' he told himself. 'There has never been an instance of a blue-stocking
being carried away by affairs of the heart'—a statement
which, though gathered from an unknown source, he
believed implicitly. Yet strange to say Borís's presence
in his wife's drawing-room (and he was almost always
there) had a physical effect upon Pierre; it constricted
his limbs and destroyed the unconsciousness and freedom
of his movements.

'What a strange antipathy,' thought Pierre, 'yet I used
to like him very much.'

In the eyes of the world Pierre was a great gentleman,
the rather blind and absurd husband of a distinguished
wife, a clever crank who did nothing, but harmed
nobody, and was a first-rate, good-natured fellow. But a
complex and difficult process of internal development was
taking place all this time in Pierre's soul, revealing much
to him and causing him many spiritual doubts and joys.

CHAPTER X

PIERRE went on with his diary, and this is what he
wrote in it during that time:

'*24th November.*

'Got up at eight, read the Scriptures, then went to
my duties.' (By Joseph Alexéevich's advice Pierre had
entered the service of the State and served on one of the

committees.) 'Returned home for dinner and dined alone—the countess had many visitors I do not like. I ate and drank moderately, and after dinner copied out some passages for the Brothers. In the evening I went down to the countess and told a funny story about B., and only remembered that I ought not to have done so when everybody laughed loudly at it.

'I am going to bed with a happy and tranquil mind. Great God, help me to walk in Thy paths, (1) to conquer anger by calmness and deliberation, (2) to vanquish lust by self-restraint and repulsion, (3) to withdraw from worldliness, but not avoid (a) the service of the State, (b) family duties, (c) relations with my friends, and (d) the management of my affairs.

'*27th November.*

'I got up late. On waking I lay long in bed yielding to sloth. O God, help and strengthen me that I may walk in Thy ways! Read the Scriptures, but without proper feeling. Brother Urúsov came and we talked about worldly vanities. He told me of the Emperor's new projects. I began to criticize them, but remembered my rules and my benefactor's words—that a true Freemason should be a zealous worker for the State when his aid is required and a quiet onlooker when not called on to assist. My tongue is my enemy. Brothers G. V. and O visited me and we had a preliminary talk about the reception of a new Brother. They laid on me the duty of Rhetor. I feel myself weak and unworthy. Then our talk turned to the interpretation of the seven pillars and steps of the Temple, the seven sciences, the seven virtues the seven vices, and the seven gifts of the Holy Spirit Brother O. was very eloquent. In the evening the admission took place. The new decoration of the premise contributed much to the magnificence of the spectacle It was Borís Drubetskóy who was admitted. I nominated him and was the Rhetor. A strange feeling agitated me all the time I was alone with him in the dark chamber I caught myself harbouring a feeling of hatred toward him which I vainly tried to overcome. That is wh I should really like to save him from evil and lead him into the path of truth, but evil thoughts of him did no

leave me. It seemed to me that his object in entering
the Brotherhood was merely to be intimate and in
favour with members of our Lodge. Apart from the
fact that he had asked me several times whether N. and
S. were members of our Lodge (a question to which
I could not reply) and that according to my observation
he is incapable of feeling respect for our holy Order and
is too preoccupied and satisfied with the outer man to
desire spiritual improvement, I had no cause to doubt
him, but he seemed to me insincere, and all the time
I stood alone with him in the dark temple it seemed to
me that he was smiling contemptuously at my words,
and I wished really to stab his bare breast with the
sword I held to it. I could not be eloquent, nor could
I frankly mention my doubts to the Brothers and to the
Grand Master. Great Architect of Nature, help me to
find the true path out of the labyrinth of lies!'

After this three pages were left blank in the diary, and
then the following was written:

'I have had a long and instructive talk alone with
Brother V., who advised me to hold fast by Brother A.
Though I am unworthy, much was revealed to me.
Adonai is the name of the creator of the world. Elohim
is the name of the ruler of all. The third name is the
name unutterable which means the *All*. Talks with
Brother V. strengthen, refresh, and support me in the
path of virtue. In his presence doubt has no place. The
distinction between the poor teachings of mundane
science and our sacred all-embracing teaching is clear
to me. Human sciences dissect everything to comprehend
it, and kill everything to examine it. In the holy science
of our Order all is one, all is known in its entirety and
life. The Trinity—the three elements of matter—are
sulphur, mercury, and salt. Sulphur is of an oily and
fiery nature; in combination with salt by its fiery nature
it arouses a desire in the latter by means of which it
attracts mercury, seizes it, holds it, and in combination
produces other bodies. Mercury is a fluid, volatile,
spiritual essence. Christ, the Holy Spirit, Him! . . .

'*3rd December.*

'Awoke late, read the Scriptures but was apathetic.

Afterwards went and paced up and down the large hall. I wished to meditate, but instead my imagination pictured an occurrence of four years ago, when Dólokhov, meeting me in Moscow after our duel, said he hoped I was enjoying perfect peace of mind in spite of my wife's absence. At the time I gave him no answer. Now I recalled every detail of that meeting and in my mind gave him the most malevolent and bitter replies. I recollected myself and drove away that thought only when I found myself glowing with anger, but I did not sufficiently repent. Afterwards Borís Drubetskóy came and began relating various adventures. His coming vexed me from the first, and I said something disagreeable to him. He replied. I flared up and said much that was unpleasant and even rude to him. He became silent, and I recollected myself only when it was too late. My God, I cannot get on with him at all. The cause of this is my egotism. I set myself above him and so become much worse than he, for he is lenient to my rudeness while I on the contrary nourish contempt for him. O God, grant that in his presence I may rather see my own vileness, and behave so that he too may benefit. After dinner I fell asleep and as I was drowsing off I clearly heard a voice saying in my left ear, "Thy day!"

'I dreamt that I was walking in the dark and was suddenly surrounded by dogs, but I went on undismayed. Suddenly a smallish dog seized my left thigh with its teeth and would not let go. I began to throttle it with my hands. Scarcely had I torn it off before another a bigger one, began biting me. I lifted it up but the higher I lifted it the bigger and heavier it grew. And suddenly Brother A. came and, taking my arm, led me to a building, to enter which we had to pass along a narrow plank. I stepped on it, but it bent and gave way and I began to clamber up a fence which I could scarcely reach with my hands. After much effort I dragged myself up, so that my legs hung down on one side and my body on the other. I looked round and saw Brother A. standing on the fence and pointing me to a broad avenue and garden, and in the garden was a large and beautiful building. I woke up. O Lord great Architect of Nature, help me to tear from myself these dogs—my passions—especially the last, which unites in itself the strength of all the former ones, and aid me to enter that temple of virtue to a vision of which I attained in my dream.

'*7th December.*

'I dreamt that Joseph Alexéevich was sitting in my house, and that I was very glad, and wished to entertain him. It seemed as if I chattered incessantly with other people and suddenly remembered that this could not please him, and I wished to come close to him and embrace him. But as soon as I drew near, I saw that his face had changed and grown young, and he was quietly telling me something about the teaching of our Order, but so softly that I could not hear it. Then it seemed that we all left the room and something strange happened. We were sitting or lying on the floor. He was telling me something, and I wished to show him my sensibility, and not listening to what he was saying, I began picturing to myself the condition of my inner man and the grace of God sanctifying me. And tears came into my eyes, and I was glad he noticed this. But he looked at me with vexation and jumped up, breaking off his remarks. I felt abashed and asked whether what he had been saying did not concern me; but he did not reply, gave me a kind look, and then we suddenly found ourselves in my bedroom where there is a double bed. He lay down on the edge of it and I burned with longing to caress him and lie down too. And he said, "Tell me frankly what is your chief temptation? Do you know it? I think you know it already." Abashed by this question, I replied that sloth was my chief temptation. He shook his head incredulously; and even more abashed, I said that though I was living with my wife as he advised, I was not living with her as her husband. To this he replied that one should not deprive a wife of one's embraces, and gave me to understand that that was my duty. But I replied that I should be ashamed to do it, and suddenly everything vanished. And I awoke and found in my mind the text from the Gospel: "The life was the light of men. And the light shineth in darkness; and the darkness comprehended it not." Joseph Alexéevich's face had looked young and bright. That day I received a letter from my benefactor in which he wrote about "conjugal duties".

'*9th December.*

'I had a dream from which I awoke with a throbbing heart. I saw that I was in Moscow in my house, in the big sitting-room, and Joseph Alexéevich came in from the drawing-room. I seemed to know at once that the process of regeneration had already taken place in him, and I rushed to meet him. I embraced him and kissed his hands, and he said, "Hast thou noticed that my face is different?" I looked at him, still holding him in my arms, and saw that his face was young, but that he had no hair on his head and his features were quite changed. And I said, "I should have known you had I met you by chance," and I thought to myself, "Am I telling the truth?" And suddenly I saw him lying like a dead body; then he gradually recovered and went with me into my study carrying a large book of sheets of drawing paper; I said, "I drew that," and he answered by bowing his head. I opened the book, and on all the pages there were excellent drawings. And in my dream I knew that these drawings represented the love adventures of the soul with its beloved. And on its pages I saw a beautiful representation of a maiden in transparent garments and with a transparent body, flying up to the clouds. And I seemed to know that this maiden was nothing else than a representation of the Song of Songs. And looking at those drawings I dreamed I felt that I was doing wrong, but could not tear myself away from them. Lord, help me! My God, if Thy forsaking me is Thy doing, Thy will be done; but if I am myself the cause, teach me what I should do! I shall perish of my debauchery if Thou utterly desertest me!'

CHAPTER XI

THE Rostóvs' monetary affairs had not improved during the two years they had spent in the country. Though Nicholas Rostóv had kept firmly to his resolution and was still serving modestly in an obscure regiment,

spending comparatively little, the way of life at Otrádnoe
—Mítinka's management of affairs, in particular—was
such that the debts inevitably increased every year. The
only resource obviously presenting itself to the old count
was to apply for an official post, so he had come to
Petersburg to look for one and also, as he said, to let the
lassies enjoy themselves for the last time.

Soon after their arrival in Petersburg, Berg proposed
to Véra and was accepted.

Though in Moscow the Rostóvs belonged to the best
society without themselves giving it a thought, yet in
Petersburg their circle of acquaintances was a mixed and
indefinite one. In Petersburg they were provincials, and
the very people they had entertained in Moscow without
inquiring to what set they belonged, here looked down
on them.

The Rostóvs lived in the same hospitable way in
Petersburg as in Moscow, and the most diverse people
met at their suppers. Country neighbours from Otrádnoe,
impoverished old squires and their daughters, Perónskaya a maid of honour, Pierre Bezúkhov, and the son
of their district postmaster, who had obtained a post in
Petersburg. Among the men who very soon became
frequent visitors at the Rostóvs' house in Petersburg were
Borís, Pierre whom the count had met in the street and
dragged home with him, and Berg who spent whole days
at the Rostóvs' and paid the eldest daughter, Countess
Véra, the attentions a young man pays when he intends
to propose.

Not in vain had Berg shown everybody his right hand
wounded at Austerlitz and held a perfectly unnecessary
sword in his left. He narrated that episode so persistently
and with so important an air that every one believed in
the merit and usefulness of his deed, and he had obtained
two decorations for Austerlitz.

In the Finnish war he also managed to distinguish
himself. He had picked up the scrap of a grenade that
had killed an aide-de-camp standing near the commander-in-chief, and had taken it to his commander.
Just as he had done after Austerlitz, he related this
occurrence at such length and so insistently that every

one again believed it had been necessary to do this, and
he received two decorations for the Finnish war also. In
1809 he was a captain in the Guards, wore medals, and
held some special lucrative posts in Petersburg.

Though some sceptics smiled when told of Berg's
merits, it could not be denied that he was a painstaking
and brave officer, on excellent terms with his superiors,
and a moral young man with a brilliant career before
him and an assured position in society.

Four years before, meeting a German comrade in the
stalls of a Moscow theatre, Berg had pointed out Véra
Rostóva to him and had said in German, 'das soll mein
Weib werden,'[1] and from that moment had made up his
mind to marry her. Now in Petersburg, having considered the Rostóvs' position and his own, he decided
that the time had come to propose.

Berg's proposal was at first received with a perplexity
that was not flattering to him. At first it seemed strange
that the son of an obscure Livonian gentleman should
propose marriage to a Countess Rostóva; but Berg's chief
characteristic was such a naïve and good-natured
egotism that the Rostóvs involuntarily came to think it
would be a good thing, since he himself was so firmly
convinced that it was good, indeed excellent. Moreover
the Rostóvs' affairs were seriously embarrassed, as the
suitor could not but know; and above all, Véra was
twenty-four, had been taken out everywhere, and though
she was certainly good-looking and sensible, no one up to
now had proposed to her. So they gave their consent.

'You see,' said Berg to his comrade, whom he called
'friend' only because he knew that every one has friends.
'You see, I have considered it all, and should not marry if
I had not thought it all out or if it were in any way unsuitable. But on the contrary, my papa and mamma are
now provided for—I have arranged that rent for them
in the Baltic Provinces—and I can live in Petersburg on
my pay, and with her fortune and my good management
we can get along nicely. I am not marrying for money—
I consider that dishonourable—but a wife should bring
her share and a husband his. I have my position in the

        [1] 'That girl shall be my wife.'

service, she has connexions and some means. In our times that is worth something, isn't it? But above all, she is a handsome, estimable girl, and she loves me . . .'

Berg blushed and smiled.

'And I love her, because her character is sensible and very good. Now the other sister, though they are the same family, is quite different—an unpleasant character and has not the same intelligence. She is so . . . you know? . . . Unpleasant . . . But my fiancée . . .! Well, you will be coming' he was going to say 'to dine', but changed his mind and said 'to take tea with us', and quickly doubling up his tongue he blew a small round ring of tobacco smoke, perfectly embodying his dream of happiness.

After the first feeling of perplexity aroused in the parents by Berg's proposal, the holiday tone of joyousness usual at such times took possession of the family, but the rejoicing was external and insincere. In the family's feeling towards this wedding a certain awkwardness and constraint was evident: as if they were ashamed of not having loved Véra sufficiently and of being so ready to get her off their hands. The old count felt this most. He would probably have been unable to state the cause of his embarrassment, but it resulted from the state of his affairs. He did not know at all how much he had, what his debts amounted to, or what dowry he could give Véra. When his daughters were born he had assigned to each of them, for her dowry, an estate with three hundred serfs; but one of those estates had already been sold, and the other was mortgaged, and the interest so much in arrears that it would have to be sold, so that it was impossible to give it to Véra. Nor had he any money.

Berg had already been engaged a month, and only a week remained before the wedding, but the count had not yet decided in his own mind the question of the dowry, nor spoken to his wife about it. At one time the count thought of giving her the Ryazán estate, or of selling a forest, at another time of borrowing money on note of hand. A few days before the wedding Berg entered the count's study early one morning, and with a pleasant smile respectfully asked his future father-in-law to let him know what Véra's dowry would be. The count was so disconcerted by this long-foreseen inquiry that without consideration he gave the first reply that came into his head. 'I like your being business-like about it . . . I like it. You shall be satisfied . . .'

And patting Berg on the shoulder he got up, wishing to end the conversation. But Berg, smiling pleasantly, explained that if he did not know for certain how much Véra would have and did not receive at least part of the dowry in advance, he would have to break matters off.

'Because, consider, Count—if I allowed myself to marry now without having definite means to maintain my wife, I should be acting badly . . .'

The conversation ended by the count, who wished to be generous and to avoid further importunity, saying that he would give a note of hand for eighty thousand rubles. Berg smiled meekly, kissed the count on the shoulder, and said that he was very grateful, but that it was impossible for him to arrange his new life without receiving thirty thousand in ready money. 'Or at least twenty thousand, Count,' he added, 'and then a note of hand for only sixty thousand.'

'Yes, yes, all right!' said the count hurriedly. 'Only excuse me, my dear fellow, I'll give you twenty thousand and a note of hand for eighty thousand as well. Yes, yes! Kiss me.'

CHAPTER XII

NATÁSHA was sixteen and it was the year 1809, the very year to which she had counted on her fingers with Borís after they had kissed four years ago. Since then she had not once seen him. Before Sónya and her mother, if Borís happened to be mentioned, she spoke quite freely of that episode as of some childish, long-forgotten matter that was not worth mentioning. But in the secret depths of her soul the question whether her engagement to Borís was a jest or an important, binding promise tormented her.

Since Borís left Moscow in 1805 to join the army he had not seen the Rostóvs. He had been in Moscow several

times, and had passed near Otrádnoe, but had never
been to see them.

Sometimes it occurred to Natásha that he did not wish
to see her, and this conjecture was confirmed by the sad
tone in which her elders spoke of him.

'Nowadays old friends are not remembered,' the
countess would say when Borís was mentioned.

Anna Mikháylovna also had of late visited them less
frequently, seemed to hold herself with particular dignity,
and always spoke rapturously and gratefully of the merits
of her son and the brilliant career on which he had
entered. When the Rostóvs came to Petersburg, Borís
called on them.

He drove to their house in some agitation. The
memory of Natásha was his most poetic recollection. But
he went with the firm intention of letting her and her
parents feel that the childish relations between himself
and Natásha could not be binding either on her or on
him. He had a brilliant position in society thanks to his
intimacy with Countess Bezúkhova, a brilliant position
in the service thanks to the patronage of an important
personage whose complete confidence he enjoyed, and he
was beginning to make plans for marrying one of the
richest heiresses in Petersburg, plans which might very
easily be realized. When he entered the Rostóvs'
drawing-room Natásha was in her own room. When she
heard of his arrival she almost ran into the drawing-room,
flushed, and beaming with a more than cordial smile.

Borís remembered Natásha in a short dress, with dark
eyes shining from under her curls and boisterous, childish
laughter, as he had known her four years before; and so
he was taken aback when quite a different Natásha
entered, and his face expressed rapturous astonishment.
This expression on his face pleased Natásha.

'Well, do you recognize your little madcap playmate?'
asked the countess.

Borís kissed Natásha's hand and said that he was
astonished at the change in her.

'How handsome you have grown!'

'I should think so!' replied Natásha's laughing eyes.

'And is Papa older?' she asked.

Natásha sat down and, without joining in Borís's conversation with the countess, silently and minutely studied her childhood's suitor. He felt the weight of that resolute and affectionate scrutiny, and glanced at her occasionally.

Borís's uniform, spurs, tie, and the way his hair was brushed, were all *comme il faut* and in the latest fashion. This Natásha noticed at once. He sat rather sideways in the arm-chair next to the countess, arranging with his right hand the cleanest of gloves that fitted his left hand like a skin, and he spoke with a particularly refined compression of his lips about the amusements of the highest Petersburg society, recalling with mild irony old times in Moscow and Moscow acquaintances. It was not accidentally, Natásha felt, that he alluded, when speaking of the highest aristocracy, to an ambassador's ball he had attended, and to invitations he had received from N. N. and S. S.

All this time Natásha sat silent, glancing up at him from under her brows. This gaze disturbed and confused Borís more and more. He looked round more frequently towards her, and broke off in what he was saying. He did not stay more than ten minutes, then rose and took his leave. The same inquisitive, challenging, and rather mocking eyes still looked at him. After his first visit Borís said to himself that Natásha attracted him just as much as ever, but that he must not yield to that feeling, because to marry her, a girl almost without fortune, would mean ruin to his career, while to renew their former relations without intending to marry her would be dishonourable. Borís made up his mind to avoid meeting Natásha, but despite that resolution he called again a few days later, and began calling often and spending whole days at the Rostóvs'. It seemed to him that he ought to have an explanation with Natásha and tell her that the old times must be forgotten, that in spite of everything . . . she could not be his wife, that he had no means, and they would never let her marry him. But he failed to do so, and felt awkward about entering on such an explanation. From day to day he became more and more entangled. It seemed to her mother and Sónya that Natásha was in love with Borís as of old. She sang him his favourite songs,

showed him her album, making him write in it, did not
allow him to allude to the past, letting it be understood
how delightful was the present; and every day he went
away in a fog, without having said what he meant to,
and not knowing what he was doing or why he came, or
how it would all end. He left off visiting Hélène and
received reproachful notes from her every day, and yet he
continued to spend whole days with the Rostóvs.

CHAPTER XIII

ONE night when the old countess, in nightcap and
dressing-jacket, without her false curls, and with her
poor little knob of hair showing under her white cotton
cap, knelt sighing and groaning on a rug and bowing to
the ground in prayer, her door creaked and Natásha, also
in a dressing-jacket with slippers on her bare feet and her
hair in curl-papers, ran in. The countess—her prayerful
mood dispelled—looked round and frowned. She was
finishing her last prayer: 'Can it be that this couch will be
my grave?' Natásha, flushed and eager, seeing her mother
in prayer suddenly checked her rush, half sat down, and
unconsciously put out her tongue as if chiding herself.
Seeing that her mother was still praying she ran on tiptoe
to the bed and, rapidly slipping one little foot against the
other, pushed off her slippers and jumped onto the bed
the countess had feared might become her grave. This
couch was high, with a feather-bed and five pillows each
smaller than the one below. Natásha jumped on it, sank
into the feather-bed, rolled over to the wall, and began
snuggling up the bedclothes as she settled down, raising
her knees to her chin, kicking out and laughing almost
inaudibly, now covering herself up head and all, and now
peeping at her mother. The countess finished her prayers
and came to the bed with a stern face, but seeing that
Natásha's head was covered, she smiled in her kind, weak
way.

'Now then, now then!' said she.

'Mamma, can we have a talk? Yes?' said Natásha.
'Now, just one on your throat and another . . . that'll do!'

And seizing her mother round the neck, she kissed her on the throat. In her behaviour to her mother Natásha seemed rough, but she was so sensitive and tactful that however she clasped her mother she always managed to do it without hurting her, or making her feel uncomfortable or displeased.

'Well, what is it to-night?' said the mother, having arranged her pillows and waited until Natásha, after turning over a couple of times, had settled down beside her under the quilt, spread out her arms, and assumed a serious expression.

These visits of Natásha's at night, before the count returned from his club, were one of the greatest pleasures of both mother and daughter.

'What is it to-night?—But I have to tell you . . .'

Natásha put her hand on her mother's mouth.

'About Borís . . . I know,' she said seriously; 'that's what I have come about. Don't say it—I know. No, do tell me!' and she removed her hand. 'Tell me, Mamma! He's nice?'

'Natásha, you are sixteen. At your age I was married. You say Borís is nice. He is very nice, and I love him like a son. But what then . . .? What are you thinking about? You have quite turned his head, I can see that . . .'

As she said this the countess looked round at her daughter. Natásha was lying looking steadily straight before her at one of the mahogany sphinxes carved on the corners of the bedstead, so that the countess only saw her daughter's face in profile. That face struck her by its peculiarly serious and concentrated expression.

Natásha was listening and considering.

'Well, what then?' said she.

'You have quite turned his head, and why? What do you want of him? You know you can't marry him.'

'Why not?' said Natásha, without changing her position.

'Because he is young, because he is poor, because he is a relation . . . and because you yourself don't love him.'

'How do you know?'

'I know. It is not right, darling!'

'But if I want to . . .' said Natásha.

'Leave off talking nonsense,' said the countess.

'But if I want to . . .'

'Natásha, I am in earnest . . .'

Natásha did not let her finish. She drew the countess's large hand to her, kissed it on the back and then on the palm, then again turned it over and began kissing first one knuckle, then the space between the knuckles, then the next knuckle, whispering, 'January, February, March, April, May. Speak, Mamma, why don't you say anything? Speak!' said she, turning to her mother, who was tenderly gazing at her daughter and in that contemplation seemed to have forgotten all she had wished to say.

'It won't do, my love! Not every one will understand this friendship dating from your childish days, and to see him so intimate with you may injure you in the eyes of other young men who visit us, and above all, it torments him for nothing. He may already have found a suitable and wealthy match, and now he's half crazy.'

'Crazy?' repeated Natásha.

'I'll tell you some things about myself. I had a cousin...'

'I know! Cyril Matvéich ... but he is old.'

'He was not always old. But this is what I'll do, Natásha, I'll have a talk with Borís. He need not come so often . . .'

'Why not, if he likes to?'

'Because I know it will end in nothing . . .'

'How can you know? No, mamma, don't speak to him! What nonsense!' said Natásha in the tone of one being deprived of her property. 'Well, I won't marry, but let him come if he enjoys it and I enjoy it.' Natásha smiled and looked at her mother. 'Not to marry, but just *so*,' she added.

'How *so*, my pet?'

'Just *so*. There's no need for me to marry him. But ... just *so*.'

'Just so, just so,' repeated the countess, and shaking all over, she went off into a good-humoured, unexpected, elderly laugh.

'Don't laugh, stop!' cried Natásha. 'You're shaking the whole bed! You're awfully like me, just such another giggler ... Wait ...' and she seized the countess's hands and kissed a knuckle of the little finger, saying, 'June,' and continued, kissing, 'July, August' on the other hand. 'But, Mamma, is he very much in love? What do you think? Was anybody ever so much in love with you? And he's very nice, very, very nice. Only not quite my taste—he is so narrow, like the dining-room clock . . . Don't you understand? Narrow, you know—grey, light grey . . .'

'What rubbish you're talking!' said the countess.

Natásha continued:

'Don't you really understand? Nicholas would under-stand . . . Bezúkhov, now, is blue, dark-blue and red, and he is square.'

'You flirt with him too,' said the countess, laughing.

'No, he is a Freemason, I have found out. He is fine, dark-blue and red . . . How can I explain it to you?'

'Little Countess!' the count's voice called from behind the door. 'You're not asleep?' Natásha jumped up, snatched up her slippers, and ran barefoot to her own room.

It was a long time before she could sleep. She kept thinking that no one could understand all that she under-stood and all there was in her.

'Sónya?' she thought, glancing at that curled-up, sleeping little kitten with her enormous plait of hair. 'No, how could she? She's virtuous. She fell in love with Nicholas and does not wish to know anything more. Even Mamma does not understand. It is wonderful how clever I am and how . . . charming she is,' she went on, speaking of herself in the third person, and imagining it was some very wise man—the wisest and best of men—who was saying it of her. 'There is everything, everything in her,' continued this man. 'She is unusually intelligent, charming . . . and then she is pretty, uncommonly pretty, and agile—she swims and rides splendidly . . . and her voice! One can really say it's a wonderful voice!'

She hummed a scrap from her favourite opera by Cherubini, threw herself on her bed, laughed at the pleasant thought that she would immediately fall asleep, called Dunyásha, the maid, to put out the candle, and before Dunyásha had left the room had already passed

into another yet happier world of dreams, where everything was as light and beautiful as in reality, and even
more so because it was different.

Next day the countess called Borís aside and had a talk
with him, after which he ceased coming to the Rostóvs.

CHAPTER XIV

ON the 31st of December, New Year's Eve 1810, an
old grandee of Catherine's day was giving a ball and
midnight supper. The diplomatic corps and the Emperor
himself were to be present.

The grandee's well-known mansion on the English
Quay glittered with innumerable lights. Police were
stationed at the brightly lit entrance which was carpeted
with red baize, and not only gendarmes, but dozens of
police officers and even the police-master himself stood at
the porch. Carriages kept driving away and fresh ones
arriving, with red-liveried footmen and footmen in plumed
hats. From the carriages emerged men wearing uniforms,
stars, and ribbons, while ladies in satin and ermine
cautiously descended the carriage steps which were let
down for them with a clatter, and then walked hurriedly
and noiselessly over the baize at the entrance.

Almost every time a new carriage drove up a whisper
ran through the crowd and caps were doffed.

'The Emperor? . . . No, a minister . . . prince . . .
ambassador. Don't you see the plumes? . . .' was
whispered among the crowd.

One person, better dressed than the rest, seemed to
know every one and mentioned by name the greatest
dignitaries of the day.

A third of the visitors had already arrived, but the
Rostóvs, who were to be present, were still hurrying to
get dressed.

There had been many discussions and preparations for
this ball in the Rostóv family, many fears that the invitation would not arrive, that the dresses would not be ready,
or that something would not be arranged as it should be.

Márya Ignátevna Perónskaya, a thin and sallow maid of honour at the court of the Dowager Empress, who was a friend and relation of the countess and piloted the provincial Rostóvs in Petersburg high society, was to accompany them to the ball.

They were to call for her at her house in the Taurida Gardens at ten o'clock, but it was already five minutes to ten and the girls were not yet dressed.

Natásha was going to her first grand ball. She had got up at eight that morning and had been in a fever of excitement and activity all day. All her powers since morning had been concentrated on ensuring that they all—she herself, Mamma, and Sónya—should be as well dressed as possible. Sónya and her mother put themselves entirely in her hands. The countess was to wear a claret-coloured velvet dress, and the two girls white gauze over pink silk slips, with roses on their bodices and their hair dressed *à la grecque*.

Everything essential had already been done; feet, hands, necks, and ears washed, perfumed, and powdered, as befits a ball; the open-work silk stockings and white satin shoes with ribbons were already on; the hair-dressing was almost done. Sónya was finishing dressing and so was the countess, but Natásha, who had bustled about helping them all, was behindhand. She was still sitting before a looking-glass with a dressing-jacket thrown over her slender shoulders. Sónya stood ready dressed in the middle of the room, and pressing the head of a pin till it hurt her dainty finger, was fixing on a last ribbon that squeaked as the pin went through it.

'That's not the way, that's not the way, Sónya!' cried Natásha turning her head and clutching with both hands at her hair which the maid, who was dressing it, had not time to release. 'That bow is not right. Come here!'

Sónya sat down and Natásha pinned the ribbon on differently.

'Allow me, Miss! I can't do it like that,' said the maid who was holding Natásha's hair.

'Oh dear! Well then, wait. That's right, Sónya.'

'Aren't you ready? It is nearly ten,' came the countess's voice.

'Directly! Directly! And you, Mamma?'

'I have only my cap to pin on.'

'Don't do it without me!' called Natásha. 'You won't do it right.'

'But it's already ten.'

They had decided to be at the ball by half-past ten, and Natásha had still to get dressed and they had to call at the Taurida Gardens.

When her hair was done, Natásha, in her short petticoat from under which her dancing shoes showed, and in her mother's dressing-jacket, ran up to Sónya, scrutinized her, and then ran to her mother. Turning her mother's head this way and that, she fastened on the cap and hurriedly kissing her grey hair ran back to the maids who were turning up the hem of her skirt.

The cause of the delay was Natásha's skirt, which was too long. Two maids were turning up the hem and hurriedly biting off the ends of thread. A third with pins in her mouth was running about between the countess and Sónya, and a fourth held the whole of the gossamer garment up high on one uplifted hand.

'Mávra, quicker, darling!'

'Give me my thimble, Miss, from there . . .'

'Whenever will you be ready?' asked the count coming to the door. 'Here is some scent. Perónskaya must be tired of waiting.'

'It's ready, Miss,' said the maid, holding up the shortened gauze dress with two fingers, and blowing and shaking something off it, as if by this to express a consciousness of the airiness and purity of what she held.

Natásha began putting on the dress.

'In a minute! In a minute! Don't come in, Papa!' she cried to her father as he opened the door—speaking from under the filmy skirt which still covered her whole face.

Sónya slammed the door to. A minute later they let the count in. He was wearing a blue swallow-tail coat, shoes and stockings, and was perfumed and his hair pomaded.

'Oh, Papa! how nice you look! Charming!' cried Natásha, as she stood in the middle of the room smoothing out the folds of the gauze.

'If you please, Miss! allow me,' said the maid, who on her knees was pulling the skirt straight and shifting the pins from one side of her mouth to the other with her tongue.

'Say what you like,' exclaimed Sónya, in a despairing voice as she looked at Natásha, 'say what you like, it is still too long.'

Natásha stepped back to look at herself in the pier-glass. The dress *was* too long.

'Really, madam, it is not at all too long,' said Mávra, crawling on her knees after her young lady.

'Well, if it's too long we'll tack it up ... we'll tack it up in one minute,' said the resolute Dunyásha taking a needle that was stuck on the front of her little shawl and, still kneeling on the floor, set to work once more.

At that moment, with soft steps, the countess came in shyly, in her cap and velvet gown.

'Oo-oo, my beauty!' exclaimed the count, 'she looks better than any of you!'

He would have embraced her but, blushing, she stepped aside fearing to be rumpled.

'Mamma, your cap, more to this side,' said Natásha. 'I'll arrange it,' and she rushed forward so that the maids who were tacking up her skirt could not move fast enough and a piece of gauze was torn off.

'Oh goodness! What has happened? Really it was not my fault!'

'Never mind, I'll run it up, it won't show,' said Dunyásha.

'What a beauty—a very queen!' said the nurse as she came to the door. 'And Sónya! They are lovely!'

At a quarter past ten they at last got into their carriages and started. But they had still to call at the Taurida Gardens.

Perónskaya was quite ready. In spite of her age and plainness she had gone through the same process as the Rostóvs, but with less flurry—for to her it was a matter of routine. Her ugly old body was washed, perfumed, and powdered, in just the same way. She had washed behind her ears just as carefully, and when she entered her drawing-room in her yellow dress, wearing her badge as maid of honour, her old lady's maid was as full of rapturous admiration as the Rostóvs' servants had been.

She praised the Rostóvs' toilets. They praised her taste and toilet, and at eleven o'clock, careful of their *coiffures* and dresses, they settled themselves in their carriages and drove off.

CHAPTER XV

NATÁSHA had not had a moment free since early morning and had not once had time to think of what lay before her.

In the damp chill air and crowded closeness of the swaying carriage, she for the first time vividly imagined what was in store for her there at the ball, in those brightly lighted rooms—with music, flowers, dances, the Emperor, and all the brilliant young people of Petersburg. The prospect was so splendid that she hardly believed it would come true, so out of keeping was it with the chill darkness and closeness of the carriage. She understood all that awaited her only when, after stepping over the red baize at the entrance, she entered the hall, took off her fur cloak and, beside Sónya and in front of her mother, mounted the brightly illuminated stairs between the flowers. Only then did she remember how she must behave at a ball, and tried to assume the majestic air she considered indispensable for a girl on such an occasion. But, fortunately for her, she felt her eyes growing misty, she saw nothing clearly, her pulse beat a hundred to the minute and the blood throbbed at her heart. She could not assume that pose, which would have made her ridiculous, and she moved on almost fainting from excitement and trying with all her might to conceal it. And this was the very attitude that became her best. Before and behind them other visitors were entering, also talking in low tones and wearing ball-dresses. The mirrors on the landing reflected ladies in white, pale blue, and pink dresses, with diamonds and pearls on their bare necks and arms.

Natásha looked in the mirrors and could not distinguish her reflection from the others. All was blent into one

brilliant procession. On entering the ball-room the regular
hum of voices, footsteps, and greetings deafened Natásha,
and the light and glitter dazzled her still more. The host
and hostess, who had already been standing at the door
for half an hour repeating the same words to the various
arrivals, '*Charmé de vous voir*,'[1] greeted the Rostóvs and
Perónskaya in the same manner.

The two girls in their white dresses, each with a rose in
her black hair, both curtsied in the same way, but the
hostess's eye involuntarily rested longer on the slim
Natásha. She looked at her and gave her alone a special
smile, in addition to her usual smile as hostess. Looking
at her she may have recalled the golden, irrevocable days
of her own girlhood and her own first ball. The host also
followed Natásha with his eyes and asked the count which
was his daughter.

'Charming!' said he, kissing the tips of his fingers.

In the ball-room guests stood crowding at the entrance
doors awaiting the Emperor. The countess took up a
position in one of the front rows of that crowd. Natásha
heard and felt that several people were asking about her
and looking at her. She realized that those noticing her
liked her, and this observation helped to calm her.

'There are some like ourselves and some worse,' she
thought.

Perónskaya was pointing out to the countess the most
important people at the ball.

'That is the Dutch ambassador, do you see? That
grey-haired man,' she said, indicating an old man with
a profusion of silver-grey curly hair, who was surrounded
by ladies laughing at something he said.

'Ah, here she is, the Queen of Petersburg, Countess
Bezúkhova,' said Perónskaya, indicating Hélène who had
just entered. 'How lovely! She is quite equal to Márya
Antónovna. See how the men, young and old, pay court
to her. Beautiful and clever . . . they say Prince —— is
quite mad about her. But see, those two, though not good-
looking, are even more run after.'

She pointed to a lady who was crossing the room
followed by a very plain daughter.

[1] 'Delighted to see you.'

'She is a splendid match, a millionairess,' said Perónskaya. 'And look, here come her suitors.'

'That is Bezúkhova's brother, Anatole Kurágin,' she said, indicating a handsome officer of the Horse Guards who passed by them with head erect, looking at something over the heads of the ladies. 'He's handsome, isn't he? I hear they will marry him to that rich girl. But your cousin, Drubetskóy, is also very attentive to her. They say she has millions. Oh yes, that's the French ambassador himself!' she replied to the countess's inquiry about Caulaincourt. 'Looks as if he were a king! All the same, the French are charming, very charming. No one more charming in society. Ah, here she is! Yes, she is still the most beautiful of them all, our Márya Antónovna! And how simply she is dressed! Lovely! And that stout one in spectacles is the universal Freemason,' she went on, indicating Pierre. 'Put him beside his wife and he looks a regular buffoon!'

Pierre, swaying his stout body, advanced making way through the crowd and nodding to right and left as casually and good-naturedly as if he were passing through a crowd at a fair. He pushed through, evidently looking for some one.

Natásha looked joyfully at the familiar face of Pierre, 'the buffoon', as Perónskaya had called him, and knew he was looking for them, and for her in particular. He had promised to be at the ball and introduce partners to her.

But before he reached them Pierre stopped beside a very handsome, dark man of middle height, and in a white uniform, who stood by a window talking to a tall man wearing stars and a ribbon. Natásha at once recognized the shorter and younger man in the white uniform: it was Bolkónski, who seemed to her to have grown much younger, happier, and better-looking.

'There's some one else we know—Bolkónski, do you see, Mamma?' said Natásha, pointing out Prince Andrew. 'You remember, he stayed a night with us at Otrádnoe.'

'Oh, you know him?' said Perónskaya. 'I can't bear him. *Il fait à présent la pluie et le beau temps.*[1] He's too

[1] 'Wet and fine weather depend now on him.' A French proverb meaning that he has great success.

proud for anything. Takes after his father. And he's
hand in glove with Speránski, writing some projects or
other. Just look how he treats the ladies! There's one
talking to him and he has turned away,' she said, pointing
at him. 'I'd give it him if he treated me as he does those
ladies.'

CHAPTER XVI

SUDDENLY everybody stirred, began talking, and
pressed forward and then back, and between the two
rows, which separated, the Emperor entered to the
sounds of music that had immediately struck up. Behind
him walked his host and hostess. He walked in rapidly,
bowing to right and left as if anxious to get the first
moments of the reception over. The band played the
polonaise in vogue at that time on account of the words
that had been set to it, beginning: 'Alexander, Elisaveta,
all our hearts you ravish quite . . .' The Emperor passed
on to the drawing-room, the crowd made a rush for the
doors, and several persons with excited faces hurried
there and back again. Then the crowd hastily retired
from the drawing-room door, at which the Emperor
reappeared talking to the hostess. A young man, looking
distraught, pounced down on the ladies, asking them to
move aside. Some ladies, with faces betraying complete
forgetfulness of all the rules of decorum, pushed forward
to the detriment of their toilets. The men began to choose
partners and take their places for the polonaise.

Every one moved back, and the Emperor came smiling
out of the drawing-room leading his hostess by the hand
but not keeping time to the music. The host followed
with Márya Antónovna Narýshkina; then came ambassadors, ministers, and various generals, whom Perónskaya
diligently named. More than half the ladies already had
partners and were taking up, or preparing to take up, their
positions for the polonaise. Natásha felt that she would
be left with her mother and Sónya among a minority of
women who crowded near the wall, not having been
invited to dance. She stood with her slender arms hanging down, her scarcely defined bosom rising and falling

regularly, and with bated breath and glittering, frightened eyes gazed straight before her, evidently prepared for the height of joy or misery. She was not concerned about the Emperor, or any of those great people whom Perónskaya was pointing out—she had but one thought: 'Is it possible no one will ask me, that I shall not be among the first to dance? Is it possible that not one of all these men will notice me? They do not even seem to see me, or if they do, they look as if they were saying, "Ah, she's not the one I'm after, so it's not worth looking at her!" No, it's impossible,' she thought. 'They must know how I long to dance, how splendidly I dance, and how they would enjoy dancing with me.'

The strains of the polonaise, which had continued for a considerable time, had begun to sound like a sad reminiscence in Natásha's ears. She wanted to cry. Perónskaya had left them. The count was at the other end of the room. She and the countess and Sónya were standing by themselves as in the depths of a forest, amid that crowd of strangers, with no one interested in them and not wanted by any one. Prince Andrew with a lady passed by, evidently not recognizing them. The handsome Anatole was smilingly talking to a partner on his arm, and looked at Natásha as one looks at a wall. Borís passed them twice and each time turned away. Berg and his wife, who were not dancing, came up to them.

This family gathering seemed humiliating to Natásha —as if there were nowhere else for the family to talk but here at the ball. She did not listen to or look at Véra, who was telling her something about her own green dress.

At last the Emperor stopped beside his last partner (he had danced with three) and the music ceased. A worried aide-de-camp ran up to the Rostóvs requesting them to stand farther back, though as it was they were already close to the wall, and from the gallery resounded the distinct, precise, enticingly rhythmical strains of a valse. The Emperor looked smilingly down the room. A minute passed but no one had yet begun dancing. An aide-de-camp, the Master of Ceremonies, went up to Countess

Bezúkhova and asked her to dance. She smilingly raised her hand and laid it on his shoulder without looking at him. The aide-de-camp, an adept in his art, grasping his partner firmly round her waist, with confident delibera-tion started smoothly, gliding first round the edge of the circle, then at the corner of the room he caught Hélène's left hand and turned her, the only sound audible, apart from the ever-quickening music, being the rhythmic click of the spurs on his rapid, agile feet, while at every third beat his partner's velvet dress spread out and seemed to flash as she whirled round. Natásha gazed at them and was ready to cry because it was not she who was dancing that first turn of the valse.

Prince Andrew, in the white uniform of a cavalry colonel, wearing stockings and dancing shoes, stood look-ing animated and bright in the front row of the circle not far from the Rostóvs. Baron Firhoff was talking to him about the first sitting of the Council of State to be held next day. Prince Andrew, as one closely connected with Speránski and participating in the work of the legis-lative commission, could give reliable information about that sitting, concerning which various rumours were current. But not listening to what Firhoff was saying, he was gazing now at the sovereign, and now at the men intending to dance who had not yet gathered courage to enter the circle.

Prince Andrew was watching these men abashed by the Emperor's presence, and the women who were breathlessly longing to be asked to dance.

Pierre came up to him and caught him by the arm.

'You always dance. I have a protégée, the young Rostóva, here. Ask her,' he said.

'Where is she?' asked Bolkónski. 'Excuse me!' he added, turning to the baron, 'we will finish this conver-sation elsewhere—at a ball one must dance.' He stepped forward in the direction Pierre indicated. The despair-ing, dejected expression of Natásha's face caught his eye. He recognized her, guessed her feelings, saw that it was her début, remembered her conversation at the window, and with an expression of pleasure on his face approached Countess Rostóva.

'Allow me to introduce you to my daughter,' said the countess, with heightened colour.

'I have the pleasure of being already acquainted, if the Countess remembers me,' said Prince Andrew with a low and courteous bow quite belying Perónskaya's remarks about his rudeness, and approaching Natásha he held out his arm to grasp her waist before he had completed his invitation. He asked her to valse. That tremulous expression on Natásha's face, prepared either for despair or rapture, suddenly brightened into a happy, grateful, childlike smile.

'I have long been waiting for you,' that frightened happy little girl seemed to say by the smile that replaced the threatened tears, as she raised her hand to Prince Andrew's shoulder. They were the second couple to enter the circle. Prince Andrew was one of the best dancers of his day and Natásha danced exquisitely. Her little feet in their white satin dancing-shoes did their work swiftly, lightly, and independently of herself, while her face beamed with ecstatic happiness. Her slender bare arms and neck were not beautiful—compared to Hélène's her shoulders looked thin and her bosom undeveloped. But Hélène seemed, as it were, hardened by a varnish left by the thousands of looks that had scanned her person, while Natásha was like a girl exposed for the first time, who would have felt very much ashamed had she not been assured that this was absolutely necessary.

Prince Andrew liked dancing, and wishing to escape as quickly as possible from the political and clever talk which every one addressed to him, wishing also to break up the circle of restraint he disliked, caused by the Emperor's presence, he danced, and had chosen Natásha because Pierre pointed her out to him and because she was the first pretty girl who caught his eye; but scarcely had he embraced that slender supple figure, and felt her stirring so close to him and smiling so near him, than the wine of her charm rose to his head, and he felt himself revived and rejuvenated when after leaving her he stood breathing deeply and watching the other dancers.

CHAPTER XVII

AFTER Prince Andrew, Borís came up to ask Natásha for a dance, and then the aide-de-camp who had opened the ball, and several other young men, so that, flushed and happy, and passing on her superfluous partners to Sónya, she did not cease dancing all the evening. She noticed and saw nothing of what occupied every one else. Not only did she fail to notice that the Emperor talked a long time with the French ambassador, and how particularly gracious he was to a certain lady, or that Prince So-and-so and So-and-so did and said this and that, and that Hélène had great success and was honoured by the special attention of So-and-so, but she did not even see the Emperor, and only noticed that he had gone because the ball became livelier after his departure. For one of the merry cotillions before supper Prince Andrew was again her partner. He reminded her of their first encounter in the Otrádnoe avenue, and how she had been unable to sleep that moonlight night, and told her how he had involuntarily overheard her. Natásha blushed at that recollection and tried to excuse herself, as if there had been something to be ashamed of in what Prince Andrew had overheard.

Like all men who have grown up in society, Prince Andrew liked meeting some one there not of the conventional society stamp. And such was Natásha, with her surprise, her delight, her shyness, and even her mistakes in speaking French. With her he behaved with special care and tenderness, sitting beside her and talking of the simplest and most unimportant matters; he admired the joyous brightness of her eyes and smile, which related not to what was said but to her own happiness. When she was chosen by a dancer, and rose with a smile and danced round the room, Prince Andrew particularly admired her shy grace. In the middle of the cotillion, having completed one of the figures, Natásha, still out of breath, was returning to her seat when another dancer chose her. She was tired and panting and evidently thought of declining, but immediately put her hand gaily on the man's shoulder, smiling at Prince Andrew.

'I'd be glad to sit beside you and rest: I'm tired; but you see how they keep asking me, and I'm glad of it, I'm happy and I love everybody, and you and I understand it all,' and much, much more was said in her smile. When her partner left her, Natásha ran across the room to choose two ladies for the figure.

'If she goes to her cousin first and then to another lady, she will be my wife,' said Prince Andrew to himself, quite to his own surprise, as he watched her. She did go first to her cousin.

'What rubbish sometimes enters one's head!' thought Prince Andrew, 'but what is certain is that that girl is so charming, so original, that she won't be dancing here a month before she will be married . . . Such as she are rare here,' he thought, as Natásha, readjusting a rose that was slipping on her bodice, settled herself beside him.

When the cotillion was over the old count in his blue coat came up to the dancers. He invited Prince Andrew to come and see them, and asked his daughter whether she was enjoying herself. Natásha did not answer at once, but only looked up with a smile that said reproachfully: 'How can you ask such a question?'

'I have never enjoyed myself so much before!' she said, and Prince Andrew noticed how her thin arms rose quickly as if to embrace her father, and instantly dropped again. Natásha was happier than she had ever been in her life. She was at that height of bliss when one becomes completely kind and good, and does not believe in the possibility of evil, unhappiness, or sorrow.

At that ball Pierre for the first time felt humiliated by the position his wife occupied in court circles. He was gloomy and absent-minded. A deep furrow ran across his forehead, and standing by a window he stared over his spectacles seeing no one.

On her way to supper Natásha passed him.

Pierre's gloomy, unhappy look struck her. She stopped in front of him. She wished to help him, to bestow on him the superabundance of her own happiness.

'How delightful it is, Count!' said she. 'Isn't it?'

Pierre smiled absent-mindedly, evidently not grasping what she said.

'Yes, I am very glad,' he said.

'How can people be dissatisfied with anything?' thought Natásha. 'Especially such a capital fellow as Bezúkhov!' In Natásha's eyes all the people at the ball alike were good, kind, and splendid people, loving one another; none of them capable of injuring another—and so they ought all to be happy.

CHAPTER XVIII

NEXT day Prince Andrew thought of the ball, but his mind did not dwell on it long. 'Yes, it was a very brilliant ball,' and then . . . 'Yes, that little Rostóva is very charming. There's something fresh, original, un-Petersburg-like about her that distinguishes her.' That was all he thought about yesterday's ball, and after his morning tea he set to work.

But either from fatigue or want of sleep he was ill-disposed for work and could get nothing done. He kept criticizing his own work as he often did, and was glad when he heard some one coming.

The visitor was Bítski, who served on various committees, frequented all the societies in Petersburg, and was a passionate devotee of the new ideas and of Speránski, and a diligent Petersburg newsmonger—one of those men who choose their opinions like their clothes, according to the fashion, but who for that very reason appear to be the warmest partisans. Hardly had he got rid of his hat before he ran into Prince Andrew's room with a preoccupied air and at once began talking. He had just heard particulars of that morning's sitting of the Council of State opened by the Emperor, and he spoke of it enthusiastically. The Emperor's speech had been extraordinary. It had been a speech such as only constitutional monarchs deliver. 'The sovereign plainly said that the Council and Senate are *estates* of the realm, he said that the government must rest not on authority but on secure bases. The Emperor said that the fiscal system must be reorganized and the accounts published,' recounted Bítski, emphasizing certain words and opening his eyes significantly.

'Ah, yes! To-day's events mark an epoch, the greatest epoch in our history,' he concluded.

Prince Andrew listened to the account of the opening of the Council of State, which he had so impatiently awaited and to which he had attached such importance, and was surprised that this event, now that it had taken place, did not affect him, and even seemed quite insignificant. He listened with quiet irony to Bítski's enthusiastic account of it. A very simple thought occurred to him: 'What does it matter to me or to Bítski what the Emperor was pleased to say at the Council? Can all that make me any happier or better?'

And this simple reflection suddenly destroyed all the interest Prince Andrew had felt in the impending reforms. He was going to dine that evening at Speránski's, 'with only a few friends,' as the host had said when inviting him. The prospect of that dinner in the intimate home circle of the man he so admired, had greatly interested Prince Andrew, especially as he had not yet seen Speránski in his domestic surroundings, but now he felt disinclined to go to it.

At the appointed hour however he entered the modest house Speránski owned in the Taurida Gardens. In the parqueted dining-room of this small house, remarkable for its extreme cleanliness (suggesting that of a monastery), Prince Andrew, who was rather late, found the friendly gathering of Speránski's intimate acquaintances already assembled at five o'clock. There were no ladies present except Speránski's little daughter (long-faced like her father) and her governess. The other guests were Gervais, Magnítski, and Stolýpin. While still in the anteroom, Prince Andrew heard loud voices and a ringing staccato laugh—a laugh such as one hears on the stage. Some one—it sounded like Speránski—was distinctly ejaculating ha-ha-ha. Prince Andrew had never before heard Speránski's famous laugh, and this ringing, high-pitched laughter from a statesman made a strange impression on him.

He entered the dining-room. The whole company were standing between two windows, at a small table laid with hors-d'œuvres. Speránski, wearing a grey swallow-tail coat with a star on the breast, and evidently still the same waistcoat and high white stock he had worn at the meeting of the Council of State, stood at the table with a beaming countenance. His guests surrounded him. Magnítski, addressing himself to Speránski, was relating an anecdote, and Speránski was laughing in advance at what Magnítski was going to say. When Prince Andrew entered the room Magnítski's words were again drowned by laughter. Stolýpin gave a deep bass guffaw as he munched a piece of bread and cheese. Gervais laughed softly with a hissing chuckle, and Speránski in a high-pitched staccato manner.

Still laughing, Speránski held out his soft white hand to Prince Andrew.

'Very pleased to see you, Prince,' he said. 'One moment . . .' he went on, turning to Magnítski and inter-rupting his story. 'We have agreed that this is a dinner for recreation, with not a word about business!' and turning again to the narrator he began to laugh afresh.

Prince Andrew looked at the laughing Speránski with astonishment, regret, and disillusionment. It seemed to him that this was not Speránski but some one else. Everything that had formerly appeared mysterious and fascinating in Speránski suddenly became plain and unattractive.

At dinner the conversation did not cease for a moment, and seemed to consist of the contents of a book of funny anecdotes. Before Magnítski had finished his story, some one else was anxious to relate something still funnier. Most of the anecdotes, if not relating to the State service, related to people in the service. It seemed that in this company the insignificance of those people was so definitely accepted that the only possible attitude towards them was one of good-humoured ridicule. Speránski related how at the Council that morning, a deaf dignitary, when asked his opinion, replied that he thought so too. Gervais gave a long account of an official revision, remarkable for the stupidity of everybody concerned. Stolýpin, stuttering, broke into the conversation and began excitedly talking of the abuses that existed under the former order of things—threatening to give a serious turn to the conversation. Magnítski starting quizzing Stolýpin about his vehemence. Gervais intervened with a joke, and the talk reverted to its former lively tone.

Evidently Speránski liked to rest after his labours and find amusement in a circle of friends, and his guests, understanding his wish, tried to enliven him and amuse themselves. But their gaiety seemed to Prince Andrew mirthless and tiresome. Speránski's high-pitched voice struck him unpleasantly, and the incessant laughter grated on him like a false note. Prince Andrew did not laugh and feared that he would be a damper on the spirits of the company, but no one took any notice of his being out of harmony with the general mood. They all seemed very gay.

He tried several times to join in the conversation, but his remarks were tossed aside each time like a cork thrown out of the water, and he could not jest with them.

There was nothing wrong or unseemly in what they said, it was witty, and might have been funny, but it lacked just that something which is the salt of mirth, and they were not even aware that such a thing existed.

After dinner Speránski's daughter and her governess rose. He patted the little girl with his white hand and kissed her. And that gesture, too, seemed unnatural to Prince Andrew.

The men remained at table over their port—English fashion. In the midst of a conversation that was started about Napoleon's Spanish affairs, which they all agreed in approving, Prince Andrew began to express a contrary opinion. Speránski smiled and, with an evident wish to prevent the conversation from taking an unpleasant course, told a story that had no connexion with the previous conversation. For a few moments all were silent.

Having sat some time at table, Speránski corked a bottle of wine, and remarking, 'Nowadays good wine rides in a carriage and pair,' passed it to the servant and got up. All rose, and continuing to talk loudly went into the

drawing-room. Two letters brought by a courier were
handed to Speránski, and he took them to his study. As
soon as he had left the room the general merriment
stopped and the guests began to converse sensibly and
quietly with one another.

'Now for the recitation!' said Speránski on returning
from his study. 'A wonderful talent!' he said to Prince
Andrew, and Magnítski immediately assumed a pose and
began reciting some humorous verses in French which he
had composed about various well-known Petersburg
people. He was interrupted several times by applause.
When the verses were finished, Prince Andrew went up
to Speránski and took his leave.

'Where are you off to so early?' asked Speránski.

'I promised to go to a reception.'

They said no more. Prince Andrew looked closely into
those mirror-like, impenetrable eyes, and felt that it had
been ridiculous of him to have expected anything from
Speránski and from any of his own activities connected
with him, or ever to have attributed importance to what
Speránski was doing. That precise, mirthless laughter
rang in Prince Andrew's ears long after he had left
the house.

When he reached home Prince Andrew began thinking
of his life in Petersburg during those last four months, as
if it were something new. He recalled his exertions and
solicitations, and the history of his project of army reform,
which had been accepted for consideration and which
they were trying to pass over in silence simply because
another, a very poor one, had already been prepared and
submitted to the Emperor. He thought of the meetings
of a committee of which Berg was a member. He remembered how carefully and at what length everything relating
to form and procedure was discussed at those meetings,
and how sedulously and promptly all that related to
the gist of the business was evaded. He recalled his
labours on the Legal Code, and how painstakingly he had
translated the articles of the Roman and French codes
into Russian, and he felt ashamed of himself. Then he
vividly pictured to himself Boguchárovo, his occupations
in the country, his journey to Ryazán, he remembered

the peasants, and Dron the village elder, and mentally applying to them the Personal Rights he had divided into paragraphs, he felt astonished that he could have spent so much time on such useless work.

CHAPTER XIX

NEXT day Prince Andrew called at a few houses he had not visited before, and among them at the Rostóvs' with whom he had renewed acquaintance at the ball. Apart from considerations of politeness which demanded the call, he wanted to see that original, eager girl who had left such a pleasant impression on his mind, in her own home.

Natásha was one of the first to meet him. She was wearing a dark blue house dress, in which Prince Andrew thought her even prettier than in her ball-dress. She and all the Rostóv family welcomed him as an old friend, simply and cordially. The whole family, whom he had formerly judged severely, now seemed to him to consist of excellent, simple, and kindly people. The old count's hospitality and good nature, which struck one especially in Petersburg as a pleasant surprise, were such that Prince Andrew could not refuse to stay to dinner. 'Yes,' he thought, 'they are capital people, who of course have not the slightest idea what a treasure they possess in Natásha; but they are kindly folk and form the best possible setting for this strikingly poetic, charming girl, overflowing with life!'

In Natásha Prince Andrew was conscious of a strange world completely alien to him and brimful of joys unknown to him, a different world that in the Otrádnoe avenue and at the window that moonlight night had already begun to disconcert him. Now this world disconcerted him no longer and was no longer alien to him, but he himself, having entered it, found in it a new enjoyment.

After dinner Natásha, at Prince Andrew's request, went to the clavichord and began singing. Prince Andrew stood by a window talking to the ladies and listened to her. In the midst of a phrase he ceased speaking and

suddenly felt tears choking him, a thing he had thought
impossible for him. He looked at Natásha as she sang,
and something new and joyful stirred in his soul. He felt
happy and at the same time sad. He had absolutely
nothing to weep about yet he was ready to weep. What
about? His former love? The little princess? His dis-
illusionments? . . . His hopes for the future? . . . Yes
and no. The chief reason was a sudden, vivid sense of
the terrible contrast between something infinitely great
and illimitable within him, and that limited and material
something that he, and even she, was. This contrast
weighed on and yet cheered him while she sang.

As soon as Natásha had finished she went up to him
and asked how he liked her voice. She asked this and
then became confused, feeling that she ought not to have
asked it. He smiled, looking at her, and said he liked
her singing as he liked everything she did.

Prince Andrew left the Rostóvs' late in the evening.
He went to bed from habit, but soon realized that he
could not sleep. Having lit his candle he sat up in bed,
then got up, then lay down again but not at all troubled by
his sleeplessness: his soul was as fresh and joyful as if he
had stepped out of a stuffy room into God's own fresh
air. It did not enter his head that he was in love with
Natásha, he was not thinking about her, but only
picturing her to himself, and in consequence all life
appeared in a new light. 'Why do I strive, why do I toil
in this narrow, confined frame, when life, all life with all
its joys, is open to me?' said he to himself. And for the
first time for a very long while he began making happy
plans for the future. He decided that he must attend to
his son's education by finding a tutor and putting the boy
in his charge, then he ought to retire from the service and
go abroad, and see England, Switzerland, and Italy. 'I
must use my freedom while I feel so much strength and
youth in me,' he said to himself. 'Pierre was right when
he said one must believe in the possibility of happiness in
order to be happy, and now I do believe in it. Let the
dead bury their dead, but while one has life one must live
and be happy!' thought he.

CHAPTER XX

ONE morning Colonel Adolf Berg, whom Pierre knew as he knew everybody in Moscow and Petersburg, came to see him. Berg arrived in an immaculate brand-new uniform, with his hair pomaded and brushed forward over his temples as the Emperor Alexander wore his hair.

'I have just been to see the countess, your wife. Unfortunately she could not grant my request, but I hope, Count, I shall be more fortunate with you,' he said with a smile.

'What is it you wish, Colonel? I am at your service.'

'I have now quite settled in my new rooms, Count,' (Berg said this with perfect conviction that this information could not but be agreeable) 'and so I wish to arrange just a small party for my own and my wife's friends.' (He smiled still more pleasantly.) 'I wished to ask the countess and you to do me the honour of coming to tea and to supper.'

Only Countess Hélène, considering the society of such people as the Bergs beneath her, could be cruel enough to refuse such an invitation. Berg explained so clearly why he wanted to collect at his house a small but select company, and why this would give him pleasure, and why though he grudged spending money on cards or anything harmful, he was prepared to run into some expense for the sake of good society—that Pierre could not refuse, and promised to come.

'But don't be late, Count, if I may venture to ask; about ten minutes to eight, please. We shall make up a rubber. Our general is coming. He is very good to me. We shall have supper, Count. So you will do me the favour.'

Contrary to his habit of being late, Pierre on that day arrived at the Bergs' house, not at ten but at fifteen minutes to eight.

Having prepared everything necessary for the party, the Bergs were ready for their guests' arrival.

In their new, clean, and light study, with its small busts and pictures and new furniture, sat Berg and his wife. Berg, closely buttoned up in his new uniform, sat beside his wife, explaining to her that one always could and should be acquainted with people above one, because only then does one get satisfaction from acquaintances.

'You can get to know something, you can ask for something. See how I managed from my first promotion.' (Berg measured his life not by years but by promotions.) 'My comrades are still nobodies, while I am only waiting for a vacancy to command a regiment, and have the happiness to be your husband.' (He rose and kissed Véra's hand, and on the way to her straightened out a turned-up corner of the carpet.) 'And how have I obtained all this? Chiefly by knowing how to choose my acquaintances. It goes without saying that one must be conscientious and methodical.'

Berg smiled with a sense of his superiority over a weak woman, and paused, reflecting that this dear wife of his was after all but a weak woman who could not understand all that constitutes a man's dignity, what it was *ein Mann zu sein.*[1] Véra at the same time was smiling with a sense of superiority over her good, conscientious husband, who all the same understood life wrongly as, according to Véra, all men did. Berg, judging by his wife, thought all women weak and foolish. Véra, judging only by her husband and generalizing from that observation, supposed that all men, though they understand nothing and are conceited and selfish, ascribe common sense to themselves alone.

Berg rose and embraced his wife carefully, so as not to crush her lace fichu for which he had paid a good price, kissing her straight on the lips.

'The only thing is, we mustn't have children too soon,' he continued, following an unconscious sequence of ideas.

'Yes,' answered Véra, 'I don't at all want that. We must live for society.'

'Princess Yusúpova wore one exactly like this,' said Berg, pointing to the fichu with a happy and kindly smile.

Just then Count Bezúkhov was announced. Husband and wife glanced at one another, both smiling with self-satisfaction, and each mentally claiming the honour of this visit.

[1] to be a man.

'This is what comes of knowing how to make acquaintances,' thought Berg. 'This is what comes of knowing how to conduct oneself.'

'But please don't interrupt me when I am entertaining the guests,' said Véra, 'because I know what interests each of them and what to say to different people.'

Berg smiled again.

'It can't be helped: men must sometimes have masculine conversation,' said he.

They received Pierre in their small, new drawing-room, where it was impossible to sit down anywhere without disturbing its symmetry, neatness, and order; so it was quite comprehensible and not strange that Berg, having generously offered to disturb the symmetry of an arm-chair or of the sofa for his dear guest, but being apparently painfully undecided on the matter himself, eventually left the visitor to settle the question of selection. Pierre disturbed the symmetry by moving a chair for himself, and Berg and Véra immediately began their evening party, interrupting each other in their efforts to entertain their guest.

Véra, having decided in her own mind that Pierre ought to be entertained with conversation about the French embassy, at once began accordingly. Berg, having decided that masculine conversation was required, interrupted his wife's remarks and touched on the question of the war with Austria, and unconsciously jumped from the general subject to personal considerations as to the proposals made him to take part in the Austrian campaign, and the reasons why he had declined them. Though the conversation was very incoherent and Véra was angry at the intrusion of the masculine element, both husband and wife felt with satisfaction that, even if only one guest was present, their evening had begun very well and was as like as two peas to every other evening party with its talk, tea, and lighted candles.

Before long Borís, Berg's old comrade, arrived. There was a shade of condescension and patronage in his treatment of Berg and Véra. After Borís came a lady with the colonel, then the general himself, then the Rostóvs, and the party became unquestionably exactly like all other evening parties. Berg and Véra could not repress their smiles of satisfaction at the sight of all this movement in their drawing-room, at the sound of the disconnected talk, the rustling of dresses, and the bowing and scraping. Everything was just as everybody always has it, especially so the general, who admired the apartment, patted Berg on the shoulder, and with parental authority superintended the setting out of the table for boston. The general sat down by Count Ilyá Rostóv, who was next to himself the most important guest. The old people sat with the old, the young with the young, and the hostess at the tea-table, on which stood exactly the same kind of cakes in a silver cake-basket as the Pánins had at their party. Everything was just as it was everywhere else.

CHAPTER XXI

PIERRE, as one of the principal guests, had to sit down to boston with Count Rostóv, the general, and the colonel. At the card-table he happened to be directly facing Natásha, and was struck by a curious change that had come over her since the ball. She was silent, and not only less pretty than at the ball, but only redeemed from plainness by her look of gentle indifference to everything around.

'What's the matter with her?' thought Pierre, glancing at her. She was sitting by her sister at the tea-table, and reluctantly, without looking at him, made some reply to Borís who sat down beside her. After playing out a whole suit and to his partner's delight taking five tricks, Pierre, hearing greetings and the steps of some one who had entered the room while he was picking up his tricks, glanced again at Natásha.

'What has happened to her?' he asked himself with still greater surprise.

Prince Andrew was standing before her, saying something to her with a look of tender solicitude. She having raised her head, was looking up at him, flushed and evidently trying to master her rapid breathing. And the bright glow of some inner fire that had been suppressed was again alight in her. She was completely transformed, and from a plain girl had again become what she had been at the ball.

Prince Andrew went up to Pierre, and the latter noticed a new and youthful expression in his friend's face.

Pierre changed places several times during the game, sitting now with his back to Natásha and now facing her, but during the whole of the six rubbers he watched her and his friend.

'Something very important is happening between them,' thought Pierre, and a feeling that was both joyful and painful agitated him and made him neglect the game.

After six rubbers the general got up, saying that it was no use playing like that, and Pierre was released. Natásha on one side was talking with Sónya and Borís, and Véra with a subtle smile was saying something to Prince Andrew. Pierre went up to his friend, and asking whether they were talking secrets, sat down beside them. Véra having noticed Prince Andrew's attentions to Natásha, decided that at a party, a real evening party, subtle allusions to the tender passion were absolutely necessary, and seizing a moment when Prince Andrew was alone, began a conversation with him about feelings in general and about her sister. With so intellectual a guest as she considered Prince Andrew to be, she felt that she had to employ her diplomatic tact.

When Pierre went up to them he noticed that Véra was being carried away by her self-satisfied talk, but that Prince Andrew seemed embarrassed, a thing that rarely happened with him.

'What do you think?' Véra was saying with an arch smile. 'You are so discerning, Prince, and understand people's characters so well at a glance. What do you think of Natalie? Could she be constant in her attachments? Could she, like other women' (Véra meant herself) 'love a man once for all and remain true to him for ever? That is what I consider true love. What do you think, Prince?'

'I know your sister too little,' replied Prince Andrew,

with a sarcastic smile under which he wished to hide his embarrassment, 'to be able to solve so delicate a question, and then I have noticed that the less attractive a woman is the more constant she is likely to be,' he added, and looked up at Pierre who was just approaching them.

'Yes, that is true, Prince. In our days,' continued Véra —mentioning 'our days' as people of limited intelligence are fond of doing, imagining that they have discovered and appraised the peculiarities of 'our days' and that human characteristics change with the times—'In our days a girl has so much freedom that the pleasure of being courted often stifles real feeling in her. And it must be confessed that Natalie is very susceptible.' This return to the subject of Natalie caused Prince Andrew to knit his brows with discomfort: he was about to rise, but Véra continued with a still more subtle smile:

'I think no one has been more courted than she,' she went on, 'but till quite lately she never cared seriously for any one. Now you know, Count,' she said to Pierre, 'even our dear cousin Borís, who, between ourselves, was very far gone in the land of tenderness . . .' (alluding to a map of love much in vogue at that time).

Prince Andrew frowned and remained silent.

'You are friendly with Borís, aren't you?' asked Véra.

'Yes, I know him . . .'

'I expect he has told you of his childish love for Natásha?'

'Oh, there was a childish love?' suddenly asked Prince Andrew, blushing unexpectedly.

'Yes, you know between cousins intimacy often leads to love. *Le cousinage est un dangereux voisinage.*[1] Don't you think so?'

'Oh, undoubtedly!' said Prince Andrew, and with sudden and unnatural liveliness he began chaffing Pierre about the need to be very careful with his fifty-year-old Moscow cousins, and in the midst of these jesting remarks he rose, taking Pierre by the arm, and drew him aside.

'Well?' asked Pierre, seeing his friend's strange animation with surprise, and noticing the glance he turned on Natásha as he rose.

[1] 'Cousinhood is a dangerous neighbourhood.'

'I must . . . I must have a talk with you,' said Prince Andrew. 'You know that pair of women's gloves?' (He referred to the Masonic gloves given to a newly initiated Brother to present to the woman he loved.) 'I . . . but no, I will talk to you later on,' and with a strange light in his eyes and restlessness in his movements, Prince Andrew approached Natásha and sat down beside her. Pierre saw how Prince Andrew asked her something and how she flushed as she replied.

But at that moment Berg came to Pierre and began insisting that he should take part in an argument between the general and the colonel on the affairs in Spain.

Berg was satisfied and happy. The smile of pleasure never left his face. The party was very successful and quite like other parties he had seen. Everything was similar: the ladies' subtle talk, the cards, the general raising his voice at the card-table, and the samovar and the tea-cakes; only one thing was lacking that he had always seen at the evening parties he wished to imitate. They had not yet had a loud conversation among the men and a dispute about something important and clever. Now the general had begun such a discussion and so Berg drew Pierre to it.

CHAPTER XXII

NEXT day, having been invited by the count, Prince Andrew dined with the Rostóvs and spent the rest of the day there.

Every one in the house realized for whose sake Prince Andrew came, and without concealing it he tried to be with Natásha all day. Not only in the soul of the frightened yet happy and enraptured Natásha, but in the whole house, there was a feeling of awe at something important that was bound to happen. The countess looked with sad and sternly serious eyes at Prince Andrew when he talked to Natásha, and timidly started some artificial conversation about trifles as soon as he looked her way. Sónya was afraid to leave Natásha and afraid of being in the way when she was with them. Natásha grew pale, in a panic of expectation, when she remained alone with him for a moment. Prince Andrew surprised her by his timidity. She felt that he wanted to say something to her but could not bring himself to do so.

In the evening, when Prince Andrew had left, the countess went up to Natásha and whispered:

'Well, what?'

'Mamma! For heaven's sake don't ask me anything now! One can't talk about that,' said Natásha.

But all the same that night Natásha, now agitated and now frightened, lay a long time in her mother's bed gazing straight before her. She told her how he had complimented her, how he told her he was going abroad, asked her where they were going to spend the summer, and then how he had asked her about Borís.

'But such a . . . such a . . . never happened to me before!' she said. 'Only I feel afraid in his presence. I am always afraid when I'm with him. What does that mean? Does it mean that it's the real thing? Yes? Mamma, are you asleep?'

'No, my love; I am frightened myself,' answered her mother. 'Now go!'

'All the same I shan't sleep. What silliness, to sleep! Mummy! Mummy! such a thing never happened to me before,' she said, surprised and alarmed at the feeling she was aware of in herself. 'And could we ever have thought! . . .'

It seemed to Natásha that even at the time she first saw Prince Andrew at Otrádnoe, she had fallen in love with him. It was as if she feared this strange, unexpected happiness of meeting again the very man she had then chosen (she was firmly convinced she had done so), and of finding him, as it seemed, not indifferent to her.

'And it had to happen that he should come specially to Petersburg while we are here. And it had to happen that we should meet at that ball. It is fate. Clearly it is fate, that everything led up to this! Already *then*, directly I saw him I felt something peculiar.'

'What else did he say to you? What are those verses? Read them, . . .' said her mother, thoughtfully, referring to some verses Prince Andrew had written in Natásha's album.

'Mamma, one need not be ashamed of his being a widower?'

'Don't, Natásha! Pray to God. "Marriages are made in heaven",' said her mother.

'Darling Mummy, how I love you! How happy I am!' cried Natásha, shedding tears of joy and excitement, and embracing her mother.

At that very time Prince Andrew was sitting with Pierre and telling him of his love for Natásha and his firm resolve to make her his wife.

That day Countess Hélène had a reception at her house. The French ambassador was there, and a foreign Prince of the Blood who had of late become a frequent visitor of hers, and many brilliant ladies and gentlemen. Pierre, who had come downstairs, walked through the rooms and struck every one by his preoccupied, absent-minded and morose air.

Since the ball he had felt the approach of a fit of nervous depression and had made desperate efforts to combat it. Since the intimacy of his wife with the royal Prince, Pierre had unexpectedly been made a gentleman of the bedchamber, and from that time he had begun to feel oppressed and ashamed in court society, and dark thoughts of the vanity of all things human came to him oftener than before. At the same time the feeling he had noticed between his protégée Natásha and Prince Andrew accentuated his gloom by the contrast between his own position and his friend's. He tried equally to avoid thinking about his wife, and about Natásha and Prince Andrew; and again everything seemed to him insignificant in comparison with eternity; again the question: For what? presented itself; and he forced himself to work day and night at Masonic labours, hoping to drive away the evil spirit that threatened him. Towards midnight, after he had left the countess's apartments, he was sitting upstairs in a shabby dressing-gown, copying out the original transactions of the Scottish Lodge of Freemasons, at a table in his low room cloudy with tobacco smoke, when some one came in. It was Prince Andrew.

'Ah, it's you!' said Pierre with a preoccupied, dis-

satisfied air. 'And I, you see, am hard at it,' he pointed
to his manuscript-book with that air of escaping from the
ills of life with which unhappy people look at their work.

Prince Andrew, with a beaming, ecstatic expression of
renewed life on his face, paused in front of Pierre and, not
noticing his sad look, smiled at him with the egotism of
joy.

'Well, dear heart,' said he, 'I wanted to tell you about
it yesterday, and I have come to do so to-day. I never
experienced anything like it before. I am in love, my
friend!'

Suddenly Pierre heaved a deep sigh and dumped his
heavy person down on the sofa beside Prince Andrew.

'With Natásha Rostóva, yes?' said he.

'Yes, yes! Who else should it be? I should never have
believed it, but the feeling is stronger than I. Yesterday
I tormented myself and suffered, but I would not
exchange even that torment for anything in the world, I
have not lived till now. At last I live, but I can't live
without her! But can she love me? . . . I am too old for
her . . . Why don't you speak?'

'I? I? What did I tell you?' said Pierre suddenly,
rising and beginning to pace up and down the room.
'I always thought it . . . That girl is such a treasure . . .
she is a rare girl . . . My dear friend, I entreat you, don't
philosophize, don't doubt, marry, marry, marry . . . And
I am sure there will not be a happier man than you.'

'But what of her?'

'She loves you.'

'Don't talk rubbish, . . .' said Prince Andrew, smiling
and looking into Pierre's eyes.

'She does, I know,' Pierre cried fiercely.

'But do listen,' returned Prince Andrew, holding him
by the arm. 'Do you know the condition I am in? I must
talk about it to some one.'

'Well, go on, go on. I am very glad,' said Pierre, and
his face really changed, his brow became smooth, and
he listened gladly to Prince Andrew. Prince Andrew
seemed, and really was, quite a different, quite a new
man. Where was his spleen, his contempt for life, his
disillusionment? Pierre was the only person to whom he

made up his mind to speak openly; and to him he told all that was in his soul. Now he boldly and lightly made plans for an extended future, said he could not sacrifice his own happiness to his father's caprice, and spoke of how he would either make his father consent to this marriage and love her, or would do without his consent; then he marvelled at the feeling that had mastered him, as at something strange, apart from and independent of himself.

'I should not have believed any one who told me that I was capable of such love,' said Prince Andrew. 'It is not at all the same feeling that I knew in the past. The whole world is now for me divided into two halves: one half is she, and there all is joy, hope, light: the other half is everything where she is not, and there all is gloom and darkness . . .'

'Darkness and gloom,' reiterated Pierre; 'yes, yes, I understand that.'

'I cannot help loving the light, it is not my fault. And I am very happy! You understand me? I know you are glad for my sake.'

'Yes, yes,' Pierre assented, looking at his friend with a touched and sad expression in his eyes. The brighter Prince Andrew's lot appeared to him, the gloomier seemed his own.

CHAPTER XXIII

PRINCE ANDREW needed his father's consent to his marriage, and to obtain this he started for the country next day.

His father received his son's communication with external composure, but inward wrath. He could not comprehend how any one could wish to alter his life or introduce anything new into it, when his own life was already ending. 'If only they would let me end my days as I want to,' thought the old man, 'then they might do as they please.' With his son however he employed the diplomacy he reserved for important occasions and, adopting a quiet tone, discussed the whole matter.

In the first place the marriage was not a brilliant one

as regards birth, wealth, or rank. Secondly, Prince Andrew was no longer as young as he had been and his health was poor (the old man laid special stress on this), while she was very young. Thirdly, he had a son whom it would be a pity to entrust to a chit of a girl. 'Fourthly and finally,' the father said, looking ironically at his son, 'I beg you to put it off for a year: go abroad, take a cure, look out, as you wanted to, for a German tutor for Prince Nicholas. Then if your love or passion or obstinacy—as you please—is still as great, marry! And that's my last word on it. Mind, the last! . . .' concluded the prince, in a tone which showed that nothing would make him alter his decision.

Prince Andrew saw clearly that the old man hoped that his feelings, or his fiancée's, would not stand a year's test, or that he (the old prince himself) would die before then, and he decided to conform to his father's wish—to propose, and postpone the wedding for a year.

Three weeks after the last evening he had spent with the Rostóvs, Prince Andrew returned to Petersburg.

Next day after her talk with her mother Natásha expected Bolkónski all day, but he did not come. On the second and third day it was the same. Pierre did not come either and Natásha, not knowing that Prince Andrew had gone to see his father, could not explain his absence to herself.

Three weeks passed in this way. Natásha had no desire to go out anywhere, and wandered from room to room like a shadow, idle and listless; she wept secretly at night and did not go to her mother in the evenings. She blushed continually and was irritable. It seemed to her that everybody knew about her disappointment, and was laughing at her and pitying her. Strong as was her inward grief, this wound to her vanity intensified her misery.

Once she came to her mother, tried to say something, and suddenly began to cry. Her tears were those of an offended child who does not know why it is being punished.

The countess began to soothe Natásha, who after first listening to her mother's words, suddenly interrupted her:

'Leave off, mamma! I don't think, and don't want to think about it! He just came and then left off, left off . . .'

Her voice trembled, and she again nearly cried, but recovered and went on quietly:

'And I don't at all want to get married. And I am afraid of him; I have now become quite, quite calm.'

The day after this conversation Natásha put on the old dress which she knew had the peculiar property of conducing to cheerfulness in the mornings, and that day she returned to the old way of life which she had abandoned since the ball. Having finished her morning tea she went to the ball-room, which she particularly liked for its loud resonance, and began singing her solfeggio. When she had finished her first exercise she stood still in the middle of the room and sang a musical phrase that particularly pleased her. She listened joyfully (as though she had not expected it) to the charm of the notes reverberating, filling the whole empty ball-room, and slowly dying away; and all at once she felt cheerful. 'What's the good of making so much of it? Things are nice as it is,' she said to herself, and she began walking up and down the room, not stepping simply on the resounding parquet but treading with each step from the heel to the toe (she had on a new and favourite pair of shoes) and listening to the regular tap of the heel and creak of the toe as gladly as she had to the sounds of her own voice. Passing a mirror she glanced into it. 'There, that's me!' the expression of her face seemed to say as she caught sight of herself. 'Well, and very nice too! I need nobody.'

A footman wanted to come in to clear away something in the room, but she would not let him, and having closed the door behind him continued her walk. That morning she had returned to her favourite mood—love of, and delight in, herself. 'How charming that Natásha is!' she said again, speaking as some third, collective, male person. 'Pretty, a good voice, young, and in nobody's way if only they leave her in peace.' But however much they left her in peace, she could not now be at peace, and immediately felt this.

In the hall the porch-door opened, and some one asked, 'At home?' and then footsteps were heard. Natásha was looking at the mirror, but did not see herself. She listened to the sounds in the hall. When she saw herself, her face was pale. It was *he*. She knew this for certain, though she hardly heard his voice through the closed doors.

Pale and agitated, Natásha ran into the drawing-room.

'Mamma! Bolkónski has come!' she said. 'Mamma, it is awful, it is unbearable! I don't want . . . to be tormented! What am I to do? . . .'

Before the countess could answer, Prince Andrew entered the room with an agitated and serious face. As soon as he saw Natásha his face brightened. He kissed the countess's hand and Natásha's, and sat down beside the sofa.

'It is long since we had the pleasure . . .' began the countess, but Prince Andrew interrupted her by answering her intended question, obviously in haste to say what he had to.

'I have not been to see you all this time because I have been at my father's. I had to talk over a very important matter with him. I only got back last night,' he said, glancing at Natásha; 'I want to have a talk with you, Countess,' he added after a moment's pause.

The countess lowered her eyes, sighing deeply.

'I am at your disposal,' she murmured.

Natásha knew that she ought to go away, but was unable to do so: something gripped her throat, and regardless of manners she stared straight at Prince Andrew with wide-open eyes.

'At once? This instant! . . . No, it can't be!' she thought.

Again he glanced at her, and that glance convinced her that she was not mistaken. Yes, at once, that very instant, her fate would be decided.

'Go, Natásha! I will call you,' said the countess in a whisper.

Natásha glanced with frightened imploring eyes at Prince Andrew and at her mother, and went out.

'I have come, Countess, to ask for your daughter's hand,' said Prince Andrew.

The countess's face flushed hotly, but she said nothing.

'Your offer . . .' she began at last sedately. He remained silent, looking into her eyes. 'Your offer . . .' (she grew confused) 'is agreeable to us, and . . . I accept your offer. I am glad. And my husband . . . I hope . . . but it will depend on her . . .'

'I will speak to her when I have your consent . . . Do you give it to me?' said Prince Andrew.

'Yes,' replied the countess. She held out her hand to him, and with a mixed feeling of estrangement and tenderness pressed her lips to his forehead as he stooped to kiss her hand. She wished to love him as a son, but felt that to her he was a stranger and a terrifying man. 'I am sure my husband will consent,' said the countess, 'but your father . . .'

'My father, to whom I have told my plans, has made it an express condition of his consent that the wedding is not to take place for a year. And I wished to tell you of that,' said Prince Andrew.

'It is true that Natásha is still young, but—so long as that? . . .'

'It is unavoidable,' said Prince Andrew with a sigh.

'I will send her to you,' said the countess, and left the room.

'Lord have mercy upon us!' she repeated while seeking her daughter.

Sónya said that Natásha was in her bedroom. Natásha was sitting on the bed, pale and dry-eyed, and was gazing at the icons and whispering something as she rapidly crossed herself. Seeing her mother, she jumped up and flew to her.

'Well, mamma? . . . Well? . . .'

'Go, go to him. He is asking for your hand,' said the countess, coldly it seemed to Natásha. 'Go . . . go,' said the mother, sadly and reproachfully, with a deep sigh, as her daughter ran away.

Natásha never remembered how she entered the drawing-room. When she came in and saw him she paused. 'Is it possible that this stranger has now become *everything* to me?' she asked herself, and immediately answered, 'Yes, everything! He alone is now dearer to me than everything in the world.' Prince Andrew came up to her with downcast eyes.

'I have loved you from the very first moment I saw you. May I hope?'

He looked at her and was struck by the serious impassioned expression of her face. Her face said: 'Why ask? Why doubt what you cannot but know? Why speak, when words cannot express what one feels?'

She drew near to him and stopped. He took her hand and kissed it.

'Do you love me?'

'Yes, yes!' Natásha murmured as if in vexation. Then she sighed loudly and, catching her breath more and more quickly, began to sob.

'What is it? What's the matter?'

'Oh, I am so happy!' she replied, smiled through her tears, bent over closer to him, paused for an instant as if asking herself whether she might, and then kissed him.

Prince Andrew held her hands, looked into her eyes, and did not find in his heart his former love for her. Something in him had suddenly changed; there was no longer the former poetic and mystic charm of desire, but there was pity for her feminine and childish weakness, fear at her devotion and trustfulness, and an oppressive yet joyful sense of the duty that now bound him to her for ever. The present feeling, though not so bright and poetic as the former, was stronger and more serious.

'Did your mother tell you that it cannot be for a year?' asked Prince Andrew, still looking into her eyes.

'Is it possible that I—the "chit of a girl", as everybody called me,' thought Natásha, 'is it possible that I am now to be the *wife* and the equal of this strange, dear, clever man, whom even my father looks up to? Can it be true? Can it be true that there can be no more playing with life, that now I am grown up, that on me now lies a responsibility for my every word and deed? Yes, but what did he ask me?'

'No,' she replied, but she had not understood his question.

'Forgive me!' he said. 'But you are so young, and I have already been through so much in life. I am afraid for you, you do not yet know yourself.'

Natásha listened with concentrated attention, trying but failing to take in the meaning of his words.

'Hard as this year which delays my happiness will be,' continued Prince Andrew, 'it will give you time to be sure of yourself. I ask you to make me happy in a year, but you are free: our engagement shall remain a secret, and should you find that you do not love me, or should you come to love ...' said Prince Andrew with an unnatural smile.

'Why do you say that?' Natásha interrupted him. 'You know that from the very day you first came to Otrádnoe I have loved you,' she cried, quite convinced that she spoke the truth.

'In a year you will learn to know yourself ...'

'A whole year!' Natásha repeated suddenly, only now realizing that the marriage was to be postponed for a year. 'But why a year? Why a year? ...'

Prince Andrew began to explain to her the reasons for this delay. Natásha did not hear him.

'And can't it be helped?' she asked. Prince Andrew did not reply, but his face expressed the impossibility of altering that decision.

'It's awful! Oh, it's awful! awful!' Natásha suddenly cried, and again burst into sobs. 'I shall die, waiting a year: it's impossible, it's awful!' She looked into her lover's face and saw in it a look of commiseration and perplexity.

'No, no! I'll do anything!' she said, suddenly checking her tears. ' I am so happy.'

The father and mother came into the room and gave the betrothed couple their blessing.

From that day Prince Andrew began to frequent the Rostóvs' as Natásha's affianced lover.

CHAPTER XXIV

NO betrothal ceremony took place and Natásha's engagement to Bolkónski was not announced; Prince Andrew insisted on that. He said that as he was responsible for the delay, he ought to bear the whole burden of it; that he had given his word and bound himself for ever, but that he did not wish to bind Natásha and gave her perfect freedom. If after six months she felt that she did

not love him, she would have full right to reject him.
Naturally neither Natásha nor her parents wished to hear
of this, but Prince Andrew was firm. He came every day
to the Rostóvs', but did not behave to Natásha as an
affianced lover: he did not use the familiar *thou*, but said
you to her, and kissed only her hand. After their engagement, quite different, intimate, and natural relations
sprang up between them. It was as if they had not
known each other till now. Both liked to recall how they
had regarded each other when as yet they were *nothing* to
one another; they felt themselves now quite different
beings: then they were artificial, now natural and sincere.
At first the family felt some constraint in intercourse with
Prince Andrew; he seemed a man from another world,
and for a long time Natásha trained the family to get used
to him, proudly assuring them all that he only appeared
to be different, but was really just like all of them, and
that she was not afraid of him and no one else ought to
be. After a few days they grew accustomed to him, and
without restraint in his presence pursued their usual way
of life, in which he took his part. He could talk about rural
economy with the count, fashions with the countess and
Natásha, and about albums and fancy-work with Sónya.
Sometimes the household both among themselves and in
his presence expressed their wonder at how it had all
happened, and at the evident omens there had been of
it: Prince Andrew's coming to Otrádnoe and their
coming to Petersburg, and the likeness between Natásha
and Prince Andrew which her nurse had noticed on his
first visit, and Andrew's encounter with Nicholas in 1805,
and many other incidents betokening that it had to be.

In the house that poetic dullness and quiet reigned
which always accompanies the presence of a betrothed
couple. Often when all sitting together everyone kept
silent. Sometimes the others would get up and go away
and the couple, left alone, still remained silent. They
rarely spoke of their future life. Prince Andrew was
afraid and ashamed to speak of it. Natásha shared this
as she did all his feelings, which she constantly divined.
Once she began questioning him about his son. Prince
Andrew blushed, as he often did now—Natásha par-

ticularly liked it in him—and said that his son would not live with them.

'Why not?' asked Natásha in a frightened tone.

'I cannot take him away from his grandfather, and besides . . .'

'How I should have loved him!' said Natásha, immediately guessing his thought; 'but I know you wish to avoid any pretext for finding fault with us.'

Sometimes the old count would come up, kiss Prince Andrew, and ask his advice about Pétya's education or Nicholas's service. The old countess sighed as she looked at them; Sónya was always getting frightened lest she should be in the way, and tried to find excuses for leaving them alone, even when they did not wish it. When Prince Andrew spoke (he could tell a story very well) Natásha listened to him with pride; when she spoke, she noticed with fear and joy that he gazed attentively and scrutinizingly at her. She asked herself in perplexity: 'What does he look for in me? He is trying to discover something by looking at me! What if what he seeks in me is not there?' Sometimes she fell into one of the mad, merry moods characteristic of her, and then she particularly loved to hear and see how Prince Andrew laughed. He seldom laughed, but when he did he abandoned himself entirely to his laughter, and after such a laugh she always felt nearer to him. Natásha would have been completely happy if the thought of the separation awaiting her and drawing near had not terrified her, just as the mere thought of it made him turn pale and cold.

On the eve of his departure from Petersburg Prince Andrew brought with him Pierre, who had not been to the Rostóvs' once since the ball. Pierre seemed disconcerted and embarrassed. He was talking to the countess, and Natásha sat down beside a little chess-table with Sónya, thereby inviting Prince Andrew to come too. He did so.

'You have known Bezúkhov a long time?' he asked. 'Do you like him?'

'Yes, he's a dear, but very absurd.'

And, as usual when speaking of Pierre, she began to tell anecdotes of his absent-mindedness, some of which had even been invented about him.

'Do you know I have entrusted him with our secret? I have known him from childhood. He has a heart of gold. I beg you, Natalie,' Prince Andrew said with sudden seriousness—'I am going away, and heaven knows what may happen. You may cease to . . . all right, I know I am not to say that. Only this, then: whatever may happen to you when I am not there . . .'

'What can happen?'

'Whatever trouble may come,' Prince Andrew continued, 'I beg you, Mademoiselle Sophie, whatever may happen, to turn to him alone for advice and help! He is a most absent-minded and absurd fellow, but he has a heart of gold.'

Neither her father, nor her mother, nor Sónya, nor Prince Andrew himself, could have foreseen how the separation from her lover would act on Natásha. Flushed and agitated she went about the house all that day, dry-eyed, occupied with most trivial matters as if not understanding what awaited her. She did not even cry when, on taking leave, he kissed her hand for the last time. 'Don't go!' she said in a tone that made him wonder whether he really ought not to stay and which he remembered long afterwards. Nor did she cry when he was gone; but for several days she sat in her room dry-eyed, taking no interest in anything and only saying now and then, 'Oh, why did he go away?'

But a fortnight after his departure, to the surprise of those around her, she recovered from her mental sickness just as suddenly and became her old self again, but with a change in her moral physiognomy, as a child gets up after a long illness with a changed expression of face.

CHAPTER XXV

DURING that year after his son's departure, Prince Nicholas Bolkónski's health and temper became much worse. He grew still more irritable, and it was Princess Mary who generally bore the brunt of his frequent fits of unprovoked anger. He seemed carefully to seek out her tender spots so as to torture her mentally as harshly as possible. Princess Mary had two passions and consequently two joys—her nephew, little Nicholas, and religion—and these were the favourite subjects of the prince's attacks and ridicule. Whatever was spoken of he would bring round to the superstitiousness of old maids, or the petting and spoiling of children. 'You want to make him'—little Nicholas—'into an old maid like yourself! A pity! Prince Andrew wants a son and not an old maid,' he would say. Or, turning to Mademoiselle Bourienne, he would ask her in Princess Mary's presence how she liked our village priests and icons, and would joke about them.

He continually hurt Princess Mary's feelings and tormented her, but it cost her no effort to forgive him. Could he be to blame towards her, or could her father, who she knew loved her in spite of it all, be unjust? And what is justice? The princess never thought of that proud word 'justice'. All the complex laws of man centred for her in one clear and simple law—the law of love and self-sacrifice taught us by Him who lovingly suffered for mankind though He Himself was God. What had she to do with the justice or injustice of other people? She had to endure and love, and that she did.

During the winter Prince Andrew had come to Bald Hills, and had been gay, gentle, and more affectionate than Princess Mary had known him for a long time past. She felt that something had happened to him, but he said nothing to her about his love. Before he left he had a long talk with his father about something, and Princess Mary noticed that before his departure they were dissatisfied with one another.

Soon after Prince Andrew had gone, Princess Mary wrote to her friend Julie Karágina in Petersburg, whom she had dreamed (as all girls dream) of marrying to her brother, and who was at that time in mourning for her own brother, killed in Turkey.

'Sorrow, it seems, is our common lot, my dear, tender friend Julie.

'Your loss is so terrible that I can only explain it to myself as a special providence of God who, loving you, wishes to try you and your excellent mother. Oh, my friend! Religion, and religion alone, can—I will not say comfort us—but save us from despair. Religion alone can explain to us what without its help man cannot comprehend: why, for what cause, kind and noble beings, able to find happiness in life—not merely harming no one, but necessary to the happiness of others—are called away to God, while cruel, useless, harmful persons, or such as are a burden to themselves and to others, are left living. The first death I saw, and one I shall never forget—that of my dear sister-in-law—left that impression on me. Just as you ask destiny why your splendid brother had to die, so I asked why that angel Lise, who not only never wronged any one, but in whose soul there were never any unkind thoughts, had to die. And what do you think, dear friend? Five years have passed since then, and already I, with my petty understanding, begin to see clearly why she had to die, and in what way that death was but an expression of the infinite goodness of the Creator, whose every action, though generally incomprehensible to us, is but a manifestation of His infinite love for His creatures. Perhaps, I often think, she was too angelically innocent to have the strength to perform all a mother's duties. As a young wife she was irreproachable; perhaps she could not have been so as a mother. As it is, not only has she left us, and particularly Prince Andrew, with the purest regrets and memories, but probably she will *there* receive a place I dare not hope for myself. But not to speak of her alone, that early and terrible death has had the most beneficent influence on me and on my brother in spite of all our grief. Then, at the moment of our loss, these thoughts could not occur to me: I should then have dismissed them with horror, but now they are very clear and certain. I write all this to you, dear friend, only to convince you of the Gospel truth which has become for me a principle of life: not a single hair of our heads will fall without His will. And His will is governed only by infinite love for us, and so whatever befalls us is for our good.

'You ask whether we shall spend next winter in Moscow. In spite of my wish to see you, I do not think so and do not want to do so. You will be surprised to hear that the reason for this is Buonaparte! The case is this: my father's health is growing noticeably worse, he cannot stand any contradiction and is becoming irritable. This irritability is, as you know, chiefly directed to political questions. He cannot endure the notion that Buonaparte is negotiating on equal terms with all the sovereigns of Europe, and particularly with our own, the grandson of the Great Catherine! As you know, I am quite indifferent to politics, but from my father's remarks and his talks with Michael Ivánovich I know all that goes on in the world, and especially about the honours conferred on Buonaparte, who only at Bald Hills in the whole world, it seems, is not accepted as a great man, still less as Emperor of France. And my father cannot stand this. It seems to me that it is chiefly because of his political views that my father is reluctant to speak of going to Moscow; for he foresees the encounters that would result from his way of expressing his views regardless of anybody. All the benefit he might derive from a course of treatment, he would lose as a result of the disputes about Buonaparte which would be inevitable. In any case it will be decided very shortly.

'Our family life goes on in the old way except for my brother Andrew's absence. He, as I wrote you before, has changed very much of late. After his sorrow he only this year quite recovered his spirits. He has again become as I used to know him when a child: kind, affectionate, with that heart of gold to which I know no equal. He has realized, it seems to me, that life is not over for him. But together with this mental change he has grown physically much weaker. He has become thinner and more nervous. I am anxious about him and glad he is taking this trip abroad which the doctors recommended long ago. I hope it will cure him. You write that in Petersburg he is spoken of as one of the most active, cultivated, and capable of the young men. Forgive my vanity as a relation, but I never doubted it. The good he has done to everybody here, from his peasants up to the gentry, is incalculable. On his arrival in Petersburg he received only his due. I always wonder at the way rumours fly from Petersburg to Moscow, especially such false ones as that you write about—I mean the report of my brother's betrothal to the little Rostóva. I do not think my brother will ever marry again, and certainly not her; and this is why: first, I know that though he rarely speaks about the wife he has lost, the grief of that loss has gone too deep in his heart for him ever to decide to give her a successor and our little angel a step-mother. Secondly because, as far as I know, that girl is not the kind of girl who could please Prince Andrew. I do not think he would choose her for a wife, and frankly I do not wish it. But I am running on too long and am at the end of my second sheet. Good-bye, my dear friend. May God keep you in His holy and mighty care. My dear friend, Mademoiselle Bourienne, sends you kisses.

'Mary.'

CHAPTER XXVI

IN the middle of the summer Princess Mary received an unexpected letter from Prince Andrew in Switzerland in which he gave her strange and surprising news. He informed her of his engagement to Natásha Rostóva. The whole letter breathed loving rapture for his betrothed and tender and confiding affection for his sister. He wrote that he had never loved as he did now, and that only now did he understand and know what life was. He asked his sister to forgive him for not having told her of his resolve when he had last visited Bald Hills, though he had spoken of it to his father. He had not done so for fear Princess Mary should ask her father to give his consent, irritating him and having to bear the brunt of his displeasure without attaining her object. 'Besides,' he wrote, 'the matter was not then so definitely settled as it is now. My father then insisted on a delay of a year and now already *six months*, half of that period, has passed, and my resolution is firmer than ever. If the doctors did not keep me here at the spas I should be back in Russia, but as it is I have to postpone my return for three months. You know me and my relations with Father. I want nothing from him. I have been and always shall be independent; but to go against his will and arouse his anger, now that he may perhaps remain with us such a short time, would destroy half my happiness. I am now writing to him about the same question, and beg you to choose a good moment to hand him the letter, and to let me know how he looks at the whole matter and whether there is hope that he may consent to reduce the term by four months.'

After long hesitations, doubts and prayers, Princess Mary gave the letter to her father. The next day the old prince said to her quietly:

'Write and tell your brother to wait till I am dead . . . It won't be long—I shall soon set him free.'

The princess was about to reply, but her father would not let her speak and raising his voice more and more, cried:

'Marry, marry, my boy! . . . A good family! . . . Clever people, eh? Rich, eh? Yes, a nice step-mother little Nicholas will have! Write and tell him that he may marry to-morrow if he likes. She will be little Nicholas's step-mother and I'll marry Bourienne! . . . Ha, ha, ha! He mustn't be without a step-mother either! Only one thing, no more women are wanted in my house—let him marry and live by himself. Perhaps you will go and live with him too?' he added, turning to Princess Mary. 'Go in heaven's name! Go out into the frost . . . the frost . . . the frost!'

After this outburst the prince did not speak any more about the matter. But repressed vexation at his son's poor-spirited behaviour found expression in his treatment of his daughter. To his former pretexts for irony a fresh one was now added—allusions to step-mothers, and amiabilities to Mademoiselle Bourienne.

'Why shouldn't I marry her?' he asked his daughter. 'She'll make a splendid princess!'

And latterly, to her surprise and bewilderment, Princess Mary noticed that her father was really associating more and more with the Frenchwoman. She wrote to Prince Andrew about the reception of his letter, but comforted him with hopes of reconciling their father to the idea.

Little Nicholas and his education, her brother Andrew, and religion, were Princess Mary's joys and consolations; but besides that, since every one must have personal hopes, Princess Mary in the profoundest depths of her heart had a hidden dream and hope that supplied the chief consolation of her life. This comforting dream and hope were given her by *God's folk*—the half-witted and other pilgrims who visited her without the prince's knowledge. The longer she lived, the more experience and observation she had of life, the greater was her wonder at the short-sightedness of men who seek enjoyment and happiness here on earth: toiling, suffering, struggling, and harming one another, to obtain that impossible, visionary, sinful happiness. Prince Andrew had loved his wife, she died, but that was not enough, he wanted to bind his happiness to another woman. Her father objected to this because he wanted a more distinguished and wealthier match for Andrew. And they all struggled and suffered and tormented one another and injured their souls, their eternal souls, for the attainment of benefits which endure but for an instant. Not only do we know this ourselves, but Christ, the Son of God, came down to earth and told us that this life is but for a moment and is a probation; yet we cling to it and think to find happiness in it. 'How is it that no one realizes this?' thought Princess Mary. 'No one except these despised *God's folk* who, wallet on back, come to me by the back door, afraid of being seen by the prince, not for fear of ill-usage by him but for fear of causing him to sin. To leave family, home, and all the cares of worldly welfare, in order without clinging to anything to wander in hempen rags from place to place under an assumed name, doing no one any harm but praying for all—for those who drive one away as well as for those who protect one: higher than that life and truth there is no life or truth!'

There was one pilgrim, a quiet pock-marked little woman of fifty called Theodosia, who for over thirty years had gone about barefoot and worn heavy chains. Princess Mary was particularly fond of her. Once when in a room with a lamp dimly lit before the icon Theodosia was talking of her life, the thought that Theodosia alone had found the true path of life suddenly came to Princess Mary with such force that she resolved to become a pilgrim herself. When Theodosia had gone to sleep Princess Mary thought about this for a long time, and at last made up her mind that, strange as it might seem, she must go on pilgrimage. She disclosed this thought to no one but to her confessor, Father Akínfi, the monk, and he approved of her intention. Under guise of a present for the pilgrims, Princess Mary prepared a pilgrim's complete costume for herself: a coarse smock, bast shoes, a rough coat and a black kerchief. Often, approaching the chest of drawers containing this secret treasure, Princess Mary paused, uncertain whether the time had not already come to put her project into execution.

Often listening to the pilgrims' tales she was so stimulated by their simple speech, mechanical to them but to her so full of deep meaning, that several times she was on the point of abandoning everything and running away from home. In imagination she already pictured herself by Theodosia's side, dressed in coarse rags, walking with a staff, a wallet on her back, along the dusty road, directing her wanderings from one saint's shrine to another, free from envy, earthly love, or desire, and reaching at last the place where there is no more sorrow or sighing, but eternal joy and bliss.

'I shall come to a place and pray there, and before having time to get used to it or getting to love it, I shall go farther. I will go on till my legs fail, and I'll lie down and die somewhere, and shall at last reach that eternal, quiet haven, where there is neither sorrow nor sighing . . .' thought Princess Mary.

But afterwards, when she saw her father and especially little Koko (Nicholas) her resolve weakened. She wept quietly, and felt that she was a sinner who loved her father and little nephew more than God.

END OF BOOK VI

BOOK VII

E

BOOK VII

CHAPTER I

THE Bible legend tells us that the absence of labour
—idleness—was a condition of the first man's blessedness before the Fall. Fallen man has retained a love of
idleness, but the curse weighs on the race not only because
we have to seek our bread in the sweat of our brows, but
because our moral nature is such that we cannot be both
idle and at ease. An inner voice tells us we are in the
wrong if we are idle. If man could find a state in which
he felt that though idle he was fulfilling his duty, he
would have found one of the conditions of man's primi-
tive blessedness. And such a state of obligatory and
irreproachable idleness is the lot of a whole class—the
military. The chief attraction of military service has
consisted and will consist in this compulsory and irreproachable idleness.

Nicholas Rostóv experienced this blissful condition to
the full when after 1807 he continued to serve in the
Pávlograd regiment, in which he already commanded
the squadron he had taken over from Denísov.

Rostóv had become a bluff, good-natured fellow, whom
his Moscow acquaintances would have considered rather
bad form, but who was liked and respected by his comrades, subordinates, and superiors, and was well contented with his life. Of late, in 1809, he found in letters
from home more frequent complaints from his mother
that their affairs were falling into greater and greater
disorder, and that it was time for him to come back to
gladden and comfort his old parents.

Reading these letters Nicholas felt a dread of their
wanting to take him away from surroundings in which,
protected from all the entanglements of life, he was
living so calmly and quietly. He felt that sooner or
later he would have to re-enter that whirlpool of life,
with its embarrassments and affairs to be straightened
out, its accounts with stewards, quarrels, and intrigues,
its ties, society, and with Sónya's love and his promise to

her. It was all dreadfully difficult and complicated; and he replied to his mother in cold, formal letters in French, beginning: 'My dear Mamma' and ending: 'Your obedient son', which said nothing of when he would return. In 1810 he received letters from his parents in which they told him of Natásha's engagement to Bolkónski, and that the wedding would be in a year's time because the old prince made difficulties. This letter grieved and mortified Nicholas. In the first place he was sorry that Natásha, for whom he cared more than for any one else in the family, should be lost to the home; and secondly, from his hussar point of view, he regretted not to have been there to show that fellow Bolkónski that connexion with him was no such great honour after all, and that if he loved Natásha he might dispense with permission from his dotard father. For a moment he hesitated whether he should not apply for leave in order to see Natásha before she was married, but then came the manœuvres, and considerations about Sónya and about the confusion of their affairs, and Nicholas again put it off. But in the spring of that year he received a letter from his mother, written without his father's knowledge, and that letter persuaded him to return. She wrote that if he did not come and take matters in hand, their whole property would be sold by auction and they would all have to go begging. The count was so weak, and trusted Mítenka so much, and was so good-natured, that everybody took advantage of him and things were going from bad to worse. 'For God's sake, I implore you, come at once, if you do not wish to make me and the whole family wretched,' wrote the countess.

This letter touched Nicholas. He had that common sense of a matter-of-fact man which showed him what he ought to do.

The right thing now was, if not to retire from the service, at any rate to go home on leave. Why he had to go he did not know; but after his after-dinner nap he gave orders to saddle Mars, an extremely vicious grey stallion that had not been ridden for a long time, and when he returned with the horse all in a lather, he informed Lavrúshka (Denísov's servant who had remained with him) and his comrades who turned up in the evening, that he was applying for leave and was going home. Difficult and strange as it was for him to reflect that he would go away without having heard from the staff—and this interested him extremely—whether he was promoted to a captaincy or would receive the Order of St. Anne for the last manœuvres; strange as it was to think that he would go away without having sold his three roans to the Polish Count Golukhovski, who was bargaining for the horses Rostóv had betted he would sell for two thousand rubles; incomprehensible as it seemed that the ball the hussars were giving in honour of the Polish Mademoiselle Przazdziecka (out of rivalry to the uhlans, who had given one in honour of their Polish Mademoiselle Borzozowska) would take place without him—he knew he must go away from this good, bright world, to somewhere where everything was stupid and confused. A week later he obtained his leave. His hussar comrades—not only those of his own regiment, but the whole brigade—gave Rostóv a dinner to which the subscription was fifteen rubles a head, and at which there were two bands and two choirs of singers. Rostóv danced the Trepák with Major Básov; the tipsy officers tossed, embraced, and dropped Rostóv; the soldiers of the third squadron tossed him too, and shouted 'hurrah!', and then they put him in his sledge and escorted him as far as the first post-station.

During the first half of the journey—from Kremenchúg to Kiev—all Rostóv's thoughts, as is usual in such cases, were behind him, with the squadron; but when he had gone more than half-way he began to forget his three roans and Dozhoyvéyko, his quartermaster, and to wonder anxiously how things would be at Otrádnoe and what he would find there. Thoughts of home grew stronger the nearer he approached it—far stronger, as though this feeling of his was subject to the law by which the force of attraction is in inverse proportion to the square of the distance. At the last post-station before Otrádnoe he gave the driver a three-ruble tip, and on arriving he ran breathlessly, like a boy, up the steps of his home.

After the rapture of meeting, and after that odd feeling of unsatisfied expectation—the feeling that 'everything is just the same, so why did I hurry?'—Nicholas began to settle down in his old home world. His father and mother were much the same, only a little older. What was new in them was a certain uneasiness and occasional discord, which there used not to be, and which, as Nicholas soon found out, was due to the bad state of their affairs. Sónya was nearly twenty, she had stopped growing prettier and promised nothing more than she was already, but that was enough. She exhaled happiness and love from the time Nicholas returned, and the faithful, unalterable love of this girl had a gladdening effect on him. Pétya and Natásha surprised Nicholas most. Pétya was a big, handsome boy of thirteen, merry, witty, and mischievous, with a voice that was already breaking. As for Natásha, for a long while Nicholas wondered and laughed whenever he looked at her.

'You're not the same at all,' he said.

'How? Am I uglier?'

'On the contrary, but what dignity! A Princess!' he whispered to her.

'Yes, yes, yes!' cried Natásha joyfully.

She told him all about her romance with Prince Andrew and of his visit to Otrádnoe, and showed him his last letter.

'Well, are you glad?' Natásha asked. 'I am so tranquil and happy now.'

'Very glad,' answered Nicholas. 'He is an excellent fellow . . . And are you very much in love?'

'How shall I put it?' replied Natásha. 'I was in love with Borís, with my teacher, and with Denísov, but this is quite different. I feel at peace and settled. I know that no better man than he exists, and I am calm and contented now. Not at all as before.'

Nicholas expressed his disapproval of the postponement of the marriage for a year; but Natásha attacked her brother with exasperation, proving to him that it could not be otherwise, and that it would be a bad thing to enter a family against the father's will, and that she herself wished it so.

'You don't at all understand,' she said.

Nicholas was silent and agreed with her.

Her brother often wondered as he looked at her. She did not seem at all like a girl in love and parted from her affianced husband. She was even-tempered and calm, and quite as cheerful as of old. This amazed Nicholas and even made him regard Bolkónski's courtship sceptically. He could not believe that her fate was sealed, especially as he had not seen her with Prince Andrew. It always seemed to him that there was something not quite right about this intended marriage.

'Why this delay? Why no betrothal?' he thought. Once, when he had touched on this topic with his mother, he discovered, to his surprise and somewhat to his satisfaction, that in the depth of her soul she too had doubts about this marriage.

'You see he writes,' said she, showing her son a letter of Prince Andrew's with that latent grudge a mother always has in regard to a daughter's future married happiness, 'he writes that he won't come before December. What can be keeping him? Illness, probably! His health is very delicate. Don't tell Natásha. And don't attach importance to her being so bright: that's because she's living through the last days of her girlhood, but I know what she is like every time we receive a letter from him! However, God grant that everything turns out well!' (she always ended with these words). 'He is an excellent man!'

CHAPTER II

AFTER reaching home Nicholas was at first serious and even dull. He was worried by the impending necessity of interfering in the stupid business matters for which his mother had called him home. To throw off this burden as quickly as possible, on the third day after his arrival he went, angry and scowling and without answering questions as to where he was going, to Mítenka's lodge, and demanded an *account of everything*. But what an *account of everything* might be Nicholas knew even less than the frightened and bewildered Mítenka. The conversation and the examination of the accounts with Mítenka did not last long. The village elder, a peasant delegate, and the village clerk, who were waiting in the passage, heard with fear and delight first the young count's voice roaring and snapping and rising louder and louder, and then words of abuse, dreadful words, ejaculated one after the other.

'Robber! . . . Ungrateful wretch! . . . I'll hack the dog to pieces! I'm not my father! . . . Robbing us! . . .' and so on.

Then with no less fear and delight they saw how the young count, red in the face and with bloodshot eyes, dragged Mítenka out by the scruff of the neck and applied his foot and knee to him behind with great agility at convenient moments between his words, shouting, 'Be off! Never let me see your face here again, you villain!'

Mítenka flew headlong down the six steps and ran away into the shrubbery. (This shrubbery was a well-known haven of refuge for culprits at Otrádnoe. Mítenka himself, returning tipsy from the town, used to hide there, and many of the residents at Otrádnoe, hiding from Mítenka, knew of its protective qualities.)

Mítenka's wife and sisters-in-law thrust their heads and frightened faces out of the door of a room where a bright samovar was boiling and where the steward's high bedstead stood with its patchwork quilt.

The young count paid no heed to them, but breathing hard passed by with resolute strides and went into the house.

The countess, who heard at once from the maids what had happened at the lodge, was calmed by the thought that now their affairs would certainly improve, but on the other hand felt anxious as to the effect this excitement might have on her son. She went several times to his door on tiptoe and listened, as he lighted one pipe after another.

Next day the old count called his son aside and with an embarrassed smile said to him:

'But you know, my dear boy, it's a pity you got excited! Mítenka has told me all about it.'

'I knew,' thought Nicholas, 'that I should never understand anything in this crazy world.'

'You were angry that he had not entered those 700 rubles. But they were carried forward—and you did not look at the other page.'

'Papa, he is a blackguard and a thief! I know he is! And what I have done, I have done; but if you like I won't speak to him again.'

'No, my dear boy' (the count, too, felt embarrassed. He knew he had mismanaged his wife's property and was to blame towards his children, but he did not know how to remedy it). 'No, I beg you to attend to the business. I am old. I . . .'

'No, papa. Forgive me if I have caused you unpleasantness. I understand it all less than you do.'

'Devil take all these peasants, and money matters, and carryings forward from page to page,' he thought. 'I used to understand what a "corner" and the stakes at cards meant, but carrying forward to another page I don't understand at all,' said he to himself, and after that he did not meddle in business affairs. But once the countess called her son and informed him that she had a promissory note from Anna Mikháylovna for two thousand rubles, and asked him what he thought of doing with it.

'This,' answered Nicholas. 'You say it rests with me. Well, I don't like Anna Mikháylovna, and I don't like Borís, but they were our friends and poor. Well then, this!' and he tore up the note, and by so doing caused the old countess to weep tears of joy. After that, young Rostóv took no further part in any business affairs, but devoted himself with passionate enthusiasm to what was to him a new pursuit—the chase—for which his father kept a large establishment.

CHAPTER III

THE weather was already growing wintry, and morning frosts congealed an earth saturated by autumn rains. The verdure had thickened, and its bright green stood out sharply against the brownish strips of winter rye trodden down by the cattle, and against the pale yellow stubble of the spring sowing and the reddish strips of buckwheat. The wooded ravines and the copses, which at the end of August had still been green islands amid black fields and stubble, had become golden and bright-red islands amid the green winter rye. The hares had already half changed their summer coats, the fox-cubs were beginning to scatter, and the young wolves were bigger than dogs. It was the best time of year for the chase. The hounds of that ardent young sportsman Rostóv had not merely reached hard winter condition, but were so jaded that at a meeting of the huntsmen it was decided to give them a three days' rest and then, on the 16th of September, to go on a distant expedition, starting from the oak grove where there was an undisturbed litter of wolf-cubs.

All that day the hounds remained at home. It was frosty and the air was sharp, but towards evening the sky became overcast and it began to thaw. On the 15th, when young Rostóv in his dressing-gown looked out of the window, he saw it was an unsurpassable morning for hunting: it was as if the sky were melting and sinking to the earth without any wind. The only motion in the air was that of the dripping, microscopic particles of drizzling mist. The bare twigs in the garden were hung with transparent drops which fell on the freshly fallen leaves. The earth in the kitchen-garden looked wet and black and glistened like poppy-seed and at a short distance merged into the dull moist veil of mist. Nicholas went out into the wet and muddy porch. There was a smell of decaying leaves and of dog. Mílka, a black-spotted broad-haunched bitch with prominent black eyes, got up on seeing her master, stretched her hind legs, lay down like a hare and then suddenly jumped up and licked him right on his nose and moustache. Another borzoi, a dog, catching sight of his master from the garden path, arched his back and rushing headlong towards the porch with lifted tail began rubbing himself against his legs.

'O-hoy!' came at that moment that inimitable hunts-man's call which unites the deepest bass with the shrillest tenor, and round the corner came Daniel the head hunts-man and head kennel-man, a grey, wrinkled old man with hair cut straight over his forehead, Ukrainian fashion, a long bent whip in his hand, and that look of independence and scorn of everything that is only seen in huntsmen. He doffed his Circassian cap to his master and looked at him scornfully. This scorn was not offensive to his master. Nicholas knew that this Daniel, disdainful of everybody and who considered himself above them, was all the same his serf and huntsman.

'Daniel!' Nicholas said timidly, conscious at the sight of the weather, the hounds, and the huntsman, that he was being carried away by that irresistible passion for sport which makes a man forget all his previous resolutions, as a lover forgets in the presence of his mistress.

'What orders, your Excellency?' said the huntsman in his deep bass, deep as a proto-deacon's and hoarse with hallooing—and two flashing black eyes gazed from under his brows at his master, who was silent. 'Can you resist it?' those eyes seemed to be asking.

'It's a good day, eh? For a hunt and a gallop, eh?' asked Nicholas, scratching Mílka behind the ears.

Daniel did not answer, but winked instead.

'I sent Uvárka at dawn to listen,' his bass boomed out after a minute's pause. 'He says *she's moved them* into the Otrádnoe enclosure. They were howling there.' (This meant that the she-wolf, about whom they both knew, had moved with her cubs to the Otrádnoe copse, a small place two versts from the house.)

'We ought to go, don't you think so?' said Nicholas. 'Come to me with Uvárka.'

'As you please.'

'Then put off feeding them.'

'Yes, sir.'

Five minutes later Daniel and Uvárka were standing in Nicholas's big study. Though Daniel was not a big man, to see him in a room was like seeing a horse or a bear on the floor among the furniture and surroundings of human life. Daniel himself felt this, and as usual stood just inside the door, trying to speak softly and not move, for fear of breaking something in the master's apartment, and he hastened to say all that was necessary so as to get from under that ceiling, out into the open under the sky once more.

Having finished his inquiries and extorted from Daniel an opinion that the hounds were fit (Daniel himself wished to go hunting), Nicholas ordered the horses to be saddled. But just as Daniel was about to go, Natásha came in with rapid steps, not having done up her hair or finished dressing, and with her old nurse's big shawl wrapped round her. Pétya ran in at the same time.

'You are going?' asked Natásha. 'I knew you would! Sónya said you wouldn't go, but I knew that to-day is the sort of day when you couldn't help going.'

'Yes, we are going,' replied Nicholas reluctantly, for to-day as he intended to hunt seriously he did not want to take Natásha and Pétya. 'We are going, but only wolf-hunting: it would be dull for you.'

'You know it is my greatest pleasure,' said Natásha. 'It's not fair; you are going by yourself, are having the horses saddled, and said nothing to us about it.'

'"No barrier bars a Russian's path"—we'll go!' shouted Pétya.

'But you can't. Mamma said you mustn't,' said Nicholas to Natásha.

'Yes, I'll go. I shall certainly go,' said Natásha decisively. 'Daniel, tell them to saddle for us, and Michael must come with my dogs,' she added to the huntsman.

It seemed to Daniel irksome and improper to be in a room at all, but to have anything to do with a young lady seemed to him impossible. He cast down his eyes and hurried out as if it were none of his business, careful as he went not to inflict any accidental injury on the young lady.

CHAPTER IV

THE old count, who had always kept up an enormous hunting establishment but had now handed it all completely over to his son's care, being in very good spirits on this 15th of September, prepared to go out with the others.

In an hour's time the whole hunting party was at the porch. Nicholas, with a stern and serious air which showed that now was no time for attending to trifles, went past

Natásha and Pétya who were trying to tell him something. He had a look at all the details of the hunt, sent a pack of hounds and huntsmen on ahead to find the quarry, mounted his chestnut Donéts, and whistling to his own leash of borzois, set off across the threshing-ground to a field leading to the Otrádnoe wood. The old count's horse, a sorrel gelding called Viflyánka, was led by the groom in attendance on him, while the count himself was to drive in a small trap straight to a spot reserved for him.

They were taking fifty-four hounds with six hunt-attendants and whippers-in. Besides the family there were eight borzoi kennel-men and more than forty borzois, so that, with the borzois on leash belonging to members of the family, there were about a hundred and thirty dogs and twenty horsemen.

Each dog knew its master and its call. Each man in the hunt knew his business, his place, and what he had to do. As soon as they had passed the fence they all spread out evenly and quietly without noise or talk, along the road and field leading to the Otrádnoe covert.

The horses stepped over the field as over a thick carpet, now and then splashing into puddles as they crossed a road. The misty sky still seemed to descend evenly and imperceptibly towards the earth, the air was still, warm, and silent. Occasionally the whistle of a huntsman, the snort of a horse, the crack of a whip, or the whine of a straggling hound, could be heard.

When they had gone about a verst, five more riders with dogs appeared out of the mist, approaching the Rostóvs. In front rode a fresh-looking handsome old man with a large grey moustache.

'Good morning, Uncle!' said Nicholas when the old man drew near.

'That's it. Come on! . . . I was sure of it,' began 'Uncle'. (He was a distant relative of the Rostóvs', a man of small means, and their neighbour.) 'I knew you wouldn't be able to resist it and it's a good thing you're going. That's it! Come on!' (This was 'Uncle's' favourite expression.) 'Take the covert at once, for my Gírchik says the Ilágins are at Kornikí with their hounds.

That's it. Come on! . . . They'll take the cubs from under your very nose.'

'That's where I'm going. Shall we join up our packs?' asked Nicholas.

The hounds were joined into one pack, and 'Uncle' and Nicholas rode on side by side. Natásha, muffled up in shawls which did not hide her eager face and shining eyes, galloped up to them. She was followed by Pétya who always kept close to her, by Michael a huntsman, and by a groom appointed to look after her. Pétya, who was laughing, whipped and pulled at his horse. Natásha sat easily and confidently on her black Arábchik and reined him in without effort with a firm hand.

'Uncle' looked round disapprovingly at Pétya and Natásha. He did not like to combine frivolity with the serious business of hunting.

'Good morning, Uncle! We are going too!' shouted Pétya.

'Good morning, good morning! But don't go over-riding the hounds,' said 'Uncle' sternly.

'Nicholas, what a fine dog Truníla is! He knew me,' said Natásha, referring to her favourite hound.

'In the first place Truníla is not a "dog," but a harrier', thought Nicholas, and looked sternly at his sister, trying to make her feel the distance that ought to separate them at that moment. Natásha understood it.

'You mustn't think we'll be in any one's way, Uncle,' she said. 'We'll go to our places and won't budge.'

'A good thing too, little Countess,' said 'Uncle', 'only mind you don't fall off your horse,' he added, 'because— that's it, come on!—you've nothing to hold on to.'

The oasis of the Otrádnoe covert came in sight a couple of hundred yards off, the huntsmen were already nearing it. Rostóv having finally settled with 'Uncle' where they should set on the hounds, and having shown Natásha where she was to stand—a spot where nothing could possibly run out—went round above the ravine.

'Well, nephew, you're going for a big wolf,' said 'Uncle'. 'Mind and don't let her slip!'

'That's as may happen,' answered Rostóv. 'Karáy, here!' he shouted, answering 'Uncle's' remark by this call to his borzoi. Karáy was a shaggy old dog with a hanging jowl, famous for having tackled a big wolf unaided. They all took up their places.

The old count, knowing his son's ardour in the hunt, hurried so as not to be late, and the huntsmen had not yet reached their places when Count Ilyá Rostóv, cheerful, flushed, and with quivering cheeks, drove up with his black horses over the winter rye to the place reserved for him where a wolf might come out. Having straightened his coat and fastened on his hunting-knives and horn, he mounted his good, sleek, well-fed and comfortable horse, Viflyánka, which was turning grey like himself. His horses and trap were sent home. Count Ilyá Rostóv, though not at heart a keen sportsman, knew the rules of the hunt well, and rode to the bushy edge of the wood where he was to stand, arranged his reins, settled himself in the saddle and, feeling that he was ready, looked about with a smile.

Beside him was Simon Chekmár, his personal attendant, an old horseman now somewhat stiff in the saddle. Chekmár held in leash three formidable wolf-hounds, who had however grown fat like their master and his horse. Two wise old dogs lay down unleashed. Some hundred paces farther along the edge of the wood stood Mítka, the count's other groom, a daring horseman and keen rider to hounds. Before the hunt, by old custom, the count had drunk a silver cupful of mulled brandy, taken a snack, and washed it down with half a bottle of his favourite Bordeaux.

He was somewhat flushed with the wine and the drive. His eyes were rather moist and glittered more than usual, and as he sat in his saddle wrapped up in his fur coat he looked like a child taken for an outing.

The thin, hollow-cheeked Chekmár, having got everything ready, kept glancing at his master with whom he had lived on the best of terms for thirty years, and understanding the mood he was in, expected a pleasant chat. A third person rode up circumspectly through the wood (it was plain that he had had a lesson) and stopped behind the count. This person was a grey-bearded old man in a woman's cloak with a tall peaked cap on his head. He was the buffoon, who went by a woman's name, Nastásya Ivánovna.

'Well, Nastásya Ivánovna!' whispered the count, winking at him. 'If you scare away the beast, Daniel'll give it you!'

'I know a thing or two myself!' said Nastásya Ivánovna.

'Hush!' whispered the count and turned to Simon. 'Have you seen the young countess?' he asked. 'Where is she?'

'With young Count Peter, by the Zhárov rank grass,' answered Simon, smiling. 'Though she's a lady she's very fond of hunting.'

'And you're surprised at the way she rides, Simon, eh?' said the count. 'She's as good as many a man!'

'Of course! It's marvellous. So bold, so easy!'

'And Nicholas? Where is he? By the Lyádov upland, isn't he?'

'Yes sir. He knows where to stand. He understands the matter so well that Daniel and I are often quite astounded,' said Simon, well knowing what would please his master.

'Rides well, eh? And how well he looks on his horse, eh?'

'A perfect picture! How he chased a fox out of the rank grass by the Zavárzinsk thicket the other day! Leapt a fearful place; what a sight when they rushed from the covert . . . the horse worth a thousand rubles and the rider beyond all price! Yes, one would have to search far to find another as smart.'

'To search far . . .' repeated the count, evidently sorry Simon had not said more. 'To search far,' he said, turning back the skirt of his coat to get at his snuff-box.

'The other day when he came out from Mass in full uniform, Michael Sidórych . . .' Simon did not finish, for on the still air he had distinctly caught the music of the hunt with only two or three hounds giving tongue. He bent down his head and listened, shaking a warning finger at his master. 'They are on the scent of the cubs . . .' he whispered, 'straight to the Lyádov uplands.'

The count, forgetting to smooth out the smile on his face, looked into the distance straight before him, down the narrow open space, holding the snuff-box in his hand but not taking any. After the cry of the hounds came the deep tones of the wolf-call from Daniel's hunting-horn; the pack joined the first three hounds and they could be heard in full cry, with that peculiar lift in the note that indicates that they are after a wolf. The whippers-in no longer set on the hounds, but changed to the cry of *ulyulyu*, and above the others rose Daniel's voice, now a deep bass, now piercingly shrill. His voice seemed to fill the whole wood and carried far beyond out into the open field.

After listening a few moments in silence the count and his attendant convinced themselves that the hounds had separated into two packs: the sound of the larger pack, eagerly giving tongue, began to die away in the distance, the other pack rushed by the wood past the count, and it was with this that Daniel's voice was heard calling *ulyulyu*. The sounds of both packs mingled and broke apart again, but both were becoming more distant.

Simon sighed and stooped to straighten the leash a young borzoi had entangled, the count too sighed, and noticing the snuff-box in his hand opened it and took a pinch. 'Back!' cried Simon to a borzoi that was pushing forward out of the wood. The count started and dropped the snuff-box. Nastásya Ivánovna dismounted to pick it up. The count and Simon were looking at him.

Then unexpectedly, as often happens, the sound of the hunt suddenly approached, as if the hounds in full cry and Daniel *ulyulyuing* were just in front of them.

The count turned and saw on his right Mítka, staring at him with eyes starting out of his head, raising his cap and pointing before him to the other side.

'Look out!' he shouted in a voice plainly showing that he had long fretted to utter that word, and letting the borzois slip he galloped towards the count.

The count and Simon galloped out of the wood, and saw on their left a wolf which, softly swaying from side to side, was coming at a quiet lope farther to the left to the very place where they were standing. The angry borzois whined, and getting free of the leash rushed past the horses' feet at the wolf.

The wolf paused, turned its heavy forehead towards the dogs awkwardly, like a man suffering from the quinsy, and still slightly swaying from side to side, gave a couple of leaps and with a swish of its tail disappeared into the skirt of the wood. At the same instant, with a cry like a wail, first one hound, then another, and then another, sprang out helter-skelter from the wood opposite and the whole pack rushed across the field towards the very spot where the wolf had disappeared. The hazel bushes parted behind the hounds, and Daniel's chestnut horse appeared, dark with sweat. On its long back sat Daniel, hunched forward, capless, his dishevelled grey hair hanging over his flushed, perspiring face.

'*Ulyulyulyu! ulyulyu! . . .*' he cried. When he caught sight of the count his eyes flashed lightning.

'Blast you!' he shouted, holding up his whip threateningly at the count.

'You've let the wolf go! . . . What sportsmen!' and as if scorning to say more to the frightened and shamefaced count, he lashed the heaving flanks of his sweating chestnut gelding with all the anger the count had aroused, and flew off after the hounds. The count, like a punished schoolboy, looked round trying by a smile to win Simon's sympathy for his plight. But Simon was no longer there. He was galloping round by the bushes while the field was coming up on both sides, all trying to head the wolf, but it vanished into the wood before they could do so.

CHAPTER V

NICHOLAS ROSTÓV meanwhile remained at his post waiting for the wolf. By the way the hunt approached and receded, by the cries of the dogs whose notes were familiar to him, by the way the voices of the huntsmen approached, receded, and rose, he realized what was happening at the copse. He knew that young and old wolves were there, that the hounds had separated into two packs, that somewhere a wolf was being chased, and that something had gone wrong. He expected the wolf to come his way any moment. He made thousands

of different conjectures as to where and from what side
the beast would come and how he would set upon it.
Hope alternated with despair. Several times he addressed
a prayer to God that the wolf should come his way. He
prayed with that passionate and shamefaced feeling with
which men pray at moments of great excitement arising
from trivial causes. 'What would it be to Thee to do this
for me?' he said to God. 'I know Thou art great, and
that it is a sin to ask this of Thee, but for God's sake do
let the old wolf come my way and let Karáy spring at it—
in sight of "Uncle" who is watching from over there—
and seize it by the throat in a death-grip!' A thousand
times during that half-hour Rostóv cast eager and restless
glances over the edge of the wood, with the two scraggy
oaks rising above the aspen undergrowth and the gully
with its water-worn side and 'Uncle's' cap just visible
above the bush on his right.

'No, I shan't have such luck,' thought Rostóv, 'yet
what wouldn't it be worth! It is not to be! Everywhere,
at cards and in war, I am always unlucky.' Memories
of Austerlitz and of Dólokhov flashed rapidly and clearly
through his mind. 'Only once in my life to get an old
wolf, I want only that!' thought he, straining eyes and ears
and looking to the left and then to the right, and listening
to the slightest variation of note in the cries of the dogs.

Again he looked to the right, and saw something running towards him across the deserted field. 'No, it can't
be!' thought Rostóv taking a deep breath, as a man does
at the coming of something long hoped for. The height of
happiness was reached—and so simply, without warning,
or noise, or display, that Rostóv could not believe his eyes
and remained in doubt for over a second. The wolf ran
forward and jumped heavily over a gully that lay in her
path. She was an old animal, with a grey back and big
reddish belly. She ran without hurry, evidently feeling
sure that no one saw her. Rostóv, holding his breath,
looked round at the borzois. They stood or lay not seeing
the wolf or understanding the situation. Old Karáy had
turned his head and was angrily searching for fleas,
baring his yellow teeth and snapping at his hind legs.

'*Ulyulyulyu!*' whispered Rostóv pouting his lips. The

borzois jumped up, jerking the rings of the leashes and pricking their ears. Karáy finished scratching his hind quarters, and cocking his ears, got up with quivering tail from which tufts of matted hair hung down.

'Shall I loose them or not?' Nicholas asked himself as the wolf approached him coming from the copse. Suddenly the wolf's whole physiognomy changed; she shuddered, seeing what she had probably never seen before—human eyes fixed upon her, and turning her head a little towards Rostóv she paused.

'Back or forward? Eh, no matter, forward . . .' the wolf seemed to say to herself, and she moved forward without again looking round, and with a quiet, long, easy yet resolute lope.

'*Ulyulyu!*' cried Nicholas in a voice not his own, and of its own accord his good horse darted headlong downhill leaping over gullies to head off the wolf, and the borzois passed it running faster still. Nicholas did not hear his own cry nor feel that he was galloping, nor see the borzois, nor the ground over which he went: he saw only the wolf, who increasing her speed bounded on in the same direction along the hollow. The first to come into view was Mílka, with her black markings and powerful quarters, gaining upon the wolf. Nearer and nearer . . . now she was ahead of it; but the wolf turned its head to face her, and instead of putting on speed as she usually did Mílka suddenly raised her tail and stiffened her forelegs.

'*Ulyulyulyulyu!*' shouted Nicholas.

The reddish Lyubím rushed forward from behind Mílka, sprang impetuously at the wolf and seized it by its hind quarters, but immediately jumped aside in terror. The wolf crouched, gnashed her teeth, and again rose and bounded forward, followed at the distance of a couple of feet by all the borzois, who did not get any closer to her.

'She'll get away! No, it's impossible!' thought Nicholas, still shouting with a hoarse voice.

'Karáy, *ulyulyu!* . . .' he shouted, looking round for the old borzoi who was now his only hope. Karáy, with all the strength age had left him, stretched himself to the utmost, and watching the wolf galloped heavily aside to intercept it. But the quickness of the wolf's lope and the borzoi's slower pace made it plain that Karáy had miscalculated. Nicholas could already see not far in front of him the wood, where the wolf would certainly escape should she reach it. But coming towards him he saw hounds and a huntsman galloping almost straight at the wolf. There was still hope. A long yellowish young borzoi, one Nicholas did not know, from another leash, rushed impetuously at the wolf in front and almost knocked her over. But the wolf jumped up more quickly than any one could have expected and, gnashing her teeth, flew at the yellowish borzoi, which with a piercing yelp fell with its head on the ground, bleeding from a gash in its side.

'Karáy! Old fellow! . . .' wailed Nicholas.

Thanks to the delay caused by this crossing of the wolf's path, the old dog with its felted hair hanging from its thigh was within five paces of it. As if aware of her danger the wolf turned her eyes on Karáy, tucked her tail yet further between her legs, and increased her speed. But here Nicholas only saw that something happened to Karáy—the borzoi was suddenly on the wolf, and they rolled together down into a gully just in front of them.

That instant when Nicholas saw the wolf struggling in the gully with the dogs, while from under them could be seen her grey hair and outstretched hind leg and her frightened choking head with ears laid back (Karáy was pinning her by the throat), was the happiest moment of his life. With his hand on his saddle-bow he was ready to dismount and stab the wolf, when she suddenly thrust her head up from among that mass of dogs, and then her fore-paws were on the edge of the gully. She clicked her teeth (Karáy no longer had her by the throat), leapt with a movement of her hind legs out of the gully, and having disengaged herself from the dogs, with tail tucked in again went forward. Karáy, his hair bristling, and probably bruised or wounded, climbed with difficulty out of the gully.

'Oh my God! Why?' Nicholas cried in despair.

'Uncle's' huntsman was galloping from the other side across the wolf's path and his borzois once more stopped the animal's advance. She was again hemmed in.

Nicholas and his attendant, with 'Uncle' and his huntsman, were all riding round the wolf, crying *ulyulyu!*, shouting and preparing to dismount each moment that the wolf crouched back, and starting forward again every time she shook herself and moved towards the wood where she would be safe.

Already at the beginning of this chase Daniel, hearing the *ulyulyuing*, had rushed out from the wood. He saw Karáy seize the wolf, and checked his horse supposing the affair to be over. But when he saw that the horsemen did not dismount and that the wolf shook herself and ran for safety, Daniel set his chestnut galloping not at the wolf but straight towards the wood, just as Karáy had run to cut the animal off. As a result of this he galloped up to the wolf just when she had been stopped a second time by 'Uncle's' borzois.

Daniel galloped up silently, holding a naked dagger in his left hand and thrashing the labouring sides of his chestnut horse with his whip as if it were a flail.

Nicholas neither saw nor heard Daniel until the chestnut, breathing heavily, panted past him, and he heard the fall of a body and saw Daniel lying on the wolf's back among the dogs trying to seize her by the ears. It was evident to the dogs, the hunters, and to the wolf herself, that all was now over. The terrified wolf pressed back her ears and tried to rise, but the borzois stuck to her. Daniel rose a little, took a step, and with his whole weight, as if lying down to rest, fell on the wolf, seizing her by the ears. Nicholas was about to stab her, but Daniel whispered, 'Don't, we'll gag her!' and changing his position set his foot on the wolf's neck. A stick was thrust between her jaws and she was fastened with a leash, as if bridled, her legs were bound together, and Daniel rolled her over once or twice from side to side.

With happy, exhausted faces they laid the old wolf, alive, on a shying and snorting horse, and accompanied by the dogs yelping at her, took her to the place where they were all to meet. The hounds had killed two of the cubs and the borzois three. The huntsmen assembled with their booty and their stories, and all came to look at the wolf, which with her broad-browed head hanging down and the bitten stick between her jaws, gazed with great glassy eyes at this crowd of dogs and men surrounding her. When she was touched, she jerked her bound legs and looked wildly yet simply at everybody. Old Count Rostóv also rode up and touched the wolf.

'Oh, what a formidable one!' said he. 'A formidable one, eh?' he asked Daniel, who was standing near.

'Yes, your Excellency,' answered Daniel quickly doffing his cap.

The count remembered the wolf he had let slip and his encounter with Daniel.

'Ah, but you are a crusty fellow, friend!' said the count.

For sole reply Daniel gave him a shy, childlike, meek and amiable smile.

CHAPTER VI

THE old count went home and Natásha and Pétya promised to return very soon, but as it was still early the hunt went farther. At midday they put the hounds into a ravine thickly overgrown with young trees. Nicholas standing in a fallow field could see all his whips.

Facing him lay a field of winter rye, and there his own huntsman stood alone in a hollow behind a hazel bush. The hounds had scarcely been loosed before Nicholas heard one he knew, Voltórn, giving tongue at intervals, other hounds joined in, now pausing and now again giving tongue. A moment later he heard a cry from the wooded ravine that a fox had been found, and the whole pack, joining together, rushed along the ravine towards the rye-field and away from Nicholas.

He saw the whips in their red caps galloping along the edge of the ravine, he even saw the hounds, and was expecting a fox to show itself at any moment on the rye-field opposite.

The huntsman standing in the hollow moved and loosed his borzois, and Nicholas saw a queer, short-legged red fox with a fine brush going hard across the field. The borzois bore down on it . . . Now they drew close to the fox which began to dodge between the field in sharper and sharper curves, trailing its brush, when suddenly a strange white borzoi dashed in followed by a black one, and everything was in confusion; the borzois formed a star-shaped figure, scarcely swaying their bodies and with tails turned away from the centre of the group. Two huntsmen galloped up to the dogs, one in a red cap, the other, a stranger, in a green coat.

'What's this?' thought Nicholas. 'Where's that huntsman from? He is not "Uncle's" man.'

The huntsmen got the fox, but stayed there a long time without strapping it to the saddle. Their horses, bridled and with high saddles, stood near them and there too the dogs were lying. The huntsmen waved their arms and did something to the fox. Then from that spot came the sound of a horn, with the signal agreed on in case of a fight.

'That's Ilágin's huntsman having a row with our Iván,' said Nicholas's groom.

Nicholas sent the man to call Natásha and Pétya to him, and rode at a foot-pace to the place where the whips were getting the hounds together. Several of the field galloped to the spot where the fight was going on.

Nicholas dismounted, and with Natásha and Pétya who had ridden up, stopped near the hounds, waiting to see how the matter would end. Out of the bushes came the huntsman who had been fighting, and rode towards his young master with the fox tied to his crupper. While still at a distance he took off his cap and tried to speak respectfully, but he was pale and breathless and his face was angry. One of his eyes was black, but he probably was not even aware of it.

'What has happened?' asked Nicholas.

'A likely thing, killing a fox our dogs had hunted! And it was my grey bitch that caught it! Go to law, indeed! . . . He snatches at the fox! I gave him one with the fox. Here it is on my saddle! Do you want a taste of this? . . .' said the huntsman, pointing to his dagger and probably imagining himself still speaking to his foe.

Nicholas, not stopping to talk to the man, asked his sister and Pétya to wait for him and rode to the spot where the enemy's, Ilágin's, hunting-party was.

The victorious huntsman rode off to join the field, and

there, surrounded by inquiring sympathizers, recounted his exploits.

The facts were that Ilágin, with whom the Rostóvs had a quarrel and were at law, hunted over places that belonged by custom to the Rostóvs, and had now, as if purposely, sent his men to the very woods the Rostóvs were hunting, and let his man snatch a fox their dogs had chased.

Nicholas, though he had never seen Ilágin, with his usual absence of moderation in judgement, hated him cordially from reports of his arbitrariness and violence, and regarded him as his bitterest foe. He rode in angry agitation towards him, firmly grasping his whip and fully prepared to take the most resolute and desperate steps to punish his enemy.

Hardly had he passed an angle of the wood before a stout gentleman in a beaver cap came riding towards him on a handsome raven-black horse, accompanied by two hunt-servants.

Instead of an enemy, Nicholas found in Ilágin a stately and courteous gentleman who was particularly anxious to make the young count's acquaintance. Having ridden up to Nicholas, Ilágin raised his beaver cap and said he much regretted what had occurred and would have the man punished who had allowed himself to seize a fox hunted by some one else's borzois. He hoped to become better acquainted with the count and invited him to draw his covert.

Natásha, afraid that her brother would do something dreadful, had followed him in some excitement. Seeing the enemies exchanging friendly greetings she rode up to them. Ilágin lifted his beaver cap still higher to Natásha, and said with a pleasant smile that the young countess resembled Diana in her passion for the chase as well as in her beauty, of which he had heard much.

To expiate his huntsman's offence Ilágin pressed the Rostóvs to come to an upland of his about a verst away which he usually kept for himself and which, he said, swarmed with hares. Nicholas agreed, and the hunt, now doubled, moved on.

The way to Ilágin's upland was across the fields. The

hunt-servants fell into line. The masters rode together, 'Uncle', Rostóv, and Ilágin, kept stealthily glancing at one another's dogs, trying not to be observed by their companions and searching uneasily for rivals to their own borzois.

Rostóv was particularly struck by the beauty of a small, pure bred, red-spotted bitch on Ilágin's leash, slender but with muscles like steel, a delicate muzzle and prominent black eyes. He had heard of the swiftness of Ilágin's borzois, and in that beautiful bitch saw a rival to his own Mílka.

In the middle of a sober conversation begun by Ilágin about the year's harvest, Nicholas pointed to the red-spotted bitch.

'A fine little bitch, that!' said he in a careless tone. 'Is she swift?'

'That one? Yes, she's a good dog, gets what she's after,' answered Ilágin indifferently of the red-spotted bitch Erzá, for which a year before he had given a neighbour three families of house-serfs. 'So in your parts, too, the harvest is nothing to boast of, Count?' he went on, continuing the conversation they had begun. And considering it polite to return the young count's compliment, Ilágin looked at his borzois and picked out Mílka, who attracted his attention by her breadth. 'That black-spotted one of yours is fine—well-shaped!' said he.

'Yes, she's fast enough,' replied Nicholas, and thought: 'If only a full-grown hare would cross the field now, I'd show you what sort of a borzoi she is,' and turning to his groom he said he would give a ruble to any one who found a hare.

'I don't understand,' continued Ilágin, 'how some sportsmen can be so jealous about game and dogs. For myself, I can tell you, Count, I enjoy riding in company such as this . . . what could be better?' (he again raised his cap to Natásha), 'but as for counting skins and what one takes, I don't care about that.'

'Of course not!'

'Or being upset because some one else's borzoi and not mine catches something. All I care about is to enjoy seeing the chase, is it not so, Count? For I consider that . . .'

'*A-tu!*' came the long-drawn cry of one of the borzoi-whippers-in who had halted. He stood on a knoll in the stubble holding his whip aloft, and again repeated his long-drawn cry, '*a-tu!*' (This call and the uplifted whip meant that he saw a sitting hare.)

'Ah, he has found one, I think,' said Ilágin carelessly. 'Well, let us course it, Count.'

'Yes, we must ride up . . . Shall we both course it?' answered Nicholas, seeing in Erzá and 'Uncle's' red Rugáy two rivals he had never yet had a chance of pitting against his own borzois. 'And suppose they outdo my Mílka at once!' he thought, as he rode with 'Uncle' and Ilágin towards the hare.

'A full-grown one?' asked Ilágin as he approached the whip who had sighted the hare—and not without agitation he looked round and whistled to Erzá.

'And you, Michael Nikanórovich?' he said, addressing 'Uncle'.

The latter was riding with a sullen expression on his face.

'How can I join in? Why you've given a village for each of your borzois! That's it, come on! Yours are worth thousands. Try yours against one another, you two, and I'll look on!'

'Rugáy, hey, hey!' he shouted. 'Rugáyushka!' he added, involuntarily by this diminutive expressing his affection and the hopes he placed on this red borzoi. Natásha saw and felt the agitation the two elderly men and her brother were trying to conceal, and was herself excited by it.

The huntsman stood half-way up the knoll holding up his whip and the gentlefolk rode up to him at a foot-pace; the hounds that were far off on the horizon turned away from the hare, and the whips, but not the gentlefolk, also moved away. All were moving slowly and sedately.

'How is it pointing?' asked Nicholas, riding a hundred paces towards the whip who had sighted the hare.

But before the whip could reply, the hare, scenting the frost coming next morning, was unable to rest and leapt up. The pack on leash rushed downhill in full cry after the hare, and from all sides the borzois that were not on leash darted after the hounds and the hare. All the hunt, who had been moving slowly, shouted 'Stop!' calling in the hounds, while the borzoi-whips, with a cry of '*A-tu!*', galloped across the field setting the borzois on the hare. The tranquil Ilágin, Nicholas, Natásha, and 'Uncle', flew, reckless of where or how they went, seeing only the borzois and the hare and fearing only to lose sight even for an instant of the chase. The hare they had started was a strong and swift one. When he jumped up he did not run at once, but pricked his ears listening to the shouting and trampling that resounded from all sides at once. He took a dozen bounds not very quickly, letting the borzois gain on him, and finally, having chosen his direction and realized his danger, laid back his ears and rushed off headlong. He had been lying in the stubble, but in front of him was the autumn-sowing where the ground was soft. The two borzois of the huntsman who had sighted him, having been the nearest, were the first to see and pursue him, but they had not gone far before Ilágin's red-spotted Erzá passed them, got within a length, flew at the hare with terrible swiftness aiming at his scut, and thinking she had seized him rolled over like a ball. The hare arched his back and bounded off yet more swiftly. From behind Erzá rushed the broad-haunched black-spotted Mílka and began rapidly gaining on the hare.

'Miláshka, dear!' rose Nicholas's triumphant cry. It looked as if Mílka would immediately pounce on the hare, but she overtook him and flew past. The hare had squatted. Again the beautiful Erzá reached him, but when close to the hare's scut paused as if measuring the distance so as not to make a mistake this time but seize his hind leg.

'Erzá, darling!' Ilágin wailed in a voice unlike his own. Erzá did not hearken to his appeal. At the very moment when she would have seized her prey, the hare moved and darted along the balk between the winter rye and the stubble. Again Erzá and Mílka were abreast, running like a pair of carriage horses, and began to overtake the hare, but it was easier for the hare to run on the balk and the borzois did not overtake him so quickly.

'Rugáy, Rugáyushka! That's it, come on!' came a
third voice just then, and 'Uncle's' red borzoi, straining
and curving its back, caught up with the two foremost
borzois, pushed ahead of them, regardless of the terrible
strain put on speed close to the hare, knocked it off the
balk onto the rye-field, again put on speed still more
viciously, sinking to his knees in the muddy field, and all
one could see was how, muddying his back, he rolled
over with the hare. A ring of borzois surrounded him.
A moment later every one had drawn up round the crowd
of dogs. Only the delighted 'Uncle' dismounted, and cut
off a pad, shaking the hare for the blood to drip off, and
anxiously glancing round with restless eyes while his
arms and legs twitched. He spoke without himself knowing whom to or what about. 'That's it, come on! That's
a dog! . . . There, it has beaten them all, the thousand-
ruble as well as the one-ruble borzois. That's it, come
on!' said he, panting and looking wrathfully around as
if he were abusing some one, and as if they were all his
enemies, had insulted him, and only now had he at last
succeeded in justifying himself. 'There are your thousand-
ruble ones . . . That's it, come on! . . .'

'Rugáy, here's a pad for you!' he said, throwing down
the hare's muddy pad. 'You've deserved it, that's it,
come on!'

'She'd tired herself out, she'd run it down three times
by herself,' said Nicholas, also not listening to any one
and regardless of whether he were heard or not.

'But what is there in running across it like that?' said
Ilágin's groom.

'Once she had missed it and turned it away, any
mongrel could take it,' Ilágin was saying at the same
time, breathless from his gallop and his excitement. At
the same moment Natásha, without drawing breath,
screamed joyously, ecstatically, and so piercingly that it
set every one's ears tingling. By that shriek she expressed
what the others expressed by all talking at once, and it
was so strange that she must herself have been ashamed
of so wild a cry, and every one else would have been
amazed at it, at any other time. 'Uncle' himself twisted
up the hare, threw it neatly and smartly across his horse's

back as if by that gesture he meant to rebuke everybody, and with an air of not wishing to speak to any one mounted his bay and rode off. The others all followed dispirited and shamefaced, and only much later were they able to regain their former affectation of indifference. For a long time they continued to look at red Rugáy who, his arched back spattered with mud and clanking the ring of his leash, walked along just behind 'Uncle's' horse with the serene air of a conqueror.

'Well, I am like any other dog as long as it's not a question of coursing. But when it is, then look out!' his appearance seemed to Nicholas to be saying.

When, much later, 'Uncle' rode up to Nicholas and began talking to him, he felt flattered that, after what had happened, 'Uncle' deigned to speak to him.

CHAPTER VII

TOWARDS evening Ilágin took leave of Nicholas, who found that they were so far from home that he accepted 'Uncle's' offer that the hunting-party should spend the night in his little village of Mikháylovna.

'And if you put up at my house that will be better still. That's it, come on!' said 'Uncle'. 'You see it's damp weather, and you could rest, and the little Countess could be driven home in a trap.'

'Uncle's' offer was accepted. A huntsman was sent to Otrádnoe for a trap, while Nicholas rode with Natásha and Pétya to 'Uncle's' house.

Some five male domestic serfs, big and little, rushed out to the front porch to meet their master. A score of women serfs old and young, as well as children, popped out from the back entrance to have a look at the hunters who were arriving. The presence of Natásha—a woman, a lady, and on horseback—raised the curiosity of the serfs to such a degree that many of them came up to her, stared her in the face, and unabashed by her presence made remarks about her as though she were some prodigy on show, and not a human being able to hear or understand what was said about her.

'Arínka! Look, she sits sideways! There she sits and her skirt dangles . . . See, she's got a little hunting-horn!'

'Goodness gracious! See her knife? . . .'

'Isn't she a Tartar!'

'How is it you didn't go head over heels?' asked the boldest of all, addressing Natásha directly.

'Uncle' dismounted at the porch of his little wooden house, which stood in the midst of an overgrown garden, and after a glance at his retainers shouted authoritatively that the superfluous ones should take themselves off and that all necessary preparations should be made to receive the guests and the visitors.

The serfs all dispersed. 'Uncle' lifted Natásha off her horse, and taking her hand led her up the rickety wooden steps of the porch. The house with its bare unplastered log-walls was not over-clean—it did not seem that those living in it aimed at keeping it spotless—but neither was it noticeably neglected. In the entry there was a smell of fresh apples, and wolf and fox skins hung about.

'Uncle' led his visitors through the ante-room into a small hall with a folding table and red chairs, then into the drawing-room with a round birch-wood table and a sofa, and finally into his private room, where there was a tattered sofa, a worn carpet, and portraits of Suvórov, of the host's father and mother, and of himself in military uniform. The study smelt strongly of tobacco and dogs. 'Uncle' asked his visitors to sit down and make themselves at home, and then went out of the room. Rugáy, his back still muddy, came into the room and lay down on the sofa, cleaning himself with his tongue and teeth. Leading from the study was a passage in which a partition with ragged curtains could be seen. From behind this came women's laughter and whispers. Natásha, Nicholas, and Pétya, took off their wraps and sat down on the sofa. Pétya, leaning on his elbow, fell asleep at once. Natásha and Nicholas were silent. Their faces glowed, they were very hungry and very cheerful. They looked at one another (now that the hunt was over and they were in the house, Nicholas no longer considered it necessary to show his manly superiority over his sister),

Natásha gave him a wink, and neither refrained long from bursting into a peal of ringing laughter even before they had a pretext ready to account for it.

After a while 'Uncle' came in, in a Cossack coat, blue trousers, and small top-boots. And Natásha felt that this costume, the very one she had regarded with surprise and amusement at Otrádnoe, was just the right thing and not at all worse than a swallow-tail or frock coat. 'Uncle' too was in high spirits, and far from being offended by the brother's and sister's laughter (it could never enter his head that they might be laughing at his way of life), he himself joined in their spontaneous merriment.

'That's right, young Countess, that's it, come on! I never saw any one like her!' said he, offering Nicholas a pipe with a long stem and with a practised motion of three fingers taking down another that had been cut short. 'She's ridden all day like a man, and is as fresh as ever!'

Soon after 'Uncle's' reappearance the door was opened, evidently from the sound by a bare-footed girl, and a stout, rosy, good-looking woman of about forty, with a double chin and full red lips, entered carrying a large loaded tray. With hospitable dignity and cordiality in her glance and in every motion, she looked at the visitors and, with a pleasant smile, bowed respectfully. In spite of her exceptional stoutness, which caused her to protrude her chest and stomach and throw back her head, this woman (who was 'Uncle's' housekeeper) trod very lightly. She went to the table, set down the tray, and with her plump white hands deftly took from it the bottles and various hors-d'œuvre and dishes, and arranged them on the table. When she had finished, she stepped aside and stopped at the door with a smile on her face. 'Here I am. I am she! Now do you understand "Uncle"?' her expression said to Rostóv. How could one help understanding? Not only Nicholas but even Natásha understood the meaning of his puckered brow and the happy complacent smile that slightly puckered his lips when Anísya Fëdorovna entered. On the tray was a bottle of herb-wine, different kinds of vodka, pickled mushrooms, rye-cakes made with buttermilk, honey in the comb, still mead and sparkling mead, apples, nuts (raw and roasted), and nut-and-honey sweets. Afterwards she brought a freshly roasted chicken, ham, preserves made with honey, and preserves made with sugar.

All this was the fruit of Anísya Fëdorovna's housekeeping, gathered and prepared by her. The smell and taste of it all had a smack of Anísya Fëdorovna herself; a savour of juiciness, cleanliness, whiteness, and pleasant smiles.

'Take this, little Lady-Countess!' she kept saying, as she offered Natásha first one thing and then another.

Natásha ate of everything and thought she had never seen or eaten such buttermilk-cakes, such aromatic jam, such honey-and-nut sweets, or such a chicken anywhere. Anísya Fëdorovna left the room.

After supper over their cherry brandy Rostóv and 'Uncle' talked of past and future hunts, of Rugáy and Ilágin's dogs, while Natásha sat upright on the sofa and listened with sparkling eyes. She tried several times to wake Pétya that he might eat something, but he only muttered incoherent words without waking up. Natásha felt so light-hearted and happy in these novel surroundings that she only feared the trap would come for her too soon. After a casual pause such as often occurs when receiving friends for the first time in one's own house, 'Uncle', answering a thought that was in his visitors' minds, said:

'This, you see, is how I am finishing my days ... Death will come. That's it, come on! Nothing will remain. Then why harm any one?'

'Uncle's' face was very significant and even handsome as he said this. Involuntarily Rostóv recalled all the good he had heard about him from his father and the neighbours. Throughout the whole province 'Uncle' had the reputation of being the most honourable and disinterested of cranks. They called him in to decide family disputes, chose him as executor, confided secrets to him, elected him to be a justice and to other posts; but he always persistently refused public appointments, passing the autumn and spring in the fields on his bay gelding, sitting at home in winter, and lying in his overgrown garden in summer.

'Why don't you enter the service, Uncle?'

'I did once, but gave it up. I am not fit for it. That's it, come on! I can't make head or tail of it. That's for you—I haven't brains enough. Now hunting is another matter—that's it, come on! Open the door, there!' he shouted. 'Why have you shut it?'

The door at the end of the passage led to the huntsmen's room, as they called the room for the hunt servants.

There was a rapid patter of bare feet, and an unseen hand opened the door into the huntsmen's room, from which came the clear sounds of a balaláyka,[1] on which some one, who was evidently a master of the art, was playing. Natásha had been listening to those strains for some time and now went out into the passage to hear better.

'That's Mítka, my coachman . . . I have got him a good balaláyka. I'm fond of it,' said 'Uncle'.

It was the custom for Mítka to play the balaláyka in the huntsmen's room when 'Uncle' returned from the chase. 'Uncle' was fond of such music.

'How good! Really very good!' said Nicholas with some unintentional superciliousness, as if ashamed to confess that the sounds pleased him very much.

'Very good?' said Natásha reproachfully, noticing her brother's tone. 'Not "very good"—it's simply delicious!'

Just as 'Uncle's' pickled mushrooms, honey, and cherry brandy, had seemed to her the best in the world, so also that song, at that moment, seemed to her the acme of musical delight.

'More, please, more!' cried Natásha at the door as soon as the balaláyka ceased. Mítka tuned up afresh, and recommenced thrumming the balaláyka to the air of *My Lady*, with trills and variations. 'Uncle' sat listening, slightly smiling with his head on one side. The air was repeated a hundred times. The balaláyka was retuned several times and the same notes were thrummed again, but the listeners did not grow weary of it and wished to hear it again and again. Anísya Fëdorovna

[1] The balaláyka is a popular Russian three-stringed instrument, which may be taken as the equivalent of the Spanish guitar.

came in and leaned her portly person against the door-post.

'You like listening?' she said to Natásha, with a smile extremely like 'Uncle's'. 'That's a good player of ours,' she added.

'He doesn't play that part right!' said 'Uncle' suddenly, with an energetic gesture. 'Here he ought to burst out—that's it, come on!—ought to burst out.'

'Do you play then?' asked Natásha.

'Uncle' did not answer, but smiled.

'Anísya, go and see if the strings of my guitar are all right. I haven't touched it for a long time. That's it—come on! I've given it up.'

Anísya Fëdorovna with her light step willingly went to fulfil her errand, and brought back the guitar.

Without looking at any one, 'Uncle' blew the dust off it, and tapping the case with his bony fingers tuned the guitar and settled himself in his arm-chair. He took the guitar a little above the finger-board, arching his left elbow with a somewhat theatrical gesture, and with a wink at Anísya Fëdorovna struck a single chord, pure and sonorous, and then quietly, smoothly, and confidently, began playing in very slow time not *My Lady*, but the well-known song: *Came a maiden down the street*. The tune played with precision and in exact time began to thrill in the hearts of Nicholas and Natásha, arousing in them the same kind of sober mirth as radiated from Anísya Fëdorovna's whole being. Anísya Fëdorovna flushed, and drawing her kerchief over her face went laughing out of the room. 'Uncle' continued to play correctly, carefully, with energetic firmness, looking with a changed and inspired expression at the spot where Anísya Fëdorovna had just stood. Something seemed to be laughing a little on one side of his face under his grey moustaches, especially as the song grew brisker and the time quicker, and when, here and there, as he ran his fingers over the strings, something seemed to snap.

'Lovely, lovely! Go on, Uncle, go on!' shouted Natásha as soon as he had finished. She jumped up and hugged and kissed him. 'Nicholas, Nicholas!' she said, turning to her brother, as if asking him: 'What is it moves me so?'

Nicholas too was greatly pleased by 'Uncle's' playing, and 'Uncle' played the piece over again. Anísya Fëdorovna's smiling face reappeared in the doorway and behind hers other faces . . .

Fetching water clear and sweet,
Stop, dear maiden, I entreat—

played 'Uncle' once more, running his fingers skilfully over the strings, and then he stopped short and jerked his shoulders.

'Go on, Uncle dear,' Natásha wailed in an imploring tone as if her life depended on it.

'Uncle' rose, and it was as if there were two men in him: one of them smiled seriously at the merry fellow, while the merry fellow struck a naïve and precise attitude preparatory to a folk-dance.

'Now then, niece!' he exclaimed, waving to Natásha the hand that had just struck a chord.

Natásha threw off the shawl from her shoulders, ran forward to face 'Uncle', and setting her arms akimbo, also made a motion with her shoulders and struck an attitude.

Where, how, and when, had this young countess, educated by an *émigrée* French governess, imbibed from the Russian air she breathed that spirit, and obtained that manner which the *pas de châle* [1] would, one would have supposed, long ago have effaced? But the spirit and the movements were those inimitable and unteachable Russian ones that 'Uncle' had expected of her. As soon as she had struck her pose and smiled triumphantly, proudly, and with sly merriment, the fear that had at first seized Nicholas and the others that she might not do the right thing was at an end, and they were already admiring her.

She did the right thing with such precision, such complete precision, that Anísya Fëdorovna, who had at once handed her the handkerchief she needed for the dance, had tears in her eyes, though she laughed as she watched this slim, graceful countess, reared in silks and velvets and so different from herself, who yet was able to under-

[1] The shawl-dance; a French dance, the style of which contrasts with the Russian folk-dances.

stand all that was in Anísya and in Anísya's father and
mother and aunt, and in every Russian man and woman.

'Well, little Countess; that's it—come on!' cried 'Uncle'
with a joyous laugh, having finished the dance. 'Well done,
niece! Now a fine young fellow must be found as husband
for you. That's it—come on!'

'He's chosen already,' said Nicholas smiling.

'Oh?' said 'Uncle' in surprise, looking inquiringly at
Natásha, who nodded her head with a happy smile.

'And such a one!' she said. But as soon as she had said
it a new train of thoughts and feelings arose in her. 'What
did Nicholas's smile mean when he said "Chosen
already"? Is he glad of it or not? It is as if he thought my
Bolkónski would not approve of or understand our gaiety.
But he would understand it all. Where is he now?' she
thought, and her face suddenly became serious. But this
lasted only a second. 'Don't dare to think about it,' she
said to herself, and sat down again smilingly beside
'Uncle', begging him to play something more.

'Uncle' played another song and a valse; then after
a pause he cleared his throat, and sang his favourite
hunting song:

> 'As 'twas growing dark last night
> Fell the snow so soft and light . . .'

'Uncle' sang as peasants sing, with full and naïve conviction that the whole meaning of a song lies in the
words, and that the tune comes of itself, and that apart
from the words there is no tune, which exists only to give
measure to the words. As a result of this the unconsidered
tune, like the song of a bird, was extraordinarily good.
Natásha was in ecstasies over 'Uncle's' singing. She resolved to give up learning the harp, and to play only the
guitar. She asked 'Uncle' for his guitar and at once
found the chords of the song.

After nine o'clock two traps and three mounted men, who
had been sent to look for them, arrived to fetch Natásha
and Pétya. The count and countess did not know where
they were and were very anxious, said one of the men.

Pétya was carried out like a log and laid in the larger
of the two traps. Natásha and Nicholas got into the other.
'Uncle' wrapped Natásha up warmly, and took leave of

her with quite a new tenderness. He accompanied them on foot as far as a bridge that could not be crossed, so that they had to go round by the ford, and he sent huntsmen to ride in front with lanterns.

'Good-bye, dear niece,' his voice called out of the darkness—not the voice Natásha had known previously, but the one that had sung *As 'twas growing dark last night*.

In the village through which they passed there were red lights and a cheerful smell of smoke.

'What a darling "Uncle" is!' said Natásha, when they had come out onto the high road.

'Yes,' returned Nicholas. 'You're not cold?'

'No. I'm quite, quite all right. I feel so comfortable!' answered Natásha, almost perplexed by her feelings. They remained silent a long while. The night was dark and damp. They could not see the horses, but only heard them splashing through the unseen mud.

What was passing in that receptive child-like soul that so eagerly caught and assimilated all the diverse impressions of life? How did they all find place in her? But she was very happy. As they were nearing home she suddenly struck up the air of *As 'twas growing dark last night*—the tune of which she had all the way been trying to get, and had at last caught.

'Got it?' said Nicholas.

'What were you thinking about just now, Nicholas?' inquired Natásha.

They were fond of asking one another that question.

'I?' said Nicholas, trying to remember. 'Well, you see, first I thought that Rugáy, the red hound, was like "Uncle", and that if he were a man he would always keep "Uncle" near him, if not for his riding then for his manner. What a good fellow "Uncle" is! Don't you think so? Well, and you?'

'I? Wait a bit, wait. Yes, first I thought that we are driving along and imagining that we are going home, but that heaven knows where we are really going in the darkness, and that we shall arrive and suddenly find that we are not in Otrádnoe but in Fairyland. And then I thought . . . No, nothing else.'

'I know, I expect you thought of him,' said

Nicholas, smiling as Natásha knew by the sound of his voice.

'No,' said Natásha, though she had in reality been thinking about Prince Andrew at the same time as of the rest, and of how he would have liked 'Uncle'. 'And then I was saying to myself all the way, "How well Anísya carried herself, how well!"' And Nicholas heard her spontaneous, happy, ringing laughter. 'And do you know,' she suddenly said, 'I know that I shall never again be as happy and tranquil as I am now.'

'Rubbish, nonsense, humbug!' exclaimed Nicholas, and he thought: 'How charming this Natásha of mine is! I have no other friend like her, and never shall have. Why should she marry? We might always drive about together!'

'What a darling this Nicholas of mine is!' thought Natásha.

'Ah, there are still lights in the drawing-room!' she said, pointing to the windows of the house that gleamed invitingly in the moist velvety darkness of the night.

CHAPTER VIII

COUNT Ilyá Rostóv had resigned the position of Marshal of the Nobility because it involved him in too much expense, but still his affairs did not improve. Natásha and Nicholas often noticed their parents conferring together anxiously and privately, and heard suggestions of selling the fine ancestral Rostóv house and estate near Moscow. It was not necessary to entertain so freely as when the count had been Marshal, and life at Otrádnoe was quieter than in former years, but still the enormous house and its lodges were full of people, and more than twenty sat down to table every day. These were all their own people who had settled down in the house almost as members of the family, or persons who were, it seemed, obliged to live in the count's house. Such were Dimmler the musician and his wife, Vogel the dancing-master and his family, Belóva, an old maiden lady, an inmate of the house, and many others such as Pétya's tutors, the girls' former governess, and other people who simply found it preferable and more advantageous to live in the count's house than at home. They had not as many visitors as before, but the old habits of life, without which the count and countess could not conceive of existence, remained unchanged. There was still the hunting establishment which Nicholas had even enlarged, the same fifty horses and fifteen grooms in the stables, the same expensive presents and dinner-parties to the whole district on name-days; there were still the count's games of whist and boston, at which—spreading out his cards so that every-one could see them—he let himself be plundered of hundreds of rubles every day by neighbours, who looked upon an opportunity to play a rubber with Count Rostóv as a most profitable source of income.

The count moved in his affairs as in a huge net, trying not to believe that he was entangled but becoming more and more so at every step, and feeling too feeble to break the meshes or to set to work carefully and patiently to disentangle them. The countess with her loving heart felt that her children were being ruined, that it was not the count's fault, for he could not help being what he was —that (though he tried to hide it) he himself suffered from the consciousness of his own and his children's ruin, and she tried to find means of remedying the position. From her feminine point of view she could see only one solution, namely, for Nicholas to marry a rich heiress. She felt this to be their last hope, and that if Nicholas refused the match she had found for him, she would have to abandon the hope of ever getting matters right. This match was with Julie Karágina, the daughter of excellent and virtuous parents, a girl the Rostóvs had known from childhood, and who had now become a wealthy heiress through the death of the last of her brothers.

The countess had written direct to Julie's mother in Moscow, suggesting a marriage between their children, and had received a favourable answer from her. Karágina had replied that for her part she was agreeable, and every-thing would depend on her daughter's inclination. She invited Nicholas to come to Moscow.

Several times the countess, with tears in her eyes, told her son that now that both her daughters were settled her only wish was to see him married. She said she could lie down in her grave peacefully if that were accomplished. Then she told him that she knew of a splendid girl, and tried to discover what he thought about marriage.

At other times she praised Julie to him, and advised him to go to Moscow during the holidays to amuse himself. Nicholas guessed what his mother's remarks were leading to, and during one of these conversations induced her to speak quite frankly. She told him that her only hope of getting their affairs disentangled, now lay in his marrying Julie Karágina.

'But, Mamma, suppose I loved a girl who has no fortune, would you expect me to sacrifice my feelings and my honour for the sake of money?' he asked his mother, not realizing the cruelty of his question and only wishing to show his noble-mindedness.

'No, you have not understood me,' said his mother, not knowing how to justify herself. 'You have not understood me, Nikólenka. It is your happiness I wish for,' she added, feeling that she was telling an untruth and was becoming entangled. She began to cry.

'Mamma, don't cry. Only tell me that you wish it, and you know I will give my life, anything, to put you at ease,' said Nicholas. 'I would sacrifice anything for you—even my feelings.'

But the countess did not want the question put like that: she did not want a sacrifice from her son, she herself wished to make a sacrifice for him.

'No, you have not understood me, don't let us talk about it,' she replied, wiping away her tears.

'Maybe I do love a poor girl,' said Nicholas to himself. 'Am I to sacrifice my feelings and my honour for money? I wonder how Mamma could speak so to me. Because Sónya is poor I must not love her,' he thought, 'must not respond to her faithful, devoted love? Yet I should certainly be happier with her than with some doll-like Julie. I can always sacrifice my feelings for my family's welfare,' he said to himself, 'but I can't coerce my feelings. If I love Sónya, that feeling is for me stronger and higher than all else.'

Nicholas did not go to Moscow, and the countess did

not renew the conversation with him about marriage.
She saw with sorrow, and sometimes with exasperation,
symptoms of a growing attachment between her son and
the portionless Sónya. Though she blamed herself for it,
she could not refrain from grumbling at and worrying
Sónya, often pulling her up without reason, addressing
her stiffly as 'my dear', and using the formal 'you'
instead of the intimate 'thou' in speaking to her. The
kind-hearted countess was the more vexed with Sónya
because that poor, dark-eyed niece of hers was so meek,
so kind, so devotedly grateful to her benefactors, and so
faithfully, unchangingly and unselfishly in love with
Nicholas, that there were no grounds for finding fault
with her.

Nicholas was spending the last of his leave at home.
A fourth letter had come from Prince Andrew, from
Rome, in which he wrote that he would have been on his
way back to Russia long ago had not his wound unexpectedly reopened in the warm climate, which
obliged him to defer his return till the beginning of the
new year. Natásha was still as much in love with her
betrothed, found the same comfort in that love, and was
still as ready to throw herself into all the pleasures of life
as before; but at the end of the fourth month of their
separation she began to have fits of depression which she
could not master. She felt sorry for herself; sorry that she
was being wasted all this time, and of no use to any one—
while she felt herself so capable of loving and being loved.

Things were not cheerful in the Rostóvs' home.

CHAPTER IX

CHRISTMAS came, and except for the ceremonial
Mass, the solemn and wearisome Christmas congratulations from neighbours and servants, and the new
dresses every one put on, there were no special festivities
though the calm frost of twenty degrees Réaumur,[1] the
dazzling sunshine by day, and the starlight of the winter
nights, seemed to call for some special celebration of the
season.

1 13 degrees below zero, Fahrenheit.

On the third day of Christmas week, after the midday dinner all the inmates of the house dispersed to various rooms. It was the dullest time of the day. Nicholas, who had been visiting some neighbours that morning, was asleep on the sitting-room sofa. The old count was resting in his study. Sónya sat in the drawing-room at the round table, copying a design for embroidery. The countess was playing patience. Nastásya Ivánovna, the buffoon, sat with a sad face at the window with two old ladies. Natásha came into the room, went up to Sónya, glanced at what she was doing, and then went up to her mother and stood without speaking.

'Why are you wandering about like an outcast?' asked her mother. 'What do you want?'

'*Him* . . . I want him . . . now, this minute! I want *him*!' said Natásha, with glittering eyes and no sign of a smile.

The countess lifted her head and looked attentively at her daughter.

'Don't look at me, Mamma! Don't look; I shall cry directly.'

'Sit down with me a little,' said the countess.

'Mamma, I want *him*. Why should I be wasted like this, Mamma?'

Her voice broke, tears gushed from her eyes, and she turned quickly to hide them and left the room.

She passed into the sitting-room, stood there thinking a while, and then went into the maids' room. There an old maid-servant was grumbling at a young girl who stood panting, having just run in through the cold from the serfs' quarters.

'Stop playing—there's a time for everything,' said the old woman.

'Let her alone, Kondrátevna,' said Natásha. 'Go, Mavrúsha, go.'

Having released Mavrúsha, Natásha crossed the dancing-hall and went to the vestibule. There an old footman and two young ones were playing cards. They broke off and rose as she entered.

'What can I do with them?' thought Natásha.

'Oh, Nikíta, please go . . . where can I send him? . . .

Yes, go to the yard and fetch a fowl, please, a cock, and you, Mísha, bring me some oats.'[1]

'Just a few oats?' said Mísha cheerfully and readily.

'Go, go quickly,' the old man urged him.

'And you, Theodore, get me a piece of chalk.'

On her way past the butler's pantry she told them to set a samovar, though it was not at all the time for tea.

Fóka, the butler, was the most ill-tempered person in the house. Natásha liked to test her power over him. He distrusted the order and asked whether the samovar was really wanted.

'Oh dear, what a young lady!' said Fóka, pretending to frown at Natásha.

No one in the house sent people about or gave them as much trouble as Natásha did. She could not see people unconcernedly, but had to send them on some errand. She seemed to be trying whether any of them would get angry or sulky with her; but the serfs fulfilled no one's orders so readily as they did hers. 'What can I do, where can I go?' thought she, as she went slowly along the passage.

'Nastásya Ivánovna, what sort of children shall I have?' she asked the buffoon, who was coming towards her in a woman's jacket.

'Why, fleas, crickets, grasshoppers,' answered the buffoon.

'O Lord, O Lord, it's always the same! Oh, where am I to go? What am I to do with myself?' And tapping with her heels she ran quickly upstairs to see Vogel and his wife who lived on the upper story.

Two governesses were sitting with the Vogels at a table on which were plates of raisins, walnuts, and almonds. The governesses were discussing whether it was cheaper to live in Moscow or Odessa. Natásha sat down, listened to their talk with a serious and thoughtful air, and then got up again.

'The island of Madagascar,' she said, 'Ma-da-gas-car,' she repeated, articulating each syllable distinctly, and

[1] Feeding a fowl with grain arranged on the floor is a way of telling fortunes at Christmas time.

not replying to Madame Schoss who asked what she was saying, she went out of the room.

Her brother Pétya was upstairs too; with the man in attendance on him he was preparing fireworks to let off that night.

'Pétya! Pétya!' she called to him. 'Carry me downstairs.'

Pétya ran up and offered her his back. She jumped on it, putting her arms round his neck, and he pranced along with her.

'No, don't . . . the island of Madagascar!' she said, and jumping off his back she went downstairs.

Having as it were reviewed her kingdom, tested her power, and made sure that every one was submissive, but that all the same it was dull, Natásha betook herself to the ball-room, picked up her guitar, sat down in a dark corner behind a bookcase and began to run her fingers over the strings in the bass, picking out a passage she recalled from an opera she had heard in Petersburg with Prince Andrew. What she drew from the guitar would have had no meaning for other listeners, but in her imagination a whole series of reminiscences arose from those sounds. She sat behind the bookcase with her eyes fixed on a streak of light escaping from the pantry door, and listened to herself and pondered. She was in a mood for brooding on the past.

Sónya passed to the pantry with a glass in her hand. Natásha glanced at her and at the crack in the pantry door, and it seemed to her that she remembered the light falling through that crack once before and Sónya passing with a glass in her hand. 'Yes, it was exactly the same,' thought Natásha.

'Sónya, what is this?' she cried, twanging a thick string.

'Oh, you are there!' said Sónya with a start, and came near and listened. 'I don't know. A storm?' she ventured timidly, afraid of being wrong.

'There! That's just how she started and just how she came up smiling timidly when all this happened before,' thought Natásha, 'and in just the same way I thought there was something lacking in her.'

'No, it's the chorus from the *Water-Carrier*,[1] listen!' and Natásha sang the air of the chorus so that Sónya should catch it. 'Where were you going?' she asked.

'To change the water in this glass. I am just finishing the design.'

'You always find something to do, but I can't,' said Natásha. 'And where's Nicholas?'

'Asleep, I think.'

'Sónya, go and wake him,' said Natásha. 'Tell him I want him to come and sing.'

She sat awhile, wondering what the meaning of it all having happened before could be, and without solving this problem, or at all regretting not having done so, she again passed in fancy to the time when she was with *him* and he was looking at her with a lover's eyes.

'Oh, if only he would come quicker! I am so afraid it will never be! And worst of all, I am growing old— that's the thing! There won't then be in me what there is now. But perhaps he'll come to-day, will come immediately. Perhaps he has come and is sitting in the drawing-room. Perhaps he came yesterday and I have forgotten it.' She rose, put down the guitar, and went to the drawing-room.

All the domestic circle, tutors, governesses, and guests, were already at the tea-table. The servants stood round the table—but Prince Andrew was not there and life was going on as before.

'Ah, here she is!' said the old count when he saw Natásha enter. 'Well, sit down by me.' But Natásha stayed by her mother and glanced round as if looking for something.

'Mamma!' she muttered, 'give him to me, give him, Mamma, quickly, quickly!' and she again had difficulty in repressing her sobs.

She sat down at the table and listened to the conversation between the elders and Nicholas, who had also come to the table. 'My God, my God! The same faces, the same talk, Papa holding his cup and blowing in the same way!' thought Natásha, feeling with horror a sense

[1] Cherubini's operatic masterpiece *Les deux Journées* or *The Water-Carrier*, 1804.

of repulsion rising up in her for the whole household because they were always the same.

After tea Nicholas, Sónya, and Natásha went to the sitting-room, to their favourite corner where their most intimate talks always began.

CHAPTER X

'DOES it ever happen to you,' said Natásha to her brother when they had settled down in the sitting-room, 'does it ever happen to you to feel as if there were nothing more to come—nothing; that everything good is past? And to feel not exactly dull, but sad?'

'I should think so!' he replied. 'I have felt like that when everything was all right and every one was cheerful. The thought has come into my mind that I was already tired of it all, and that we must all die. Once in the regiment I had not gone to some merrymaking where there was music . . . and suddenly I felt so depressed . . .'

'Oh yes, I know, I know, I know!' Natásha interrupted him. 'When I was quite little that used to be so with me. Do you remember when I was punished once about some plums? You were all dancing, and I sat sobbing in the school-room? I shall never forget it: I felt sad and sorry for every one, for myself, and for every one. And I was innocent—that was the chief thing,' said Natásha. 'Do you remember?'

'I remember,' answered Nicholas. 'I remember that I came to you afterwards and wanted to comfort you but, do you know, I felt ashamed to. We were terribly absurd. I had a funny doll then and wanted to give it you. Do you remember?'

'And do you remember,' Natásha asked with a pensive smile, 'how once, long long ago, when we were quite little, uncle called us into the study—that was in the old house—and it was dark—we went in and suddenly there stood . . .'

'A negro,' chimed in Nicholas with a smile of delight. 'Of course I remember. Even now I don't know whether there really was a negro, or if we only dreamt it or were told about him.'

'He was grey, you remember, and had white teeth, and stood and looked at us . . .'

'Sónya, do *you* remember?' asked Nicholas.

'Yes, yes, I do remember something too,' Sónya answered timidly.

'You know I have asked Papa and Mamma about that negro,' said Natásha, 'and they say there was no negro at all. But you see, you remember!'

'Of course I do, I remember his teeth as if I had just seen them.'

'How strange it is! It's as if it were a dream! I like that.'

'And do you remember how we rolled hard-boiled eggs in the ball-room, and suddenly two old women began spinning round on the carpet? Was that real or not? Do you remember what fun it was?'

'Yes, and you remember how Papa in his blue overcoat fired a gun in the porch?'

So they went through their memories, smiling with pleasure: not the sad memories of old age, but poetic, youthful ones—those impressions of one's most distant past in which dreams and realities blend—and they laughed with quiet enjoyment.

Sónya, as always, did not quite keep pace with them, though they shared the same reminiscences.

Much that they remembered had slipped from her mind, and what she recalled did not arouse the same poetic feeling as they experienced. She simply enjoyed their pleasure and tried to fit in with it.

She only really took part when they recalled Sónya's first arrival. She told them how afraid she had been of Nicholas because he had on a corded jacket, and her nurse had told her that she, too, would be sewn up with cords.

'And I remember their telling me that you had been born under a cabbage,' said Natásha, 'and I remember that I dared not disbelieve it then, but knew it was not true, and I felt so uncomfortable.'

While they were talking a maid thrust her head in at the other door of the sitting-room.

'They have brought the cock, Miss,' she said in a whisper.

'It isn't wanted, Pólya. Tell them to take it away,' replied Natásha.

In the middle of their talk in the sitting-room, Dimmler came in and went up to the harp that stood there in a corner. He took off its cloth covering, and the harp gave out a jarring sound.

'Mr. Dimmler, please play my favourite nocturne by Field,' came the old countess's voice from the drawing-room.

Dimmler struck a chord, and turning to Natásha, Nicholas, and Sónya, remarked: 'How quiet you young people are!'

'Yes, we're philosophizing,' said Natásha, glancing round for a moment and then continuing the conversation. They were now discussing dreams.

Dimmler began to play, Natásha went on tiptoe noiselessly to the table, took up a candle, carried it out and returned, seating herself quietly in her former place. It was dark in the room, especially where they were sitting on the sofa, but through the big windows the silvery light of the full moon fell on the floor. Dimmler had finished the piece but still sat softly running his fingers over the strings, evidently uncertain whether to stop or to play something else.

'Do you know,' said Natásha in a whisper, moving closer to Nicholas and Sónya, 'that when one goes on and on recalling memories, one at last begins to remember what happened before one was in the world . . .'

'That is metempsychosis,' said Sónya, who had always learned well, and remembered everything. 'The Egyptians believed that our souls have lived in animals, and will go back into animals again.'

'No, I don't believe we ever were in animals,' said Natásha, still in a whisper though the music had ceased. 'But I am certain that we were angels somewhere *there*, and have been here, and that is why we remember . . .'

'May I join you?' said Dimmler who had come up quietly, and he sat down by them.

'If we have been angels, why have we fallen lower?' said Nicholas. 'No, that can't be!'

'Not lower, who said we were lower? . . . How do I

know what I was before?' Natásha rejoined with conviction. 'The soul is immortal—well then, if I shall always live I must have lived before, lived for a whole eternity.'

'Yes, but it is hard for us to imagine eternity,' remarked Dimmler, who had joined the young folk with a mildly condescending smile but now spoke as quietly and seriously as they.

'Why is it hard to imagine eternity?' said Natásha. 'It is now to-day, and it will be to-morrow, and always; and there was yesterday, and the day before . . .'

'Natásha! Now it's your turn. Sing me something,' they heard the countess say. 'Why are you sitting there like conspirators?'

'Mamma, I don't at all want to,' replied Natásha, but all the same she rose.

None of them, not even the middle-aged Dimmler, wanted to break off their conversation and quit that corner in the sitting-room, but Natásha got up and Nicholas sat down at the clavichord. Standing as usual in the middle of the hall, and choosing the place where the resonance was best, Natásha began to sing her mother's favourite song.

She had said she did not want to sing, but it was long since she had sung, and long before she again sang, as she did that evening. The count, from his study where he was talking to Mítenka, heard her, and like a schoolboy in a hurry to run out to play, blundered in his talk while giving orders to the steward, and at last stopped, while Mítenka stood in front of him, also listening and smiling. Nicholas did not take his eyes off his sister and drew breath in time with her. Sónya, as she listened, thought of the immense difference there was between herself and her friend, and how impossible it was for her to be anything like as bewitching as her cousin. The old countess sat with a blissful yet sad smile and with tears in her eyes, occasionally shaking her head. She thought of Natásha and of her own youth, and of how there was something unnatural and dreadful in this impending marriage of Natásha and Prince Andrew.

Dimmler, who had seated himself beside the countess, listened with closed eyes.

'Ah, Countess,' he said at last, 'that's a European

talent, she has nothing to learn—what softness, tenderness, and strength . . .'

'Ah, how afraid I am for her, how afraid I am!' said the countess, not realizing to whom she was speaking. Her maternal instinct told her that Natásha had too much of something, and that because of this she would not be happy. Before Natásha had finished singing, fourteen-year-old Pétya rushed in delightedly to say that some mummers had arrived.

Natásha stopped abruptly.

'Idiot!' she screamed at her brother and running to a chair threw herself on it sobbing so violently that she could not stop for a long time.

'It's nothing, Mamma, really it's nothing; only Pétya startled me,' she said trying to smile, but her tears still flowed and sobs still choked her.

The mummers (some of the house-serfs) dressed up as bears, Turks, inn-keepers, and ladies—frightening and funny—bringing in with them the cold from outside and a feeling of gaiety, crowded, at first timidly, in the anteroom, then hiding behind one another they pushed into the ball-room where, shyly at first and then more and more merrily and heartily, they started singing, dancing, and playing Christmas games. The countess, when she had identified them and laughed at their costumes, went into the drawing-room. The count sat in the ball-room smiling radiantly and applauding the players. The young people had disappeared.

Half an hour later there appeared among the other mummers in the ball-room an old lady in a hooped skirt —this was Nicholas. A Turkish girl was Pétya. A clown was Dimmler. An hussar was Natásha, and a Circassian was Sónya with burnt-cork moustache and eyebrows.

After the condescending surprise, non-recognition, and praise, of those who were not themselves dressed up, the young people decided that their costumes were so good that they ought to be shown elsewhere.

Nicholas, who as the roads were in splendid condition wanted to take them all for a drive in his troyka, proposed to take with them about a dozen of the serf-mummers and drive to 'Uncle's'.

'No, why disturb the old fellow?' said the countess, 'besides, you wouldn't have room to turn round there. If you must go, go to the Melyukóvs'.'

Melyukóva was a widow, who with her family and their tutors and governesses lived three miles from the Rostóvs.

'That's right, my dear,' chimed in the old count, thoroughly aroused. 'I'll dress up at once and go with them. I'll make Pashette open her eyes.'

But the countess would not agree to his going; he had had a bad leg all these last days. It was decided that the count must not go, but that if Louisa Ivánovna (Madame Schoss) would go with them, the young ladies might go to the Melyukóvs', Sónya, generally so timid and shy, begging Louisa Ivánovna not to refuse more urgently than any one.

Sónya's costume was the best of all. Her moustache and eyebrows were extraordinarily becoming. Every one told her she looked very handsome, and she was in a spirited and energetic mood unusual with her. Some inner voice told her that now or never her fate would be decided, and in her male attire she seemed quite a different person. Louisa Ivánovna consented to go, and in half an hour four troyka-sledges with large and small bells, their runners squeaking and whistling over the frozen snow, drove up to the porch.

Natásha was foremost in setting a merry holiday tone, which passing from one to another grew stronger and stronger and reached its climax when they all came out into the frost and got into the sledges, talking, calling to one another, laughing and shouting.

Two of the troykas were the usual household sledges, the third was the old count's with a trotter from the Orlóv stud as shaft-horse, the fourth was Nicholas's own with a short shaggy black shaft-horse. Nicholas, in his old lady's dress, over which he had belted his hussar over-coat, stood in the middle of the sledge reins in hand.

It was so light that he could see the moonlight reflected from the metal harness disks and from the eyes of the horses, who looked round in alarm at the noisy party under the shadow of the porch-roof.

Natásha, Sónya, Madame Schoss and two maids got

into Nicholas's sledge, Dimmler, his wife, and Pétya, into the old count's, and the rest of the mummers seated themselves in the other two sledges.

'You go ahead, Zakhár!' shouted Nicholas to his father's coachman, wishing for a chance to race past him.

The old count's troyka, with Dimmler and his party, started forward squeaking on its runners as though freezing to the snow, its deep-toned bell clanging. The side-horses, pressing against the shafts of the middle horse, sank in the snow which was dry and glittered like sugar, and threw it up.

Nicholas set off following the first sledge: behind him the others moved noisily, their runners squeaking. At first they drove at a steady trot along the narrow road. While they drove past the garden, the shadows of the bare trees often fell across the road and hid the brilliant moonlight, but as soon as they were past the fence, the snowy plain, bathed in moonlight and motionless, spread out before them glittering like diamonds and dappled with bluish shadows. *Bang, bang!* went the first sledge over a cradle-hole in the snow of the road, and each of the other sledges jolted in the same way, and rudely breaking the frost-bound stillness the troykas began to speed along the road one after the other.

'A hare's track, a lot of tracks!' rang out Natásha's voice through the frost-bound air.

'How light it is, Nicholas!' came Sónya's voice.

Nicholas glanced round at Sónya, and bent down to see her face closer. Quite a new, sweet face with black eyebrows and moustaches peeped up at him from her sable furs—so close and yet so distant—in the moonlight.

'That used to be Sónya,' thought he, and looked at her closer and smiled.

'What is it, Nicholas?'

'Nothing,' said he and turned again to the horses.

When they came out onto the beaten high road—polished by sledge-runners and cut up by rough-shod hoofs, the marks of which were visible in the moonlight—the horses began to tug at the reins of their own accord and increased their pace. The near side-horse, arching his head and breaking into a short canter, tugged at his traces. The shaft-horse swayed from side to side moving his ears as if asking: 'Isn't it time to begin now?' In front, already far ahead, the deep bell of the sledge ringing farther and farther off, the black horses driven by Zakhár could be clearly seen against the white snow. From that sledge one could hear the shouts, laughter, and voices of the mummers.

'Gee up, my darlings!' shouted Nicholas pulling the reins to one side and flourishing the whip.

It was only by the keener wind that met them and the jerks given by the side-horses who pulled harder—ever increasing their gallop—that one noticed how fast the troyka was flying. Nicholas looked back. With screams, squeals, and waving of whips, that caused even the shaft-horses to gallop—the other sledges followed. The shaft-horse swung steadily beneath the bow over its head, with no thought of slackening pace and ready to put on speed when required.

Nicholas overtook the first sledge. They were driving down hill and coming out upon a broad trodden track across a meadow near a river.

'Where are we?' thought he. 'It's the Kosóy meadow, I suppose. But no—this is something new I've never seen before. This isn't the Kosóy meadow, nor the Dëmkin hill, and heaven only knows what it is! It is something new and enchanted. Well, whatever it may be . . .' And shouting to his horses he began to pass the first sledge.

Zakhár held back his horses and turned his face, which was already covered with hoar-frost to his eyebrows.

Nicholas gave the horses the rein, and Zakhár, stretching out his arms, clucked his tongue and let his horses go.

'Now, look out, Master!' he cried.

Faster still the two troykas flew, side by side, and faster moved the feet of the galloping side-horses. Nicholas began to draw ahead. Zakhár, while still keeping his arms extended, raised one hand with the reins.

'No you won't, Master!' he shouted.

Nicholas put all his horses to a gallop and passed Zakhár. The horses showered the fine dry snow on the faces of those in the sledge—beside them sounded quick

ringing bells and they caught confused glimpses of swiftly
moving legs and the shadows of the troyka they were
passing. The whistling sound of the runners on the snow
and the voices of girls shrieking, were heard from
different sides.

Again checking his horses, Nicholas looked around
him. They were still surrounded by the magic plain
bathed in moonlight and spangled with stars.

'Zakhár is shouting that I should turn to the left, but
why to the left?' thought Nicholas. 'Are we getting to
the Melyukóvs'? Is this Melyukóvka? Heaven only
knows where we are going, and heaven knows what is
happening to us—but it is very strange and pleasant
whatever it is.' And he looked round in the sledge.

'Look, his moustache and eyelashes are all white!' said
one of the strange, pretty, unfamiliar people—the one
with fine eyebrows and moustache.

'I think this used to be Natásha,' thought Nicholas,
'and that was Madame Schoss, but perhaps it's not, and
this Circassian with the moustache I don't know, but I
love her.'

'Aren't you cold?' he asked.

They did not answer but began to laugh. Dimmler
from the sledge behind shouted something—probably
something funny—but they could not make out what he
said.

'Yes, yes!' some voices answered, laughing.

'But here was a fairy forest with black moving shadows,
and a glitter of diamonds and a flight of marble steps and
the silver roofs of fairy buildings and the shrill yells of
some animals. And if this is really Melyukóvka it is still
stranger that we drove heaven knows where and have
come to Melyukóvka,' thought Nicholas.

It really was Melyukóvka, and maids and footmen with
merry faces came running out to the porch, carrying
candles.

'Who is it?' asked some one in the porch.

'The mummers from the count's. I know by the
horses,' replied some voices.

CHAPTER XI

PELAGÉYA Danílovna Melyukóva, a broadly built, energetic woman wearing spectacles, sat in the drawing-room in a loose dress surrounded by her daughters whom she was trying to keep from feeling dull. They were quietly dropping melted wax into snow and looking at the shadows the wax figures would throw on the wall, when they heard the steps and voices of new arrivals in the vestibule.

Hussars, ladies, witches, clowns and bears, after clearing their throats and wiping the hoar-frost from their faces in the vestibule, came into the ball-room where candles were hurriedly lighted. The clown—Dimmler—and the lady—Nicholas—started a dance. Surrounded by the screaming children the mummers, covering their faces and disguising their voices, bowed to their hostess and arranged themselves about the room.

'Dear me! there's no recognizing them! And Natásha! See whom she looks like! She really reminds me of somebody. But Herr Dimmler—isn't he good! I didn't know him! And how he dances. Dear me, there's a Circassian. Really how becoming it is to dear Sónya. And who is that? Well you have cheered us up! Nikíta and Ványa—clear away the tables! And we were sitting so quietly. Ha, ha, ha! . . . The hussar, the hussar! Just like a boy! And the legs! . . . I can't look at him . . .' different voices were saying.

Natásha, the young Melyukóvs's favourite, disappeared with them into the back rooms where a cork, and various dressing-gowns and male garments were called for, and received from the footman by bare girlish arms from behind the door. Ten minutes later all the young Melyukóvs joined the mummers.

Pelagéya Danílovna, having given orders to clear the rooms for the visitors, and arranged about refreshments for the gentry and the serfs, went about among the mummers without removing her spectacles, peering into their faces with a suppressed smile and failing to recognize any of them. It was not merely Dimmler and the Rostóvs she failed to recognize, she did not even recog-

nize her own daughters, or her late husband's dressing-
gowns and uniforms, which they had put on.

'And who is this?' she asked her governess, peering into
the face of her own daughter dressed up as a Kazán-Tartar.
'I suppose it is one of the Rostóvs! Well, Mr. Hussar, and
what regiment do you serve in?' she asked Natásha.
'Here, hand some fruit-jelly to the Turk!' she ordered
the butler who was handing things round. 'That's not
forbidden by his law.'

Sometimes, as she looked at the strange but amusing
capers cut by the dancers, who—having decided once for
all that being disguised no one would recognize them—
were not at all shy, Pelagéya Danílovna hid her face in
her handkerchief, and her whole stout body shook with
irrepressible, kindly, elderly laughter.

'My little Sásha! Look at Sásha!' she said.

After Russian country-dances and chorus-dances,
Pelagéya Danílovna made the serfs and gentry join in
one large circle: a ring, a string, and a silver ruble, were
fetched, and they all played games together.

In an hour all the costumes were crumpled and disordered. The corked eyebrows and moustaches were
smeared over the perspiring, flushed, and merry faces.
Pelagéya Danílovna began to recognize the mummers,
admired their cleverly contrived costumes, and particularly how they suited the young ladies, and she thanked
them all for having entertained her so well. The visitors
were invited to supper in the drawing-room, and the serfs
had something served to them in the ball-room.

'Now to tell one's fortune in the empty bath-house is
frightening!' said an old maid who lived with the
Melyukóvs, during supper.

'Why?' asked the eldest Melyukóv girl.

'You wouldn't go, it takes courage . . .'

'I'll go,' said Sónya.

'Tell what happened to the young lady!' said the
second Melyukóv girl.

'Well,' began the old maid, 'a young lady once went
out, took a cock, laid the table for two, all properly, and
sat down. After sitting a while, she suddenly hears some
one coming . . . a sledge drives up with harness bells;

she hears him coming! He comes in, just in the shape of a man, like an officer—comes in and sits down to table with her.'

'Ah! ah!' screamed Natásha, rolling her eyes with horror.

'Yes? And how . . . did he speak?'

'Yes, like a man. Everything quite all right, and he began persuading her; and she should have kept him talking till cock-crow, but she got frightened, just got frightened and hid her face in her hands. Then he caught her up. It was lucky the maids ran in just then . . .'

'Now, why frighten them?' said Pelagéya Danílovna.

'Mamma, you used to try your fate yourself . . .' said her daughter.

'And how does one do it in a barn?' inquired Sónya.

'Well, say you went to the barn now, and listened. It depends on what you hear; hammering and knocking—that's bad; but a sound of shifting grain is good, and one sometimes hears that, too.'

'Mamma, tell us what happened to you in the barn.'

Pelagéya Danílovna smiled.

'Oh, I've forgotten . . .' she replied. 'But none of you would go?'

'Yes, I will, Pelagéya Danílovna, let me! I'll go,' said Sónya.

'Well why not, if you're not afraid?'

'Louisa Ivánovna, may I?' asked Sónya.

Whether they were playing the ring and string game, or the ruble game, or talking as now, Nicholas did not leave Sónya's side, and gazed at her with quite new eyes. It seemed to him that it was only to-day, thanks to that burnt cork moustache, that he had fully learnt to know her. And really that evening Sónya was brighter, more animated, and prettier, than Nicholas had ever seen her before.

'So that's what she is like; what a fool I have been!' he thought, gazing at her sparkling eyes, and under the moustache a happy, rapturous smile dimpled her cheeks, a smile he had never seen before.

'I'm not afraid of anything,' said Sónya. 'May I go at once?' She got up.

They told her where the barn was and how she should stand silent and listen, and they handed her a fur cloak. She threw this over her head and shoulders and glanced at Nicholas.

'What a darling that girl is!' thought he. 'And what have I been thinking of till now?'

Sónya went out into the passage to go to the barn. Nicholas went hastily to the front porch, saying he felt too hot. The crowd of people really had made the house stuffy.

Outside there was the same cold stillness, and the same moon, but even brighter than before. The light was so strong and the snow sparkled with so many stars, that one did not wish to look up at the sky and the real stars were unnoticed. The sky was black and dreary, while the earth was gay.

'I am a fool, a fool! what have I been waiting for?' thought Nicholas, and running out from the porch he went round the corner of the house and along the path that led to the back porch. He knew Sónya would pass that way. Half-way lay some snow-covered piles of firewood, and across and along them a network of shadows from the bare old lime trees fell on the snow and on the path. This path led to the barn. The log walls of the barn and its snow-covered roof, that looked as if hewn out of some precious stone, sparkled in the moonlight. A tree in the garden snapped with the frost, and then all was again perfectly silent. His bosom seemed to inhale not air, but the strength of eternal youth and gladness.

From the back porch came the sound of feet descending the steps, the bottom step, upon which snow had fallen, gave a ringing creak and he heard the voice of an old maidservant saying, 'Straight, straight along the path, Miss. Only don't look back.'

'I am not afraid,' answered Sónya's voice, and along the path towards Nicholas came the crunching, whistling sound of Sónya's feet in her thin shoes.

Sónya came along wrapped in her cloak. She was only a couple of paces away when she saw him, and to her too he was not the Nicholas she had known and always slightly feared. He was in a woman's dress, with tousled hair and a happy smile new to Sónya. She ran rapidly towards him.

'Quite different and yet the same,' thought Nicholas looking at her face all lit up by the moonlight. He slipped his arms under the cloak that covered her head, embraced her, pressed her to him, and kissed her on the lips that wore a moustache and had a smell of burnt cork. Sónya kissed him full on the lips, and disengaging her little hands, pressed them to his cheeks.

'Sónya!' . . . 'Nicholas!' . . . was all they said. They ran to the barn and then back again, re-entering, he by the front and she by the back porch.

CHAPTER XII

WHEN they all drove back from Pelagéya Danílovna's, Natásha, who always saw and noticed everything, arranged that she and Madame Schoss should go back in the sledge with Dimmler, and Sónya with Nicholas and the maids.

On the way back Nicholas drove at a steady pace instead of racing, and kept peering by that fantastic all-transforming light into Sónya's face and searching beneath the eyebrows and moustache for his former and his present Sónya from whom he had resolved never to be parted again. He looked, and recognizing in her both the old and the new Sónya, and being reminded by the smell of burnt cork of the sensation of her kiss, inhaled the frosty air with a full breast and, looking at the ground flying beneath him and at the sparkling sky, felt himself again in fairyland.

'Sónya, is it well with *thee*?' he asked from time to time.

'Yes!' she replied. 'And with *thee*?'

When half-way home, Nicholas handed the reins to the coachman and ran for a moment to Natásha's sledge and stood on its wing.

'Natásha!' he whispered in French, 'do you know I have made up my mind about Sónya?'

'Have you told her?' asked Natásha, suddenly beaming all over with joy.

'Oh, how strange you are with that moustache and those eyebrows! . . . Natásha—are you glad?'

'I am so glad, so glad! I was beginning to be vexed with you. I did not tell you, but you have been treating her badly. What a heart she has, Nicholas! I am horrid sometimes but I was ashamed to be happy while Sónya was not,' continued Natásha. 'Now I am so glad! Well, run back to her.'

'No, wait a bit . . . Oh, how funny you look!' cried Nicholas peering into her face and finding in his sister too something new, unusual, and bewitchingly tender, that he had not seen in her before. 'Natásha, it's magical, isn't it?'

'Yes,' she replied. 'You have done splendidly.'

'Had I seen her before as she is now,' thought Nicholas, 'I should long ago have asked her what to do, and have done whatever she told me, and all would have been well.'

'So you are glad, and I have done right?'

'Oh, quite right! I had a quarrel with Mamma some time ago about it. Mamma said she was angling for you. How could she say such a thing! I nearly stormed at Mamma. I will never let any one say anything bad of Sónya, for there is nothing but good in her.'

'Then it's all right?' said Nicholas again scrutinizing the expression of his sister's face to see if she was in earnest. Then he jumped down and, his boots scrunching the snow, ran back to his sledge. The same happy smiling Circassian with moustache and beaming eyes looking up from under a sable hood, was still sitting there, and that Circassian was Sónya, and that Sónya was certainly his future happy and loving wife.

When they reached home and had told their mother how they had spent the evening at the Melyukóvs', the girls went to their bed-room. When they had undressed, but without washing off the cork moustaches, they sat a long time talking of their happiness. They talked of how they would live when they were married, how their husbands would be friends, and how happy they would be. On Natásha's table stood two looking-glasses which Dunyásha had prepared before-hand.

'Only when will all that be? I am afraid never . . . It

would be too good!' said Natásha, rising and going to the looking-glasses.

'Sit down, Natásha; perhaps you'll see him,' said Sónya.

Natásha lit the candles, one on each side of one of the looking-glasses, and sat down.

'I see some one with a moustache,' said Natásha, seeing her own face.

'You musn't laugh, Miss,' said Dunyásha.

With Sónya's help and the maid's, Natásha got the glass she held into the right position opposite the other; her face assumed a serious expression, and she sat silent. She sat a long time looking at the receding line of candles reflected in the glasses and expecting (from tales she had heard) to see a coffin, or *him*, Prince Andrew, in that last dim, indistinctly outlined, square. But ready as she was to take the smallest speck for the image of a man or of a coffin, she saw nothing. She began blinking rapidly and moved away from the looking-glasses.

'Why is it others see things and I don't?' she said. 'You sit down now, Sónya. You absolutely must, to-night! Do it for me . . . To-day I feel so frightened!'

Sónya sat down before the glasses, got the right position, and began looking.

'Now, Miss Sónya is sure to see something,' whispered Dunyásha; 'while you do nothing but laugh.'

Sónya heard this and Natásha's whisper:

'I know she will. She saw something last year.'

For about three minutes all were silent.

'Of course she will!' whispered Natásha, but did not finish . . . suddenly Sónya pushed away the glass she was holding and covered her eyes with her hand.

'Oh, Natásha!' she cried.

'Did you see? Did you? What was it?' exclaimed Natásha, holding up the looking-glass.

Sónya had not seen anything, she was just wanting to blink and to get up when she heard Natásha say, 'Of course she will!' She did not wish to disappoint either Dunyásha or Natásha, but it was hard to sit still. She did not herself know how or why the exclamation escaped her when she covered her eyes.

'You saw him?' urged Natásha, seizing her hand.

'Yes. Wait a bit . . . I . . . saw him,' Sónya could not help saying, not yet knowing whom Natásha meant by *him*, Nicholas or Prince Andrew.

'But why shouldn't I say I saw something? Others do see! Besides who can tell whether I saw anything or not?' flashed through Sónya's mind.

'Yes, I saw him,' she said.

'How? Standing or lying?'

'No, I saw . . . At first there was nothing, then I saw him lying down.'

'Andrew lying? Is he ill?' asked Natásha, her frightened eyes fixed on her friend.

'No, on the contrary, on the contrary! His face was cheerful, and he turned to me.' And when saying this she herself fancied she had really seen what she described.

'Well and then, Sónya? . . .'

'After that, I could not make out what there was; something blue and red . . .'

'Sónya! When will he come back? When shall I see him! O, God, how afraid I am for him and for myself and about everything! . . .' Natásha began, and without replying to Sónya's words of comfort she got into bed, and long after her candle was out lay open-eyed and motionless, gazing at the moonlight through the frosty window-panes.

CHAPTER XIII

SOON after the Christmas holidays Nicholas told his mother of his love for Sónya and of his firm resolve to marry her. The countess who had long noticed what was going on between them and was expecting this declaration, listened to him in silence, and then told her son that he might marry whom he pleased, but that neither she nor his father would give their blessing to such a marriage. Nicholas, for the first time, felt that his mother was displeased with him and that, despite her love for him, she would not give way. Coldly, without looking at her son, she sent for her husband, and when he came tried briefly and coldly to inform him of the facts, in her son's

presence, but unable to restrain herself she burst into
tears of vexation and left the room. The old count began
irresolutely to admonish Nicholas and beg him to abandon
his purpose. Nicholas replied that he could not go back
on his word, and his father, sighing and evidently disconcerted, very soon became silent and went in to the
countess. In all his encounters with his son the count
was always conscious of his own guilt towards him for
having wasted the family fortune, and so he could not be
angry with him for refusing to marry an heiress and
choosing the dowerless Sónya. On this occasion he was
only more vividly conscious of the fact that if his affairs
had not been in disorder, no better wife for Nicholas than
Sónya could have been wished for, and that no one but
himself, with his Mítenka and his unconquerable habits,
was to blame for the condition of the family finances.

The father and mother did not speak of the matter to
their son again, but a few days later the countess sent for
Sónya and, with a cruelty neither of them expected,
reproached her niece for trying to catch Nicholas and for
ingratitude. Sónya listened silently with downcast eyes
to the countess's cruel words, without understanding
what was required of her. She was ready to sacrifice
everything for her benefactors. Self-sacrifice was her
most cherished idea; but in this case she could not see
what she ought to sacrifice, or for whom. She could not
help loving the countess and the whole Rostóv family,
but neither could she help loving Nicholas and knowing
that his happiness depended on that love. She was silent
and sad, and did not reply. Nicholas felt the situation to
be intolerable and went to have an explanation with his
mother. He first implored her to forgive him and Sónya
and consent to their marriage, then he threatened that if
she molested Sónya he would at once marry her secretly.

The countess, with a coldness her son had never seen
in her before, replied that he was of age, that Prince
Andrew was marrying without his father's consent, and
he could do the same, but that she would never receive
that *intriguer* as her daughter.

Exploding at the word *intriguer*, Nicholas, raising his
voice, told his mother he had never expected her to try

to force him to sell his feelings, but if that were so, he would say for the last time . . . But he had no time to utter the decisive word which the expression of his face caused his mother to await with terror, and which would perhaps have for ever remained a cruel memory to them both. He had not time to say it, for Natásha, with a pale and set face, entered the room from the door at which she had been listening.

'Nicholas, you are talking nonsense! Be quiet, be quiet, be quiet, I tell you! . . .' she almost screamed, so as to drown his voice.

'Mamma darling, it's not at all so . . . my poor, sweet darling,' she said to her mother, who conscious that they had been on the brink of a rupture, gazed at her son with terror, but in the obstinacy and excitement of the conflict could not and would not give way.

'Nicholas, I'll explain to you. Go away! Listen, Mamma darling,' said Natásha.

Her words were incoherent, but they attained the purpose at which she was aiming.

The countess, sobbing heavily, hid her face on her daughter's breast, while Nicholas rose, clutching his head, and left the room.

Natásha set to work to effect a reconciliation, and so far succeeded that Nicholas received a promise from his mother that Sónya should not be troubled, while he on his side promised not to undertake anything without his parents' knowledge.

Firmly resolved, after putting his affairs in order in the regiment, to retire from the army and return and marry Sónya, Nicholas, serious, sorrowful, and at variance with his parents, but as it seemed to him passionately in love, left at the beginning of January to rejoin his regiment.

After Nicholas had gone things in the Rostóv household were more depressing than ever, and the countess fell ill from mental agitation.

Sónya was unhappy at the separation from Nicholas, and still more so on account of the hostile tone the countess could not help adopting towards her. The count was more perturbed than ever by the condition of his affairs, which called for some decisive action. Their town house and estate near Moscow had inevitably to be sold, and for this they had to go to Moscow. But the countess's health obliged them to delay their departure from day to day.

Natásha, who had borne the first period of separation from her betrothed lightly and even cheerfully, now grew more agitated and impatient every day. The thought that her best days, which she would have employed in loving him, were being vainly wasted with no advantage to any one, tormented her incessantly. His letters for the most part irritated her. It hurt her to think that while she lived only in the thought of him, he was living a real life, seeing new places and new people that interested him. The more interesting his letters were the more vexed she felt. Her letters to him, far from giving her any comfort, seemed to her a wearisome and artificial obligation. She could not write, because she could not conceive the possibility of expressing sincerely in a letter even a thousandth part of what she expressed by voice, smile, and glance. She wrote to him formal, monotonous, and dry letters, to which she attached no importance herself, and in the rough copies of which the countess corrected her mistakes in spelling.

There was still no improvement in the countess's health, but it was impossible to defer the journey to Moscow any longer. Natásha's trousseau had to be ordered and the house sold. Moreover Prince Andrew was expected in Moscow, where old Prince Bolkónski was spending the winter, and Natásha felt sure he had already arrived.

So the countess remained in the country, and the count, taking Sónya and Natásha with him, went to Moscow at the end of January.

END OF BOOK VII

BOOK VIII

BOOK VIII

CHAPTER I

AFTER Prince Andrew's engagement to Natásha, Pierre without any apparent cause suddenly felt it impossible to go on living as before. Firmly convinced as he was of the truths revealed to him by his benefactor, and happy as he had been in perfecting his inner man, to which he had devoted himself with such ardour—all the zest of such a life vanished after the engagement of Andrew and Natásha, and the death of Joseph Alexéevich, the news of which reached him almost at the same time. Only the skeleton of life remained: his house, a brilliant wife who now enjoyed the favours of a very important personage, acquaintance with all Petersburg, and his Court service with its dull formalities. And this life suddenly seemed to Pierre unexpectedly loathsome. He ceased keeping a diary, avoided the company of the Brothers, began going to the Club again, drank a great deal, and came once more in touch with the bachelor sets, leading such a life that the Countess Hélène thought it necessary to speak severely to him about it. Pierre felt that she was right, and to avoid compromising her went away to Moscow.

In Moscow as soon as he entered his huge house in which the faded and fading princesses still lived, with its enormous retinue: as soon as, driving through the town, he saw the Iberian shrine with innumerable tapers burning before the golden settings of the icons, the Kremlin Square with its snow undisturbed by vehicles, the sledge-drivers and hovels of the Sívtsev Vrazhók,[1] those old Moscovites who desired nothing, hurried nowhere, and were ending their days leisurely; when he saw those old Moscow ladies, the Moscow balls and the English Club, he felt himself at home in a quiet haven. In Moscow he felt at peace, at home, warm and dirty as in an old dressing-gown.

Moscow society, from the old women down to the

[1] A slum district in Moscow.

children, received Pierre like a long-expected guest whose place was always ready, awaiting him. For Moscow society Pierre was the nicest, kindest, most intellectual, merriest, and most magnanimous of cranks, a heedless, genial nobleman of the old Russian type. His purse was always empty because it was open to every one.

Benefit performances, poor pictures, statues, benevolent societies, gipsy choirs, schools, subscription dinners, sprees, Freemasons, churches, and books—no one and nothing met with a refusal from him, and had it not been for two friends who had borrowed large sums from him and taken him under their protection, he would have given everything away. There was never a dinner or soirée at the club without him. As soon as he sank into his place on the sofa after two bottles of Margaux he was surrounded, and talking, disputing, and joking began. When there were quarrels, his kindly smile and well-timed jests reconciled the antagonists. The Masonic dinners were dull and dreary when he was not there.

When after a bachelor supper he rose with his amiable and kindly smile, yielding to the entreaties of the festive company to drive off somewhere with them, shouts of delight and triumph arose among the young men. At balls he danced if a partner was needed. Young ladies, married and unmarried, liked him because, without making love to any one of them, he was equally amiable to all, especially after supper. '*Il est charmant; il n'a pas de sexe,*'[1] they said of him.

Pierre was one of those retired gentlemen-in-waiting of whom there were hundreds, good-humouredly ending their days in Moscow.

How horrified he would have been seven years before, when he first arrived from abroad, had he been told that there was no need for him to seek or plan anything, that his rut had long been shaped, eternally predetermined, and that wriggle as he might, he would be what all in his position were. He could not have believed it! Had he not at one time longed with all his heart to establish a republic in Russia; then himself to be a Napoleon; then to be a philosopher; and then a strategist and the

[1] 'He is charming; he has no sex.'

conqueror of Napoleon? Had he not seen the possibility of, and passionately desired, the regeneration of the sinful human race, and his own progress to the highest degree of perfection? Had he not established schools and hospitals and liberated his serfs?

But instead of all that—here he was, the wealthy husband of an unfaithful wife, a retired gentleman-in-waiting, fond of eating and drinking and, as he unbuttoned his waistcoat, of abusing the government a bit, a member of the Moscow English Club and a universal favourite in Moscow society. For a long time he could not reconcile himself to the idea that he was one of those same retired Moscow gentlemen-in-waiting he had so despised seven years before.

Sometimes he consoled himself with the thought that he was only living this life temporarily; but then he was shocked by the thought of how many, like himself, had entered that life and that Club temporarily, with all their teeth and hair, and had only left it when not a single tooth or hair remained.

In moments of pride, when he thought of his position it seemed to him that he was quite different and distinct from those other retired gentlemen-in-waiting he had formerly despised: they were empty, stupid, contented fellows, satisfied with their position, 'while I am still discontented and want to do something for mankind. But perhaps all these comrades of mine struggled just like me and sought something new, a path in life of their own, and like me were brought by force of circumstances, society, and race—by that elemental force against which man is powerless—to the condition I am in,' said he to himself in moments of humility; and after living some time in Moscow he no longer despised, but began to grow fond of, to respect, and to pity, his comrades in destiny, as he pitied himself.

Pierre no longer suffered moments of despair, hypochondria, and disgust with life, but the malady that had formerly found expression in such acute attacks was driven inwards and never left him for a moment. 'What for? Why? What is going on in the world?' he would ask himself in perplexity several times a day, involuntarily beginning to reflect anew on the meaning of the phenomena of life; but knowing by experience that there were no answers to these questions he made haste to turn away from them, and took up a book, or hurried off to the Club or to Apollón Nikoláevich's, to exchange the gossip of the town.

'Hélène, who has never cared for anything but her own body and is one of the stupidest women in the world,' thought Pierre, 'is regarded by people as the acme of intelligence and refinement, and they pay homage to her. Napoleon Bonaparte was despised by all as long as he was great, but now that he has become a wretched comedian the Emperor Francis wants to offer him his daughter in an illegal marriage. The Spaniards, through the Catholic clergy, offer praise to God for their victory over the French on the 14th of June, and the French, also through the Catholic clergy, offer praise because on that same 14th of June they defeated the Spaniards. My brother Masons swear by the blood that they are ready to sacrifice everything for their neighbour, but they do not give a ruble each to the collections for the poor, and they intrigue, the Astræa Lodge against the Manna Seekers, and fuss about an authentic Scotch carpet and a charter that nobody needs, and the meaning of which the very man who wrote it does not understand. We all profess the Christian law of forgiveness of injuries and love of our neighbours, the law in honour of which we have built in Moscow forty times forty churches—but yesterday a deserter was knouted to death and a minister of that same law of love and forgiveness, a priest, gave the soldier a cross to kiss before his execution.' So thought Pierre, and the whole of this general deception which every one accepts, accustomed as he was to it, astonished him each time as if it were something new. 'I understand the deception and confusion,' he thought, 'but how am I to tell them all that I see? I have tried, and have always found that they too in the depths of their souls understand it as I do, and only try not to see it. So it appears that it must be so! But I—what is to become of me?' thought he. He had the unfortunate capacity many men, especially Russians, have of seeing and believing in the possibility of goodness and truth, but of seeing the evil and falsehood of life too clearly to be able to take a serious part in it. Every sphere of work was connected, in his eyes, with evil and deception. Whatever he tried to be, whatever he engaged in, the evil and falsehood of it repulsed him and blocked every path of activity. Yet he had to live and to find occupation. It was too dreadful to be under the burden of these insoluble problems, so he abandoned himself to any distraction in order to forget them. He frequented every kind of society, drank much, bought pictures, engaged in building, and above all—read.

He read, and read everything that came to hand. On coming home, while his valets were still taking off his things, he picked up a book and began to read. From reading he passed to sleeping, from sleeping to gossip in drawing-rooms of the Club, from gossip to carousals and women; from carousals back to gossip, reading, and wine. Drinking became more and more a physical and also a moral necessity. Though the doctors warned him that with his corpulence wine was dangerous for him, he drank a great deal. He was only quite at ease when, having poured several glasses of wine mechanically into his large mouth, he felt a pleasant warmth in his body, an amiability towards all his fellows, and a readiness to respond superficially to every ideal without probing it deeply. Only after emptying a bottle or two did he feel dimly that the terribly tangled skein of life which previously had terrified him was not as dreadful as he had thought. He was always conscious of some aspect of that skein, as with a buzzing in his head after dinner or supper he chatted or listened to conversation, or read. But under the influence of wine he said to himself: 'It doesn't matter. I'll get it unravelled. I have a solution ready, but have no time now—I'll think it all out later on!' But the *later on* never came.

In the morning, on an empty stomach, all the old questions appeared as insoluble and terrible as ever, and Pierre hastily picked up a book, and if any one came to see him he was glad.

Sometimes he remembered how he had heard that soldiers in war when entrenched under the enemy's fire, if they have nothing to do, try hard to find some occupation the more easily to bear the danger. To Pierre all men seemed like those soldiers, seeking refuge from life: some in ambition, some in cards, some in framing laws, some in women, some in toys, some in horses, some in politics, some in sport, some in wine, and some in governmental affairs. 'Nothing is trivial, and nothing is important, it's all the same—only to save oneself from it as best one can,' thought Pierre. 'Only not to see *it*, that dreadful *it*!'

CHAPTER II

AT the beginning of winter Prince Nicholas Bolkónski and his daughter moved to Moscow. At that time enthusiasm for the Emperor Alexander's régime had weakened, and a patriotic and anti-French tendency prevailed there, and this together with his past and his intellect and his originality, at once made Prince Nicholas Bolkónski an object of particular respect to the Moscovites, and the centre of the Moscow opposition to the government.

The prince had aged very much that year. He showed marked signs of senility by a tendency to fall asleep, forgetfulness of quite recent events, remembrance of remote ones, and the childish vanity with which he accepted the role of head of the Moscow opposition. In spite of this the old man inspired in all his visitors alike a feeling of respectful veneration—especially of an evening when he came in to tea in his old-fashioned coat and powdered wig and, aroused by any one, told his abrupt stories of the past, or uttered yet more abrupt and scathing criticisms of the present. For them all, that old-fashioned house with its gigantic mirrors, pre-Revolution furniture, powdered footmen, and the stern shrewd old man (himself a relic of the past century) with his gentle daughter and the pretty Frenchwoman who were reverently devoted to him, presented a majestic and agreeable spectacle. But the visitors did not reflect that besides the couple of hours during which they saw their host, there were also twenty-two hours in the day during which the private and intimate life of the house continued.

Latterly that private life had become very trying for Princess Mary. There in Moscow she was deprived of her greatest pleasures—talks with the pilgrims and the solitude which refreshed her at Bald Hills—and she had none of the advantages and pleasures of city life. She did not go out into society; every one knew that her father would not let her go anywhere without him, and his failing health prevented his going out himself, so that she was not invited to dinners and evening parties. She had quite abandoned the hope of getting married. She saw the coldness and malevolence with which the old prince received and dismissed the young men, possible suitors, who sometimes appeared at their house. She had no friends: during this visit to Moscow she had been disappointed in the two who had been nearest to her. Mademoiselle Bourienne, with whom she had never been able to be quite frank, had now become unpleasant to her, and for various reasons Princess Mary avoided her. Julie, with whom she had corresponded for the last five years, was in Moscow, but proved to be quite alien to her when they met. Just then Julie, who by the death of her brothers had become one of the richest heiresses in Moscow, was in the full whirl of society pleasures. She was surrounded by young men who, she fancied, had suddenly learnt to appreciate her worth. Julie was at that stage in the life of a society woman when she feels that her last chance of marrying has come, and that her fate must be decided now or never. On Thursdays Princess Mary remembered with a mournful smile that she now had no one to write to, since Julie—whose presence gave her no pleasure—was here and they met every week. Like the old *émigré* who declined to marry the lady with whom he had spent his evenings for years, she regretted Julie's presence and having no one to write to. In Moscow Princess Mary had no one to talk to, no one to whom to confide her sorrow, and much sorrow fell to her lot just then. The time for Prince Andrew's return and marriage was approaching, but his request to her to prepare his father for it had not been carried out; in fact it seemed as if matters were quite hopeless, for at every mention of the young Countess Rostóva the old prince (who apart from that was usually in a bad temper) lost control of himself. Another lately added sorrow arose from the lessons she gave her six-year-old nephew. To her consternation she detected in herself in relation to little Nicholas, some symptoms of her father's irritability. However often she told herself that she must not get irritable when teaching her nephew, almost every time that, pointer in hand, she sat down to show him the French alphabet, she so longed to pour her own knowledge quickly and easily into the child—who was already afraid that Auntie might at any moment get angry—that at his slightest inattention she trembled, became flustered and heated, raised her voice, and sometimes pulled him by the arm and put him in the corner. Having put him in the corner she would herself begin to cry over her cruel, evil nature, and little Nicholas, following her example, would sob, and without permission would leave his corner, come to her, pull her wet hands from her face, and comfort her. But what distressed the princess most of all was her father's irritability, which was always directed against her and had of late amounted to cruelty. Had he forced her to prostrate herself to the ground all night, had he beaten her, or made her fetch wood or water, it would never have entered her mind to think her position hard; but this loving despot—the more cruel because he loved her and for that reason tormented himself and her—knew how not merely to hurt and humiliate her deliberately, but to show her that she was always to blame for everything. Of late he had exhibited a new trait that tormented Princess Mary more than anything else; this was his ever-increasing intimacy with Mademoiselle Bourienne. The idea that at the first moment of receiving the news of his son's intentions had occurred to him in jest—that if Andrew got married, he himself would marry Bourienne—had evidently pleased him, and latterly he had persistently, and as it seemed to Princess Mary merely to offend her, shown special endearments to the companion, and expressed his dissatisfaction with his daughter by demonstrations of love of Bourienne.

One day in Moscow in Princess Mary's presence (she thought her father did it purposely when she was there) the old prince kissed Mademoiselle Bourienne's hand and, drawing her to him, embraced her affectionately. Princess Mary flushed and ran out of the room. A few minutes later Mademoiselle Bourienne came into Princess Mary's room smiling and making cheerful remarks in her agreeable voice. Princess Mary hastily wiped away her tears, went resolutely up to Mademoiselle Bourienne, and evidently unconscious of what she was doing began shouting in angry haste at the Frenchwoman, her voice breaking: 'It's horrible, vile, inhuman, to take advantage of the weakness . . .' She did not finish. 'Leave my room,' she exclaimed, and burst into sobs.

Next day the prince did not say a word to his daughter, but she noticed that at dinner he gave orders that Mademoiselle Bourienne should be served first. After dinner, when the footman handed coffee, and from habit began with the princess, the prince suddenly grew furious, threw his stick at Philip, and instantly gave instructions to have him conscripted for the army.

'He doesn't obey . . . I said it twice . . . and he doesn't obey! She is the first person in this house; she's my best friend,' cried the prince. 'And if you allow yourself,' he screamed in a fury, addressing Princess Mary for the first time, 'to forget yourself again before her as you dared to do yesterday, I will show you who is master in this house. Go! Don't let me set eyes on you; beg her pardon!'

Princess Mary asked Mademoiselle Bourienne's pardon, and also her father's pardon for herself and for Philip the footman, who had begged for her intervention.

At such moments something like a pride of sacrifice gathered in her soul. And suddenly that father, whom she had judged, would look for his spectacles in her presence, fumbling near them and not seeing them, or would forget something that had just occurred, or take a false step with his failing legs and turn to see if any one had noticed his feebleness, or, worst of all, at dinner when there were no visitors to excite him, would suddenly fall asleep, letting his napkin drop and his shaking head sink over his plate. 'He is old and feeble, and I dare to condemn him!' she thought at such moments, with a feeling of revulsion against herself.

CHAPTER III

IN 1811 there was living in Moscow a French doctor—Métivier—who had rapidly become the fashion. He was enormously tall, handsome, amiable as Frenchmen are, and was, as all Moscow said, an extraordinarily clever doctor. He was received in the best houses not merely as a doctor, but as an equal.

Prince Nicholas had always ridiculed medicine, but latterly on Mademoiselle Bourienne's advice had allowed this doctor to visit him and had grown accustomed to him. Métivier came to see the prince about twice a week.

On December 6th—St. Nicholas's day and the prince's name-day—all Moscow came to the prince's front door, but he gave orders to admit no one, and to invite to dinner only a small number, a list of whom he gave to Princess Mary.

Métivier, who came in the morning with his felicitations, considered it proper in his quality of doctor *de forcer la consigne*,[1] as he told Princess Mary, and went in to see the prince. It happened that on that morning of his name-day the prince was in one of his worst moods. He had been going about the house all the morning finding fault with every one and pretending not to understand what was said to him and not to be understood himself. Princess Mary well knew this mood of quiet absorbed querulousness, which generally culminated in a burst of rage, and she went about all that morning as though facing a cocked and loaded gun and awaited the inevitable explosion. Until the doctor's arrival the morning had passed off safely. After admitting the doctor, Princess Mary sat down with a book in the drawing-room near the door through which she could hear all that passed in the study.

At first she only heard Métivier's voice, then her father's, then both voices began speaking at the same time, the door was flung open, and on the threshold appeared the handsome figure of the terrified Métivier with his shock of black hair, and the prince in his dressing-

---

[1] To force the guard.

gown and fez, his face distorted with fury and the pupils of his eyes rolled downwards.

'You don't understand?' shouted the prince, 'but I do! French spy, slave of Buonaparte, spy, get out of my house! Be off, I tell you . . .' and he slammed the door.

Métivier, shrugging his shoulders, went up to Mademoiselle Bourienne, who at the sound of shouting had run in from an adjoining room.

'The prince is not very well: bile and rush of blood to the head. Keep calm, I will call again to-morrow,' said Métivier; and putting his fingers to his lips he hastened away.

Through the study-door came the sound of slippered feet and the cry: 'Spies, traitors, traitors everywhere! Not a moment's peace in my own house!'

After Métivier's departure the old prince called his daughter in, and the whole weight of his wrath fell on her. She was to blame that a spy had been admitted. Had he not told her, yes, told her to make a list, and not to admit any one who was not on that list? Then why was that scoundrel admitted? She was the cause of it all. With her, he said, he could not have a moment's peace, and could not die quietly.

'No, ma'am! We must part, we must part! Understand that, understand it! I cannot endure any more,' he said, and left the room. Then, as if afraid she might find some means of consolation, he returned and trying to appear calm added: 'And don't imagine I have said this in a moment of anger. I am calm, I have thought it over, and it will be carried out—we must part; so find some place for yourself! . . .' But he could not restrain himself and, with the virulence of which only one who loves is capable, evidently suffering himself, he shook his fists at her and screamed:

'If only some fool would marry her!' Then he slammed the door, sent for Mademoiselle Bourienne and subsided in his study.

At two o'clock the six chosen guests assembled for dinner.

These guests—the famous Count Rostopchín, Prince Lopukhín and his nephew, General Chatróv, an old war comrade of the prince's, and of the younger generation Pierre and Borís Drubetskóy—awaited the prince in the drawing-room.

Borís, who had come to Moscow on leave a few days before, had been anxious to be presented to Prince Nicholas Bolkónski, and had contrived to ingratiate himself so well that the old prince in his case made an exception to the rule of not receiving bachelors in his house.

The prince's house did not belong to what is known as *fashionable society*, but his little circle—though not much talked about in town—was one it was more flattering to be received in than any other. Borís had realized this the week before, when the commander-in-chief in his presence invited Rostopchín to dinner on St. Nicholas's day, and Rostopchín had replied that he could not come:

'On that day I always go to pay my devotions to the relics of Prince Nicholas Bolkónski.'

'Oh, yes, yes!' replied the commander-in-chief. 'How is he? . . .'

The small group that assembled before dinner in the lofty old-fashioned drawing-room, with its old furniture, resembled the solemn gathering of a Court of Justice. All were silent or talked in low tones. Prince Nicholas came in serious and taciturn. Princess Mary seemed even quieter and more diffident than usual. The guests were reluctant to address her, feeling that she was in no mood for their conversation. Count Rostopchín alone kept the conversation going, now relating the latest town news, and now the latest political gossip.

Lopukhín and the old general occasionally took part in the conversation. Prince Bolkónski listened as a presiding judge receives a report, only now and then, silently or by a brief word, showing that he took heed of what was being reported to him. The tone of the conversation was such as indicated that no one approved of what was being done in the political world. Incidents were related evidently confirming the opinion that everything was going from bad to worse, but whether telling a story or giving an opinion the speaker always stopped, or was stopped, at the point beyond which his criticism might touch the sovereign himself.

At dinner the talk turned on the latest political news: Napoleon's seizure of the Duke of Oldenburg's territory, and the Russian Note, hostile to Napoleon, which had been sent to all the European courts.

'Bonaparte treats Europe as a pirate does a captured vessel,' said Count Rostopchín, repeating a phrase he had uttered several times before. 'One only wonders at the long-suffering or blindness of the crowned heads. Now the Pope's turn has come, and Bonaparte doesn't scruple to depose the head of the Catholic Church—yet all keep silent! Our sovereign alone has protested against the seizure of the Duke of Oldenburg's territory, and even…' Count Rostopchín paused, feeling that he had reached the limit beyond which censure was impossible.

'Other territories have been offered in exchange for the Duchy of Oldenburg,' said Prince Bolkónski. 'He shifts the Dukes about as I might move my serfs from Bald Hills to Boguchárovo or my Ryazán estates.'

'The Duke of Oldenburg bears his misfortunes with admirable strength of character and resignation,' remarked Borís, joining in respectfully.

He said this because on his journey from Petersburg he had had the honour of being presented to the Duke. Prince Bolkónski glanced at the young man as if about to say something in reply, but changed his mind, evidently considering him too young.

'I have read our protest about the Oldenburg affair and was surprised how badly the Note was worded,' remarked Count Rostopchín in the casual tone of a man dealing with a subject quite familiar to him.

Pierre looked at Rostopchín with naïve astonishment, not understanding why he should be disturbed by the bad composition of the Note.

'Does it matter, Count, how the Note is worded,' he asked, 'so long as its substance is forcible?'

'My dear fellow, with our five hundred thousand troops it should be easy to have a good style,' returned Count Rostopchín.

Pierre now understood the count's dissatisfaction with the wording of the Note.

'One would have thought quill-drivers enough had

sprung up,' remarked the old prince. 'There in Petersburg they are always writing—not Notes only but even new laws. My Andrew there has written a whole volume of laws for Russia. Nowadays they are always writing!' and he laughed unnaturally.

There was a momentary pause in the conversation; the old general cleared his throat to draw attention.

'Did you hear of the last event at the review in Petersburg? The figure cut by the new French ambassador.'

'Eh? Yes, I heard something: he said something awkward in his Majesty's presence.'

'His Majesty drew his attention to the Grenadier division and to the march past,' continued the general, 'and it seems the ambassador took no notice and allowed himself to reply that: "We in France pay no attention to such trifles!" The Emperor did not condescend to reply. At the next review, they say, the Emperor did not once deign to address him.'

All were silent. On this fact relating to the Emperor personally, it was impossible to pass any judgement.

'Impudent fellows!' said the prince. 'You know Métivier? I turned him out of my house this morning. He was here; they admitted him in spite of my request that they should let no one in,' he went on, glancing angrily at his daughter.

And he narrated his whole conversation with the French doctor and the reasons that convinced him that Métivier was a spy. Though these reasons were very insufficient and obscure, no one made any rejoinder.

After the roast, champagne was served. The guests rose to congratulate the old prince. Princess Mary, too, went round to him.

He gave her a cold, angry look, and offered her his wrinkled, clean-shaven cheek to kiss. The whole expression of his face told her that he had not forgotten the morning's talk, that his decision remained in force, and only the presence of visitors hindered his speaking of it to her now.

When they went into the drawing-room where coffee was served, the old men sat together.

Prince Nicholas grew more animated and expressed his views on the impending war.

He said that our wars with Bonaparte would be disastrous so long as we sought alliances with the Germans and thrust ourselves into European affairs, into which we had been drawn by the Peace of Tilsit. 'We ought not to fight either for or against Austria. Our political interests are all in the East, and in regard to Bonaparte the only thing is to have an armed frontier and a firm policy, and he will never dare to cross the Russian frontier, as was the case in 1807!'

'How can we fight the French, Prince?' said Count Rostopchín. 'Can we arm ourselves against our teachers and divinities? Look at our youths, look at our ladies! The French are our Gods: Paris is our Kingdom of Heaven.'

He began speaking louder, evidently to be heard by every one.

'French dresses, French ideas, French feelings! There now, you turned Métivier out by the scruff of his neck because he is a Frenchman and a scoundrel, but our ladies crawl after him on their knees. I went to a party last night, and there out of five ladies three were Roman Catholics and had the Pope's indulgence for doing wool-work on Sundays. And they themselves sit there nearly naked, like the sign-boards at our Public Baths, if I may say so. Ah, when one looks at our young people, Prince, one would like to take Peter the Great's old cudgel out of the museum and belabour them in the Russian way till all the nonsense jumps out of them.'

All were silent. The old Prince looked at Rostopchín with a smile and wagged his head approvingly.

'Well, good-bye, your Excellency, keep well!' said Rostopchín, getting up with characteristic briskness and holding out his hand to the prince.

'Good-bye, my dear fellow . . . His words are music, I never tire of hearing him!' said the old prince, keeping hold of the hand and offering his cheek to be kissed.

Following Rostopchín's example the others also rose.

CHAPTER IV

PRINCESS Mary, as she sat listening to the old men's talk and fault-finding, understood nothing of what she heard; she only wondered whether the guests had all observed her father's hostile attitude towards her. She did not even notice the special attentions and amiabilities shown her during dinner by Borís Drubetskóy, who was visiting them for the third time already.

Princess Mary turned with an absent-minded questioning look to Pierre, who hat in hand and with a smile on his face was the last of the guests to approach her after the old prince had gone out and they were left alone in the drawing-room.

'May I stay a little longer?' he said, letting his stout body sink into an arm-chair beside her.

'Oh yes,' she answered. 'You noticed nothing?' her look asked.

Pierre was in an agreeable after-dinner mood. He looked straight before him and smiled quietly.

'Have you known that young man long, Princess?' he asked.

'Who?'

'Drubetskóy.'

'No, not long . . .'

'Do you like him?'

'Yes, he is an agreeable young man . . . Why do you ask me that?' said Princess Mary, still thinking of that morning's conversation with her father.

'Because I have noticed that when a young man comes on leave from Petersburg to Moscow it is usually with the object of marrying an heiress.'

'You have observed that?' said Princess Mary.

'Yes,' returned Pierre with a smile, 'and this young man now manages matters so that where there is a wealthy heiress, there he is too. I can read him like a book. At present he is hesitating whom to lay siege to— you or Mademoiselle Julie Karágina. He is very attentive to her.'

'He visits them?'

'Yes, very often. And do you know the new way of

courting?' said Pierre with an amused smile, evidently in that cheerful mood of good-humoured raillery for which he so often reproved himself in his diary.

'No,' replied Princess Mary.

'To please Moscow girls nowadays one has to be melancholy. He is very melancholy with Mademoiselle Karágina,' said Pierre.

'Really?' asked Princess Mary, looking into Pierre's kindly face and still thinking of her own sorrow. 'It would be a relief,' thought she, 'if I ventured to confide what I am feeling to some one. I should like to tell everything to Pierre. He is kind and generous. It would be a relief. He would give me advice.'

'Would you marry him?'

'Oh, my God, Count, there are moments when I would marry anybody!' she cried suddenly to her own surprise and with tears in her voice. 'Ah, how bitter it is to love some one near to you and to feel that . . .' she went on in a trembling voice, 'that you can do nothing for him but grieve him, and to know that you cannot alter this. Then there is only one thing left—to go away, but where could I go?'

'What is wrong? What is it, Princess?'

But without finishing what she was saying, Princess Mary burst into tears.

'I don't know what is the matter with me to-day. Don't take any notice—forget what I have said!'

Pierre's gaiety vanished completely. He anxiously questioned the princess, asked her to speak out fully and confide her grief to him; but she only repeated that she begged him to forget what she had said, that she did not remember what she had said, and that she had no trouble except the one he knew of—that Prince Andrew's marriage threatened to cause a rupture between father and son.

'Have you any news of the Rostóvs?' she asked, to change the subject. 'I was told they are coming soon. I am also expecting Andrew any day. I should like them to meet here.'

'And how does he now regard the matter?' asked Pierre, referring to the old prince.

Princess Mary shook her head.

'What is to be done? In a few months the year will be

up. The thing is impossible. I only wish I could spare my brother the first moments. I wish they would come sooner. I hope to be friends with her. You have known them a long time,' said Princess Mary. 'Tell me honestly the whole truth: what sort of a girl is she, and what do you think of her?—The real truth, because you know Andrew is risking so much doing this against his father's will, that I should like to know . . .'

An undefined instinct told Pierre that these explanations, and repeated requests to be told the *whole truth*, expressed ill will on the princess's part towards her future sister-in-law, and a wish that he should disapprove of Andrew's choice; but in reply he said what he felt rather than what he thought.

'I don't know how to answer your question,' he said, blushing without knowing why. 'I really don't know what sort of girl she is; I can't analyse her at all. She is enchanting, but what makes her so I don't know. That is all one can say about her.'

Princess Mary sighed, and the expression on her face said: 'Yes, that's what I expected and feared.'

'Is she clever?' she asked.

Pierre considered.

'I think not,' he said, 'and yet—yes. She does not deign to be clever . . . Oh no, she is simply enchanting, and that is all.'

Princess Mary again shook her head disapprovingly.

'Ah, I so long to like her! Tell her so, if you see her before I do.'

'I hear they are expected very soon,' said Pierre.

Princess Mary told Pierre of her plan to become intimate with her future sister-in-law as soon as the Rostóvs arrived and to try to accustom the old prince to her.

CHAPTER V

BORÍS had not succeeded in making a wealthy match in Petersburg, so with the same object in view he came to Moscow. There he wavered between the two richest heiresses, Julie and Princess Mary. Though Princess Mary despite her plainness seemed to him more attractive than Julie, he, without knowing why, felt awkward about paying court to her. When they had last met, on the old prince's name-day, she had answered at random all his attempts to talk sentimentally, evidently not listening to what he was saying.

Julie on the contrary accepted his attentions readily, though in a manner peculiar to herself.

She was twenty-seven. After the death of her brothers she had become very wealthy. She was by now decidedly plain, but thought herself not merely as good-looking as before but even far more attractive. She was confirmed in this delusion by the fact that she had become a very wealthy heiress and also by the fact that the older she grew the less dangerous she became to men, and the more freely they could associate with her and avail themselves of her suppers, soirées, and the animated company that assembled at her house, without incurring any obligation. A man who would have been afraid ten years before of going every day to the house when there was a girl of seventeen there, for fear of compromising her and committing himself, would now go boldly every day and treat her not as a marriageable girl but as a sexless acquaintance.

That winter the Karágins' house was the most agreeable and hospitable in Moscow. In addition to the formal evening and dinner parties, a large company, chiefly of men, gathered there every day, supping at midnight and staying till three in the morning. Julie never missed a ball, a promenade, or a play. Her dresses were always of the latest fashion. But in spite of that she seemed to be disillusioned about everything, and told every one that she did not believe either in friendship or in love, or any of the joys of life, and expected peace only 'yonder'. She adopted the tone of one who has suffered a great disappointment, like a girl who has either lost the man she loved or been cruelly deceived by him. Though nothing of the kind had happened to her, she was regarded in that light and had even herself come to believe that she had suffered much in life. This melancholy, which did not prevent her amusing herself, did not hinder the young people who came to her house from passing the time pleasantly. Every visitor who came to

the house paid his tribute to the melancholy mood of the
hostess, and then amused himself with society gossip,
dancing, intellectual games, and *bouts rimés*, which were
in vogue at the Karágins'. Only a few of these young
men, among them Borís, entered more deeply into
Julie's melancholy, and with these she had prolonged
conversations in private on the vanity of all worldly
things, and to them she showed her albums, filled with
mournful sketches, maxims, and verses.

To Borís Julie was particularly gracious: she regretted
his early disillusionment with life, offered him such
consolation of friendship as she, who had herself suffered
so much, could render, and showed him her album.
Borís sketched two trees in the album, and wrote:
'Rustic trees, your dark branches shed gloom and
melancholy upon me.'

On another page he drew a tomb, and wrote:

> *La mort est secourable et la mort est tranquille.*
> *Ah! contre les douleurs il n'y a pas d'autre asile.*[1]

Julie said this was charming.

'There is something so enchanting in the smile of
melancholy,' she said to Borís, repeating word for word
a passage she had copied from a book. 'It is a ray of
light in the darkness, a shade between sadness and despair,
showing the possibility of consolation.'

In reply Borís wrote these lines:

> *Aliment de poison d'une âme trop sensible,*
> *Toi, sans qui le bonheur me serait impossible,*
> *Tendre mélancholie, ah, viens me consoler,*
> *Viens calmer les tourments de ma sombre retraite*
> *Et mêle une douceur secrète*
> *A ces pleurs, que je sens couler.*[2]

[1] Death gives relief and death is peaceful.
  Ah, from suffering there is no other refuge!

[2] Poisonous nourishment of a too sensitive soul,
  Thou, without whom happiness would be for me impos-
  sible,
  Tender melancholy, ah, come to console me,
  Come to calm the torments of my gloomy retreat,
  And mingle a secret sweetness
  With these tears that I feel to be flowing.

For Borís Julie played most doleful nocturnes on her harp. Borís read *Poor Liza* aloud to her, and more than once interrupted the reading because of the emotions that choked him. Meeting at large gatherings Julie and Borís looked on one another as the only souls who understood one another in a world of indifferent people.

Anna Mikháylovna, who often visited the Karágins, while playing cards with the mother made careful inquiries as to Julie's dowry (she was to have two estates in Pénza and the Nizhegórod forests). Anna Mikháylovna regarded the refined sadness that united her son to the wealthy Julie with emotion and resignation to the Divine will.

'You are always charming and melancholy, my dear Julie,' she said to the daughter. 'Borís says his soul finds repose at your house. He has suffered so many disappointments and is so sensitive,' said she to the mother. 'Ah, my dear, I can't tell you how fond I have grown of Julie latterly,' she said to her son. 'But who could help loving her? She is an angelic being! Ah, Borís, Borís!'— she paused. 'And how I pity her mother,' she went on; 'to-day she showed me her accounts and letters from Pénza (they have enormous estates there) and she, poor thing, has no one to help her, and they do cheat her so!'

Borís smiled almost imperceptibly while listening to his mother. He laughed blandly at her naïve diplomacy but listened to what she had to say, and sometimes questioned her carefully about the Pénza and Nizhegórod estates.

Julie had long been expecting a proposal from her melancholy adorer and was ready to accept it; but some secret feeling of repulsion for her, for her passionate desire to get married, for her artificiality, and a feeling of horror at renouncing the possibility of real love, still restrained Borís. His leave was expiring. He spent every day and whole days at the Karágins', and every day on thinking the matter over told himself that he would propose to-morrow. But in Julie's presence, looking at her red face and chin (nearly always powdered), her moist eyes, and her expression of continual readiness to pass at once from melancholy to an unnatural rapture of married

bliss, Borís could not utter the decisive words, though in
imagination he had long regarded himself as the possessor
of those Pénza and Nizhegórod estates and had apportioned the use of the income from them. Julie saw Borís's
indecision and sometimes the thought occurred to her
that she was repulsive to him, but her feminine self-
deception immediately supplied her with consolation,
and she told herself that he was only shy from love. Her
melancholy however began to turn to irritability, and
not long before Borís's departure she formed a definite
plan of action. Just as Borís's leave of absence was
expiring, Anatole Kurágin made his appearance in
Moscow, and of course in the Karágins' drawing-room,
and Julie, suddenly abandoning her melancholy, became
cheerful and very attentive to Kurágin.

'My dear,' said Anna Mikháylovna to her son, 'I know
from a reliable source that Prince Vasíli has sent his son
to Moscow to get him married to Julie. I am so fond of
Julie that I should be sorry for her. What do you think
of it, my dear?'

The idea of being made a fool of, and of having thrown
away that whole month of arduous melancholy service
to Julie, and of seeing all the revenue from the Pénza
estates, which he had already mentally apportioned and
put to proper use, fall into the hands of another and
especially into the hands of that idiot Anatole, pained
Borís. He drove to the Karágins' with the firm intention
of proposing. Julie met him in a gay, careless manner,
spoke casually of how she had enjoyed yesterday's ball,
and asked when he was leaving. Though Borís had come
intentionally to speak of his love and therefore meant
to be tender, he began speaking irritably of feminine
inconstancy, of how easily women can turn from sadness
to joy, and how their moods depend solely on who
happens to be paying court to them. Julie was offended,
and replied that it was true that a woman needs variety,
and the same thing over and over again would weary
any one.

'Then I should advise you . . .' Borís began, wishing
to sting her; but at that instant the galling thought
occurred to him that he might have to leave Moscow

without having accomplished his aim, and have vainly
wasted his efforts—which was a thing he never allowed
to happen.

He checked himself in the middle of the sentence,
lowered his eyes to avoid seeing her unpleasantly irritated
and irresolute face, and said:

'I did not come here at all to quarrel with you. On the
contrary . . .'

He glanced at her to make sure that he might go on.
Her irritability had suddenly quite vanished, and her
anxious, imploring eyes were fixed on him with greedy
expectation. 'I can always arrange so as not to see her
often,' thought Borís. 'The affair has been begun and
must be finished!' He blushed hotly, raised his eyes to
hers, and said:

'You know my feelings for you!'

There was no need to say more: Julie's face shone with
triumph and self-satisfaction; but she forced Borís to say
all that is said on such occasions—that he loved her and
had never loved any other woman more than her. She
knew that for the Pénza estates and Nizhegórod forests
she could demand this, and she received what she
demanded.

The affianced couple, no longer alluding to trees that
shed gloom and melancholy upon them, planned the
arrangements of a splendid house in Petersburg, paid
calls, and prepared everything for a brilliant wedding.

CHAPTER VI

AT the end of January old Count Rostóv went to
Moscow with Natásha and Sónya. The countess was
still unwell and unable to travel but it was impossible to
wait for her recovery. Prince Andrew was expected in
Moscow any day, the trousseau had to be ordered and
the estate near Moscow had to be sold, besides which the
opportunity of presenting his future daughter-in-law to
old Prince Bolkónski while he was in Moscow could not
be missed. The Rostóvs' Moscow house had not been
heated that winter and, as they had come only for a short

time and the countess was not with them, the count decided to stay with Márya Dmítrievna Akhrosímova, who had long been pressing her hospitality on them.

Late one evening the Rostóvs' four sledges drove into Márya Dmítrievna's courtyard in the old Konyúsheny street. Márya Dmítrievna lived alone. She had already married off her daughter, and her sons were all in the service.

She held herself as erect, told every one her opinion as candidly, loudly, and bluntly, as ever, and her whole bearing seemed a reproach to others for any weakness, passion, or temptation—the possibility of which she did not admit. From early in the morning, wearing a dressing-jacket, she attended to her household affairs, and then she drove out: on holy days to church, and after the service to jails and prisons on affairs of which she never spoke to any one.[1] On ordinary days, after dressing, she received petitioners of various classes, of whom there were always some. Then she had dinner, a substantial and appetizing meal at which there were always three or four guests; after dinner she played a game of boston, and at night she had the newspapers or a new book read to her while she knitted. She rarely made an exception and went out to pay visits, and then only to the most important persons in the town.

She had not yet gone to bed when the Rostóvs arrived and the pulley of the hall-door squeaked as it let in the Rostóvs and their servants from the cold. Márya Dmítrievna, with her spectacles hanging down on her nose and her head flung back, stood in the hall doorway looking with a stern, grim face at the new arrivals. One might have thought she was angry with the traveller and would immediately turn them out, had she not at the same time been giving careful instructions to the servants for the accommodation of the visitors and their belongings.

'The Count's things? Bring them here,' she said, pointing to the portmanteaux and not greeting any one

[1] In Russia the fate of prisoners was a hard one. They suffered much want, and to contribute to their needs was a recognized Christian duty.

'The young ladies'? There to the left. Now what are
you dawdling for?' she cried to the maids. 'Get the
samovár ready! ... You've grown plumper and prettier,'
she remarked, drawing Natásha (whose cheeks were
glowing from the cold) to her by the hood. 'Foo! You *are*
cold! Now take off your things, quick!' she shouted to the
count who was going to kiss her hand. 'You're half
frozen, I'm sure! Bring some rum for tea! ... *Bonjour*,
Sónya dear!' she added, turning to Sónya and indicating
by this French greeting her slightly contemptuous though
affectionate attitude towards her.

When they came in to tea, having taken off their out-
door things and tidied themselves up after their journey,
Márya Dmítrievna kissed them all in due order.

'I'm heartily glad you have come and are staying with
me. It was high time,' she said, giving Natásha a significant look. 'The old man is here and his son's expected
any day. You'll have to make his acquaintance. But we'll
speak of that later on,' she added, glancing at Sónya with
a look that showed she did not want to speak of it in her
presence. 'Now listen,' she said to the count. 'What do
you want to-morrow? Whom will you send for? Shinshín?' She crooked one of her fingers. 'The snivelling
Anna Mikháylovna? That's two. She's here with her son.
The son is getting married! Then Bezúkhov, eh? He is
here too, with his wife. He ran away from her and she
came galloping after him. He dined with me on Wednesday. As for them'—and she pointed to the girls—'to-
morrow I'll take them first to the Iberian shrine of the
Mother of God, and then we'll drive to the Super-
Rogue's.[1] I suppose you'll have everything new. Don't
judge by me: sleeves nowadays are this size! The other
day young Princess Irína Vasílevna came to see me; she
was an awful sight—looked as if she had put two barrels
on her arms. You know not a day passes now without
some new fashion. And what have you to do yourself?'
she asked the count sternly.

[1] A pun is usually a trial to translators. In this case, as the
dressmaker's name does not appear on this page, it seems to
necessitate a footnote to let the reader know that a pun is
intended.

'One thing has come on top of another: her rags to buy, and now a purchaser has turned up for the Moscow estate and for the house. If you will be so kind, I'll fix a time and go down to the estate just for a day, and leave my lassies with you.'

'All right. All right. They'll be safe with me, as safe as in Chancery! I'll take them where they must go, scold them a bit, and pet them a bit,' said Márya Dmítrievna, touching her god-daughter and favourite, Natásha, on the cheek with her large hand.

Next morning Márya Dmítrievna took the young ladies to the Iberian shrine of the Mother of God and to Madame Suppert-Roguet, who was so afraid of Márya Dmítrievna that she always let her have costumes at a loss merely to get rid of her. Márya Dmítrievna ordered almost the whole trousseau. When they got home she turned everybody out of the room except Natásha, and then called her pet to her arm-chair.

'Well, now we'll talk. I congratulate you on your betrothed. You've hooked a fine fellow! I am glad for your sake, and I've known him since he was so high.' She held her hand a couple of feet from the ground. Natásha blushed happily. 'I like him and all his family. Now listen! You know that old Prince Nicholas much dislikes his son's marrying. The old fellow's crotchety! Of course Prince Andrew is not a child and can shift without him, but it's not nice to enter a family against a father's will. One wants to do it peacefully and lovingly. You're a clever girl and you'll know how to manage. Be kind, and use your wits. Then all will be well.'

Natásha remained silent, from shyness Márya Dmítrievna supposed, but really because she disliked any one interfering in what touched her love of Prince Andrew, which seemed to her so apart from all human affairs that no one could understand it. She loved and knew Prince Andrew, he loved her only, and was to come one of these days and take her. She wanted nothing more.

'You see, I have known him a long time and am also fond of Mary, your future sister-in-law. "Husbands' sisters bring up blisters", but this one wouldn't hurt a fly. She has asked me to bring you two together.

To-morrow you'll go with your father to see her. Be very nice and affectionate to her: you're younger than she. When *he* comes, he'll find you already know his sister and father and are liked by them. Am I right or not? Won't that be best?'

'Yes, it will,' Natásha answered reluctantly.

CHAPTER VII

NEXT day, by Márya Dmítrievna's advice, Count Rostóv took Natásha to call on Prince Nicholas Bolkónski. The count did not set out cheerfully on this visit, at heart he felt afraid. He well remembered the last interview he had had with the old prince, at the time of the enrolment, when in reply to an invitation to dinner he had had to listen to an angry reprimand for not having provided his full quota of men. Natásha, on the other hand, having put on her best gown was in the highest spirits. 'They can't help liking me,' she thought. 'Everybody always has liked me, and I am so willing to do anything they wish, so ready to be fond of him—for being *his* father—and of her—for being *his* sister—that there is no reason for them not to like me . . .'

They drove up to the gloomy old house on the Vozdvízhenka and entered the vestibule.

'Well, the Lord have mercy on us!' said the count, half in jest, half in earnest; but Natásha noticed that her father was flurried on entering the ante-room, and inquired timidly and softly whether the prince and princess were at home.

When they had been announced a perturbation was noticeable among the servants. The footman who had gone to announce them was stopped by another in the large hall and they whispered to one another. Then a maidservant ran into the hall and hurriedly said something, mentioning the princess. At last an old, cross-looking footman came and announced to the Rostóvs that the prince was not receiving, but that the princess begged them to walk up. The first person who came to meet the visitors was Mademoiselle Bourienne. She greeted the father and daughter with special politeness, and showed them to the princess's room. The princess, looking excited and nervous, her face flushed in patches, ran in to meet the visitors, treading heavily, and vainly trying to appear cordial and at ease. From the first glance Princess Mary did not like Natásha. She thought her too fashionably dressed, frivolously gay, and vain. She did not at all realize that before having seen her future sister-in-law she was prejudiced against her by involuntary envy of her beauty, youth, and happiness, as well as by jealousy of her brother's love for her. Apart from this insuperable antipathy to her, Princess Mary was agitated just then because on the Rostóvs being announced, the old prince had shouted that he did not wish to see them, that Princess Mary might do so if she chose, but they were not to be admitted to him. She had decided to receive them, but feared lest the prince might at any moment indulge in some freak, as he seemed much upset by the Rostóvs' visit.

'There, my dear Princess, I've brought you my songstress,' said the count, bowing, and looking round uneasily as if afraid the old prince might appear. 'I am so glad you should get to know one another ... very sorry the prince is still ailing,' and after a few more commonplace remarks he rose. 'If you'll allow me to leave my Natásha in your hands for a quarter of an hour, Princess, I'll drive round to see Anna Seménovna, it's quite near, in the Dogs' Square, and then I'll come back for her.'

The count had devised this diplomatic ruse (as he afterwards told his daughter) to give the future sisters-in-law an opportunity to talk to one another freely, but another motive was to avoid the danger of encountering the old prince, of whom he was afraid. He did not mention this to his daughter, but Natásha noticed her father's nervousness and anxiety and felt mortified by it. She blushed for him, grew still angrier at having blushed, and looked at the princess with a bold and defiant expression which said that she was not afraid of anybody. The princess told the count that she would be delighted, and only begged him to stay longer at Anna Seménovna's, and he departed.

Despite the uneasy glances thrown at her by Princess Mary—who wished to have a tête-à-tête with Natásha—Mademoiselle Bourienne remained in the room and persistently talked about Moscow amusements and theatres. Natásha felt offended by the hesitation she had noticed in the ante-room, by her father's nervousness, and by the unnatural manner of the princess who—she thought—was making a favour of receiving her, and so everything displeased her. She did not like Princess Mary, whom she thought very plain, affected, and dry. Natásha suddenly shrank into herself, and involuntarily assumed an off-hand air which alienated Princess Mary still more. After five minutes of irksome, constrained conversation, they heard the sound of slippered feet rapidly approaching. Princess Mary looked frightened. The door opened, and the old prince, in a dressing-gown and a white night-cap, came in.

'Ah, madam!' he began. 'Madam, Countess . . . Countess Rostóva, if I am not mistaken . . . I beg you to excuse me, to excuse me . . . I did not know, madam. God is my witness, I did not know you had honoured us with a visit, and I came in such a costume only to see my daughter. I beg you to excuse me . . . God is my witness, I didn't know—' he repeated, stressing the word 'God' so unnaturally and so unpleasantly that Princess Mary stood with downcast eyes, not daring to look either at her father or at Natásha.

Nor did the latter, having risen and curtsied, know what to do. Mademoiselle Bourienne alone smiled agreeably.

'I beg you to excuse me, excuse me! God is my witness, I did not know,' muttered the old man, and after looking Natásha over from head to foot he went out.

Mademoiselle Bourienne was the first to recover herself after this apparition, and began speaking about the prince's indisposition. Natásha and Princess Mary looked at one another in silence, and the longer they did so, without saying what they wanted to say, the greater grew their antipathy to one another.

When the count returned, Natásha was impolitely pleased, and hastened to get away: at that moment she hated the stiff, elderly princess, who could place her in such an embarrassing position and had spent half an hour with her without once mentioning Prince Andrew. 'I couldn't begin talking about him in the presence of that Frenchwoman,' thought Natásha. The same thought was meanwhile tormenting Princess Mary. She knew what she ought to have said to Natásha, but she had been unable to say it because Mademoiselle Bourienne was in the way, and because, without knowing why, she felt it very difficult to speak of the marriage. When the count was already leaving the room, Princess Mary went up hurriedly to Natásha, took her by the hand, and said with a deep sigh:

'Wait, I must . . .'

Natásha glanced at her ironically, without knowing why.

'Dear Natalie,' said Princess Mary, 'I want you to know that I am glad my brother has found happiness . . .'

She paused, feeling that she was not telling the truth. Natásha noticed this and guessed its reason.

'I think, Princess, it is not convenient to speak of that now,' she said with external dignity and coldness, though she felt the tears choking her.

'What have I said and what have I done?' thought she, as soon as she was out of the room.

They waited a long time for Natásha to come to dinner that day. She sat in her room crying like a child, blowing her nose and sobbing. Sónya stood beside her, kissing her hair.

'Natásha, what is it about?' she asked. 'What do they matter to you? It will all pass, Natásha.'

'But if you only knew how offensive it was . . . as if I . . .'

'Don't talk about it, Natásha. It wasn't your fault, so why should you mind? Kiss me,' said Sónya.

Natásha raised her head and, kissing her friend on the lips, pressed her wet face against her.

'I can't tell you, I don't know. No one's to blame,' said Natásha—'It's my fault. But it all hurts terribly. Oh, why doesn't he come? . . .'

She came in to dinner with red eyes. Márya Dmítrievna, who knew how the prince had received the Rostóvs, pretended not to notice how upset Natásha was, and jested resolutely and loudly at table with the count and the other guests.

CHAPTER VIII

THAT evening the Rostóvs went to the Opera, for which Márya Dmítrievna had taken a box.

Natásha did not want to go, but could not refuse Márya Dmítrievna's kind offer which was intended expressly for her. When she came ready dressed into the ball-room to await her father and looking in the large mirror there saw that she was pretty, very pretty, she felt even more sad, but it was a sweet, tender sadness.

'O, God, if he were here now I would not behave as I did then, but differently. I would not be silly and afraid of things, I would simply embrace him, cling to him, and make him look at me with those searching inquiring eyes with which he has so often looked at me, and then I would make him laugh as he used to laugh. And his eyes—how I see those eyes!' thought Natásha. 'And what do his father and sister matter to me? I love him alone, him, him, with that face and those eyes, with his smile, manly and yet child-like ... No, I had better not think of him; not think of him but forget him, quite forget him for the present. I can't bear this waiting and I shall cry in a minute!' and she turned away from the glass, making an effort not to cry. 'And how can Sónya love Nicholas so calmly and quietly and wait so long and so patiently?' thought she, looking at Sónya, who also came in quite ready, with a fan in her hand. 'No, she's altogether different. I can't!'

Natásha at that moment felt so softened and tender that it was not enough for her to love and know she was beloved, she wanted now, at once, to embrace the man she loved, to speak and hear from him words of love such as filled her heart. While she sat in the carriage beside her father, pensively watching the lights of the street-lamps flickering on the frozen window, she felt still

sadder and more in love, and forgot where she was
going and with whom. Having fallen into the line of
carriages, the Rostóvs' carriage drove up to the theatre,
its wheels squeaking over the snow. Natásha and Sónya,
holding up their dresses, jumped out quickly. The count
got out helped by the footmen, and, passing among men
and women who were entering, and the programme
sellers, they all three went along the corridor to the first
row of boxes. Through the closed doors the music was
already audible.

'Natásha, your hair!' . . . whispered Sónya.

An attendant deferentially and quickly slipped before
the ladies and opened the door of their box. The music
sounded louder, and through the door rows of brightly
lit boxes in which ladies sat with bare arms and shoulders,
and noisy stalls brilliant with uniforms, glittered before
their eyes. A lady entering the next box shot a glance
of feminine envy at Natásha. The curtain had not yet
risen and the overture was being played. Natásha,
smoothing her gown, went in with Sónya and sat down,
scanning the brilliant tiers of boxes opposite. A sensation
she had not experienced for a long time—that of hundreds
of eyes looking at her bare arms and neck—suddenly
affected her both agreeably and disagreeably and called
up a whole crowd of memories, desires, and emotions
associated with that feeling.

The two remarkably pretty girls, Natásha and Sónya,
with Count Rostóv who had not been seen in Moscow
for a long time, attracted general attention. Moreover,
everybody knew vaguely of Natásha's engagement to
Prince Andrew, and knew that the Rostóvs had lived in
the country ever since, and all looked with curiosity at a
fiancée who was making one of the best matches in Russia.

Natásha's looks, as every one told her, had improved in
the country, and that evening thanks to her agitation
she was particularly pretty. She struck those who saw
her by her fullness of life and beauty, combined with her
indifference to everything about her. Her black eyes
looked at the crowd without seeking any one, and her
delicate arm, bare to above the elbow, lay on the velvet
edge of the box, while, evidently unconsciously, she

opened and closed her hand in time to the music, crumpling her programme.

'Look, there's Alénina,' said Sónya, 'with her mother, isn't it?'

'Dear me, Michael Kirílovich has grown still stouter!' remarked the count.

'Look at our Anna Mikháylovna—what a head-dress she has on!'

'The Karágins, Julie—and Borís with them. One can see at once that they're engaged . . .'

'Drubetskóy has proposed?'

'Oh yes, I heard it to-day,' said Shinshín, coming into the Rostóvs' box.

Natásha looked in the direction in which her father's eyes were turned, and saw Julie sitting beside her mother with a happy look on her face and a string of pearls round her thick red neck—which Natásha knew was covered with powder. Behind them, wearing a smile and leaning over with an ear to Julie's mouth, was Borís's handsome smoothly brushed head. He looked at the Rostóvs from under his brows and said something, smiling, to his betrothed.

'They are talking about us, about me and him!' thought Natásha. 'And he no doubt is calming her jealousy of me. They needn't trouble themselves! If only they knew how little I am concerned about any of them.'

Behind them sat Anna Mikháylovna wearing a green head-dress, and with a happy look of resignation to the will of God on her face. Their box was pervaded by that atmosphere of an affianced couple which Natásha knew so well and liked so much. She turned away and suddenly remembered all that had been so humiliating in her morning's visit.

'What right has he not to wish to receive me into his family? Oh, better not think of it—not till he comes back!' she told herself, and began looking at the faces, some strange and some familiar, in the stalls. In the front, in the very centre, leaning back against the orchestra-rail, stood Dólokhov in a Persian dress, his curly hair brushed up into a huge shock. He stood in full view of the audience, well aware that he was attracting every one's attention, yet as much at ease as though he were in his own room. Around him thronged Moscow's most brilliant young men, whom he evidently dominated.

The count, laughing, nudged the blushing Sónya and pointed to her former adorer.

'Do you recognize him?' said he. 'And where has he sprung from?' he asked, turning to Shinshín. 'Didn't he vanish somewhere?'

'He did,' replied Shinshín. 'He was in the Caucasus and ran away from there. They say he has been acting as minister to some ruling prince in Persia, where he killed the Shah's brother. Now all the Moscow ladies are mad about him! It's "Dólokhov the Persian" that does it! We never hear a word but Dólokhov is mentioned. They swear by him, they offer him to you as they would a dish of choice sterlet. Dólokhov and Anatole Kurágin have turned all our ladies' heads.'

A tall, beautiful woman with a mass of plaited hair and much exposed plump white shoulders and neck, round which she wore a double string of large pearls, entered the adjoining box rustling her heavy silk dress, and took a long time settling into her place.

Natásha involuntarily gazed at that neck, those shoulders and pearls and *coiffure*, and admired the beauty of the shoulders and the pearls. While Natásha was fixing her gaze on her for the second time the lady looked round, and meeting the count's eyes nodded to him and smiled. She was the Countess Bezúkhova, Pierre's wife, and the count, who knew every one in society, leaned over and spoke to her.

'Have you been here long, Countess?' he inquired. 'I'll call, I'll call to kiss your hand. I'm here on business and have brought my girls with me. They say Seménova acts marvellously. Count Pierre never used to forget us. Is he here?'

'Yes, he meant to look in,' answered Hélène, and glanced attentively at Natásha.

Count Rostóv resumed his seat.

'Handsome, isn't she?' he whispered to Natásha.

'Wonderful!' answered Natásha. 'She's a woman one could easily fall in love with.'

Just then the last chords of the overture were heard and the conductor tapped with his stick. Some late comers took their seats in the stalls and the curtain rose.

As soon as it rose every one in the boxes and stalls became silent, and all the men, old and young, in uniform and evening dress, and all the women with gems on their bare flesh, turned their whole attention with eager curiosity to the stage. Natásha too began to look at it.

CHAPTER IX

THE floor of the stage consisted of smooth boards, at the sides was some painted cardboard representing trees, and at the back was a cloth stretched over boards. In the centre of the stage sat some girls in red bodices and white skirts. One very fat girl in a white silk dress sat apart on a low bench, to the back of which a piece of green cardboard was glued. They all sang something. When they had finished their song the girl in white went up to the prompter's box, and a man with tight silk trousers over his stout legs, and holding a plume and a dagger, went up to her and began singing, waving his arms about.

First the man in the tight trousers sang alone, then she sang, then they both paused while the orchestra played and the man fingered the hand of the girl in white, obviously awaiting the beat to start singing with her. They sang together and every one in the theatre began clapping and shouting, while the man and woman on the stage—who represented lovers—began smiling, spreading out their arms, and bowing.

After her life in the country, and in her present serious mood, all this seemed grotesque and amazing to Natásha. She could not follow the opera nor even listen to the music, she saw only the painted cardboard and the queerly dressed men and women who moved, spoke, and sang, so strangely in that brilliant light. She knew what it was all meant to represent, but it was so pretentiously false and unnatural that she first felt ashamed for the actors and then amused at them. She looked at the faces of the audience, seeking in them the same sense of ridicule and perplexity she herself experienced, but they all seemed attentive to what was happening on the stage, and expressed delight which to Natásha seemed feigned. 'I suppose it has to be like this!' she thought. She kept looking round in turn at the rows of pomaded heads in the stalls and then at the semi-nude women in the boxes, especially at Hélène in the next box, who—apparently quite unclothed—sat with a quiet tranquil smile, not taking her eyes off the stage. And feeling the bright light that flooded the whole place and the warm air heated by the crowd, Natásha little by little began to pass into a state of intoxication she had not experienced for a long while. She did not realize who and where she was, nor what was going on before her. As she looked and thought, the strangest fancies unexpectedly and disconnectedly passed through her mind: the idea occurred to her of jumping onto the edge of the box and singing the air the actress was singing, then she wished to touch with her fan an old gentleman sitting not far from her, then to lean over to Hélène and tickle her.

At a moment when all was quiet before the commencement of a song, a door leading to the stalls on the side nearest the Rostóvs' box creaked, and the steps of a belated arrival were heard. 'There's Kurágin!' whispered Shinshín. Countess Bezúkhova turned smiling to the new-comer, and Natásha, following the direction of that look, saw an exceptionally handsome adjutant approaching their box with a self-assured yet courteous bearing. This was Anatole Kurágin whom she had seen and noticed long ago at the ball in Petersburg. He was now in an adjutant's uniform with one épaulette and a shoulder-knot. He moved with a restrained swagger which would have been ridiculous had he not been so good-looking and had his handsome face not worn such an expression of good-humoured complacency and gaiety. Though the performance was proceeding, he walked deliberately down the carpeted gangway, his sword and spurs slightly jingling and his handsome perfumed head held high. Having looked at Natásha he approached his sister, laid his well-gloved hand on the edge of her box, nodded to her, and leaning forward asked a question, with a motion towards Natásha.

'*Mais charmante!*' said he, evidently referring to Natásha, who did not exactly hear his words but understood them from the movement of his lips. Then he took his place in the first row of the stalls and sat down beside Dólokhov, nudging with his elbow in a friendly and off-hand way that Dólokhov whom others treated so fawningly. He winked at him gaily, smiled, and rested his foot against the orchestra-screen.

'How like the brother is to the sister,' remarked the count. 'And how handsome they both are!'

Shinshín, lowering his voice, began to tell the count of some intrigue of Kurágin's in Moscow, and Natásha tried to overhear it just because he had said she was '*charmante*'.

The first act was over. In the stalls every one began moving about, going out and coming in.

Borís came to the Rostóvs' box, received their congratulations very simply, and raising his eyebrows with an absent-minded smile conveyed to Natásha and Sónya his fiancée's invitation to her wedding, and went away. Natásha with a gay coquettish smile talked to him, and congratulated on his approaching wedding that same Borís with whom she had formerly been in love. In the state of intoxication she was in everything seemed simple and natural.

The scantily clad Hélène was sitting near her, smiling at every one with the same smile, and Natásha gave Borís just such a smile.

Hélène's box was filled, and surrounded from the stalls, by the most distinguished and intellectual men, who seemed to vie with one another in their wish to let every one see that they knew her.

During the whole of that *entr'acte* Kurágin stood with Dólokhov in front of the orchestra partition looking at the Rostóvs' box. Natásha knew he was talking about her and this afforded her pleasure. She even turned so that he should see her profile in what she thought was its most becoming aspect. Before the beginning of the second act Pierre appeared in the stalls. The Rostóvs

202 WAR AND PEACE

had not seen him since their arrival. His face looked sad,
and he had grown still stouter since Natásha last saw him.
He passed up to the front rows not noticing any one.
Anatole went up to him and began speaking to him,
looking at and indicating the Rostóvs' box. On seeing
Natásha Pierre grew animated and, hastily passing
between the rows, came towards their box. When he
got there he leaned on his elbows and, smiling, talked to
her for a long time. While conversing with Pierre
Natásha heard a man's voice in Countess Bezúkhova's
box and something told her it was Kurágin. She turned
and their eyes met. Almost smiling, he gazed straight
into her eyes with such an enraptured caressing look
that it seemed strange to be so near him, to look at him
like that, to be so sure he admired her, and not to be
acquainted with him.

In the second act there was scenery representing
tombstones, and there was a round hole in the canvas to
represent the moon, shades were raised over the foot-
lights, and from horns and contrabass came deep notes
while many people appeared from right and left wearing
black cloaks and holding things like daggers in their
hands. They began waving their arms. Then some other
people ran in and began dragging away the maiden who
had been in white and was now in light blue. They
did not drag her away at once, but sang with her for
a long time, and then at last dragged her off, and behind
the scenes something metallic was struck three times and
every one knelt down and sang a prayer. All these things
were repeatedly interrupted by the enthusiastic shouts
of the audience.

During this act every time Natásha looked towards the
stalls she saw Anatole Kurágin, with an arm thrown
across the back of his chair, staring at her. She was
pleased to see that he was captivated by her and it did
not occur to her that there was anything wrong in it.

When the second act was over Countess Bezúkhova
rose, turned to the Rostóvs' box—her whole bosom completely exposed—beckoned the old count with a gloved
finger, and paying no attention to those who had entered
her box, began talking to him with an amiable smile.

'Do make me acquainted with your charming daughters,' said she. 'The whole town is singing their praises and I don't even know them.'

Natásha rose and curtsied to the splendid countess. She was so pleased by praise from this brilliant beauty that she blushed with pleasure.

'I want to become a Moscovite too, now,' said Hélène. 'How is it you're not ashamed to bury such pearls in the country?'

Countess Bezúkhova quite deserved her reputation of being a fascinating woman. She could say what she did not think—especially what was flattering—quite simply and naturally.

'Dear Count, you must let me look after your daughters! Though I am not staying here long this time—nor are you—I will try to amuse them. I have already heard much of you in Petersburg and wanted to get to know you,' said she to Natásha with her stereotyped and lovely smile. 'I had heard about you from my page, Drubetskóy. Have you heard he is getting married? And also from my husband's friend, Bolkónski, Prince Andrew Bolkónski,' she went on with special emphasis, implying that she knew of his relation to Natásha. To get better acquainted she asked that one of the young ladies should come into her box for the rest of the performance, and Natásha moved over to it.

The scene of the third act represented a palace in which many candles were burning and pictures of knights with short beards hung on the walls. In the middle stood what were probably a king and a queen. The king waved his right arm and, evidently nervous, sang something badly and sat down on a crimson throne. The maiden who had been first in white and then in light blue, now wore only a smock, and stood beside the throne with her hair down. She sang something mournfully, addressing the queen, but the king waved his arm severely, and men and women with bare legs came in from both sides and began dancing all together. Then the violins played very shrilly and merrily and one of the women with thick bare legs and thin arms, separating from the others, went behind the wings, adjusted her bodice,

returned to the middle of the stage, and began jumping
and striking one foot rapidly against the other. In the
stalls every one clapped and shouted 'bravo!' Then
one of the men went into a corner of the stage. The
cymbals and horns in the orchestra struck up more
loudly, and this man with bare legs jumped very high
and waved his feet about very rapidly. (He was Duport,
who received sixty thousand rubles a year for this art.)
Everybody in the stalls, boxes, and galleries began
clapping and shouting with all their might, and the man
stopped and began smiling and bowing to all sides. Then
other men and women danced with bare legs. Then
the king again shouted to the sound of music and they all
began singing. But suddenly a storm came on, chromatic
scales and diminished sevenths were heard in the
orchestra, every one ran off, again dragging one of their
number away, and the curtain dropped. Once more
there was a terrible noise and clatter among the audience,
and with rapturous faces every one began shouting:
'Duport! Duport! Duport!' Natásha no longer thought
this strange. She looked about with pleasure, smiling
joyfully.

'Isn't Duport delightful?' Hélène asked her.

'Oh yes,' replied Natásha.

CHAPTER X

DURING the *entr'acte* a whiff of cold air came into
Hélène's box, the door opened and Anatole entered,
stooping and trying not to brush against any one.

'Let me introduce my brother to you,' said Hélène,
her eyes shifting uneasily from Natásha to Anatole.

Natásha turned her pretty little head towards the
elegant young officer, and smiled at him over her bare
shoulder. Anatole, who was as handsome at close
quarters as at a distance, sat down beside her and told
her he had long wished to have this happiness—ever
since the Naryshkins' ball, in fact, at which he had had
the well-remembered pleasure of seeing her. Kurágin was
much more sensible and simple with women than among

men. He talked boldly and naturally, and Natásha was strangely and agreeably struck by the fact that there was nothing formidable in this man about whom there was so much talk, but that on the contrary his smile was most naïve, cheerful, and good-natured.

Kurágin asked her opinion of the performance, and told her how at a previous performance Semënova had fallen down on the stage.

'And do you know, Countess,' he said, suddenly addressing her as an old, familiar acquaintance, 'we are getting up a costume-tournament; you ought to take part in it! It will be great fun. We shall all meet at the Karágins! Please come! No! Really, eh?' said he.

While saying this he never removed his smiling eyes from her face, her neck, and her bare arms. Natásha knew for certain that he was enraptured by her. This pleased her, yet his presence made her feel constrained and oppressed. When she was not looking at him she felt that he was looking at her shoulders, and she involuntarily caught his eye so that he should look into hers rather than this. But looking into his eyes she was frightened, realizing that there was not that barrier of modesty she had always felt between herself and other men. She did not know how it was that within five minutes she had come to feel herself terribly near to this man. When she turned away she feared he might seize her from behind by her bare arm and kiss her on the neck. They spoke of most ordinary things, yet she felt that they were closer to one another than she had ever been to any man. Natásha kept turning to Hélène and to her father, as if asking what it all meant, but Hélène was engaged in conversation with a general, and did not answer her look, and her father's eyes said nothing but what they always said: 'Having a good time? Well, I'm glad of it!'

During one of these moments of awkward silence when Anatole's prominent eyes were gazing calmly and fixedly at her, Natásha, to break the silence, asked him how he liked Moscow. She asked the question and blushed. She felt all the time that by talking to him she was doing something improper. Anatole smiled as though to encourage her.

'At first I did not like it much, because what makes a town pleasant *ce sont les jolies femmes,*[1] isn't that so? But now I like it very much indeed,' he said, looking at her significantly. 'You'll come to the costume-tournament, Countess? Do come!' and putting out his hand to her bouquet and dropping his voice, he added, 'You will be the prettiest there. Do come, dear Countess, and give me this flower as a pledge!'

Natásha did not understand what he was saying any more than he did himself, but she felt that his incomprehensible words had an improper intention. She did not know what to say, and turned away as if she had not heard his remark. But as soon as she had turned away she felt that he was there, behind, so close behind her.

'How is he now? Confused? Angry? Ought I to put it right?' she asked herself, and she could not refrain from turning round. She looked straight into his eyes, and his nearness, self-assurance, and the good-natured tenderness of his smile, vanquished her. She smiled just as he was doing, gazing straight into his eyes. And again she felt with horror that no barrier lay between him and her.

The curtain rose again. Anatole left the box, serene and gay. Natásha went back to her father in the other box, now quite submissive to the world she found herself in. All that was going on before her now seemed quite natural, but on the other hand all her previous thoughts of her betrothed, of Princess Mary, or of life in the country, did not once recur to her mind and were as if belonging to a remote past.

In the fourth act there was some sort of a devil who sang, waving his arm about, till the boards were withdrawn from under him and he disappeared down below. That was the only part of the fourth act that Natásha saw. She felt agitated and tormented, and the cause of this was Kurágin, whom she could not help watching. As they were leaving the theatre Anatole came up to them, called their carriage and helped them in. As he was putting Natásha in he pressed her arm above the elbow. Agitated and flushed she turned round. He was looking at her with glittering eyes, smiling tenderly.

[1] 'Are the pretty women.'

Only after she had reached home was Natásha able clearly to think over what had happened to her, and suddenly remembering Prince Andrew she was horrified, and at tea to which all had sat down after the opera, she gave a loud exclamation, flushed, and ran out of the room.

'O God! I am lost!' she said to herself. 'How could I let him?' She sat for a long time hiding her flushed face in her hands trying to realize what had happened to her, but was unable either to understand what had happened or what she felt. Everything seemed dark, obscure, and terrible. There in that enormous, illuminated theatre where the bare-legged Duport, in a tinsel-decorated jacket, jumped about to the music on wet boards, and young girls and old men, and the nearly naked Hélène with her proud, calm smile, rapturously cried 'bravo!'— there in the presence of that Hélène it had all seemed clear and simple; but now, alone, by herself, it was incomprehensible. 'What is it? What was that terror I felt of him? What is this gnawing of conscience I am feeling now?' she thought.

Only to the old countess at night in bed could Natásha have told all she was feeling. She knew that Sónya with her severe and simple views would either not understand it at all or would be horrified at such a confession. So Natásha tried to solve what was torturing her by herself.

'Am I spoilt for Andrew's love or not?' she asked herself, and with soothing irony replied: 'What a fool I am to ask that! What did happen to me? Nothing! I have done nothing, I didn't lead him on at all. Nobody will know and I shall never see him again;' she told herself. 'So it is plain that nothing has happened and there if nothing to repent of, and Andrew can love me still. But why "still"? O God, O God, why isn't he here?' Natásha quieted herself for a moment but again some instinct told her that though all this was true, and though nothing had happened, yet the former purity of her love for Prince Andrew had perished. And again in imagination she went over her whole conversation with Kurágin, and again saw the face, gestures, and tender smile, of that bold handsome man when he pressed her arm.

CHAPTER XI

ANATOLE KURÁGIN was staying in Moscow because his father had sent him away from Petersburg, where he had been spending twenty thousand rubles a year in cash, besides running up debts for as much more which his creditors demanded from his father.

His father announced to him that he would now pay half his debts for the last time, but only on condition that he went to Moscow as adjutant to the commander-in-chief—a post his father had procured for him—and would at last try to make a good match there. He indicated to him Princess Mary and Julie Karágin.

Anatole consented and went to Moscow, where he put up at Pierre's house. Pierre received him unwillingly at first, but got used to him after a while, sometimes even accompanied him on his carousals, and gave him money under the guise of loans.

As Shinshín had remarked, from the time of his arrival Anatole had turned the heads of the Moscow ladies, especially by the fact that he slighted them and plainly preferred the gipsy-girls and French actresses—with the chief of whom, Mademoiselle Georges, he was said to be on intimate relations. He never missed a carousal at Danílov's or other Moscow revellers, drank whole nights through, outvying every one else, and was at all the balls and parties of the best society. There was talk of his intrigues with some of the ladies, and he flirted with a few of them at the balls. But he did not run after the unmarried girls, especially the rich heiresses who were most of them plain. There was a special reason for this, as he had got married two years before—a fact known only to his most intimate friends. At that time, while with his regiment in Poland, a Polish landowner of small means had forced him to marry his daughter. Anatole had very soon abandoned his wife, and for a payment which he agreed to send to his father-in-law had arranged to be free to pass himself off as a bachelor.

Anatole was always content with his position, with himself, and with others. He was instinctively and thoroughly convinced that it was impossible for him to live otherwise than as he did, and that he had never in his life done anything base. He was incapable of considering how his actions might affect others, or what the consequences of this or that action of his might be. He was convinced that, as a duck is so made that it must live in water, so God had made him such that he must spend thirty thousand rubles a year and always occupy a prominent position in society. He believed this so firmly that others, looking at him, were persuaded of it too, and did not refuse him either a leading place in society, or money, which he borrowed from any one and every one and evidently would not repay.

He was not a gambler, at any rate he did not care about winning. He was not vain. He did not mind what people thought of him. Still less could he be accused of ambition. More than once he had vexed his father by spoiling his own career, and he laughed at distinctions of all kinds. He was not mean, and did not refuse any one who asked of him. All he cared about was gaiety and women, and as according to his ideas there was nothing dishonourable in these tastes, and he was incapable of considering what the gratification of his tastes entailed for others, he honestly considered himself irreproachable, sincerely despised rogues and bad people, and with a tranquil conscience carried his head high.

Rakes, those male Magdalenes, have a secret feeling of innocence similar to that which female Magdalenes have, based on the same hope of forgiveness. 'All will be forgiven her, for she loved much; and all will be forgiven him, for he enjoyed much.'

Dólokhov, who had reappeared that year in Moscow after his exile and his Persian adventures, and was leading a life of luxury, gambling and dissipation, associated with his old Petersburg comrade Kurágin and made use of him for his own ends.

Anatole was sincerely fond of Dólokhov for his cleverness and audacity. Dólokhov, who needed Anatole Kurágin's name, position, and connexions as a bait to draw rich young men into his gambling set, made use of him and amused himself at his expense without letting the other feel it. Apart from the advantage he derived from Anatole, the very process of dominating another's will was in itself a pleasure, a habit, and a necessity to Dólokhov.

Natásha had made a strong impression on Kurágin. At supper after the opera he described to Dólokhov, with the air of a connoisseur, the attractions of her arms, shoulders, feet and hair, and expressed his intention of making love to her. Anatole had no notion, and was incapable of considering, what might come of such love-making, as he never had any notion of the outcome of any of his actions.

'She's first-rate, my dear fellow, but not for us,' replied Dólokhov.

'I will tell my sister to ask her to dinner,' said Anatole, 'Eh?'

'You'd better wait till she's married . . .'

'You know, I adore little girls, they lose their heads at once,' pursued Anatole.

'You have been caught once already by a "little girl",' said Dólokhov, who knew of Kurágin's marriage. 'Take care!'

'Well, that can't happen twice! Eh?' said Anatole, with a good-humoured laugh.

CHAPTER XII

THE day after the opera the Rostóvs went nowhere and nobody came to see them. Márya Dmítrievna talked to the count about something which they concealed from Natásha. Natásha guessed they were talking about the old prince and planning something, and this disquieted and offended her. She was expecting Prince Andrew any moment, and twice that day sent a man-servant to the Vozdvízhenka to ascertain whether he had come. He had not arrived. She suffered more now than during her first days in Moscow. To her impatience and pining for him were now added the unpleasant recollection of her interview with Princess Mary and the old prince, and a fear and anxiety of which she did not understand the cause. She continually fancied that either he would never come, or that something would happen to her before he came. She could no longer think of him by herself calmly and continuously as she had done before. As soon as she began to think of him, the recollection of the old prince, of Princess Mary, of the theatre, and of Kurágin, mingled with her thoughts. The question again presented itself whether she was not guilty, whether she had not already broken faith with Prince Andrew, and again she found herself recalling to the minutest detail, every word, every gesture, and every shade in the play of expression on the face of the man who had been able to arouse in her such an incomprehensible and terrifying feeling. To the family Natásha seemed livelier than usual, but she was far less tranquil and happy than before.

On Sunday morning Márya Dmítrievna invited her visitors to Mass at her parish church—the Church of the Assumption built over the graves of victims of the plague. 'I don't like those fashionable churches,' she said, evidently priding herself on her independence of thought. 'God is the same everywhere. We have an excellent priest, he conducts the service decently and with dignity, and the deacon is the same. What holiness is there in giving concerts in the choir? I don't like it, it's just self-indulgence!'

Márya Dmítrievna liked Sundays and knew how to keep them. Her whole house was scrubbed and cleaned on Saturdays; neither she nor the servants worked, and they all wore holiday dress and went to church. At her table there were extra dishes at dinner, and the servants had vodka and roast goose or sucking-pig. But in nothing in the house was the holiday so noticeable as in Márya Dmítrievna's broad, stern face, which on that day wore an invariable look of solemn festivity.

After Mass, when they had finished their coffee, in the dining-room where the loose covers had been removed from the furniture, a servant announced that the carriage was ready, and Márya Dmítrievna rose with a stern air. She wore her holiday shawl, in which she paid calls, and announced that she was going to see Prince Nicholas Bolkónski to have an explanation with him about Natásha.

After she had gone, a dressmaker from Madame Suppert-Roguet waited on the Rostóvs, and Natásha, very glad of this diversion, having shut herself into a room adjoining the drawing-room, occupied herself trying on the new dresses. Just as she had put on a bodice without sleeves and only tacked together, and was turning her head to see in the glass how the back fitted, she heard in the drawing-room the animated sounds of her father's voice and another's—a woman's—that made her flush. It was Hélène. Natásha had not time to take off the bodice before the door opened and Countess Bezúkhova, dressed in a purple velvet gown with a high collar, came into the room beaming with good-humoured amiable smiles.

'Oh, my enchantress!' she cried to the blushing Natásha. 'Charming! No, this is really beyond anything, my dear Count,' said she to Count Rostóv who had followed her in. 'How can you live in Moscow and go nowhere? No, I won't let you off! Mademoiselle Georges will recite at my house to-night, and there'll be some people, and if you don't bring your lovely girls—who are prettier than Mademoiselle Georges—I won't know you! My husband is away in Tver or I would send him to fetch you. You must come. You positively must! Between eight and nine.'

She nodded to the dressmaker, whom she knew and who had curtsied respectfully to her, and seated herself in an arm-chair beside the looking-glass draping the folds of her velvet dress picturesquely. She did not cease chattering good-naturedly and gaily, continually praising Natásha's beauty. She looked at Natásha's dresses and praised them, as well as a new dress of her own, made of 'metallic gauze', which she had received from Paris, and advised Natásha to have one like it.

'But anything suits you, my charmer!' she remarked.

A smile of pleasure never left Natásha's face. She felt happy and as if she were blossoming, under the praise of this dear Countess Bezúkhova who had formerly seemed to her so unapproachable and important and was now so kind to her. Natásha brightened up and felt almost in love with this woman, who was so beautiful and so kind

Hélène for her part was sincerely delighted with Natásha and wished to give her a good time. Anatole had asked her to bring him and Natásha together, and she was calling on the Rostóvs for that purpose. The idea of throwing her brother and Natásha together amused her.

Though at one time, in Petersburg, she had been annoyed with Natásha for drawing Borís away, she did not think of that now, and in her own way heartily wished Natásha well. As she was leaving the Rostóvs she called her protégée aside.

'My brother dined with me yesterday—we nearly died of laughter—he ate nothing and kept sighing for you, my charmer! He is madly, quite madly, in love with you, my dear.'

Natásha blushed scarlet when she heard this.

'How she blushes, how she blushes, my pretty!' said Hélène. 'You must certainly come. If you love somebody, my charmer, that is not a reason to shut yourself up. Even if you are engaged, I am sure your fiancé would wish you to go into society rather than be bored to death.'

'So she knows I am engaged, and she and her husband Pierre—that good Pierre—have talked and laughed about this. So it's all right.' And again, under Hélène's influence, what had seemed terrible now seemed simple and natural. 'And she is such a *grande dame*, so kind, and evidently likes me so much. And why not enjoy myself?' thought Natásha gazing at Hélène with wide-open, wondering eyes.

Márya Dmítrievna came back to dinner taciturn and serious, having evidently suffered a defeat at the old prince's. She was still too agitated by the encounter to be able to talk of the affair calmly. In answer to the count's inquiries she replied that things were all right and that she would tell about it next day. On hearing of Countess Bezúkhova's visit and the invitation for that evening, Márya Dmítrievna remarked:

'I don't care to have anything to do with Bezúkhova and don't advise you to; however, if you've promised—go. It will divert your thoughts,' she added, addressing Natásha.

CHAPTER XIII

COUNT ROSTÓV took the girls to Countess Bezúkhova's. There were a good many people there, but nearly all strangers to Natásha. Count Rostóv was displeased to see that the company consisted almost entirely of men and women known for the freedom of their conduct. Mademoiselle Georges was standing in a corner of the drawing-room surrounded by young men. There were several Frenchmen present, among them Métivier, who from the time Hélène reached Moscow had been an intimate in her house. The count decided not to sit down to cards or let his girls out of his sight, and to get away as soon as Mademoiselle Georges's performance was over.

Anatole was at the door, evidently on the look-out for the Rostóvs. Immediately after greeting the count he went up to Natásha and followed her. As soon as she saw him she was seized by the same feeling she had had at the opera—gratified vanity at his admiration of her, and fear at the absence of a moral barrier between them.

Hélène welcomed Natásha delightedly and was loud in admiration of her beauty and her dress. Soon after their arrival Mademoiselle Georges went out of the room to change her costume. In the drawing-room people began arranging the chairs and taking their seats. Anatole moved a chair for Natásha and was about to sit down beside her, but the count, who never lost sight of her, took the seat himself. Anatole sat down behind her.

Mademoiselle Georges, with her bare, fat, dimpled arms, and a red shawl draped over one shoulder, came into the space left vacant for her, and assumed an unnatural pose. Enthusiastic whispering was audible.

Mademoiselle Georges looked sternly and gloomily at the audience, and began reciting some French verses describing her guilty love for her son. In some places she raised her voice, in others she whispered, lifting her head triumphantly, sometimes she paused and uttered hoarse sounds, rolling her eyes.

'Adorable! divine! delicious!' was heard from every side.

Natásha looked at the fat actress, but neither saw nor heard nor understood anything of what went on before her. She only felt herself again completely borne away into this strange senseless world—so remote from her old world—a world in which it was impossible to know what was good or bad, reasonable or senseless. Behind her sat Anatole, and conscious of his proximity she experienced a frightened sense of expectancy.

After the first monologue the whole company rose and surrounded Mademoiselle Georges, expressing their enthusiasm.

'How beautiful she is!' Natásha remarked to her father, who had also risen and was moving through the crowd towards the actress.

'I don't think so when I look at you!' said Anatole, following Natásha. He said this at a moment when she alone could hear him. 'You are enchanting . . . from the moment I saw you I have never ceased . . .'

'Come, come, Natásha!' said the count, as he turned back for his daughter. 'How beautiful she is!'

Natásha without saying anything stepped up to her father and looked at him with surprised inquiring eyes.

After giving several recitations, Mademoiselle Georges left, and Countess Bezúkhova asked her visitors into the ball-room.

The count wished to go home, but Hélène entreated him not to spoil her improvised ball, and the Rostóvs stayed on. Anatole asked Natásha for a valse and as they danced he pressed her waist and hand and told her she was bewitching and that he loved her. During the Écossaise, which she also danced with him, Anatole said nothing when they happened to be by themselves, but merely gazed at her. Natásha lifted her frightened eyes to him, but there was such confident tenderness in his affectionate look and smile that she could not, whilst looking at him, say what she had to say. She lowered her eyes.

'Don't say such things to me. I am betrothed and love another,' she said rapidly . . . She glanced at him.

Anatole was not upset or pained by what she had said.

'Don't speak to me of that! What can I do?' said he.

'I tell you I am madly, madly, in love with you! Is it my fault that you are enchanting? . . . It's our turn to begin.'

Natásha, animated and excited, looked about her with wide-open frightened eyes and seemed merrier than usual. She understood hardly anything that went on that evening. They danced the Écossaise and the *Grossvater*. Her father asked her to come home, but she begged to remain. Wherever she went and whomever she was speaking to, she felt *his* eyes upon her. Later on she recalled how she had asked her father to let her go to the dressing-room to rearrange her dress, that Hélène had followed her and spoken laughingly of her brother's love, and that she again met Anatole in the little sitting-room. Hélène had disappeared leaving them alone, and Anatole had taken her hand and said in a tender voice:

'I cannot come to visit you but is it possible that I shall never see you? I love you madly. Can I never . . .?' and, blocking her path, he brought his face close to hers.

His large, glittering, masculine eyes were so close to hers that she saw nothing but them.

'Natalie?' he whispered inquiringly while she felt her hands being painfully pressed. 'Natalie?'

'I don't understand. I have nothing to say,' her eyes replied.

Burning lips were pressed to hers, and at the same instant she felt herself released, and Hélène's footsteps and the rustle of her dress were heard in the room. Natásha looked round at her, and then, red and trembling, threw a frightened look of inquiry at Anatole and moved towards the door.

'One word, just one, for God's sake!' cried Anatole.

She paused. She so wanted a word from him that would explain to her what had happened, and to which she could find an answer.

'Natalie, just a word, only one!' he kept repeating, evidently not knowing what to say—and he repeated it till Hélène came up to them.

Hélène returned with Natásha to the drawing-room. The Rostóvs went away without staying for supper.

After reaching home Natásha did not sleep all night. She was tormented by the insoluble question whether she

loved Anatole or Prince Andrew. She loved Prince
Andrew—she remembered distinctly how deeply she
loved him. But she also loved Anatole, of that there was
no doubt. 'Else how could all this have happened?'
thought she. 'If, after that, I could return his smile
when saying good-bye, if I was able to let it come to that,
it means that I loved him from the first. It means that
he is kind, noble, and splendid, and I could not help loving
him. What am I to do if I love him and the other one
too?' she asked herself, unable to find an answer to these
terrible questions.

CHAPTER XIV

MORNING came with its cares and bustle. Every
one got up and began to move about and talk,
dressmakers came again, Márya Dmítrievna appeared,
and they were called to breakfast. Natásha kept looking uneasily at everybody with wide-open eyes, as if
wishing to intercept every glance directed towards her,
and tried to appear the same as usual.

After breakfast, which was her best time, Márya
Dmítrievna sat down in her arm-chair and called Natásha
and the count to her.

'Well, friends, I have now thought the whole matter
over and this is my advice,' she began. 'Yesterday, as you
know, I went to see Prince Bolkónski. Well, I had a talk
with him ... He took it into his head to begin shouting,
but I am not one to be shouted down. I said what I had
to say!'

'Well, and he?' asked the count.

'He? He's crazy ... he did not want to listen. But
what's the use of talking? As it is we have worn the poor
girl out,' said Márya Dmítrievna. 'My advice to you is,
finish your business and go back home to Otrádnoe ...
and wait there.'

'Oh, no!' exclaimed Natásha.

'Yes, go back,' said Márya Dmítrievna, 'and wait there.
If your betrothed comes here now—there will be no
avoiding a quarrel; but alone with the old man he will
talk things over and then come on to you.'

Count Rostóv approved of this suggestion, appreciating its reasonableness. If the old man came round it would be all the better to visit him in Moscow or at Bald Hills later on; and if not, the wedding, against his wishes, could only be arranged at Otrádnoe.

'That is perfectly true. And I am sorry I went to see him and took her,' said the old count.

'No, why be sorry! Being here you had to pay your respects. But if he won't—that's his affair,' said Márya Dmítrievna, looking for something in her reticule. 'Besides, the trousseau is ready, so there is nothing to wait for; and what is not ready I'll send after you. Though I don't like letting you go, it is the best way. So go, with God's blessing!'

Having found what she was looking for in the reticule she handed it to Natásha. It was a letter from Princess Mary.

'She has written to you. How she torments herself, poor thing! She's afraid you might think that she does not like you.'

'But she doesn't like me,' said Natásha.

'Don't talk nonsense!' cried Márya Dmítrievna.

'I shan't believe any one, I know she doesn't like me,' replied Natásha boldly as she took the letter, and her face expressed a cold and angry resolution that caused Márya Dmítrievna to look at her more intently and to frown.

'Don't answer like that, my good girl!' she said. 'What I say is true! Write an answer!'

Natásha did not reply, and went to her own room to read Princess Mary's letter.

Princess Mary wrote that she was in despair at the misunderstanding that had occurred between them. Whatever her father's feelings might be, she begged Natásha to believe that she could not help loving her as the one chosen by her brother, for whose happiness she was ready to sacrifice everything.

'Do not think however,' she wrote, 'that my father is ill-disposed towards you. He is an invalid and an old man who must be forgiven; but he is good and magnanimous, and will love her who makes his son happy.' Princess

Mary went on to ask Natásha to fix a time when she could see her again.

After reading the letter Natásha sat down at the writing-table to answer it. 'Dear Princess,' she wrote in French quickly and mechanically, and then paused. What more could she write after all that had happened the evening before? 'Yes, yes! All that has happened, and now all is changed,' she thought as she sat with the letter she had begun before her. 'Must I break off with him? Must I really? That's awful! . . .' and to escape from these dreadful thoughts she went to Sónya and began sorting patterns with her.

After dinner Natásha went to her room and again took up Princess Mary's letter. 'Can it be that it is all over?' she thought. 'Can it be that all this has happened so quickly and has destroyed all that went before?' She recalled her love for Prince Andrew in all its former strength, and at the same time felt that she loved Kurágin. She vividly pictured herself as Prince Andrew's wife, and the scenes of happiness with him she had so often repeated in her imagination, and at the same time, aglow with excitement, recalled every detail of yesterday's interview with Anatole.

'Why could that not be as well?' she sometimes asked herself in complete bewilderment. 'Only so could I be completely happy; but now I have to choose, and I can't be happy without either of them. Only,' she thought, 'to tell Prince Andrew what has happened or to hide it from him are both equally impossible. But with *that one* nothing is spoilt. But am I really to abandon for ever the joy of Prince Andrew's love, in which I have lived so long?'

'Please, Miss!' whispered a maid entering the room with a mysterious air. 'A man told me to give you this—' and she handed Natásha a letter.

'Only, for Christ's sake . . .' the girl went on, as Natásha, without thinking, mechanically broke the seal and read a love-letter from Anatole, of which without taking in a word, she understood only that it was a letter from him —from the man she loved. Yes, she loved him, or else how could that have happened which had happened?

And how could she have a love-letter from him in her hand?

With trembling hands Natásha held that passionate love-letter which Dólokhov had composed for Anatole, and as she read it, she found in it an echo of all that she herself imagined she was feeling.

'Since yesterday evening my fate has been sealed; to be loved by you or to die. There is no other way for me,' the letter began. Then he went on to say that he knew her parents would not give her to him—for this there were secret reasons he could reveal only to her—but that if she loved him, she need only say the word *Yes*, and no human power could hinder their bliss. Love would conquer all. He would steal her away and carry her off to the ends of the earth.

'Yes, yes! I love him!' thought Natásha, reading the letter for the twentieth time and finding some peculiarly deep meaning in each word of it.

That evening Márya Dmítrievna was going to the Akhárovs' and proposed to take the girls with her. Natásha, pleading a headache, remained at home.

CHAPTER XV

ON returning late in the evening Sónya went to Natásha's room, and to her surprise found her still dressed, and asleep on the sofa. Open on the table beside her lay Anatole's letter. Sónya picked it up and read it.

As she read she glanced at the sleeping Natásha, trying to find in her face an explanation of what she was reading, but did not find it. Her face was calm, gentle, and happy. Clutching her breast to keep herself from choking, Sónya, pale and trembling with fear and agitation, sat down in an arm-chair and burst into tears.

'How was it I noticed nothing? How could it go so far? Can she have left off loving Prince Andrew? And how could she let Kurágin go to such lengths? He is a deceiver and a villain, that's plain! What will Nicholas dear noble Nicholas, do when he hears of it? So this is

the meaning of her excited, resolute, unnatural look the
day before yesterday, yesterday, and to-day,' thought
Sónya. 'But it can't be that she loves him! She probably
opened the letter without knowing who it was from.
Probably she is offended by it. She could not do such
a thing!'

Sónya wiped away her tears and went up to Natásha,
again scanning her face.

'Natásha!' she said, just audibly.

Natásha awoke and saw Sónya.

'Ah, you're back?'

And with the decision and tenderness that often come
at the moment of awakening, she embraced her friend,
but noticing Sónya's look of embarrassment, her own
face expressed confusion and suspicion.

'Sónya, you've read that letter?' she demanded.

'Yes,' answered Sónya softly.

Natásha smiled rapturously.

'No, Sónya, I can't any longer!' she said. 'I can't hide
it from you any longer. You know we love one another!
Sónya, darling, he writes. . . Sónya . . .'

Sónya stared open-eyed at Natásha, unable to believe
her ears.

'And Bolkónski?' she asked.

'Ah, Sónya, if you only knew how happy I am!' cried
Natásha. 'You don't know what love is . . .'

'But, Natásha, can *that* be all over?'

Natásha looked at Sónya with wide-open eyes as if she
could not grasp the question.

'Well then, are you refusing Prince Andrew?' said
Sónya.

'Oh, you don't understand anything! Don't talk
nonsense, just listen!' said Natásha, with momentary
vexation.

'But I can't believe it,' insisted Sónya. 'I don't understand. How is it you have loved a man for a whole year
and suddenly . . . Why, you have only seen him three
times! Natásha, I don't believe you, you're joking! In
three days to forget everything and so . . .'

'Three days?' said Natásha. 'It seems to me I've
loved him a hundred years. It seems to me that I have

never loved any one before. You can't understand it. Sónya, wait a bit, sit here,' and Natásha embraced and kissed her.

'I had heard that it happens like this, and you must have heard it too, but it's only now that I feel such love. It's not the same as before. As soon as I saw him I felt he was my master and I his slave, and that I could not help loving him. Yes, his slave! Whatever he orders I shall do. You don't understand that. What can I do? What can I do, Sónya?' cried Natásha with a happy yet frightened expression.

'But think what you are doing,' cried Sónya. 'I can't leave it like this. This secret correspondence . . . How could you let him go so far?' she went on, with a horror and disgust she could hardly conceal.

'I told you that I have no will,' Natásha replied. 'Why can't you understand? I love him!'

'Then I won't let it come to that . . . I shall tell!' cried Sónya, bursting into tears.

'What do you mean? For God's sake . . . If you tell, you are my enemy!' declared Natásha. 'You want me to be miserable, you want us to be separated . . .'

When she saw Natásha's fright, Sónya shed tears of shame and pity for her friend.

'But what has happened between you?' she asked. 'What has he said to you? Why doesn't he come to the house?'

Natásha did not answer her questions.

'For God's sake, Sónya, don't tell any one, don't torture me,' Natásha entreated. 'Remember no one ought to interfere in such matters! I have confided in you . . .'

'But why this secrecy? Why doesn't he come to the house?' asked Sónya. 'Why doesn't he openly ask for your hand? You know Prince Andrew gave you complete freedom—if it is really so; but I don't believe it! Natásha, have you considered what these *secret reasons* can be?'

Natásha looked at Sónya with astonishment. Evidently this question presented itself to her mind for the first time and she did not know how to answer it.

'I don't know what the reasons are. But there must be reasons!'

Sónya sighed and shook her head incredulously.

'If there were reasons . . .' she began.

But Natásha, guessing her doubts, interrupted her in alarm.

'Sónya, one can't doubt him! One can't, one can't! Don't you understand?' she cried.

'Does he love you?'

'Does he love me?' Natásha repeated with a smile of pity at her friend's lack of comprehension. 'Why, you have read his letter and you have seen him.'

'But if he is dishonourable?'

'*He!* dishonourable? If you only knew!' exclaimed Natásha.

'If he is an honourable man he should either declare his intentions, or cease seeing you; and if you won't do this, I will. I will write to him, and I will tell Papa!' said Sónya resolutely.

'But I can't live without him!' cried Natásha.

'Natásha, I don't understand you. And what are you saying! Think of your father and of Nicholas.'

'I don't want any one, I don't love any one but him. How dare you say he is dishonourable? Don't you know that I love him?' screamed Natásha. 'Go away, Sónya! I don't want to quarrel with you, but go, for God's sake go! You see how I am suffering!' Natásha cried angrily, in a voice of despair and repressed irritation. Sónya burst into sobs and ran from the room.

Natásha went to the table and without a moment's reflection wrote that answer to Princess Mary which she had been unable to write all the morning. In this letter she said briefly that all their misunderstandings were at an end; that availing herself of the magnanimity of Prince Andrew, who when he went abroad had given her her freedom, she begged Princess Mary to forget everything and forgive her if she had been to blame towards her, but that she could not be his wife. At that moment this all seemed quite easy, simple, and clear to Natásha.

On Friday the Rostóvs were to return to the country, but on Wednesday the count went with the prospective purchaser to his estate near Moscow.

On the day the count left, Sónya and Natásha were invited to a big dinner-party at the Karágins', and Márya Dmítrievna took them there. At that party Natásha again met Anatole, and Sónya noticed that she spoke to him, trying not to be overheard, and that all through dinner she was more agitated than ever. When they got home Natásha was the first to begin the explanation Sónya expected.

'There, Sónya, you were talking all sorts of nonsense about him,' Natásha began in a mild voice such as children use when they wish to be praised. 'We have had an explanation to-day.'

'Well, what happened? What did he say? Natásha, how glad I am you're not angry with me! Tell me everything—the whole truth. What did he say?'

Natásha became thoughtful.

'Oh, Sónya, if you knew him as I do! He said . . . He asked me what I had promised Bolkónski. He was glad I was free to refuse him.'

Sónya sighed sorrowfully.

'But you haven't refused Bolkónski?' said she.

'Perhaps I have. Perhaps all is over between me and Bolkónski. Why do you think so badly of me?'

'I don't think anything, only I don't understand this . . .'

'Wait a bit, Sónya, you'll understand everything. You'll see what a man he is! Don't think badly of me or of him. I don't think badly of any one: I love and pity everybody. But what am I to do?'

Sónya did not succumb to the tender tone Natásha used towards her. The more emotional and ingratiating the expression of Natásha's face became, the more serious and stern grew Sónya's.

'Natásha,' said she, 'you asked me not to speak to you, and I haven't spoken, but now you yourself have begun. I don't trust him, Natásha. Why this secrecy?'

'Again, again!' interrupted Natásha.

'Natásha, I am afraid for you!'

'Afraid of what?'

'I am afraid you're going to your ruin,' said Sónya resolutely, and was herself horrified at what she had said.

Anger again showed in Natásha's face.

'And I'll go to my ruin, I will, as soon as possible! It's not your business! It won't be you, but I, who'll suffer. Leave me alone, leave me alone! I hate you!'

'Natásha!' moaned Sónya, aghast.

'I hate you, I hate you! You're my enemy for ever!' And Natásha ran out of the room.

Natásha did not speak to Sónya again, and avoided her. With the same expression of agitated surprise and guilt she went about the house, taking up now one occupation, now another, and at once abandoning them.

Hard as it was for Sónya, she watched her friend and did not let her out of her sight.

The day before the count was to return, Sónya noticed that Natásha sat by the drawing-room window all the morning, as if expecting something, and that she made a sign to an officer who drove past, whom Sónya took to be Anatole.

Sónya began watching her friend still more attentively, and noticed that at dinner and all that evening Natásha was in a strange and unnatural state. She answered questions at random, began sentences she did not finish, and laughed at everything.

After tea Sónya noticed a housemaid at Natásha's door timidly waiting to let her pass. She let the girl go in, and then listening at the door, learnt that another letter had been delivered.

Then suddenly it became clear to Sónya that Natásha had some dreadful plan for that evening. Sónya knocked at her door. Natásha did not let her in.

'She will run away with him!' thought Sónya. 'She is capable of anything. There was something particularly pathetic and resolute in her face to-day. She cried as she said good-bye to Uncle,' Sónya remembered. 'Yes, that's it, she means to elope with him, but what am I to do?' thought she, recalling all the signs that clearly indicated that Natásha had some terrible intention. 'The count is away. What am I to do? Write to Kurágin demanding an explanation? But what is there to oblige him to reply? Write to Pierre, as Prince Andrew asked me to in case of some misfortune? . . . But perhaps she really has

already refused Bolkónski—she sent a letter to Princess
Mary yesterday. And Uncle is away . . .' To tell Márya
Dmítrievna who had such faith in Natásha, seemed to
Sónya terrible. 'Well anyway,' thought Sónya as she
stood in the dark passage, 'now or never I must prove
that I remember the family's goodness to me and that
I love Nicholas. Yes! If I don't sleep for three nights
I'll not leave this passage, and will hold her back by
force and not let the family be disgraced,' she thought.

CHAPTER XVI

ANATOLE had lately moved to Dólokhov's. The plan
for Natalie Rostóva's abduction had been arranged
and the preparations made by Dólokhov a few days
before, and on the day that Sónya, after listening at
Natásha's door, resolved to safeguard her, it was to have
been put into execution. Natásha had promised to come
out to Kurágin at the back porch at ten that evening.
Kurágin was to put her into a troyka he would have
ready, and to drive her forty miles to the village of
Kámenka, where an unfrocked priest was in readiness to
perform a marriage ceremony over them. At Kámenka
a relay of horses was to wait which would take them to
the Warsaw high road, and from there they would hasten
abroad with post-horses.

Anatole had a passport, an order for post-horses, ten
thousand rubles he had taken from his sister and another
ten thousand borrowed with Dólokhov's help.

Two witnesses for the mock marriage—Khvóstikov, a
retired petty official whom Dólokhov made use of in his
gambling transactions, and Makárin, a retired hussar,
a kindly, weak fellow who had an unbounded affection
for Kurágin—were sitting at tea in Dólokhov's front
room.

In his large study, the walls of which were hung to the
ceiling with Persian rugs, bearskins, and weapons, sat
Dólokhov in a travelling cloak and high boots, at an open
desk on which lay an abacus and some bundles of paper
money. Anatole, with uniform unbuttoned, walked

and fro between the room where the witnesses were sitting, the study, and the room behind, where his French valet and others were packing the last of his things. Dólokhov was counting the money and noting something down.

'Well,' he said, 'Khvóstikov must have two thousand.'

'Give it him, then,' said Anatole.

'Makárka' (their name for Makárin) 'will go through fire and water for you for nothing. So here are our accounts all settled,' said Dólokhov, showing him the memorandum. 'Is that right?'

'Yes, of course,' returned Anatole, evidently not listening to Dólokhov and looking straight before him with a smile that did not leave his face.

Dólokhov banged down the lid of his desk, and turned to Anatole with an ironic smile:

'Do you know? You'd really better drop it all. There's still time!'

'Fool,' retorted Anatole. 'Don't talk nonsense! If you only knew . . . it's the devil knows what!'

'No, really, give it up!' said Dólokhov. 'I am speaking seriously. It's no joke, this plot you've hatched.'

'What, teasing again? Go to the devil! Eh?' said Anatole, making a grimace. 'Really it's no time for your stupid jokes,' and he left the room.

Dólokhov smiled contemptuously and condescendingly when Anatole had gone out.

'You wait a bit,' he called after him. 'I'm not joking, I'm talking sense. Come here, come here!'

Anatole returned and looked at Dólokhov, trying to give him his attention and evidently submitting to him involuntarily.

'Now listen to me. I'm telling you this for the last time. Why should I joke about it? Did I hinder you? Who arranged everything for you? Who found the priest and got the passport? Who raised the money? I did it all.'

'Well, thank you for it. Do you think I am not grateful?' And Anatole sighed and embraced Dólokhov.

'I helped you, but all the same I must tell you the truth; it is a dangerous business, and if you think about it—a stupid business. Well, you'll carry her off—all right! Will they let it stop at that? It will come out that you're already married. Why, they'll have you in the criminal court . . .'

'Oh, nonsense, nonsense!' Anatole ejaculated and again made a grimace. 'Didn't I explain to you? What?' And Anatole, with the partiality dull-witted people have for any conclusion they have reached by their own reasoning, repeated the argument he had already put to Dólokhov a hundred times. 'Didn't I explain to you that I have come to this conclusion: if this marriage is invalid,' he went on, crooking one finger, 'then I have nothing to answer for; but if it is valid, no matter! Abroad no one will know anything about it. Isn't that so? And don't talk to me, don't, don't!'

'Seriously, you'd better drop it! You'll only get yourself into a mess!'

'Go to the devil!' cried Anatole and clutching his hair left the room, but returned at once and dropped into an arm-chair in front of Dólokhov with his feet tucked under him. 'It's the very devil! What? Feel how it beats!' He took Dólokhov's hand and put it on his heart. 'What a foot, my dear fellow! What a glance! A goddess!' he added in French. 'What?'

Dólokhov with a cold smile and a gleam in his hand-some insolent eyes looked at him—evidently wishing to get some more amusement out of him.

'Well, and when the money's gone, what then?'

'What then? Eh?' repeated Anatole, sincerely perplexed by a thought of the future. 'What then? . . . Then I don't know . . . But why talk nonsense!' He glanced at his watch. 'It's time!'

Anatole went into the back room.

'Now then! Nearly ready? You're dawdling!' he shouted to the servants.

Dólokhov put away the money, called a footman whom he ordered to bring something for them to eat and drink before the journey, and went into the room where Khvóstikov and Makárin were sitting.

Anatole lay on the sofa in the study leaning on his elbow and smiling pensively, while his handsome lips muttered tenderly to himself.

'Come and eat something. Have a drink!' Dólokhov
shouted to him from the other room.

'I don't want to,' answered Anatole continuing to smile.

'Come! Balagá is here.'

Anatole rose and went into the dining-room. Balagá
was a famous troyka driver who had known Dólokhov
and Anatole some six years and had given them good
service with his troykas. More than once when Anatole's
regiment was stationed at Tver he had taken him from
Tver in the evening, brought him to Moscow by day-
break, and driven him back again the next night. More
than once he had enabled Dólokhov to escape when pursued. More than once he had driven them through the
town with gipsies and 'ladykins' as he called the *cocottes*.
More than once in their service he had run over pedes-
trians and upset vehicles in the streets of Moscow, and
had always been protected from the consequences by 'my
gentlemen' as he called them. He had ruined more than
one horse in their service. More than once they had
beaten him, and more than once they had made him
drunk on champagne and madeira, which he loved; and
he knew more than one thing about each of them which
would long ago have sent an ordinary man to Siberia.
They often called Balagá into their orgies and made him
drink and dance at the gipsies', and more than one
thousand rubles of their money had passed through his
hands. In their service he risked his skin and his life
twenty times a year, and in their service had lost more
horses than the money he had from them would buy.
But he liked them; liked that mad driving at twelve miles
an hour, liked upsetting a driver, or running down a
pedestrian, and flying at full gallop through the Moscow
streets. He liked to hear those wild, tipsy shouts behind
him: 'Get on! Get on!' when it was impossible to go any
faster. He liked giving a painful lash on the neck to some
peasant who, more dead than alive, was already hurrying
out of his way. 'Real gentlemen!' he considered them.

Anatole and Dólokhov liked Balagá too, for his masterly driving and because he liked the things they liked.
With others Balagá bargained, charging twenty-five
rubles for a two-hours' drive, and rarely drove himself,

generally letting his young men do so. But with 'his gentlemen' he always drove himself, and never demanded anything for his work. Only a couple of times a year— when he knew from their valets that they had money in hand—he would turn up of a morning quite sober, and with a deep bow would ask them to help him. The gentlemen always made him sit down.

'Do help me out, Theodore Iványch, sir,' or 'your Excellency,' he would say. 'I am quite out of horses. Let me have what you can to go to the fair.'

And Anatole and Dólokhov, when they had money, would give him a thousand or a couple of thousand rubles.

Balagá was a fair-haired, short, and snub-nosed peasant of about twenty-seven, red-faced, with a particularly red thick neck, glittering little eyes, and a small beard. He wore a fine, dark-blue, silk-lined cloth coat over a sheepskin.

On entering the room now, he crossed himself, turning towards the front corner of the room, and went up to Dólokhov holding out a small, black hand.

'Theodore Iványch!' he said, bowing.

'How d'you do, friend? Well, here he is!'

'Good day, your Excellency!' he said, again holding out his hand to Anatole who had just come in.

'I say, Balagá,' said Anatole, putting his hands on the man's shoulders, 'do you care for me or not? Eh? Now, do me a service . . . What horses have you come with? Eh?'

'As your messenger ordered, your special beasts,' replied Balagá.

'Well, listen, Balagá! Drive all three to death, but get me there in three hours. Eh?'

'When they are dead, what shall I drive?' said Balagá with a wink.

'Mind, I'll smash your face in! Don't make jokes!' cried Anatole, suddenly rolling his eyes.

'Why joke?' said the driver, laughing. 'As if I'd grudge my gentlemen anything! As fast as ever the horses can gallop, so fast we'll go!'

'Ah!' said Anatole. 'Well, sit down.'

'Yes, sit down!' said Dólokhov.

'I'll stand, Theodore Iványch.'

'Sit down; nonsense! Have a drink!' said Anatole, and filled a large glass of madeira for him.

The driver's eyes sparkled at the sight of the wine. After refusing it for manners' sake, he drank it and wiped his mouth with a red silk handkerchief he took out of his cap.

'And when are we to start, your Excellency?'

'Well . . .' Anatole looked at his watch. 'We'll start at once. Mind, Balagá! You'll get there in time? Eh?'

'That depends on our luck in starting, else why shouldn't we be there in time?' replied Balagá. 'Didn't we get you to Tver in seven hours? I think you remember that, your Excellency?'

'Do you know, one Christmas I drove from Tver,' said Anatole, smiling at the recollection and turning to Makárin who gazed rapturously at him with wide-open eyes. 'Will you believe it, Makárka, it took one's breath away, the rate we flew. We came across a train of loaded sledges, and drove right over two of them. Eh?'

'Those were horses!' Balagá continued the tale. 'That time I'd harnessed two young side-horses with the bay in the shafts,' he went on, turning to Dólokhov. 'Will you believe it, Theodore Iványch, those animals flew forty miles? I couldn't hold them in, my hands grew numb in the sharp frost so that I threw down the reins—"Catch hold yourself, your Excellency!" says I, and I just tumbled on the bottom of the sledge and sprawled there. It wasn't a case of urging them on, there was no holding them in till we reached the place. The devils took us there in three hours! Only the near one died of it.'

CHAPTER XVII

ANATOLE went out of the room and returned a few minutes later wearing a fur coat girt with a silver belt and a sable cap jauntily set on one side and very becoming to his handsome face. Having looked in a mirror, and standing before Dólokhov in the same pose he had assumed before it, he lifted a glass of wine.

'Well, good-bye, Theodore. Thank you for everything and farewell!' said Anatole. 'Well, comrades and friends . . .' he considered for a moment, '. . . of my youth, farewell!' he said, turning to Makárin and the others.

Though they were all going with him, Anatole evidently wished to make something touching and solemn out of this address to his comrades. He spoke slowly in a loud voice, and throwing out his chest slightly swayed one leg.

'All take glasses; you too, Balagá. Well, comrades and friends of my youth, we've had our fling and lived and revelled. Eh? And now, when shall we meet again? I am going abroad. We have had a good time—now farewell, lads! To our health! Hurrah! . . .' he cried, and emptying his glass flung it on the floor.

'To your health!' said Balagá who also emptied his glass, and wiped his mouth with his handkerchief.

Makárin embraced Anatole with tears in his eyes.

'Ah, Prince, how sorry I am to part from you!'

'Let's go. Let's go!' cried Anatole.

Balagá was about to leave the room.

'No, stop!' said Anatole. 'Shut the door; we have first to sit down. That's the way.'

They shut the door and all sat down.[1]

'Now, quick march, lads!' said Anatole, rising.

Joseph, his valet, handed him his sabretache and sabre, and they all went out into the vestibule.

'And where's the fur cloak?' asked Dólokhov. 'Hey, Ignátka! Go to Matrëna Matrévna and ask her for the sable cloak. I have heard what elopements are like,' continued Dólokhov with a wink. 'Why, she'll rush out more dead than alive just in the things she is wearing; if you delay at all, there'll be tears and "papa" and "mamma", and she's frozen in a minute and must go back—but you wrap the fur cloak round her first thing and carry her to the sledge.'

The valet brought a woman's fox-lined cloak.

'Fool, I told you the sable one! Hey, Matrëna, the sable!' he shouted, so that his voice rang far through the rooms.

[1] This is in accord with a Russian superstition as to what should be done when starting on a journey.

A handsome, slim, and pale-faced gipsy-girl with glittering black eyes and curly blue-black hair, wearing a red shawl, ran out with a sable mantle on her arm.

'Here, I don't grudge it—take it!' she said, evidently afraid of her master and yet regretful of her cloak.

Dólokhov, without answering, took the cloak, threw it over Matrëna and wrapped her up in it.

'That's the way,' said Dólokhov, 'and then so!' and he turned the collar up round her head, leaving only a little of the face uncovered. 'And then so, do you see?' and he pushed Anatole's head forward to meet the gap left by the collar, through which Matrëna's brilliant smile was seen.

'Well, good-bye, Matrëna,' said Anatole, kissing her. 'Ah, my revels here are over. Remember me to Stëshka. There, good-bye! Good-bye, Matrëna, wish me luck!'

'Well, Prince, may God give you great luck!' said Matrëna in her gipsy accent.

Two troykas were standing before the porch and two young drivers were holding the horses. Balagá took his seat in the front one, and holding his elbows high arranged the reins deliberately. Anatole and Dólokhov got in with him. Makárin, Khvóstikov, and a valet seated themselves in the other sledge.

'Well, are you ready?' asked Balagá.

'Go!' he cried, twisting the reins round his hands, and the troyka tore down the Nikítski Boulevard.

'Tproo! Get out of the way! Hi! . . . Tproo! . . .' The shouting of Balagá and of the sturdy young fellow seated on the box was all that could be heard. On the Arbát Square the troyka caught against a carriage; something cracked, shouts were heard, and the troyka flew along the Arbát Street.

After taking a turn along the Podnovínski Boulevard, Balagá began to rein in, and turning back drew up at the crossing of the old Konyúsheny Street.

The young fellow on the box jumped down to hold the horses, and Anatole and Dólokhov went along the pavement. When they reached the gate Dólokhov whistled. The whistle was answered, and a maid-servant ran out.

'Come into the courtyard or you'll be seen; she'll come out directly,' said she.

Dólokhov stayed by the gate. Anatole followed the maid into the courtyard, turned the corner, and ran up into the porch.

He was met by Gabriel, Márya Dmítrievna's gigantic footman.

'Come to the mistress, please,' said the footman in his deep bass, intercepting any retreat.

'To what mistress? Who are you?' asked Anatole in a breathless whisper.

'Kindly step in, my orders are to bring you in.'

'Kurágin! Come back!' shouted Dólokhov. 'Betrayed! Back!'

Dólokhov, after Anatole entered, had remained at the wicket-gate, and was struggling with the yard-porter who was trying to lock it. With a last desperate effort Dólokhov pushed the porter aside, and when Anatole ran back seized him by the arm, pulled him through the wicket, and ran back with him to the troyka.

CHAPTER XVIII

MÁRYA DMÍTRIEVNA having found Sónya weeping in the corridor, made her confess everything, and intercepting the note to Natásha she read it and went into Natásha's room with it in her hand.

'You shameless good-for-nothing!' said she. 'I won't hear a word.'

Pushing back Natásha, who looked at her with astonished but tearless eyes, she locked her in, and having given orders to the yard-porter to admit the persons who would be coming that evening, but not to let them out again, and having told the footman to bring them up to her, she seated herself in the drawing-room to await the abductors.

When Gabriel came to inform her that the men who had come had run away again, she rose frowning, and clasping her hands behind her paced through the rooms a long time considering what she should do. Towards

midnight she went to Natásha's room fingering the key
in her pocket. Sónya was sitting sobbing in the corridor.
'Márya Dmítrievna, for God's sake let me in to her!' she
pleaded, but Márya Dmítrievna unlocked the door and
went in without giving her an answer . . .'Disgusting,
abominable . . . In my house . . . horrid girl, hussy! I'm
only sorry for her father!' thought she, trying to restrain
her wrath. 'Hard as it may be, I'll tell them all to hold
their tongues, and will hide it from the count.' She
entered the room with resolute steps. Natásha was lying
on the sofa, her head hidden in her hands, and she did
not stir. She was in just the same position in which
Márya Dmítrievna had left her.

'A nice girl! Very nice!' said Márya Dmítrievna.
'Arranging meetings with lovers in my house! It's no use
pretending: you listen when I speak to you!' And Márya
Dmítrievna touched her arm. 'Listen when I speak!
You've disgraced yourself like the lowest of hussies. I'd
treat you differently, but I'm sorry for your father, so I
will conceal it.'

Natásha did not change her position, but her whole
body heaved with noiseless, convulsive sobs which choked
her. Márya Dmítrievna glanced round at Sónya and
seated herself on the sofa beside Natásha.

'It's lucky for him that he escaped me; but I'll find
him!' she said in her rough voice. 'Do you hear what I
am saying or not?' she added.

She put her large hand under Natásha's face and
turned it towards her. Both Márya Dmítrievna and
Sónya were amazed when they saw how Natásha looked.
Her eyes were dry and glistening, her lips compressed,
her cheeks sunken.

'Let me be! . . . What is it to me? . . . I shall die!' she
muttered, wrenching herself from Márya Dmítrievna's
hands with a vicious effort and sinking down again into
her former position.

'Natalie!' said Márya Dmítrievna. 'I wish for your
good. Lie still, stay like that then, I won't touch you.
But listen. I won't tell you how guilty you are. You
know that yourself. But when your father comes back
to-morrow—what am I to tell him? Eh?'

Again Natásha's body shook with sobs.

'Suppose he finds out, and your brother, and your betrothed?'

'I have no betrothed: I have refused him!' cried Natásha.

'That's all the same,' continued Márya Dmítrievna. 'If they hear of this will they let it pass? He, your father, I know him . . . if he challenges him to a duel will that be all right? Eh?'

'Oh, let me be! Why have you interfered at all? Why? Why? Who asked you to?' shouted Natásha, raising herself on the sofa and looking malignantly at Márya Dmítrievna.

'But what did you want?' cried Márya Dmítrievna, growing angry again. 'Were you kept under lock and key? Who hindered his coming to the house? Why carry you off as if you were some gipsy singing-girl? . . . Well, if he had carried you off . . . do you think they wouldn't have found him? Your father, or brother, or your betrothed? And he's a scoundrel, a wretch—that's a fact!'

'He is better than any of you!' exclaimed Natásha getting up. 'If you hadn't interfered . . . Oh, my God! What is it all? What is it? Sónya, why . . .? Go away!'

And she burst into sobs with the despairing vehemence with which people bewail disasters they feel they have themselves caused. Márya Dmítrievna was about to speak again, but Natásha cried out:

'Go away! Go away! You all hate and despise me!' and she threw herself back on the sofa.

Márya Dmítrievna went on admonishing her for some time, enjoining on her that it must all be kept from her father and assuring her that nobody would know anything about it if only Natásha herself would undertake to forget it all and not let any one see that something had happened. Natásha did not reply, nor did she sob any longer, but she grew cold and had a shivering fit. Márya Dmítrievna put a pillow under her head, covered her with two quilts, and herself brought her some lime-flower water, but Natásha did not respond to her.

'Well, let her sleep,' said Márya Dmítrievna as she went out of the room supposing Natásha to be asleep.

But Natásha was not asleep; with pale face and fixed wide-open eyes she looked straight before her. All that night she did not sleep or weep, and did not speak to Sónya who got up and went to her several times.

Next day Count Rostóv returned from his estate near Moscow in time for lunch as he had promised. He was in very good spirits; the affair with the purchaser was going on satisfactorily, and there was nothing to keep him any longer in Moscow, away from the countess whom he missed. Márya Dmítrievna met him and told him that Natásha had been very unwell the day before and that they had sent for the doctor, but that she was better now. Natásha had not left her room that morning. With compressed and parched lips, and dry fixed eyes, she sat at the window, uneasily watching the people who drove past, and hurriedly glancing round at any one who entered the room. She was evidently expecting news of him and that he would come or would write to her.

When the count came to see her she turned anxiously round at the sound of a man's footstep, and then her face resumed its cold and malevolent expression. She did not even get up to greet him.

'What is the matter with you, my angel? Are you ill?' asked the count.

After a moment's silence Natásha answered: 'Yes, ill.'

In reply to the count's anxious inquiries as to why she was so dejected and whether anything had happened to her betrothed, she assured him that nothing had happened and asked him not to worry. Márya Dmítrievna confirmed Natásha's assurances that nothing had happened. From the pretence of illness, from his daughter's distress, and by the embarrassed faces of Sónya and Márya Dmítrievna, the count saw clearly that something had gone wrong during his absence, but it was so terrible for him to think that anything disgraceful had happened to his beloved daughter, and he so prized his own cheerful tranquillity, that he avoided inquiries and tried to assure himself that nothing particular had happened, and he was only dissatisfied that her indisposition delayed their return to the country.

CHAPTER XIX

FROM the day his wife arrived in Moscow Pierre had been intending to go away somewhere, so as not to be near her. Soon after the Rostóvs came to Moscow the effect Natásha had on him made him hasten to carry out his intention. He went to Tver to see Joseph Alexéevich's widow, who had long since promised to hand over to him some papers of her deceased husband's.

When he returned to Moscow Pierre was handed a letter from Márya Dmítrievna asking him to come and see her on a matter of great importance relating to Andrew Bolkónski and his betrothed. Pierre had been avoiding Natásha because it seemed to him that his feeling for her was stronger than a married man's should be for his friend's fiancée. Yet some fate constantly threw them together.

'What can have happened? And what can they want with me?' thought he as he dressed to go to Márya Dmítrievna's. 'If only Prince Andrew would hurry up and come and marry her!' thought he on his way to the house.

On the Tverskóy Boulevard a familiar voice called to him.

'Pierre! Been back long?' some one shouted. Pierre raised his head. In a sledge drawn by two grey trotting-horses that were bespattering the dashboard with snow, Anatole and his constant companion Makárin dashed past. Anatole was sitting upright in the classic pose of military dandies, the lower part of his face hidden by his beaver collar and his head slightly bent. His face was fresh and rosy, his white-plumed hat, tilted to one side, disclosed his curled and pomaded hair besprinkled with powdery snow.

'Yes, indeed, that's a true sage,' thought Pierre. 'He sees nothing beyond the pleasure of the moment, nothing troubles him and so he is always cheerful, satisfied, and serene. What wouldn't I give to be like him!' he thought enviously.

In Márya Dmítrievna's ante-room the footman who helped him off with his fur coat said that the mistress asked him to come to her bedroom.

When he opened the ball-room door Pierre saw Natásha sitting at the window, with a thin, pale, and spiteful face. She glanced round at him, frowned, and left the room with an expression of cold dignity.

'What has happened?' asked Pierre, entering Márya Dmítrievna's room.

'Fine doings!' answered Márya Dmítrievna. 'For fifty-eight years have I lived in this world and never known anything so disgraceful.'

And having put him on his honour not to repeat anything she told him, Márya Dmítrievna informed him that Natásha had refused Prince Andrew without her parents' knowledge, and that the cause of this was Anatole Kurágin into whose society Pierre's wife had thrown her, and with whom Natásha had tried to elope during her father's absence, in order to be married secretly.

Pierre raised his shoulders and listened open-mouthed to what was told him, scarcely able to believe his own ears. That Prince Andrew's deeply loved affianced wife —the same Natásha Rostóva who used to be so charming —should give up Bolkónski for that fool Anatole who was already secretly married (as Pierre knew), and should be so in love with him as to agree to run away with him, was something Pierre could not conceive and could not imagine.

He could not reconcile the charming impression he had of Natásha, whom he had known from a child, with this new conception of her baseness, folly, and cruelty. He thought of his wife. 'They are all alike!' he said to himself, reflecting that he was not the only man unfortunate enough to be tied to a bad woman. But still he pitied Prince Andrew to the point of tears and sympathized with his wounded pride, and the more he pitied his friend the more did he think with contempt and even with disgust of that Natásha who had just passed him in the ballroom with such a look of cold dignity. He did not know that Natásha's soul was overflowing with despair, shame, and humiliation, and that it was not her fault that her face happened to assume an expression of calm dignity and severity.

'But how get married?' said Pierre, in answer to Márya Dmítrievna. 'He could not marry—he is married!'

'Things get worse from hour to hour!' ejaculated Márya Dmítrievna. 'A nice youth! What a scoundrel! And she's expecting him—expecting him since yesterday. She must be told! Then at least she won't go on expecting him.'

After hearing the details of Anatole's marriage from Pierre, and giving vent to her anger against Anatole in words of abuse, Márya Dmítrievna told Pierre why she had sent for him. She was afraid that the count or Bolkónski, who might arrive at any moment, if they knew of this affair (which she hoped to hide from them) might challenge Anatole to a duel, and she therefore asked Pierre to tell his brother-in-law in her name to leave Moscow and not dare to let her set eyes on him again. Pierre—only now realizing the danger to the old count, Nicholas, and Prince Andrew—promised to do as she wished. Having briefly and exactly explained her wishes to him, she let him go to the drawing-room.

'Mind, the count knows nothing. Behave as if you know nothing either,' she said. 'And I will go and tell her it is no use expecting him! And stay to dinner if you care to!' she called after Pierre.

Pierre met the old count, who seemed nervous and upset. That morning Natásha had told him that she had rejected Bolkónski.

'Troubles, troubles, my dear fellow!' he said to Pierre. 'What troubles one has with these girls without their mother! I do so regret having come here. I will be frank with you. Have you heard she has broken off her engagement without consulting anybody? It's true this engagement never was much to my liking. Of course he is an excellent man, but still, with his father's disapproval they wouldn't have been happy, and Natásha won't lack suitors. Still, it has been going on so long, and to take such a step without father's or mother's consent! And now she's ill, and God knows what! It's hard, Count, hard to manage daughters in their mother's absence . . .'

Pierre saw that the count was much upset, and tried to change the subject, but the count returned to his troubles.

Sónya entered the room with an agitated face.

'Natásha is not quite well; she's in her room and would like to see you. Márya Dmítrievna is with her and she too asks you to come.'

'Yes, you are a great friend of Bolkónski's, no doubt she wants to send him a message,' said the count. 'Oh dear! Oh dear! How happy it all was!'

And clutching the spare grey locks on his temples the count left the room.

When Márya Dmítrievna told Natásha that Anatole was married, Natásha did not wish to believe it, and insisted on having it confirmed by Pierre himself. Sónya told Pierre this as she led him along the corridor to Natásha's room.

Natásha, pale and stern, was sitting beside Márya Dmítrievna, and her eyes, glittering feverishly, met Pierre with a questioning look the moment he entered. She did not smile or nod, but only gazed fixedly at him, and her look asked only one thing: was he a friend, or like the others an enemy in regard to Anatole? As for himself, Pierre evidently did not exist for her.

'He knows all about it,' said Márya Dmítrievna pointing to Pierre and addressing Natásha. 'Let him tell you whether I have told you the truth.'

Natásha looked from one to the other as a hunted and wounded animal looks at the approaching dogs and sportsmen.

'Natálya Ilyníchna,' Pierre began, dropping his eyes with a feeling of pity for her and loathing for the thing he had to do, 'whether it is true or not should make no difference to you, because . . .'

'Then it is not true that he's married!'

'Yes, it is true.'

'Has he been married long?' she asked. 'On your honour? . . .'

Pierre gave his word of honour.

'Is he still here?' she asked, quickly.

'Yes, I have just seen him.'

She was evidently unable to speak, and made a sign with her hands that they should leave her alone.

CHAPTER XX

PIERRE did not stay for dinner, but left the room and went away at once. He drove through the town seeking Anatole Kurágin, at the thought of whom now the blood rushed to his heart and he felt a difficulty in breathing. He was not at the ice-hills, nor at the gipsies', nor at Komoneno's. Pierre drove to the club. In the club all was going on as usual. The members who were assembling for dinner were sitting about in groups; they greeted Pierre and spoke of the town news. The footman having greeted him, knowing his habits and his acquaintances, told him there was a place left for him in the small dining-room, and that Prince Michael Zakhárych was in the library, but Paul Timoféevich had not yet arrived. One of Pierre's acquaintances, while they were talking about the weather, asked if he had heard of Kurágin's abduction of Rostóva which was talked of in the town, and was it true? Pierre laughed and said it was nonsense for he had just come from the Rostóvs'. He asked every one about Anatole. One man told him he had not come yet, and another that he was coming to dinner. Pierre felt it strange to see this calm, indifferent crowd of people unaware of what was going on in his soul. He paced through the ball-room, waited till every one had come, and as Anatole had not turned up, did not stay for dinner but drove home.

Anatole, for whom Pierre was looking, dined that day with Dólokhov, consulting him as to how to remedy this unfortunate affair. It seemed to him essential to see Natásha. In the evening he drove to his sister's to discuss with her how to arrange a meeting. When Pierre returned home after vainly hunting all over Moscow, his valet informed him that Prince Anatole was with the countess. The countess's drawing-room was full of guests.

Pierre without greeting his wife whom he had not seen since his return—at that moment she was more repulsive to him than ever—entered the drawing-room and seeing Anatole went up to him.

'Ah, Pierre,' said the countess going up to her husband 'You don't know what a plight our Anatole . . .'

She stopped, seeing in the forward thrust of her husband's head, in his glowing eyes and his resolute gait, the terrible indications of that rage and strength which she knew, and had herself experienced after his duel with Dólokhov.

'Where you are, there is vice and evil!' said Pierre to his wife. 'Anatole, come with me! I must speak to you,' he added in French.

Anatole glanced round at his sister and rose submissively, ready to follow Pierre. Pierre, taking him by the arm, pulled him towards himself and was leading him from the room.

'If you allow yourself in my drawing-room...' whispered Hélène, but Pierre did not reply and went out of the room.

Anatole followed him with his usual jaunty step but his face betrayed anxiety.

Having entered his study Pierre closed the door, and addressed Anatole without looking at him.

'You promised Countess Rostóva to marry her and were about to elope with her, is that so?'

'*Mon cher*,' answered Anatole (their whole conversation was in French), 'I don't consider myself bound to answer questions put to me in that tone.'

Pierre's face, already pale, became distorted by fury. He seized Anatole by the collar of his uniform with his big hand, and shook him from side to side till Anatole's face showed a sufficient degree of terror.

'When I tell you that I must talk to you!...' repeated Pierre.

'Come now, this is stupid. What?' said Anatole, fingering a button of his collar that had been wrenched loose with a bit of the cloth.

'You're a scoundrel and a blackguard, and I don't know what restrains me from the pleasure of smashing your head with this,' said Pierre, expressing himself so artificially because he was talking French.

He took a heavy paper-weight and lifted it threateningly, but at once put it back in its place.

'Did you promise to marry her?'

'I ... I ... I didn't think of it. I never promised, because ...'

Pierre interrupted him.

'Have you any letters of hers? Any letters?' he said, moving towards Anatole.

Anatole glanced at him and immediately thrust his hand into his pocket and drew out his pocket-book.

Pierre took the letter Anatole handed him, and pushing aside a table that stood in his way, threw himself on the sofa.

'I shan't be violent, don't be afraid,' said Pierre in answer to a frightened gesture of Anatole's. 'First, the letters,' said he, as if repeating a lesson to himself. 'Secondly,' he continued after a short pause, again rising and again pacing the room, 'to-morrow you must get out of Moscow.'

'But how can I . . .?'

'Thirdly,' Pierre continued without listening to him, 'you must never breathe a word of what has passed between you and Countess Rostóva. I know I can't prevent your doing so, but if you have a spark of conscience . . .' Pierre paced the room several times in silence.

Anatole sat at a table frowning and biting his lips.

'After all, you must understand that besides your pleasure there is such a thing as other people's happiness and peace, and that you are ruining a whole life for the sake of amusing yourself! Amuse yourself with women like my wife—with them you are within your rights, for they know what you want of them. They are armed against you by the same experience of debauchery; but to promise *a maid* to marry her . . . to deceive, to kidnap . . . Don't you understand that it is as mean as beating an old man or a child? . . .'

Pierre paused and looked at Anatole no longer with an angry, but with a questioning look.

'I don't know about that, eh?' said Anatole, growing more confident as Pierre mastered his wrath. 'I don't know that and don't want to,' he said, not looking at Pierre, and with a slight tremor of his lower jaw, 'but you have used such words to me—"mean" and so on, which as a man of honour I can't allow any one to use.'

Pierre glanced at him with amazement, unable to understand what he wanted.

'Though it was tête-à-tête,' Anatole continued, 'still I can't . . .'

'Is it satisfaction you want?' said Pierre ironically.

'You could at least take back your words. What? If you want me to do as you wish, eh?'

'I take them back, I take them back!' said Pierre, 'and I ask you to forgive me.' Pierre involuntarily glanced at the loose button. 'And if you require money for your journey . . .'

Anatole smiled. The expression of that base and cringing smile, which Pierre knew so well in his wife, revolted him.

'Oh, vile and heartless brood!' he exclaimed, and left the room.

Next day Anatole left for Petersburg.

CHAPTER XXI

PIERRE drove to Márya Dmítrievna's to tell her of the fulfilment of her wish that Kurágin should be banished from Moscow. The whole house was in a state of alarm and commotion. Natásha was very ill, having, as Márya Dmítrievna told him in secret, poisoned herself the night after she had been told that Anatole was married, with some arsenic she had stealthily procured. After swallowing a little she had been so frightened that she woke Sónya and told her what she had done. The necessary antidotes had been administered in time and she was now out of danger, though still so weak that it was out of the question to move her to the country, and so the countess had been sent for. Pierre saw the distracted count and Sónya, who had a tear-stained face, but he could not see Natásha.

Pierre dined at the club that day and heard on all sides gossip about the attempted abduction of Rostóva. He resolutely denied these rumours, assuring every one that nothing had happened except that his brother-in-law had proposed to her and been refused. It seemed to Pierre that it was his duty to conceal the whole affair and re-establish Natásha's reputation.

He was awaiting Prince Andrew's return with dread, and went every day to the old prince's for news of him.

Old Prince Bolkónski heard all the rumours current in the town from Mademoiselle Bourienne, and had read the note to Princess Mary in which Natásha had broken off her engagement. He seemed in better spirits than usual and awaited his son with great impatience.

Some days after Anatole's departure Pierre received a note from Prince Andrew, informing him of his arrival and asking him to come to see him.

Directly he reached Moscow Prince Andrew had received from his father Natásha's note to Princess Mary breaking off her engagement (Mademoiselle Bourienne had purloined it from Princess Mary and given it to the old prince) and he heard from him the story of Natásha's elopement, with additions.

Prince Andrew had arrived in the evening and Pierre came to see him next morning. Pierre expected to find Prince Andrew in almost the same state as Natásha, and was therefore surprised on entering the drawing-room to hear him in the study talking in a loud animated voice about some intrigue going on in Petersburg. The old prince's voice and another now and then interrupted him. Princess Mary came out to meet Pierre. She sighed, looking towards the door of the room where Prince Andrew was, evidently intending to express her sympathy with his sorrow, but Pierre saw by her face that she was glad both at what had happened and at the way her brother had taken the news of Natásha's faithlessness.

'He says he expected it,' she remarked. 'I know his pride will not let him express his feelings, but still he has taken it better, far better, than I expected. Evidently it had to be . . .'

'But is it possible that all is really ended?' asked Pierre.

Princess Mary looked at him with astonishment. She did not understand how he could ask such a question. Pierre went into the study. Prince Andrew, greatly changed and plainly in better health, but with a fresh horizontal wrinkle between his brows, stood in civilian dress facing his father and Prince Meshchérski, warmly disputing and vigorously gesticulating. The conversation was about Speránski—the news of whose sudden exile and alleged treachery had just reached Moscow.

'Now he is censured and accused by all who were enthusiastic about him a month ago,' Prince Andrew was saying, 'and by those who were unable to understand his aims. To judge a man who is in disfavour and to throw on him all the blame of other men's mistakes is very easy, but I maintain that if anything good has been accomplished in this reign it was done by him, by him alone.'

He paused at the sight of Pierre. His face quivered and immediately assumed a vindictive expression.

'Posterity will do him justice,' he concluded, and at once turned to Pierre.

'Well, how are you? Still getting stouter?' he said with animation, but the new wrinkle on his forehead deepened. 'Yes, I am well,' he said in answer to Pierre's question, and smiled.

To Pierre that smile said plainly: 'I am well, but my health is now of no use to any one.'

After a few words to Pierre about the awful roads from the Polish frontier, about people he had met in Switzerland who knew Pierre, and about M. Dessalles, whom he had brought from abroad to be his son's tutor, Prince Andrew again joined warmly in the conversation about Speránski which was still going on between the two old men.

'If there were treason, or proofs of secret relations with Napoleon, they would have been made public,' he said with warmth and haste. 'I do not, and never did, like Speránski personally, but I like justice!'

Pierre now recognized in his friend a need with which he was only too familiar, to get excited and to have arguments about extraneous matters in order to stifle thoughts that were too oppressive and too intimate.

When Prince Meshchérski had left, Prince Andrew took Pierre's arm and asked him into the room that had been assigned him. A bed had been made up there, and some open portmanteaux and trunks stood about. Prince Andrew went to one and took out a small casket, from which he drew a packet wrapped in paper. He did it all silently and very quickly. He stood up and coughed. His face was gloomy and his lips compressed.

'Forgive me for troubling you . . .'

Pierre saw that Prince Andrew was going to speak of Natásha, and his broad face expressed pity and sympathy. This expression irritated Prince Andrew, and in a determined, ringing, and unpleasant tone he continued:

'I have received a refusal from Countess Rostóva, and have heard reports of your brother-in-law having sought her hand, or something of that kind. Is that true?'

'Both true and untrue,' Pierre began; but Prince Andrew interrupted him.

'Here are her letters and her portrait,' said he.

He took the packet from the table and handed it to Pierre.

'Give this to the countess . . . if you see her.'

'She is very ill,' said Pierre.

'Then she is here still?' said Prince Andrew. 'And Prince Kurágin?' he added quickly.

'He left long ago. She has been at death's door.'

'I much regret her illness,' said Prince Andrew; and he smiled like his father, coldly, maliciously, and unpleasantly.

'So Monsieur Kurágin has not honoured Countess Rostóva with his hand?' said Prince Andrew, and he snorted several times.

'He could not marry, for he was married already,' said Pierre.

Prince Andrew laughed disagreeably, again reminding one of his father.

'And where is your brother-in-law now, if I may ask?' he said.

'He has gone to Peters. . . . But I don't know,' said Pierre.

'Well, it doesn't matter,' said Prince Andrew. 'Tell Countess Rostóva that she was and is perfectly free, and that I wish her all that is good.'

Pierre took the packet. Prince Andrew, as if trying to remember whether he had something more to say, or waiting to see if Pierre would say anything, looked fixedly at him.

'I say, do you remember our discussion in Petersburg?' asked Pierre, 'about . . .'

'Yes,' returned Prince Andrew hastily. 'I said that a fallen woman should be forgiven, but I didn't say I could forgive her. I can't.'

'But can this be compared . . .?' said Pierre.

Prince Andrew interrupted him, and cried sharply:

'Yes, ask her hand again, be magnanimous, and so on? . . . Yes, that would be very noble, but I am unable to follow in that gentleman's footsteps. If you wish to be my friend never speak to me of that . . . of all that! Well, good-bye. So you'll give her the packet?'

Pierre left the room and went to the old prince and Princess Mary.

The old man seemed livelier than usual. Princess Mary was the same as always, but beneath her sympathy for her brother Pierre noticed her satisfaction that the engagement had been broken off. Looking at them Pierre realized what contempt and animosity they all felt for the Rostóvs, and that it was impossible in their presence even to mention the name of her who could give up Prince Andrew for any one else.

At dinner the talk turned on the war, the approach of which was becoming evident. Prince Andrew talked incessantly, arguing now with his father, now with the Swiss tutor Dessalles, and showing an unnatural animation, the cause of which Pierre so well understood.

CHAPTER XXII

THAT same evening Pierre went to the Rostóvs' to fulfil the commission entrusted to him. Natásha was in bed, the count at the club, and Pierre, after giving the letters to Sónya, went to Márya Dmítrievna who was interested to know how Prince Andrew had taken the news. Ten minutes later Sónya came to Márya Dmítrievna.

'Natásha insists on seeing Count Peter Kirílovich,'[1] said she.

[1] Peter Kirílovich is a form of address at once formal, correct, and polite. Kirílovich is the patronymic, and means son-of-Cyril.

'But how? Are we to take him up to her? The room there has not been tidied up.'

'No, she has dressed and gone into the drawing-room,' said Sónya.

Márya Dmítrievna only shrugged her shoulders.

'When will her mother come? She has worried me to death! Now mind, don't tell her everything!' said she to Pierre. 'One hasn't the heart to scold her, she is so much to be pitied, so much to be pitied.'

Natásha was standing in the middle of the drawing-room, emaciated, with a pale set face, but not at all shamefaced as Pierre expected to find her. When he appeared at the door she grew flurried, evidently undecided whether to go to meet him or to wait till he came up.

Pierre hastened to her. He thought she would give him her hand as usual; but she, stepping up to him, stopped, breathing heavily, her arms hanging lifelessly just in the pose she used to stand in when she went to the middle of the ball-room to sing, but with quite a different expression of face.

'Peter Kirílovich,' she began rapidly, 'Prince Bolkónski was your friend—is your friend,' she corrected herself. (It seemed to her that everything that had once been, must now be different.) 'He told me once to apply to you . . .'

Pierre sniffed as he looked at her, but did not speak. Till then he had reproached her in his heart and tried to despise her, but he now felt so sorry for her that there was no room in his soul for reproach.

'He is here now: tell him . . . to for . . . forgive me!'

She stopped and breathed still more quickly, but did not shed tears.

'Yes . . . I will tell him,' answered Pierre; 'but . . .'

He did not know what to say.

Natásha was evidently dismayed at the thought of what he might think she had meant.

'No, I know all is over,' she said hurriedly. 'No, that can never be. I'm only tormented by the wrong I have done him. Tell him only that I beg him to forgive, forgive, forgive me for everything . . .'

She trembled all over and sat down on a chair.

A sense of pity he had never before known overflowed Pierre's heart.

'I will tell him, I will tell him everything once more,' said Pierre. 'But . . . I should like to know one thing . . .'

'Know what?' Natásha's eyes asked.

'I should like to know, did you love . . .' Pierre did not know how to refer to Anatole and flushed at the thought of him—'did you love that bad man?'

'Don't call him bad!' said Natásha. 'But I don't know, don't know at all . . .'

She began to cry, and a still greater sense of pity, tenderness, and love, welled up in Pierre. He felt the tears trickle under his spectacles and hoped they would not be noticed.

'We won't speak of it any more, my dear,' said Pierre, and his gentle, cordial tone suddenly seemed very strange to Natásha.

'We won't speak of it, my dear—I'll tell him everything; but one thing I beg of you, consider me your friend and if you want help, advice, or simply to open your heart to some one—not now but when your mind is clearer—think of me!' He took her hand and kissed it. 'I shall be happy if it's in my power . . .'

Pierre grew confused.

'Don't speak to me like that. I am not worth it!' exclaimed Natásha and turned to leave the room, but Pierre held her hand.

He knew he had something more to say to her. But when he said it he was amazed at his own words.

'Stop, stop! You have your whole life before you,' said he to her.

'Before me? No! All is over for me,' she replied with shame and self-abasement.

'All over?' he repeated. 'If I were not myself, but the handsomest, cleverest, and best man in the world, and were free, I would this moment ask on my knees for your hand and your love!'

For the first time for many days Natásha wept tears of gratitude and tenderness, and glancing at Pierre she went out of the room.

Pierre, too, when she had gone almost ran into the

ante-room, restraining tears of tenderness and joy that
choked him, and without finding the sleeves of his fur
cloak threw it on and got into his sledge.

'Where to now, your Excellency?' asked the coachman.

'Where to?' Pierre asked himself. 'Where can I go
now? Surely not to the club or to pay calls?' All men
seemed so pitiful, so poor, in comparison with this feeling
of tenderness and love he experienced: in comparison
with that softened, grateful, last look she had given him
through her tears.

'Home!' said Pierre, and despite ten degrees [1] of frost he
threw open the bearskin cloak from his broad chest and
inhaled the air with joy.

It was clear and frosty. Above the dirty ill-lit streets,
above the black roofs, stretched the dark starry sky. Only
looking up at the sky did Pierre cease to feel how sordid
and humiliating were all mundane things compared with
the heights to which his soul had just been raised. At the
entrance to the Arbát Square an immense expanse of dark
starry sky presented itself to his eyes. Almost in the centre
of it, above the Prechístenka Boulevard, surrounded and
sprinkled on all sides by stars but distinguished from them
all by its nearness to the earth, its white light, and its long
uplifted tail, shone the enormous and brilliant comet of
the year 1812—the comet which was said to portend all
kinds of woes and the end of the world. In Pierre, however,
that comet with its long luminous tail aroused no feeling
of fear. On the contrary he gazed joyfully, his eyes moist
with tears, at this bright comet which, having travelled in
its orbit with inconceivable velocity through immeasurable space, seemed suddenly—like an arrow piercing the
earth—to remain fixed in a chosen spot, vigorously
holding its tail erect, shining, and displaying its white
light amid countless other scintillating stars. It seemed
to Pierre that this comet fully responded to what was
passing in his own softened and uplifted soul, now blossoming into a new life.

[1] Réaumur: equal to about ten degrees above zero, or say
22½ degrees of frost, Fahrenheit.

END OF BOOK VIII

BOOK IX

BOOK IX

CHAPTER I

FROM the close of the year 1811 an intensified arming and concentrating of the forces of Western Europe began, and in 1812 these forces—millions of men reckoning those transporting and feeding the army—moved from the west eastwards to the Russian frontier, towards which since 1811 Russian forces had been similarly drawn. On the 12th of June 1812 the forces of Western Europe crossed the Russian frontier and war began, that is, an event took place opposed to human reason and to human nature. Millions of men perpetrated against one another such innumerable crimes, frauds, treacheries, thefts, forgeries, issues of false money, burglaries, incendiarisms, and murders, as in whole centuries are not recorded in the annals of all the law courts of the world, but which those who committed them did not at the time regard as being crimes.

What produced this extraordinary occurrence? What were its causes? The historians tell us with naïve assurance that its causes were the wrongs inflicted on the Duke of Oldenburg, the non-observance of the Continental System, the ambition of Napoleon, the firmness of Alexander, the mistakes of the diplomatists, and so on.

Consequently it would only have been necessary for Metternich, Rumyántsev, or Talleyrand, between a levée and an evening party, to have taken proper pains and written a more adroit note, or for Napoleon to have written to Alexander: 'My respected Brother, I consent to restore the duchy to the Duke of Oldenburg'—and there would have been no war.

We can understand that the matter seemed like that to contemporaries. It naturally seemed to Napoleon that the war was caused by England's intrigues (as in fact he said on the island of St. Helena). It naturally seemed to members of the English Parliament that the cause of the war was Napoleon's ambition; to the Duke of Oldenburg that the cause of the war was the violence done to him;

to business men that the cause of the war was the Continental System which was ruining Europe; to the generals and old soldiers that the chief reason for the war was the necessity of giving them employment; to the legitimists of that day that it was the need of re-establishing *les bons principes*, and to the diplomatists of that time that it all resulted from the fact that the alliance between Russia and Austria in 1809 had not been sufficiently well concealed from Napoleon, and from the awkward wording of Memorandum No. 178. It is natural that these and a countless and infinite quantity of other reasons, the number depending on the endless diversity of points of view, presented themselves to the men of that day; but to us, to posterity who view the thing that happened in all its magnitude and perceive its plain and terrible meaning, these causes seem insufficient. To us it is incomprehensible that millions of Christian men killed and tortured each other either because Napoleon was ambitious or Alexander was firm, or because England's policy was astute or the Duke of Oldenburg wronged. We cannot grasp what connexion such circumstances have with the actual fact of slaughter and violence: why because the Duke was wronged, thousands of men from the other side of Europe killed and ruined the people of Smolénsk and Moscow and were killed by them.

To us their descendants, who are not historians and are not carried away by the process of research, and can therefore regard the event with unclouded common sense, an incalculable number of causes present themselves. The deeper we delve in search of these causes the more of them we find; and each separate cause or whole series of causes appears to us equally valid in itself and equally false by its insignificance compared to the magnitude of the events, and by its impotence—apart from the co-operation of all the other coincident causes—to occasion the event. To us the wish or objection of this or that French corporal to serve a second term appears as much a cause as Napoleon's refusal to withdraw his troops beyond the Vistula and to restore the duchy of Oldenburg; for had he not wished to serve, and had a second, a third, and a thousandth corporal and private also refused, there would have been so many less men in Napoleon's army and the war could not have occurred.

Had Napoleon not taken offence at the demand that he should withdraw beyond the Vistula, and not ordered his troops to advance, there would have been no war; but had all his sergeants objected to serving a second term then also there could have been no war. Nor could there have been a war had there been no English intrigues and no Duke of Oldenburg, and had Alexander not felt insulted, and had there not been an autocratic government in Russia, or a Revolution in France and a subsequent dictatorship and Empire, or all the things that produced the French Revolution, and so on. Without each of these causes nothing could have happened. So all these causes —myriads of causes—coincided to bring it about. And so there was no one cause for that occurrence, but it had to occur because it had to. Millions of men, renouncing their human feelings and reason, had to go from west to east to slay their fellows, just as some centuries previously hordes of men had come from the east to the west slaying their fellows.

The actions of Napoleon and Alexander, on whose words the event seemed to hang, were as little voluntary as the actions of any soldier who was drawn into the campaign by lot or by conscription. This could not be otherwise, for in order that the will of Napoleon and Alexander (on whom the event seemed to depend) should be carried out, the concurrence of innumerable circumstances was needed without any one of which the event could not have taken place. It was necessary that millions of men in whose hands lay the real power—the soldiers who fired, or transported provisions and guns— should consent to carry out the will of these weak individuals, and should have been induced to do so by an infinite number of diverse and complex causes.

We are forced to fall back on fatalism as an explanation of irrational events (that is to say, events the reasonableness of which we do not understand). The more we try to explain such events in history reasonably, the more unreasonable and incomprehensible do they become to us.

Each man lives for himself, using his freedom to attain

his personal aims, and feels with his whole being that he
can now do or abstain from doing this or that action;
but as soon as he has done it, that action performed
at a certain moment in time becomes irrevocable and
belongs to history, in which it has not a free but a predestined significance.

There are two sides to the life of every man, his
individual life which is the more free the more abstract
its interests, and his elemental swarm-life in which he
inevitably obeys laws laid down for him.

Man lives consciously for himself, but is an unconscious
instrument in the attainment of the historic, universal
aims of humanity. A deed done is irrevocable, and its
result coinciding in time with the actions of millions of
other men assumes an historic significance. The higher
a man stands on the social ladder, the more people he is
connected with and the more power he has over others,
the more evident is the predestination and inevitability
of his every action.

'The king's heart is in the hands of the Lord.'

A king is history's slave.

History, that is, the unconscious, general, swarm-life
of mankind, uses every moment of the life of kings as a
tool for its own purposes.

Though Napoleon at that time, in 1812, was more
convinced than ever that it depended on him, *verser (ou
ne pas verser) le sang de ses peuples* [1]—as Alexander expressed
it in the last letter he wrote him—he had never been so
much in the grip of inevitable laws, which compelled
him, while thinking that he was acting on his own
volition, to perform for the swarm-life—that is to say for
history—whatever had to be performed.

The people of the west moved eastwards to slay their
fellow men, and by the law of coincidence thousands of
minute causes fitted in and co-ordinated to produce that
movement and war: reproaches for the non-observance
of the Continental System, the Duke of Oldenburg's
wrongs, the movement of troops into Prussia—undertaken
(as it seemed to Napoleon) only for the purpose of

[1] 'To shed (or not to shed) the blood of his people.'

securing an armed peace, the French Emperor's love and habit of war coinciding with his people's inclinations, allurement by the grandeur of the preparations, and the expenditure on those preparations, and the need of obtaining advantages to compensate for that expenditure, the intoxicating honours he received in Dresden, the diplomatic negotiations which in the opinion of contemporaries were carried on with a sincere desire to attain peace but which only wounded the self-love of both sides, and millions and millions of other causes that adapted themselves to the event that was happening or coincided with it.

When an apple has ripened and falls, why does it fall? Because of its attraction to the earth, because its stalk withers, because it is dried by the sun, because it grows heavier, because the wind shakes it, or because the boy standing below wants to eat it?

Nothing is the cause. All this is only the coincidence of conditions in which all vital organic and elemental events occur. And the botanist who finds that the apple falls because the cellular tissue decays and so forth, is equally right with the child who stands under the tree and says the apple fell because he wanted to eat it and prayed for it. Equally right or wrong is he who says that Napoleon went to Moscow because he wanted to, and perished because Alexander desired his destruction, and he who says that an undermined hill weighing a million tons fell because the last navvy struck it for the last time with his mattock. In historic events the so-called great men are labels giving names to events, and like labels they have but the smallest connexion with the event itself.

Every act of theirs, which appears to them an act of their own will, is in an historical sense involuntary, and is related to the whole course of history and predestined from eternity.

CHAPTER II

ON the 29th of May Napoleon left Dresden, where he had spent three weeks surrounded by a court that included princes, dukes, kings, and even an emperor. Before leaving, Napoleon showed favour to the emperor,

kings and princes who had deserved it, reprimanded
the kings and princes with whom he was dissatisfied, presented pearls and diamonds of his own—that is which he
had taken from other kings—to the Empress of Austria,
and having, as his historian tells us, tenderly embraced the
Empress Marie Louise—who regarded him as her husband though he had left another wife in Paris—left her
grieved by the parting which she seemed hardly able to
bear. Though the diplomatists still firmly believed in the
possibility of peace, and worked zealously to that end,
and though the Emperor Napoleon himself wrote a letter
to Alexander calling him *Monsieur mon frère*, and sincerely
assured him that he did not want war and would always
love and honour him—yet he set off to join his army,
and at every station gave fresh orders to accelerate the
movement of his troops from west to east. He went in
a travelling coach with six horses, surrounded by pages,
aides-de-camp, and an escort, along the road to Posen,
Thorn, Danzig, and Königsberg. At each of these towns
thousands of people met him with excitement and enthusiasm.

The army was moving from west to east and relays of
six horses carried him in the same direction. On the 10th
of June, coming up with the army, he spent the night in
apartments prepared for him on the estate of a Polish
count in the Vilkavisski forest.

Next day, overtaking the army, he went in a carriage
to the Niemen, and changing into a Polish uniform in
order to select a place for the crossing, he drove to the
river bank.

Seeing on the other side some Cossacks (*les Cosaques*)
and the wide-spreading steppes in the midst of which lay
the holy city of Moscow (*Moscou, la ville sainte*), the
capital of a realm such as the Scythia into which Alexander the Great had marched—Napoleon unexpectedly
and contrary alike to strategic and diplomatic considerations, ordered an advance, and the next day his army
began to cross the Niemen.

Early in the morning of the 12th of June he came out
of his tent which was pitched that day on the steep left
bank of the Niemen, and looked through a spy-glass a

the streams of his troops pouring out of the Vilkavisski forest and flowing over the three bridges thrown across the river. The troops, knowing of the Emperor's presence, were on the look-out for him, and when they caught sight of a figure in an overcoat and a cocked hat standing apart from his suite in front of his tent on the hill, they threw up their caps and shouted: '*Vive l'Empereur!*' and one after another poured in a ceaseless stream out of the vast forest that had concealed them and, separating, flowed on and on by the three bridges to the other side.

'Now we'll go into action. Oh, when he takes it in hand himself things get hot . . . by heaven! . . . There he is! . . . *Vive l'Empereur!* So these are the steppes of Asia! It's a nasty country all the same. *Au revoir*, Beauché; I'll keep the best palace in Moscow for you! *Au revoir.* Good luck! . . . Did you see the Emperor? *Vive l'Empereur!* . . . *preur!*—If they make me Governor of India, Gérard, I'll make you Minister of Kashmir—that's settled. *Vive l'Empereur!* Hurrah! hurrah! hurrah! The Cossacks—those rascals—see how they run! *Vive l'Empereur!* There he is, do you see him? I've seen him twice, as I see you now. The little corporal . . . I saw him give the cross to one of the veterans . . . *Vive l'Empereur!*' came the voices of men, old and young, of most diverse characters and social positions. On the faces of all was one common expression of joy at the commencement of the long-expected campaign and of rapture and devotion to the man in the grey coat who was standing on the hill.

On the 13th of June a rather small, thoroughbred Arab horse was brought to Napoleon. He mounted it and rode at a gallop to one of the bridges over the Niemen, deafened continually by incessant and rapturous acclamations which he evidently endured only because it was impossible to forbid the soldiers to express their love of him by such shouting, but the shouting which accompanied him everywhere disturbed him and distracted his mind from the military cares that had occupied him from the time he joined the army. He rode across one of the swaying pontoon bridges to the farther side, turned sharply to the left and galloped in the direction of Kóvno, preceded by enraptured, mounted chasseurs of the Guard who, breathless with delight, galloped ahead to clear a path for him through the troops. On reaching the broad river Víliya he stopped near a regiment of Polish Uhlans stationed by the river.

'*Vivat!*' shouted the Poles ecstatically, breaking their ranks and pressing against one another to see him.

Napoleon looked up and down the river, dismounted, and sat down on a log that lay on the bank. At a mute sign from him a telescope was handed him which he rested on the back of a happy page who had run up to him, and he gazed at the opposite bank. Then he became absorbed in a map laid out on the logs. Without lifting his head he said something and two of his aides-de-camp galloped off to the Polish Uhlans.

'What? What did he say?' was heard in the ranks of the Polish Uhlans when one of the aides-de-camp rode up to them.

The order was to find a ford and to cross the river. The colonel of Polish Uhlans, a handsome old man, flushed, and fumbling in his speech from excitement asked the aide-de-camp whether he would be permitted to swim the river with his Uhlans instead of seeking a ford. In evident fear of refusal, like a boy asking for permission to get on a horse, he begged to be allowed to swim across the river before the Emperor's eyes. The aide-de-camp replied that probably the Emperor would not be displeased at this excess of zeal.

As soon as the aide-de-camp had said this, the old moustached officer with a happy face and sparkling eyes raised his sabre, shouted '*Vivat!*' and, commanding the Uhlans to follow him, spurred his horse and galloped into the river. He gave an angry thrust to his horse which had grown restive under him, and plunged into the water, heading for the deepest part where the current was swift. Hundreds of Uhlans galloped in after him. It was cold and uncanny in the rapid current in the middle of the stream, and the Uhlans caught hold of one another as they fell off their horses. Some of the horses were drowned and some of the men, the others tried to swim on, some in the saddle and some clinging to their horses' manes. They tried to make their way forward to the opposite bank, and though there was a ford half a verst away, were proud that they were swimming and drowning in this river under the eyes of the man who sat on the log and was not even looking at what they were doing. When the aide-de-camp having returned and choosing an opportune moment ventured to draw the Emperor's attention to the devotion of the Poles to his person, the little man in the grey overcoat got up and having summoned Berthier began pacing up and down the bank with him, giving him instructions and occasionally glancing disapprovingly at the drowning Uhlans who distracted his attention.

For him it was no new conviction that his presence in any part of the world, from Africa to the steppes of Muscovy alike, was enough to dumbfound people and impel them to insane self-oblivion. He called for his horse and rode to his quarters.

Some forty Uhlans were drowned in the river though boats were sent to their assistance. The majority struggled back to the bank from which they had started. The colonel and some of his men got across, and with difficulty clambered out on the further bank. And as soon as they had got out, in their soaked and streaming clothes, they shouted '*Vivat!*' and looked ecstatically at the spot where Napoleon had been but where he no longer was, and at that moment considered themselves happy.

That evening, between issuing one order that the forged Russian paper money prepared for use in Russia should be delivered as quickly as possible, and another that a Saxon on whom a letter containing information about the orders to the French army had been found should be shot, Napoleon also gave instructions that the Polish colonel who had needlessly plunged into the river should be enrolled in the *Légion d'honneur* of which Napoleon was himself the head.

Quos vult perdere dementat.[1]

---

[1] Those whom (God) wishes to destroy he drives mad.

CHAPTER III

THE Emperor of Russia had meanwhile been in Vílna for more than a month, reviewing troops and holding manœuvres. Nothing was ready for the war that every one expected and to prepare for which the Emperor had come from Petersburg. There was no general plan of action. The vacillation between the various plans that were proposed had even increased after the Emperor had been at head-quarters for a month. Each of the three armies had its own commander-in-chief, but there was no supreme commander of all the forces, and the Emperor did not assume that responsibility himself.

The longer the Emperor remained in Vílna the less did everybody—tired of waiting—prepare for the war. All the efforts of those who surrounded the sovereign seemed directed merely to making him spend his time pleasantly and forget that war was impending.

In June, after many balls and fêtes given by the Polish magnates, by the courtiers, and by the Emperor himself, it occurred to one of the Polish aides-de-camp in attendance that a dinner and ball should be given for the Emperor by his aides-de-camp. This idea was eagerly received. The Emperor gave his consent. The aides-de-camp collected money by subscription. The lady who was thought to be most pleasing to the Emperor was invited to act as hostess. Count Bennigsen, being a land-owner in the Vílna province, offered his country house for the fête, and the 13th of June was fixed for a ball, dinner, regatta, and fireworks at Zakret, Count Bennigsen's country seat.

The very day that Napoleon issued the order to cross the Niemen, and his vanguard, driving off the Cossacks, crossed the Russian frontier, Alexander spent the evening at the entertainment given by his aides-de-camp at Bennigsen's country house.

It was a gay and brilliant fête. Connoisseurs of such matters declared that rarely had so many beautiful women been assembled in one place. Countess Bezúkhova was present among other Russian ladies who had followed the sovereign from Petersburg to Vílna, and eclipsed the refined Polish ladies by her massive, so-called Russian, type of beauty. The Emperor noticed her, and honoured her with a dance.

Borís Drubetskóy, having left his wife in Moscow and being for the present *en garçon* (as he phrased it), was also there and, though not an aide-de-camp, had subscribed a large sum towards the expenses. Borís was now a rich man who had risen to high honours, and no longer sought patronage but stood on an equal footing with the highest of those of his own age. He was meeting Hélène in Vílna after not having seen her for a long time, and did not recall the past, but as Hélène was enjoying the favours of a very important personage and Borís had only recently married, they met as good friends of long standing.

At midnight dancing was still going on. Hélène, not having a suitable partner, herself offered to dance the mazurka with Borís. They were the third couple. Borís, coolly looking at Hélène's dazzling bare shoulders which emerged from a dark, gold-embroidered, gauze gown, talked to her of old acquaintances, and at the same time, unaware of it himself and unnoticed by others, never for an instant ceased to observe the Emperor who was in the same room. The Emperor was not dancing, he stood in the doorway, stopping now one pair and now another with gracious words that he alone knew how to utter.

As the mazurka began, Borís saw that Adjutant-General Baláshev, one of those in closest attendance on the Emperor, went up to him, and contrary to court etiquette stood near him while he was talking to a Polish lady. Having finished speaking to her, the Emperor looked inquiringly at Baláshev and, evidently understanding that he only acted thus because there were important reasons for so doing, nodded slightly to the lady and turned to him. Hardly had Baláshev begun to speak before a look of amazement appeared on the Emperor's face. He took Baláshev by the arm and crossed the room with him, unconsciously clearing a path seven yards wide as the people on both sides made way for him. Borís noticed Arakchéev's excited face when the sovereign went out with Baláshev. Arakchéev looked at the Emperor from under his brow, and sniffing with his red nose stepped forward from the crowd as if expecting the Emperor to address him. (Borís understood that Arakchéev envied Baláshev and was displeased that evidently important news had reached the Emperor otherwise than through himself.)

But the Emperor and Baláshev passed out into the illuminated garden without noticing Arakchéev who, holding his sword and glancing wrathfully around, followed some twenty paces behind them.

All the time Borís was going through the figures of the mazurka he was worried by the question of what news Baláshev had brought, and how he could find it out before others.

In the figure in which he had to choose two ladies, he whispered to Hélène that he meant to choose Countess Potocka who he thought had gone out onto the veranda, and glided over the parquet to the door opening into the garden, where, seeing Baláshev and the Emperor returning to the veranda, he stood still. They were moving towards the door. Borís, fluttering as if he had not had time to withdraw, respectfully pressed close to the door-post with bowed head.

The Emperor, with the agitation of one who has been personally affronted, was finishing with these words:

'To enter Russia without declaring war! I will not make peace as long as a single armed enemy remains in my country!'

It seemed to Borís that it gave the Emperor pleasure to utter these words. He was satisfied with the form in which he had expressed his thought, but displeased that Borís had overheard it.

'Let no one know of it!' the Emperor added with a frown.

Borís understood that this was meant for him, and closing his eyes slightly bowed his head. The Emperor re-entered the ball-room and remained there about another half-hour.

Borís was thus the first to learn the news that the French army had crossed the Niemen, and thanks to this was able to show certain important personages that much that was concealed from others was usually known to him, and by this means he rose higher in their estimation.

The unexpected news of the French having crossed the Niemen was particularly startling after a month of unfulfilled expectations, and at a ball. On first receiving the news, under the influence of indignation and resentment the Emperor had found a phrase that pleased him, fully expressed his feelings, and has since become famous. On returning home at two o'clock that night he sent for his secretary, Shishkóv, and told him to write an order to the troops and a rescript to Field-Marshal Prince Saltykóv, in which he insisted on the words being inserted that he would not make peace so long as a single armed Frenchman remained on Russian soil.

Next day the following letter was sent to Napoleon:

'*Monsieur mon frère,*

Yesterday I learnt that, despite the loyalty with which I have kept my engagements with your Majesty, your troops have crossed the Russian frontier, and I have this moment received from Petersburg a note in which Count Lauriston informs me, as a reason for this aggression, that your Majesty has considered yourself to be in a state of war with me from the time Prince Kurákin asked for his passports. The reasons on which the Duc de Bassano based his refusal to deliver them to him would never have led me to suppose that that incident could serve as a pretext for aggression. In fact the ambassador, as he himself has declared, was never authorized to make that demand, and as soon as I was informed of it I let him know how much I disapproved of it, and ordered him to remain at his post. If your Majesty does not intend to shed the blood of our peoples for such a misunderstanding, and consents to withdraw your troops from Russian territory, I will regard what has passed as not having occurred and an understanding between us will be possible. In the contrary case, your Majesty, I shall see myself forced to repel an attack that nothing on my part has provoked. It still depends on your Majesty to preserve humanity from the calamity of another war.

I am, &c.,

(Signed) Alexander.'

CHAPTER IV

AT two in the morning of the 14th of June the Emperor, having sent for Baláshev and read him his letter to Napoleon, ordered him to take it and hand it personally to the French Emperor. When dispatching Baláshev the Emperor repeated to him the words that he would not make peace so long as a single armed enemy remained on Russian soil, and told him to transmit those words to Napoleon. Alexander did not insert them in his letter to Napoleon because, with his characteristic tact, he felt it would be injudicious to use them at a moment when a last attempt at reconciliation was being made, but he definitely instructed Baláshev to repeat them personally to Napoleon.

Having set off in the small hours of the 14th, accompanied by a bugler and two Cossacks, Baláshev reached the French outposts at the village of Rykónty, on the Russian side of the Niemen, by dawn. There he was stopped by French cavalry sentinels.

A French non-commissioned officer of hussars, in crimson uniform and a shaggy cap, shouted to the approaching Baláshev to halt. Baláshev did not do so at once, but continued to advance along the road at a walking pace.

The non-commissioned officer frowned, and muttering words of abuse advanced his horse's chest against Baláshev, put his hand to his sabre, and shouted rudely at the Russian general, asking: was he deaf that he did not do as he was told? Baláshev mentioned who he was. The non-commissioned officer began talking with his comrades about regimental matters without looking at the Russian general.

After living at the seat of the highest authority and power, after conversing with the Emperor less than three hours before, and in general being accustomed to the respect due to his rank in the service, Baláshev found it very strange here on Russian soil to encounter this hostile, and still more this disrespectful, application of brute force to himself.

The sun was only just appearing from behind the clouds, the air was fresh and dewy. A herd of cattle was being driven along the road from the village, and over the fields the larks rose trilling, one after another, like bubbles rising in water.

Baláshev looked around him awaiting the arrival of an officer from the village. The Russian Cossacks and bugler and the French hussars looked silently at one another from time to time.

A French colonel of hussars, who had evidently just left his bed, came riding from the village on a handsome sleek grey horse, accompanied by two hussars. The officer, the soldiers, and their horses, all looked smart and well-kept.

It was that first period of a campaign when troops are still in full trim almost like that of peace-time manœuvres, but with a shade of martial swagger in their clothes, and a touch of the gaiety and spirit of enterprise which always accompany the opening of a campaign.

The French colonel with difficulty repressed a yawn, but was polite and evidently understood Baláshev's importance. He led him past his soldiers and behind the outposts, and told him that his wish to be presented to the Emperor would most likely be satisfied immediately, as the Emperor's quarters were, he believed, not far off.

They rode through the village of Rykónty, past tethered French hussar horses, past sentinels and men who saluted their colonel and stared with curiosity at a Russian uniform, and came out at the other end of the village. The colonel said that the commander of the division was a mile and a quarter away and would receive Baláshev and conduct him to his destination.

The sun had by now risen and shone gaily on the bright verdure.

They had hardly ridden up a hill, past a tavern, before they saw a group of horsemen coming towards them. In front of the group, on a black horse with trappings that glittered in the sun, rode a tall man with plumes in his hat and black hair curling down to his shoulders. He wore a red mantle, and stretched his long legs forward in French fashion. This man rode towards Baláshev at a gallop, his plumes flowing and his gems and gold lace glittering in the bright June sunshine.

Baláshev was only two horses' length from the equestrian with the bracelets, plumes, necklaces, and gold embroidery, who was galloping towards him with a theatrically solemn countenance, when Julner, the French colonel, whispered respectfully: 'The King of Naples!' It was in fact Murat, now called 'King of Naples'. Though it was quite incomprehensible why he should be King of Naples he was called so, and was himself convinced that he was so, and therefore assumed a more solemn and important air than formerly. He was so sure that he really was the King of Naples that when on the eve of his departure from that city, while walking through the streets with his wife, some Italians called out to him: '*Viva il re!*'[1] he turned to his wife with a pensive smile and said: 'Poor fellows, they don't know that I am leaving them to-morrow!'

But though he firmly believed himself to be King of Naples, and pitied the grief felt by the subjects he was abandoning, latterly, after he had been ordered to return to military service, and especially since his last interview with Napoleon in Danzig, when his august brother-in-law had told him: 'I made you King that you should reign in my way, but not in yours!'—he had cheerfully taken up his familiar business, and—like a well-fed but not over-fat horse that feels himself in harness and grows skittish between the shafts—he dressed up in clothes as variegated and expensive as possible, and gaily and contentedly galloped along the roads of Poland, without himself knowing why or where.

On seeing the Russian general he threw back his head, with its long hair curling to his shoulders, in a majestically royal manner, and looked inquiringly at the French colonel. The colonel respectfully informed his Majesty of Baláshev's mission, whose name he could not pronounce.

'De Bal-machève!' said the King (overcoming by his assurance the difficulty that had presented itself to the colonel). 'Charmed to make your acquaintance, General!' he added with a gesture of kingly condescension.

As soon as the King began to speak loud and fast his royal dignity instantly forsook him, and without noticing

[1] 'Long live the King!'

it he passed into his natural tone of good-natured familiarity. He laid his hand on the withers of Baláshev's horse
and said:

'Well, General, it all looks like war,' as if regretting a
circumstance of which he was unable to judge.

'Your Majesty,' replied Baláshev, 'my master, the
Emperor, does not desire war and as your Majesty sees
. . .' said Baláshev, using the words *your Majesty* at every
opportunity, with the affectation unavoidable in frequently addressing one to whom the title was still a
novelty.

Murat's face beamed with stupid satisfaction as he
listened to 'Monsieur de Balachoff'. But *royauté oblige*![1]
and he felt it incumbent on him, as a king and an ally, to
confer on state affairs with Alexander's envoy. He dismounted, took Baláshev's arm, and moving a few steps
away from his suite which waited respectfully, began to
pace up and down with him trying to speak significantly.
He referred to the fact that the Emperor Napoleon had
resented the demand that he should withdraw his troops
from Prussia, especially when that demand became
generally known and the dignity of France was thereby
offended.

Baláshev replied that there was nothing offensive in the
demand, because . . . but Murat interrupted him.

'Then you don't consider the Emperor Alexander the
aggressor?' he asked unexpectedly, with a kindly and
foolish smile.

Baláshev told him why he considered Napoleon to be
the originator of the war.

'Oh, my dear General!' Murat again interrupted him,
'with all my heart I wish the Emperors may arrange the
affair between them, and that the war begun by no wish
of mine may finish as quickly as possible!' said he, in the
tone of a servant who wants to remain good friends with
another despite a quarrel between their masters.

And he went on to inquiries about the Grand Duke
and the state of his health, and to reminiscences of the gay
and amusing times he had spent with him in Naples.
Then suddenly, as if remembering his royal dignity,

[1] Royalty has its obligations.

Murat solemnly drew himself up, assumed the pose in which he had stood at his coronation, and waving his right arm, said:

'I won't detain you longer, General. I wish success to your mission,' and with his embroidered red mantle, his flowing feathers, and his glittering ornaments, he rejoined his suite who were respectfully awaiting him.

Baláshev rode on, supposing from Murat's words that he would very soon be brought before Napoleon himself. But instead of that, at the next village the sentinels of Davoût's infantry corps detained him, as the pickets of the vanguard had done, and an adjutant of the corps-commander, who was fetched, conducted him into the village to Marshal Davoût.

CHAPTER V

DAVOÛT was to Napoleon what Arakchéev was to Alexander—though not a coward like Arakchéev, he was as precise, as cruel, and as unable to express his devotion to his monarch except by cruelty.

In the organism of States such men are necessary, as wolves are necessary in the organism of Nature, and they always exist, always appear and hold their own, however incongruous their presence and their proximity to the head of the government may be. This inevitability alone can explain how the cruel Arakchéev, who tore out a grenadier's moustache with his own hands, whose weak nerves rendered him unable to face danger, and who was neither an educated man nor a courtier, was able to maintain his powerful position with Alexander, whose own character was chivalrous, noble, and gentle.

Baláshev found Davoût seated on a barrel in the shed of a peasant's hut writing—he was auditing accounts. Better quarters could have been found him, but Marshal Davoût was one of those men who purposely put themselves in most depressing conditions to have a justification for being gloomy. For the same reason they are always hard at work and in a hurry. 'How can I think of the bright side of life when, as you see, I am sitting on a barrel and working in a dirty shed?' the expression of his face seemed to say. The chief pleasure and necessity of such men, when they encounter any one who shows animation, is to flaunt their own dreary, persistent activity. Davoût allowed himself that pleasure when Baláshev was brought in. He became still more absorbed in his task when the Russian general entered, and after glancing over his spectacles at Baláshev's face, which was animated by the beauty of the morning and by his talk with Murat, he did not rise or even stir, but scowled still more and sneered malevolently.

When he noticed in Baláshev's face the disagreeable impression this reception produced, Davoût raised his head and coldly asked what he wanted.

Thinking he could have been received in such a manner only because Davoût did not know that he was adjutant-general to the Emperor Alexander and even his envoy to Napoleon, Baláshev hastened to inform him of his rank and mission. Contrary to his expectation, Davoût after hearing him became still surlier and ruder.

'Where is your dispatch?' he inquired. 'Give it to me. I will send it to the Emperor.'

Baláshev replied that he had been ordered to hand it personally to the Emperor.

'Your Emperor's orders are obeyed in your army, but here,' said Davoût, 'you must do as you're told.'

And as if to make the Russian general still more conscious of his dependence on brute force, Davoût sent an adjutant to call the officer on duty.

Baláshev took out the packet containing the Emperor's letter and laid it on the table (made of a door with its hinges still hanging on it, laid across two barrels). Davoût took the packet and read the inscription.

'You are perfectly at liberty to treat me with respect or not,' protested Baláshev, 'but permit me to observe that I have the honour to be adjutant-general to his Majesty . . .'

Davoût glanced at him silently and plainly derived pleasure from the signs of agitation and confusion which appeared on Baláshev's face.

'You will be treated as is fitting,' said he, and putting the packet in his pocket left the shed.

A minute later the marshal's adjutant, de Castrés, came in and conducted Balashev to the quarters assigned him.

That day he dined with the marshal, at the same board on the barrels.

Next day Davoût rode out early, and after asking Balashev to come to him peremptorily requested him to remain there, to move on with the baggage-train should orders come for it to move, and to talk to no one except Monsieur de Castrés.

After four days of solitude, ennui, and consciousness of his impotence and insignificance—particularly acute by contrast with the sphere of power in which he had so lately moved—and after several marches with the marshal's baggage and the French army, which occupied the whole district, Balashev was brought to Vílna—now occupied by the French—through the very gate by which he had left it four days previously.

Next day the imperial gentleman-in-waiting, Comte de Turenne, came to Balashev and informed him of the Emperor Napoleon's wish to honour him with an audience.

Four days before, sentinels of the Preobrazhénsk regiment had stood in front of the house to which Balashev was conducted, and now two French grenadiers stood there, in blue uniforms unfastened in front and with shaggy caps on their heads, and an escort of hussars and uhlans and a brilliant suite of aides-de-camp, pages, and generals, who were waiting for Napoleon to come out, were standing at the porch round his saddle-horse and his Mameluke, Rustan. Napoleon received Balashev in the very house in Vílna from which Alexander had dispatched him on his mission.

CHAPTER VI

THOUGH Balashev was used to imperial pomp he was amazed at the luxury and magnificence of Napoleon's court.

Comte de Turenne showed him into a large reception room, where many generals, gentlemen-in-waiting, and

Polish magnates—several of whom Baláshev had seen at
the court of the Emperor of Russia—were waiting. Duroc
said that Napoleon would receive the Russian general
before going for his ride.

After some minutes the gentleman-in-waiting who was
on duty came into the great reception room and bowing
politely, asked Baláshev to follow him.

Baláshev went into a small reception room one door
of which led into a study, the very one from which the
Russian Emperor had dispatched him on his mission.
He stood a minute or two waiting. He heard hurried
footsteps beyond the door, both halves of it were opened
rapidly; all was silent and then from the study the sound
was heard of other steps, firm and resolute—they were
those of Napoleon. He had just finished dressing for his
ride, and wore a blue uniform opening in front over
a white waistcoat, so long that it covered his rotund
stomach, white leather breeches tightly fitting the fat
thighs of his short legs, and Hessian boots. His short hair
had evidently just been brushed, but one lock hung
down in the middle of his broad forehead. His plump
white neck stood out sharply above the black collar of
his uniform, and he smelt of eau-de-cologne. His full
face, rather young-looking, with its prominent chin, wore
a gracious and majestic expression of imperial welcome.

He entered briskly, with a jerk at every step and his
head slightly thrown back. His whole short corpulent
figure with broad thick shoulders, and chest and stomach
involuntarily protruding, had that imposing and stately
appearance one sees in men of forty who live in comfort.
It was evident, too, that he was in the best of spirits that
day.

He nodded in answer to Baláshev's low and respectful
bow, and coming up to him at once began speaking like
a man who values every moment of his time and does
not condescend to prepare what he has to say, but is sure
he will always say the right thing and say it well.

'Good day, General!' said he. 'I have received the
letter you brought from the Emperor Alexander and am
very glad to see you.' He glanced with his large eyes into
Baláshev's face and immediately looked past him.

It was plain that Balashev's personality did not interest him at all. Evidently only what took place within *his own* mind interested him. Nothing outside himself had any significance for him because everything in the world, it seemed to him, depended entirely on his will.

'I do not, and did not, desire war,' he continued, 'but it has been forced on me. Even *now*' (he emphasized the word), 'I am ready to receive any explanations you can give me.'

And he began clearly and concisely to explain his reasons for dissatisfaction with the Russian government. Judging by the calmly moderate and amicable tone in which the French Emperor spoke, Balashev was firmly persuaded that he wished for peace and intended to enter into negotiations.

When Napoleon having finished speaking looked inquiringly at the Russian envoy, Balashev began a speech he had prepared long before: 'Sire! The Emperor, my master . . .' but the sight of the Emperor's eyes bent on him confused him. 'You are flurried—compose yourself!' Napoleon seemed to say, as with a scarcely perceptible smile he looked at Balashev's uniform and sword.

Balashev recovered himself and began to speak. He said that the Emperor Alexander did not consider Kurakin's demand for his passports a sufficient cause for war; that Kurakin had acted on his own initiative and without his sovereign's assent, that the Emperor Alexander did not desire war, and had no relations with England.

'Not *yet*!' interposed Napoleon, and, as if fearing to give vent to his feelings, he frowned and nodded slightly as a sign that Balashev might proceed.

After saying all he had been instructed to say, Balashev added that the Emperor Alexander wished for peace, but would not enter into negotiations except on condition that . . . Here Balashev hesitated: he remembered the words the Emperor Alexander had not written in his letter, but had specially inserted in the rescript to Saltykov and had told Balashev to repeat to Napoleon. Balashev remembered these words, 'So long as a single armed foe remains on Russian soil,' but some complex feeling restrained him. He could not utter them, though he wished to do so. He grew confused, and said: 'On condition that the French army retires beyond the Niemen.'[1]

Napoleon noticed Baláshev's embarrassment when uttering these last words: his face twitched and the calf of his left leg began to quiver rhythmically. Without moving from where he stood he began speaking in a louder tone and more hurriedly than before. During the speech that followed Baláshev, who more than once lowered his eyes, involuntarily noticed the quivering of Napoleon's left leg which increased the more, the more Napoleon raised his voice.

'I desire peace no less than the Emperor Alexander,' he began. 'Have I not for eighteen months been doing everything to obtain it? I have waited eighteen months for explanations. But in order to begin negotiations what is demanded of me?' he said frowning and making an energetic gesture of inquiry with his small, white, plump hand.

'The withdrawal of your army beyond the Niemen, Sire,' replied Baláshev.

'The Niemen?' repeated Napoleon. 'So now you want me to retire beyond the Niemen—only the Niemen?' repeated Napoleon, looking straight at Baláshev.

The latter bowed his head respectfully.

Instead of the demand of four months earlier to withdraw from Pomerania, only a withdrawal beyond the Niemen was now demanded. Napoleon turned quickly and began to pace the room.

'You say the demand now is that I am to withdraw beyond the Niemen before commencing negotiations, but in just the same way two months ago the demand was that I should withdraw beyond the Vistula and the Oder, and yet you are willing to negotiate.'

He went in silence from one corner of the room to the other and again stopped in front of Baláshev. Baláshev noticed that his left leg was quivering faster than before and his face seemed petrified in its stern expression. This quivering of his left leg was a thing Napoleon was

[1] The Niemen, in 1812, was the frontier between Russia and Poland.

conscious of. 'The vibration of my left calf is a great sign with me,' he remarked at a later date.

'Such demands as to retreat beyond the Vistula and Oder may be made to a Prince of Baden, but not to me!' Napoleon almost screamed, quite to his own surprise. 'If you gave me Petersburg and Moscow I could not accept such conditions. You say I have begun this war! But who first joined his army? The Emperor Alexander, not I! And you offer me negotiations when I have expended millions, when you are in alliance with England, and when your position is a bad one. You offer me negotiations! But what is the aim of your alliance with England? What has she given you?' he continued hurriedly, evidently no longer trying to show the advantages of peace and discuss its possibility, but only to prove his own rectitude and power and Alexander's errors and duplicity.

The commencement of his speech had obviously been made with the intention of demonstrating the advantages of his position and showing that he was nevertheless willing to negotiate. But he had begun talking, and the more he talked the less could he control his words.

The whole purport of his remarks now was evidently to exalt himself and insult Alexander—just what he had least desired at the commencement of the interview.

'I hear you have made peace with Turkey?'

Baláshev bowed his head affirmatively.

'Peace has been concluded . . .' he began.

But Napoleon did not let him speak. He evidently wanted to do all the talking himself and continued to talk with the sort of eloquence and unrestrained irritability to which spoilt people are so prone.

'Yes, I know you have made peace with the Turks without obtaining Moldavia and Wallachia; I would have given your sovereign those provinces as I gave him Finland. Yes,' he went on, 'I promised and would have given the Emperor Alexander Moldavia and Wallachia, and now he won't have those splendid provinces. Yet he might have united them to his empire and in a single reign would have extended Russia from the Gulf of Bothnia to the mouths of the Danube. Catherine the

Great could not have done more,' said Napoleon, growing
more and more excited as he paced up and down the
room repeating to Baláshev almost the very words he had
used to Alexander himself at Tilsit. 'All that, he would
have owed to my friendship. Oh, what a splendid reign!'
he repeated several times, then paused, drew from his
pocket a gold snuff-box, lifted it to his nose, and greedily
sniffed at it.

'What a splendid reign the Emperor Alexander's *might
have been*!'

He looked compassionately at Baláshev, and as soon as
the latter tried to make some rejoinder hastily interrupted
him.

'What could he wish or look for that he would not have
obtained through my friendship?' demanded Napoleon,
shrugging his shoulders in perplexity. 'But no, he has
preferred to surround himself with my enemies, and with
whom? With Steins, Armfelts, Bennigsens, and Wintzin-
gerodes! Stein, a traitor expelled from his own country;
Armfelt, a rake and an intriguer; Wintzingerode, a fugi-
tive French subject; Bennigsen, rather more of a soldier
than the others, but all the same an incompetent, who
was unable to do anything in 1807 and who should
awaken terrible memories in the Emperor Alexander's
mind ... Granted that were they competent they might
be made use of,' continued Napoleon—hardly able to
keep pace in words with the rush of thoughts that
incessantly sprang up proving how right and strong he
was (in his perception the two were one and the same)—
'but they are not even that! They are neither fit for war
nor peace! Barclay is said to be the most capable of them
all, but I cannot say so judging by his first movements.
And what are they doing, all these courtiers? Pfuel
proposes, Armfelt disputes, Bennigsen considers, and
Barclay, called on to act, does not know what to decide
on, and time passes bringing no result. Bagratión
alone is a military man. He's stupid, but he has experience, a quick eye, and resolution ... And what role is
your young monarch playing in that monstrous crowd?
They compromise him and throw on him the responsibility for all that happens. A sovereign should not be with

the army unless he is a general!' said Napoleon, evidently uttering these words as a direct challenge to the Emperor. He knew how Alexander desired to be a military commander.

'The campaign only began a week ago, and you haven't even been able to defend Vílna. You are cut in two and have been driven out of the Polish provinces. Your army is grumbling.'

'On the contrary, your Majesty,' said Baláshev, hardly able to remember what had been said to him, and following these verbal fireworks with difficulty, 'the troops are burning with eagerness . . .'

'I know everything!' Napoleon interrupted him. 'I know everything. I know the number of your battalions as exactly as I know my own. You have not two hundred thousand men, and I have three times that number. I give you my word of honour,' said Napoleon, forgetting that his word of honour could carry no weight—'I give you my word of honour that I have five hundred and thirty thousand men this side of the Vistula. The Turks will be of no use to you; they are worth nothing and have shown it by making peace with you. As for the Swedes— it is their fate to be governed by mad kings. Their king was insane and they changed him for another—Bernadotte, who promptly went mad—for no Swede would ally himself with Russia unless he were mad.'

Napoleon grinned maliciously and again raised his snuff-box to his nose.

Baláshev knew how to reply to each of Napoleon's remarks, and would have done so; he continually made the gesture of a man wishing to say something, but Napoleon always interrupted him. To the alleged insanity of the Swedes, Baláshev wished to reply that when Russia is on her side Sweden is practically an island; but Napoleon gave an angry exclamation to drown his voice. Napoleon was in that state of irritability in which a man has to talk, talk, and talk, merely to convince himself that he is in the right. Baláshev began to feel uncomfortable: as envoy he feared to demean his dignity and felt the necessity of replying; but as a man he shrank before the transport of groundless wrath that had evidently seized Napoleon.

He knew that none of the words now uttered by Napoleon had any significance, and that Napoleon himself would be ashamed of them when he came to his senses. Baláshev stood with downcast eyes, looking at the movements of Napoleon's stout legs and trying to avoid meeting his eyes.

'But what do I care about your allies?' said Napoleon. 'I have allies—the Poles. There are eighty thousand of them and they fight like lions! And there will be two hundred thousand of them.'

And probably still more perturbed by the fact that he had uttered this obvious falsehood, and that Baláshev still stood silently before him in the same attitude of submission to fate, Napoleon abruptly turned round, drew close to Baláshev's face, and gesticulating rapidly and energetically with his white hands almost shouted:

'Know that if you stir up Prussia against me, I'll wipe it off the map of Europe!' he declared, his face pale and distorted by anger, and he struck one of his small hands energetically with the other. 'Yes, I will throw you back beyond the Dvína and beyond the Dnieper, and will re-erect against you that barrier[1] which it was criminal and blind of Europe to allow to be destroyed. Yes, that is what will happen to you. That is what you have gained by alienating me!' And he walked silently several times up and down the room, his fat shoulders twitching.

He put his snuff-box into his waistcoat pocket, took it out again, lifted it several times to his nose, and stopped in front of Baláshev. He paused, looked ironically straight into Baláshev's eyes, and said in a quiet voice:

'And yet what a splendid reign your master *might have had*!'

Baláshev, feeling it incumbent on him to reply, said that from the Russian side things did not appear in so gloomy a light. Napoleon was silent, still looking derisively at him and evidently not listening to him. Baláshev said that in Russia the best results were expected from the war. Napoleon nodded condescendingly, as if to say, 'I know it's your duty to say that, but you don't believe it yourself. I have convinced you.'

---

[1] Namely, a large Polish state.

When Balashev had ended, Napoleon again took out his snuff-box, sniffed at it, and stamped his foot twice on the floor as a signal. The door opened, a gentleman-in-waiting, bending respectfully, handed the Emperor his hat and gloves, another brought him a pocket-handkerchief. Napoleon, without giving them a glance, turned to Balashev:

'Assure the Emperor Alexander from me,' said he, taking his hat, 'that I am as devoted to him as before: I know him thoroughly and very highly esteem his lofty qualities. I will detain you no longer, General; you shall receive my letter to the Emperor.'

And Napoleon went quickly to the door. Every one in the reception-room rushed forward and descended the staircase.

CHAPTER VII

AFTER all that Napoleon had said to him—those bursts of anger and the last dryly spoken words: 'I will detain you no longer, General; you shall receive my letter,' Balashev felt convinced that Napoleon would not wish to see him, and would even avoid another meeting with him—an insulted envoy—especially as he had witnessed his unseemly anger. But to his surprise Balashev received, through Duroc, an invitation to dine with the Emperor that day.

Bessières, Caulaincourt, and Berthier were present at that dinner.

Napoleon met Balashev cheerfully and amiably. He not only showed no sign of constraint or self-reproach on account of his outburst that morning, but on the contrary tried to reassure Balashev. It was evident that he had long been convinced that it was impossible for him to make a mistake, and that in his perception whatever he did was right, not because it harmonized with any idea of right and wrong, but because he did it.

The Emperor was in very good spirits after his ride through Vílna,[1] where crowds of people had rapturously greeted and followed him. From all the windows of the

[1] In 1812 Vílna was within the frontier of Russia, but had only been so for a short time, and its sympathies were still Polish.

streets through which he rode rugs, flags, and his monogram, were displayed, and the Polish ladies welcoming him, waved their handkerchiefs to him.

At dinner, having placed Baláshev beside him, Napoleon not only treated him amiably but behaved as if Baláshev were one of his own courtiers, one of those who sympathized with his plans and ought to rejoice at his success. In the course of conversation he mentioned Moscow, and questioned Baláshev about the Russian capital, not merely as an interested traveller asks about a new city he intends to visit, but as if convinced that Baláshev, as a Russian, must be flattered by his curiosity.

'How many inhabitants are there in Moscow? How many houses? Is it true that Moscow is called "Holy Moscow"? How many churches are there in Moscow?' he asked.

And receiving the reply that there were more than two hundred churches, he remarked:

'Why such a quantity of churches?'

'The Russians are very devout,' replied Baláshev.

'But a large number of monasteries and churches is always a sign of the backwardness of a people,' said Napoleon, turning to Caulaincourt for appreciation of this remark.

Baláshev respectfully ventured to disagree with the French Emperor.

'Every country has its own character,' said he.

'But nowhere in Europe is there anything like that,' said Napoleon.

'I beg your Majesty's pardon,' returned Baláshev, 'besides Russia there is Spain, where there are also many churches and monasteries.'

This reply of Baláshev's, which hinted at the recent defeats of the French in Spain, was much appreciated when he related it at Alexander's court, but it was not much appreciated at Napoleon's dinner, where it passed unnoticed.

The uninterested and perplexed faces of the marshals showed that they were puzzled as to what Baláshev's tone suggested. 'If there is a point we don't see it, or it is not at all witty,' their expressions seemed to say. So

little was his rejoinder appreciated that Napoleon did
not notice it at all, and naïvely asked Baláshev through
what towns the direct road from there to Moscow passed.
Baláshev, who was on the alert all through the dinner,
replied that just as 'all roads lead to Rome,' so all roads
lead to Moscow: there were many roads, and 'among them
the road through *Poltáva*, which Charles XII chose'.
Baláshev involuntarily flushed with pleasure at the apt-
ness of this reply, but hardly had he uttered the word
Poltáva before Caulaincourt began speaking of the bad-
ness of the road from Petersburg to Moscow and of his
Petersburg reminiscences.

After dinner they went to drink coffee in Napoleon's
study, which four days previously had been that of the
Emperor Alexander. Napoleon sat down, toying with
his Sèvres coffee cup, and motioned Baláshev to a chair
beside him.

Napoleon was in that well-known after-dinner mood
which, more than any reasoned cause, makes a man
contented with himself and disposed to consider every
one his friend. It seemed to him that he was surrounded
by men who adored him; and he felt convinced that,
after his dinner, Baláshev too was his friend and wor-
shipper. Napoleon turned to him with a pleasant though
slightly ironic smile.

'They tell me this is the room the Emperor Alexander
occupied? Strange, isn't it, General?' he said, evidently
not doubting that this remark would be agreeable to his
hearer since it went to prove his, Napoleon's, superiority
to Alexander.

Baláshev could make no reply and bowed his head in
silence.

'Yes. Four days ago in this room, Wintsingerode and
Stein were deliberating,' continued Napoleon with the
same derisive and self-confident smile. 'What I can't
understand,' he went on, 'is that the Emperor Alexander
has surrounded himself with my personal enemies. That
I do not . . . understand. Has he not thought that I may
do the same?' and he turned inquiringly to Baláshev, and
evidently this thought turned him back on to the track
of his morning's anger, which was still fresh in him.

'And let him know that I will do so!' said Napoleon, rising and pushing his cup away with his hand. 'I'll drive all his Würtemberg, Baden, and Weimar relations out of Germany ... Yes. I'll drive them out. Let him prepare an asylum for them in Russia!'

Baláshev bowed his head with an air indicating that he would like to make his bow and leave, and only listened because he could not help hearing what was said to him. Napoleon did not notice this expression; he treated Baláshev not as an envoy from his enemy, but as a man now fully devoted to him and who must rejoice at his former master's humiliation.

'And why has the Emperor Alexander taken command of the armies? What is the good of that? War is my profession, but his business is to reign and not to command armies! Why has he taken on himself such a responsibility?'

Again Napoleon brought out his snuff-box, paced several times up and down the room in silence, and then suddenly and unexpectedly went up to Baláshev, and with a slight smile as confidently, quickly, and simply as if he were doing something not merely important but pleasing to Baláshev, he raised his hand to the forty-year-old Russian general's face, and taking him by the ear pulled it gently, smiling with his lips only.

To have one's ear pulled by the Emperor was considered the greatest honour and mark of favour at the French court.

'Well, adorer and courtier of the Emperor Alexander, why don't you say anything?' said he, as if it was ridiculous, in his presence, to be the adorer and courtier of any one but himself, Napoleon. 'Are the horses ready for the General?' he added, with a slight inclination of his head in reply to Baláshev's bow. 'Let him have mine, he has *a long way to go!*'

The letter taken by Baláshev was the last Napoleon sent to Alexander. Every detail of the interview was communicated to the Russian monarch, and the war began ...

CHAPTER VIII

AFTER his interview with Pierre in Moscow, Prince Andrew went to Petersburg, on business as he told his family, but really to meet Anatole Kurágin whom he felt it necessary to encounter. On reaching Petersburg he inquired for Kurágin but the latter had already left the city. Pierre had warned his brother-in-law that Prince Andrew was on his track. Anatole Kurágin promptly obtained an appointment from the Minister of War and went to join the army in Moldavia. While in Petersburg Prince Andrew met Kutúzov, his former commander who was always well disposed towards him, and Kutúzov suggested that he should accompany him to the army in Moldavia to which the old general had been appointed commander-in-chief. So Prince Andrew, having received an appointment on the head-quarters staff, left for Turkey.

Prince Andrew did not think it proper to write and challenge Kurágin. He thought that if he challenged him without some fresh cause it might compromise the young Countess Rostóva, and so he wanted to meet Kurágin personally in order to find a fresh pretext for a duel. But he again failed to meet Kurágin in Turkey, for soon after Prince Andrew arrived the latter returned to Russia. In a new country, amid new conditions, Prince Andrew found life easier to bear. After his betrothed had broken faith with him—which he felt the more acutely the more he tried to conceal its effects—the surroundings in which he had been happy became trying to him, and the freedom and independence he had once prized so highly were still more so. Not only could he no longer think the thoughts that had first come to him as he lay gazing at the sky on the field of Austerlitz and had later enlarged upon with Pierre, and which had filled his solitude at Boguchárovo and then in Switzerland and Rome, but he even dreaded to recall them and the bright and boundless horizons they had revealed. He was now concerned only with the nearest practical matters unrelated to his past interests, and he seized on these the more eagerly the more those past interests were closed to him. It was as if that lofty infinite canopy of heaven that had once towered above him had suddenly turned into a low solid vault that weighed him down, in which all was clear, but nothing eternal or mysterious.

Of the activities that presented themselves to him, army service was the simplest and most familiar. As a general on duty on Kutúzov's staff he applied himself to business with zeal and perseverance, and surprised Kutúzov by his willingness and accuracy in work. Not having found Kurágin in Turkey, Prince Andrew did not think it necessary to rush back to Russia after him, but all the same he knew that however long it might be before he met Kurágin, despite his contempt for him and despite all the proofs he deduced to convince himself that it was not worth stooping to a conflict with him—he knew that when he did meet him he would not be able to resist calling him out, any more than a ravenous man can help snatching at food. And the consciousness that the insult was not yet avenged, that his rancour was still unspent, weighed on his heart and poisoned the artificial tranquillity which he managed to obtain in Turkey by means of restless, plodding, and rather vainglorious and ambitious activity.

In the year 1812, when news of the war with Napoleon reached Bucharest—where Kutúzov had been living for two months passing his days and nights with a Wallachian woman—Prince Andrew asked Kutúzov to transfer him to the Western Army. Kutúzov, who was already weary of Bolkónski's activity which seemed to reproach his own idleness, very readily let him go, and gave him a mission to Barclay de Tolly.

Before joining the Western Army which was then, in May, encamped at Drissa,[1] Prince Andrew visited Bald Hills which was directly on his way, being only three versts off the Smolénsk high road. During the last three years there had been so many changes in his life, he had thought, felt, and seen, so much (having travelled both in the east and the west) that on reaching Bald Hills it

[1] A provincial town, situated where the river Drissa flows into the Western Dvína. A fortified camp had been constructed there, chiefly to guard the road to Petersburg.

struck him as strange and unexpected to find the way of life there unchanged and still the same in every detail. He entered through the gates with their stone pillars, and drove up the avenue leading to the house as if he were entering an enchanted, sleeping castle. The same old stateliness, the same cleanliness, the same stillness reigned there, and inside there was the same furniture, the same walls, sounds, and smell, and the same timid faces, only somewhat older. Princess Mary was still the same timid, plain, maiden getting on in years, uselessly and joylessly passing the best years of her life in fear and constant suffering. Mademoiselle Bourienne was the same coquettish, self-satisfied girl, enjoying every moment of her existence and full of joyous hopes for the future. She had merely become more self-confident, Prince Andrew thought. Dessalles, the tutor he had brought from Switzerland, was wearing a coat of Russian cut and talking broken Russian to the servants, but was still the same narrowly intelligent, conscientious, and pedantic preceptor. The old prince had changed in appearance only by the loss of a tooth, which left a noticeable gap on one side of his mouth: in character he was the same as ever, only showing still more irritability and scepticism as to what was happening in the world. Little Nicholas alone had changed. He had grown, become rosier, had curly dark hair, and when merry and laughing quite unconsciously lifted the upper lip of his pretty little mouth just as the little princess used to do. He alone did not obey the law of immutability in the enchanted sleeping castle. But though externally all remained as of old, the inner relations of all these people had changed since Prince Andrew had seen them last. The household was divided into two alien and hostile camps, who changed their habits for his sake and only met because he was there. To the one camp belonged the old prince, Mademoiselle Bourienne, and the architect; to the other Princess Mary, Dessalles, little Nicholas, and all the old nurses and maids.

During his stay at Bald Hills all the family dined together, but they were ill at ease and Prince Andrew felt that he was a visitor for whose sake an exception was being made, and that his presence made them all feel awkward. Involuntarily feeling this at dinner on the first day he was taciturn, and the old prince noticing this also became morosely dumb, and retired to his apartments directly after dinner. In the evening when Prince Andrew went to him, and, trying to rouse him, began to tell him of the young Count Kámensky's campaign, the old prince began unexpectedly to talk about Princess Mary, blaming her for her superstitions and her dislike of Mademoiselle Bourienne, who he said was the only person truly attached to him.

The old prince said that if he was ill it was only because of Princess Mary: that she purposely worried and irritated him, and that by indulgence and silly talk she was spoiling little Prince Nicholas. The old prince knew very well that he tormented his daughter and that her life was very hard, but he also knew that he could not help tormenting her and that she deserved it. 'Why does Prince Andrew, who sees this, say nothing to me about his sister? Does he think me a scoundrel, or an old fool who without any reason keeps his own daughter at a distance and attaches his Frenchwoman to himself? He doesn't understand, so I must explain it, and he must hear me out,' thought the old prince. And he began explaining why he could not put up with his daughter's unreasonable character.

'If you ask me,' said Prince Andrew without looking up (he was censuring his father for the first time in his life), 'I did not wish to speak about it, but as you ask me I will give you my frank opinion. If there is any misunderstanding and discord between you and Mary, I can't blame her for it at all. I know how she loves and respects you. Since you ask me,' continued Prince Andrew, becoming irritable—as he was always liable to do of late— 'I can only say that if there are any misunderstandings they are caused by that worthless woman, who is not fit to be my sister's companion.'

The old man at first stared fixedly at his son, and an unnatural smile disclosed the fresh gap between his teeth to which Prince Andrew could not get accustomed.

'What companion, my dear boy? Eh? You've already been talking it over! Eh?'

'Father, I did not want to judge,' said Prince Andrew in

a hard and bitter tone, 'but you challenged me, and I have said, and always shall say, that Mary is not to blame, but those to blame—the one to blame—is that Frenchwoman.'

'Ah, he has passed judgement . . . passed judgement!' said the old man in a low voice and, as it seemed to Prince Andrew, with some embarrassment, but then he suddenly jumped up and cried: 'Be off, be off! Let not a trace of you remain here! . . .'

Prince Andrew wished to leave at once, but Princess Mary persuaded him to stay another day. That day he did not see his father, who did not leave his room and admitted no one but Mademoiselle Bourienne and Tíkhon, but asked several times whether his son had gone. Next day before leaving Prince Andrew went to his son's rooms. The boy, curly-headed like his mother and glowing with health, sat on his knee, and Prince Andrew began telling him the story of Bluebeard, but fell into a reverie without finishing the story. He thought not of this pretty child, his son whom he held on his knee, but of himself. He sought in himself either remorse for having angered his father, or regret at leaving home for the first time in his life on bad terms with him, and was horrified to find neither. What meant still more to him was, that he sought and did not find in himself the former tenderness for his son which he had hoped to reawaken by caressing the boy and taking him on his knee.

'Well, go on!' said his son.

Prince Andrew without replying put him down from his knee and went out of the room.

As soon as Prince Andrew had given up his daily occupations, and especially on returning to the old condition of life amid which he had been happy, weariness of life overcame him with its former intensity, and he hastened to escape from these memories and to find some work as soon as possible.

'So you've decided to go, Andrew?' asked his sister.

'Thank God that I can,' replied Prince Andrew. 'I am very sorry you can't.'

'Why do you say that?' replied Princess Mary. 'Why do you say that, when you are going to this terrible war and he is so old? Mademoiselle Bourienne says he has been asking about you ...'

As soon as she began to speak of that, her lips trembled and her tears began to fall. Prince Andrew turned away and began pacing the room.

'Ah, my God! my God! When one thinks who and what—what trash—can cause people misery!' he said with a malignity that alarmed Princess Mary.

She understood that when speaking of 'trash' he referred not only to Mademoiselle Bourienne, the cause of her misery, but also to the man who had ruined his own happiness.

'Andrew! One thing I beg, I entreat of you!' she said, touching his elbow and looking at him with eyes that shone through her tears. 'I understand you' (she looked down). 'Don't imagine that sorrow is the work of men. Men are His tools.' She looked a little above Prince Andrew's head with the confident, accustomed look with which one looks at the place where a familiar portrait hangs. 'Sorrow is sent by *Him*, not by men. Men are His instruments, they are not to blame. If you think some one has wronged you, forget it and forgive! We have no right to punish. And then you will know the happiness of forgiving.'

'If I were a woman I would do so, Mary. That is a woman's virtue. But a man should not and cannot forgive and forget,' he replied; and though till that moment he had not been thinking of Kurágin all his unexpended anger suddenly swelled up in his heart.

'If Mary is already persuading me to forgive, it means that I ought long ago to have punished him,' he thought. And giving her no further reply, he began thinking of the glad vindictive moment when he would meet Kurágin who he knew was now in the army.

Princess Mary begged him to stay one day more, saying that she knew how unhappy her father would be if Andrew left without being reconciled to him, but Prince Andrew replied that he would probably soon be back again from the army, and would certainly write to his father, but that the longer he stayed now the more embittered their difference would become.

'Good-bye, Andrew! Remember that misfortunes come from God, and men are never to blame,' were the last words he heard from his sister when he took leave of her.

'Then it must be so!' thought Prince Andrew as he drove out of the avenue from the house at Bald Hills. 'She, poor innocent creature, is left to be victimized by an old man who has outlived his wits. The old man feels he is guilty, but cannot change himself. My boy is growing up and rejoices in life, in which like everybody else he will deceive or be deceived. And I am off to the army. Why? I myself don't know. I want to meet that man whom I despise, so as to give him a chance to kill and laugh at me!'

These conditions of life had been the same before, but then they were all connected, while now they had all tumbled to pieces. Only senseless things, lacking coherence, presented themselves one after another to Prince Andrew's mind.

CHAPTER IX

PRINCE ANDREW reached the general head-quarters of the army at the end of June. The first army with which was the Emperor, occupied the fortified camp at Drissa, the second army[1] was retreating, trying to effect a junction with the first one from which it was said to be cut off by large French forces. Every one was dissatisfied with the general course of affairs in the Russian army, but no one anticipated any danger of an invasion of the Russian provinces, and no one thought the war would extend farther than the western, the Polish provinces.[2]

Prince Andrew found Barclay de Tolly, to whom he had been assigned, on the bank of the Drissa. As there was not a single town or large village in the vicinity of the camp, the immense number of generals and courtiers

---

[1] Bagratión's.
[2] The provinces west of Smolénsk—even those annexed to Russia several years before—were still called 'Polish provinces'.

accompanying the army were living in the best houses of the villages on both sides of the river, over a radius of six miles. Barclay de Tolly was quartered nearly three miles from the Emperor. He received Bolkónski stiffly and coldly, and told him in his foreign accent that he would mention him to the Emperor for a decision as to his employment, but asked him meanwhile to remain on his staff. Anatole Kurágin, whom Prince Andrew had hoped to find with the army, was not there. He had gone to Petersburg, but Prince Andrew was glad to hear this. His mind was occupied by the interests of the centre that was conducting a gigantic war, and he was glad to be free for a while from the distraction caused by the thought of Kurágin. During the first four days, while no duties were required of him, Prince Andrew rode round the whole fortified camp and, by the aid of his own knowledge and by talks with experts, tried to form a definite opinion about it. But the question whether the camp was advantageous or disadvantageous remained for him undecided. Already from his military experience and what he had seen in the Austrian campaign, he had come to the conclusion that in war the most deeply considered plans have no significance, and that all depends on the way unexpected movements of the enemy—that cannot be foreseen—are met, and on how and by whom the whole matter is handled. To clear up this last point for himself Prince Andrew, utilizing his position and acquaintances, tried to fathom the character of the control of the army and of the men and parties engaged in it, and he deduced for himself the following idea of the state of affairs.

While the Emperor had still been at Vílna the forces had been divided into three armies. First, the army under Barclay de Tolly, secondly, the army under Bagratión, and thirdly the one commanded by Tormásov. The Emperor was with the first army but not as commander-in-chief. In the orders issued it was stated, not that the Emperor would take command, but only that he would be with the army. The Emperor moreover had with him not a commander-in-chief's staff but the imperial headquarters staff. In attendance on him was the head of the imperial staff, Quartermaster-General Prince Volkónski,

as well as generals, imperial aides-de-camp, diplomatic
officials, and a large number of foreigners, but not the
army staff. Besides these there were in attendance on the
Emperor without any definite appointments: Arakchéev,
the ex-Minister of War; Count Bennigsen, the senior
general in rank; the Grand Duke Tsarévich Constantine
Pávlovich; Count Rumyántsev, the Chancellor; Stein, a
former Prussian minister; Armfelt, a Swedish general;
Pfuel, the chief author of the plan of campaign; Paulucci,
an adjutant-general and Sardinian *émigré*; Wolzogen—
and many others. Though these men had no military
appointment in the army their position gave them influence, and often a corps commander, or even the commander-in-chief, did not know in what capacity he was
questioned by Bennigsen, the Grand Duke, Arakchéev,
or Prince Volkónski, or was given this or that advice, and
did not know whether a certain order received in the
form of advice emanated from the man who gave it or
from the Emperor, and whether it had to be executed or
not. But this was only the external condition; the essential significance of the presence of the Emperor and of all
these people, from a courtier's point of view (and in an
Emperor's vicinity all become courtiers), was clear to
every one. It was this: the Emperor did not assume the
title of commander-in-chief but disposed of all the armies;
the men around him were his assistants. Arakchéev was
a faithful custodian to enforce order, and acted as the
sovereign's bodyguard. Bennigsen was a landlord in the
Vílna province who appeared to be doing the honours of
the district, but was in reality a good general, useful as an
adviser and ready at hand to replace Barclay. The
Grand Duke was there because it suited him to be. The
ex-Minister Stein was there because his advice was useful
and the Emperor Alexander held him in high esteem
personally. Armfelt virulently hated Napoleon and was
a general full of self-confidence, a quality that always
influenced Alexander. Paulucci was there because he
was bold and decided in speech. The adjutants-general
were there because they always accompanied the Emperor, and lastly and chiefly Pfuel was there because he
had drawn up the plan of campaign against Napoleon

and, having induced Alexander to believe in the efficacy of that plan, was directing the whole business of the war. With Pfuel was Wolzogen, who expressed Pfuel's thought in a more comprehensible way than Pfuel himself—who was a harsh, bookish theorist, self-confident to the point of despising every one else—was able to do.

Besides these Russians and foreigners who propounded new and unexpected ideas every day—especially the foreigners, who did so with a boldness characteristic of people employed in a country not their own—there were many secondary personages accompanying the army because their principals were there.

Among the opinions and voices in this immense, restless, brilliant, and proud sphere, Prince Andrew noticed the following sharply defined sub-divisions of tendencies and parties.

The first party consisted of Pfuel and his adherents—military theorists who believed in a science of war with immutable laws—laws of oblique movements, outflankings, and so forth. Pfuel and his adherents demanded a retirement into the depths of the country in accordance with precise laws defined by a pseudo-theory of war, and they saw only barbarism, ignorance, or evil intention, in every deviation from that theory. To this party belonged the foreign nobles, Wolzogen, Wintzingerode, and others, chiefly Germans.

The second party was directly opposed to the first, one extreme, as always happens, was met by representatives of the other. The members of this party were those who had demanded an advance from Vílna into Poland, and freedom from all prearranged plans. Besides being advocates of bold action, this section also represented nationalism, which made them still more one-sided in the dispute. They were Russians: Bagratión, Ermólov who was beginning to come to the front), and others. At that time a famous joke of Ermólov's was being circulated, that as a great favour he had petitioned the Emperor to make him a German. The men of that party, remembering Suvórov, said that what one had to do was not to reason, or stick pins into maps, but to fight, beat the enemy, keep him out of Russia and not let the army get discouraged.

To the third party—in which the Emperor had most confidence—belonged the courtiers who tried to arrange compromises between the other two. The members of this party, chiefly civilians, and to whom Arakchéev belonged, thought and said what men who have no convictions but wish to seem to have some, generally say. They said that undoubtedly war, particularly against such a genius as Bonaparte (they called him Bonaparte again now), needs most deeply devised plans and profound scientific knowledge, and in that respect Pfuel was a genius, but at the same time it had to be acknowledged that theorists are often one-sided, and therefore one should not trust them absolutely, but should also listen to what Pfuel's opponents and practical men of experience in warfare had to say, and then choose a middle course. They insisted on the retention of the camp at Drissa according to Pfuel's plan, but on changing the movements of the other armies. Though by this course neither one aim nor the other could be attained, yet it seemed best to the adherents of this third party.

Of a fourth opinion the most conspicuous representative was the Tsarévich, who could not forget his disillusionment at Austerlitz, where he had ridden out at the head of the Guards, in his casque and cavalry uniform as to a review, expecting to crush the French gallantly; but unexpectedly finding himself in the front line had narrowly escaped amid the general confusion. The men of this party had both the quality and the defect of frankness in their opinions. They feared Napoleon, recognized his strength and their own weakness, and frankly said so. They said: 'Nothing but sorrow, shame, and ruin, will come of all this! We have abandoned Vílna and Vítebsk and shall abandon Drissa. The only reasonable thing left to do is to conclude peace as soon as possible, before we are turned out of Petersburg.'

This view was very general in the upper army circles, and found support also in Petersburg, and from the chancellor, Rumyántsev, who for other reasons of state was in favour of peace.

The fifth party consisted of those who were adherents of Barclay de Tolly, not so much as a man but as minister of war and commander-in-chief. 'Be he what he may' (they always began like that), 'he is an honest, practical man and we have nobody better. Give him real power, for war cannot be conducted successfully without unity of command, and he will show what he can do, as he did in Finland. If our army is well organized and strong and has withdrawn to Drissa without suffering any defeats, we owe this entirely to Barclay. If Barclay is now to be superseded by Bennigsen all will be lost, for Bennigsen showed his incapacity already in 1807.'

The sixth party, the Bennigsenites, said, on the contrary, that at any rate there was no one more active and experienced than Bennigsen: 'and twist about as you may you will have to come to Bennigsen eventually. Let the others make mistakes now!' said they, arguing that our retirement to Drissa was a most shameful reverse and an unbroken series of blunders. 'The more mistakes that are made the better. It will at any rate be understood all the sooner that things cannot go on like this. What is wanted is not some Barclay or other, but a man like Bennigsen, who made his mark in 1807, and to whom Napoleon himself did justice—a man whose authority would be willingly recognized, and Bennigsen is the only such man.'

The seventh party consisted of the sort of people who are always to be found, especially around young sovereigns, and of whom there were particularly many round Alexander—generals and imperial aides-de-camp passionately devoted to the Emperor, not merely as a monarch but as a man, adoring him sincerely and disinterestedly, as Rostóv had done in 1805, and who saw in him not only all the virtues but all human capabilities as well. These men, though enchanted with the sovereign for refusing the command of the army, yet blamed him for such excessive modesty, and only desired and insisted that their adored sovereign should abandon his diffidence and openly announce that he would place himself at the head of the army, gather round him a commander-in-chief's staff and, consulting experienced theoreticians and practical men where necessary, would himself lead the troops, whose spirits would thereby be raised to the highest pitch.

The eighth and largest group, which in its enormous numbers was to the others as ninety-nine to one, consisted of men who desired neither peace nor war, neither an advance nor a defensive camp at the Drissa or anywhere else, neither Barclay nor the Emperor, neither Pfuel nor Bennigsen, but only the one most essential thing—as much advantage and pleasure for themselves as possible. In the troubled waters of conflicting and intersecting intrigues that eddied about the Emperor's head-quarters, it was possible to succeed in many ways unthinkable at other times. A man who simply wished to retain his lucrative post would to-day agree with Pfuel, to-morrow with his opponent, and the day after, merely to avoid responsibility or to please the Emperor, would declare that he had no opinion at all on the matter. Another who wished to gain some advantage would attract the Emperor's attention by loudly advocating the very thing the Emperor had hinted at the day before, and would dispute and shout at the council, beating his breast and challenging those who did not agree with him to duels, thereby proving that he was prepared to sacrifice himself for the common good. A third, in the absence of opponents, between two councils would simply solicit a special gratuity for his faithful services, well knowing that at that moment people would be too busy to refuse him. A fourth would continually come accidentally under the Emperor's eye while overwhelmed with work. A fifth, to achieve his long-cherished aim of dining with the Emperor, would stubbornly insist on the correctness or falsity of some newly emerging opinion, and for this object would produce arguments more or less forcible and correct.

All the men of this party were fishing for rubles, decorations, and promotions, and in this pursuit watched only the weather-cock of imperial favour, and directly they noticed it turning in any direction, this whole drone-population of the army began blowing hard that way, so that it was all the harder for the Emperor to turn it else-where. Amid the uncertainties of the position, with the menace of serious danger giving a peculiarly threatening character to everything, amid this vortex of intrigue egotism, conflict of views and feelings, and the diversity of race among these people—this eighth and largest party of those preoccupied with personal interests imparted great confusion and obscurity to the common task. Whatever question arose, a swarm of these drones, without having finished their buzzing on a previous theme, flew over to the new one and by their hum drowned and obscured the voices of those who were disputing honestly.

From among all these parties, just at the time Prince Andrew reached the army, another, a ninth party, was being formed and was beginning to raise its voice. This was the party of the elders, reasonable men experienced and capable in state affairs, who without sharing any of those conflicting opinions were able to take a detached view of what was going on at the staff at head-quarters, and to consider means of escape from this muddle, indecision, intricacy, and weakness.

The men of this party said and thought that what was wrong resulted chiefly from the Emperor's presence in the army with his military court, and from the consequent presence there of an indefinite, conditional, and unsteady fluctuation of relations, which is in place at court but harmful in an army; that a sovereign should reign but not command the army, and that the only way out of the position would be for the Emperor and his court to leave the army; that the mere presence of the Emperor paralysed the action of fifty thousand men required to secure his personal safety, and that the worst commander-in-chief if independent would be better than the very best one trammelled by the presence and authority of the monarch.

Just at the time Prince Andrew was living unoccupied at Drissa, Shishkóv, the Secretary of State and one of the chief representatives of this party, wrote a letter to the Emperor which Arakchéev and Baláshev agreed to sign. In this letter, availing himself of permission given him by the Emperor to discuss the general course of affairs, he respectfully suggested—on the plea that it was necessary for the sovereign to arouse a warlike spirit in the people of the capital—that the Emperor should leave the army.

That arousing of the people by their sovereign, and his

call to them to defend their country—the very incitement which was the chief cause of Russia's triumph in so far as it was produced by the Tsar's personal presence in Moscow—was suggested to the Emperor, and accepted by him, as a pretext for quitting the army.

CHAPTER X

THIS letter had not yet been presented to the Emperor when Barclay one day at dinner informed Bolkónski that the sovereign wished to see him personally, to question him about Turkey, and that Prince Andrew was to present himself at Bennigsen's quarters at six that evening.

News was received at the Emperor's quarters that very day of a fresh movement by Napoleon which might endanger the army—news subsequently found to be false. And that morning Colonel Michaud had ridden round the Drissa fortifications with the Emperor and had pointed out to him that this fortified camp constructed by Pfuel, and till then considered a *chef-d'œuvre* of tactical science which would ensure Napoleon's destruction, was an absurdity, threatening the destruction of the Russian army.

Prince Andrew arrived at Bennigsen's quarters—a country gentleman's house of moderate size situated on the very banks of the river. Neither Bennigsen nor the Emperor was there, but Chernýshev, the Emperor's aide-de-camp, received Bolkónski and informed him that the Emperor, accompanied by General Bennigsen and Marquis Paulucci, had gone a second time that day to inspect the fortifications of the Drissa camp, of the suitability of which serious doubts were beginning to be felt.

Chernýshev was sitting at a window in the first room with a French novel in his hand. This room had probably been a music-room, there was still an organ in it on which some rugs were piled, and in one corner stood the folding bedstead of Bennigsen's adjutant. This adjutant was also there, and sat dozing on the rolled-up bedding, evidently exhausted by work or by feasting. Two doors led from the room, one straight on into what had been the drawing-

room, and another on the right to the study. Through
the first door came the sound of voices conversing in
German and occasionally in French. In that drawing-
room were gathered by the Emperor's wish, not a military council (the Emperor preferred indefiniteness) but
certain persons whose opinions he wished to know in view
of the impending difficulties. It was not a council of war,
but, as it were, a council to elucidate certain questions
for the Emperor personally. To this semi-council had
been invited the Swedish General Armfelt, Adjutant-
General Wolzogen, Wintzingerode (whom Napoleon had
referred to as a renegade French subject), Michaud, Toll,
Count Stein who was not a military man at all, and Pfuel
himself, who as Prince Andrew had heard was the main-
spring of the whole affair. Prince Andrew had an opportunity of getting a good look at him, for Pfuel arrived
soon after himself, and in passing through to the drawing-
room stopped a minute to speak to Chernýshev.

At first sight Pfuel, in his ill-made uniform of a Russian
general, which fitted him badly like a fancy costume,
seemed familiar to Prince Andrew though he saw him
now for the first time. There was about him something of Weyrother, Mack, and Schmidt, and many
other German theorist-generals whom Prince Andrew
had seen in 1805, but he was more typical than any of
them. Prince Andrew had never yet seen a German
theorist in whom all the characteristics of those others
were united to such an extent.

Pfuel was short and very thin but broad-boned, of
coarse, robust build, broad in the hips and with prominent shoulder-blades. His face was much wrinkled and
his eyes deep set. His hair had evidently been hastily
brushed smooth in front on the temples, but stuck up
behind in quaint little tufts. He entered the room looking
restlessly and angrily around, as if afraid of everything in
that large apartment. Awkwardly holding up his sword
he addressed Chernýshev, and asked in German where
the Emperor was. One could see that he wished to pass
through the rooms as quickly as possible, finish with the
bows and greetings, and sit down to business in front of a
map, where he would feel at home. He nodded hurriedly

in reply to Chernýshev, and smiled ironically on hearing that the sovereign was inspecting the fortifications that he, Pfuel, had planned in accord with his theory. He muttered something to himself abruptly and in a bass voice, as self-assured Germans do—it might have been 'stupid fellow' . . . or 'the whole affair will be ruined', or 'something absurd will come of it' . . . Prince Andrew did not catch what he said and would have passed on, but Chernýshev introduced him to Pfuel, remarking that Prince Andrew was just back from Turkey where the war had terminated so fortunately. Pfuel barely glanced —not so much at Prince Andrew as past him—and said with a laugh: 'That must have been a fine tactical war'; and laughing contemptuously went on into the room from which the sound of voices was heard.

Pfuel, always inclined to be irritably sarcastic, was particularly disturbed that day, evidently by the fact that they had dared to inspect and criticize his camp in his absence. From this short interview with Pfuel, Prince Andrew, thanks to his Austerlitz experiences, was able to form a clear conception of the man. Pfuel was one of those hopelessly and immutably self-confident men, self-confident to the point of martyrdom as only Germans are, because only Germans are self-confident on the basis of an abstract notion—science, that is, the supposed knowledge of absolute truth. A Frenchman is self-assured because he regards himself personally both in mind and body as irresistibly attractive to men and women. An Englishman is self-assured as being a citizen of the best-organized state in the world and therefore, as an Englishman, always knows what he should do and knows that all he does as an Englishman is undoubtedly correct. An Italian is self-assured because he is excitable and easily forgets himself and other people. A Russian is self-assured just because he knows nothing and does not want to know anything, since he does not believe that anything can be known. The German's self-assurance is worst of all, stronger and more repulsive than any other, because he imagines that he knows the truth—science— which he himself has invented but which is for him the absolute truth.

Pfuel was evidently of that sort. He had a science—the theory of oblique movements deduced by him from the history of Frederick the Great's wars, and all he came across in the history of more recent warfare seemed to him absurd and barbarous—monstrous collisions in which so many blunders were committed by both sides that these wars could not be called wars, they did not accord with the theory, and therefore could not serve as material for science.

In 1806 Pfuel had been one of those responsible for the plan of campaign that ended in Jena and Auerstadt, but he did not see the least proof of the fallibility of his theory in the disasters of that war. On the contrary, the deviations made from his theory were, in his opinion, the sole cause of the whole disaster, and with characteristically gleeful sarcasm he would remark, 'There, I said the whole affair would go to the devil!' Pfuel was one of those theoreticians who so love their theory that they lose sight of the theory's object—its practical application. His love of theory made him hate everything practical, and he would not listen to it. He was even pleased by failure, for failures resulting from deviations in practice from the theory, only proved to him the accuracy of his theory.

He said a few words to Prince Andrew and Chernýshev about the present war, with the air of a man who knows beforehand that all will go wrong, and who is not displeased that it should be so. The unbrushed tufts of hair sticking up behind and the hastily brushed hair on his temples expressed this most eloquently.

He passed into the next room, and the deep, querulous sounds of his voice were at once heard from there.

CHAPTER XI

PRINCE ANDREW'S eyes were still following Pfuel out of the room when Count Bennigsen entered hurriedly, and nodding to Bolkónski, but not pausing, went into the study giving instructions to his adjutant as he went. The Emperor was following him, and Bennigsen had hastened on to make some preparations and to be ready to receive the sovereign. Chernýshev and Prince Andrew went out into the porch, where the Emperor, who looked fatigued, was dismounting. Marquis Paulucci was talking to him with particular warmth and the Emperor, with his head bent to the left, was listening with a dissatisfied air. The Emperor moved forward evidently wishing to end the conversation, but the flushed and excited Italian oblivious of decorum followed him and continued to speak.

'And as for the man who advised forming this camp— the Drissa camp,' said Paulucci as the Emperor mounted the steps and noticing Prince Andrew scanned his unfamiliar face, 'as to that person, Sire . . .' continued Paulucci desperately, apparently unable to restrain himself, 'the man who advised the Drissa camp—I see no alternative but the lunatic asylum or the gallows!'

Without heeding the end of the Italian's remarks, and as though not hearing them, the Emperor, recognizing Bolkónski, addressed him graciously:

'I am very glad to see you! Go in there where they are meeting, and wait for me.'

The Emperor went into the study. He was followed by Prince Peter Mikháylovich Volkónski and Baron Stein, and the door closed behind them. Prince Andrew, taking advantage of the Emperor's permission, accompanied Paulucci, whom he had known in Turkey, into the drawing-room where the council was assembled.

Prince Peter Mikháylovich Volkónski occupied the position as it were of chief of the Emperor's staff. He came out of the study into the drawing-room with some maps which he spread on a table, and put questions on which he wished to hear the opinion of the gentlemen present. What had happened was that news (which afterwards proved to be false) had been received during the night of a movement by the French to outflank the Drissa camp.

The first to speak was General Armfelt who, to meet the difficulty that presented itself, unexpectedly proposed a perfectly new position away from the Petersburg and Moscow roads. The reason for this was inexplicable (unless he wished to show that he, too, could have an opinion), but he urged that at this point the army should unite and there await the enemy. It was plain that Armfelt had thought out that plan long ago, and now expounded it not so much to answer the questions put— which in fact his plan did not answer—as to avail himself of the opportunity to air it. It was one of the millions of proposals, one as good as another, that could be made as long as it was quite unknown what character the war would take. Some disputed his arguments, others defended them. Young Count Toll objected to the Swedish general's views more warmly than any one else, and in the course of the dispute drew from his side pocket a well-filled note-book which he asked permission to read to them. In these voluminous notes Toll suggested another scheme, totally different from Armfelt's or Pfuel's plan of campaign. In answer to Toll, Paulucci suggested an advance and an attack, which, he urged, could alone extricate us from the present uncertainty and from the trap (as he called the Drissa camp) in which we were situated. During all these discussions Pfuel and his interpreter Wolzogen (his 'bridge' in court relations) were silent. Pfuel only snorted contemptuously and turned away, to show that he would never demean himself by replying to such nonsense as he was now hearing. So when Prince Volkónski, who was in the chair, called on him to give his opinion, he merely said:

'Why ask me? General Armfelt has proposed a splendid position with an exposed rear, or why not this Italian gentleman's attack—very fine, or a retreat, also good! Why ask me?' said he. 'Why, you yourselves know everything better than I do.'

But when Volkónski said with a frown that it was in the Emperor's name that he asked his opinion, Pfuel rose and, suddenly growing animated, began to speak:

'Everything has been spoilt, everything muddled, everybody thought they knew better than I did, and now you come to me! How mend matters? There is nothing to mend! The principles laid down by me must be strictly adhered to,' said he, drumming on the table with his bony fingers. 'What is the difficulty? Nonsense, childishness!'

He went up to the map, and speaking rapidly began proving that no eventuality could alter the efficiency of the Drissa camp, that everything had been foreseen, and that if the enemy were really going to outflank it, the enemy would inevitably be destroyed.

Paulucci, who did not know German, began questioning him in French. Wolzogen came to the assistance of his chief, who spoke French badly, and began translating for him, hardly able to keep pace with Pfuel, who was rapidly demonstrating that not only all that had happened, but all that could happen, had been foreseen in his scheme, and that if there were now any difficulties the whole fault lay in the fact that his plan had not been precisely executed. He kept laughing sarcastically, he demonstrated, and at last contemptuously ceased to demonstrate, like a mathematician who ceases to prove in various ways the accuracy of a problem that has already been proven. Wolzogen took his place and continued to explain his views in French, every now and then turning to Pfuel and saying, 'Is it not so, your Excellency?' But Pfuel, like a man heated in a fight who strikes those on his own side, shouted angrily at his own supporter, Wolzogen:

'Well, of course, what more is there to explain?'

Paulucci and Michaud both attacked Wolzogen simultaneously in French. Armfelt addressed Pfuel in German. Toll explained to Volkónski in Russian. Prince Andrew listened and observed in silence.

Of all these men Prince Andrew sympathized most with Pfuel, angry, determined, and absurdly self-confident as he was. Of all those present evidently he alone was not seeking anything for himself, nursed no hatred against any one, and only desired that the plan, formed on a theory arrived at by years of toil, should be carried out. He was ridiculous, and unpleasantly sarcastic, but yet he inspired involuntary respect by his boundless devotion to an idea. Besides this, the remarks of all except Pfuel had one common trait that had not been noticeable at the council of war in 1805: there was now a panic fear of Napoleon's genius, which though concealed was noticeable in every rejoinder. Everything was assumed to be possible for Napoleon, they expected him from every side, and invoked his terrible name to shatter each other's proposals. Pfuel alone seemed to consider Napoleon a barbarian like every one else who opposed his theory. But besides this feeling of respect, Pfuel evoked pity in Prince Andrew. From the tone in which the courtiers addressed him, and the way Paulucci had allowed himself to speak of him to the Emperor, but above all from a certain desperation in Pfuel's own expressions, it was clear that the others knew, and Pfuel himself felt, that his fall was at hand. And despite his self-confidence and grumpy German sarcasm he was pitiable, with his hair smoothly brushed on the temples and sticking up in tufts behind. Though he concealed the fact under a show of irritation and contempt, he was evidently in despair that the sole remaining chance of verifying his theory by a huge experiment and proving its soundness to the whole world, was slipping away from him.

The discussions continued a long time, and the longer they lasted the more heated became the disputes, culminating in shouts and personalities, and the less was it possible to arrive at any general conclusion from all that had been said. Prince Andrew, listening to this polyglot talk and to these surmises, plans, refutations and shouts, felt nothing but amazement at what they were saying. A thought that had long since and often occurred to him during his military activities—the idea that there is not, and cannot be, any science of war, and that therefore there can be no such thing as a military genius—now appeared to him an obvious truth. 'What theory and science is possible about a matter the conditions and circumstances of which are unknown and cannot be defined, especially when the strength of the acting forces cannot be ascertained? No one was or is able to foresee in what condition our or the enemy's armies will be in a day's time, and no one can gauge the force of this or that detachment. Sometimes—when there is not a coward at the front to shout, "We are cut off" and start running, but a brave and jolly lad who shouts "Hurrah!"—a detachment of five thousand is worth thirty thousand, as at Schön Grabern, while at times fifty thousand run from eight thousand as at Austerlitz. What science can there be in a matter in which, as in all practical matters, nothing can be defined, and everything depends on innumerable conditions the significance of which is determined at a particular moment which arrives no one knows when? Armfelt says our army is cut in half, and Paulucci says we have got the French army between two fires, Michaud says that the worthlessness of the Drissa camp lies in having the river behind it, and Pfuel says that is what constitutes its strength, Toll proposes one plan, Armfelt another, and they are all good and all bad, and the advantages of any suggestion can only be seen at the moment of trial. And why do they all speak of a "military genius"? Is a man a genius who can order bread to be brought up at the right time and say who is to go to the right and who to the left? It is only because military men are invested with pomp and power, and crowds of sycophants flatter power, attributing to it qualities of genius it does not possess. The best generals I have known were, on the contrary, stupid or absent-minded men. Bagratión was the best, Napoleon himself admitted that. And Bonaparte himself! I remember his limited, self-satisfied face on the field of Austerlitz. Not only does a good army commander not need any special qualities, on the contrary he needs the absence of the highest and best human attributes—love, poetry, tenderness, and philosophic inquiring doubt. He should be limited, firmly convinced that what he is doing is very important (otherwise he will not have sufficient patience), and only then will he be a brave leader. God forbid that he should be humane, should love, or pity, or think of what is just and unjust. It is understandable that a theory of their "genius" was invented for them long ago because they have power! The success of a military action depends not on them, but on the man in the ranks who shouts "We are lost!" or who shouts "Hurrah!" And only in the ranks can one serve with assurance of being useful.'

So thought Prince Andrew as he listened to the talking, and he roused himself only when Paulucci called him and every one was leaving.

At the review next day the Emperor asked Prince Andrew where he would like to serve, and Prince Andrew lost his standing in court circles for ever by not asking to remain attached to the sovereign's person, but for permission to serve in the army.

CHAPTER XII

BEFORE the beginning of the campaign Rostóv had received a letter from his parents in which they told him briefly of Natásha's illness and the breaking off of her engagement to Prince Andrew (which they explained by Natásha's having rejected him) and again asked Nicholas to retire from the army and return home. On receiving this letter Nicholas did not even make any attempt to get leave of absence or to retire from the army, but wrote to his parents that he was sorry Natásha was ill and her engagement broken off, and that he would do all he could to meet their wishes. To Sónya he wrote separately.

'Adored friend of my soul!' he wrote. 'Nothing but honour could keep me from returning to the country. But now, at the commencement of the campaign, I should feel dishonoured not only in my comrades' eyes but in my own if I preferred my own happiness to my love and duty to the Fatherland. But this shall be our last separation. Believe me, directly the war is over, if I am still alive and still loved by you, I will throw up everything and fly to you, to press you for ever to my ardent breast.'

It was, in fact, only the commencement of the campaign that prevented Rostóv from returning home as he had promised, and marrying Sónya. The autumn in Otrádnoe with the hunting, and the winter with the Christmas holidays and Sónya's love, had opened out to him a vista of tranquil rural joys and peace such as he had never known before, and which now allured him. 'A splendid wife, children, a good pack of hounds, a dozen leashes of smart borzois, agriculture, neighbours, service by election [1] . . .' thought he. But now the cam-

[1] He meant that he might be elected by the local nobility to some administrative post.

paign was beginning and he had to remain with his regiment. And since it had to be so, Nicholas Rostóv, as was natural to him, felt contented with the life he led in the regiment, and was able to find pleasure in that life.

On his return from his furlough Nicholas, having been joyfully welcomed by his comrades, was sent to obtain remounts, and brought back from the Ukraine excellent horses which pleased him and earned him commendation from his commanders. During his absence he had been promoted Captain, and when the regiment was put on war-footing with an increase in numbers, he was again allotted his old squadron.

The campaign began, the regiment was moved into Poland on double pay, new officers arrived, new men and horses, and above all, everybody was infected with the merrily excited mood that goes with the commencement of a war, and Rostóv, conscious of his advantageous position in the regiment, devoted himself entirely to the pleasures and interests of military service, though he knew that sooner or later he would have to relinquish them.

The troops retired from Vílna for various complicated reasons of state, political and strategic. Each step of the retreat was accompanied by a complicated interplay of interests, arguments, and passions, at head-quarters. For the Pávlograd Hussars however the whole of this retreat during the finest period of summer and with sufficient supplies, was a very simple and agreeable business.

It was only at head-quarters that there was depression, uneasiness, and intriguing; in the body of the army they did not ask themselves where they were going or why. If they regretted having to retreat, it was only because they had to leave billets they had grown accustomed to, or some pretty young Polish lady. If the thought that things looked bad chanced to enter any one's head, he tried to be cheerful as befits a good soldier, and not to think of the general trend of affairs, but only of the task nearest to hand. First they camped gaily before Vílna, making acquaintance with the Polish landowners, preparing for reviews, and being reviewed by the Emperor and other high commanders. Then came an order to retreat to Sventsyáni and destroy any provisions they could not carry away with them. Sventsyáni was remembered by the hussars only as the *drunken camp*, a name the whole army gave to their encampment there, and because many complaints were made against the troops, who taking advantage of the order to collect provisions, took also horses, carriages, and carpets, from the Polish proprietors. Rostóv remembered Sventsyáni because on the first day of their arrival at that small town he changed his sergeant-major, and was unable to manage all the drunken men of the squadron who, unknown to him, had appropriated five barrels of old beer. From Sventsyáni they retired farther and farther to Drissa, and thence again beyond Drissa, drawing near to the frontier of Russia proper.

On the 13th of July the Pávlograds took part in a serious action for the first time.

On the 12th of July, on the eve of that action, there was a heavy storm of rain and hail. In general the summer of 1812 was remarkable for its storms.

The two Pávlograd squadrons were bivouacking on a field of rye, which was already in ear but had been completely trodden down by cattle and horses. The rain was descending in torrents, and Rostóv with a young officer named Ilyín, his protégé, was sitting in a hastily constructed shelter. An officer of their regiment, with long moustaches extending onto his cheeks, who after riding to the staff had been overtaken by the rain, entered Rostóv's shelter.

'I have come from the staff, Count. Have you heard of Raévski's exploit?'

And the officer gave them details of the Saltánov battle, which he had heard at the staff.

Rostóv, smoking his pipe and turning his head about as the water trickled down his neck, listened inattentively, with an occasional glance at Ilyín who was pressing close to him. This officer, a lad of sixteen who had recently joined the regiment, was now in the same relation to Nicholas that Nicholas had been to Denísov seven years before. Ilyín tried to imitate Rostóv in everything, and adored him as a girl might have done.

Zdrzhinski, the officer with the long moustache, spoke

grandiloquently of the Saltánov dam being 'a Russian Thermopylae,' and of how a deed worthy of antiquity had been performed by General Raévski. He recounted how Raévski had led his two sons onto the dam under terrific fire, and had charged with them beside him. Rostóv heard the story and not only said nothing to encourage Zdrzhinski's enthusiasm, but on the contrary looked like a man ashamed of what he was hearing, though with no intention of contradicting it. Since the campaigns of Austerlitz and of 1807 Rostóv knew by experience that men always lie when describing military exploits, as he himself had done when recounting them; besides that, he had experience enough to know that nothing happens in war at all as we can imagine or relate it. And so he did not like Zdrzhinski's tale, nor did he like Zdrzhinski himself who, with his moustaches extending over his cheeks, bent low over the face of his hearer, as was his habit, and crowded Rostóv in the narrow shanty. Rostóv looked at him in silence. 'In the first place, there must have been such a confusion and crowding on the dam that was being attacked, that if Raévski did lead his sons there it could have had no effect except perhaps on some dozen men nearest to him,' thought he, 'the rest could not have seen how or with whom Raévski came onto the dam. And even those who did see it would not have been much stimulated by it, for what had they to do with Raévski's tender paternal feelings when their own skins were in danger? And besides, the fate of the Fatherland did not depend on whether they took the Saltánov dam or not, as we are told was the case at Thermopylae. So why should he have made such a sacrifice? And why expose his own children in the battle? I would not have taken my brother Pétya there, or even Ilyín, who's a stranger to me but a nice lad, but would have tried to put them somewhere under cover,' Nicholas continued to think, as he listened to Zdrzhinski. But he did not express his thoughts for in such matters, too, he had gained experience. He knew that this tale redounded to the glory of our arms and so one had to pretend not to doubt it. And he acted accordingly.

'I can't stand this any more,' said Ilyín, noticing that

Rostóv did not relish Zdrzhinski's conversation. 'My stockings and shirt . . . and the water is running on my seat! I'll go and look for shelter. The rain seems less heavy.'

Ilyín went out and Zdrzhinski rode away.

Five minutes later Ilyín, splashing through the mud, came running back to the shanty.

'Hurrah! Rostóv, come quick! I've found it! About two hundred yards away there's a tavern where *ours* have already gathered. We can at least get dry there, and Mary Hendríkhovna's there.'

Mary Hendríkhovna was the wife of the regimental doctor, a pretty young German woman he had married in Poland. The doctor, whether from lack of means or because he did not like to part from his young wife in the early days of their marriage, took her about with him wherever the hussar regiment went, and his jealousy had become a standing joke among the hussar officers.

Rostóv threw his cloak over his shoulders, shouted to Lavrúshka to follow with the things, and—now slipping in the mud, now splashing right through it—set off with Ilyín in the lessening rain, and the darkness that was occasionally rent by distant lightning.

'Rostóv, where are you?'

'Here. What lightning!' they called to one another.

CHAPTER XIII

IN the tavern, before which stood the doctor's covered cart, there were already some five officers. Mary Hendríkhovna, a plump little blonde German, in a dressing-jacket and night-cap, was sitting on a broad bench in the front corner. Her husband, the doctor, lay asleep behind her. Rostóv and Ilyín on entering the room were welcomed with merry shouts and laughter.

'Dear me, how jolly we are!' said Rostóv laughing.

'And why do you stand there gaping?'

'What swells they are! Why, the water streams from them! Don't make our drawing-room so wet.'

'Don't mess Mary Hendríkhovna's dress!' cried other voices.

Rostóv and Ilyín hastened to find a corner where they could change into dry clothes without offending Mary Hendríkhovna's modesty. They were going into a tiny recess behind a partition to change, but found it completely filled by three officers who sat playing cards by the light of a solitary candle on an empty box, and these officers would on no account yield their position. Mary Hendríkhovna obliged them with the loan of a petticoat, to be used as a curtain, and behind that screen Rostóv and Ilyín, helped by Lavrúshka who had brought their kits, changed their wet things for dry ones.

A fire was made up in the dilapidated brick stove. A board was found, fixed on two saddles and covered with a horse-cloth, a small samovar was produced and a cellaret and half a bottle of rum, and having asked Mary Hendríkhovna to preside they all crowded round her. One offered her a clean handkerchief to wipe her charming hands, another spread a jacket under her little feet to keep them from the damp, another hung his coat over the window to keep out the draught, and yet another waved the flies off her husband's face lest he should wake up.

'Leave him alone,' said Mary Hendríkhovna, smiling timidly and happily. 'He is sleeping well as it is, after a sleepless night.'

'Oh, no, Mary Hendríkhovna,' replied the officer, 'one must look after the doctor. Perhaps he'll take pity on me some day, when it comes to cutting off a leg or an arm for me.'

There were only three tumblers, the water was so muddy that one could not make out whether the tea was strong or weak, and the samovar held only six tumblers of water, but this made it all the pleasanter to take turns in order of seniority to receive one's tumbler from Mary Hendríkhovna's plump little hands with their short and not over-clean nails. All the officers appeared to be and really were in love with her that evening. Even those playing cards behind the partition soon left their game and came over to the samovar, yielding to the general mood of courting Mary Hendríkhovna. She, seeing herself surrounded by such brilliant and polite young men, beamed with satisfaction, try as she might to hide it, and perturbed as she evidently was each time her husband moved in his sleep behind her.

There was only one spoon, sugar was more plentiful than anything else but it took too long to dissolve, so it was decided that Mary Hendríkhovna should stir the sugar for every one in turn. Rostóv received his tumbler, and adding some rum to it asked Mary Hendríkhovna to stir it.

'But you take it without sugar?' she said, smiling all the time as if everything she said and everything the others said was very amusing and had a double meaning.

'It is not the sugar I want, but only that your little hand should stir my tea.'

Mary Hendríkhovna assented and began looking for the spoon which some one meanwhile had pounced on.

'Use your finger, Mary Hendríkhovna, it will be still nicer,' said Rostóv.

'Too hot!' she replied, blushing with pleasure.

Ilyín put a few drops of rum into the bucket of water and brought it to Mary Hendríkhovna asking her to stir it with her finger.

'This is my cup,' said he. 'Only dip your finger in it and I'll drink it all up.'

When they had emptied the samovar Rostóv took a pack of cards and proposed that they should play 'Kings' with Mary Hendríkhovna. They drew lots to settle who should make up her set. At Rostov's suggestion it was agreed that whoever became 'King' should have the right to kiss Mary Hendríkhovna's hand, and that the 'Booby' should go to refill and reheat the samovar for the doctor when the latter awoke.

'Well, but supposing Mary Hendríkhovna is "King"?' asked Ilyín.

'As it is, she is Queen, and her word is law!'

They had hardly begun to play before the doctor's dishevelled head suddenly appeared from behind Mary Hendríkhovna. He had been awake some time, listening to what was being said, and evidently found nothing entertaining or amusing in what was going on. His face was sad and depressed. Without greeting the officers, he scratched himself and asked to be allowed to pass as they were blocking the way. As soon as he had left the room all the officers burst into loud laughter, and Mary Hendríkhovna blushed till her eyes filled with tears and thereby became still more attractive to them. Returning from the yard the doctor told his wife (who had ceased to smile so happily, and looked at him in alarm awaiting her sentence) that the rain had ceased and they must go to sleep in their covered cart, or everything in it would be stolen.

'But I'll send an orderly . . . Two of them!' said Rostóv. 'What an idea, doctor!'

'I'll stand guard on it myself!' said Ilyín.

'No, gentlemen, you have had your sleep, but I have not slept for two nights,' replied the doctor, and he sat down morosely beside his wife waiting for the game to end.

Seeing his gloomy face as he frowned at his wife, the officers grew still merrier, and some of them could not refrain from laughter, for which they hurriedly sought plausible pretexts. When he had gone, taking his wife with him, and had settled down with her in their covered cart, the officers lay down in the tavern, covering themselves with their wet cloaks, but they did not sleep for a long time; now they exchanged remarks, recalling the doctor's uneasiness and his wife's delight, now they ran out into the porch and reported what was taking place in the covered trap. Several times Rostóv, covering his head, tried to go to sleep, but some remark would arouse him and conversation would be resumed, to the accompaniment of unreasoning, merry, childlike laughter.

CHAPTER XIV

IT was nearly three o'clock but no one was yet asleep, when the quartermaster appeared with an order to move on to the little town of Ostróvna.

Still laughing and talking, the officers began hurriedly getting ready, and again boiled some muddy water in the samovar. But Rostóv went off to his squadron without waiting for tea. Day was breaking, the rain had ceased and the clouds were dispersing. It felt damp and cold, especially in clothes that were still moist. As they left the tavern in the twilight of the dawn Rostóv and Ilyín both glanced under the wet and glistening leather hood of the doctor's cart, from under the apron of which his feet were sticking out, and in the middle of which his wife's night-cap was visible and her sleepy breathing audible.

'She really is a dear little thing,' said Rostóv to Ilyín who was following him.

'A charming woman!' said Ilyín with all the gravity of a boy of sixteen.

Half an hour later the squadron was lined up on the road. The command was heard to 'mount' and the soldiers crossed themselves and mounted. Rostóv riding in front gave the order 'Forward!' and the hussars, with clanking sabres and subdued talk, their horses' hoofs splashing in the mud, defiled in fours and moved along the broad road planted with birch-trees on each side, following the infantry and a battery that had gone on in front.

Tattered, blue-purple clouds, reddening in the east, were scudding before the wind. It was growing lighter and lighter. That curly grass which always grows by country roadsides became clearly visible, still wet with the night's rain, the drooping branches of the birches, also wet, swayed in the wind and flung down bright drops of water to one side. The soldiers' faces were more and more clearly visible. Rostóv, always closely followed by Ilyín, rode along the side of the road between two rows of birch-trees.

When campaigning, Rostóv allowed himself the indulgence of riding not a regimental but a Cossack horse. A judge of horses and a sportsman, he had lately procured himself a large, fine, mettlesome, Donéts horse, duncoloured with light mane and tail, and when he rode it no one could out-gallop him. To ride this horse was a pleasure to him, and he thought of the horse, of the morning, of the doctor's wife, but not once of the impending danger.

Formerly, when going into action, Rostóv had felt afraid, now he had not the least feeling of fear. He was fearless not because he had grown used to being under fire (one cannot grow used to danger), but because he had learned how to manage his thoughts when in danger. He had grown accustomed when going into action to think about anything but what would seem most likely to interest him—the impending danger. During the first period of his service, hard as he tried and much as he reproached himself with cowardice, he had not been able to do this, but with time it had come of itself. Now he rode beside Ilyín under the birch-trees, occasionally plucking leaves from a branch that met his hand, sometimes touching his horse's side with his foot, or without turning round handing a pipe he had finished to an hussar riding behind him, with as calm and careless an air as though he were merely out for a ride. He glanced with pity at the excited face of Ilyín, who talked much and in great agitation. He knew from experience the tormenting expectation of terror and death the cornet was suffering, and knew that only time could help him.

As soon as the sun appeared in a clear strip of sky beneath the clouds, the wind fell, as if it dared not spoil the beauty of the summer morning after the storm; drops still continued to fall, but vertically now, and all was still. The whole sun appeared on the horizon and disappeared behind a long, narrow cloud that hung above it. A few minutes later it reappeared brighter still from behind the top of the cloud, tearing its edge. Everything grew bright and glittered. And with that light, and as if in reply to it, came the sound of guns ahead of them.

Before Rostóv had had time to consider and determine the distance of that firing, Count Ostermann-Tolstóy's adjutant came galloping from Vítebsk with orders to advance at a trot along the road.

The squadron overtook and passed the infantry and the battery—which had also quickened their pace—rode down a hill, and passing through an empty and deserted village again ascended. The horses began to lather and the men to flush.

'Halt! Dress your ranks!' the order of the regimental commander was heard ahead. 'Forward by the left. Walk, march!' came the order from in front.

And the hussars, passing along the line of troops on the left flank of our position, halted behind our uhlans who were in the front line. To the right stood our infantry in a dense column: they were the reserve. Higher up the hill, on the very horizon, our guns were visible through the wonderfully clear air, brightly illuminated by slanting morning sunbeams. In front, beyond a hollow dale, could be seen the enemy's columns and guns. Our advanced line, already in action, could be heard briskly exchanging shots with the enemy in the dale.

At these sounds, long unheard, Rostóv's spirits rose as at the strains of the merriest music. *Trap-ta-ta-tap!* cracked the shots, now together, now several quickly one after another. Again all was silent, and then again it sounded as if some one were walking on detonators and exploding them.

The hussars remained in the same place for about an hour. A cannonade began. Count Ostermann with his suite rode up behind the squadron, halted, spoke to the commander of the regiment, and rode up the hill to the guns.

After Ostermann had gone a command rang out to the uhlans.

'Form column! Prepare to charge!'

The infantry in front of them parted into platoons to allow the cavalry to pass. The uhlans started, the streamers on their spears fluttering, and trotted downhill towards the French cavalry which was seen below to the left.

As soon as the uhlans descended the hill the hussars were ordered up the hill to support the battery. As they took the places vacated by the uhlans, bullets came from the front, whining and whistling, but fell spent without taking effect.

These sounds, which he had not heard for so long, had an even more pleasurable and exhilarating effect on Rostóv than the previous sounds of firing. Drawing himself up he viewed the field of battle opening out before him from the hill, and with his whole soul followed the movement of the uhlans. They swooped down close to the French dragoons, something confused happened there amid the smoke, and five minutes later our uhlans were galloping back, not to the place they had occupied but more to the left, and among the orange-coloured uhlans on chestnut horses and behind them in a large group, blue French dragoons on grey horses could be seen.

CHAPTER XV

ROSTÓV, with his keen sportsman's eye, was one of the first to catch sight of these blue French dragoons pursuing our uhlans. Nearer and nearer in disorderly crowds came the uhlans and the French dragoons pursuing them. He could already see how these men, who looked so small at the foot of the hill, jostled and overtook one another waving their arms and their sabres in the air.

Rostóv gazed at what was happening before him as at a hunt. He felt instinctively that if the hussars struck at the French dragoons now, the latter could not withstand them, but if a charge was to be made it must be done now, that very moment, or it would be too late. He looked round. A captain, standing beside him, was gazing like himself with eyes fixed on the cavalry below them.

'Andrew Sevastyánych!' said Rostóv. 'You know, we could crush them . . .'

'A fine thing, too!' replied the captain, 'and really . . .'

Rostóv without waiting to hear him out touched his horse, galloped to the front of the squadron, and before he had time to finish giving the word of command, the whole squadron, sharing his feeling, was following him. Rostóv himself did not know how or why he did it. He acted as he did when hunting, without reflecting or considering. He saw the dragoons near, and that they were galloping in disorder; he knew they could not withstand an attack—knew there was only that moment, and that if he let it slip it would not return. The bullets were whining and whistling so stimulatingly around him

and his horse was so eager to go, that he could not restrain
himself. He touched his horse, gave the word of command, and immediately, hearing behind him the tramp
of the horses of his deployed squadron, rode at full trot
downhill towards the dragoons. Hardly had they reached
the bottom of the hill before their pace instinctively
changed to a gallop, which grew faster and faster as they
drew nearer to our uhlans and the French dragoons who
galloped after them. The dragoons were now close at
hand. On seeing our hussars the foremost began to turn,
while those behind began to halt. With the same feeling
with which he had galloped across the path of a wolf,
Rostóv gave rein to his Donéts horse and galloped to
intersect the path of the dragoons' disordered lines. One
uhlan stopped, another who was on foot flung himself
to the ground to avoid being knocked over, and a rider-
less horse fell in among the hussars. Nearly all the
French dragoons were galloping back. Rostóv, picking
out one on a grey horse, dashed after him. On the way he
came upon a bush, his gallant horse cleared it, and almost
before he had righted himself in his saddle he saw that he
would immediately overtake the enemy he had selected.
That Frenchman, by his uniform an officer, was going at
a gallop crouching on his grey horse and urging it on with
his sabre. In another moment Rostóv's horse dashed its
breast against the hind quarters of the officer's horse almost
knocking it over, and at the same instant Rostóv, without knowing why, raised his sabre and struck the Frenchman with it.

The instant he had done this, all Rostóv's animation
vanished. The officer fell, not so much from the blow—
which had but slightly cut his arm above the elbow—as
from the shock to his horse and from fright. Rostóv
reined in his horse, and his eyes sought his foe to see whom
he had vanquished. The French dragoon officer was
hopping with one foot on the ground, the other being
caught in the stirrup. His eyes, screwed up with fear as
if he every moment expected another blow, gazed up at
Rostóv with shrinking terror. His pale and mud-stained
face—fair and young, with a dimple in the chin and light
blue eyes—was not an enemy's face at all suited to

a battle-field, but a most ordinary, homelike face. Before
Rostóv had decided what to do with him the officer cried,
'I surrender!' He hurriedly but vainly tried to get his
foot out of the stirrup, and did not remove his frightened
blue eyes from Rostóv's face. Some hussars who galloped
up disengaged his foot and helped him into the saddle.
On all sides the hussars were busy with the dragoons;
one was wounded, but though his face was bleeding he
would not give up his horse; another was perched up
behind an hussar with his arms round him; a third was
being helped by an hussar to mount his horse. In front
the French infantry were firing as they ran. The hussars
galloped hastily back with their prisoners. Rostóv galloped back with the rest, aware of an unpleasant feeling
of depression in his heart. Something vague and confused, which he could not at all account for, had come
over him with the capture of that officer and the blow he
had dealt him.

Count Ostermann-Tolstóy met the returning hussars,
sent for Rostóv, thanked him, and said he would report
his gallant deed to the Emperor and would recommend
him for a St. George's Cross. When sent for by Count
Ostermann, Rostóv, remembering that he had charged
without orders, felt sure his commander was sending for
him to punish him for breach of discipline. Ostermann's
flattering words and promise of a reward should therefore have struck him all the more pleasantly, but he still
felt that same vaguely disagreeable feeling of moral
nausea. 'But what on earth is worrying me?' he asked
himself as he rode back from the general. 'Ilyín? No,
he's safe. Have I disgraced myself in any way? No,
that's not it.' Something else, resembling remorse,
tormented him. 'Yes, oh yes, that French officer with
the dimple. And I remember how my arm paused when
I raised it.'

Rostóv saw the prisoners being led away, and galloped
after them to have a look at his Frenchman with the
dimple on his chin. He was sitting in his foreign uniform
on an hussar pack-horse and looked anxiously about him.
The sword-cut on his arm could scarcely be called a
wound. He glanced at Rostóv with a feigned smile, and

waved his hand in greeting. Rostóv still had the same indefinite feeling, as of shame.

All that day and the next his friends and comrades noticed that Rostóv, without being dull or angry, was silent, thoughtful, and preoccupied. He drank reluctantly, tried to remain alone, and kept turning something over in his mind.

Rostóv was always thinking about that brilliant exploit of his, which to his amazement had gained him the St. George's Cross and even given him a reputation for bravery, and there was something he could not at all understand. 'So others are even more afraid than I am!' he thought. 'So that's all there is in what is called heroism! And did I do it for my country's sake? And how was he to blame, with his dimple and blue eyes? And how frightened he was! He thought I should kill him. Why should I kill him? My hand trembled. And they have given me a St. George's Cross. I can't make it out at all.'

But while Nicholas was considering these questions and still could reach no clear solution of what puzzled him so, the wheel of fortune in the service, as often happens, turned in his favour. After the affair at Ostróvna he was brought into notice, received command of an hussar battalion, and when a brave officer was needed he was chosen.

CHAPTER XVI

ON receiving news of Natásha's illness, the countess, though not quite well yet and still weak, went to Moscow with Pétya and the rest of the household, and the whole family moved from Márya Dmítrievna's house to their own, and settled down in town.

Natásha's illness was so serious that, fortunately for her and for her parents, the consideration of all that had caused the illness, her conduct and the breaking off of her engagement, receded into the background. She was so ill that it was impossible for them to consider in how far she was to blame for what had happened. She could not eat or sleep, grew visibly thinner, coughed and, as the doctors made them feel, was in danger. They could

not think of anything but how to help her. Doctors
came to see her singly and in consultation, talked much
in French, German, and Latin, blamed one another, and
prescribed a great variety of medicines for all the diseases
known to them, but the simple idea never occurred to
any of them that they could not know the disease Natásha
was suffering from, as no disease suffered by a live man
can be known, for every living person has his own
peculiarities and always has his own peculiar, personal, novel, complicated disease, unknown to medicine
—not a disease of the lungs, liver, skin, heart, nerves,
and so on mentioned in medical books, but a disease
consisting of one of the innumerable combinations of the
maladies of those organs. This simple thought could not
occur to the doctors (as it cannot occur to a wizard that
he is unable to work charms) because the business of their
lives was to cure, and they received money for it and had
spent the best years of their lives on that business. But
above all that thought was kept out of their minds by
the fact that they saw they were really useful, as in fact
they were to the whole Rostóv family. Their usefulness
did not depend on making the patient swallow substances
for the most part harmful (the harm was scarcely perceptible as they were given in small doses) but they were
useful, necessary, and indispensable, because they satisfied
a mental need of the invalid and of those who loved her—
and that is why there are, and always will be, pseudo-
healers, wise women, homoeopaths, and allopaths. They
satisfied that eternal human need for hope of relief, for
sympathy, and that something should be done, which
is felt by those who are suffering. They satisfied the need
seen in its most elementary form in a child, when it wants
to have a place rubbed that has been hurt. A child
knocks itself and runs at once to the arms of its mother
or nurse to have the aching spot rubbed or kissed, and it
feels better when this is done. The child cannot believe that
the strongest and wisest of its people have no remedy for
its pain, and the hope of relief and the expression of its
mother's sympathy while she rubs the bump, comforts it.
The doctors were of use to Natásha because they kissed
and rubbed her bump, assuring her that it would soon

pass if only the coachman went to the chemist's in the Arbát and got a powder and some pills in a pretty box for a ruble and seventy kopeks, and if she took those powders in boiled water at intervals of precisely two hours, neither more nor less.

What would Sónya and the count and countess have done, how would they have looked, if nothing had been done, if there had not been those pills to give by the clock, the warm drinks, the chicken cutlets, and all the other details of life ordered by the doctors, the carrying out of which supplied an occupation and consolation to the family circle? How would the count have borne his dearly loved daughter's illness had he not known that it was costing him a thousand rubles, and that he would not grudge thousands more to benefit her, or had he not known that if her illness continued he would not grudge yet other thousands and would take her abroad for consultations there, and had he not been able to explain the details of how Métivier and Feller had not understood the symptoms, but Frise had, and Múdrov had diagnosed them even better? What would the countess have done had she not been able sometimes to scold the invalid for not strictly obeying the doctor's orders?

'You'll never get well like that,' she would say, forgetting her grief in her vexation, 'if you won't obey the doctor and take your medicine at the right time! You musn't trifle with it, you know, or it may turn to *pneumonia*,' she would go on, deriving much comfort from the utterance of that foreign word, incomprehensible to others as well as to herself.

What would Sónya have done without the glad consciousness that she had not undressed during the first three nights, in order to be ready to carry out all the doctor's injunctions with precision, and that she still kept awake at night so as not to miss the proper time when the slightly harmful pills in the little gilt box had to be administered? Even to Natásha herself it was pleasant to see that so many sacrifices were being made for her sake, and to know that she had to take medicine at certain hours, though she declared that no medicine would cure her and that it was all nonsense. And it was even pleasant to be able to show, by disregarding the orders, that she did not believe in medical treatment and did not value her life.

The doctor came every day, felt her pulse, looked at her tongue, and regardless of her grief-stricken face joked with her. But when he had gone into another room, to which the countess hurriedly followed him, he assumed a grave air and thoughtfully shaking his head said that though there was danger, he had hopes of the effect of this last medicine and one must wait and see, that the malady was chiefly mental, but . . .' And the countess, trying to conceal the action from herself and from him, slipped a gold coin into his hand, and always returned to the patient with a more tranquil mind.

The symptoms of Natásha's illness were that she ate little, slept little, coughed, and was always low-spirited. The doctors said that she could not get on without medical treatment, so they kept her in the stifling atmosphere of the town, and the Rostóvs did not move to the country that summer of 1812.

In spite of the many pills she swallowed and the drops and powders out of the little bottles and boxes of which Madame Schoss, who was fond of such things, made a large collection, and in spite of being deprived of the country life to which she was accustomed, youth prevailed. Natásha's grief began to be overlaid by the impressions of daily life, it ceased to press so painfully on her heart, it gradually faded into the past, and she began to recover physically.

CHAPTER XVII

NATÁSHA was calmer but no happier. She not merely avoided all external forms of pleasure—balls, promenades, concerts, and theatres—but she never laughed without a sound of tears in her laughter. She could not sing. As soon as she began to laugh, or tried to sing by herself, tears choked her: tears of remorse, tears at the recollection of those pure times which could never return, tears of vexation that she should so uselessly have ruined her young life which might have been so

happy. Laughter and singing in particular seemed to
her like a blasphemy, in face of her sorrow. Without any
need of self-restraint no wish to coquet ever entered her
head. She said and felt at that time that no man was
more to her than Nastásya Ivánovna, the buffoon. Something stood sentinel within her and forbade her every
joy. Besides, she had lost all the old interests of her care-
free girlish life that had been so full of hope. The previous
autumn, the hunting, 'Uncle', and the Christmas holidays
spent with Nicholas at Otrádnoe, were what she recalled
oftenest and most painfully. What would she not have
given to bring back even a single day of that time! But
it was gone for ever. Her presentiment at the time had
not deceived her—that that state of freedom and readiness for any enjoyment would not return again. Yet it
was necessary to live on.

It comforted her to reflect that she was not better, as
she had formerly imagined, but worse, much worse,
than anybody else in the world. But this was not enough.
She knew that, and asked herself, 'What next?' But there
was nothing to come. There was no joy in life, yet life was
passing. Natásha apparently tried not to be a burden
or a hindrance to any one, but wanted nothing for herself.
She kept away from every one in the house, and only felt
at ease with her brother Pétya. She liked to be with him
better than with the others, and when alone with him
she sometimes laughed. She hardly ever left the house,
and of those who came to see them was only glad to see one
person, Pierre. It would have been impossible to treat
her with more delicacy, greater care, and at the same
time more seriously, than did Count Bezúkhov. Natásha
unconsciously felt this delicacy, and so found great
pleasure in his society. But she was not even grateful to
him for it, nothing good on Pierre's part seemed to her
to be an effort, it seemed so natural for him to be kind to
every one that there was no merit in his kindness. Sometimes Natásha noticed embarrassment and awkwardness
on his part in her presence, especially when he wanted
to do something to please her, or feared that something
they spoke of would awaken memories distressing to her.
She noticed this and attributed it to his general kindness

and shyness, which she imagined must be the same towards every one as it was to her. After those involuntary words—that if he were free he would have asked on his knees for her hand and her love—uttered at a moment when she was so strongly agitated, Pierre never spoke to Natásha of his feelings; and it seemed plain to her that those words, which had then so comforted her, were spoken as all sorts of meaningless words are spoken to comfort a crying child. It was not because Pierre was a married man, but because Natásha very strongly felt with him that moral barrier the absence of which she had experienced with Kurágin, that it never entered her head that the relations between him and herself could lead to love on her part, still less on his, or even to the kind of tender, self-conscious, romantic friendship between a man and a woman of which she had known several instances.

Before the end of the fast of St. Peter,[1] Agraféna Ivánovna Belóva, a country neighbour of the Rostóvs, came to Moscow to pay her devotions at the shrines of the Moscow saints. She suggested that Natásha should fast and prepare for Holy Communion, and Natásha gladly welcomed the idea. Despite the doctor's orders that she should not go out early in the morning, Natásha insisted on fasting and preparing for the sacrament, not as they generally prepared for it in the Rostóv family by attending three services in their own house, but as Agraféna Ivánovna did, by going to church every day for a week and not once missing Vespers, Matins, or Mass.

The countess was pleased with Natásha's zeal; after the poor results of the medical treatment, in the depths of her heart she hoped that prayer might help her daughter more than medicines and, though not without fear, and concealing it from the doctor, she agreed to Natásha's wish and entrusted her to Belóva. Agraféna Ivánovna used to come to wake Natásha at three in the morning, but generally found her already awake. She was afraid of being late for Matins. Hastily washing, and meekly

[1] That is, for two weeks before St. Peter's day (29th June, old style) and seventeen days after Napoleon had crossed the Russian frontier.

putting on her shabbiest dress and an old mantilla, Natásha, shivering in the fresh air, went out into the deserted streets lit by the clear light of dawn. By Agraféna Ivánovna's advice Natásha prepared herself not in their own parish, but at a church where according to the devout Agraféna Ivánovna the priest was a man of very severe and lofty life. There were never many people in the church; Natásha always stood beside Belóva in the customary place before an icon of the Blessed Virgin let into the screen before the choir on the left side, and a feeling, new to her, of humility before something great and incomprehensible, seized her when at that unusual morning hour, gazing at the dark face of the Virgin illuminated by the candles burning before it and by the morning light falling from the window, she listened to the words of the service which she tried to follow with understanding. When she understood them, her personal feeling became interwoven in the prayers with shades of its own. When she did not understand, it was sweeter still to think that the wish to understand everything is pride, that it is impossible to understand all, that it is only necessary to believe and to commit oneself to God, whom she felt guiding her soul at those moments. She crossed herself, bowed low, and when she did not understand, in horror at her own vileness, simply asked God to forgive her everything, everything, and to have mercy upon her. The prayers to which she surrendered herself most of all were those of repentance. On her way home at an early hour when she met no one but bricklayers going to work or men sweeping the street, and everybody within the houses was still asleep, Natásha experienced a feeling new to her, a sense of the possibility of correcting her faults, the possibility of a new, clean life, and of happiness.

During the whole week she spent in this way, that feeling grew every day. And the happiness of taking communion, or 'communing' as Agraféna Ivánovna, joyously playing with the word, called it, seemed to Natásha so great that she felt she should never live till that blessed Sunday.

But the happy day came, and on that memorable Sunday, when dressed in white muslin she returned home after communion, for the first time for many months she felt calm and not oppressed by the thought of the life that lay before her.

The doctor who came to see her that day ordered her to continue the powders he had prescribed a fortnight previously.

'She must certainly go on taking them morning and evening,' said he, evidently sincerely satisfied with his success. 'Only, please be particular about it.'

'Be quite easy,' he continued playfully, as he adroitly took the gold coin in his palm. 'She will soon be singing and frolicking about. The last medicine has done her a very great deal of good. She has freshened up very much.'

The countess, with a cheerful expression on her face, looked down at her nails and spat a little for luck as she returned to the drawing-room.[1]

CHAPTER XVIII

AT the beginning of July more and more disquieting reports about the war began to spread in Moscow; people spoke of an appeal by the Emperor to the people, and of his coming himself from the army to Moscow. And as up to the 11th of July no manifesto or appeal had been received, exaggerated reports became current about them, and about the position of Russia. It was said that the Emperor was leaving the army because it was in danger, it was said that Smolénsk had surrendered, that Napoleon had an army of a million and only a miracle could save Russia.

On the 11th of July, which was Saturday, the manifesto was received but was not yet in print, and Pierre, who was at the Rostóvs', promised to come to dinner next day, Sunday, and bring a copy of the manifesto and appeal, which he would obtain from Count Rostopchín.

That Sunday the Rostóvs went to Mass at the Razumóvskis' private chapel as usual. It was a hot July day.

[1] As some people in England 'touch wood' for luck to avert the ill results of over-confidence, so in Russia people spat for the same purpose.

Even at ten o'clock, when the Rostóvs got out of their carriage at the chapel, the sultry air, the shouts of hawkers, the light and gay summer clothes of the crowd, the dusty leaves of the trees on the boulevard, the sounds of the band and the white trousers of a battalion marching to parade, the rattling of wheels on the cobble-stones, and the brilliant, hot sunshine, were all full of that summer languor, that content and discontent with the present, which is most strongly felt on a bright hot day in town. All the Moscow notabilities, all the Rostóvs' acquaintances, were at the Razumóvskis' chapel, for as if expecting something to happen, many wealthy families who usually left town for their country estates had not gone away that summer. As Natásha, at her mother's side, passed through the crowd behind a liveried footman who cleared the way for them, she heard a young man speaking about her in too loud a whisper.

'That's Rostóva, the one who . . . '

'She's much thinner, but all the same she's pretty!'

She heard or thought she heard the names of Kurágin and Bolkónski. But she was always imagining that. It always seemed to her that every one who looked at her was thinking only of what had happened to her. With a sinking heart, wretched as she always was now when she found herself in a crowd, Natásha, in her lilac silk dress trimmed with black lace, walked—as women can walk—with the more repose and stateliness the greater the pain and shame in her soul. She knew for certain that she was pretty, but this no longer gave her satisfaction as it used to. On the contrary it had tormented her more than anything else of late, and particularly so on this bright, hot summer day in town. 'It's Sunday again—another week past,' she thought, recalling that she had been here the Sunday before, 'and always the same life that is no life, and the same surroundings in which it used to be so easy to live. I'm pretty, I'm young, and I know that now I am good. I used to be bad, but now I know I am good,' she thought, 'but yet my best years are slipping by and are no good to any one.' She stood by her mother's side and exchanged nods with acquaintances near her. From habit she scrutinized the ladies' dresses, condemned the bearing of a lady standing close by who was not crossing herself properly but in a cramped manner, and again she thought with vexation that she was herself being judged and was judging others, and suddenly, at the sound of the service, she felt horrified at her own vileness, horrified that the former purity of her soul was again lost to her.

A comely fresh-looking old man was conducting the service with that mild solemnity which has so elevating and soothing an effect on the souls of the worshippers. The gates of the sanctuary-screen were closed, the curtain was slowly drawn, and from behind it a soft mysterious voice pronounced some words. Tears, the cause of which she herself did not understand, made Natásha's breast heave, and a joyous but oppressive feeling agitated her.

'Teach me what I should do, how to live my life, how I may grow good for ever, for ever!' she pleaded.

The deacon came out onto the raised space before the altar-screen, and holding his thumb extended, drew his long hair from under his dalmatic, and making the sign of the cross on his breast, began in a loud and solemn voice to recite the words of the prayer . . .

'In peace let us pray unto the Lord.'

'As one community,[1] without distinction of class, without enmity, united by brotherly love—let us pray!' thought Natásha.

'For the peace that is from above, and for the salvation of our souls.'

'For the world of angels and all the spirits who dwell above us,' prayed Natásha.

When they prayed for the warriors, she thought of her brother and Denísov. When they prayed for all travelling by land and sea she remembered Prince Andrew, prayed for him, and asked God to forgive her all the wrong she had done him. When they prayed for those who love us, she prayed for the members of her own family, her father and mother and Sónya, realizing for the first time how

---

[1] The Russian word *mir* has two meanings. Sometimes—and especially in the Church service—it means peace, concord and union. Natásha takes it in the popular sense, as meaning the universe, the world, the commune, the village assembly, and so on.

wrongly she had acted towards them, and feeling all the strength of her love for them. When they prayed for those who hate us, she tried to think of her enemies and people who hated her, in order to pray for them. She included among her enemies the creditors and all who had business dealings with her father, and always at the thought of enemies and those who hated her, she remembered Anatole who had done her so much harm—and though he did not hate her, she gladly prayed for him as for an enemy. Only at prayer did she feel able to think clearly and calmly of Prince Andrew and Anatole, as men for whom her feelings were as nothing compared with her awe and devotion to God. When they prayed for the Imperial family and the Synod, she bowed very low and made the sign of the cross, saying to herself that even if she did not understand, still she could not doubt, and at any rate loved the governing Synod and prayed for it.

When he had finished the Litany the deacon crossed the stole over his breast and said,

'Let us commit ourselves and our whole lives to Christ the Lord!'

'Commit ourselves to God,' Natásha inwardly repeated. 'Lord God, I submit myself to Thy will!' she thought. 'I want nothing, wish for nothing; teach me what to do and how to use my will! Take me, take me!' prayed Natásha with impatient emotion in her heart, not crossing herself but letting her slender arms hang down as if expecting some invisible power at any moment to take her and deliver her from herself, from her regrets, desires, remorse, hopes, and sins.'

The countess looked round several times at her daughter's softened face and shining eyes, and prayed God to help her.

Unexpectedly, in the middle of the service, and not in the usual order Natásha knew so well, the deacon brought out a small stool, the one he knelt on when praying on Trinity Sunday, and placed it before the doors of the sanctuary-screen. The priest came out, with his purple velvet biretta [1] on his head, adjusted his

---

[1] It is not strictly accurate to use the word biretta for this head-gear used in the Russo-Greek church, but is the nearest word available in English.

hair, and knelt down with an effort. Everybody followed his example and looked at one another in surprise. Then came the prayer just received from the Synod—a prayer for the deliverance of Russia from hostile invasion.

'Lord God of might, God of our salvation!' began the priest in that voice, clear, not grandiloquent but mild, in which only the Slav clergy read and which acts so irresistibly on a Russian heart.

'Lord God of might, God of our salvation! Look this day in mercy and blessing on Thy humble people, and graciously hear us, spare us, and have mercy upon us! This foe confounding Thy land, desiring to lay waste the whole world, rises against us; these lawless men are gathered together to overthrow Thy kingdom, to destroy Thy dear Jerusalem, Thy beloved Russia: to defile Thy temples, to overthrow Thine altars and to desecrate our holy shrines. How long, O Lord, how long shall the wicked triumph? How long shall they wield unlawful power?

'Lord God! Hear us when we pray to Thee; strengthen with Thy might our most gracious sovereign lord the Emperor Alexander Pávlovich; be mindful of his uprightness and meekness, reward him according to his righteousness, and let it preserve us, Thy chosen Israel! Bless his counsels, his undertakings, and his work; strengthen his kingdom by Thine almighty hand, and give him victory over his enemy, even as Thou gavest Moses the victory over Amalek, Gideon over Midian, and David over Goliath. Preserve his army, put a bow of brass in the hands of those who have armed themselves in Thy Name, and gird their loins with strength for the fight. Take up the spear and shield and arise to help us; confound and put to shame those who have devised evil against us, may they be before the faces of Thy faithful warriors as dust before the wind, and may Thy mighty Angel confound them and put them to flight; may they be ensnared when they know it not, and may the plots they have laid in secret be turned against them; let them fall before Thy servants' feet and be laid low by our hosts! Lord, Thou art able to save both great and small; Thou art God, and man cannot prevail against Thee!

'God of our fathers! Remember Thy bounteous mercy and loving kindness which are from of old; turn not Thy face from us, but be gracious to our unworthiness, and in Thy great goodness and Thy many mercies regard not our transgressions and iniquities! Create in us a clean heart and renew a right spirit within us, strengthen us all in Thy faith, fortify our hope, inspire us with true love one for another, arm us with unity of spirit in the righteous defence of the heritage Thou gavest to us and to our fathers, and let not the sceptre of the wicked be exalted against the destiny of those Thou hast sanctified.

'O Lord our God, in whom we believe and in whom we put our trust, let us not be confounded in our hope of Thy mercy, and give us a token of Thy blessing, that those who hate us and our Orthodox faith may see it, and be put to shame and perish, and may all the nations know that Thou art the Lord and we are Thy people. Show Thy mercy upon us this day, O Lord, and grant us Thy salvation; make the hearts of Thy servants to rejoice in Thy mercy; smite down our enemies and destroy them swiftly beneath the feet of Thy faithful servants! For Thou art the defence, the succour, and the victory of them that put their trust in Thee, and to Thee be all glory, to Father, Son, and Holy Ghost, now and for ever, world without end. Amen.'

In Natásha's receptive condition of soul this prayer affected her strongly. She listened to every word about the victory of Moses over Amalek, of Gideon over Midian, and of David over Goliath, and about the destruction of 'Thy Jerusalem', and she prayed to God with the tenderness and emotion with which her heart was over-flowing, but without fully understanding what she was asking of God in that prayer. She shared with all her heart in the prayer for the spirit of righteousness, for the strengthening of the heart by faith and hope, and its animation by love. But she could not pray that her enemies might be trampled under foot when but a few minutes before she had been wishing she had more of them that she might pray for them. But neither could she doubt the righteousness of the prayer that was being read on bended knees. She felt in her heart a devout and tremulous awe at the thought of the punishment that overtakes men for their sins, and especially of her own sins, and she prayed to God to forgive them all, and her too, and to give them all, and her too, peace and happiness. And it seemed to her that God heard her prayer.

CHAPTER XIX

FROM the day when Pierre, after leaving the Rostóvs' with Natásha's grateful look fresh in his mind, had gazed at the comet that seemed to be fixed in the sky and felt that something new was appearing on his own horizon—from that day the problem of the vanity and uselessness of all earthly things, that had incessantly tormented him, no longer presented itself. That terrible question 'Why?' 'Wherefore?' which had come to him amid every occupation, was now replaced, not by another question or by a reply to the former question, but by *her* image. When he listened to, or himself took part in, trivial conversations, when he read or heard of human baseness or folly, he was not horrified as formerly, and did not ask himself why men struggled so about these things, when all is so transient and incomprehensible— but he remembered her as he had last seen her, and all his doubts vanished—not because she had answered the questions that had haunted him, but because his conception of her transferred him instantly to another, a brighter, realm of spiritual activity in which no one could be justified or guilty—a realm of beauty and love which it was worth living for. Whatever worldly baseness presented itself to him he said to himself:

'Well, supposing N. N. has swindled the country and the Tsar, and the country and the Tsar confer honours upon him, what does that matter? She smiled at me yesterday and asked me to come again, and I love her, and no one will ever know it.' And his soul felt calm and peaceful.

Pierre still went into society, drank as much, and led the same idle and dissipated life, because besides the hours he spent at the Rostóvs' there were other hours he had to spend somehow, and the habits and acquaintances he had made in Moscow formed a current that bore him along irresistibly. But latterly, when more and more disquieting reports came from the seat of war and Natásha's health began to improve and she no longer aroused in him the former feeling of careful pity, an ever-increasing restlessness, which he could not explain, took possession of him. He felt that the condition he was in could not continue long, that a catastrophe was coming which would change his whole life, and he impatiently sought everywhere for signs of that approaching catastrophe. One of his brother Masons had revealed to Pierre the following prophecy concerning Napoleon, drawn from the Revelation of St. John.

In chapter xiii, verse 18, of the Apocalypse, it is said:

Here is wisdom. Let him that hath understanding count the number of the beast: for it is the number of a man; and his number is Six hundred threescore and six.

And in the fifth verse of the same chapter:

And there was given unto him a mouth speaking great things and blasphemies; and power was given unto him to continue forty and two months.

The French alphabet, written out with the same numerical values as the Hebrew, in which the first nine letters denote units and the others tens, will have the following significance:

a	b	c	d	e	f	g	h	i	k	l	m	n	o	p
1	2	3	4	5	6	7	8	9	10	20	30	40	50	60

q	r	s	t	u	v	w	x	y	z
70	80	90	100	110	120	130	140	150	160.

Writing the words *L'Empereur Napoléon* in numbers, it appears that the sum of them is 666,[1] and that Napoleon was therefore the beast foretold in the Apocalypse. Moreover by applying the same system to the words *quarante-deux* (forty-two), which was the term allowed to the beast that 'spoke great things and blasphemies', the same number 666 was obtained; from which it followed that the

[1] Including a 5 for the letter *e* dropped by elision from the *le* before *Empereur*.

limit fixed for Napoleon's power had come in the year
1812, when the French emperor was forty-two.[1] This
prophecy pleased Pierre very much, and he often asked
himself what would put an end to the power of the beast,
that is, of Napoleon, and tried by the same system of
using letters as numbers and adding them up, to find an
answer to the question that engrossed him. He wrote the
words *L'Empereur Alexandre, La nation russe* and added up
their numbers, but the sums were either more or less than
666. Once when making such calculations he wrote
down his own name in French, Comte Pierre Besouhoff,
but the sum of the numbers did not come right. Then he
changed the spelling, substituting a *z* for the *s* and adding
de and the article *le*, still without obtaining the desired
result. Then it occurred to him that if the answer to the
question were contained in his name, his nationality
would also be given in the answer. So he wrote *Le russe
Besuhof* and adding up the numbers got 671. This was
only five too much, and five was represented by *e*, the
very letter elided from the article *le* before the word
Empereur. By omitting the *e*, though incorrectly, Pierre
got the answer he sought. *L'russe Besuhof* made 666.[2]
This discovery excited him. How, or by what means, he
was connected with the great event foretold in the
Apocalypse he did not know, but he did not doubt
that connexion for a moment. His love for Natásha,
Antichrist, Napoleon, the invasion, the comet, 666,
L'Empereur Napoléon, and *L'russe Besuhof*—all this had to

[1] Apparently the correspondence of *quarante-deux* with 666
was sufficient for Pierre, and it did not trouble him that the
text spoke of months, while to fit the 42 to Napoleon it was
necessary to take years. Napoleon's forty-second birthday was
on 15 August 1811; so that till August 1812 he was, in ordinary parlance, forty-two.

[2] Russians transliterating their names into the Latin alphabet have generally followed no fixed rule but have adopted
such spelling as, in this or that country, seemed to them most
likely to cause people to pronounce the name correctly. So
it occurs that the name which on the system now usually
adopted in England is spelt Bezúkhov, could be written by
Pierre in French in more than one way, and he found Besuhof
most convenient for the purpose of his calculation.

mature and culminate, to lift him out of that spellbound, petty sphere of Moscow habits in which he felt himself held captive, and lead him to a great achievement and great happiness.

On the eve of the Sunday when the special prayer was read, Pierre had promised the Rostóvs to bring them, from Count Rostopchín whom he knew well, both the appeal to the people and the latest news from the army. In the morning, when he went to call at Rostopchín's he met there a courier fresh from the army, an acquaintance of his own, who often danced at Moscow balls.

'Do, please, for heaven's sake relieve me of something!' said the courier. 'I have a sackful of letters to parents.'

Among these letters was one from Nicholas Rostóv to his father. Pierre took that letter, and Rostopchín also gave him the Emperor's appeal to Moscow which had just been printed, the last army orders, and his own most recent bulletin. Glancing through the army orders Pierre found in one of them, in the lists of killed, wounded, and rewarded, the name of Nicholas Rostóv, awarded a St. George's Cross of the Fourth Class for courage shown in the Ostróvna affair, and in the same order the name of Prince Andrew Bolkónski, appointed to the command of a regiment of Chasseurs. Though he did not want to remind the Rostóvs of Bolkónski, Pierre could not refrain from making them happy by the news of their son's having received a decoration, so he sent that printed army order and Nicholas's letter to the Rostóvs, keeping the appeal, the bulletin, and the other orders, to take with him when he went to dinner.

His conversation with Count Rostopchín and the latter's tone of anxious hurry, the meeting with the courier who talked casually of how badly things were going in the army, the rumours of the discovery of spies in Moscow and of a leaflet in circulation stating that Napoleon promised to be in both the Russian capitals by the autumn, and the talk of the Emperor's being expected to arrive next day—all aroused with fresh force that feeling of agitation and expectation in Pierre which he had been conscious of ever since the appearance of the comet, and especially since the beginning of the war.

He had long been thinking of entering the army and would have done so had he not been hindered, first, by his membership of the Society of Freemasons to which he was bound by oath and which preached perpetual peace and the abolition of war, and secondly, by the fact that when he saw the great mass of Moscovites who had donned uniform and were talking patriotism, he somehow felt ashamed to take the step. But the chief reason for not carrying out his intention to enter the army lay in the vague idea that he was *L'russe Besuhof* who had the number of the beast, 666; that his part in the great affair of setting a limit to the power of the beast that spoke great and blasphemous things had been predestined from eternity, and that therefore he ought not to undertake anything, but wait for what was bound to come to pass.

CHAPTER XX

A FEW intimate friends were dining with the Rostóvs that day, as usual on Sundays.

Pierre came early so as to find them alone.

He had grown so stout this year that he would have been abnormal had he not been so tall, so broad of limb, and so strong that he carried his bulk with evident ease.

He went up the stairs puffing and muttering something. His coachman did not even ask whether he was to wait. He knew that when his master was at the Rostóvs he stayed till midnight. The Rostóvs' footman rushed eagerly forward to help him off with his cloak and take his hat and stick. Pierre, from club habit, always left both hat and stick in the ante-room.

The first person he saw in the house was Natásha. Even before he saw her, while taking off his cloak, he heard her. She was practising sol-fa exercises in the music-room. He knew that she had not sung since her illness, and so the sound of her voice surprised and delighted him. He opened the door softly and saw her, in the lilac dress she had worn at church, walking about the room

singing. She had her back to him when he opened the
door, but when, turning quickly, she saw his broad,
surprised face, she blushed and came rapidly up to him:

'I want to try to sing again,' she said, adding as if by
way of excuse, 'it is at least something to do.'

'That's capital!'

'How glad I am you've come! I am so happy to-day,'
she said, with the old animation Pierre had not seen in
her for a long time. 'You know Nicholas has received a
St. George's Cross? I am so proud of him.'

'Oh yes, I sent that announcement. But I don't want
to interrupt you,' he added, and was about to go to the
drawing-room.

Natásha stopped him.

'Count, is it wrong of me to sing?' she said blushing,
and fixing her eyes inquiringly on him.

'No . . . Why should it be? On the contrary . . . But
why do you ask me?'

'I don't know myself,' Natásha answered quickly, 'but
I should not like to do anything you disapproved of.
I believe in you completely. You don't know how important you are to me, how much you've done for me . . .'
She spoke rapidly and did not notice how Pierre flushed
at her words. 'I saw in that same army order that *he*,
Bolkónski' (she whispered the name hastily), 'is in Russia,
and in the army again. What do you think?'—she was
speaking hurriedly, evidently afraid her strength might
fail her—'Will he ever forgive me? Will he not always
have a bitter feeling towards me? What do you think?
What do you think?'

'I think . . .' Pierre replied, 'that he has nothing to
forgive . . . If I were in his place . . .'

By association of ideas Pierre was at once carried back
to the day when, trying to comfort her, he had said that
if he were not himself but the best man in the world and
free, he would ask on his knees for her hand; and the same
feeling of pity, tenderness, and love, took possession of
him and the same words rose to his lips. But she did not
give him time to say them.

'Yes, you . . . you . . .' she said, uttering the word *you*
rapturously—'that's a different thing. I know no one

kinder, more generous, or better than you; nobody could be! Had you not been there then, and now too, I don't know what would have become of me, because...'

Tears suddenly rose in her eyes, she turned away, lifted her music before her eyes, began singing again, and again began walking up and down the room.

Just then Pétya came running in from the drawing-room.

Pétya was now a handsome rosy lad of fifteen, with full red lips, and resembled Natásha. He was preparing to enter the university, but he and his friend Obolénski had lately, in secret, agreed to join the hussars.

Pétya had come rushing out to talk to his namesake [1] about this affair. He had asked Pierre to find out whether he would be accepted in the hussars.

Pierre walked up and down the drawing-room not listening to what Pétya was saying.

Pétya pulled him by the arm to attract his attention.

'Well, what about my plan? Peter Kirílych, for heaven's sake! You are my only hope!' said Pétya.

'Oh yes, your plan. To join the hussars? I'll mention it, I'll bring it all up to-day.'

'Well, *mon cher*, have you got the manifesto?' asked the old count. 'The countess has been to Mass at the Razumóvskis' and heard the new prayer. She says it's very fine.'

'Yes, I've got it,' said Pierre. 'The Emperor is to be here to-morrow . . . there's to be an Extraordinary Meeting of the nobility, and they are talking of a levy of ten men per thousand. Oh yes, let me congratulate you!'

'Yes, yes, thank God! Well, and what news from the army?'

'We are again retreating. They say we're already near Smolénsk,' replied Pierre.

'O Lord, O Lord!' exclaimed the count. 'Where is the manifesto?'

'The Emperor's appeal? Oh yes!'

Pierre began feeling in his pockets for the papers, but could not find them. Still slapping his pockets, he kissed the hand of the countess who entered the room, and

[1] Pétya is the diminutive of Pëtr, which is the Russian equivalent of Pierre, or Peter.

glanced uneasily around evidently expecting Natásha, who had left off singing but had not yet come into the drawing-room.

'On my word, I don't know what I've done with it,' he said.

'There he is, always losing everything!' remarked the countess.

Natásha entered with a softened and agitated expression of face, and sat down looking silently at Pierre. As soon as she entered, Pierre's features, which had been gloomy, suddenly lighted up, and while still searching for the papers he glanced at her several times.

'No, really! I'll drive home, I must have left them there. I'll certainly . . .'

'But you'll be late for dinner.'

'Oh! And my coachman has gone.'

But Sónya, who had gone to look for the papers in the ante-room, had found them in Pierre's hat, where he had carefully tucked them under the lining. Pierre was about to begin reading.

'No, after dinner,' said the old count, evidently expecting much enjoyment from that reading.

At dinner, at which champagne was drunk to the health of the new chevalier of St. George, Shinshín told them the town news, of the illness of the old Georgian princess, of Métivier's disappearance from Moscow, and of how some German fellow had been brought to Rostopchín and accused of being a French 'spyer' (so Count Rostopchín had told the story), and how Rostopchín let him go and assured the people that he was 'not a spire at all, but only an old German ruin'.

'People are being arrested . . .' said the count. 'I've told the countess she should not speak French so much. It's not the time for it now.'

'And have you heard?' Shinshín asked. 'Prince Golítsin has engaged a master to teach him Russian. It is becoming dangerous to speak French in the streets.' [1]

[1] It was so customary for the Russian aristocracy of those days to speak French that many of them could neither write nor speak Russian correctly, though the mass of the people spoke nothing but Russian.

'And how about you, Count Peter Kirílych? If they call up the militia, you too will have to mount a horse,' remarked the old count, addressing Pierre.

Pierre had been silent and preoccupied all through dinner, seeming not to grasp what was said. He looked at the count.

'Oh yes, the war,' he said. 'No! What sort of a warrior should I make? And yet everything is so strange, so strange! I can't make it out. I don't know, I am very far from having military tastes, but in these times no one can answer for himself.'

After dinner the count settled himself comfortably in an easy-chair and with a serious face asked Sónya, who was considered an excellent reader, to read the appeal.

'To Moscow, our ancient Capital!

'The enemy has entered the borders of Russia with immense forces. He comes to despoil our beloved country,' Sónya read painstakingly in her high-pitched voice. The count listened with closed eyes, heaving abrupt sighs at certain passages.

Natásha sat erect gazing with a searching look now at her father and now at Pierre.

Pierre felt her eyes on him and tried not to look round. The countess shook her head disapprovingly and angrily at every solemn expression in the manifesto. In all these words she saw only that the danger threatening her son would not soon be over. Shinshín, with a sarcastic smile on his lips, was evidently preparing to make fun of anything that gave him the opportunity: Sónya's reading, any remark of the count's, or even the manifesto itself should no better pretext present itself.

After reading about the dangers that threatened Russia, the hopes the Emperor placed on Moscow and especially on its illustrious nobility, Sónya, with a quiver in her voice due chiefly to the attention that was being paid to her, read the last words: 'We ourselves will not delay to appear among our people in that Capital and in other parts of our realm for consultation, and for the direction of all our levies, both those now barring the enemy's path and those freshly formed to defeat him wherever he may appear. May the ruin he hopes to bring upon us recoil on his own head, and may Europe delivered from bondage glorify the name of Russia!'

'Yes, that's it!' cried the count, opening his moist eyes and sniffing repeatedly as if a strong vinaigrette had been held to his nose; and he added, 'Let the Emperor but say the word and we'll sacrifice everything and begrudge nothing.'

Before Shinshín had time to utter the joke he was ready to make on the count's patriotism, Natásha jumped up from her place and ran to her father.

'What a darling our Papa is!' she cried kissing him, and she again looked at Pierre with the unconscious coquetry that had returned to her with her better spirits.

'There! Here's a patriot for you!' said Shinshín.

'Not a patriot at all, but simply . . .' Natásha replied in an injured tone. 'Everything seems funny to you, but this isn't at all a joke . . .'

'A joke indeed!' put in the count. 'Let him but say the word and we'll all go . . . We're not Germans!'

'But did you notice, it says, "for consultation"?' said Pierre.

'Never mind what it's for . . .'

At this moment Pétya, to whom nobody was paying any attention, came up to his father with a very flushed face, and said in his breaking voice that was now deep and now shrill:

'Well Papa, I tell you definitely, and Mamma too, it's as you please, but I say definitely that you must let me enter the army, because I can't . . . that is all . . .'

The countess, in dismay, looked up to heaven, clasped her hands, and turned angrily to her husband.

'That comes of your talking!' said she.

But the count had already recovered from his excitement.

'Come, come!' said he. 'Here's a fine warrior! No! Nonsense! You must study.'

'It's not nonsense, Papa! Fédya Obolénski is younger than I, and he's going too. Besides, all the same, I can't study now when . . .' Pétya stopped short, flushed till he perspired, but still got out the words, 'when our Fatherland is in danger.'

'That'll do, that'll do—nonsense . . .'

'But you said yourself that we would sacrifice everything.'

'Pétya! Be quiet, I tell you!' cried the count with a glance at his wife, who had turned pale and was staring fixedly at her son.

'And I tell you—Peter Kirílych here will also tell you . . .'

'Nonsense, I tell you. Your mother's milk has hardly dried on your lips and you want to go into the army! There, there, I tell you,' and the count moved to go out of the room, taking the papers, probably to re-read them in his study before having a nap.

'Well, Peter Kirílych, let's go and have a smoke,' he said.

Pierre was agitated and undecided. Natásha's unwontedly brilliant eyes, continually glancing at him with a more than cordial look, had reduced him to this condition.

'No, I think I'll go home.'

'Home? Why, you meant to spend the evening with us . . . You don't often come nowadays as it is, and this girl of mine,' said the count good-naturedly, pointing to Natásha, 'only brightens up when you're here.'

'Yes, I had forgotten . . . I really must go home . . . business . . .' said Pierre hurriedly.

'Well then, *au revoir*!' said the count and went out of the room.

'Why are you going? Why are you upset?' asked Natásha, and she looked challengingly into Pierre's eyes.

'Because I love you!' was what he wanted to say, but he did not say it, and only blushed till the tears came, and lowered his eyes.

'Because it is better for me to come less often . . . because . . . No, simply I have business . . .'

'Why? No, tell me!' Natásha began resolutely, and suddenly stopped.

They looked at each other with dismayed and embarrassed faces. He tried to smile but could not: his smile expressed suffering, and he silently kissed her hand and went out.

Pierre made up his mind not to go to the Rostóvs' any more.

CHAPTER XXI

AFTER the definite refusal he had received, Pétya went to his room and there locked himself in and wept bitterly. When he came in to tea, silent, morose, and with tear-stained face, everybody pretended not to notice anything.

Next day the Emperor arrived in Moscow, and several of the Rostóvs' domestic serfs begged permission to go to have a look at him. That morning Pétya was a long time dressing and arranging his hair and collar to look like a grown-up man. He frowned before his looking-glass, gesticulated, shrugged his shoulders, and finally without saying a word to any one took his cap and left the house by the back door, trying to avoid notice. Pétya had decided to go straight to where the Emperor was and to explain frankly to some gentleman-in-waiting (he imagined the Emperor to be always surrounded by gentlemen-in-waiting) that he, Count Rostóv, in spite of his youth, wished to serve his country; that youth could be no hindrance to loyalty, and that he was ready to . . . While dressing, Pétya had prepared many fine things he meant to say to the gentleman-in-waiting.

It was on the very fact of being so young that Pétya counted for success in reaching the Emperor—he even thought how surprised every one would be at his youthfulness—and yet in the arrangement of his collar and hair and by his sedate deliberate walk he wished to appear a grown-up man. But the farther he went and the more his attention was diverted by the ever-increasing crowds moving towards the Krémlin, the less he remembered to walk with the sedateness and deliberation of a man. As he approached the Krémlin he even began to avoid being crushed, and resolutely stuck out his elbows in a menacing way. But within the Trinity Gateway he was so pressed to the wall by people who probably were unaware of the patriotic intentions with which he had come, that in spite of all his determination he had to give in, and stop while carriages passed in, rumbling beneath the archway. Beside Pétya stood a peasant woman, a footman, two tradesmen, and a discharged soldier. After standing some time in the gateway, Pétya tried to move forward in front of the others without waiting for all the carriages to pass, and he began resolutely working his way with his elbows, but the woman just in front of him, who was the first against whom he directed his efforts, angrily shouted at him:

'What are you shoving for, young lordling? Don't you see we're all standing still? Then why push?'

'Anybody can shove,' said the footman, and also began working his elbows to such effect that he pushed Pétya into a very filthy corner of the gateway.

Pétya wiped his perspiring face with his hands, and pulled up the damp collar which he had arranged so well at home to seem like a man's.

He felt that he no longer looked presentable, and feared that if he presented himself to the gentlemen-in-waiting in that plight he would not be admitted to the Emperor. But it was impossible to smarten oneself up, or move to another place, because of the crowd. One of the generals who drove past was an acquaintance of the Rostóvs' and Pétya thought of asking his help, but came to the conclusion that that would not be a manly thing to do. When the carriages had all passed in, the crowd, carrying Pétya with it, streamed forward into the Krémlin Square which was already full of people. There were people not only in the square, but everywhere—on the slopes and on the roofs. As soon as Pétya found himself in the square he clearly heard the sound of the bells and the joyous voices of the crowd that filled the whole Krémlin.

For a while the crowd was less dense, but suddenly all heads were bared, and every one rushed forward in one direction. Pétya was being pressed so that he could scarcely breathe, and everybody shouted 'hurrah! hurrah! hurrah!' Pétya stood on tiptoe, and pushed and pinched, but could see nothing except the people about him.

All the faces bore the same expression of excitement and enthusiasm. A tradesman's wife standing beside Pétya sobbed, and the tears ran down her cheeks.

'Father! Angel! Dear one!' she kept repeating, wiping away her tears with her fingers.

'Hurrah!' was heard on all sides.

For a moment the crowd stood still, but then it made another rush forward.

Quite beside himself, Pétya, clenching his teeth and rolling his eyes ferociously, pushed forward, elbowing his way and shouting 'hurrah!' as if he were prepared that instant to kill himself and every one else, but on both sides of him other people with similarly ferocious faces pushed forward and everybody shouted 'hurrah!'

'So this is what the Emperor is!' thought Pétya. 'No, I can't petition him myself—that would be too bold.' But in spite of this he continued to struggle desperately forward, and from between the backs of those in front he caught glimpses of an open space with a strip of red cloth spread out on it; but just then the crowd swayed back—the police in front were pushing back those who had pressed too close to the procession: the Emperor was passing from the palace to the Cathedral of the Assumption—and Pétya unexpectedly received such a blow on his side and ribs, and was squeezed so hard, that suddenly everything grew dim before his eyes and he lost consciousness. When he came to himself a man of clerical appearance with a tuft of grey hair at the back of his head and wearing a shabby blue cassock—probably a church clerk and chanter—was holding him under the arm with one hand, while warding off the pressure of the crowd with the other.

'You've crushed the young gentleman!' said the clerk. 'What are you up to? Gently! . . . They've crushed him, crushed him!'

The Emperor entered the Cathedral of the Assumption. The crowd spread out again more evenly, and the clerk led Pétya—pale and breathless—to the Tsar-cannon.[1] Several people were sorry for Pétya, and suddenly a crowd

---

[1] The Tsar-cannon (*Tsar-púshka*), a very large cannon cast in 1488, which is preserved in the Moscow Krémlin as a curiosity.

turned towards him and crushed round him. Those who
stood nearest attended to him, unbuttoned his coat,
seated him on the raised platform of the cannon, and
reproached those others (whoever they might be) who
had crushed him.

'One might easily get killed that way! What do they
mean by it? Killing people! Poor dear, he's as white as
a sheet!'—various voices were heard saying.

Pétya soon came to himself, the colour returned to his
face, the pain had passed, and at the cost of that temporary
unpleasantness he had obtained a place by the cannon,
from where he hoped to see the Emperor who would be
returning that way. Pétya no longer thought of presenting his petition. If he could only see the Emperor he
would be happy!

While the service was proceeding in the Cathedral of
the Assumption—it was a combined service of prayer on
the occasion of the Emperor's arrival and of thanksgiving
for the conclusion of peace with the Turks—the crowd
outside spread out and hawkers appeared, selling kvas,
gingerbread, and poppy-seed sweets (of which Pétya was
particularly fond), and ordinary conversation could again
be heard. A tradesman's wife was showing a rent in her
shawl and telling how much the shawl had cost; another
was saying that all silk goods had now got dear. The
clerk who had rescued Pétya was talking to a functionary
about the priests who were officiating that day with the
bishop. The clerk several times used the word 'plenary'
(of the service), a word Pétya did not understand. Two
young citizens were joking with some serf-girls who were
cracking nuts. All these conversations, especially the
joking with the girls, were such as might have had a
particular charm for Pétya at his age, but they did not
interest him now. He sat on his elevation—the pedestal
of the cannon—still agitated as before by the thought of
the Emperor and by his love for him. The feeling of pain
and fear he had experienced when he was being crushed,
together with that of rapture, still further intensified his
sense of the importance of the occasion.

Suddenly the sound of a firing of cannon was heard
from the embankment, to celebrate the signing of peace

with the Turks, and the crowd rushed impetuously towards the embankment to watch the firing. Pétya too would have run there, but the clerk who had taken the young gentleman under his protection stopped him. The firing was still proceeding when officers, generals, and gentlemen-in-waiting, came running out of the cathedral, and after them others in a more leisurely manner: caps were again raised, and those who had run to look at the cannon ran back again. At last four men in uniforms and sashes emerged from the cathedral doors. 'Hurrah! hurrah!' shouted the crowd again.

'Which is he? Which?' asked Pétya in a tearful voice of those around him, but no one answered him, everybody was too excited; and Pétya, fixing on one of those four men, whom he could not clearly see for the tears of joy that filled his eyes, concentrated all his enthusiasm on him—though it happened not to be the Emperor—frantically shouted 'Hurrah!' and resolved that tomorrow, come what might, he would join the army.

The crowd ran after the Emperor, followed him to the palace, and began to disperse. It was already late, and Pétya had not eaten anything and was drenched with perspiration, yet he did not go home but stood with that diminishing, but still considerable, crowd before the palace while the Emperor dined—looking in at the palace windows, expecting he knew not what, and envying alike the notables he saw arriving at the entrance to dine with the Emperor and the court footmen who served at table, glimpses of whom could be seen through the windows.

While the Emperor was dining, Valúev, looking out of the window, said:

'The people are still hoping to see your Majesty again.'

The dinner was nearly over, and the Emperor, munching a biscuit, rose and went out onto the balcony. The people, with Pétya among them, rushed towards the balcony.

'Angel! Dear one! Hurrah! Father!' . . . cried the crowd, and Pétya with it, and again the women and men of weaker mould, Pétya among them, wept with joy.

A largish piece of the biscuit the Emperor was holding in his hand broke off, fell on the balcony parapet, and then to the ground. A coachman in a jerkin, who stood nearest, sprang forward and snatched it up. Several people in the crowd rushed at the coachman. Seeing this the Emperor had a plateful of biscuits brought him, and began throwing them down from the balcony. Pétya's eyes grew bloodshot, and still more excited by the danger of being crushed, he rushed at the biscuits. He did not know why, but he had to have a biscuit from the Tsar's hand and he felt that he must not give way. He sprang forward and upset an old woman who was catching at a biscuit, the old woman did not consider herself defeated though she was lying on the ground—she grabbed at some biscuits but her hand did not reach them. Pétya pushed her hand away with his knee, seized a biscuit, and as if fearing to be too late, again shouted 'Hurrah!' with a voice already hoarse.

The Emperor went in, and after that the greater part of the crowd began to disperse.

'There! I said if only we waited—and so it was!' was being joyfully said by various people.

Happy as Pétya was, he felt sad at having to go home knowing that all the enjoyment of that day was over. He did not go straight home from the Krémlin, but called on his friend Obolénski, who was fifteen and was also entering the regiment. On returning home Pétya announced resolutely and firmly that if he was not allowed to enter the service he would run away. And next day Count Ilyá Rostóv—though he had not yet quite yielded—went to inquire how he could arrange for Pétya to serve where there would be least danger.

CHAPTER XXII

TWO days later, on the 15th of July, an immense number of carriages were standing outside the Slobóda Palace.

The great halls were full. In the first were the nobility and gentry in their uniforms, in the second bearded merchants in full-skirted coats of blue cloth and wearing medals. In the noblemen's hall there was an incessant movement and buzz of voices. The chief magnates sat on high-backed chairs at a large table under the portrait of the Emperor, but most of the gentry were strolling about the room.

All these nobles, whom Pierre met every day at the club or in their own houses, were in uniform—some in that of Catherine's day, others in that of the Emperor Paul, others again in the new uniforms of Alexander's time, or the ordinary uniform of the nobility, and the general characteristic of being in uniform imparted something strange and fantastic to these diverse and familiar personalities, both old and young. The old men, dim-eyed, toothless, bald, sallow and bloated, or gaunt and wrinkled, were especially striking. For the most part they sat quietly in their places and were silent, or if they walked about and talked, attached themselves to some one younger. On all these faces, as on the faces of the crowd Pétya had seen in the Square, there was a striking contradiction: the general expectation of a solemn event, and at the same time the everyday interests in a boston card-party, Peter the cook, Zinaída Dmítrievna's health, and so on.

Pierre was there too, buttoned up since early morning in a nobleman's uniform that had become too tight for him. He was agitated: this extraordinary gathering not only of nobles but also of the merchant-class—*les états généraux* (States-General)—evoked in him a whole series of ideas he had long laid aside but which were deeply graven in his soul: thoughts of the *Contrat Social* and the French Revolution. The words that had struck him in the Emperor's appeal—that the sovereign was coming to the capital for consultation with his people—strengthened this idea. And imagining that in this direction something important which he had long awaited was drawing near, he strolled about, watching and listening to conversations, but nowhere finding any confirmation of the ideas that occupied him.

The Emperor's manifesto was read, evoking enthusiasm, and then all moved about discussing it. Besides the ordinary topics of conversation, Pierre heard questions of where the marshals of the nobility were to stand when the Emperor entered, when a ball should be given in the Emperor's honour, whether they should group themselves by districts or by whole provinces . . . and so on; but as soon as the war was touched on, or what the nobility had been convened for, the talk became undecided and indefinite. Then all preferred listening to speaking

A middle-aged man, handsome and virile, in the uniform of a retired naval officer, was speaking in one of the rooms, and a small crowd was pressing round him. Pierre went up to the circle that had formed round the speaker, and listened. Count Ilyá Rostóv, in a military uniform of Catherine's time, was sauntering with a pleasant smile among the crowd, with all of whom he was acquainted. He too approached that group and listened with a kindly smile and nods of approval, as he always did, to what the speaker was saying. The retired naval man was speaking very boldly, as was evident from the expression on the faces of the listeners and from the fact that some people Pierre knew as the meekest and quietest of men walked away disapprovingly, or expressed disagreement with him. Pierre pushed his way into the middle of the group, listened, and convinced himself that the man was indeed a Liberal, but of views quite different from his own. The naval officer spoke in a particularly sonorous, musical, and aristocratic baritone voice, pleasantly swallowing his r's and generally slurring his consonants: the voice of a man calling out to his servant, 'Heah! Bwing me my pipe!' It was indicative of dissipation and the exercise of authority.

'What if the Smolénsk people have offahd to waise militia for the Empewah? Ah we to take Smolénsk as our patte'n? If the noble awistocwacy of the pwovince of Moscow thinks fit, it can show its loyalty to our sov'weign the Empewah in othah ways. Have we fo'gotten the waising of the militia in the yeah 'seven? All that did was to enwich the pwiests' sons, and thieves and wobbahs . . .'

Count Ilyá Rostóv smiled blandly and nodded approval.

'And was our militia of any use to the Empia? Not at all! It only wuined our farming! Bettah have another conscwiption . . . o' ou' men will wetu'n neithah soldiers no' peasants, and we'll get only depwavity fwom them. The nobility don't gwudge theah lives—evewy one of us will go and bwing in more wecwuits, and the sov'weign' (that was the way he referred to the Emperor) 'need only say the word and we'll all die fo' him!' added the orator with animation.

Count Rostóv's mouth watered with pleasure and he nudged Pierre, but Pierre wanted to speak himself. He pushed forward, feeling stirred, but not yet sure what stirred him or what he would say. Scarcely had he opened his mouth when one of the senators, a man without a tooth in his head, with a shrewd though angry expression, standing near the first speaker, interrupted him. Evidently accustomed to managing debates and to maintaining an argument, he began in low but distinct tones:

'I imagine, Sir,' said he, mumbling with his toothless mouth, 'that we have been summoned here not to discuss whether it's best for the empire at the present moment to adopt conscription or to call out the militia. We have been summoned to reply to the appeal with which our sovereign the Emperor has honoured us. But to judge what is best—conscription or the militia—we can leave to the supreme authority ...'

Pierre suddenly saw an outlet for his excitement. He hardened his heart against the senator who was introducing this set and narrow attitude into the deliberations of the nobility. Pierre stepped forward and interrupted him. He himself did not yet know what he would say, but he began to speak eagerly, occasionally lapsing into French or expressing himself in bookish Russian.

'Excuse me, your Excellency,' he began. (He was well acquainted with the senator, but thought it necessary on this occasion to address him formally.) 'Though I don't agree with the gentleman ...' (He hesitated: he wished to say '*Mon très honorable préopinant*' ('My very honourable opponent') 'with the gentleman ... whom I have not the honour of knowing, I suppose that the nobility have been summoned not merely to express their sympathy and enthusiasm but also to consider the means by which we can assist our Fatherland! I imagine,' he went on, warming to his subject, 'that the Emperor him-

self would not be satisfied to find in us merely owners of
serfs whom we are willing to devote to his service, and
chair à canon[1] we are ready to make of ourselves—and
not to obtain from us any co-co-counsel.'

Many persons withdrew from the circle, noticing the
senator's sarcastic smile and the freedom of Pierre's
remarks. Only Count Rostóv was pleased with them as
he had been pleased with those of the naval officer, the
senator, and in general with whatever speech he had last
heard.

'I think that before discussing these questions,' Pierre
continued, 'we should ask the Emperor—most respectfully ask his Majesty—to let us know the number of our
troops and the position in which our army and our forces
now are, and then . . .'

But scarcely had Pierre uttered these words before he
was attacked from three sides. The most vigorous attack
came from an old acquaintance, a boston player who had
always been well disposed towards him, Stepán Stepáno-
vich Adráksin. Adráksin was in uniform, and whether as
a result of the uniform or from some other cause Pierre
saw before him quite a different man. With a sudden
expression of malevolence on his aged face Adráksin
shouted at Pierre:

'In the first place, I tell you we have no right to
question the Emperor about that, and secondly, if the
Russian nobility had that right, the Emperor could not
answer such a question. The troops move according to
the enemy's movements and the number of men increases
and decreases . . .'

Another voice, that of a nobleman of medium height
and about forty years of age, whom Pierre had formerly
met at the gipsies' and knew as a bad card-player, and
who, also transformed by his uniform, came up to Pierre,
interrupted Adráksin.

'Yes, and this is not a time for discussing,' he continued,
'but for acting: there is war in Russia! The enemy is
advancing to destroy Russia, to desecrate the tombs of
our fathers, to carry off our wives and children.' The
nobleman smote his breast. 'We will all arise, every one

_____
[1] Food for cannon.

of us will go, for our father the Tsar!'[1] he shouted, rolling his bloodshot eyes. Several approving voices were heard in the crowd. 'We are Russians and will not grudge our blood in defence of our faith, the throne, and the Fatherland! We must cease raving if we are sons of our Fatherland! We will show Europe how Russia rises to the defence of Russia!'

Pierre wished to reply, but could not get in a word. He felt that his words, apart from what meaning they conveyed, were less audible than the sound of his opponent's voice.

Count Rostóv at the back of the crowd was expressing approval, several persons, briskly turning a shoulder to the orator at the end of a phrase, said:

'That's right, quite right! Just so!'

Pierre wished to say that he was ready to sacrifice his money, his serfs, or himself, only one ought to know the state of affairs in order to be able to improve it, but he was unable to speak. Many voices shouted and talked at the same time, so that Count Rostóv had not time to signify his approval of them all, and the group increased, dispersed, re-formed, and then moved with a hum of talk into the largest hall and to the big table. Not only was Pierre's attempt to speak unsuccessful but he was rudely interrupted, pushed aside, and people turned away from him as from a common enemy. This happened not because they were displeased by the substance of his speech, which had even been forgotten after the many subsequent speeches, but to animate it the crowd needed a tangible object to love and a tangible object to hate. Pierre became the latter. Many other orators spoke after the excited nobleman, and all in the same tone. Many spoke eloquently and with originality.

Glínka, the editor of the *Russian Messenger*, who was recognized (cries of 'author! author!' were heard in the crowd), said that 'hell must be repulsed by hell,' and that

[1] The ruler of Russia was officially and properly speaking the 'Autocrat and Emperor', but in poetry and popular speech it was still permissible to refer to him as the 'Tsar', though that word was more in place in fairy-tales, as, for instance, when speaking of the 'Tsar-Maid'.

he had seen a child smiling at lightning flashes and thunderclaps, but 'we will not be that child'.

'Yes, yes, at thunderclaps!' was repeated approvingly in the back rows of the crowd.

The crowd drew up to the large table, at which sat grey-haired or bald seventy-year-old magnates, uniformed and besashed, almost all of whom Pierre had seen in their own homes with their buffoons, or playing boston at the clubs. With an incessant hum of voices the crowd advanced to the table. Pressed by the throng against the high backs of the chairs, the orators spoke one after another and sometimes two together. Those standing behind noticed what a speaker omitted to say and hastened to supply it. Others in that heat and crush racked their brains to find some thought and hastened to utter it. The old magnates, whom Pierre knew, sat and turned to look first at one and then at another, and their faces for the most part only expressed the fact that they found it very hot. Pierre however felt excited, and the general desire to show that they were ready to go to all lengths—which found expression in the tones and looks more than in the substance of the speeches—infected him too. He did not renounce his opinions, but felt himself in some way to blame and wished to justify himself.

'I only said that it would be more to the purpose to make sacrifices when we know what is needed!' said he, trying to be heard above the other voices.

One of the old men nearest to him looked round, but his attention was immediately diverted by an exclamation at the other side of the table.

'Yes, Moscow will be surrendered! She will be our expiation!' shouted one man.

'He is the enemy of mankind!' cried another. 'Allow me to speak . . .' 'Gentlemen, you are crushing me! . . .

CHAPTER XXIII

AT that moment Count Rostopchín with his protruding chin and alert eyes, wearing the uniform of a general with sash over his shoulder, entered the room stepping briskly to the front of the crowd of gentry.

'Our sovereign the Emperor will be here in a moment,' said Rostopchín. 'I am straight from the palace. Seeing the position we are in, I think there is little need for discussion. The Emperor has deigned to summon us and the merchants. Millions will pour forth from there'— he pointed to the merchants' hall—'but our business is to supply men and not spare ourselves . . . That is the least we can do!'

A conference took place confined to the magnates sitting at the table. The whole consultation passed more than quietly. After all the preceding noise the sound of their old voices saying one after another, 'I agree' or for variety, 'I too am of that opinion' and so on, had even a mournful effect.

The secretary was told to write down the resolution of the Moscow nobility and gentry, that they would furnish ten men fully equipped out of every thousand serfs, as the Smolénsk gentry had done. Their chairs made a scraping noise as the gentlemen who had conferred rose with apparent relief, and began walking up and down arm in arm to stretch their legs and converse in couples.

'The Emperor! The Emperor!' a sudden cry resounded through the halls, and the whole throng hurried to the entrance.

The Emperor entered the hall through a broad path between two lines of nobles. Every face expressed respectful, awe-struck curiosity. Pierre stood rather far off, and could not hear all that the Emperor said. From what he did hear he understood that the Emperor spoke of the danger threatening the empire and of the hopes he placed on the Moscow nobility. He was answered by a voice which informed him of the resolution just arrived at.

'Gentlemen!' said the Emperor with a quivering voice. There was a rustling among the crowd and it again subsided, so that Pierre distinctly heard the pleasantly human voice of the Emperor saying with emotion:

'I never doubted the devotion of the Russian nobles, but to-day it has surpassed my expectations. I thank you in the name of the Fatherland! Gentlemen, let us act! Time is most precious . . .'

The Emperor ceased speaking, the crowd began pressing round him, and rapturous exclamations were heard from all sides.

'Yes, most precious . . . a royal word,' said Count Rostóv with a sob. He stood at the back, and though he had heard hardly anything, understood everything in his own way.

From the hall of the nobility the Emperor went to that of the merchants. There he remained about ten minutes. Pierre was among those who saw him come out from the merchants' hall with tears of emotion in his eyes. As became known later, he had scarcely begun to address the merchants before tears gushed from his eyes and he concluded in a trembling voice. When Pierre saw the Emperor he was coming out accompanied by two merchants, one of whom Pierre knew, a fat *otkupshchík*.[1] The other was the mayor, a man with a thin sallow face and narrow beard. Both were weeping. Tears filled the thin man's eyes, and the fat *otkupshchík* sobbed outright like a child, and kept repeating:

'Our lives and property—take them, your Majesty!'

Pierre's one feeling at the moment was a desire to show that he was ready to go all lengths and was prepared to sacrifice everything. He now felt ashamed of his speech with its constitutional tendency and sought an opportunity of effacing it. Having heard that Count Mamónov was furnishing a regiment, Bezúhkov at once informed Rostopchín that he would give a thousand men and their maintenance.

Old Rostóv could not tell his wife of what had passed without tears, and at once consented to Pétya's request and went himself to enter his name.

Next day the Emperor left Moscow. The assembled nobles all took off their uniforms and settled down again in their homes and clubs, and not without some groans gave orders to their stewards about the enrolment, feeling amazed themselves at what they had done.

[1] A dealer in spirits—one who leased from the government the monopoly of the sale of spirits for a certain district.

END OF BOOK IX

BOOK X

BOOK X

CHAPTER I

NAPOLEON began the war with Russia because he could not resist going to Dresden, could not help having his head turned by the homage he received, could not help donning a Polish uniform and yielding to the stimulating influence of a June morning, and could not refrain from bursts of anger in the presence of Kurákin and then of Balá shev.

Alexander refused negotiations because he felt himself to be personally insulted. Barclay de Tolly tried to command the army in the best way because he wished to fulfil his duty and earn fame as a great commander. Rostóv charged the French because he could not restrain his wish for a gallop across a level field; and in the same way the innumerable people who took part in the war acted in accord with their personal characteristics, habits, circumstances, and aims. They were moved by fear or vanity, rejoiced or were indignant, reasoned, imagining that they knew what they were doing and did it of their own free will, but they all were involuntary tools of history, carrying on a work concealed from them but comprehensible to us. Such is the inevitable fate of men of action, and the higher they stand in the social hierarchy the less are they free.

The actors of 1812 have long since left the stage, their personal interests have vanished leaving no trace, and nothing remains of that time but its historic results.

Providence compelled all these men, striving to attain personal aims, to further the accomplishment of a stupendous result no one of them at all expected—neither Napoleon, nor Alexander, and still less any of those who did the actual fighting.

The cause of the destruction of the French army in 1812 is clear to us now. No one will deny that that cause was, on the one hand its advance into the heart of Russia late in the season without any preparation for a winter campaign, and on the other the character given to the

war by the burning of Russian towns and the hatred of the
foe this aroused among the Russian people. But no one
at the time foresaw (what now seems so evident) that
this was the only way an army of eight hundred thousand
men—the best in the world and led by the best general—
could be destroyed in conflict with a raw army of half
its numerical strength, and led by inexperienced commanders as the Russian army was. *Not only did no one see
this*, but *on the Russian side* every effort was made to hinder
the only thing that could save Russia, while *on the French
side*, despite Napoleon's experience and so-called military
genius, every effort was directed to pushing on to Moscow
at the end of the summer, that is, to doing the very thing
that was bound to lead to destruction.

In historical works on the year 1812 French writers are
very fond of saying that Napoleon felt the danger of extending his line, that he sought a battle, and that his
marshals advised him to stop at Smolénsk, and of making
similar statements to show that the danger of the campaign was even then understood. Russian authors are
still fonder of telling us that from the commencement of
the campaign a Scythian war-plan was adopted to lure
Napoleon into the depths of Russia, and this plan some
of them attribute to Pfuel, others to a certain Frenchman,
others to Toll, and others again to Alexander himself—
pointing to notes, projects, and letters, which contain
hints of such a line of action. But all these hints at what
happened, both from the French side and the Russian,
are advanced only because they fit in with the event.
Had that event not occurred these hints would have been
forgotten, as we have forgotten the thousands and
millions of hints and expectations to the contrary which
were current then but have now been forgotten because
the event falsified them. There are always so many
conjectures as to the issue of any event, that however
it may end there will always be people to say: 'I said
then that it would be so,' quite forgetting that amid
their innumerable conjectures many were to quite the
contrary effect.

Conjectures as to Napoleon's awareness of the danger
of extending his line, and (on the Russian side) as to

luring the enemy into the depths of Russia, are evidently of that kind, and only by much straining can historians attribute such conceptions to Napoleon and his marshals, or such plans to the Russian commanders. All the facts are in flat contradiction to such conjectures. During the whole period of the war not only was there no wish on the Russian side to draw the French into the heart of the country, but from their first entry into Russia, everything was done to stop them. And not only was Napoleon not afraid to extend his line, but he welcomed every step forward as a triumph, and did not seek battle as eagerly as in former campaigns, but very lazily.

At the very beginning of the war our armies were divided, and our sole aim was to unite them, though uniting the armies was no advantage if we meant to retire and lure the enemy into the depths of the country. Our Emperor joined the army to encourage it to defend every inch of Russian soil and not to retreat. The enormous Drissa camp was formed on Pfuel's plan, and there was no intention of retiring farther. The Emperor reproached the commanders-in-chief for every step they retired. He could not bear the idea of letting the enemy even reach Smolénsk, still less could he contemplate the burning of Moscow, and when our armies did unite he was displeased that Smolénsk was abandoned and burnt without a general engagement having been fought under its walls.

So thought the Emperor, and the Russian commanders and people were still more provoked at the thought that our forces were retreating into the depths of the country.

Napoleon having cut our armies apart advanced far into the country and missed several chances of forcing an engagement. In August he was at Smolénsk, and thought only of how to advance farther, though as we now see that advance was evidently ruinous to him.

The facts clearly show that Napoleon did not foresee the danger of the advance on Moscow, nor did Alexander and the Russian commanders then think of luring Napoleon on, but quite the contrary. The luring of Napoleon into the depths of the country was not the result of any plan, for no one believed it to be possible;

it resulted from a most complex interplay of intrigues, aims, and wishes, among those who took part in the war and had no perception whatever of the inevitable, or of the one way of saving Russia. Everything came about fortuitously. The armies were divided at the commencement of the campaign. We tried to unite them, with the evident intention of giving battle and checking the enemy's advance, and by this effort to unite them while avoiding battle with a much stronger enemy, and necessarily withdrawing the armies at an acute angle—we led the French on to Smolénsk. But we withdrew at an acute angle not only because the French advanced between our two armies; the angle became still more acute and we withdrew still farther, because Barclay de Tolly was an unpopular foreigner disliked by Bagratión (who would come under his command), and Bagratión—being in command of the second army—tried to postpone joining up and coming under Barclay's command as long as he could. Bagratión was slow in effecting the junction —though that was the chief aim of all at head-quarters— because, as he alleged, he exposed his army to danger on this march, and it was best for him to retire more to the left and more to the south, worrying the enemy from flank and rear and securing from the Ukraine recruits for his army ; and it looks as if he planned this in order not to come under the command of the detested foreigner Barclay, whose rank was inferior to his own.

The Emperor was with the army to encourage it, but his presence and ignorance of what steps to take, and the enormous number of advisers and plans, destroyed the first army's energy and it retired.

The intention was to make a stand at the Drissa camp, but Paulucci, aiming at becoming commander-in-chief, unexpectedly employed his energy to influence Alexander, and Pfuel's whole plan was abandoned and the command entrusted to Barclay. But as Barclay did not inspire confidence his power was limited. The armies were divided, there was no unity of command, and Barclay was unpopular; but from this confusion, division, and the unpopularity of the foreign commander-in-chief, there resulted on the one hand indecision and the avoidance of a battle (which we could not have refrained from had the armies been united and had some one else, instead of Barclay, been in command) and on the other an ever-increasing indignation against the foreigners and an increase of patriotic zeal.

At last the Emperor left the army, and as the most convenient and indeed the only pretext for his departure it was decided that it was necessary for him to inspire the people in the capitals and arouse the nation in general to a patriotic war. And by this visit of the Emperor to Moscow the strength of the Russian army was trebled.

He left in order not to obstruct the commander-in-chief's undivided control of the army, and hoping that more decisive action would then be taken, but the command of the armies became still more confused and enfeebled. Bennigsen, the Tsarévich, and a swarm of adjutants-general, remained with the army to keep the commander-in-chief under observation and arouse his energy, and Barclay, feeling less free than ever under the observation of all these 'eyes of the Emperor', became still more cautious of undertaking any decisive action, and avoided giving battle.

Barclay stood for caution. The Tsarévich hinted at treachery and demanded a general engagement. Lubomírski, Bronnítski, Wlocki, and the others of that group, stirred up so much trouble that Barclay, under pretext of sending papers to the Emperor, dispatched these Polish adjutants-general to Petersburg, and plunged into an open struggle with Bennigsen and the Tsarévich.

At Smolénsk the armies at last reunited, much as Bagratión disliked it.

Bagratión drove up in a carriage to the house occupied by Barclay. Barclay donned his sash and came out to meet and report to his senior officer Bagratión.

Despite his seniority in rank, Bagratión, in this contest of magnanimity, took his orders from Barclay, but having submitted, agreed with him less than ever. By the Emperor's orders Bagratión reported direct to him. He wrote to Arakchéev, the Emperor's confidant: 'It must be as my Sovereign pleases, but I cannot work with the *Minister* (meaning Barclay). For God's sake send me somewhere else, if only in command of a regiment. I cannot stand it here. Head-quarters are so full of Germans that a Russian cannot exist and there is no sense in anything. I thought I was really serving my Sovereign and the Fatherland, but it turns out that I am serving Barclay. I confess I do not want to.'

The swarm of Bronnítskis and Wintsingerodes and their like still further embittered the relations between the commanders-in-chief, and even less unity resulted. Preparations were made to fight the French before Smolénsk. A general was sent to survey the position. This general, hating Barclay, rode to visit a friend of his own, a corps-commander, and having spent the day with him, returned to Barclay and condemned, as unsuitable from every point of view, the battleground he had not seen.

While disputes and intrigues were going on about the future field of battle, and while we were looking for the French—having lost touch with them—the French stumbled upon Nevérovski's division and reached the walls of Smolénsk.

It was necessary to fight an unexpected battle at Smolénsk to save our lines of communication. The battle was fought, and thousands were killed on both sides.

Smolénsk was abandoned contrary to the wishes of the Emperor and of the whole people. But Smolénsk was burnt by its own inhabitants who had been misled by their governor. And these ruined inhabitants, setting an example to other Russians, went to Moscow thinking only of their own losses but kindling hatred of the foe. Napoleon advanced farther and we retired, thus arriving at the very result which caused his destruction.

CHAPTER II

THE day after his son had left, Prince Nicholas sent for Princess Mary to come to his study.

'Well? Are you satisfied now?' said he. 'You've made me quarrel with my son! Satisfied, are you? That's all you wanted! Satisfied? . . . It hurts me, it hurts. I'm old and weak and this is what you wanted. Well then, gloat over it! Gloat over it!'

After that Princess Mary did not see her father for a whole week. He was ill and did not leave his study.

Princess Mary noticed to her surprise that during this illness the old prince not only excluded her from his room, but did not admit Mademoiselle Bourienne either. Tíkhon alone attended him.

At the end of the week the prince reappeared and resumed his former way of life, devoting himself with special activity to building operations and the arrangement of the gardens, and completely breaking off his relations with Mademoiselle Bourienne. His looks and his cold tone to his daughter seemed to say: 'There, you see? You plotted against me, you lied to Prince Andrew about my relations with that Frenchwoman and made me quarrel with him, but you see I need neither her nor you!'

Princess Mary spent half of every day with little Nicholas, watching his lessons, teaching him Russian and music herself, and talking to Dessalles; the rest of the day she spent over her books, with her old nurse, or with 'God's folk' who sometimes came by the back door to see her.

Of the war Princess Mary thought as women do think about wars. She feared for her brother who was in it, was horrified by and amazed at the strange cruelty that impels men to kill one another, but she did not understand the significance of this war, which seemed to her like all previous wars. She did not realize the significance of this war, though Dessalles with whom she constantly conversed was passionately interested in its progress and tried to explain his own conception of it to her, and though the 'God's folk' who came to see her reported, in their own way, the rumours current among the people of an invasion by Antichrist, and though Julie (now Princess Drubetskáya), who had resumed correspondence with her, wrote patriotic letters from Moscow.

'I write you in Russian, my good friend,' wrote Julie in her Frenchified Russian, 'because I have a detestation for all the French, and the same for their language which

I cannot support to hear spoken . . . We in Moscow are elated by enthusiasm for our adored Emperor.

'My poor husband is enduring pains and hunger in Jewish taverns, but the news which I have inspires me yet more.

'You heard probably of the heroic exploit of Raévski, embracing his two sons and saying: "I will perish with them but we will not shake!" And truly though the enemy was twice stronger than we, we were unshakeable. We pass the time as we can, but in war as in war! The princesses Aline and Sophie sit whole days with me, and we, unhappy widows of live men, make beautiful conversations over our *charpie*, only you my friend are missing . . .' and so on.

The chief reason Princess Mary did not realize the full significance of this war was because the old prince never spoke of it, did not recognize it, and laughed at Dessalles when he mentioned it at dinner. The prince's tone was so calm and confident that Princess Mary unhesitatingly believed him.

All that July the old prince was exceedingly active and even animated. He planned another garden and began a new building for the domestic serfs. The only thing that made Princess Mary anxious about him was that he slept very little and, instead of sleeping in his study as usual, changed his sleeping place every day. One day he would order his camp-bed to be set up in the glass-gallery, another day he remained on the couch or on the lounge-chair in the drawing-room and dozed there without undressing, while—instead of Mademoiselle Bourienne—a serf-boy read to him. Then again he would spend a night in the dining-room.

On August 1st a second letter was received from Prince Andrew. In his first letter which came soon after he had left home Prince Andrew had dutifully asked his father's forgiveness for what he had allowed himself to say, and begged to be restored to his favour. To this letter the old prince had replied affectionately, and from that time had kept the Frenchwoman at a distance. Prince Andrew's second letter, written near Vítebsk after the French had occupied that town, gave a brief account of the whole campaign with a plan he had drawn in the letter and forecasts as to the further progress of the war. In this letter Prince Andrew pointed out to his father the danger of staying at Bald Hills, so near the theatre of war and on the army's direct line of march, and advised him to move to Moscow.

At dinner that day, on Dessalles's mentioning that the French were said to have already entered Vítebsk, the old prince remembered his son's letter.

'There was a letter from Prince Andrew to-day,' he said to Princess Mary—'Haven't you read it?'

'No, father,' she replied in a frightened voice.

She could not have read the letter as she did not even know it had arrived.

'He writes about this war,' said the prince, with the ironic smile that had become habitual to him in speaking of the present war.

'That must be very interesting,' said Dessalles. 'Prince Andrew is in a position to know . . .'

'Oh, very interesting!' said Mademoiselle Bourienne.

'Go and get it for me,' said the old prince to Mademoiselle Bourienne. 'You know—under the paper-weight on the little table.'

Mademoiselle Bourienne jumped up eagerly.

'No, don't!' he exclaimed with a frown. 'You go, Michael Ivánovich.'

Michael Ivánovich rose and went to the study. But as soon as he had left the room the old prince, looking uneasily round, threw down his napkin and went himself.

'They can't do anything . . . always make some muddle,' he muttered.

While he was away Princess Mary, Dessalles, Mademoiselle Bourienne, and even little Nicholas, exchanged looks in silence. The old prince returned with quick steps, accompanied by Michael Ivánovich, bringing the letter and a plan. These he put down beside him—not letting any one read them at dinner.

On moving to the drawing-room he handed the letter to Princess Mary and, spreading out before him the plan of the new building and fixing his eyes upon it, told her to read the letter aloud. When she had done so Princess

Mary looked inquiringly at her father. He was examining the plan, evidently engrossed in his own ideas.

'What do you think of it, Prince?' Dessalles ventured to ask.

'I? I? . . .' said the prince as if unpleasantly awakened, and not taking his eyes from the plan of the building.

'Very possibly the theatre of war will move so near to us that . . .'

'Ha ha ha! The theatre of war!' said the prince. 'I have said and still say, that the theatre of war is Poland and the enemy will never get beyond the Niemen.'

Dessalles looked in amazement at the prince, who was talking of the Niemen when the enemy was already at the Dnieper, but Princess Mary, forgetting the geographical position of the Niemen, thought that what her father was saying was correct.

'When the snow melts they'll sink in the Polish swamps. Only they could fail to see it,' the prince continued, evidently thinking of the campaign of 1807 which seemed to him so recent. 'Bennigsen should have advanced into Prussia sooner, then things would have taken a different turn . . .'

'But, Prince,' Dessalles began timidly, 'the letter mentions Vítebsk . . .'

'Ah, the letter? Yes . . .' replied the prince, peevishly. 'Yes . . . yes . . .' His face suddenly took on a morose expression. He paused. 'Yes, he writes that the French were beaten at . . . at . . . what river is it?'

Dessalles dropped his eyes.

'The prince says nothing about that,' he remarked gently.

'Doesn't he? But I didn't invent it myself.'

No one spoke for a long time.

'Yes . . . yes . . . Well, Michael Ivánovich,' he suddenly went on, raising his head and pointing to the plan of the building, 'tell me how you mean to alter it . . .'

Michael Ivánovich went up to the plan, and the prince after speaking to him about the new building looked angrily at Princess Mary and Dessalles and went to his own room.

Princess Mary saw Dessalles's embarrassed and astonished look fixed on her father, noticed his silence, and was struck by the fact that her father had forgotten his son's letter on the drawing-room table, but she was not only afraid to speak of it and ask Dessalles the reason of his confusion and silence, but was afraid even to think about it.

In the evening Michael Ivánovich, sent by the prince, came to Princess Mary for Prince Andrew's letter which had been forgotten in the drawing-room. She gave it to him and, unpleasant as it was to her to do so, ventured to ask him what her father was doing.

'Always busy,' replied Michael Ivánovich with a respectfully ironic smile which caused Princess Mary to turn pale. 'He's worrying very much about the new building. He has been reading a little, but now'— Michael Ivánovich went on, lowering his voice—'now he's at his desk, busy with his will I expect.' (One of the prince's favourite occupations of late had been the preparation of some papers he meant to leave at his death and which he called his 'will'.)

'And Alpátych is being sent to Smolénsk?' asked Princess Mary.

'Oh, yes, he has been waiting to start for some time.'

CHAPTER III

WHEN Michael Ivánovich returned to the study with the letter, the old prince, with spectacles on and a shade over his eyes, was sitting at his open bureau with screened candles, holding a paper in his outstretched hand, and in a somewhat dramatic attitude was reading his manuscript—his 'Remarks' as he termed it—which was to be transmitted to the Emperor after his death.

When Michael Ivánovich went in there were tears in the prince's eyes evoked by the memory of the time when the paper he was now reading had been written. He took the letter from Michael Ivánovich's hand, put it in his pocket, folded up his papers, and called in Alpátych who had long been waiting.

The prince had a list of things to be bought in

Smolénsk, and walking up and down the room past Alpátych who stood by the door, he gave his instructions.

'First, notepaper—do you hear? Eight quires, like this sample, gilt-edged . . . it must be exactly like the sample. Varnish, sealing-wax, as in Michael Ivánovich's list.'

He paced up and down for a while and glanced at his notes.

'Then hand to the governor in person a letter about the deed.'

Next bolts for the doors of the new building were wanted and had to be of a special shape the prince had himself designed, and a bound case had to be ordered to keep the 'will' in.

The instructions to Alpátych took over two hours and still the prince did not let him go. He sat down, sank into thought, closed his eyes, and dozed off. Alpátych made a slight movement.

'Well, go, go! If anything more is wanted I'll send after you.'

Alpátych went out. The prince again went to his bureau, glanced into it, fingered his papers, closed the bureau again, and sat down at the table to write to the governor.

It was already late when he rose after sealing the letter. He wished to sleep, but he knew he would not be able to, and that most depressing thoughts came to him in bed. So he called Tíkhon and went through the rooms with him to show him where to set up the bed for that night.

He went about looking at every corner. Every place seemed unsatisfactory, but worst of all was his customary couch in the study. That couch was dreadful to him, probably because of the oppressive thoughts he had had when lying there. It was unsatisfactory everywhere, but the corner behind the piano in the sitting-room was better than other places: he had never slept there yet.

With the help of a footman Tíkhon brought in the bedstead and began putting it up.

'That's not right! That's not right!' cried the prince, and himself pushed it a few inches from the corner and then closer in again.

'Well, at last I've finished, now I'll rest,' thought the prince, and let Tíkhon undress him.

Frowning with vexation at the effort necessary to divest himself of his coat and trousers, the prince undressed, sat down heavily on the bed, and appeared to be meditating as he looked contemptuously at his withered yellow legs. He was not meditating, but only deferring the moment of making the effort to lift those legs up and turn over on the bed. 'Ugh, how hard it is! Oh, that this toil might end and *you* would release me!' thought he. Pressing his lips together he made that effort for the twenty-thousandth time and lay down. But hardly had he done so before he felt the bed rocking backwards and forwards beneath him as if it were breathing heavily and jolting. This happened to him almost every night. He opened his eyes as they were closing.

'No peace, damn them!' he muttered, angry he knew not with whom. 'Ah yes, there was something else important, very important, that I was keeping till I should be in bed. The bolts? No, I told him about them. No, it was something, something in the drawing-room. Princess Mary talked some nonsense. Dessalles, that fool, said something. Something in my pocket—can't remember.'

'Tíkhon, what did we talk about at dinner?'

'About Prince Michael . . .'

'Be quiet, quiet!' The prince slapped his hand on the table. 'Yes, I know, Prince Andrew's letter! Princess Mary read it. Dessalles said something about Vítebsk. Now I'll read it.'

He had the letter taken from his pocket, and the table —on which stood a glass of lemonade and a spiral wax candle—moved close to the bed, and putting on his spectacles he began reading. Only now in the stillness of the night, reading it by the faint light under the green shade, did he grasp its meaning for a moment.

'The French at Vítebsk, in four days' march they may be at Smolénsk; perhaps are already there! Tíkhon!' Tíkhon jumped up. 'No, no, I don't want anything!' he shouted.

He put the letter under the candlestick and closed his eyes. And there rose before him the Danube at bright noonday: reeds, the Russian camp, and himself a young

general without a wrinkle on his ruddy face, vigorous and
alert, entering Potëmkin's gaily-coloured tent, and a burning sense of jealousy of 'the favourite' agitated him now
as strongly as it had done then. He recalled all the words
spoken at that first meeting with Potëmkin. And he saw
before him a plump, rather sallow-faced, short, stout
woman, the Empress-Mother, with her smile and her words
at her first gracious reception of him, and then that same
face on the catafalque, and the encounter he had with
Zúbov over her coffin about his right to kiss her hand.

'Oh, quicker, quicker! To get back to that time and
have done with all the present! Quicker, quicker—and
that they should leave me in peace!'

CHAPTER IV

BALD HILLS, Prince Nicholas Bolkónski's estate, lay
forty miles east from Smolénsk and two miles from the
main road to Moscow.

The same evening that the prince gave his instructions
to Alpátych, Dessalles having asked to see Princess Mary
told her that, as the prince was not very well and was
taking no steps to secure his safety, though from Prince
Andrew's letter it was evident that to remain at Bald
Hills might be dangerous, he respectfully advised her to
send a letter by Alpátych to the Provincial Governor at
Smolénsk, asking him to let her know the state of affairs
and the extent of the danger to which Bald Hills was
exposed. Dessalles wrote this letter to the governor for
Princess Mary, she signed it, and it was given to Alpátych
with instructions to hand it to the Governor and to come
back as quickly as possible if there was danger.

Having received all his orders Alpátych, wearing a
white beaver hat—a present from the prince—and carrying
a stick as the prince did, went out accompanied by his
family. Three well-fed roans stood ready harnessed to a
small conveyance with a leather hood.

The larger bell was muffled and the little bells on the
harness stuffed with paper. The prince allowed no one
at Bald Hills to drive with ringing bells, but on a long

journey Alpátych liked to have them. His satellites—the senior clerk, a counting-house clerk, a scullery maid, a cook, two old women, a little page boy, the coachman, and various domestic serfs—were seeing him off.

His daughter placed chintz-covered down-cushions for him to sit on and behind his back. His old sister-in-law popped in a small bundle, and one of the coachmen helped him into the vehicle.

'There! There! Women's fuss! Women, women!' said Alpátych, puffing and speaking rapidly just as the prince did, and he climbed into the trap.

After giving the clerk orders about the work to be done, Alpátych, not trying to imitate the prince now, lifted the hat from his bald head and crossed himself three times.

'If there is anything . . . come back, Yákov Alpátych. For Christ's sake think of us!' cried his wife, referring to the rumours of war and the enemy.

'Women, women! Women's fuss!' muttered Alpátych to himself and started on his journey, looking round at the fields of yellow rye and the still green, thickly growing oats, and at other quite black fields just being ploughed a second time.

As he went along he looked with pleasure at the year's splendid crop of corn, scrutinized the strips of rye-field which here and there were already being reaped, made his calculations as to the sowing and the harvest, and asked himself whether he had not forgotten any of the prince's orders.

Having baited the horses twice on the way, he arrived at the town towards evening on the 4th of August.

Alpátych kept meeting and overtaking baggage-trains and troops on the road. As he approached Smolénsk he heard the sounds of distant firing, but these did not impress him. What struck him most was the sight of a splendid field of oats in which a camp had been pitched, and which was being mown down by the soldiers evidently for fodder. This fact impressed Alpátych, but in thinking about his own business he soon forgot it.

All the interests of his life for more than thirty years had been bounded by the will of the prince, and he never went beyond that limit. Everything not connected with the execution of the prince's orders did not interest and did not even exist for Alpátych.

On reaching Smolénsk on the evening of the 4th of August he put up in the Gáchina suburb, across the Dnieper, at the inn kept by Ferapóntov, where he had been in the habit of putting up for the last thirty years. Some thirty years ago, Ferapóntov, by Alpátych's advice, had bought a wood from the prince, had begun to trade, and now had a house, an inn, and a corn-dealer's shop in that province. He was a stout, dark, red-faced peasant in the forties, with thick lips, a broad knob of a nose, similar knobs over his black frowning brows, and a round belly.

Wearing a waistcoat over his cotton shirt, Ferapóntov was standing before his shop which opened onto the street. On seeing Alpátych he went up to him.

'You're welcome, Yákov Alpátych. Folks are leaving the town, but you have come to it,' said he.

'Why are they leaving the town?' asked Alpátych.

'That's what I say. Folks are foolish! Always afraid of the French.'

'Women's fuss, women's fuss!' said Alpátych.

'Just what I think, Yákov Alpátych. What I say is: orders have been given not to let them in, so that must be right. And the peasants are asking three rubles for carting—it isn't Christian!'

Yákov Alpátych heard without heeding. He asked for a samovar, and for hay for his horses, and when he had had his tea he went to bed.

All night long troops were moving past the inn. Next morning Alpátych donned a jacket he only wore in town, and went out on business. It was a sunny morning and by eight o'clock it was already hot. 'A good day for harvesting,' thought Alpátych.

From beyond the town firing had been heard since early morning. At eight o'clock the booming of cannon was added to the sound of musketry. Many people were hurrying through the streets and there were many soldiers, but cabs were still driving about, tradesmen stood at their shops, and service was being held in the churches as usual. Alpátych went to the shops, to government offices, to the post office, and to the Governor's. In the offices and shops and at the post office every one was talking about the army and about the enemy who was already attacking the town, everybody was asking what should be done, and all were trying to calm one another.

In front of the Governor's house Alpátych found a large number of people, Cossacks, and a travelling carriage belonging to the Governor. At the porch he met two of the landed gentry, one of whom he knew. This man, an ex-captain of police, was saying angrily:

'It's no joke, you know! It's all very well if you're single. "One man though undone is but one," as the proverb says, but with thirteen in family and all the property. . . . They've brought us to utter ruin! What sort of Governors are they to do that? They ought to be hanged —the brigands! . . .'

'Oh come, that's enough!' said the other.

'What do I care? Let him hear! We're not dogs,' said the ex-captain of police, and looking round he noticed Alpátych.

'Oh, Yákov Alpátych! What have you come for?'

'To see the Governor, by his Excellency's order,' answered Alpátych, lifting his head and proudly thrusting his hand into the bosom of his coat as he always did when he mentioned the prince . . . 'He has ordered me to inquire into the position of affairs,' he added.

'Yes, go and find out!' shouted the angry gentleman. 'They've brought things to such a pass that there are no carts or anything! . . . There it is again, do you hear?' said he, pointing in the direction whence came the sounds of firing.

'They've brought us all to ruin . . . the brigands!' he repeated, and descended the porch steps.

Alpátych swayed his head and went upstairs. In the waiting-room were tradesmen, women, and officials, looking silently at one another. The door of the Governor's room opened and they all rose and moved forward. An official ran out, said some words to a merchant, called a stout official with a cross hanging on his neck to follow him, and vanished again, evidently wishing to avoid the inquiring looks and questions addressed to him. Alpátych moved forward and next time the official came out addressed him, one hand placed in the breast of his buttoned coat, and handed him two letters.

'To his Honour Baron Asch, from General-in-Chief Prince Bolkónski,' he announced with such solemnity and significance that the official turned to him and took the letters.

A few minutes later the Governor received Alpátych and hurriedly said to him:

'Inform the prince and princess that I knew nothing: I acted on the highest instructions—here . . .' and he handed a paper to Alpátych. 'Still, as the prince is unwell, my advice is that they should go to Moscow. I am just starting myself. Inform them . . .'

But the Governor did not finish: a dusty perspiring officer ran into the room and began to say something in French. The Governor's face expressed terror.

'Go,' he said, nodding his head to Alpátych, and began questioning the officer.

Eager, frightened, helpless glances were turned on Alpátych when he came out of the Governor's room. Involuntarily listening now to the firing, which had drawn nearer and was increasing in strength, Alpátych hurried to his inn. The paper handed to him by the Governor was this:

'I assure you that the town of Smolénsk is not in the slightest danger as yet and it is unlikely that it will be threatened with any. I from the one side and Prince Bagratión from the other are marching to unite our forces before Smolénsk, which junction will be effected on the 22nd instant, and both armies with their united forces will defend our compatriots of the province entrusted to your care till our efforts shall have beaten back the enemies of our Fatherland, or till the last warrior in our valiant ranks has perished. From this you will see that you have a perfect right to reassure the inhabitants of Smolénsk, for those defended by two such brave armies may feel assured of victory.' (Instructions from Barclay de Tolly to the civil governor of Smolénsk, Baron Asch, 1812.)

People were anxiously roaming about the streets.

Carts piled high with household utensils, chairs, and

cupboards, kept emerging from the gates of the yards and moving along the streets. Loaded carts stood at the house next to Ferapóntov's and women were wailing and lamenting as they said good-bye. A small watch-dog ran round barking in front of the harnessed horses.

Alpátych entered the inn yard at a quicker pace than usual and went straight to the shed where his horses and trap were. The coachman was asleep. He woke him up, told him to harness, and went into the passage. From the host's room came the sounds of a child crying, the despairing sobs of a woman, and the hoarse angry shouting of Ferapóntov. The cook began running hither and thither in the passage like a frightened hen, just as Alpátych entered.

'He's done her to death. Killed the mistress! . . . Beat her . . . dragged her about so! . . .'

'What for?' asked Alpátych.

'She kept begging to go away. She's a woman! "Take me away," says she, "don't let me perish with my little children; folks," she says, "are all gone, so why", she says, "don't we go?" And he began beating and pulling her about so!'

At these words Alpátych nodded as if in approval and not wishing to hear more went to the door of the room opposite the innkeeper's, where he had left his purchases.

'You brute, you murderer!' screamed a thin, pale woman who, with a baby in her arms and her kerchief torn from her head, burst through the door at that moment and down the steps into the yard.

Ferapóntov came out after her, but on seeing Alpátych, adjusted his waistcoat, smoothed his hair, yawned, and followed Alpátych into the opposite room.

'Going already?' said he.

Alpátych, without answering or looking at his host, sorted his packages and asked how much he owed.

'We'll reckon up! Well, have you been to the Governor's?' asked Ferapóntov. 'What has been decided?'

Alpátych replied that the Governor had not told him anything definite.

'With our business, how can we get away?' said Ferapóntov. 'We'd have to pay seven rubles a cartload to Dorogobúzh and I tell them they're not Christians to ask it! Selivánov, now, did a good stroke last Thursday— sold flour to the army at nine rubles a sack. Will you have some tea?' he added.

While the horses were being harnessed Alpátych and Ferapóntov over their tea talked of the price of corn, the crops, and the good weather for harvesting.

'Well, it seems to be getting quieter,' remarked Ferapóntov, finishing his third cup of tea and getting up. 'Ours must have got the best of it. The orders were not to let them in. So we're in force, it seems . . . They say the other day Matthew Iványch Plátov drove them into the river Márina and drowned some eighteen thousand in one day.'

Alpátych collected his parcels, handed them to the coachman who had come in, and settled up with the innkeeper. The noise of wheels, hoofs, and bells, was heard from the gateway as a little trap passed out.

It was by now late in the afternoon. Half the street was in shadow, the other half brightly lit by the sun. Alpátych looked out of the window and went to the door. Suddenly the strange sound of a far-off whistling and thud was heard, followed by a boom of cannon blending into a dull roar that set the windows rattling.

He went out into the street: two men were running past towards the bridge. From different sides came whistling sounds and the thud of cannon-balls and bursting shells falling on the town. But these sounds were hardly heard in comparison with the noise of the firing outside the town, and attracted little attention from the inhabitants. The town was being bombarded by a hundred and thirty guns which Napoleon had ordered up after four o'clock. At first the people did not realize the meaning of this bombardment.

At first the noise of the falling bombs and shells only aroused curiosity. Ferapóntov's wife who till then had not ceased wailing under the shed, became quiet, and with the baby in her arms went to the gate listening to the sounds and looking in silence at the people.

The cook and a shop-assistant came to the gate. With lively curiosity every one tried to get a glimpse of the projectiles as they flew over their heads. Several people came round the corner talking eagerly.

'What force!' remarked one. 'Knocked the roof and ceiling all to splinters!'

'Routed up the earth like a pig,' said another.

'That's grand, it bucks one up!' laughed the first. 'Lucky you jumped aside, or it would have wiped you out!'

Others joined those men, and stopped and told how cannon-balls had fallen on a house close to them. Meanwhile still more projectiles, now with the swift sinister whistle of a cannon ball, now with the agreeable intermittent whistle of a shell, flew over the people's heads incessantly, but not one fell close by, they all flew over. Alpátych was getting into his trap. The innkeeper stood at the gate.

'What are you staring at?' he shouted to the cook, who in her red skirt, with sleeves rolled up, swinging her bare elbows, had stepped to the corner to listen to what was being said.

'What marvels!' she exclaimed, but hearing her master's voice she turned back pulling down her tucked-up skirt.

Once more something whistled, but this time quite close, swooping downwards like a little bird; a flame flashed in the middle of the street, something exploded, and the street was shrouded in smoke.

'Scoundrel, what are you doing?' shouted the inn-keeper, rushing to the cook.

At that moment the pitiful wailing of women was heard from different sides, the frightened baby began to cry, and people crowded silently with pale faces round the cook. The loudest sound in that crowd was her wailing.

'Oh-h-h! Dear souls, dear kind souls! Don't let me die! My good souls! . . .'

Five minutes later no one remained in the street. The cook, with her thigh broken by a shell-splinter, had been carried into the kitchen. Alpátych, his coachman, Fera-póntov's wife and children, and the house-porter, were all sitting in the cellar listening. The roar of guns, the whistling of projectiles, and the piteous moaning of the

cook, which rose above the other sounds, did not cease for
a moment. The mistress rocked and hushed her baby
and when any one came into the cellar asked in a pathetic
whisper what had become of her husband who had remained in the street. A shopman who entered told her
that her husband had gone with others to the cathedral,
whence they were fetching the wonder-working icon of
Smolénsk.

Towards dusk the cannonade began to subside. Alpátych left the cellar and stopped in the doorway. The
evening sky that had been so clear was clouded with
smoke, through which, high up, the sickle of the new
moon shone strangely. Now that the terrible din of the
guns had ceased a hush seemed to reign over the town,
broken only by the rustle of footsteps, the moaning, the
distant cries, and the crackle of fires which seemed wide-
spread everywhere. The cook's moans had now subsided.
On two sides black curling clouds of smoke rose and
spread from the fires. Through the streets soldiers in
various uniforms walked or ran confusedly in different
directions like ants from a ruined ant-hill. Several of
them ran into Ferapóntov's yard before Alpátych's eyes.
Alpátych went out to the gate. A retreating regiment,
thronging and hurrying, blocked the street.

Noticing him, an officer said: 'The town is being
abandoned. Get away, get away!' and then turning to
the soldiers, shouted:

'I'll teach you to run into the yards!'

Alpátych went back to the house, called the coachman,
and told him to set off. Ferapóntov's whole household
came out too, following Alpátych and the coachman.
The women, who had been silent till then, suddenly
began to wail as they looked at the fires—the smoke and
even the flames of which could be seen in the failing
twilight—and as if in reply the same kind of lamentation
was heard from other parts of the street. Inside the shed
Alpátych and the coachman arranged the tangled reins
and traces of their horses with trembling hands.

As Alpátych was driving out of the gate he saw some
ten soldiers in Ferapóntov's open shop, talking loudly and
filling their bags and knapsacks with flour and sunflower

seeds. Just then Ferapóntov returned and entered his shop. On seeing the soldiers he was about to shout at them, but suddenly stopped, and clutching at his hair burst into sobs and laughter:

'Loot everything, lads! Don't let those devils get it!' he cried, taking some bags of flour himself and throwing them into the street.

Some of the soldiers were frightened and ran away, others went on filling their bags. On seeing Alpátych Ferapóntov turned to him:

'Russia is done for!' he cried. 'Alpátych, I'll set the place on fire myself. We're done for! . . .' and Ferapóntov ran into the yard.

Soldiers were passing in a constant stream along the street blocking it completely, so that Alpátych could not pass out and had to wait. Ferapóntov's wife and children were also sitting in a cart waiting till it was possible to drive out.

Night had come. There were stars in the sky and the new moon shone out amid the smoke that screened it. On the sloping descent to the Dnieper Alpátych's cart and that of the innkeeper's wife, which were slowly moving amid the rows of soldiers and of other vehicles, had to stop. In a side street near the cross-roads where the vehicles had stopped a house and some shops were on fire. This fire was already burning itself out. The flames now died down and were lost in the black smoke, now suddenly flared up again brightly, lighting up with strange distinctness the faces of the people crowding at the cross-roads. Black figures flitted about before the fire and through the incessant crackling of the flames talking and shouting could be heard. Seeing that his cart would not be able to move on for some time, Alpátych got down and turned into the side street to look at the fire. Soldiers were continually rushing backwards and forwards near it, and he saw two of them and a man in a frieze coat dragging burning beams into another yard across the street, while others carried bundles of hay.

Alpátych went up to a large crowd standing before a high barn which was blazing briskly. The walls were all in fire and the back wall had fallen in, the wooden roof was collapsing and the rafters were alight. The crowd was evidently watching for the roof to fall in, and Alpátych watched for it too.

'Alpátych!' a familiar voice suddenly hailed the old man.

'Mercy on us! Your Excellency!' answered Alpátych, immediately recognizing the voice of his young prince.

Prince Andrew in his riding cloak, mounted on a black horse, was looking at Alpátych from the back of the crowd.

'Why are you here?' he asked.

'Your . . . your Excellency,' stammered Alpátych and broke into sobs. 'Are we really lost? Master! . . .'

'Why are you here?' Prince Andrew repeated.

At that moment the flames flared up and showed his young master's pale worn face. Alpátych told how he had been sent there and how difficult it was to get away.

'Are we really quite lost, your Excellency?' he asked again.

Prince Andrew without replying took out a note-book, and raising his knee began writing in pencil on a page he tore out. He wrote to his sister:

'Smolénsk is being abandoned. Bald Hills will be occupied by the enemy within a week. Set off immediately for Moscow. Let me know at once when you will start. Send by special messenger to Usvyázh.'

Having written this and given the paper to Alpátych, he told him how to arrange for the departure of the prince, the princess, his son, and the boy's tutor, and how and where to let him know immediately. Before he had had time to finish giving these instructions, a chief of staff followed by a suite galloped up to him.

'You are a colonel?' shouted the chief of staff with a German accent, in a voice familiar to Prince Andrew. 'Houses are set on fire in your presence and you stand by! What does this mean? You will answer for it!' shouted Berg, who was now assistant to the chief of staff of the commander of the left flank of the infantry of the First Army, a place, as Berg said, 'very agreeable and well in evidence.'

Prince Andrew looked at him and without replying went on speaking to Alpátych.

'So tell them that I shall await a reply till the 10th and if by the 10th I don't receive news that they have all got away, I shall have to throw up everything and come myself to Bald Hills.'

'Prince,' said Berg, recognizing Prince Andrew, 'I only spoke because I have to obey orders, because I always do obey exactly . . . You must please excuse me,' he went on apologetically.

Something cracked in the flames. The fire died down for a moment and wreaths of black smoke rolled from under the roof. There was another terrible crash and something huge collapsed.

'Ou-rou-rou!' yelled the crowd, echoing the crash of the collapsing roof of the barn, the burning grain in which diffused a cake-like aroma all around. The flames flared up again, lighting the animated, delighted, exhausted faces of the spectators.

The man in the frieze coat raised his arms and shouted: 'It's fine, lads! Now it's raging. It's fine!'

'That's the owner himself,' cried several voices.

'Well then,' continued Prince Andrew to Alpátych, 'report to them as I have told you'; and not replying a word to Berg, who was now mute beside him, he touched his horse and rode down the side street.

CHAPTER V

FROM Smolénsk the troops continued to retreat, followed by the enemy. On the 10th of August the regiment Prince Andrew commanded was marching along the high road past the avenue leading to Bald Hills. Heat and drought had continued for more than three weeks. Each day fleecy clouds floated across the sky and occasionally veiled the sun, but towards evening the sky cleared again and the sun set in reddish-brown mist. Heavy night-dews alone refreshed the earth. The unreaped corn was scorched and shed its grain. The marshes dried up. The cattle lowed from hunger, finding no food on the sun-parched meadows. Only at night and in the forests while the dew lasted was there any freshness. But on the road, the high road along which the troops marched, there was no such freshness even at night or when the road passed through the forest: the dew was imperceptible on the sandy dust churned up more than six inches deep. As soon as day dawned the march began. The artillery and baggage-wagons moved noiselessly through the deep dust that rose to the very hubs of the wheels, and the infantry sank ankle deep in that soft, choking, hot dust that never cooled even at night. Some of this dust was kneaded by the feet and wheels, while the rest rose and hung like a cloud over the troops, settling in eyes, ears, hair and nostrils, and worst of all in the lungs of the men and beasts as they moved along that road. The higher the sun rose the higher rose that cloud of dust, and through the screen of its hot fine particles one could look with naked eye at the sun, which showed like a huge crimson ball in the unclouded sky. There was no wind, and the men choked in that motionless atmosphere. They marched with handkerchiefs tied over their noses and mouths. When they passed through a village they all rushed to the wells and fought for the water, and drank it down to the mud.

Prince Andrew was in command of a regiment, and the management of that regiment, the welfare of the men and the necessity of receiving and giving orders, engrossed him. The burning of Smolénsk and its abandonment made an epoch in his life. A novel feeling of anger against the foe made him forget his own sorrow. He was entirely devoted to the affairs of his regiment and was considerate and kind to his men and officers. In the regiment they called him 'our Prince', were proud of him and loved him. But he was kind and gentle only to those of his regiment, to Timókhin and the like—people quite new to him, belonging to a different world, and who could not know and understand his past. As soon as he came across a former acquaintance, or any one from the staff, he bristled up immediately, and grew spiteful, ironical, and contemptuous. Everything that reminded him of his past was repugnant to him, and so in his relations with that former circle he confined himself to trying to do his duty and not to be unfair.

In truth everything presented itself in a dark and
gloomy light to Prince Andrew, especially after the
abandonment of Smolénsk on the 6th of August (he considered that it could and should have been defended) and
after his sick father had had to flee to Moscow, abandoning to pillage his dearly beloved Bald Hills which he had
built and peopled. But despite this, thanks to his regiment, Prince Andrew had something to think about
entirely apart from general questions. Two days previously he had received news that his father, son, and
sister had left for Moscow; and though there was nothing
for him to do at Bald Hills, Prince Andrew with a
characteristic desire to foment his own grief decided that
he must ride there.

He ordered his horse to be saddled and, leaving his
regiment on the march, rode to his father's estate, where
he had been born and spent his childhood. Riding past
the pond where there used always to be dozens of women
chattering as they rinsed their linen or beat it with
wooden beetles, Prince Andrew noticed that there was
not a soul about, and that the little washing-wharf, torn
from its place and half submerged, was floating on its
side in the middle of the pond. He rode to the keeper's
lodge. No one was at the stone entrance-gates of the
drive and the door stood open. Grass had already begun
to grow on the garden paths, and horses and calves were
straying in the English park. Prince Andrew rode up to
the hot-house; some of the glass panes were broken, and
of the trees in tubs some were overturned and others
dried up. He called for Tarás the gardener, but no one
replied. Having gone round the corner of the hot-house
to the ornamental garden, he saw that the carved garden
fence was broken and branches of the plum trees had
been torn off with the fruit. An old peasant whom Prince
Andrew in his childhood had often seen at the gate, was
sitting on a green garden-seat, plaiting a bast shoe.

He was deaf and did not hear Prince Andrew ride up.
He was sitting on the seat the old prince used to like to
sit on, and beside him strips of bast were hanging on the
broken and withered branch of a magnolia.

Prince Andrew rode up to the house. Several limes in

the old garden had been cut down and a piebald ma
and her foal were wandering in front of the house amo
the rose bushes. The shutters were all closed, except
one window which was open. A little serf boy, see
Prince Andrew, ran into the house. Alpátych, havi
sent his family away, was alone at Bald Hills and v
sitting indoors reading the *Lives of the Saints*. On heari
that Prince Andrew had come, he went out with
spectacles on his nose, buttoning his coat, and hast
stepping up without a word began weeping and kissi
Prince Andrew's knee.

Then, vexed at his own weakness, he turned away a
began to report on the position of affairs. Everythi
precious and valuable had been removed to Bogucháro
Seventy quarters of grain had also been carted awa
The hay and the spring corn, of which Alpátych sa
there had been a remarkable crop that year, had be
commandeered by the troops and mown down wh
still green. The peasants were ruined; some of them t
had gone to Boguchárovo, only a few remained.

Without waiting to hear him out, Prince Andrew aske
'When did my father and sister leave?' meaning wh
did they leave for Moscow.

Alpátych, understanding the question to refer to th
departure for Boguchárovo, replied that they had left
the 7th, and again went into details concerning the est
management, asking for instructions.

'Am I to let the troops have the oats, and to take
receipt for them? We have still six hundred quart
left,' he inquired.

'What am I to say to him?' thought Prince Andre
looking down on the old man's bald head shining in t
sun and seeing by the expression on his face that the
man himself understood how untimely such questio
were, and only asked them to allay his grief.

'Yes, let them have it,' replied Prince Andrew.

'If you noticed some disorder in the garden,' said Al
tych, 'it was impossible to prevent it. Three regime
have been here and spent the night, dragoons mostly.
took down the name and rank of their commandi
officer, to hand in a complaint about it.'

'Well, and what are you going to do? Will you stay
re if the enemy occupies the place?' asked Prince
drew.

Alpatych turned his face to Prince Andrew, looked at
n, and suddenly with a solemn gesture raised his arm.

'He is my refuge! His will be done!' he exclaimed.

A group of bareheaded peasants was approaching
ross the meadow towards the prince.

'Well, good-bye!' said Prince Andrew, bending over to
pátych. 'You must go away too, take away what you
n, and tell the serfs to go to the Ryázan estate or to the
e near Moscow.'

Alpátych clung to Prince Andrew's leg and burst into
os. Gently disengaging himself, the prince spurred his
rse and rode down the avenue at a gallop.

The old man was still sitting in the ornamental garden,
e a fly impassive on the face of a loved one who is
ad, tapping the last on which he was making the bast
be, and two little girls, running out from the hot-house
rrying in their skirts plums they had plucked from
e trees there, came upon Prince Andrew. On seeing
e young master the elder one, with frightened look,
tched her younger companion by the hand and hid
h her behind a birch tree, not stopping to pick up some
en plums they had dropped.

Prince Andrew turned away with startled haste, un-
lling to let them see that they had been observed. He
s sorry for the pretty frightened little girl, was afraid
looking at her, and yet felt an irresistible desire to do
A new sensation of comfort and relief came over him
en, seeing these girls, he realized the existence of other
man interests entirely aloof from his own and just as
itimate as those that occupied him. Evidently these
ls passionately desired one thing—to carry away and
those green plums without being caught—and Prince
drew shared their wish for the success of their enter-
se. He could not resist looking at them once more.
ieving their danger past, they sprang from their am-
sh and chirruping something in their shrill little voices
l holding up their skirts, their bare little sunburnt feet
mpered merrily and quickly across the meadow grass.

Prince Andrew was somewhat refreshed by havin
ridden off the dusty high road along which the troo
were moving. But not far from Bald Hills he again can
out on the road and overtook his regiment at its haltin
place by the dam of a small pond. It was past one o'cloc
The sun, a red ball through the dust, burnt and scorche
his back intolerably through his black coat. The du
always hung motionless above the buzz of talk that can
from the resting troops. There was no wind. As
crossed the dam Prince Andrew smelt the ooze an
freshness of the pond. He longed to get into that wat
however dirty it might be, and he glanced round at th
pool from whence came sounds of shrieks and laughte
The small, muddy, green pond had risen visibly mo
than a foot, flooding the dam, because it was full of th
naked white bodies of soldiers with brick-red hand
necks, and faces, who were splashing about in it. All th
naked white human flesh, laughing and shriekin
floundered about in that dirty pool like carp stuffed in
a watering can, and the suggestion of merriment in th
floundering mass rendered it specially pathetic.

One fair-haired young soldier of the third compan
whom Prince Andrew knew and who had a strap roun
the calf of one leg, crossed himself, stepped back to get
good run, and plunged into the water; another, a da
non-commissioned officer who was always shaggy, stoo
up to his waist in the water joyfully wriggling his musc
lar figure and snorted with satisfaction as he poured th
water over his head with hands blackened to the wrist
There were sounds of men slapping one another, yellin
and puffing.

Everywhere on the bank, on the dam, and in the pon
there was healthy, white, muscular flesh. The office
Timókhin, with his red little nose, standing on the da
wiping himself with a towel, felt confused at seeing th
prince, but made up his mind to address him nevertheless

'It's very nice, your Excellency! Wouldn't you li
to?' said he.

'It's dirty,' replied Prince Andrew, making a grimac

'We'll clear it out for you in a minute,' said Timókhi
and, still undressed, ran off to clear the men out of the pon

'The Prince wants to bathe.'

'What Prince? Ours?' said many voices, and the men
[we]re in such haste to clear out that the prince could hardly
[sto]p them. He decided that he would rather souse him-
[sel]f with water in the barn.

'Flesh, bodies, cannon-fodder!' he thought, and he
[lo]oked at his own naked body and shuddered, not
[fro]m cold but from a sense of disgust and horror he did
[no]t himself understand, aroused by the sight of that
[im]mense number of bodies splashing about in the dirty
[po]nd.

On the 7th of August Prince Bagratión wrote as fol-
[lo]ws from his quarters at Mikháylovka on the Smolénsk
[roa]d:

'Dear Count Aléxis Andréevich,'—(He was writing to
[Ar]akchéev but knew that his letter would be read by the
[Em]peror, and therefore weighed every word in it to the
[be]st of his ability.)

'I expect the Minister' (Barclay de Tolly) 'has already
[rep]orted the abandonment of Smolénsk to the enemy.
[It i]s pitiable and sad, and the whole army is in despair
[tha]t this most important place has been wantonly aban-
[don]ed. I, for my part, begged him personally most
[urg]ently and finally wrote him, but nothing would induce
[hi]m to consent. I swear to you on my honour that
[Na]poleon was in such a fix as never before, and might
[hav]e lost half his army but could not have taken Smo-
[lén]sk. Our troops fought, and are fighting, as never
[bef]ore. With fifteen thousand men I held the enemy at
[bay] for thirty-five hours and beat him; but he would not
[hol]d out even for fourteen hours. It is disgraceful, a
[stai]n on our army, and as for him, he ought, it seems to
[me,] not to live. If he reports that our losses were great, it
[is n]ot true; perhaps about four thousand, not more, and
[not] even that; but even were they ten thousand, that's
[war!] But the enemy has lost masses . . .

[W]hat would it have cost him to hold out for another
[two] days? They would have had to retire of their own
[acco]rd, for they had no water for men or horses. He
[gav]e me his word he would not retreat, but suddenly

sent instructions that he was retiring that night. W
cannot fight in this way, or we may soon bring the enem
to Moscow . . .

'There is a rumour that you are thinking of peac
God forbid that you should make peace after all o
sacrifices and such insane retreats! You would set
Russia against you and every one of us would feel asham
to wear the uniform. If it has come to this—we must fig
as long as Russia can and as long as there are men ab
to stand . . .

'One man ought to be in command, and not two. Yo
Minister may perhaps be good as a Minister, but as
General he is not merely bad but execrable, yet to h
is entrusted the fate of our whole country . . . I am rea
frantic with vexation; forgive my writing boldly. It
clear that the man who advocates the conclusion o
peace, and that the Minister should command the arn
does not love our Sovereign and desires the ruin of us
So I write you frankly: call out the militia. For
Minister is leading these visitors after him to Moscow
a most masterly way. The whole army feels gr
suspicion of the Imperial aide-de-camp Wolzogen. H
said to be more Napoleon's man than ours, and he
always advising the Minister. I am not merely civil
him but obey him like a corporal, though I am
senior. This is painful, but loving my benefactor a
Sovereign I submit. Only I am sorry for the Empe
that he entrusts our fine army to such as he. Consi
that on our retreat we have lost by fatigue and left in
hospital more than fifteen thousand men, and had
attacked this would not have happened. Tell me,
God's sake, what will Russia, our mother Russia, say
our being so frightened, and why are we abandon
our good and gallant Fatherland to such rabble,
implanting feelings of hatred and shame in all our s
jects? What are we scared at and of whom are we afra
I am not to blame that the Minister is vacillating
coward, dense, dilatory, and has all bad qualities.
whole army bewails it and calls down curses upon him

CHAPTER VI

AMONG the innumerable categories applicable to the phenomena of human life one may discriminate between those in which substance prevails and those in which form prevails. To the latter—as distinguished from village, country, provincial, or even Moscow life—we may allot Petersburg life, and especially the life of its salons. That life of the salons is unchanging. Since the year 1805 we had made peace and had again quarrelled with Bonaparte and had made constitutions and unmade them again, but the salons of Anna Pávlovna and Hélène remained just as they had been—the one seven and the other five years before. At Anna Pávlovna's they talked with perplexity of Bonaparte's successses just as before, and saw in them and in the subservience shown to him by the European sovereigns a malicious conspiracy the sole object of which was to cause unpleasantness and anxiety to the court circle of which Anna Pávlovna was the representative. And in Hélène's salon, which Rumyántsev himself honoured with his visits, regarding Hélène as a remarkably intelligent woman, they talked with the same ecstasy in 1812 as in 1808 of the 'great nation' and the 'great man', and regretted our rupture with France, a rupture which according to them ought to be promptly terminated by peace.

Of late, since the Emperor's return from the army, there had been some excitement in these conflicting salon-circles and some demonstrations of hostility to one another, but each camp retained its own tendency. In Anna Pávlovna's circle only those Frenchmen were admitted who were deep-rooted legitimists, and patriotic views were expressed to the effect that one ought not to go to the French theatre, and that to maintain the French troupe was costing the government as much as a whole army corps. The progress of the war was eagerly followed, and only the reports most flattering to our army were circulated. In the French circle of Hélène and Rumyántsev the reports of the cruelty of the enemy and of the war were contradicted and all Napoleon's attempts at conciliation were discussed. In that circle they dis-

countenanced those who advised hurried preparati[ons]
for a removal to Kazán of the Court and the g[reat]
educational establishments under the patronage of [the]
Dowager Empress. In Hélène's circle the war in gen[eral]
was regarded as a series of formal demonstrations wh[ich]
would very soon end in peace, and the view preva[iled]
expressed by Bilíbin—who now in Petersburg was q[uite]
at home in Hélène's house, which every clever man [was]
obliged to visit—that not by gunpowder but by those w[ho]
invented it would matters be settled. In that circle [the]
Moscow enthusiasm—news of which had reached Pet[ers]-
burg simultaneously with the Emperor's return—[was]
ridiculed sarcastically and very cleverly, though with m[uch]
caution.

Anna Pávlovna's circle on the contrary was en[rap]-
tured by this enthusiasm, and spoke of it as Pluta[rch]
speaks of the deeds of the ancients. Prince Vasíli, [who]
still occupied his former important posts, formed a c[on]-
necting link between these two circles. He visited [his]
'good friend, Anna Pávlovna' as well as his daught[er's]
'diplomatic salon', and often in his constant comings a[nd]
goings between the two camps became confused, a[nd]
said at Hélène's what he should have said at A[nna]
Pávlovna's and vice versa.

Soon after the Emperor's return Prince Vasíli i[n]
conversation about the war at Anna Pávlovna's sever[ely]
condemned Barclay de Tolly, but was undecided a[s to]
who ought to be appointed commander-in-chief. O[ne]
of the visitors, usually spoken of as 'a man of great me[rit]',
having described how he had that day seen Kutúzov, [the]
newly chosen chief of the Petersburg militia, presid[ing]
over the enrolment of recruits at the Treasury, cautio[usly]
ventured to suggest that Kutúzov would be the ma[n to]
satisfy all requirements.

Anna Pávlovna remarked with a melancholy smile t[hat]
Kutúzov had done nothing but cause the Empe[ror]
annoyance.

'I have talked and talked at the Assembly of [the]
Nobility,' Prince Vasíli interrupted, 'but they did [not]
listen to me. I told them his election as chief of the mil[itia]
would not please the Emperor. They did not listen to m[e.]

'It's all this mania for opposition,' he went on. 'And who for? It is all because we want to ape the foolish enthusiasm of those Muscovites,' Prince Vasíli continued, forgetting for a moment that though at Hélène's one had to ridicule the Moscow enthusiasm, at Anna Pávlovna's one had to be ecstatic about it. But he retrieved his mistake at once. 'Now, is it suitable that Count Kutúzov, the oldest general in Russia, should preside at that tribunal? He will get nothing for his pains! How could they make a man commander-in-chief who cannot mount a horse, who drops asleep at a council, and has the very worst morals! A good reputation he made for himself at Bucharest! I don't speak of his capacity as a general, but at a time like this how can they appoint a decrepit, blind old man, positively blind? A fine idea to have a blind general! He can't see anything. To play blindman's buff? He can't see at all!'

No one replied to his remarks.

This was quite correct on the 24th of July. But on the 29th of July Kutúzov received the title of Prince. This might indicate a wish to get rid of him, and therefore Prince Vasíli's opinion continued to be correct though he was not now in any hurry to express it. But on the 8th of August a committee, consisting of Field-Marshal Saltykóv, Arakchéev, Vyazmítinov, Lopukhín, and Kochubéy met to consider the progress of the war. This committee came to the conclusion that our failures were due to a want of unity in the command, and though the members of the committee were aware of the Emperor's dislike of Kutúzov, after a short deliberation they agreed to advise his appointment as Commander-in-Chief. That same day Kutúzov was appointed Commander-in-Chief with full powers over the armies and over the whole region occupied by them.

On the 9th of August Prince Vasíli at Anna Pávlovna's again met the 'man of great merit'. The latter was very attentive to Anna Pávlovna because he wanted to be appointed director of one of the educational establishments for young ladies. Prince Vasíli entered the room with the air of a happy conqueror who has attained the object of his desires.

'Well, have you heard the great news? Prince Kutúzov is field-marshal! All dissensions are at an end! I am so glad, so delighted! At last we have a man!' said he, glancing sternly and significantly round at every one in the drawing-room.

The 'man of great merit', despite his desire to obtain the post of director, could not refrain from reminding Prince Vasíli of his former opinion. Though this was impolite to Prince Vasíli in Anna Pávlovna's drawing-room, and also to Anna Pávlovna herself who had received the news with delight, he could not resist the temptation.

'But, Prince, they say he is blind!' said he, reminding Prince Vasíli of his own words.

'Eh? Nonsense! He sees well enough,' said Prince Vasíli rapidly, in a deep voice and with a slight cough—the voice and cough with which he was wont to dispose of all difficulties.

'He sees well enough,' he added. 'And what I am so pleased about,' he went on, 'is that our Sovereign has given him full powers over all the armies and the whole region—powers no commander-in-chief ever had before. He is a second autocrat,' he concluded with a victorious smile.

'God grant it! God grant it!' said Anna Pávlovna.

The 'man of great merit', who was still a novice in court circles, wishing to flatter Anna Pávlovna by defending her former position on this question observed:

'It is said that the Emperor was reluctant to give Kutúzov those powers. They say he blushed like a girl to whom *Joconde*[1] is read, when he said to Kutúzov: "Your Emperor and the Fatherland award you this honour."'

'Perhaps the heart took no part in that speech,' said Anna Pávlovna.

'Oh, no, no!' warmly rejoined Prince Vasíli, who would not now yield Kutúzov to any one: in his opinion Kutúzov was not only admirable himself, but was adored by everybody. 'No, that's impossible,' said he, 'for our Sovereign appreciated him so highly before.'

'God grant only that Prince Kutúzov assumes real

[1] *Joconde*—Lafontaine's first *Contés* in verse, which are considered improper.

power and does not allow *any one* to put a spoke in his wheel,' observed Anna Pávlovna.

Understanding at once to whom she alluded, Prince Vasíli said in a whisper:

'I know for a fact that Kutúzov made it an absolute condition that the Tsarévich should not be with the army. Do you know what he said to the Emperor?'

And Prince Vasíli repeated the words supposed to have been spoken by Kutúzov to the Emperor. 'I can neither punish him if he does wrong nor reward him if he does right.'

'Oh, a very wise man is Prince Kutúzov! I have known him a long time!'

'They even say,' remarked the 'man of great merit' who did not yet possess courtly tact, 'that his Excellency made it an express condition that the Sovereign himself should not be with the army.'

As soon as he said this both Prince Vasíli and Anna Pávlovna turned away from him and glanced sadly at one another with a sigh at his naïveté.

CHAPTER VII

WHILE this was taking place in Petersburg the French had already passed Smolénsk and were drawing nearer and nearer to Moscow. Napoleon's historian, Thiers, like other of his historians, trying to justify his hero says that he was drawn to the walls of Moscow against his will. He is as right as other historians who look for the explanation of historic events in the will of one man; he is as right as the Russian historians who maintain that Napoleon was drawn to Moscow by the skill of the Russian commanders. Here besides the law of retrospection, which regards all the past as a preparation for events that subsequently occur, the law of reciprocity comes in, confusing the whole matter. A good chess-player having lost a game is sincerely convinced that his loss resulted from a mistake he made, and looks for that mistake in the opening, but forgets that at each stage of the game there were similar mistakes and that none of his moves were perfect. He only notices the mistake to which he pays attention, because his opponent took advantage of it. How much more complex than this is the game of war, which occurs under certain limits of time, and where it is not one will that manipulates lifeless objects, but everything results from innumerable conflicts of various wills!

After Smolénsk Napoleon sought a battle beyond Dorogobúzh at Vyázma, and then at Tsárevo-Zaymíshche, but it happened that owing to a conjunction of innumerable circumstances the Russians could not give battle till they reached Borodinó, seventy miles from Moscow. From Vyázma Napoleon ordered a direct advance on Moscow.

Moscou, la capitale asiatique de ce grand empire, la ville sacrée des peuples d'Alexandre, Moscou avec ses innombrables églises en forme de pagodes chinoises,[1] this Moscow gave Napoleon's imagination no rest. On the march from Vyázma to Tsárevo-Zaymíshche he rode his light bay bob-tailed ambler accompanied by his Guards, his bodyguard, his pages, and aides-de-camp. Berthier, his chief of staff, dropped behind to question a Russian prisoner captured by the cavalry. Followed by Lelorgne d'Ideville, an interpreter, he overtook Napoleon at a gallop and reined in his horse with an amused expression.

'Well?' asked Napoleon.

'One of Plátov's Cossacks says that Plátov's corps is joining up with the main army and that Kutúzov has been appointed commander-in-chief. He is a very shrewd and garrulous fellow.'

Napoleon smiled and told them to give the Cossack a horse and bring the man to him. He wished to talk to him himself. Several adjutants galloped off, and an hour later, Lavrúshka, the serf Denísov had handed over to Rostóv, rode up to Napoleon in an orderly's jacket and on a French cavalry saddle, with a roguish, merry, and tipsy face. Napoleon told him to ride by his side, and began questioning him.

[1] Moscow, the Asiatic capital of this great empire, the sacred city of Alexander's people, Moscow with its innumerable churches resembling Chinese pagodas.

'You are a Cossack?'

'Yes, a Cossack, your Honour.'

'The Cossack, not knowing in what company he was, for Napoleon's plain appearance had nothing about it that would reveal the presence of a monarch to an oriental mind, talked with extreme familiarity of the incidents of the war,' says Thiers, narrating this episode. In reality Lavrúshka having got drunk the day before and left his master dinnerless, had been whipped and sent to the village in quest of chickens, where he engaged in looting till the French took him prisoner. Lavrúshka was one of those coarse, bare-faced lackeys who have seen all sorts of things, consider it necessary to do everything in a mean and cunning way, are ready to render any sort of service to their master, and are keen at guessing their master's baser impulses, especially those prompted by vanity and pettiness.

Finding himself in the company of Napoleon, whose identity he had easily and surely recognized, Lavrúshka was not in the least abashed but merely did his utmost to gain his new master's favour.

He knew very well that this was Napoleon, but Napoleon's presence could no more intimidate him than Rostóv's, or a sergeant-major's with the rods, would have done, for he had nothing that either the sergeant-major or Napoleon could deprive him of.

So he rattled on, telling all the gossip he had heard among the orderlies. Much of it was true. But when Napoleon asked him whether the Russians thought they would beat Bonaparte or not, Lavrúshka screwed up his eyes and considered.

In this question he saw subtle cunning, as men of his type see cunning in everything, so he frowned and did not answer immediately.

'It's like this,' he said thoughtfully, 'if there's a battle soon, yours will win. That's right. But if three days pass, then after that, well then that same battle will not soon be over.'

Lelorgne d'Ideville smilingly interpreted this speech to Napoleon thus: 'If a battle takes place within the next three days the French will win, but if later, God knows

what will happen.' Napoleon did not smile, though he
was evidently in high good humour, and he ordered these
words to be repeated.

Lavrúshka noticed this and to entertain him further,
pretending not to know who Napoleon was, added:

'We know that you have Bonaparte and that he has
beaten everybody in the world, but we are a different
matter . . .'— without knowing why or how this bit of
boastful patriotism slipped out at the end.

The interpreter translated these words without the last
phrase, and Bonaparte smiled. 'The young Cossack
made his mighty interlocutor smile,' says Thiers. After
riding a few paces in silence, Napoleon turned to Berthier
and said he wished to see how the news that he was talking to the Emperor himself, to that very Emperor who had
written his immortally victorious name on the Pyramids,
would affect this *enfant du Don*.[1]

The fact was accordingly conveyed to Lavrúshka.

Lavrúshka, understanding that this was done to perplex
him and that Napoleon expected him to be frightened,
to gratify his new masters promptly pretended to be
astonished and awestruck, opened his eyes wide, and
assumed the expression he usually put on when taken to
be whipped. 'As soon as Napoleon's interpreter had
spoken,' says Thiers, 'the Cossack, seized by amazement,
did not utter another word, but rode on, his eyes fixed
on the conqueror whose fame had reached him across
the steppes of the East. All his loquacity was suddenly
arrested and replaced by a naïve and silent feeling of
admiration. Napoleon, after making the Cossack a
present, had him set free like a bird restored to its native
fields.'

Napoleon rode on, dreaming of the Moscow that so
appealed to his imagination, and 'the bird restored to
its native fields' galloped to our outposts, inventing on the
way all that had not taken place but that he meant to
relate to his comrades. What had really taken place he
did not wish to relate because it seemed to him not worth
telling. He found the Cossacks, inquired for the regiment
operating with Plátov's detachment, and by evening

[1] Child of the Don.

found his master, Nicholas Rostóv, quartered at Yankóvo. Rostóv was just mounting to go for a ride round the neighbouring villages with Ilyín; he let Lavrúshka have another horse and took him along with him.

CHAPTER VIII

PRINCESS MARY was not in Moscow and out of danger as Prince Andrew supposed.

After the return of Alpátych from Smolénsk the old prince suddenly seemed to awake as from a dream. He ordered the militiamen to be called up from the villages and armed, and wrote a letter to the commander-in-chief informing him that he had resolved to remain at Bald Hills to the last extremity and to defend it, leaving to the commander-in-chief's discretion to take measures or not for the defence of Bald Hills, where one of Russia's oldest generals would be captured or killed, and he announced to his household that he would remain at Bald Hills.

But while himself remaining, he gave instructions for the departure of the princess and Dessalles with the little prince to Boguchárovo and thence to Moscow. Princess Mary, alarmed by her father's feverish and sleepless activity after his previous apathy, could not bring herself to leave him alone, and for the first time in her life ventured to disobey him. She refused to go away and her father's fury broke over her in a terrible storm. He repeated every injustice he had ever inflicted on her. Trying to convict her, he told her she had worn him out, had caused his quarrel with his son, had harboured nasty suspicions of him making it the object of her life to poison his existence, and he drove her from his study telling her that if she did not go away it was all the same to him. He declared that he did not wish to remember her existence and warned her not to dare to let him see her. The fact that he did not, as she had feared, order her to be carried away by force but only told her not to let him see her, cheered Princess Mary. She knew it was a proof that in the depth of his soul he was glad she was remaining at home and had not gone away.

The morning after little Nicholas had left, the old prince donned his full uniform and prepared to visit the commander-in-chief. His calèche was already at the door. Princess Mary saw him walk out of the house in his uniform, wearing all his Orders, and go down the garden to review his armed peasants and domestic serfs. She sat by the window listening to his voice which reached her from the garden. Suddenly several men came running up the avenue with frightened faces.

Princess Mary ran out to the porch, down the flower-bordered path and into the avenue. A large crowd of militiamen and domestics was moving towards her, and in their midst several men were supporting by the arm-pits and dragging along a little old man in a uniform and decorations. She ran up to him and, in the play of the sunlight that fell in small round spots through the shade of the lime-tree avenue, could not be sure what change there was in his face. All she could see was that his former stern and determined expression had altered to one of timidity and submission. On seeing his daughter he moved his helpless lips and made a hoarse sound. It was impossible to make out what he wanted. He was lifted up, carried to his study, and laid on the very couch he had so feared of late.

The doctor, who was fetched that same night, bled him, and said that the prince had had a seizure paralysing his right side.

It was becoming more and more dangerous to remain at Bald Hills, and next day they moved the prince to Boguchárovo, the doctor accompanying him.

By the time they reached Boguchárovo, Dessalles and the little prince had already left for Moscow.

For three weeks the old prince lay stricken by paralysis in the new house Prince Andrew had built at Boguchárovo, ever in the same state, getting neither better nor worse. He was unconscious and lay like a distorted corpse. He muttered unceasingly, his eyebrows and lips twitching, and it was impossible to tell whether he understood what was going on around him or not. One thing was certain—that he was suffering and wished to say something. But what it was, no one could tell: it might be some caprice of a sick and half-crazy man, or it might relate to public affairs, or possibly to family concerns.

The doctor said this restlessness did not mean anything and was due to physical causes; but Princess Mary thought he wished to tell her something, and the fact that her presence always increased his restlessness confirmed her opinion.

He was evidently suffering both physically and mentally. There was no hope of recovery. It was impossible for him to travel, it would not do to let him die on the road. 'Would it not be better if the end did come, the very end?' Princess Mary sometimes thought. Night and day, hardly sleeping at all, she watched him, and terrible to say, often watched him not with hope of finding signs of improvement but wishing to find symptoms of the approach of the end.

Strange as it was to her to acknowledge this feeling in herself, yet there it was. And what seemed still more terrible to her was that since her father's illness began (perhaps even sooner, when she stayed with him expecting something to happen), all the personal desires and hopes that had been forgotten or sleeping within her had reawakened. Thoughts that had not entered her mind for years—thoughts of a life free from the fear of her father, and even the possibility of love and of family happiness—floated continually in her imagination like temptations of the devil. Thrust them aside as she would, questions continually recurred to her as to how she would order her life now, after *that*. These were temptations of the devil and Princess Mary knew it. She knew that the sole weapon against *him* was prayer, and she tried to pray. She assumed an attitude of prayer, looked at the icons, repeated the words of a prayer, but she could not pray. She felt that a different world had now taken possession of her—the life of a world of strenuous and free activity, quite opposed to the spiritual world in which till now she had been confined and in which her greatest comfort had been prayer. She could not pray, could not weep, and worldly cares took possession of her.

It was becoming dangerous to remain in Boguchárovo. News of the approach of the French came from all sides, and in one village, ten miles from Boguchárovo, a homestead had been looted by French marauders.

The doctor insisted on the necessity of moving the prince; the provincial Marshal of the Nobility sent an official to Princess Mary to persuade her to get away as quickly as possible, and the head of the rural police having come to Boguchárovo urged the same thing, saying that the French were only some twenty-five miles away, that French proclamations were circulating in the villages, and that if the princess did not take her father away before the 15th, he could not answer for the consequences.

The princess decided to leave on the 15th. The cares of preparation and giving orders, for which every one came to her, occupied her all day. She spent the night of the 14th as usual, without undressing, in the room next to the one where the prince lay. Several times, waking up, she heard his groans and muttering, the creak of his bed, and the steps of Tíkhon and the doctor when they turned him over. Several times she listened at the door, and it seemed to her that his mutterings were louder than usual and that they turned him over oftener. She could not sleep, and several times went to the door and listened, wishing to enter but not deciding to do so. Though he did not speak, Princess Mary saw and knew how unpleasant every sign of anxiety on his account was to him. She had noticed with what dissatisfaction he turned from the look she sometimes involuntarily fixed on him. She knew that her going in during the night at an unusual hour would irritate him.

But never had she felt so grieved for him or so much afraid of losing him. She recalled all her life with him, and in every word and act of his found an expression of his love of her. Occasionally amid these memories temptations of the devil would surge into her imagination: thoughts of how things would be after his death, and how her new, liberated life would be ordered. But she drove these thoughts away with disgust. Towards morning he became quiet and she fell asleep.

She woke late. That sincerity which often comes with waking showed her clearly what chiefly concerned her about her father's illness. On waking she listened to what was going on behind the door and, hearing him groan, said to herself with a sigh that things were still the same.

'But what could have happened? What did I want? I want his death!' she cried with a feeling of loathing for herself.

She washed, dressed, said her prayers, and went out to the porch. In front of it stood carriages without horses, and things were being packed in the vehicles.

It was a warm, grey morning. Princess Mary stopped at the porch, still horrified by her spiritual baseness and trying to arrange her thoughts before going to her father.

The doctor came downstairs and went out to her.

'He is a little better to-day,' said he. 'I was looking for you. One can make out something of what he is saying. His head is clearer. Come in, he is asking for you . . .'

Princess Mary's heart beat so violently at this news that she grew pale and leant against the wall to keep from falling. To see him, talk to him, feel his eyes on her now that her whole soul was overflowing with those dreadful, wicked temptations—was a torment of joy and terror.

'Come,' said the doctor.

Princess Mary entered her father's room and went up to his bed. He was lying on his back propped up high, and his small bony hands with their knotted purple veins were lying on the quilt; his left eye gazed straight before him, his right eye was awry and his brows and lips motionless. He seemed altogether so thin, small, and pathetic. His face seemed to have shrivelled or melted, his features had grown smaller. Princess Mary went up and kissed his hand. His left hand pressed hers so that she understood that he had long been waiting for her to come. He twitched her hand, and his brows and lips quivered angrily.

She looked at him in dismay trying to guess what he wanted of her. When she changed her position so that his left eye could see her face he calmed down, not taking his eyes off her for some seconds. Then his lips and tongue moved, sounds came, and he began to speak, gazing timidly and imploringly at her, evidently afraid that she might not understand.

Straining all her faculties Princess Mary looked at him. The comic efforts with which he moved his tongue made her drop her eyes and with difficulty repress the sobs that rose to her throat. He said something, repeating the same words several times. She could not understand them, but tried to guess what he was saying, and inquiringly repeated the words he uttered.

'Mmm . . . ar . . . ate . . . ate . . .' he repeated several times.

It was quite impossible to understand these sounds. The doctor thought he had guessed them, and inquiringly repeated: *'Mary, are you afraid?'* The prince shook his head, and again repeated the same sounds.

'My mind, my mind aches?' questioned Princess Mary.

He made a mumbling sound in confirmation of this, took her hand and began pressing it to different parts of his breast as if trying to find the right place for it.

'Always thoughts . . . about you . . . thoughts . . .' he then uttered much more clearly than he had done before, now that he was sure of being understood.

Princess Mary pressed her head against his hand trying to hide her sobs and tears.

He moved his hand over her hair.

'I have been calling you all night . . .' he brought out.

'If only I had known . . .' she said through her tears. 'I was afraid to come in.'

He pressed her hand.

'Weren't you asleep?'

'No, I did not sleep,' said Princess Mary, shaking her head.

Unconsciously imitating her father, she now tried to express herself as he did, as much as possible by signs, and her tongue too seemed to move with difficulty.

'Dear one . . . Dearest . . .' Princess Mary could not quite make out what he said, but from his look it was clear that he had uttered a tender caressing word such as he had never used to her before. 'Why didn't you come in?'

'And I, I was wishing for his death!' thought Princess Mary.

He was silent awhile.

'Thank you . . . daughter dear! . . . for all, for all . . .
forgive! . . . thank you! . . . forgive! . . . thank you! . . .'
and tears began to flow from his eyes. 'Call Andrew!' he
said suddenly, and a childish, timid expression of doubt
showed itself on his face as he spoke.

He himself seemed aware that his demand was meaningless. So at least it seemed to Princess Mary.

'I have a letter from him,' she replied.

He glanced at her with timid surprise.

'Where is he?'

'He's with the army, Father, at Smolénsk.'

He closed his eyes and remained silent a long time.
Then as if in answer to his doubts and to confirm the fact
that now he understood and remembered everything, he
nodded his head and reopened his eyes.

'Yes,' he said, softly and distinctly. 'Russia has
perished. They've destroyed her.'

And he began to sob, and again tears flowed from his
eyes. Princess Mary could no longer restrain herself and
wept while she gazed at his face.

Again he closed his eyes. His sobs ceased, he pointed
to his eyes, and Tíkhon, understanding him, wiped away
the tears.

Then he again opened his eyes and said something
none of them could understand for a long time, till at
last Tíkhon understood and repeated it. Princess Mary
had sought the meaning of his words in the mood in
which he had just been speaking. She thought he was
speaking of Russia, or Prince Andrew, of herself, of his
grandson, or of his own death, and so she could not guess
his words.

'Put on your white dress. I like it,' was what he said.

Having understood this, Princess Mary sobbed still
louder, and the doctor taking her arm led her out to the
veranda, soothing her and trying to persuade her to prepare for her journey. When she had left the room, the
prince again began speaking about his son, about the
war, and about the Emperor, angrily twitching his brows
and raising his hoarse voice, and then he had a second
and final stroke.

Princess Mary stayed on the veranda. The day had

cleared, it was hot and sunny. She could understand nothing, think of nothing, and feel nothing, except passionate love for her father, love such as she thought she had never felt till that moment. She ran out sobbing into the garden and as far as the pond, along the avenues of young lime trees Prince Andrew had planted.

'Yes . . . I . . . I . . . I wished for his death! Yes, I wanted it to end quicker . . . I wished to be at peace . . . And what will become of me? What use will peace be when he is no longer here?' Princess Mary murmured, pacing the garden with hurried steps and pressing her hands to her bosom which heaved with convulsive sobs.

When she had completed the tour of the garden, which brought her again to the house, she saw Mademoiselle Bourienne—who had remained at Boguchárovo and did not wish to leave it—coming towards her with a stranger. This was the Marshal of the Nobility of the district, who had come personally to point out to the princess the necessity for her prompt departure. Princess Mary listened without understanding him; she led him to the house, offered him lunch, and sat down with him. Then, excusing herself, she went to the door of the old prince's room. The doctor came out with an agitated face and said she could not enter.

'Go away, Princess! Go away . . . go away!'

She returned to the garden and sat down on the grass at the foot of the slope by the pond, where no one could see her. She did not know how long she had been there when she was aroused by the sound of a woman's footsteps running along the path. She rose and saw Dunyásha, her maid, who was evidently looking for her, and who stopped suddenly as if in alarm on seeing her mistress.

'Please come, Princess . . . The Prince . . .' said Dunyásha in a breaking voice.

'Immediately, I'm coming, I'm coming!' replied the princess hurriedly, not giving Dunyásha time to finish what she was saying, and trying to avoid seeing the girl she ran towards the house.

'Princess, it's God's will! You must be prepared for everything,' said the Marshal, meeting her at the house door.

'Let me alone; it's not true!' she cried angrily to him. The doctor tried to stop her. She pushed him aside and ran to her father's door. 'Why are these people with frightened faces stopping me? I don't want any of them! And what are they doing here?' she thought. She opened the door and the bright daylight in that previously darkened room startled her. In the room were her nurse and other women. They all drew back from the bed, making way for her. He was still lying on the bed as before, but the stern expression of his quiet face made Princess Mary stop short on the threshold.

'No, he's not dead—it's impossible!' she told herself and approached him, and repressing the terror that seized her, she pressed her lips to his cheek. But she stepped back immediately. All the force of the tenderness she had been feeling for him vanished instantly and was replaced by a feeling of horror at what lay there before her. 'No, he is no more! He is not, but here where he was, is something unfamiliar and hostile, some dreadful terrifying and repellent mystery!' And hiding her face in her hands, Princess Mary sank into the arms of the doctor, who held her up.

In the presence of Tíkhon and the doctor the women washed what had been the prince, tied his head up with a handkerchief that the mouth should not stiffen while open, and with another handkerchief tied together the legs that were already spreading apart. Then they dressed him in uniform with his decorations, and placed his shrivelled little body on a table. Heaven only knows who arranged all this and when, but it all got done as if of its own accord. Towards night candles were burning round his coffin, a pall was spread over it, the floor was strewn with sprays of juniper, a printed band was tucked in under his shrivelled head, and in a corner of the room sat a chanter reading the psalms.

Just as horses shy and snort and gather about a dead horse, so the inmates of the house and strangers crowded into the drawing-room round the coffin—the Marshal, the village Elder, peasant women—and all with fixed and frightened eyes, crossing themselves, bowed, and kissed the old prince's cold and stiffened hand.

CHAPTER IX

UNTIL Prince Andrew settled in Boguchárovo its
owners had always been absentees, and its peasants
were of quite a different character from those of Bald
Hills. They differed from them in speech, dress, and disposition. They were called Steppe-peasants. The old
prince used to approve of them for their endurance at
work when they came to Bald Hills to help with the
harvest or to dig ponds and ditches, but he disliked them
for their boorishness.

Prince Andrew's last stay at Boguchárovo, when he
introduced hospitals and schools and reduced the quit-
rent the peasants had to pay, had not softened their disposition but had on the contrary strengthened in them
the traits of character the old prince called boorishness.
Various obscure rumours were always current among
them: at one time a rumour that they would all be enrolled as Cossacks; at another of a new religion to which
they were all to be converted; then of some proclamation
of the Tsar's and of an oath to the Tsar Paul in 1797 (in
connexion with which it was rumoured that freedom had
been granted them but the landowners had stopped it),
then of Peter Fëdorovich's[1] return to the throne in seven
years' time, when everything would be made free and
so 'simple' that there would be no restrictions. Rumours
of the war with Bonaparte and his invasion were connected in their minds with the same sort of vague notions
of Antichrist, the end of the world, and 'pure freedom'.

In the vicinity of Boguchárovo were large villages belonging to the crown or to owners whose serfs paid quit-
rent and could work where they pleased. There were
very few resident landlords in the neighbourhood and
also very few domestic or literate serfs, and in the lives of
the peasantry of those parts the mysterious undercurrents
in the life of the Russian people, the causes and meaning

---

[1] The Emperor Peter III was assassinated, or died, on the
accession of his wife, Catherine II, to the throne in 1762; but
Tsars often long survived in the minds of the peasants, who
refused to believe in their death.

of which are so baffling to contemporaries, were more clearly and strongly noticeable than among others. One instance, which had occurred some twenty years before, was a movement among the peasants to emigrate to some unknown 'warm rivers'. Hundreds of peasants, among them the Boguchárovo folk, suddenly began selling their cattle and moving in whole families towards the southeast. As birds migrate to somewhere beyond the sea, so these men with their wives and children streamed to the south-east, to parts where none of them had ever been. They set off in caravans, bought their freedom one by one or ran away, and drove or walked towards the 'warm rivers'. Many of them were punished, some sent to Siberia, many died of cold and hunger on the road, many returned of their own accord, and the movement died down of itself just as it had sprung up, without apparent reason. But such undercurrents still existed among the people and gathered new forces ready to manifest themselves just as strangely, unexpectedly, and at the same time simply, naturally, and forcibly. Now, in 1812, to any one living in close touch with these people it was apparent that these undercurrents were acting strongly and nearing an eruption.

Alpátych, who had reached Boguchárovo shortly before the old prince's death, noticed an agitation among the peasants, and that contrary to what was happening in the Bald Hills district, where over a radius of sixty versts all the peasants were moving away and leaving their villages to be devastated by the Cossacks, the peasants in the steppe region round Boguchárovo were, it was rumoured, in touch with the French, received leaflets from them that passed from hand to hand, and did not migrate. He learnt from domestic serfs loyal to him, that the peasant Karp, who possessed great influence in the village commune and had recently been away driving a government transport, had returned with news that the Cossacks were destroying deserted villages, but that the French did not harm them. Alpátych also knew that on the previous day another peasant had even brought from the village of Vislóukhovo, which was occupied by the French, a proclamation by a French general that no harm would be done to the inhabitants, and if they remained they would be paid for anything taken from them. As proof of this the peasant had brought from Vislouќhovo a hundred rubles in notes (he did not know that they were false) paid to him in advance for hay.

More important still, Alpátych learnt that on the morning of the very day he gave the village Elder orders to collect carts to move the princess's luggage from Boguchárovo, there had been a village meeting at which it had been decided not to move but to wait. Yet there was no time to waste. On the 15th, the day of the old prince's death, the Marshal had insisted on Princess Mary's leaving at once, as it was becoming dangerous. He had told her that after the 16th he could not be responsible for what might happen. On the evening of the day the old prince died the Marshal went away, promising to return next day for the funeral. But this he was unable to do, for he received tidings that the French had unexpectedly advanced, and had barely time to remove his own family and valuables from his estate.

For some thirty years Boguchárovo had been managed by the village Elder, Dron, whom the old prince called by the diminutive 'Drónushka'.

Dron was one of those physically and mentally vigorous peasants who grow big beards as soon as they are of age, and go on unchanged till they are sixty or seventy, without a grey hair or the loss of a tooth, as straight and strong at sixty as at thirty.

Soon after the migration to the 'warm rivers', in which he had taken part like the rest, Dron was made village Elder and overseer of Boguchárovo, and had since filled that post irreproachably for twenty-three years. The peasants feared him more than they did their master. The masters, both the old prince and the young and the steward, respected him, and jestingly called him 'the Minister'. During the whole time of his service Dron had never been drunk or ill, never after sleepless nights or the hardest tasks had he shown the least fatigue, and though he could not read, he had never forgotten a single money account, or the number of quarters of flour in any of the endless cartloads he sold for the prince, nor a single shock of the whole corn crop on any single acre of the Bogu-chárovo fields.

Alpátych, arriving from the devastated Bald Hills estate, sent for this Dron on the day of the prince's funeral, and told him to have twelve horses got ready for the princess's carriages and eighteen carts for the things to be removed from Boguchárovo. Though the peasants paid quit-rent, Alpátych thought no difficulty would be made about complying with this order, for there were two hundred and thirty households at work in Boguchárovo and the peasants were well-to-do. But on hearing the order Dron lowered his eyes and remained silent. Alpàtych named certain peasants he knew, from whom he told him to take the carts.

Dron replied that the horses of these peasants were away carting. Alpátych named others, but they too, according to Dron, had no horses available: some horses were carting for the government, others were too weak, and others had died for want of fodder. It seemed that no horses could be had even for the carriages, much less for the carting.

Alpátych looked intently at Dron and frowned. Just as Dron was a model village Elder, so Alpátych had not managed the prince's estates in vain for twenty years. He was a model steward, possessing in the highest degree the faculty of divining the needs and instincts of those he dealt with. Having glanced at Dron he at once understood that his answers did not express his personal views, but the general mood of the Boguchárovo commune, by which the Elder had already been carried away. But he also knew that Dron, who had acquired property and was hated by the commune, must be hesitating between the two camps: the masters' and the serfs'. He noticed this hesitation in Dron's look, and therefore frowned and moved closer up to him.

'Now just listen, Drónushka,' said he. 'Don't talk non-sense to me. His excellency Prince Andrew himself gave me orders to move all the people away and not leave them with the enemy, and there is an order from the Tsar about it too. Any one who stays is a traitor to the Tsar. Do you hear?'

'I hear,' Dron answered without lifting his eyes.

Alpátych was not satisfied with this reply.

'Eh, Dron, it will turn out badly!' he said, shaking his head.

'The power is in your hands,' Dron rejoined sadly.

'Eh, Dron, drop it!' Alpátych repeated, withdrawing his hand from his bosom and solemnly pointing to the floor at Dron's feet. 'I can see through you and three yards into the ground under you,' he continued, gazing at the floor in front of Dron.

Dron was disconcerted, glanced furtively at Alpátych, and again lowered his eyes.

'You drop this nonsense and tell the people to get ready to leave their homes and go to Moscow, and to get carts ready for to-morrow morning for the princess's things. And don't go to any meeting yourself, do you hear?'

Dron suddenly fell on his knees.

'Yákov Alpátych, discharge me! Take the keys from me and discharge me, for Christ's sake!'

'Stop that!' cried Alpátych sternly. 'I see through you and three yards under you,' he repeated, knowing that his skill in bee-keeping, his knowledge of the right time to sow the oats, and the fact that he had been able to retain the old prince's favour for twenty years, had long since gained him the reputation of being a wizard, and that the power of seeing three yards under a man is considered an attribute of wizards.

Dron got up and was about to say something, but Alpátych interrupted him.

'What is it you have got into your heads, eh? . . . What are you thinking of, eh?'

'What am I to do with the people?' said Dron. 'They're quite beside themselves; I have already told them . . .'

' "Told them," I daresay!' said Alpátych. 'Are they drinking?' he asked abruptly.

'Quite beside themselves, Yákov Alpátych; they've fetched another barrel.'

'Well, then, listen! I'll go to the police officer, and you tell them so, and that they must stop this and the carts must be got ready.'

'I understand.'

Alpátych did not insist further. He had managed people for a long time, and knew that the chief way to make them obey is to show no suspicion that they can possibly disobey. Having wrung a submissive 'I understand' from Dron, Alpátych contented himself with that, though he not only doubted but felt almost certain that without the help of troops the carts would not be forthcoming.

And so it was, for when evening came no carts had been provided. In the village, outside the drink-shop, another meeting was being held, which decided that the horses should be driven out into the woods and the carts should not be provided. Without saying anything of this to the princess, Alpátych had his own belongings taken out of the carts which had arrived from Bald Hills, and had those horses got ready for the princess's carriages. Meanwhile he went himself to the police authorities.

CHAPTER X

AFTER her father's funeral Princess Mary shut herself up in her room and did not admit any one. A maid came to the door to say that Alpátych was asking for orders about their departure. (This was before his talk with Dron.) Princess Mary raised herself on the sofa on which she had been lying and replied through the closed door that she did not mean to go away and begged to be left in peace.

The windows of the room in which she was lying looked westward. She lay on the sofa with her face to the wall, fingering the buttons of the leather cushion and seeing nothing but that cushion, and her confused thoughts were centred on one subject—the irrevocability of death and her own spiritual baseness, which she had not suspected, but which had shown itself during her father's illness. She wished to pray but did not dare to, dared not in her present state of mind address herself to God. She lay for a long time in that position.

The sun had reached the other side of the house, and

its slanting rays shone into the open window, lighting up the room and part of the morocco cushion at which Princess Mary was looking. The flow of her thoughts suddenly stopped. Unconsciously she sat up, smoothed her hair, got up, and went to the window, involuntarily inhaling the freshness of the clear but windy evening.

'Yes, you can well enjoy the evening now! He is gone and no one will hinder you,' she said to herself, and sinking into a chair she let her head fall on the window-sill.

Some one spoke her name in a soft and tender voice from the garden, and kissed her head. She looked up. It was Mademoiselle Bourienne in a black dress and weepers. She softly approached Princess Mary, sighed, kissed her, and immediately began to cry. The princess looked up at her. All their former disharmony and her own jealousy recurred to her mind. But she remembered too how *he* had changed of late towards Mademoiselle Bourienne and could not bear to see her, thereby showing how unjust were the reproaches Princess Mary had mentally addressed to her. 'Besides, is it for me, for me who desired his death, to condemn any one?' she thought.

Princess Mary vividly pictured to herself the position of Mademoiselle Bourienne, whom she had of late kept at a distance, but who yet was dependent on her and living in her house. She felt sorry for her, and held out her hand with a glance of gentle inquiry. Mademoiselle Bourienne at once began crying again and kissed that hand, speaking of the princess's sorrow and making herself a partner in it. She said her only consolation was the fact that the princess allowed her to share her sorrow, that all the old misunderstandings should sink into nothing before this great grief; that she felt herself blameless in regard to every one, and that *he*, from above, saw her affection and gratitude. The princess heard her, not heeding her words but occasionally looking up at her and listening to the sound of her voice.

'Your position is doubly terrible, dear Princess,' said Mademoiselle Bourienne after a pause. 'I understand that you could not, and cannot, think of yourself, but with my love for you I must do so . . . Has Alpátych been to you? Has he spoken to you of going away?' she asked.

Princess Mary did not answer. She did not understand who was to go or where to. 'Is it possible to plan or think of anything now? Is it not all the same?' she thought, and did not reply.

'You know, *chère Marie*,' said Mademoiselle Bourienne, 'that we are in danger—are surrounded by the French. It would be dangerous to move now. If we go we are almost sure to be taken prisoners, and God knows . . .'

Princess Mary looked at her companion without understanding what she was talking about.

'Oh, if any one knew how little anything matters to me now,' she said. 'Of course I would on no account wish to go away from him . . . Alpátych did say something about going . . . Speak to him; I can do nothing, nothing, and don't want to . . .'

'I've spoken to him. He hopes we should be in time to get away to-morrow, but I think it would now be better to stay here,' said Mademoiselle Bourienne. 'Because, you will agree, *chère Marie*, to fall into the hands of the soldiers or of riotous peasants would be terrible.'

Mademoiselle Bourienne took from her reticule a proclamation (not printed on ordinary Russian paper) of General Rameau's, telling people not to leave their homes and that the French authorities would afford them proper protection. She handed this to the princess.

'I think it would be best to appeal to that general,' she continued, 'and I am sure that all due respect would be shown you.'

Princess Mary read the paper, and her face began to quiver with stifled sobs.

'From whom did you get this?' she asked.

'They probably recognized that I am French, by my name,' replied Mademoiselle Bourienne, blushing.

Princess Mary, with the paper in her hand, rose from the window, and with a pale face went out of the room and into what had been Prince Andrew's study.

'Dunyásha, send Alpátych, or Drónushka, or somebody to me!' she said, 'and tell Mademoiselle Bourienne not to come to me,' she added, hearing Mademoiselle Bourienne's voice. 'We must go at once, at once!' she said, appalled at the thought of being left in the hands of the French.

'If Prince Andrew heard that I was in the power of the French! That I, the daughter of Prince Nicholas Bolkónski, asked General Rameau for protection and accepted his favour!' This idea horrified her, made her shudder, blush, and feel such a rush of anger and pride as she had never experienced before. All that was distressing, and especially all that was humiliating, in her position rose vividly to her mind. 'They, the French, would settle in this house: M. le Général Rameau would occupy Prince Andrew's study and amuse himself by looking through and reading his letters and papers. Mademoiselle Bourienne would do the honours of Boguchárovo for him. I should be given a small room as a favour, the soldiers would violate my father's newly dug grave to steal his crosses and stars, they would tell me of their victories over the Russians, and would pretend to sympathize with my sorrow . . .' thought Princess Mary, not thinking her own thoughts, but feeling bound to think like her father and her brother. For herself she did not care where she remained or what happened to her, but she felt herself the representative of her dead father and of Prince Andrew. Involuntarily she thought their thoughts and felt their feelings. What they would have said and what they would have done she felt bound to say and do. She went into Prince Andrew's study trying to enter completely into his ideas, and considered her position.

The demands of life, which had seemed to her annihilated by her father's death, all at once rose before her with a new, previously unknown force, and took possession of her.

Agitated and flushed she paced the room, sending now for Michael Ivánovich and now for Tíkhon or Dron. Dunyásha, the nurse, and the other maids, could not say in how far Mademoiselle Bourienne's statement was correct. Alpátych was not at home, he had gone to the police. Neither could the architect, Michael Ivánovich, who came in with sleepy eyes on being sent for, tell Princess Mary anything. With just the same smile of agreement with which for fifteen years he had been accustomed to answer the old prince without expressing views of his own, he now replied to Princess Mary, so that nothing definite could be got from his answers. The old valet, Tíkhon, with sunken, emaciated face that bore the stamp of inconsolable grief, replied: 'Yes, Princess' to all Princess Mary's questions, and hardly refrained from sobbing as he looked at her.

At length the village Elder, Dron, entered the room, and with a deep bow to Princess Mary came to a halt by the doorpost.

Princess Mary walked up and down the room and stopped in front of him.

'Drónushka,' she said, regarding as a sure friend this Drónushka who always used to bring a special kind of ginger-bread from his visit to the fair at Vyázma every year and smilingly offer it to her. 'Drónushka, now since our misfortune . . .' she began, but could not go on.

'We are all in God's hands,' said he, with a sigh.

They were silent for awhile.

'Drónushka, Alpátych has gone off somewhere and I have no one to turn to. Is it true, as they tell me, that I can't even go away?'

'Why shouldn't you go away, your Excellency? You can go,' said Dron.

'I was told it would be dangerous because of the enemy. Dear friend, I can do nothing. I understand nothing. I have nobody. I want to go away to-night or early to-morrow morning.'

Dron paused. He looked askance at Princess Mary and said:

'There are no horses; I told Yákov Alpátych so.'

'Why are there none?' asked the princess.

'It's all God's scourge,' said Dron. 'What horses we had have been taken for the army or have died—this is such a year! It's not a case of feeding horses—we may die of hunger ourselves! As it is, some go three days without eating. We've nothing, we've been ruined.'

Princess Mary listened attentively to what he told her.

'The peasants are ruined? They have no bread?' she asked.

'They're dying of hunger,' said Dron. 'It's not a case of carting.'

'But why didn't you tell me, Drónushka? Isn't it possible to help them? I'll do all I can . . .'

To Princess Mary it was strange that now, at a moment when such sorrow was filling her soul, there could be rich people and poor, and the rich could refrain from helping the poor. She had heard vaguely that there was such a thing as 'landlord's corn' which was sometimes given to the peasants. She also knew that neither her father nor her brother would refuse to help the peasants in need, she only feared to make some mistake in speaking about the distribution of the grain she wished to give. She was glad such cares presented themselves, enabling her without scruple to forget her own grief. She began asking Dron about the peasants' needs, and what there was in Boguchárovo that belonged to the landlord.

'But we have grain belonging to my brother?' she said.

'The landlord's grain is all safe,' replied Dron proudly. 'Our prince did not order it to be sold.'

'Give it to the peasants, let them have all they need; I give you leave in my brother's name,' said she.

Dron made no answer but sighed deeply.

'Give them that corn if there is enough of it. Distribute it all. I give this order in my brother's name; and tell them that what is ours is theirs. We do not grudge them anything. Tell them so.'

Dron looked intently at the princess while she was speaking.

'Discharge me, little Mother, for God's sake! Order the keys to be taken from me,' said he. 'I have served twenty-three years and have done no wrong. Discharge me, for God's sake!'

Princess Mary did not understand what he wanted of her, or why he was asking to be discharged. She replied that she had never doubted his devotion and that she was ready to do anything for him and for the peasants.

CHAPTER XI

AN hour later Dunyásha came to tell the princess that Dron had come, and all the peasants had assembled at the barn by the princess's order and wished to have word with their mistress.

'But I never told them to come,' said Princess Mary. 'I only told Dron to let them have the grain.'

'Only, for God's sake, Princess dear, have them sent away and don't go out to them. It's all a trick,' said Dunyásha, 'and when Yákov Alpátych returns let us get away . . . and please don't . . .'

'What is a trick?' asked Princess Mary in surprise.

'I know it is, only listen to me, for God's sake! Ask nurse too. They say they don't agree to leave Boguchárovo as you ordered.'

'You're making some mistake. I never ordered them to go away,' said Princess Mary. 'Call Drónushka.'

Dron came and confirmed Dunyásha's words; the peasants had come by the princess's order.

'But I never sent for them,' declared the princess. 'You must have given my message wrong. I only said that you were to give them the grain.'

Dron only sighed in reply.

'If you order it, they will go away,' said he.

'No, no. I'll go out to them,' said Princess Mary, and in spite of the nurse's and Dunyásha's protests she went out into the porch; Dron, Dunyásha, the nurse, and Michael Ivánovich, following her.

'They probably think I am offering them the grain to bribe them to remain here, while I myself go away leaving them to the mercy of the French,' thought Princess Mary. 'I will offer them monthly rations and housing at our Moscow estate. I am sure Andrew would do even more in my place,' she thought as she went out in the twilight towards the crowd standing on the pasture by the barn.

The men crowded closer together, stirred, and rapidly took off their hats. Princess Mary lowered her eyes and, tripping over her skirt, came close up to them. So many different eyes, old and young, were fixed on her, and there were so many different faces, that she could not distinguish any of them, and feeling that she must speak to them all at once, did not know how to do it. But again the sense that she represented her father and her brother gave her courage, and she boldly began her speech.

'I am very glad you have come,' she said without

raising her eyes, and feeling her heart beating quickly and violently. 'Drónushka tells me that the war has ruined you. That is our common misfortune, and I shall grudge nothing to help you. I am myself going away because it is dangerous here . . . the enemy is near . . . because . . . I am giving you everything, my friends, and I beg you to take everything, all our grain, so that you may not suffer want! And if you have been told that I am giving you the grain to keep you here—that is not true. On the contrary, I ask you to go with all your belongings to our estate near Moscow, and I promise you I will see to it that there you shall want for nothing. You shall be given food and lodging.'

The princess stopped. Sighs were the only sound heard in the crowd.

'I am not doing this on my own account,' she continued, 'I do it in the name of my dead father, who was a good master to you, and of my brother and his son.'

Again she paused. No one broke the silence.

'Ours is a common misfortune and we will share it together. All that is mine is yours,' she concluded, scanning the faces before her.

All eyes were gazing at her with one and the same expression. She could not fathom whether it was curiosity, devotion, gratitude, or apprehension and distrust—but the expression on all the faces was identical.

'We are very thankful for your bounty, but it won't do for us to take the landlord's grain,' said a voice at the back of the crowd.

'But why not?' asked the princess.

No one replied, and Princess Mary, looking round at the crowd, found that every eye she met now was immediately dropped.

'But why don't you want to take it?' she asked again.

No one answered.

The silence began to oppress the princess, and she tried to catch some one's eye.

'Why don't you speak?' she inquired of a very old man who stood just in front of her leaning on his stick. 'If you think something more is wanted, tell me! I will do anything,' said she, catching his eye.

But as if this angered him, he bent his head quite low and muttered:

'Why should we agree? We don't want the grain.'

'Why should we give up everything? We don't agree. Don't agree . . . We are sorry for you, but we're not willing. Go away yourself, alone . . .' came from various sides of the crowd.

And again all the faces in that crowd bore an identical expression, though now it was certainly not an expression of curiosity or gratitude, but of angry resolve.

'But you can't have understood me,' said Princess Mary with a sad smile. 'Why don't you want to go? I promise to house and feed you, while here the enemy would ruin you . . .'

But her voice was drowned by the voices of the crowd.

'We're not willing. Let them ruin us! We won't take your grain. We don't agree!'

Again Princess Mary tried to catch some one's eye, but not a single eye in the crowd was turned to her; evidently they were all trying to avoid her look. She felt strange and awkward.

'Oh yes, an artful tale! Follow her into slavery! Pull down your houses and go into bondage! I daresay! "I'll give you grain, indeed!" she says', voices in the crowd were heard saying.

With drooping head Princess Mary left the crowd and went back to the house. Having repeated her order to Dron to have horses ready for her departure next morning, she went to her room and remained alone with her own thoughts.

CHAPTER XII

FOR a long time that night Princess Mary sat by the open window of her room hearing the sound of the peasants' voices that reached her from the village, but it was not of them she was thinking. She felt that she could not understand them however much she might think about them. She thought only of one thing, her sorrow, which after the break caused by cares for the present, seemed already to belong to the past. Now she could remember it and weep or pray.

After sunset the wind had dropped. The night was calm and fresh. Towards midnight the voices began to subside, a cock crowed, the full moon began to show from behind the lime trees, a fresh white dewy mist began to rise, and stillness reigned over the village and the house.

Pictures of the near past—her father's illness and last moments—rose one after another to her memory. With mournful pleasure she now lingered over these images, repelling with horror only the last one, the picture of his death, which she felt she could not contemplate even in imagination at this still and mystic hour of night. And these pictures presented themselves to her so clearly and in such detail that they seemed now present, now past, and now future.

She vividly recalled the moment when he had his first stroke and was being dragged along by his armpits through the garden at Bald Hills, muttering something with his helpless tongue, twitching his grey eyebrows, and looking uneasily and timidly at her.

'Even then he wanted to tell me what he told me the day he died,' she thought. 'He had always thought what he said then.' And she recalled in all its detail the night at Bald Hills before he had the last stroke, when with a foreboding of disaster she had remained at home against his will. She had not slept, and had stolen downstairs on tiptoe, and going to the door of the conservatory where he slept that night had listened at the door. In a suffering and weary voice he was saying something to Tíkhon, speaking of the Crimea and its warm nights and of the Empress. Evidently he had wanted to talk. 'And why didn't he call me? Why did'nt he let me be there instead of Tíkhon?' Princess Mary had thought and thought again now. 'Now he will never tell any one what he had in his soul. Never will that moment return for him or for me when he might have said all he longed to say, and not Tíkhon but I might have heard and understood him. Why didn't I enter the room?' she thought. 'Perhaps he would then have said to me what he said the day he died. While talking to Tíkhon he asked about me twice. He wanted to see me, and I was standing close by, outside the door. It was sad and painful for him to talk to Tíkhon who did not understand him. I remember how he began speaking to him about Lise as if she were alive—he had forgotten she was dead—and Tíkhon reminded him that she was no more, and he shouted "Fool!" He was greatly depressed. From behind the door I heard how he lay down on his bed groaning and loudly exclaimed "My God!" Why didn't I go in then? What could he have done to me? What could I have lost? And perhaps he would then have been comforted and would have said that word to me.' And Princess Mary uttered aloud the caressing word he had said to her on the day of his death. 'Dear-est!' she repeated, and began sobbing, with tears that relieved her soul. She now saw his face before her. And not the face she had known ever since she could remember and had always seen at a distance, but the timid feeble face she had seen for the first time quite closely, with all its wrinkles and details, when she stooped near to his mouth to catch what he said.

'Dear-est!' she repeated again.

'What was he thinking when he uttered that word? What is he thinking now?' This question suddenly presented itself to her, and in answer she saw him before her with the expression that was on his face as he lay in his coffin with his chin bound up with a white handkerchief. And the horror that had seized her when she touched him and convinced herself that *that* was not *he*, but something mysterious and horrible, seized her again. She tried to think of something else and to pray, but could do neither. With wide-open eyes she gazed at the moonlight and the shadows, expecting every moment to see his dead face, and she felt that the silence brooding over the house and within it held her fast.

'Dunyásha,' she whispered. 'Dunyásha!' she screamed wildly, and tearing herself out of this silence she ran to the servants' quarters to meet her old nurse and the maidservants who came running towards her.

CHAPTER XIII

ON the 17th of August Rostóv and Ilyín, accompanied by Lavrúshka who had just returned from captivity and by an hussar orderly, left their quarters at Yankóvo, ten miles from Boguchárovo, and went for a ride—to try a new horse Ilyín had bought and to find out whether there was any hay to be had in the villages.

For the last three days Boguchárovo had lain between the two hostile armies, so that it was as easy for the Russian rearguard to get to it as for the French vanguard, so Rostóv, as a careful squadron-commander, wished to take such provisions as remained at Boguchárovo before the French could get them.

Rostóv and Ilyín were in the merriest of moods. On the way to Boguchárovo, a princely estate with a dwelling house and farm where they hoped to find many domestic serfs and pretty girls, they questioned Lavrúshka about Napoleon and laughed at his stories, and raced one another to try Ilyín's horse.

Rostóv had no idea that the village he was entering was the property of that very Bolkónski who had been engaged to his sister.

Rostóv and Ilyín gave rein to their horses for a last race along the incline before reaching Boguchárovo, and Rostóv, outstripping Ilyín, was the first to gallop into the village street.

'You're first!' cried Ilyín, flushed.

'Yes, always first both on the grass-land and here,' answered Rostóv, stroking his heated Donéts horse.

'And I'd have won on my Frenchy, your Excellency,' said Lavrúshka from behind, alluding to his shabby cart-horse, 'only I didn't wish to mortify you.'

They rode at a foot-pace to the barn, where a large crowd of peasants was standing.

Some of the men bared their heads, others stared at the new arrivals without doffing their caps. Two tall old peasants with wrinkled faces and scanty beards emerged from the tavern, smiling, staggering, and singing some incoherent song, and approached the officers.

'Fine fellows!' said Rostóv, laughing. 'Is there any hay here?'

'And how like one another,' said Ilyín.

'A mo-o-st me-r-r-y co-o-m-pa . . . !' sang one of the peasants with a blissful smile.

One of the men came out of the crowd and went up to Rostóv.

'Who do you belong to?' he asked.

'The French,' replied Ilyín jestingly, 'and here is Napoleon himself'—and he pointed to Lavrúshka.

'Then you are Russians?' the peasant asked again.

'And is there a large force of you here?' said another, a short man, coming up.

'Very large,' answered Rostóv. 'But why have you collected here?' he added. 'Is it a holiday?'

'The old men have met to talk over the business of the commune,' replied the peasant moving away.

At that moment, on the road leading from the big house, two women and a man in a white hat were seen coming towards the officers.

'The one in pink is mine, so keep off!' said Ilyín on seeing Dunyásha running resolutely towards him.

'She'll be ours!' said Lavrúshka to Ilyín, winking.

'What do you want, my pretty?' said Ilyín with a smile.

'The princess ordered me to ask your regiment and your name.'

'This is Count Rostóv, squadron-commander, and I am your humble servant.'

'Co-o-m-pa-ny!' roared the tipsy peasant with a beatific smile as he looked at Ilyín talking to the girl. Following Dunyásha, Alpátych advanced to Rostóv, having bared his head while still at a distance.

'May I make bold to trouble your Honour?' said he respectfully, but with a shade of contempt for the youthfulness of this officer and with a hand thrust into his bosom. 'My mistress, daughter of General-in-Chief Prince Nicholas Bolkónski who died on the 15th of this month, finding herself in difficulties owing to the boorishness of these people'—he pointed to the peasants—'asks you to come up to the house . . . Won't you, please, ride on a little farther,' said Alpátych with a melancholy

smile, 'as it is not convenient in the presence of . . . ?' He
pointed to the two peasants who kept as close to him as
horseflies to a horse.

'Ah! . . . Alpátych . . . Ah, Yákov Alpátych . . . Grand!
Forgive us for Christ's sake, eh?' said the peasants,
smiling joyfully at him.

Rostóv looked at the tipsy peasants and smiled.

'Or perhaps they amuse your Honour?' remarked
Alpátych with a staid air, as he pointed at the old men
with his free hand.

'No, there's not much to be amused at here,' said
Rostóv, and rode on a little way. 'What's the matter?'
he asked.

'I make bold to inform your Honour that the rude
peasants here don't wish to let the mistress leave the
estate, and threaten to unharness her horses, so that
though everything has been packed since morning, her
Excellency cannot get away.'

'Impossible!' exclaimed Rostóv.

'I have the honour to report to you the actual truth,'
said Alpátych.

Rostóv dismounted, gave his horse to the orderly, and
followed Alpátych to the house, questioning him as to
the state of affairs. It appeared that the princess's offer
of corn to the peasants the previous day, and her talk
with Dron and at the meeting, had actually had so bad
an effect that Dron had finally given up the keys and
joined the peasants, and had not appeared when Alpátych
sent for him, and that in the morning when the princess
gave orders to harness for her journey, the peasants had
come in a large crowd to the barn and sent word that
they would not let her leave the village: that there was
an order not to move, and that they would unharness the
horses. Alpátych had gone out to admonish them, but
was told (it was chiefly Karp who did the talking, Dron
not showing himself in the crowd) that they could not
let the princess go, that there was an order to the contrary, but that if she stayed they would serve her as
before and obey her in everything.

At the moment when Rostóv and Ilyín were galloping
along the road, Princess Mary, despite the dissuasions of

Alpátych, her nurse, and the maids, had given orders to harness and intended to start, but when the cavalrymen were espied they were taken for Frenchmen, the coachman ran away, and the women in the house began to wail.

'Father! Benefactor! God has sent you!' exclaimed deeply moved voices as Rostóv passed through the anteroom.

Princess Mary was sitting, helpless and bewildered, in the large sitting-room when Rostóv was shown in. She could not grasp who he was and why he had come, or what was happening to her. When she saw his Russian face, and by his walk and the first words he uttered recognized him as a man of her own class, she glanced at him with her deep radiant look and began speaking in a voice that faltered and trembled with emotion. This meeting immediately struck Rostóv as a romantic event. 'A helpless girl overwhelmed with grief, left to the mercy of coarse rioting peasants! And what a strange fate sent me here! What gentleness and nobility there is in her features and expression!' thought he as he looked at her and listened to her timid story.

When she began to tell him that all this had happened the day after her father's funeral, her voice trembled. She turned away, and then, as if fearing he might take her words as meant to move him to pity, looked at him with an apprehensive glance of inquiry. There were tears in Rostóv's eyes. Princess Mary noticed this, and glanced gratefully at him with that radiant look which caused the plainness of her face to be forgotten.

'I cannot express, Princess, how glad I am that I happened to ride here and am able to show my readiness to serve you,' said Rostóv, rising. 'Go when you please, and I give you my word of honour that no one shall dare to cause you annoyance if only you will allow me to act as your escort.' And bowing respectfully, as if to a lady of royal blood, he moved towards the door.

Rostóv's deferential tone seemed to indicate that though he would consider himself happy to be acquainted with her, he did not wish to take advantage of her misfortunes to intrude upon her.

Princess Mary understood this and appreciated his delicacy.

'I am very, very grateful to you,' she said in French, 'but I hope it was all a misunderstanding and that no one is to blame for it.' She suddenly began to cry.

'Excuse me!' she said.

Rostóv, knitting his brows, left the room with another low bow.

CHAPTER XIV

'WELL, is she pretty? Ah, friend—my pink one is delicious; her name is Dunyásha . . .'

But on glancing at Rostóv's face Ilyín stopped short. He saw that his hero and commander was following quite a different train of thought.

Rostóv glanced angrily at Ilyín and without replying strode off with rapid steps to the village.

'I'll show them; I'll give it them, the brigands!' said he to himself.

Alpátych at a gliding trot, only just managing not to run, kept up with him with difficulty.

'What decision have you been pleased to come to?' said he.

Rostóv stopped and, clenching his fists, suddenly and sternly turned on Alpátych.

'Decision? What decision? Old dotard! . . .' cried he. 'What have you been about? Eh? The peasants are rioting, and you can't manage them? You're a traitor yourself! I know you. I'll flay you all alive!' . . . And as if afraid of wasting his store of anger, he left Alpátych and went rapidly forward. Alpátych, mastering his offended feelings, kept pace with Rostóv at a gliding gait and continued to impart his views. He said the peasants were obdurate and that at the present moment it would be imprudent to 'over-resist' them without an armed force, and would it not be better first to send for the military?

'I'll give them armed force . . . I'll "over-resist" them!' uttered Rostóv meaninglessly, breathless with irrational animal fury and the need to vent it.

Without considering what he would do he moved unconsciously with quick resolute steps towards the crowd. And the nearer he drew to it the more Alpátych felt that this unreasonable action might produce good results. The peasants in the crowd were similarly impressed when they saw Rostóv's rapid firm steps and resolute frowning face.

After the hussars had come to the village and Rostóv had gone to see the princess, a certain confusion and dissension had arisen among the crowd. Some of the peasants said that these new arrivals were Russians and might take it amiss that the mistress was being detained. Dron was of this opinion, but as soon as he expressed it Karp and others attacked their ex-Elder.

'How many years have you been fattening on the commune?' Karp shouted at him. 'It's all one to you! You'll dig up your pot of money and take it away with you . . . What does it matter to you whether our homes are ruined or not?'

'We've been told to keep order, and that no one is to leave their homes or take away a single grain, and that's all about it!' cried another.

'It was your son's turn to be conscripted, but no fear! You begrudged your lump of a son,' a little old man suddenly began attacking Dron—'and so they took my Vánka to be shaved for a soldier! But we all have to die.'

'To be sure, we all have to die. I'm not against the commune,' said Dron.

'That's it—not against it! You've filled your belly . . .'

The two tall peasants had their say. As soon as Rostóv followed by Ilyín, Lavrúska, and Alpátych, came up to the crowd, Karp, thrusting his fingers into his belt and smiling a little, walked to the front. Dron on the contrary retired to the rear, and the crowd drew closer together.

'Who is your Elder here? Hey?' shouted Rostóv, coming up to the crowd with quick steps.

'The Elder? What do you want with him? . . .' asked Karp.

But before the words were well out of his mouth, his cap flew off and a fierce blow jerked his head to one side.

'Caps off, traitors!' shouted Rostóv in a wrathful voice. 'Where's the Elder?' he cried furiously.

'The Elder . . . He wants the Elder! . . . Dron Zakhárych,[1] you!' meek and flustered voices here and there were heard calling, and the caps began to come off their heads.

'We don't riot, we're following the orders,' declared Karp, and at that moment several voices began speaking together.

'It's as the old men have decided—there's too many of you giving orders.'

'Arguing? Mutiny! . . . Brigands! Traitors!' cried Rostóv unmeaningly in a voice not his own, gripping Karp by the collar. 'Bind him, bind him!' he shouted, though there was no one to bind him but Lavrúshka and Alpátych.

Lavrúshka however ran up to Karp and seized him by the arms from behind.

'Shall I call up our men from beyond the hill?' he called out.

Alpátych turned to the peasants and ordered two of them by name to come and bind Karp. The men obediently came out of the crowd, and began taking off their belts.

'Where's the Elder?' demanded Rostóv in a loud voice.

With a pale and frowning face Dron stepped out of the crowd.

'Are you the Elder? Bind him, Lavrúshka!' shouted Rostóv, as if that order, too, could not possibly meet with any opposition.

And in fact two more peasants began binding Dron, who took off his own belt and handed it to them, as if to aid them.

'And you all listen to me,' said Rostóv to the peasants. 'Be off to your houses at once, and don't let one of your voices be heard!'

'Why, we've not done any harm. We did it just out

---

[1] The use of Dron's patronymic, Zakhárych (son of Zacharias), indicates that the peasants were no longer speaking familiarly, but wished to be as formal and ceremonious as possible.

of foolishness. It's all nonsense . . . I said then that it was not in order,' voices were heard bickering with one another.

'There! What did I say?' said Alpátych, coming into his own again. 'It's wrong, lads!'

'All our stupidity, Yákov Alpátych,' came the answers, and the crowd began at once to disperse through the village.

The two bound men were led off to the master's house. The two drunken peasants followed them.

'Aye, when I look at you!' said one of them to Karp.

'How can one talk to the masters like that? What were you thinking of, you fool?' added the other—'A real fool!'

Two hours later the carts were standing in the court-yard of the Boguchárovo house. The peasants were briskly carrying out the proprietor's goods and packing them on the carts, and Dron, liberated at Princess Mary's wish from the cupboard where he had been confined, was standing in the yard directing the men.

'Don't put it in so carelessly,' said one of the peasants, a man with a round smiling face, taking a casket from a housemaid. 'You know it has cost money! How can you chuck it in like that or shove it under the cord where it'll get rubbed? I don't like that way of doing things. Let it all be done properly, according to rule. Look here, put it under the bast-matting and cover it with hay—that's the way!'

'Eh, books, books!' said another peasant bringing out Prince Andrew's library cupboards. 'Don't catch up against it! It's heavy, lads—solid books.'

'Yes, they worked all day and didn't play!' remarked the tall, round-faced peasant gravely, pointing with a significant wink at the dictionaries that were on the top.

Unwilling to obtrude himself on the princess, Rostóv did not go back to the house but remained in the village awaiting her departure. When her carriage drove out of the house, he mounted, and accompanied her eight miles from Boguchárovo to where the road was occupied by our troops. At the inn at Yankóvo he respectfully took leave of her, for the first time permitting himself to kiss her hand.

'How can you speak so!' he blushingly replied to Princess Mary's expressions of gratitude for her deliverance, as she termed what had occurred. 'Any police officer would have done as much! If we had had only peasants to fight, we should not have let the enemy come so far,' said he with a sense of shame and wishing to change the subject. 'I am only happy to have had the opportunity of making your acquaintance. Good-bye, Princess. I wish you happiness and consolation, and hope to meet you again in happier circumstances. If you don't want to make me blush, please don't thank me!'

But the princess, if she did not again thank him in words, thanked him with the whole expression of her face, radiant with gratitude and tenderness. She could not believe that there was nothing to thank him for. On the contrary it seemed to her certain that had he not been there she would have perished at the hands of the mutineers and of the French, and that he had exposed himself to terrible and obvious danger to save her, and even more certain was it that he was a man of lofty and noble soul, able to understand her position and her sorrow. His kind, honest eyes, with the tears rising in them when she herself had begun to cry as she spoke of her loss, did not leave her memory.

When she had taken leave of him and remained alone she suddenly felt her eyes filling with tears, and then not for the first time the strange question presented itself to her: did she love him?

On the rest of the way to Moscow, though the princess's position was not a cheerful one, Dunyásha, who went with her in the carriage, more than once noticed that her mistress leaned out of the window and smiled at something with an expression of mingled joy and sorrow.

'Well, supposing I do love him?' thought Princess Mary.

Ashamed as she was of acknowledging to herself that she had fallen in love with a man who would perhaps never love her, she comforted herself with the thought that no one would ever know it, and that she would not be to blame if, without ever speaking of it to any one, she continued to the end of her life to love the man with whom she had fallen in love for the first and last time in her life.

Sometimes when she recalled his looks, his sympathy, and his words, happiness did not appear impossible to her. It was at those moments that Dunyásha noticed her smiling as she looked out of the carriage window.

'Was it not fate that brought him to Boguchárovo, and at that very moment?' thought Princess Mary, 'and that caused his sister to refuse my brother?'[1] And in all this Princess Mary saw the hand of Providence.

The impression the princess made on Rostóv was a very agreeable one. To remember her gave him pleasure, and when his comrades, hearing of his adventure at Boguchárovo, rallied him on having gone to look for hay and having picked up one of the wealthiest heiresses in Russia, he grew angry. It made him angry just because the idea of marrying the gentle Princess Mary, who was attractive to him and had an enormous fortune, had against his will more than once entered his head. For himself personally Nicholas could not wish for a better wife: by marrying her he would make the countess his mother happy, would be able to put his father's affairs in order, and would even—he felt it—ensure Princess Mary's happiness.

But Sónya? And his plighted word? That was why Rostóv grew angry when he was rallied about Princess Bolkónskaya.

CHAPTER XV

ON receiving command of the armies Kutúzov remembered Prince Andrew and sent an order for him to report at headquarters.

Prince Andrew arrived at Tsárevo-Zaymíshche on the very day and at the very hour that Kutúzov was review-

[1] A woman might not marry her brother's or sister's brother-in-law and vice versa, so that if Natásha had married Prince Andrew it would have been an obstacle to marriage between Mary and Nicholas.

ing the troops for the first time. He stopped in the village
at the priest's house in front of which stood the commander-in-chief's carriage, and he sat down on the
bench at the gate awaiting his Serene Highness, as every
one now called Kutúzov. From the field beyond the
village came, now sounds of regimental music and now
the roar of many voices shouting 'Hurrah!' to the new
commander-in-chief. Two orderlies, a courier, and a
major-domo, stood near by, some ten paces from Prince
Andrew, availing themselves of Kutúzov's absence and
of the fine weather. A short, swarthy lieutenant-colonel
of hussars with thick moustaches and whiskers rode up
to the gate and, glancing at Prince Andrew, inquired
whether his Serene Highness was putting up there and
whether he would soon be back.

Prince Andrew replied that he was not on his Serene
Highness's staff but was himself a new arrival. The
lieutenant-colonel turned to a smart orderly, who with
the peculiar contempt with which a commander-in-
chief's orderly speaks to officers, replied:

'What? His Serene Highness? I expect he'll be here
soon. What do you want?'

The lieutenant-colonel of hussars smiled beneath his
moustache at the orderly's tone, dismounted, gave his
horse to a dispatch-runner, and approached Bolkónski
with a slight bow. Bolkónski made room for him on the
bench and the lieutenant-colonel sat down beside him.

"You're also waiting for the commander-in-chief?'
said he. 'They say he weceives evewyone, thank God! . . .
It's awful with those sausage-eaters! Ermolóv had
weason to ask to be pwomoted to be a German! Now
p'waps Wussians will get a look in. As it was, devil only
knows what was happening. We kept wetweating and
wetweating. Did you take part in the campaign?' he
asked.

'I had the pleasure,' replied Prince Andrew, 'not only
of taking part in the retreat but of losing in that retreat
all I held dear—not to mention the estate and home of
my birth—my father, who died of grief. I belong to the
province of Smolénsk.'

'Ah? You're Pwince Bolkónski? Vewy glad to make

your acquaintance! I'm Lieutenant-Colonel Denísov, better known as "Váska",' said Denísov, pressing Prince Andrew's hand and looking into his face with a particularly kindly attention. 'Yes, I heard,' said he sympathetically, and after a short pause added: 'Yes, it's Scythian warfare. It's all vewy well—only not for those who get it in the neck. So you are Pwince Andwew Bolkónski?' He swayed his head. 'Vewy pleased, Pwince, to make your acquaintance!' he repeated again, smiling sadly, and he again pressed Prince Andrew's hand.

Prince Andrew knew Denísov from what Natásha had told him of her first suitor. This memory carried him sadly and sweetly back to those painful feelings of which he had not thought lately, but which still found place in his soul. Of late he had received so many new and very serious impressions—such as the retreat from Smolénsk, his visit to Bald Hills, and the recent news of his father's death—and had experienced so many emotions, that for a long time past those memories had not entered his mind, and now that they did, they did not act on him with nearly their former strength. For Denísov, too, the memories awakened by the name of Bolkónski belonged to a distant, romantic past, when after supper and after Natásha's singing he had proposed to a little girl of fifteen without realizing what he was doing. He smiled at the recollection of that time and of his love for Natásha, and passed at once to what now interested him passionately and exclusively. This was a plan of campaign he had devised while serving at the outposts during the retreat. He had proposed that plan to Barclay de Tolly and now wished to propose it to Kutúzov. The plan was based on the fact that the French line of operation was too extended, and it proposed that instead of, or concurrently with, action on the front to bar the advance of the French, we should attack their line of communication. He began explaining his plan to Prince Andrew.

'They can't hold all that line. It's impossible. I will undertake to bweak thwough. Give me five hundwed men and I will bweak the line, that's certain! There's only one way—guewilla warfare!'

Denísov rose and began gesticulating as he explained

440

his plan to Bolkónski. In the midst of his explanation shouts were heard from the army, growing more incoherent and more diffused, mingling with music and songs, and coming from the field where the review was held. Sounds of hoofs and shouts were nearing the village.

'He's coming! He's coming!' shouted a Cossack standing at the gate.

Bolkónski and Denísov moved to the gate, at which a knot of soldiers (a guard of honour) was standing, and they saw Kutúzov coming down the street mounted on a rather small sorrel horse. A huge suite of generals rode behind him. Barclay was riding almost beside him, and a crowd of officers ran after and around them shouting 'Hurrah!'

His adjutants galloped into the yard before him. Kutúzov was impatiently urging on his horse, which ambled smoothly under his weight, and he raised his hand to his white horseguard's cap with a red band and no peak, nodding his head continually. When he came up to the guard of honour, a fine set of Grenadiers mostly wearing decorations, who were giving him the salute, he looked at them silently and attentively for nearly a minute with the steady gaze of a commander and then turned to the crowd of generals and officers surrounding him. Suddenly his face assumed a subtle expression, he shrugged his shoulders with an air of perplexity.

'And with such fine fellows to retreat and retreat! Well, good-bye, General,' he added, and rode into the yard past Prince Andrew and Denísov.

'Hurrah! hurrah! hurrah!' shouted those behind him.

Since Prince Andrew had last seen him Kutúzov had grown still more corpulent, flaccid, and fat. But the bleached eyeball, the scar, and the familiar weariness of his expression were still the same. He was wearing the white horseguard's cap and a military overcoat with a whip hanging over his shoulder by a thin strap. He sat heavily and swayed limply on his brisk little horse.

'Whew . . . whew . . . whew!' he whistled just audibly as he rode into the yard. His face expressed the relief of relaxed strain felt by a man who means to rest after a ceremony. He drew his left foot out of the stirrup and, lurching with his whole body and puckering his face with the effort, raised it with difficulty onto the saddle, leaned on his knee, groaned, and slipped down into the arms of the Cossacks and adjutants who stood ready to assist him.

He pulled himself together, looked round screwing up his eyes, glanced at Prince Andrew and, evidently not recognizing him, moved with his waddling gait to the porch. 'Whew . . . whew . . . whew!' he whistled, and again glanced at Prince Andrew. As often occurs with old men, it was only after some seconds that the impression produced by Prince Andrew's face linked itself up with Kutúzov's remembrance of his personality.

'Ah, how do you do, my dear Prince? How do you do, my dear boy? Come along . . .' said he glancing wearily round, and he stepped onto the porch which creaked under his weight.

He unbuttoned his coat and sat down on a bench in the porch.

'And how's your father?'

'I received news of his death yesterday,' replied Prince Andrew abruptly.

Kutúzov looked at him with eyes wide open with dismay, and then took off his cap and crossed himself:

'May the kingdom of Heaven be his! God's will be done to us all!' He sighed deeply, his whole chest heaving, and was silent for awhile. 'I loved him and respected him, and sympathize with you with all my heart.'

He embraced Prince Andrew, pressing him to his fat breast, and for some time did not let him go. When he released him Prince Andrew saw that Kutúzov's flabby lips were trembling and that tears were in his eyes. He sighed and pressed on the bench with both hands to raise himself.

'Come! Come with me, we'll have a talk,' said he.

But at that moment Denísov, no more intimidated by his superiors than by the enemy, came with jingling spurs up the steps of the porch, despite the angry whispers of the adjutants who tried to stop him. Kutúzov, his hands still pressed on the seat, glanced at him glumly. Denísov, having given his name, announced that he had to communicate to his Serene Highness a matter of great

importance for their country's welfare. Kutúzov looked
wearily at him, and lifting his hands with a gesture of
annoyance folded them across his stomach repeating the
words: 'For our country's welfare? Well, what is it?
Speak!' Denísov blushed like a girl (it was strange to see
the colour rise in that shaggy, bibulous, time-worn face)
and boldly began to expound his plan of cutting the
enemy's lines of communication between Smolénsk and
Vyázma. Denísov came from those parts and knew the
country well. His plan seemed decidedly a good one,
especially from the strength of conviction with which he
spoke. Kutúzov looked down at his own legs, occasionally
glancing at the door of the adjoining hut as if expecting
something unpleasant to emerge from it. And from that
hut, while Denísov was speaking, a general with a port-
folio under his arm really did appear.

'What?' said Kutúzov, in the midst of Denísov's explanations, 'are you ready so soon?'

'Ready, your Serene Highness,' replied the general.

Kutúzov swayed his head, as much as to say: 'How is
one man to deal with it all?' and again listened to
Denísov.

'I give my word of honour as a Wussian officer,' said
Denísov, 'that I can bweak Napoleon's line of communication!'

'What relation are you to Intendant-General Kiríl
Andréevich Denísov?' asked Kutúzov, interrupting him.

'He is my uncle, your Serene Highness.'

'Ah, we were friends,' said Kutúzov cheerfully. 'All
right, all right, friend, stay here at the staff and to-morrow
we'll have a talk.'

With a nod to Denísov he turned away and put out his
hand for the papers Konovnítsyn had brought him.

'Would not your Serene Highness like to come inside?'
said the general on duty in a discontented voice, 'the
plans must be examined and several papers have to be
signed.'

An adjutant came out and announced that everything was in readiness within. But Kutúzov evidently did
not wish to enter that room till he was disengaged. He
made a grimace . . .

'No, tell them to bring a small table out here, my dear boy. I'll look at them here,' said he. 'Don't go away,' he added turning to Prince Andrew, who remained in the porch and listened to the general's report.

While this was being given, Prince Andrew heard the whisper of a woman's voice and the rustle of a silk dress behind the door. Several times on glancing that way he noticed behind that door a plump, rosy, handsome woman in a pink dress with a lilac silk kerchief on her head, holding a dish and evidently awaiting the entrance of the commander-in-chief. Kutúzov's adjutant whispered to Prince Andrew that this was the wife of the priest whose home it was, and that she intended to offer his Serene Highness bread and salt.[1] 'Her husband has welcomed his Serene Highness with the cross at the church, and she intends to welcome him in the house... She's very pretty,' added the adjutant with a smile. At those words Kutúzov looked round. He was listening to the general's report—which consisted chiefly of a criticism of the position at Tsárevo-Zaymíshche—as he had listened to Denísov, and seven years previously had listened to the discussion at the Austerlitz council of war. He evidently listened only because he had ears which, though there was a piece of tow in one of them, could not help hearing; but it was evident that nothing the general could say would surprise or even interest him, that he knew all that would be said beforehand, and heard it all only because he had to, as one has to listen to the chanting of a service of prayer. All that Denísov had said was clever and to the point. What the general was saying was even more clever and to the point, but it was evident that Kutúzov despised knowledge and cleverness, and knew of something else that would decide the matter—something independent of cleverness and knowledge. Prince Andrew watched the commander-in-chief's face attentively, and the only expression he could see there was one of boredom, curiosity as to the meaning of the feminine whispering

[1] It is a Russian custom to present 'bread and salt' to any one who is taking up residence in a new place. In practice the 'bread and salt' is often represented by a cake and a silver dish of white powdered sugar.

behind the door, and a desire to observe propriety. It was evident that Kutúzov despised cleverness and learning and even the patriotic feeling shown by Denísov, but despised them not because of his own intellect, feelings, or knowledge—he did not try to display any of these—but because of something else. He despised them because of his old age and experience of life. The only instruction Kutúzov gave of his own accord during that report referred to looting by the Russian troops. At the end of the report the general put before him for signature a paper relating to the recovery of payment from army commanders for green oats mown down by the soldiers, when landowners lodged petitions for compensation.

After hearing the matter, Kutúzov smacked his lips together and shook his head.

'Into the stove . . . into the fire with it! I tell you once for all, my dear fellow,' said he, 'into the fire with all such things! Let them cut the crops and burn wood to their hearts' content. I don't order it or allow it, but I don't exact compensation either. One can't get on without it. "When wood is chopped, the chips will fly."' He looked at the paper again. 'Oh, this German precision!' he muttered, shaking his head.

CHAPTER XVI

'WELL, that's all!' said Kutúzov as he signed the last of the documents, and rising heavily and smoothing out the folds in his fat white neck he moved towards the door with a more cheerful expression.

The priest's wife, flushing rosy red, caught up the dish she had not managed to present at the right moment after all, though she had so long been preparing for it, and with a low bow offered it to Kutúzov.

He screwed up his eyes, smiled, lifted her chin with his hand and said:

'Ah, what a beauty! Thank you, sweetheart!'

He took some gold pieces from his trouser pocket and put them on the dish for her. 'Well, my dear, and how are we getting on?' he asked, moving to the door of the room assigned to him. The priest's wife smiled, and with dimples in her rosy cheeks followed him into the room. The adjutant came out to the porch and asked Prince Andrew to lunch with him. Half an hour later Prince Andrew was again called to Kutúzov. He found him reclining in an arm-chair, still in the same unbuttoned overcoat. He had in his hand a French book which he closed as Prince Andrew entered, marking the place with a knife. Prince Andrew saw by the cover that it was *Les Chevaliers du Cygne* by Madame de Genlis.

'Well, sit down, sit down here. Let's have a talk,' said Kutúzov. 'It's sad, very sad. But remember, my dear fellow, that I am a father to you, a second father . . .'

Prince Andrew told Kutúzov all he knew of his father's death, and what he had seen at Bald Hills when he passed through it.

'What . . . what they have brought us to!' Kutúzov suddenly cried in an agitated voice, evidently picturing vividly to himself from Prince Andrew's story the condition Russia was in. 'But give me time, give me time!' he said with a grim look evidently not wishing to continue this agitating conversation, and added: 'I sent for you to keep you with me.'

'I thank your Serene Highness, but I fear I am no longer fit for the staff,' replied Prince Andrew with a smile which Kutúzov noticed.

Kutúzov glanced inquiringly at him.

'But above all,' added Prince Andrew, 'I have grown used to my regiment, am fond of the officers, and I fancy the men also like me. I should be sorry to leave the regiment. If I decline the honour of being with you, believe me . . .'

A shrewd, kindly, yet subtly derisive expression lit up Kutúzov's podgy face. He cut Bolkónski short.

'I am sorry, for I need you. But you're right, you're right! It's not here that men are needed. Advisers are always plentiful, but men are not. The regiments would not be what they are if the would-be advisers served there as you do. I remember you at Austerlitz . . . I remember, yes, I remember you with the standard!' said Kutúzov, and a flush of pleasure suffused Prince Andrew's face at this recollection.

Taking his hand and drawing him downwards, Kutúzov offered his cheek to be kissed, and again Prince Andrew noticed tears in the old man's eyes. Though Prince Andrew knew that Kutúzov's tears came easily and that he was particularly tender to and considerate of him from a wish to show sympathy with his loss, yet this reminder of Austerlitz was both pleasant and flattering to him.

'Go your way and God be with you. I know your path is the path of honour!' He paused. 'I missed you at Bucharest, but I needed some one to send.' And changing the subject, Kutúzov began to speak of the Turkish war and the peace that had been concluded. 'Yes, I have been much blamed,' he said, 'both for that war and the peace . . . but everything came at the right time. *Tout vient à point à celui qui sait attendre.*[1] And there were as many advisers there as here . . .' he went on, returning to the subject of 'advisers' which evidently occupied him. 'Ah, those advisers,' said he. 'If we had listened to them all we should not have made peace with Turkey and should not have been through with that war. Everything in haste, but more haste less speed. Kámenski would have been lost if he had not died. He stormed fortresses with thirty thousand men. It is not difficult to capture a fortress but it is difficult to win a campaign. For that, not storming and attacking but *patience and time* are wanted. Kámenski sent soldiers to Rustchuk, but I only employed these two things and took more fortresses than Kámenski and made the Turks eat horse-flesh!' He swayed his head. 'And the French shall too, believe me,' he went on, growing warmer and beating his chest, 'I'll make them eat horse-flesh!' And tears again dimmed his eyes.

'But shan't we have to accept battle?' remarked Prince Andrew.

'We shall if everybody wants it, it can't be helped . . . But believe me, my dear boy, there is nothing stronger than those two, *patience and time*, they will do it all. But

[1] Everything comes in time to him who knows how to wait.

the advisers *n'entendent pas de cette oreille, voilà le mal.*[1]
Some want a thing—others don't. What's one to do?'
he asked, evidently expecting an answer. 'Well, what do
you want us to do?' he repeated and his eye shone with
a deep, shrewd look. 'I'll tell you what to do,' he continued, as Prince Andrew still did not reply: 'I will tell
you what to do, and what I do. *Dans le doute, mon cher,*' he
paused, '*abstiens-toi,*'[2] he articulated the French proverb
deliberately.

'Well, good-bye, my dear fellow; remember that with
all my heart I share your sorrow, and that for you I am not
a Serene Highness, nor a prince, nor a commander-in-
chief, but a father! If you want anything, come straight
to me. Good-bye, my dear boy.'

Again he embraced and kissed Prince Andrew, but
before the latter had left the room Kutúzov gave a sigh of
relief and went on with his unfinished novel, *Les Chevaliers
du Cygne,* by Madame de Genlis.

Prince Andrew could not have explained how or why
it was, but after that interview with Kutúzov he went
back to his regiment reassured as to the general course of
affairs and as to the man to whom it had been entrusted.
The more he realized the absence of all personal motive
in that old man—in whom there seemed to remain only
the habit of passions, and in place of an intellect
(grouping events and drawing conclusions) only the
capacity calmly to contemplate the course of events—the
more reassured he was that everything would be as it
should. 'He will not bring in any plan of his own. He
will not devise or undertake anything,' thought Prince
Andrew, 'but he will hear everything, remember everything, and put everything in its place. He will not hinder
anything useful nor allow anything harmful. He understands that there is something stronger and more important than his own will—the inevitable course of events,
and he can see them and grasp their significance, and
seeing that significance can refrain from meddling and
renounce his personal wish directed to something else.
And above all,' thought Prince Andrew, 'one believes in

[1] Don't listen with that ear—that's the trouble.

[2] When in doubt, my dear fellow, do nothing.

him because he's Russian, despite the novel by Genlis and the French proverbs, and because his voice shook when he said: "What they have brought us to!" and had a sob in it when he said he would "make them eat horse-flesh!" '

On such feelings, more or less dimly shared by all, the unanimity and general approval were founded with which, despite court influences, the popular choice of Kutúzov as commander-in-chief was received.

CHAPTER XVII

AFTER the Emperor had left Moscow, life flowed on there in its usual course, and its course was so very usual that it was difficult to remember the recent days of patriotic elation and ardour, hard to believe that Russia was really in danger and that the members of the English Club were also sons of the Fatherland ready to sacrifice everything for it. The one thing that recalled the patriotic fervour every one had displayed during the Emperor's stay was the call for contributions of men and money, a necessity that as soon as the promises had been made, assumed a legal, official form and became unavoidable.

With the enemy's approach to Moscow the Moscovites' view of their situation did not grow more serious but on the contrary became even more frivolous, as always happens with people who see a great danger approaching. At the approach of danger there are always two voices that speak with equal power in the human soul: one very reasonably tells a man to consider the nature of the danger and the means of escaping it; the other, still more reasonably, says that it is too depressing and painful to think of the danger since it is not in man's power to foresee everything and avert the general course of events, and it is therefore better to disregard what is painful till it comes, and to think about what is pleasant. In solitude a man generally listens to the first voice, but in society to the second. So it was now with the inhabitants of Moscow. It was long since people had been as gay in Moscow as that year.

Rostopchín's broadsheets, headed by woodcuts of a drink-shop, a potman, and a Moscow burgher called Karpúshka Chigírin, '*who—having been a militiaman and having had rather too much at the pub—heard that Napoleon wished to come to Moscow, grew angry, abused the French in very bad language, came out of the drink-shop and, under the sign of the eagle, began to address the assembled people*', were read and discussed, together with the latest of Vasíli Lvóvich Púshkin's *bout-rimés*.

In the corner room at the Club, members gathered to read these broadsheets and some liked the way Karpúshka jeered at the French, saying: '*They will swell up with Russian cabbage, burst with our buck-wheat porridge, and choke themselves with cabbage-soup. They are all dwarfs, and one peasant woman will toss three of them with a hay-fork.*' Others did not like that tone and said it was stupid and vulgar. It was said that Rostopchín had expelled all Frenchmen and even all foreigners from Moscow, and that there had been some spies and agents of Napoleon among them, but this was told chiefly to introduce Rostopchín's witty remark on that occasion. The foreigners were deported to Nízhni by boat, and Rostopchín had said to them in French: '*Rentrez en vous-même, entrez dans la barque et n'en faites pas une barque de Charon.*' There was talk of all the government offices having been already removed from Moscow, and to this Shinshín's witticism was added—that for that alone Moscow ought to be grateful to Napoleon. It was said that Mamónov's regiment would cost him eight hundred thousand rubles, and that Bezúkhov had spent even more on his, but that the best thing about Bezúkhov's action was that he himself was going to don a uniform and ride at the head of his regiment without charging anything for the show.

'You don't spare any one,' said Julie Drubetskáya as she collected and pressed together a bunch of ravelled lint with her thin, beringed fingers.

Julie was preparing to leave Moscow next day and was giving a farewell soirée.

¹ 'Keep yourselves to yourselves. Get into the barque, and take care not to make it a barque of Charon.'

'*Bezúkhov est ridicule*,[1] but he is so kind and good-natured. What pleasure is there to be so *caustique*?'

'A forfeit!' cried a young man in militia uniform, whom Julie called '*mon chevalier*,' and who was going with her to Nízhni.

In Julie's set, as in many other circles in Moscow, it had been agreed that they would speak nothing but Russian, and that those who made a slip and spoke French should pay fines to the Committee of Voluntary Contributions.

'Another forfeit for a Gallicism,' said a Russian writer who was present. ' "What pleasure is there to be" is not Russian!'

'You spare no one,' continued Julie to the young man without heeding the author's remark.

'For *caustique*—I am guilty and will pay, and I am prepared to pay again for the pleasure of telling you the truth. For Gallicisms I won't be responsible,' she remarked, turning to the author: 'I have neither the money nor the time, like Prince Galítsin, to engage a master to teach me Russian!'

'Ah, here he is!' she added. '*Quand on* . . . No, no,' she said to the militia officer, 'you won't catch me. Speak of the sun and you see its rays!' and she smiled amiably at Pierre. 'We were just talking of you,' she said with the facility in lying natural to a society woman. 'We were saying that your regiment would be sure to be better than Mamónov's.'

'Oh, don't talk to me of my regiment,' replied Pierre, kissing his hostess's hand and taking a seat beside her. 'I am so sick of it.'

'You will, of course, command it yourself?' said Julie, directing a sly, sarcastic glance towards the militia officer.

The latter in Pierre's presence had ceased to be caustic and his face expressed perplexity as to what Julie's smile might mean. In spite of his absent-mindedness and good nature, Pierre's personality immediately checked any attempt to ridicule him to his face.

'No,' said Pierre, with a laughing glance at his big stout body. 'I should make too good a target for the

[1] Bezúkhov is absurd.

French, besides I am afraid I should hardly be able to climb onto a horse.'

Among those whom Julie's guests happened to choose to gossip about were the Rostóvs.

'I hear that their affairs are in a very bad way,' said Julie. 'And he is so unreasonable, the count himself I mean. The Razumóvskis wanted to buy his house and his estate near Moscow, but it drags on and on. He asks too much.'

'No, I think the sale will come off in a few days,' said some one. 'Though it is madness to buy anything in Moscow now.'

'Why?' asked Julie. 'You don't think Moscow is in danger?'

'Then why are you leaving?'

'I? What a question! I am going because . . . well, because every one is going; and besides—I am not Joan of Arc, or an Amazon.'

'Well, of course, of course! Let me have some more strips of linen.'

'If he manages the business properly he will be able to pay off all his debts,' said the militia officer, speaking of Rostóv.

'A kindly old man but not up to much. And why do they stay on so long in Moscow? They meant to leave for the country long ago. Natalie is quite well again now, isn't she?' Julie asked Pierre with a knowing smile.

'They are waiting for their younger son,' Pierre replied. 'He joined Obolénski's Cossacks and went to Bélaya Tsérkov where the regiment is being formed. But now they have had him transferred to my regiment and are expecting him every day. The count wanted to leave long ago, but the countess won't on any account leave Moscow till her son returns.'

'I met them the day before yesterday at the Arkhárovs'. Natalie has recovered her looks and is brighter. She sang a song. How easily some people get over everything!'

'Get over what?' inquired Pierre looking displeased. Julie smiled.

'You know, Count, such knights as you are only found in Madame de Souza's novels.'

'What knights? What do you mean?' demanded Pierre blushing.

'Oh, come, my dear Count! *C'est la fable de tout Moscou. Je vous admire, ma parole d'honneur.*[1]

'Forfeit, forfeit!' cried the militia officer.

'All right, one can't talk—how tiresome!'

'What is "the talk of all Moscow"?' Pierre asked angrily, rising to his feet.

'Come now, Count, you know!'

'I don't know anything about it,' said Pierre.

'I know you were friendly with Natalie, and so . . . but I was always more friendly with Véra—that dear Véra.'

'No, Madame!' Pierre continued in a tone of displeasure, 'I have not taken on myself the role of Natalie Rostóva's knight at all, and have not been to their house for nearly a month. But I cannot understand the cruelty . . .'

'*Qui s'excuse, s'accuse,*[2] said Julie, smiling and waving the lint triumphantly, and to have the last word she promptly changed the subject. 'Do you know what I heard to-day? Poor Mary Bolkónskaya arrived in Moscow yesterday. Do you know that she has lost her father?'

'Really? Where is she? I should very much like to see her,' said Pierre.

'I spent the evening with her yesterday. She is going to their estate near Moscow either to-day or to-morrow morning, with her nephew.'

'Well, and how is she?' asked Pierre.

'She is well, but sad. But do you know who rescued her? It is quite a romance. Nicholas Rostóv. She was surrounded, and they wanted to kill her, and had wounded some of her people. He rushed in and saved her . . .'

'Another romance,' said the militia officer. 'Really, this general flight has been arranged to get all the old maids married off. Catiche is one and Princess Bolkónskaya another.'

---

[1] It is the talk of all Moscow. I am surprised at you, on my word.

[2] Who excuses himself, accuses himself.

'Do you know, I really believe she is *un petit peu amoureuse du jeune homme?*'[1]

'Forfeit, forfeit, forfeit!'

'But how could one say that in Russian?'

CHAPTER XVIII

WHEN Pierre returned home he was handed two of Rostopchín's broadsheets that had been brought that day.

The first declared that the report that Count Rostopchín had forbidden people to leave Moscow was false; on the contrary he was glad that ladies and tradesmen's wives were leaving the city. 'There will be less panic and less gossip,' ran the broadsheet, 'but I will stake my life on it that that scoundrel will not enter Moscow.' These words showed Pierre clearly for the first time that the French would enter Moscow. The second broadsheet stated that our head-quarters were at Vyázma, that Count Wittgenstein had defeated the French, but that as many of the inhabitants of Moscow wished to be armed, weapons were ready for them at the arsenal: sabres, pistols, and muskets, which could be had at a low price. The tone of this proclamation was not as jocose as in the former Chigírin talks. Pierre pondered over these broadsheets. Evidently the terrible storm-cloud he had desired with the whole strength of his soul, but which yet aroused involuntary horror in him, was drawing near.

'Shall I join the army and enter the service or wait?' he asked himself for the hundredth time. He took a pack of cards that lay on the table and began to lay them out for a game of patience.

'If this patience comes out,' he said to himself after shuffling the cards, holding them in his hand and lifting his head, 'if it comes out, it means ... what does it mean?'

He had not decided what it should mean when he heard the voice of the eldest princess at the door asking whether she might come in.

'Then it will mean that I must go to the army,' said

[1] A little bit in love with the young man.

Pierre to himself. 'Come in, come in!' he added to the princess.

Only the eldest princess, the one with the stony face and long waist, was still living in Pierre's house. The two younger ones had both married.

'Excuse my coming to you, Cousin,' she said in a reproachful and agitated voice. 'You know some decision must be come to. What is going to happen? Every one has left Moscow and the people are rioting. How is it that we are staying on?'

'On the contrary things seem satisfactory, *ma cousine*,' said Pierre in the bantering tone he habitually adopted towards her, always feeling uncomfortable in the role of her benefactor.

'Satisfactory, indeed! Very satisfactory! Barbara Ivánovna told me to-day how our troops are distinguishing themselves. It certainly does them credit! And the people, too, are quite mutinous—they no longer obey, even my maid has taken to being rude. At this rate they will soon begin beating us. One can't walk in the streets. But, above all, the French will be here any day now, so what are we waiting for? I ask just one thing of you, cousin,' she went on, 'arrange for me to be taken to Petersburg. Whatever I may be, I can't live under Bonaparte's rule.'

'Oh, come, *ma cousine*! Where do you get your information from? On the contrary . . .'

'I won't submit to your Napoleon! Others may if they please . . . If you don't want to do this . . .'

'But I will, I'll give the order at once.'

The princess was apparently vexed at not having any one to be angry with. Muttering to herself, she sat down on a chair.

'But you have been misinformed,' said Pierre. 'Everything is quiet in the city and there is not the slightest danger. See! I've just been reading . . .' He showed her the broadsheet. 'Count Rostopchín writes that he will stake his life on it that the enemy will not enter Moscow.'

'Oh, that Count of yours!' said the princess malevolently. 'He is a hypocrite, a rascal who has himself roused the people to riot. Didn't he write in those idiotic broadsheets that any one "whoever it might be, should be dragged to the lock-up by his hair?" (How silly!) "And honour and glory to whoever captures him," he says. This is what his cajolery has brought us to! Barbara Ivánovna told me the mob nearly killed her because she said something in French.'

'Oh, but it's so . . . You take everything so to heart,' said Pierre, and began laying out his cards for patience.

Although that patience did come out, Pierre did not join the army, but remained in deserted Moscow ever in the same state of agitation, irresolution, and alarm, yet at the same time joyfully expecting something terrible.

Next day towards evening the princess set off, and Pierre's head steward came to inform him that the money needed for the equipment of his regiment could not be found without selling one of the estates. In general the head steward made out to Pierre that his project of raising a regiment would ruin him. Pierre listened to him, scarcely able to repress a smile.

'Well then, sell it,' said he. 'What's to be done? I can't draw back now!'

The worse everything became, especially his own affairs, the better was Pierre pleased and the more evident was it that the catastrophe he expected was approaching. Hardly any one he knew was left in town. Julie had gone, and so had Princess Mary. Of his intimate friends only the Rostóvs remained, but he did not go to see them.

To distract his thoughts he drove that day to the village of Vorontsóvo to see the great balloon Leppich was constructing to destroy the foe, and a trial balloon that was to go up next day. The balloon was not yet ready, but Pierre learnt that it was being constructed by the Emperor's desire. The Emperor had written to Count Rostopchín as follows:

'As soon as Leppich is ready, get together a crew of reliable and intelligent men for his car and send a courier to General Kutúzov to let him know. I have informed him of the matter.

'Please impress upon Leppich to be very careful where he descends for the first time, that he may not make a mistake and fall into the enemy's hands. It is essential for him to combine his movements with those of the commander-in-chief.'

On his way home from Vorontsóvo, as he was passing the Bolótnoe Place, Pierre, seeing a large crowd round the Lóbnoe Place,[1] stopped and got out of his trap. A French cook accused of being a spy was being flogged. The flogging was only just over, and the executioner was releasing from the flogging-bench a stout man with red whiskers, in blue stockings and a green jacket, who was moaning piteously. Another criminal, thin and pale, stood near. Judging by their faces they were both Frenchmen. With a frightened and suffering look resembling that on the thin Frenchman's face, Pierre pushed his way in through the crowd.

'What is it? Who is it? What is it for?' he kept asking. But the attention of the crowd—officials, burghers, shopkeepers, peasants, and women in cloaks and in pelisses—was so eagerly centred on what was passing in Lóbnoe Place that no one answered him. The stout man rose, frowned, shrugged his shoulders, and evidently trying to appear firm began to pull on his jacket without looking about him, but suddenly his lips trembled and he began to cry, in the way full-blooded grown-up men cry, though angry with himself for doing so. In the crowd people began talking loudly, to stifle their feelings of pity as it seemed to Pierre.

'He's cook to some prince.'

'Eh, mounseer, Russian sauce seems to be sour to a Frenchman . . . sets his teeth on edge!' said a wrinkled clerk who was standing behind Pierre, when the Frenchman began to cry.

The clerk glanced round, evidently hoping that his joke would be appreciated. Some people began to laugh, others continued to watch in dismay the executioner who was undressing the other man.

Pierre choked, his face puckered, and he turned hastily away, went back to his trap muttering something to him-

[1] The place of execution in Moscow, formerly situated on the Red Square, facing the Kremlin, but before 1812 it had been removed to another part of the town.

self as he went, and took his seat. As they drove along he shuddered, and exclaimed several times so audibly that the coachman asked him:

'What is your pleasure?'

'Where are you going?' shouted Pierre to the man, who was driving to Lubyánka Street.

'To the Governor's, as you ordered,' answered the coachman.

'Fool! Idiot!' shouted Pierre, abusing his coachman—a thing he rarely did. 'Home, I told you! And drive faster, blockhead!' 'I must get away this very day,' he murmured to himself.

At the sight of the tortured Frenchman and the crowd surrounding the Lóbnoe Place, Pierre had so definitely made up his mind that he could no longer remain in Moscow, and would leave for the army that very day, that it seemed to him that either he had told the coachman this or that the man ought to have known it of himself.

On reaching home Pierre gave orders to Evstáfey—his head coachman who knew everything, could do anything, and was known to all Moscow—that he would leave that night for the army at Mozháysk, and that his saddle-horses should be sent there. This could not all be arranged that day, so on Evstáfey's representation Pierre had to put off his departure till next day to allow time for the relay horses to be sent on in advance.

On the 24th the weather cleared up after a spell of rain, and after dinner Pierre left Moscow. When changing horses that night, in Perkhúshkovo, he learnt that there had been a great battle that evening. (This was the battle of Shevárdino.) He was told that there in Perkhúshkovo the earth had trembled from the firing, but nobody could answer his questions as to who had won. At dawn next day Pierre was approaching Mozháysk.

Every house in Mozháysk had soldiers quartered in it, and at the hostel where Pierre was met by his groom and coachman there was no room to be had. It was full of officers.

Everywhere in Mozháysk and beyond it troops were stationed or on the march. Cossacks, foot and horse soldiers, wagons, caissons and cannon, were everywhere. Pierre pushed forward as fast as he could, and the farther he left Moscow behind and the deeper he plunged into that sea of troops the more was he overcome by restless agitation and a new and joyful feeling he had not experienced before. It was a feeling akin to what he had felt at the Slobóda Palace during the Emperor's visit—a sense of the necessity of undertaking something and sacrificing something. He now experienced a glad consciousness that everything that constitutes men's happiness—the comforts of life, wealth, even life itself—is rubbish it is pleasant to throw away, compared with something . . . With what? Pierre could not say, and he did not try to determine for whom and for what he felt such particular delight in sacrificing everything. He was not occupied with the question of what to sacrifice for, the fact of sacrificing in itself afforded him a new and joyous sensation.

CHAPTER XIX

ON the 24th of August the battle of the Shevárdino Redoubt was fought, on the 25th not a shot was fired by either side, and on the 26th the battle of Borodinó itself took place.

Why and how were the battles at Shevárdino and Borodinó given and accepted? Why was the battle of Borodinó fought? There was not the least sense in it for either the French or the Russians. Its immediate result for the Russians was, and was bound to be, that we were brought nearer to the destruction of Moscow—which we feared more than anything in the world; and for the French its immediate result was that they were brought nearer to the destruction of their whole army—which they feared more than anything in the world. What the result must be was quite obvious, and yet Napoleon offered and Kutúzov accepted that battle.

If the commanders had been guided by reason it would seem that it must have been obvious to Napoleon that by advancing thirteen hundred miles and giving battle with a probability of losing a quarter of his army, he was advancing to certain destruction, and it must have been equally clear to Kutúzov that by accepting battle and risking the loss of a quarter of his army he would certainly lose Moscow. For Kutúzov this was mathematically clear, as it is that if when playing draughts, I have one man less and go on exchanging, I shall certainly lose, and therefore should not exchange. When my opponent has sixteen men and I have fourteen, I am only one-eighth weaker than he, but when I have exchanged thirteen more men he will be three times as strong as I.

Before the battle of Borodinó our strength in proportion to the French was approximately as five to six, but after that battle as one to two: that is to say, before the battle we had a hundred thousand against a hundred and twenty thousand, and after the battle fifty thousand against a hundred thousand. Yet the shrewd and experienced Kutúzov accepted the battle, while Napoleon, who was said to be a commander of genius, gave it, losing a quarter of his army and lengthening his lines of communication still more. If it is said that he expected to end the campaign by occupying Moscow, as he had ended a previous campaign by occupying Vienna, there is much evidence to the contrary. Napoleon's historians themselves tell us that from Smolénsk onwards he wished to stop, knew the danger of his extended position, and knew that the occupation of Moscow would not be the end of the campaign, for he had seen at Smolénsk the state in which Russian towns were left to him, and had not received a single reply to his repeated announcements of his wish to negotiate.

In giving and accepting battle at Borodinó Kutúzov acted involuntarily and irrationally. But later on, to fit what had occurred, the historians provided cunningly devised evidence of the foresight and genius of the generals who of all the blind tools of history were the most enslaved and involuntary.

The ancients have left us model heroic poems in which the heroes furnish the whole interest of the story, and we are still unable to accustom ourselves to the fact that for our epoch histories of that kind are meaningless.

On the other question, how the battle of Borodinó and

the preceding battle of Shevárdino were fought, there also exists a definite and well-known, but quite false, conception. All the historians describe the affair as follows:

The Russian army, they say, *in its retreat from Smolénsk sought out for itself the best position for a general engagement and found such a position at Borodinó.*

The Russians, they say, *fortified this position in advance on the left of the high road (from Moscow to Smolénsk) and almost at a right angle to it, from Borodinó to Utítsa, at the very place where the battle was fought.*

In front of this position, they say, *a fortified outpost was set up on the Shevárdino mound to observe the enemy. On the 24th,* we are told, *Napoleon attacked this advanced post and took it, and on the 26th attacked the whole Russian army, which was in position on the field of Borodinó.*

So the histories say, and it is all quite wrong, as any one who cares to look into the matter can easily convince himself.

The Russians did not seek out the best position but on the contrary during the retreat passed many positions better than Borodinó. They did not stop at any one of these positions because Kutúzov did not wish to occupy a position he had not himself chosen, because the popular demand for a battle had not yet expressed itself strongly enough, and because Milorádovich had not yet arrived with the militia, and for many other reasons. The fact is that other positions they had passed were stronger, and that the position at Borodinó (the one where the battle was fought) far from being strong, was no more a *position* than any other spot one might find in the Russian Empire by sticking a pin into the map at hazard.

Not only did the Russians not fortify the position on the field of Borodinó to the left of, and at a right angle to, the high road (that is, the position on which the battle took place) but never till the 25th of August 1812, did they think that a battle might be fought there. This is shown first by the fact that there were no entrenchments there by the 25th, and that those begun on the 25th and 26th were not completed, and secondly, by the position of the Shevárdino Redoubt. That redoubt was quite senseless in front of the position where the battle was accepted. Why was it more strongly fortified than any other post? And why were all efforts exhausted and six thousand men sacrificed to defend it till late at night on the 24th? A Cossack patrol would have sufficed to observe the enemy. Thirdly, as proof that the position on which the battle was fought had not been foreseen and that the Shevárdino Redoubt was not an advanced post of that position, we have the fact that up to the 25th Barclay de Tolly and Bagratión were convinced that the Shevárdino Redoubt was the *left flank* of the position, and that Kutúzov himself in his report written in hot haste after the battle, speaks of the Shevárdino Redoubt as the *left flank* of the position. It was much later, when reports on the battle of Borodinó were written at leisure, that the incorrect and extraordinary statement was invented (probably to justify the mistakes of a commander-in-chief who had to be represented as infallible) that the Shevárdino Redoubt was an *advanced* post—whereas in reality it was simply a fortified point on the left flank—and that the battle of Borodinó was fought by us on an entrenched position previously selected, whereas it was fought on a quite unexpected spot which was almost unentrenched.

The case was evidently this: a position was selected along the river Kolochá—which crosses the high road not at a right angle but at an acute angle—so that the left flank was at Shevárdino, the right flank near the village of Nóvoe, and the centre at Borodinó at the confluence of the rivers Kolochá and Vóyna.

To any one who looks at the field of Borodinó without thinking of how the battle was actually fought, this position, protected by the river Kolochá, presents itself as obvious for an army whose object was to prevent an enemy from advancing along the Smolénsk road to Moscow.

Napoleon, riding to Valuévo on the 24th, did not see (as the history books say he did) the position of the Russians from Utítsa to Borodinó (he could not have seen that position because it did not exist) nor did he see an advanced post of the Russian army, but while pursuing the Russian rearguard he came upon the left flank of the Russian position—at the Shevárdino Redoubt—and unexpectedly for the Russians moved his army across the

Kolochá. And the Russians, not having time to begin a general engagement, withdrew their left wing from the position they had intended to occupy and took up a new position which had not been foreseen and was not fortified. By crossing to the other side of the Kolochá to the left of the high road, Napoleon shifted the whole forthcoming battle from right to left (looking from the Russian side) and transferred it to the plain between Utítsa, Semënovsk, and Borodinó—a plain no more advantageous as a position than any other plain in Russia—and there the whole battle of the 26th of August took place. A rough outline of the plan of the intended battle and of the battle that actually took place is given on the next page.

Had Napoleon not ridden out on the evening of the 24th to the Kolochá, and had he not then ordered an immediate attack on the redoubt but had begun the attack next morning, no one would have doubted that the Shevárdino Redoubt was the left flank of our position, and the battle would have taken place where we expected it. In that case we should probably have defended the Shevárdino Redoubt—our left flank—still more obstinately. We should have attacked Napoleon in the centre or on the right, and the general engagement would have taken place on the 25th, on the position we intended and had fortified. But as the attack on our left flank took place in the evening after the retreat of our rearguard (that is, immediately after the fight at Gridnëva), and as the Russian commanders did not wish, or were not in time, to begin a general engagement then on the evening of the 24th, the first and chief action of the battle of Borodinó was already lost on the 24th, and obviously led to the loss of the one fought on the 26th.

After the loss of the Shevárdino Redoubt we found ourselves on the morning of the 25th without a position for our left flank, and were forced to bend it back and hastily entrench it where it chanced to be.

But not only was the Russian army on the 26th defended by weak, unfinished entrenchments, the disadvantage of that position was increased by the fact that the Russian commanders—not having fully realized what had happened, namely, the loss of our position on the left flank and the shifting of the whole field of the forthcoming battle from right to left—maintained their extended position from the village of Nóvoe to Utítsa, and consequently had to move their forces from right to left during the battle. So it happened that throughout the whole battle the Russians opposed the entire French army launched against our left flank with but half as many men. (Poniatowski's action against Utítsa, and Uvárov's on the right flank against the French, were actions distinct from the main course of the battle.) So the battle of Borodinó did not take place at all as (in an effort to conceal our commanders' mistakes even at the cost of diminishing the glory due to the Russian army and people) it has been described. The battle of Borodinó was not fought on a chosen and entrenched position with forces only slightly weaker than those of the enemy, but, as a result of the loss of the Shevárdino Redoubt, the Russians fought the battle of Borodinó on an open and almost unentrenched position, with forces only half as numerous as the French; that is to say, under conditions in which it was not merely unthinkable to fight for ten hours and secure an indecisive result, but unthinkable to keep an army even for three hours from complete disintegration and flight.

CHAPTER XX

ON the morning of the 25th Pierre was leaving Mozháysk. At the descent of the high steep hill, down which a winding road led out of the town past the cathedral on the right, where a service was being held and the bells were ringing, Pierre got out of his vehicle and proceeded on foot. Behind him a cavalry regiment was coming down the hill preceded by its singers. Coming up towards him was a train of carts carrying men who had been wounded in the engagement the day before. The peasant drivers, shouting and lashing their horses, kept crossing from side to side. The carts, in each of which three or four wounded soldiers were lying or sitting, jolted over the stones that had been thrown on the steep incline to make it something like a road. The wounded, bandaged with rags, with pale cheeks, compressed lips, and knitted brows, held on to the sides of the carts as they were jostled and jolted against one another. Almost all of them stared with naïve, childlike curiosity at Pierre's white hat and green swallow-tail coat.

Pierre's coachman shouted angrily at the convoy of wounded to keep to one side of the road. The cavalry regiment, as it descended the hill with its singers, surrounded Pierre's carriage and blocked the road. Pierre stopped, being pressed against the side of the cutting in which the road ran. The sunshine from behind the hill did not penetrate into the cutting, and there it was cold and damp, but above Pierre's head was the bright August sunshine and the bells sounded merrily. One of the carts with wounded stopped by the side of the road close to Pierre. The driver in his bast shoes ran panting up to it, placed a stone under one of its tyreless hind wheels, and began arranging the breeching on his little horse, which had stopped.

One of the wounded, an old soldier with a bandaged arm, who was following the cart on foot, caught hold of it with his sound hand and turned to look at Pierre.

'I say, fellow countryman, will they set us down here or take us on to Moscow?' he asked.

Pierre was so deep in thought that he did not hear the question. He was looking, now at the cavalry regiment that had met the convoy of wounded, now at the cart by which he was standing, in which two wounded men were sitting and one was lying. One of those sitting up in the cart had probably been wounded in the cheek. His whole head was wrapped in rags and one cheek was swollen to the size of a baby's head. His nose and mouth were twisted to one side. This soldier was looking at the cathedral and crossing himself. Another, a young lad, a fair-haired recruit as white as though there was no blood in his thin face, looked at Pierre kindly, with a fixed smile. The third lay prone so that his face was not visible. The cavalry singers were passing close by:

'Ah lost, quite lost . . . is my head so keen,
    Living in a foreign land . . .'

they sang their soldiers' dance-song.

As if responding to them, but with a different sort of merriment, the metallic sound of the bells reverberated high above, and the hot rays of the sun bathed the top of the opposite slope with yet another sort of merriment. But beneath the slope, by the cart with the wounded near the panting little nag where Pierre stood, it was damp, sombre, and sad.

The soldier with the swollen cheek looked angrily at the cavalry singers.

'Oh, the coxcombs!' he muttered reproachfully.

'It's not the soldiers only, but I've seen peasants to-day, too . . . The peasants—even they have to go,' said the soldier behind the cart, addressing Pierre with a sad smile. 'No distinctions made nowadays . . . They want the whole nation to fall on them—in a word, it's Moscow! They want to make an end of it.'

In spite of the obscurity of the soldier's words Pierre understood what he wanted to say, and nodded approval.

The road was clear again; Pierre descended the hill and drove on.

He kept looking to either side of the road for familiar faces, but only saw everywhere the unfamiliar faces of various military men of different branches of the service, who all looked with astonishment at his white hat and green tail-coat.

Having gone nearly three miles he at last met an acquaintance and eagerly addressed him. This was one of the head army-doctors. He was driving towards Pierre in a covered gig, sitting beside a young surgeon, and on recognizing Pierre he told the Cossack who occupied the driver's seat to pull up.

'Count! Your Excellency, how come you to be here?' asked the doctor.

'Well, you know, I wanted to see . . .'

'Yes, yes, there will be something to see . . .'

Pierre got out and talked to the doctor, explaining his intention of taking part in the battle.

The doctor advised him to apply direct to Kutúzov.

'Why should you be God knows where, out of sight, during the battle?' he said, exchanging glances with his young companion. 'Anyhow, his Serene Highness knows you and will receive you graciously. That's what you must do.'

The doctor seemed tired and in a hurry.

'You think so? . . . Ah, I also wanted to ask you where our position is exactly?' said Pierre.

'The position?' repeated the doctor. 'Well, that's not my line. Drive past Tatárinova, a lot of digging is going on there. Go up the hillock and you'll see.'

'Can one see from there? . . . If you would . . .'

But the doctor interrupted him and moved towards his gig.

'I would go with you but on my honour I'm up to here'—and he pointed to his throat. 'I'm galloping to the commander of the corps. How do matters stand? . . . You know, Count, there'll be a battle to-morrow. Out of an army of a hundred thousand we must expect at least twenty thousand wounded, and we haven't stretchers, or bunks, or dressers, or doctors enough for six thousand. We have ten thousand carts, but we need other things as well—we must manage as best we can!'

The strange thought, that of the thousands of men, young and old, who had stared with merry surprise at his hat (perhaps the very men he had noticed) twenty thousand were inevitably doomed to wounds and death, amazed Pierre.

'They may die to-morrow; why are they thinking of anything but death?' And by some latent sequence of thought the descent of the Mozháysk hill, the carts with the wounded, the ringing bells, the slanting rays of the sun, and the songs of the cavalrymen, vividly recurred to his mind.

'The cavalry ride to battle and meet the wounded and do not for a moment think of what awaits them, but pass by, winking at the wounded. Yet from among these men twenty thousand are doomed to die, and they wonder at my hat! Strange!' thought Pierre, continuing his way to Tatárinova.

In front of a landowner's house to the left of the road stood carriages, wagons, and crowds of orderlies and sentinels. The commander-in-chief was putting up there, but just when Pierre arrived he was not in, and hardly any of the staff were there—they had gone to the church service. Pierre drove on towards Górki.

When he had ascended the hill and reached the little village street, he saw for the first time peasant militiamen in their white shirts and with crosses on their caps, who, talking and laughing loudly, animated and perspiring, were at work on a huge knoll overgrown with grass to the right of the road.

Some of them were digging, others were wheeling barrow-loads of earth along planks, while others stood about doing nothing.

Two officers were standing on the knoll, directing the men. On seeing these peasants, who were evidently still amused by the novelty of their position as soldiers, Pierre once more thought of the wounded men at Mozháysk, and understood what the soldier had meant when he said: 'They want the whole nation to fall on them.' The sight of these bearded peasants at work on the battlefield, with their queer, clumsy boots and perspiring necks, and their shirts, opening from the left towards the middle, unfastened, exposing their sunburnt collar-bones, impressed Pierre more strongly with the solemnity and importance of the moment than anything he had yet seen or heard.

CHAPTER XXI

PIERRE stepped out of his carriage and, passing the toiling militiamen, ascended the knoll from which according to the doctor the battle-field could be seen.

It was about eleven o'clock. The sun shone somewhat to the left and behind him, and brightly lit up the enormous panorama which, rising like an amphitheatre, extended before him in the clear rarified atmosphere.

From above on the left, bisecting that amphitheatre, wound the Smolénsk high road, passing through a village with a white church some five hundred paces in front of the knoll and below it. This was Borodinó. Below the village the road crossed the river by a bridge, and winding

down and up, rose higher and higher to the village of
Valúevo visible about four miles away, where Napoleon
was then stationed. Beyond Valúevo the road disappeared into a yellowing forest on the horizon. Far in the
distance in that birch and fir forest to the right of the
road, the cross and belfry of the Kolochá Monastery
gleamed in the sun. Here and there over the whole of
that blue expanse, to right and left of the forest and the
road, smoking camp-fires could be seen and indefinite
masses of troops—ours and the enemy's. The ground to
the right—along the course of the Kolochá and Moskvá
rivers—was broken and hilly. Between the hollows the
villages of Bezzúbova and Zakhárino showed in the
distance. On the left the ground was more level; there
were fields of grain, and the smoking village of Seménovsk,
which had been burnt down, could be seen.

All that Pierre saw was so indefinite that neither the
left nor the right side of the field fully satisfied his expectations. Nowhere could he see the battle-field he had
expected to find, but only fields, meadows, troops, woods,
the smoke of camp-fires, villages, mounds, and streams;
and try as he would he could descry no military 'position'
in this place which teemed with life, nor could he even
distinguish our troops from the enemy's.

'I must ask some one who knows,' he thought, and
addressed an officer who was looking with curiosity at
his huge unmilitary figure.

'May I ask you,' said Pierre, 'what village that is in
front?'

'Búrdino, isn't it?' said the officer, turning to a companion.

'Borodinó,' the other corrected him.

The officer, evidently glad of an opportunity for a talk,
moved up to Pierre.

'Are those our men there?' Pierre inquired.

'Yes, and there further on are the French,' said the
officer. 'There they are, there, you can see them.'

'Where? Where?' asked Pierre.

'One can see them with the naked eye . . . Why,
there!'

The officer pointed with his hand to the smoke visible

on the left beyond the river, and the same stern and serious expression that Pierre had noticed on many of the faces he had met came into his face.

'Ah, so those are the French! And over there?' . . . Pierre pointed to a knoll on the left, near which some troops could be seen.

'Those are ours.'

'Ah, ours! And there?' . . . Pierre pointed to another knoll in the distance with a big tree on it, near a village that lay in a hollow where some camp-fires were smoking too, and something black was visible.

'That's *his* again,' said the officer. (It was the Shevár-dino Redoubt.) 'It was ours yesterday, but now it is *his*.'

'Then how about our position?'

'Our position?' replied the officer with a smile of satisfaction. 'I can tell you quite clearly, because I constructed nearly all our entrenchments. There, you see? There's our centre, at Borodinó, just there,' and he pointed to the village in front of them with the white church. 'That's where one crosses the Kolochá. You see down there where the rows of hay are lying in the hollow, there's the bridge. That's our centre. Our right flank is over there'—he pointed sharply to the right, far away in the broken ground—'That's where the Moskvá river is, and we have thrown up three redoubts there, very strong ones. The left flank . . .' here the officer paused. 'Well, you see, that's difficult to explain . . . Yesterday our left flank was there at Shevárdino, you see, where the oak is, but now we have withdrawn our left wing—now it is over there, do you see that village and the smoke? That's Semënovsk, yes, there,' he pointed to Raévski's knoll. 'But the battle will hardly be there. *His* having moved his troops there is only a ruse; *he* will probably pass round to the right of the Moskvá. But wherever it may be, many a man will be missing to-morrow!' he remarked.

An elderly sergeant who had approached the officer while he was giving these explanations had waited in silence for him to finish speaking, but at this point, evidently not liking the officer's remark, interrupted him.

'Gabions must be sent for,' said he sternly.

The officer appeared abashed, as though he understood that one might think of how many men would be missing to-morrow but ought not to speak of it.

'Well, send number three company again,' the officer replied hurriedly.

'And you, are you one of the doctors?'

'No, I've come on my own,' answered Pierre, and he went down the hill again passing the militiamen.

'Oh, those damned fellows!' muttered the officer, who followed him holding his nose as he ran past the men at work.

'There they are . . . bringing her, coming . . . There they are . . . They'll be here in a minute . . .' voices were suddenly heard saying; and officers, soldiers, and militiamen began running forward along the road.

A church procession was coming up the hill from Borodinó. First along the dusty road came the infantry in ranks, bareheaded and with arms reversed. From behind them came the sound of church singing.

Soldiers and militiamen ran bareheaded past Pierre towards the procession.

'They are bringing her, our Protectress! . . . The Iberian Mother of God!' some one cried.[1]

'The Smolénsk Mother of God,' another corrected him.

The militiamen, both those who had been in the village and those who had been at work on the battery, threw down their spades and ran to meet the church procession. Following the battalion that marched along the dusty road, came priests in their vestments—one little old man in a hood with attendants and singers. Behind them soldiers and officers bore a large, dark-faced icon with an embossed metal cover. This was the icon that had been brought from Smolénsk and had since accompanied the army. Behind, before, and on both sides, crowds of militiamen with bared heads walked, ran, and bowed to the ground.

At the summit of the hill they stopped with the icon; the men who had been holding it up by the linen bands attached to it were relieved by others, the chanters relit their censers and service began. The hot rays of the sun

[1] Names of an icon of the Holy Virgin Mother.

beat down vertically, and a fresh soft wind played with the hair of the bared heads and with the ribbons decorating the icon. The singing did not sound loud under the open sky. An immense crowd of bareheaded officers, soldiers, and militiamen, surrounded the icon. Behind the priest and a chanter stood the notabilities, on a spot reserved for them. A bald general with a St. George's Cross on his neck stood just behind the priest's back, and without crossing himself (he was evidently a German) patiently awaited the end of the service, which he considered it necessary to hear to the end, probably to arouse the patriotism of the Russian people. Another general stood in a martial pose, crossing himself by shaking his hand in front of his chest while looking about him. Standing among the crowd of peasants, Pierre recognized several acquaintances among these notables, but did not look at them—his whole attention was absorbed in watching the serious expression on the faces of the crowd of soldiers and militiamen who were all gazing eagerly at the icon. As soon as the tired chanters, who were singing the service for the twentieth time that day, began lazily and mechanically to sing: 'Save from calamity Thy servants, O Mother of God,' and the priest and deacon chimed in: 'For to Thee under God we all flee as to an inviolable bulwark and protection,' there again kindled in all those faces the same expression of consciousness of the solemnity of the impending moment that Pierre had seen on the faces at the foot of the hill at Mozháysk, and momentarily on many and many faces he had met that morning; and heads were bowed more frequently and hair tossed back, and sighs and the sound men made as they crossed themselves were heard.

The crowd round the icon suddenly parted, and pressed against Pierre. Some one, a very important personage judging by the haste with which way was made for him, was approaching the icon.

It was Kutúzov, who had been riding round the position and on his way back to Tatárinova had stopped where the service was being held. Pierre recognized him at once by his peculiar figure, which distinguished him from everybody else.

With a long overcoat on his exceedingly stout, round-shouldered body, with uncovered white head and puffy face showing the white ball of the eye he had lost, Kutúzov walked with plunging, swaying gait into the crowd and stopped behind the priest. He crossed himself with an accustomed movement, bent till he touched the ground with his hand, and bowed his white head with a deep sigh. Behind Kutúzov was Bennigsen and the suite. Despite the presence of the commander-in-chief who attracted the attention of all the superior officers, the militiamen and soldiers continued their prayers without looking at him.

When the service was over Kutúzov stepped up to the icon, sank heavily to his knees, bowed to the ground, and for a long time tried vainly to rise, but could not do so on account of his weakness and weight. His white head twitched with the effort. At last he rose, kissed the icon as a child does with naïvely pouting lips, and again bowed till he touched the ground with his hand. The other generals followed his example, then the officers, and after them with excited faces, pressing on one another, crowding, panting, and pushing, scrambled the soldiers and militiamen.

CHAPTER XXII

STAGGERING amid the crush Pierre looked about him.

'Count Peter Kirílovich! How did you get here?' said a voice.

Pierre looked round. Borís Drubetskóy, brushing his knees with his hand (he had probably soiled them when he, too, had knelt before the icon) came up to him smiling. Borís was elegantly dressed, with a slightly martial touch appropriate to a campaign. He wore a long coat, and like Kutúzov had a whip slung across his shoulder.

Meanwhile Kutúzov had reached the village and seated himself in the shade of the nearest house, on a bench which one Cossack had run to fetch and another had hastily covered with a rug. An immense and brilliant suite surrounded him.

The icon was carried further, accompanied by the throng. Pierre stopped some thirty paces from Kutúzov, talking to Borís.

He explained his wish to be present at the battle and to see the position.

'This is what you must do,' said Borís. 'I will do the honours of the camp for you. You will see everything best from where Count Bennigsen will be. I am in attendance on him, you know; I'll mention it to him. But if you want to ride round the position, come along with us. We are just going to the left flank. Then when we get back, do spend the night with me and we'll arrange a game of cards. Of course you know Dmítri Sergéevich? Those are his quarters,' and he pointed to the third house in the village of Górki.

'But I should like to see the right flank. They say it's very strong,' said Pierre. 'I should like to start from the Moskvá river and ride round the whole position.'

'Well, you can do that later, but the chief thing is the left flank.'

'Yes, yes. But where is Prince Bolkónski's regiment? Can you point it out to me?'

'Prince Andrew's? We shall pass it and I'll take you to him.'

'What about the left flank?' asked Pierre.

'To tell you the truth, between ourselves, God only knows what state our left flank is in,' said Borís, confidentially lowering his voice. 'It is not at all what Count Bennigsen intended. He meant to fortify that knoll quite differently, but . . .' Borís shrugged his shoulders, 'his Serene Highness would not have it, or some one persuaded him. You see . . .' but Borís did not finish, for at that moment Kaysárov, Kutúzov's adjutant, came up to Pierre. 'Ah, Kaysárov!' said Borís, addressing him with an unembarrassed smile, 'I was just trying to explain our position to the Count. It is amazing how his Serene Highness could so foresee the intentions of the French!'

'You mean the left flank?' asked Kaysárov.

'Yes, exactly; the left flank is now extremely strong.'

Though Kutúzov had dismissed all unnecessary men from the staff, Borís had contrived to remain at head-quarters after the changes. He had established himself with Count Bennigsen, who, like all on whom Borís had been in attendance, considered young Prince Drubetskóy an invaluable man.

In the higher command there were two sharply defined parties: Kutúzov's party and that of Bennigsen, the chief of staff. Borís belonged to the latter, and no one else, while showing servile respect to Kutúzov, could so create an impression that the old fellow was not much good, and that Bennigsen managed everything. Now the decisive moment of battle had come when Kutúzov would be destroyed and the power pass to Bennigsen, or even if Kutúzov won the battle it would be felt that everything was done by Bennigsen. In any case many great rewards would have to be given for to-morrow's action, and new men would come to the front. So Borís was full of nervous vivacity all that day.

After Kaysárov, others whom Pierre knew came up to him, and he had not time to reply to all the questions about Moscow that were showered upon him, or to listen to all that was told him. The faces all expressed animation and apprehension, but it seemed to Pierre that the cause of the excitement shown in some of these faces lay chiefly in questions of personal success; his mind, however, was occupied by the different expression he saw on other faces—an expression that spoke not of personal matters but of the universal questions of life and death. Kutúzov noticed Pierre's figure and the group gathered round him.

'Call him to me,' said Kutúzov.

An adjutant told Pierre of his Serene Highness's wish, and Pierre went towards Kutúzov's bench. But a militia-man got there before him. It was Dólokhov.

'How did that fellow get here?' asked Pierre.

'He's a creature that wriggles in anywhere!' was the answer. 'He has been degraded, you know. Now he wants to bob up again. He's been proposing some scheme or other and has crawled into the enemy's piquet line at night . . . He's a brave fellow.'

Pierre took off his hat and bowed respectfully to Kutúzov.

'I concluded that if I reported to your Serene Highness, you might send me away or say that you knew what I was reporting, but then I shouldn't lose anything . . .' Dólokhov was saying.

'Yes, yes.'

'But if I were right, I should be rendering a service to my Fatherland for which I am ready to die.'

'Yes, yes.'

'And should your Serene Highness require a man who will not spare his skin, please think of me . . . Perhaps I may prove useful to your Serene Highness.'

'Yes . . . Yes . . .' Kutúzov repeated, his laughing eye narrowing more and more as he looked at Pierre.

Just then Borís, with his courtier-like adroitness, stepped up to Pierre's side near Kutúzov, and in a most natural manner, without raising his voice, said to Pierre as though continuing an interrupted conversation:

'The militia have put on clean white shirts to be ready to die. What heroism, Count!'

Borís evidently said this to Pierre in order to be overheard by his Serene Highness. He knew Kutúzov's attention would be caught by those words, and so it was.

'What are you saying about the militia?' he asked Borís.

'Preparing for to-morrow, your Serene Highness—for death—they have put on clean shirts.'

'Ah . . . a wonderful, a matchless people!' said Kutúzov; and he closed his eyes and swayed his head. 'A matchless people!' he repeated with a sigh.

'So you want to smell gunpowder?' he said to Pierre. 'Yes, it's a pleasant smell. I have the honour to be one of your wife's adorers. Is she well? My quarters are at your service.'

And as often happens with old people, Kutúzov began looking about absent-mindedly as if forgetting all he wanted to say or do.

Then, evidently remembering what he wanted, he beckoned to Andrew Kaysárov, his adjutant's brother.

'Those verses . . . those verses of Márin's . . . how do they go, eh? Those he wrote about Gerákov: "Lectures for the corps inditing". . . . Recite them, recite them!' said he, evidently preparing to laugh.

Kaysárov recited . . . Kutúzov smilingly nodded his head to the rhythm of the verses.

When Pierre had left Kutúzov, Dólokhov came up to him and took his hand.

'I am very glad to meet you here, Count,' he said aloud, regardless of the presence of strangers and in a particularly resolute and solemn tone. 'On the eve of a day when God alone knows who of us is fated to survive, I am glad of this opportunity to tell you that I regret the misunderstandings that occurred between us, and should wish you not to have any ill feeling for me. I beg you to forgive me.'

Pierre looked at Dólokhov with a smile, not knowing what to say to him. With tears in his eyes Dólokhov embraced Pierre and kissed him.

Borís said a few words to his general, and Count Bennigsen turned to Pierre and proposed that he should ride with him along the line.

'It will interest you,' said he.

'Yes, very much,' replied Pierre.

Half an hour later Kutúzov left for Tatárinova, and Bennigsen and his suite, with Pierre among them, set out on their ride along the line.

CHAPTER XXIII

FROM Górki Bennigsen descended the high road to the bridge which, when they had looked at it from the hill, the officer had pointed out as being the centre of our position and where rows of fragrant new-mown hay lay by the riverside. They rode across that bridge into the village of Borodinó and thence turned to the left, passing an enormous number of troops and guns, and came to a high knoll where militiamen were digging. This was the redoubt, as yet unnamed, which afterwards became known as the Raévski Redoubt, or the Knoll-Battery, but Pierre paid no special attention to it. He did not know that it would become more memorable to him than any other spot on the plain of Borodinó. They then crossed the hollow to Seménovsk, where the soldiers were dragging away the last logs from the huts and barns. Then they rode downhill and uphill, across a rye-field trodden and beaten down as if by hail, following a track freshly made by the artillery over the furrows of the ploughed land, and reached some flèches[1] which were still being dug.

At the flèches Bennigsen stopped, and began looking at the Shevárdino Redoubt opposite, which had been ours the day before and where several horsemen could be descried. The officers said that either Napoleon or Murat was there, and they all gazed eagerly at this little group of horsemen. Pierre also looked at them, trying to guess which of the scarcely discernible figures was Napoleon. At last those mounted men rode away from the mound and disappeared.

Bennigsen spoke to a general who approached him, and began explaining the whole position of our troops. Pierre listened to him, straining each faculty to understand the essential points of the impending battle, but was mortified to feel that his mental capacity was inadequate for the task. He could make nothing of it. Bennigsen stopped speaking, and noticing that Pierre was listening, suddenly said to him:

'I don't think this interests you?'

'On the contrary it's very interesting!' replied Pierre not quite truthfully.

From the flèches they rode still farther to the left, along a road winding through a thick, low-growing birch wood. In the middle of the wood a brown hare with white feet sprang out and, scared by the tramp of the many horses, grew so confused that it leapt along the road in front of them for some time, arousing general attention and laughter, and only when several voices shouted at it did it dart to one side and disappear in the thicket. After going through the wood for about a mile and a half they came out on a glade where troops of Túchkov's corps were stationed to defend the left flank.

Here, at the extreme left flank, Bennigsen talked a great deal and with much heat, and, as it seemed to Pierre, gave orders of great military importance. In front of

[1] A kind of entrenchment. L. T.

Túchkov's troops was some high ground not occupied by troops. Bennigsen loudly criticized this mistake, saying that it was madness to leave a height which commanded the country around unoccupied and to place troops below it. Some of the generals expressed the same opinion. One in particular declared with martial heat that they were put there to be slaughtered. Bennigsen on his own authority ordered the troops to occupy the high ground.

This disposition on the left flank increased Pierre's doubt of his own capacity to understand military matters. Listening to Bennigsen and the generals criticizing the position of the troops behind the hill, he quite understood them and shared their opinion, but for that very reason he could not understand how the man who put them there behind the hill could have made so gross and palpable a blunder.

Pierre did not know that these troops were not, as Bennigsen supposed, put there to defend the position, but were in a concealed position, as an ambush, that they should not be seen and might be able to strike an approaching enemy unexpectedly. Bennigsen did not know this, and moved the troops forward according to his own ideas without mentioning the matter to the commander-in-chief.

CHAPTER XXIV

ON that bright evening of August the 25th, Prince Andrew lay leaning on his elbow in a broken-down shed in the village of Knyazkóvo at the further end of his regiment's encampment. Through a gap in the broken wall he could see, beside the wooden fence, a row of thirty-year-old birches with their lower branches lopped off, a field on which shocks of oats were standing, and some bushes near which rose the smoke of camp-fires—the soldiers' kitchens.

Narrow and burdensome and useless to any one as his life now seemed to him, Prince Andrew on the eve of battle felt agitated and irritable, as he had done seven years before at Austerlitz.

He had received and given the orders for next day's

battle, and had nothing more to do. But his thoughts—the simplest, clearest, and therefore most terrible thoughts—would give him no peace. He knew that to-morrow's battle would be the most terrible of all he had taken part in, and for the first time in his life the possibility of death presented itself to him—not in relation to any worldly matter or with reference to its effect on others, but simply in relation to himself, to his own soul—vividly, plainly, terribly, and almost as a certainty. And from the height of this perception all that had previously tormented and preoccupied him suddenly became illumined by a cold white light without shadows, without perspective, and without distinction of outline. All life appeared to him like magic-lantern pictures at which he had long been gazing by artificial light through a glass. Now he suddenly saw those badly daubed pictures in clear daylight and without a glass. 'Yes, yes! There they are, those false images that agitated, enraptured, and tormented me,' said he to himself, passing in review the principal pictures of the magic lantern of life and regarding them now in the cold white daylight of his clear perception of death. 'There they are, those rudely painted figures that once seemed splendid and mysterious. Glory, the good of society, love of a woman, the Fatherland itself—how important these pictures appeared to me, with what profound meaning they seemed to be filled! And it is all so simple, pale, and crude in the cold white light of this morning which I feel is dawning for me.' The three great sorrows of his life held his attention in particular: his love for a woman, his father's death, and the French invasion which had overrun half Russia. 'Love! . . . that little girl who seemed to me brimming over with mystic forces! Yes, indeed I loved her. I made romantic plans of love and happiness with her! Oh, what a boy I was!' he said aloud bitterly. 'Ah me! I believed in some ideal love which was to keep her faithful to me for the whole year of my absence! Like the gentle dove in the fable she was to pine apart from me . . . But it was much simpler really . . . It was all very simple and horrible.

'When my father built Bald Hills he thought the place

was his, his land, his air, his peasants. But Napoleon came and swept him aside, unconscious of his existence, as he might brush a chip from his path, and his Bald Hills and his whole life fell to pieces. Princess Mary says it is a trial sent from above. What is the trial for, when he is not here and will never return? He is not here! For whom then is the trial intended? The Fatherland, the destruction of Moscow! And to-morrow I shall be killed, perhaps not even by a Frenchman but by one of our own men, by a soldier discharging a musket close to my ear, as one of them did yesterday, and the French will come and take me by head and heels and fling me into a hole that I may not stink under their noses, and new conditions of life will arise, which will seem quite ordinary to others and about which I shall know nothing. I shall not exist.'

He looked at the row of birches shining in the sunshine with their motionless green and yellow foliage and white bark. 'To die . . . to be killed to-morrow . . . That I should not exist . . . That all this should still be, but no me . . .'

And the birches with their light and shade, the curly clouds, the smoke of the camp-fires, and all that was around him, changed and seemed terrible and menacing. A cold shiver ran down his spine. He rose quickly, went out of the shed, and began to walk about.

After he had returned, voices were heard outside the shed. 'Who's that?' he cried.

The red-nosed Captain Timókhin, formerly Dólokhov's squadron-commander, but now from lack of officers a battalion-commander, shyly entered the shed, followed by an adjutant and the regimental paymaster.

Prince Andrew rose hastily, listened to the business they had come about, gave them some further instructions, and was about to dismiss them when he heard a familiar, lisping voice behind the shed.

'Devil take it!' said the voice of a man stumbling over something.

Prince Andrew looked out of the shed and saw Pierre, who had tripped over a pole on the ground and had nearly fallen, coming his way. It was unpleasant to Prince

Andrew to meet people of his own set in general, and Pierre especially, for he reminded him of all the painful moments of his last visit to Moscow.

'You? What a surprise!' said he. 'What brings you here? This is unexpected!'

As he said this his eyes and face expressed more than coldness—they expressed hostility, which Pierre noticed at once. He had approached the shed full of animation, but on seeing Prince Andrew's face he felt constrained and ill at ease.

'I have come . . . simply . . . you know . . . come . . . it interests me,' said Pierre, who had so often that day senselessly repeated that word 'interesting'. 'I wish to see the battle.'

'Oh yes, and what do the Masonic brothers say about war? How would they stop it?' said Prince Andrew sarcastically. 'Well, and how's Moscow? And my people? Have they reached Moscow at last?' he asked seriously.

'Yes, they have. Julie Drubetskáya told me so. I went to see them, but missed them. They have gone to your estate near Moscow.'

CHAPTER XXV

THE officers were about to take leave, but Prince Andrew, apparently reluctant to be left alone with his friend, asked them to stay and have tea. Seats were brought in and so was the tea. The officers gazed with surprise at Pierre's huge stout figure, and listened to his talk of Moscow and the position of our army, round which he had ridden. Prince Andrew remained silent, and his expression was so forbidding that Pierre addressed his remarks chiefly to Timókhin, the good-natured battalion-commander.

'So you understand the whole position of our troops?' Prince Andrew interrupted him.

'Yes—that is, how do you mean?' said Pierre. 'Not being a military man I can't say I have understood it fully, but I understand the general position.'

'Well, then, you know more than any one else, be it who it may,' said Prince Andrew.

'Oh!' said Pierre, looking over his spectacles in perplexity at Prince Andrew. 'Well, and what do you think of Kutúzov's appointment?' he asked.

'I was very glad of his appointment, that's all I know,' replied Prince Andrew.

'And tell me your opinion of Barclay de Tolly. In Moscow they are saying heaven knows what about him... What do you think of him?'

'Ask them,' replied Prince Andrew, indicating the officers.

Pierre looked at Timókhin with the condescendingly interrogative smile with which everybody involuntarily addressed that officer.

'We see light[1] again, since his Serenity has been appointed, your Excellency,' said Timókhin, timidly and continually turning to glance at his colonel.

'Why so?' asked Pierre.

'Well, to mention only fire-wood and fodder, let me inform you. Why, when we were retreating from Sventsyáni we dare not touch a stick, or a wisp of hay or anything. You see, we were going away, so he[2] would get it all; wasn't it so, your Excellency?' and again Timókhin turned to the prince. 'But we daren't. In our regiment two officers were court-martialled for that kind of thing. But when his Serenity took command everything became straightforward. Now we see light...'

'Then why was it forbidden?'

Timókhin looked about in confusion, not knowing what or how to answer such a question. Pierre put the same question to Prince Andrew.

'Why, so as not to lay waste the country we were abandoning to the enemy,' said Prince Andrew with venomous irony. 'It is very sound: one can't permit the land to be pillaged and accustom the troops to marauding. At Smolénsk too he judged correctly that the French might outflank us, as they had larger forces. But he could

---

[1] There is an untranslatable play on words. Kutúzov was addressed as 'Serenity', *svetléyshi*, the first syllable of which in Russian means *light*. So Timókhin says that at the appointment of his Serenity they saw light again.

[2] The enemy was always *he* to the Russians.

not understand this,' cried Prince Andrew in a shrill voice that seemed to escape him involuntarily: 'He could not understand that there, for the first time, we were fighting for Russian soil, and that there was a spirit in the men such as I had never seen before, that we had held the French for two days, and that that success had increased our strength tenfold. He ordered us to retreat, and all our efforts and losses went for nothing. He had no thought of betraying us, he tried to do the best he could, he thought out everything, and that is why he is unsuitable. He is unsuitable now, just because he plans out everything very thoroughly and accurately as every German has to. How can I explain? . . . Well, say your father has a German valet, and he is a splendid valet and satisfies your father's requirements better than you could, then it's all right to let him serve. But if your father is mortally sick you'll send the valet away and attend to your father with your own unpractised, awkward hands, and will soothe him better than a skilled man who is a stranger could. So it has been with Barclay. While Russia was well, a foreigner could serve her and be a splendid Minister; but as soon as she is in danger she needs one of her own kin. But in your Club they have been making him out a traitor! They slander him as a traitor, and the only result will be that afterwards, ashamed of their false accusations, they will make him out a hero or a genius instead of a traitor, and that will be still more unjust. He is an honest and very punctilious German.'

'And they say he's a skilful commander,' rejoined Pierre.

'I don't understand what is meant by "a skilful commander",' replied Prince Andrew ironically.

'A skilful commander?' replied Pierre. 'Why, one who foresees all contingencies . . . and foresees the adversary's intentions.'

'But that's impossible,' said Prince Andrew as if it were a matter settled long ago.

Pierre looked at him in surprise.

'And yet they say that war is like a game of chess?' he remarked.

'Yes', replied Prince Andrew, 'but with this little difference, that in chess you may think over each move as long as you please and are not limited for time, and with this difference too, that a knight is always stronger than a pawn, and two pawns are always stronger than one, while in war a battalion is sometimes stronger than a division and sometimes weaker than a company. The relative strength of bodies of troops can never be known to any one. Believe me,' he went on, 'if things depended on arrangements made by the staff, I should be there making arrangements, but instead of that I have the honour to serve here in the regiment with these gentlemen, and I consider that on us to-morrow's battle will depend and not on those others . . . Success never depends, and never will depend, on position, or equipment, or even on numbers, and least of all on position.'

'But on what then?'

'On the feeling that is in me and in him,' he pointed to Timókhin, 'and in each soldier.'

Prince Andrew glanced at Timókhin, who looked at his commander in alarm and bewilderment. In contrast to his former reticent taciturnity Prince Andrew now seemed excited. He could apparently not refrain from expressing the thoughts that had suddenly occurred to him.

'A battle is won by those who firmly resolve to win it! Why did we lose the battle at Austerlitz? The French losses were almost equal to ours, but very early we said to ourselves that we were losing the battle, and we did lose it. And we said so because we had nothing to fight for there, we wanted to get away from the battle-field as soon as we could. "We've lost, so let us run," and we ran. If we had not said that till the evening, heaven knows what might not have happened. But to-morrow we shan't say it. You talk about our position, the left flank weak and the right flank too extended,' he went on. 'That's all nonsense, there's nothing of the kind. But what awaits us to-morrow? A hundred million most diverse chances which will be decided on the instant by the fact that our men or theirs run or do not run, and that this man or that man is killed; but all that is being done at present is only play. The fact is that those men with whom you have ridden round the position not only do not help matters, but hinder. They are only concerned with their own petty interests.'

'At such a moment?' said Pierre reproachfully.

'*At such a moment!*' Prince Andrew repeated. 'To them it is only a moment affording opportunities to undermine a rival and obtain an extra cross or ribbon. For me to-morrow means this: a Russian army of a hundred thousand and a French army of a hundred thousand have met to fight, and the thing is that these two hundred thousand men *will* fight, and the side that fights more fiercely and spares itself least will win. And if you like I will tell you that whatever happens, and whatever muddles those at the top may make, we shall win to-morrow's battle. To-morrow, happen what may, we shall win!'

'There now, your Excellency! That's the truth, the real truth,' said Timókhin. 'Who would spare himself now? The soldiers in my battalion, believe me, wouldn't drink their vodka! "It's not the day for that!" they say.'

All were silent. The officers rose. Prince Andrew went out of the shed with them, giving final orders to the adjutant. After they had gone, Pierre approached Prince Andrew and was about to start a conversation when they heard the clatter of three horses' hoofs on the road not far from the shed, and looking in that direction Prince Andrew recognized Wolzogen and Clausewitz accompanied by a Cossack. They rode close by, continuing to converse, and Prince Andrew involuntarily heard these words:

'*Der Krieg muss in Raum verlegt werden. Der Ansicht kann ich nicht genug Preis geben,*'[1] said one of them.

'*Oh, ja,*' said the other, '*der Zweck ist nur den Feind zu schwächen, so kann man gewiss nicht den Verlust der Privat-Personen in Achtung nehmen.*'[2]

'Oh, no,' agreed the other.

[1] 'The war must be extended widely. I cannot sufficiently commend that view.'

[2] 'Oh yes, the only aim is to weaken the enemy, so one cannot, of course, take into account the losses of private persons.'

'Extend widely!' said Prince Andrew with an angry snort, when they had ridden past. 'In that "extent" were my father, son, and sister, at Bald Hills. That's all the same to him! That's what I was saying to you—those German gentlemen won't win the battle to-morrow but will only make all the mess they can, because they have nothing in their German heads but theories not worth an empty egg-shell, and haven't in their hearts the one thing needed to-morrow—that which Timókhin has. They have yielded up all Europe to *him*, and have now come to teach us. Fine teachers!' and again his voice grew shrill.

'So you think we shall win to-morrow's battle?' asked Pierre.

'Yes, yes,' answered Prince Andrew absently. 'One thing I would do if I had the power,' he began again, 'I would not take prisoners. Why take prisoners? It's chivalry! The French have destroyed my home and are on their way to destroy Moscow, they have outraged and are outraging me every moment. They are my enemies. In my opinion they are all criminals. And so thinks Timókhin and the whole army. They should be executed! Since they are my foes they cannot be my friends, whatever may have been said at Tilsit.'

'Yes, yes,' muttered Pierre, looking with shining eyes at Prince Andrew. 'I quite agree with you!'

The question that had perturbed Pierre on the Mozháysk hill and all that day now seemed to him quite clear and completely solved. He now understood the whole meaning and importance of this war and of the impending battle. All he had seen that day, all the significant and stern expressions on the faces he had seen in passing, were lit up for him by a new light. He understood that latent heat (as they say in physics) of patriotism which was present in all these men he had seen, and this explained to him why they all prepared for death calmly, and as it were light-heartedly.

'Not take prisoners,' Prince Andrew continued. 'That by itself would quite change the whole war and make it less cruel. As it is we have played at war—that's what's vile! We play at magnanimity and all that stuff. Such magnanimity and sensibility are like the magnanimity and sensibility of a lady who faints when she sees a calf being killed: she is so kind-hearted that she can't look at blood, but enjoys eating the calf served up with sauce. They talk to us of the rules of war, of chivalry, of flags of truce, of mercy to the unfortunate, and so on. It's all rubbish. I saw chivalry and flags of truce in 1805; they humbugged us and we humbugged them. They plunder other people's houses, issue false paper money, and worst of all they kill my children and my father, and then talk of rules of war and magnanimity to foes! Take no prisoners, but kill and be killed! He who has come to this as I have through the same sufferings . . .'

Prince Andrew, who had thought it was all the same to him whether or not Moscow was taken as Smolénsk had been, was suddenly checked in his speech by an unexpected cramp in his throat. He paced up and down a few times in silence, but his eyes glittered feverishly and his lips quivered as he began to speak again.

'If there was none of this magnanimity in war, we should go to war only when it was worth while going to certain death, as now. Then there would not be war because Paul Ivánovich had offended Michael Ivánovich. And when there was a war, like this one, it would be war! And then the determination of the troops would be quite different. Then all these Westphalians and Hessians whom Napoleon is leading would not follow him into Russia, and we should not go to fight in Austria and Prussia without knowing why. War is not courtesy but the most horrible thing in life; and we ought to understand that, and not play at war. We ought to accept this terrible necessity sternly and seriously. It all lies in that: get rid of falsehood and let war be war and not a game. As it is now, war is the favourite pastime of the idle and frivolous. The military calling is the most highly honoured.

'But what is war? What is needed for success in warfare? What are the habits of the military? The aim of war is murder; the methods of war are spying, treachery, and their encouragement, the ruin of a country's inhabitants, robbing them or stealing to provision the army, and fraud and falsehood termed military craft. The habits of the military class are the absence of freedom, that is, discipline, idleness, ignorance, cruelty, debauchery and drunkenness. And in spite of all this it is the highest class, respected by every one. All the kings, except the Chinese, wear military uniforms, and he who kills most people receives the highest rewards.

'They meet, as we shall meet to-morrow, to murder one another; they kill and maim tens of thousands, and then have thanksgiving services for having killed so many people (they even exaggerate the number), and they announce a victory, supposing that the more people they have killed the greater their achievement. How does God above look at them and hear them?' exclaimed Prince Andrew in a shrill, piercing voice. 'Ah, my friend, it has of late become hard for me to live. I see that I have begun to understand too much. And it doesn't do for man to taste of the tree of knowledge of good and evil . . . Ah, well, it's not for long!' he added.

'However, you're sleepy, and it's time for me to sleep. Go back to Górki!' said Prince Andrew suddenly.

'Oh, no!' Pierre replied, looking at Prince Andrew with frightened, compassionate eyes.

'Go, go! Before a battle one must have one's sleep out,' repeated Prince Andrew.

He came quickly up to Pierre and embraced and kissed him.

'Good-bye, be off!' he shouted. 'Whether we meet again or not . . .' and turning away hurriedly he entered the shed.

It was already dark, and Pierre could not make out whether the expression of Prince Andrew's face was angry or tender.

For some time he stood in silence considering whether he should follow him or go away. 'No, he does not want it!' Pierre concluded, 'and I know that this is our last meeting!' He sighed deeply and rode back to Górki.

On re-entering the shed Prince Andrew lay down on a rug, but he could not sleep.

He closed his eyes. One picture succeeded another in his imagination. On one of them he dwelt long and joyfully. He vividly recalled an evening in Petersburg. Natásha with animated and excited face was telling him how she had gone to look for mushrooms the previous summer and had lost her way in the big forest. She incoherently described the depths of the forest, her feelings, and a talk with a bee-keeper she met, and constantly interrupted her story to say: 'No, I can't, I'm not telling it right; no, you don't understand,' though he encouraged her by saying that he did understand, and he really had understood all she wanted to say. But Natásha was not satisfied with her own words: she felt that they did not convey the passionately poetic feeling she had experienced that day and wished to convey. 'He was such a delightful old man, and it was so dark in the forest . . . and he had such kind . . . No, I can't describe it,' she had said, flushed and excited. Prince Andrew smiled now the same happy smile as then when he had looked into her eyes. 'I understood her,' he thought. 'I not only understood her, but it was just that inner, spiritual force, that sincerity, that frankness of soul—that very soul of hers which seemed to be fettered by her body—it was that soul I loved in her . . . loved so strongly and happily . . .' and suddenly he remembered how his love had ended. 'He did not need anything of that kind. He neither saw nor understood anything of the sort. He only saw in her a pretty and fresh young girl, with whom he did not deign to unite his fate. And I? . . . and he is still alive and gay!'

Prince Andrew jumped up as if some one had burnt him, and again began pacing up and down in front of the shed.

CHAPTER XXVI

ON August 25th, the eve of the battle of Borodinó, M. de Beausset, prefect of the French Emperor's palace, arrived at Napoleon's quarters at Valúevo with Colonel Fabvier, the former from Paris and the latter from Madrid.

Donning his court uniform, M. de Beausset ordered a box he had brought for the Emperor to be carried before him, and entered the first compartment of Napoleon's tent, where he began opening the box while conversing with Napoleon's aides-de-camp who surrounded him.

Fabvier, not entering the tent, remained at the entrance talking to some generals of his acquaintance.

The Emperor Napoleon had not yet left his bedroom and was finishing his toilet. Slightly snorting and grunting, he presented now his back and now his plump hairy chest to the brush with which his valet was rubbing him down. Another valet, with his finger over the mouth of a bottle, was sprinkling eau-de-Cologne on the Emperor's pampered body with an expression which seemed to say that he alone knew where and how much eau-de-Cologne should be sprinkled. Napoleon's short hair was wet and matted on the forehead, but his face, though puffy and yellow, expressed physical satisfaction. 'Go on, harder, go on!' he muttered to the valet who was rubbing him, slightly twitching and grunting. An aide-de-camp, who had entered the bedroom to report to the Emperor the number of prisoners taken in yesterday's action, was standing by the door after delivering his message, awaiting permission to withdraw. Napoleon, frowning, looked at him from under his brows.

'No prisoners!' said he, repeating the aide-de-camp's words. 'They are forcing us to exterminate them. So much the worse for the Russian army . . . Go on . . . harder, harder!' he muttered, hunching his back and presenting his fat shoulders.

'All right. Let Monsieur de Beausset enter, and Fabvier too,' he said, nodding to the aide-de-camp.

'Yes, Sire,' and the aide-de-camp disappeared through the door of the tent.

Two valets rapidly dressed his Majesty, and wearing the blue uniform of the Guards he went with firm quick steps to the reception room.

De Beausset's hands meanwhile were busily engaged arranging the present he had brought from the Empress, on two chairs directly in front of the entrance. But Napoleon had dressed and come out with such unexpected rapidity that he had not time to finish arranging the surprise.

Napoleon noticed at once what they were about and guessed that they were not ready. He did not wish to deprive them of the pleasure of giving him a surprise, so he pretended not to see de Beausset and called Fabvier to him, listening silently and with a stern frown to what Fabvier told him of the heroism and devotion of his troops fighting at Salamanca, at the other end of Europe, with but one thought—to be worthy of their Emperor, and but one fear—to fail to please him. The result of that battle had been deplorable. Napoleon made ironic remarks during Fabvier's account, as if he had not expected that matters could go otherwise in his absence.

'I must make up for that in Moscow,' said Napoleon. 'I'll see you later,' he added, and summoned de Beausset, who by that time had prepared the surprise, having placed something on the chairs and covered it with a cloth.

De Beausset bowed low, with that courtly French bow which only the old retainers of the Bourbons knew how to make, and approached him, presenting an envelope.

Napoleon turned to him gaily and pulled his ear.

'You have hurried here. I am very glad. Well, what is Paris saying?' he asked, suddenly changing his former stern expression for a most cordial tone.

'Sire, all Paris regrets your absence,' replied de Beausset as was proper.

But though Napoleon knew that de Beausset had to say something of this kind, and though in his lucid moments he knew it was untrue, he was pleased to hear it from him. Again he honoured him by touching his ear.

'I am very sorry to have made you travel so far,' said he.

'Sire, I expected nothing less than to find you at the gates of Moscow,' replied de Beausset.

Napoleon smiled, and lifting his head absent-mindedly looked to the right. An aide-de-camp approached with gliding steps and offered him a gold snuff-box, which he took.

'Yes, it has happened luckily for you,' he said, raising the open snuff-box to his nose. 'You are fond of travel, and in three days you will see Moscow. You surely did not expect to see that Asiatic capital. You will have a pleasant journey.'

De Beausset bowed gratefully at this regard for his taste for travel (of which he had not till then been aware).

'Ha, what's this?' asked Napoleon, noticing that all the courtiers were looking at something concealed under a cloth.

With courtly adroitness de Beausset half turned, and without turning his back to the Emperor retired two steps, twitching off the cloth at the same time, and said:

'A present to your Majesty from the Empress.'

It was a portrait, painted in bright colours by Gérard, of the son borne to Napoleon by the daughter of the Emperor of Austria, the boy whom for some reason every one called 'The King of Rome'.

A very pretty curly-headed boy, with a look of the Christ in the Sistine Madonna, was depicted playing at stick and ball. The ball represented the terrestrial globe and the stick in his other hand a sceptre.

Though it was not clear what the artist meant to express by depicting the so-called King of Rome spiking the earth with a stick, the allegory apparently seemed to Napoleon, as it had done to all who had seen it in Paris, quite clear and very pleasing.

'The King of Rome!' he said, pointing to the portrait with a graceful gesture. 'Admirable!'

With the natural capacity of an Italian for changing the expression of his face at will, he drew nearer to the portrait and assumed a look of pensive tenderness. He felt that what he said now and did would be historical, and it seemed to him that it would now be best for him—whose grandeur enabled his son to play stick and ball with the terrestrial globe—to show, in contrast to that grandeur, the simplest paternal tenderness. His eyes grew dim, he moved forward, glanced round at a chair (which seemed to place itself under him), and sat down on it before the portrait. At a single gesture from him every one went out on tiptoe, leaving the great man to himself and his emotion.

Having sat still for a while he touched—himself not knowing why—the thick spot of paint representing the highest light in the portrait, rose, and recalled de Beausset and the officer on duty. He ordered the portrait to be carried outside his tent, that the Old Guard, stationed round it, might not be deprived of the pleasure of seeing the King of Rome, the son and heir of their adored monarch.

And while he was doing M. de Beausset the honour of breakfasting with him, they heard, as Napoleon had anticipated, the rapturous cries of the officers and men of the Old Guard who had run up to see the portrait.

'*Vive l'Empereur! Vive le roi de Rome! Vive l'Empereur!*' came those ecstatic cries.

After breakfast Napoleon in de Beausset's presence dictated his order of the day to the army.

'Short and energetic!' he remarked when he had read over the proclamation which he had dictated straight off without corrections. It ran:

'Soldiers! This is the battle you have so longed for. Victory depends on you. It is essential for us; it will give us all we need, comfortable quarters and a speedy return to our country. Behave as you did at Austerlitz, Friedland, Vitebsk, and Smolensk. Let our remotest posterity recall your achievements this day with pride. Let it be said of each of you: "He was in the great battle before Moscow!"'

'Before Moscow!' repeated Napoleon, and inviting M. de Beausset, who was so fond of travel, to accompany him on his ride, he went out of the tent to where the horses stood saddled.

'Your Majesty is too kind!' replied de Beausset to the invitation to accompany the Emperor: he wanted to sleep, did not know how to ride, and was afraid of doing so.

But Napoleon nodded to the traveller, and de Beausset had to mount. When Napoleon came out of the tent the shouting of the Guards before his son's portrait grew still louder. Napoleon frowned.

'Take him away!' he said, pointing with a gracefully majestic gesture to the portrait. 'It is too soon for him to see a field of battle.'

De Beausset closed his eyes, bowed his head, and sighed deeply, to indicate how profoundly he valued and comprehended the Emperor's words.

CHAPTER XXVII

ON the 25th of August, so his historians tell us, Napoleon spent the whole day on horseback inspecting the locality, considering plans submitted to him by his marshals, and personally giving commands to his generals.

The original line of the Russian forces along the river Kolochá had been dislocated by the capture of the Shevárdino Redoubt on the 24th, and part of the line—the left flank—had been drawn back. That part of the line was not entrenched and in front of it the ground was more open and level than elsewhere. It was evident to any one, military or not, that it was here the French should attack. It would seem that not much consideration was needed to reach this conclusion, nor any particular care or trouble on the part of the Emperor and his marshals, nor was there any need of that special and supreme quality called genius, that people are so apt to ascribe to Napoleon; yet the historians who described the event later and the men who then surrounded Napoleon, and he himself, thought otherwise.

Napoleon rode over the plain and surveyed the locality with a profound air and in silence, nodded with approval or shook his head dubiously, and without communicating to the generals around him the profound course of ideas which guided his decisions merely gave them his final conclusions in the form of commands. Having listened to a suggestion from Davoût, who was now called Prince d'Eckmühl, to turn the Russian left wing, Napoleon said it should not be done, without explaining why not. To a proposal made by General Campan (who was to attack the flèches) to lead his division through the woods, Napoleon agreed, though the so-called Duke of Elchingen (Ney) ventured to remark that a movement through the woods was dangerous and might disorder the division.

Having inspected the country opposite the Shevárdino Redoubt, Napoleon pondered a little in silence and then indicated the spots where two batteries should be set up by the morrow to act against the Russian entrenchments, and the places where, in line with them, the field artillery should be placed.

After giving these and other commands he returned to his tent, and the dispositions for the battle were written down from his dictation.

These dispositions, of which the French historians write with enthusiasm and other historians with profound respect, were as follows:

'At dawn the two new batteries established during the night on the plain occupied by the Prince d'Eckmühl will open fire on the two opposing batteries of the enemy.

'At the same time the commander of the artillery of the 1st Corps, General Pernetti, with thirty cannon of Campan's division and all the howitzers of Dessaix's and Friant's divisions, will move forward, open fire, and overwhelm with shell-fire the enemy's battery, against which will operate:

	24 guns of the artillery of the Guards
	30 guns of Campan's division
and	8 guns of Friant's and Dessaix's divisions

in all 62 guns.

'The commander of the artillery of the 3rd Corps, General Fouché, will place the howitzers of the 3rd and 8th Corps, sixteen in all, on the flanks of the battery that is to bombard the entrenchment on the left, which will have forty guns in all directed against it.

'General Sorbier must be ready at the first order to advance with all the howitzers of the Guards' artillery against either one or other of the entrenchments.

'During the cannonade Prince Poniatowski is to advance through the wood on the village and turn the enemy's position.

'General Campan will move through the wood to seize the first fortification.

'After the advance has begun in this manner, orders will be given in accordance with the enemy's movements.

'The cannonade on the left flank will begin as soon as the guns of the right wing are heard. The sharpshooters of Morand's division and of the vice-King's[1] division will

[1] The vice-King referred to is Murat, whom Napoleon had made King of Naples.

open a heavy fire on seeing the attack commence on the right wing.

'The vice-King will occupy the village[1] and cross by its three bridges, advancing to the same heights as Morand's and Gérard's divisions, which under his leadership will be directed against the redoubt and come into line with the rest of the forces.

'All this must be done in good order (*le tout se fera avec ordre et méthode*) as far as possible retaining troops in reserve.

'The Imperial Camp near Mozhaysk,
    6th September[2] 1812.'

These dispositions, which are very obscure and confused if one allows oneself to regard the arrangements without religious awe of his genius, related to Napoleon's orders to deal with four points—four different orders. Not one of these was, or could be, carried out.

In the disposition it is said first, *that the batteries placed on the spot chosen by Napoleon, with the guns of Pernetti and Fouché which were to come in line with them, 102 guns in all, were to open fire and shower shells on the Russian flèches and redoubts.* This could not be done, as from the spots selected by Napoleon the projectiles did not carry to the Russian works, and those 102 guns shot into the air until the nearest commander, contrary to Napoleon's instructions, moved them forward.

The second order was that *Poniatowski, moving to the village through the wood, should turn the Russian left flank.* This could not be done and was not done, because Poniatowski, advancing on the village through the wood, met Tuchkóv there barring his way, and could not and did not turn the Russian position.

The third order was: *General Campan will move through the wood to seize the first fortification.* General Campan's division did not seize the first fortification, but was driven back, for on emerging from the wood it had to re-form under grape-shot, of which Napoleon was unaware.

[1] Borodinó.
[2] The date of this French proclamation is new style, and corresponds to August 25th, old style.

The fourth order was: *The vice-King will occupy the village* (Borodinó) *and cross by its three bridges, advancing to the same heights as Morand's and Gérard's divisions* (for whose movements no directions are given), *which under his leadership will be directed against the redoubt and come into line with the rest of the forces.*

As far as one can make out, not so much from this unintelligible sentence as from the attempts the vice-King made to execute the orders given him, he was to advance from the left through Borodinó to the redoubt, while the divisions of Morand and Gérard were to advance simultaneously from the front.

All this, like the other parts of the disposition, was not and could not be executed. After passing through Borodinó the vice-King was driven back to the Kolochá and could get no farther; while the divisions of Morand and Gérard did not take the redoubt but were driven back, and the redoubt was only taken at the end of the battle by the cavalry (a thing probably unforeseen and not heard of by Napoleon). So not one of the orders in the disposition was, or could be, executed. But in the disposition it is said that, *after the fight has commenced in this manner, orders will be given in accordance with the enemy's movements*, and so it might be supposed that all necessary arrangements would be made by Napoleon during the battle. But this was not and could not be done, for during the whole battle Napoleon was so far away that, as appeared later, he could not know the course of the battle, and not one of his orders during the fight could be executed.

CHAPTER XXVIII

MANY historians say that the French did not win the battle of Borodinó because Napoleon had a cold, and that if he had not had a cold the orders he gave before and during the battle would have been still more full of genius and Russia would have been lost and the face of the world have been changed. To historians who believe that Russia was shaped by the will of one man— Peter the Great—and that France from a republic became an empire and French armies went to Russia at the will of one man—Napoleon—to say that Russia remained a power because Napoleon had a bad cold on the 24th of August may seem logical and convincing.

If it had depended on Napoleon's will to fight or not to fight the battle of Borodinó, and if this or that other arrangement depended on his will, then evidently a cold affecting the manifestation of his will might have saved Russia, and consequently the valet who omitted to bring Napoleon his waterproof-boots on the 24th would have been the saviour of Russia. Along that line of thought such a deduction is indubitable, as indubitable as the deduction Voltaire made in jest (without knowing what he was jesting at) when he said that the Massacre of St. Bartholomew was due to Charles the Ninth's stomach being deranged. But to men who do not admit that Russia was formed by the will of one man, Peter I, or that the French Empire was formed and the war with Russia begun by the will of one man, Napoleon, that argument seems not merely untrue and irrational, but contrary to all human reality. To the question of what causes historic events, another answer presents itself, namely, that the course of human events is predetermined from on high—depends on the coincidence of the wills of all who take part in the events, and that a Napoleon's influence on the course of these events is purely external and fictitious.

Strange as at first glance it may seem to suppose that the Massacre of St. Bartholomew was not due to Charles IX's will, though he gave the order for it and thought it was done as a result of that order; and strange as it may seem to suppose that the slaughter of eighty thousand men at Borodinó was not due to Napoleon's will, though he ordered the commencement and conduct of the battle and thought it was done because he ordered it; strange as these suppositions appear, yet human dignity—which tells me that each of us is, if not more, at least not less a man than the great Napoleon—demands the acceptance of that solution of the question, and historic investigation abundantly confirms it.

At the battle of Borodinó Napoleon shot at no one and killed no one. That was all done by the soldiers. Therefore it was not he who killed people.

The French soldiers went to kill and be killed at the battle of Borodinó not because of Napoleon's orders, but by their own volition. The whole army—French, Italian, German, Polish, and Dutch—hungry, ragged, and weary of the campaign, felt at the sight of an army blocking their road to Moscow, that the wine was drawn and must be drunk. Had Napoleon then forbidden them to fight the Russians, they would have killed him and have proceeded to fight the Russians because it was inevitable.

When they heard Napoleon's proclamation offering them, as compensation for mutilation and death, the words of posterity about their having been in the battle before Moscow, they cried *'Vive l'Empereur!'* just as they had cried *'Vive l'Empereur!'* at the sight of the portrait of the boy piercing the terrestrial globe with a toy stick, and just as they would have cried *'Vive l'Empereur!'* at any nonsense that might be told them. There was nothing left for them to do but cry *'Vive l'Empereur!'* and go to fight in order to get food and rest as conquerors in Moscow. So it was not because of Napoleon's commands that they killed their fellow men.

And it was not Napoleon who directed the course of the battle, for none of his orders were executed and during the battle he did not know what was going on before him. So the way in which these people killed one another was not decided by Napoleon's will but occurred independently of him, in accord with the will of hundreds of thousands of people who took part in the common action. It *only seemed* to Napoleon that it all took place by his will. And so the question whether he had or had not a cold has no more historic interest than the cold of the least of the transport soldiers.

Moreover the assertion made by various writers that his cold was the cause of his dispositions not being as well planned as on former occasions, and of his orders during the battle not being as good as previously, is quite baseless, which again shows that Napoleon's cold on the 26th of August was unimportant.

The dispositions cited above are not at all worse, but are even better, than previous dispositions by which he had won victories. His pseudo-orders during the battle were also no worse than formerly, but much the same as usual. These dispositions and orders only seem worse than previous ones because the battle of Borodinó was the first Napoleon did not win. The profoundest and most excellent dispositions and orders seem very bad, and every learned militarist criticizes them with looks of importance, when they relate to a battle that has been lost, and the very worst dispositions and orders seem very good, and serious people fill whole volumes to demonstrate their merits, when they relate to a battle that has been won.

The dispositions drawn up by Weyrother for the battle of Austerlitz were a model of perfection for that kind of composition, but still they were criticized—criticized for their very perfection, for their excessive minuteness.

Napoleon at the battle of Borodinó fulfilled his office as representative of authority as well as, and even better than, at other battles. He did nothing harmful to the progress of the battle; he inclined to the most reasonable opinions, he made no confusion, did not contradict himself, did not get frightened or run away from the field of battle, but with his great tact and military experience carried out his role of appearing to command, calmly and with dignity.

CHAPTER XXIX

ON returning from a second careful inspection of the lines, Napoleon remarked:

'The chessmen are set up, the game will begin tomorrow!'

Having ordered punch and summoned de Beausset, he began to talk to him about Paris and about some changes he meant to make in the Empress's household, surprising the prefect by his memory of minute details relating to the Court.

He showed an interest in trifles, joked about de Beausset's love of travel, and chatted carelessly, as a famous, self-confident surgeon who knows his job does when turning up his sleeves and putting on his apron while a patient is being strapped to the operating-table.

'The matter is in my hands and is clear and definite in my head. When the time comes to set to work I shall do it as no one else could, but now I can jest, and the more I jest and the calmer I am the more tranquil and confident you ought to be, and the more amazed at my genius.'

Having finished his second glass of punch, Napoleon went to rest before the serious business which, he considered, awaited him next day. He was so much interested in that task that he was unable to sleep, and in spite of his cold which had grown worse from the dampness of the evening, he went into the large division of the tent at three o'clock in the morning, loudly blowing his nose. He asked whether the Russians had not withdrawn, and was told that the enemy's fires were still in the same places. He nodded approval.

The adjutant in attendance came into the tent.

'Well, Rapp, do you think we shall do good business to-day?' Napoleon asked him.

'Without doubt, Sire,' replied Rapp.

Napoleon looked at him.

'Do you remember, Sire, what you did me the honour to say at Smolénsk?' continued Rapp. 'The wine is drawn and must be drunk.'

Napoleon frowned, and sat silent for a long time leaning his head on his hand.

'This poor army!' he suddenly remarked. 'It has diminished greatly since Smolénsk. Fortune is frankly a courtesan, Rapp. I have always said so and I am beginning to experience it. But the Guards, Rapp, the Guards are intact?' he remarked interrogatively.

'Yes, Sire,' replied Rapp.

Napoleon took a lozenge, put it in his mouth, and glanced at his watch. He was not sleepy and it was still not nearly morning. It was impossible to give further orders for the sake of killing time, for the orders had all been given and were now being executed.

'Have the biscuits and rice been served out to the regiments of the Guards?' asked Napoleon sternly.

'Yes, Sire.'

'The rice too?'

Rapp replied that he had given the Emperor's order

about the rice, but Napoleon shook his head in dissatisfaction as if not believing that his order had been executed. An attendant came in with punch. Napoleon
ordered another glass to be brought for Rapp, and
silently sipped his own.

'I have neither taste nor smell,' he remarked, sniffing
at his glass. 'This cold is tiresome. They talk about
medicine—what is the good of medicine when it can't
cure a cold! Corvisart[1] gave me these lozenges but they
don't help at all. What can doctors cure? One can't
cure anything. Our body is a machine for living. It is
organized for that, it is its nature. Let life go on in it
unhindered and let it defend itself, it will do more than if
you paralyse it by encumbering it with remedies. Our
body is like a perfect watch that should go for a certain
time; the watchmaker cannot open it, he can only adjust
it by fumbling, and that blindfold . . . Yes, our body is
a machine for living, that is all.'

And having entered on the path of definition, of which
he was fond, Napoleon suddenly and unexpectedly gave
a new one.

'Do you know, Rapp, what military art is?' asked he.
'It is the art of being stronger than the enemy at a given
moment. That's all.'

Rapp made no reply.

'To-morrow we shall have to deal with Kutúzov!' said
Napoleon. 'We shall see! Do you remember at Braunau
he commanded an army for three weeks and did not
once mount a horse to inspect his entrenchments . . . We
shall see!'

He looked at his watch. It was still only four o'clock.
He did not feel sleepy. The punch was finished and there
was still nothing to do. He rose, walked to and fro, put
on a warm overcoat and a hat, and went out of the tent.
The night was dark and damp, a scarcely perceptible
moisture was descending from above. Near by, the camp-
fires were dimly burning among the French Guards, and
in the distance those of the Russian line shone through
the smoke. The weather was calm, and the rustle and

[1] Baron J. N. de Corvisart-Demarets (1755–1821), a famous
French doctor, physician to Napoleon.

tramp of the French troops already beginning to move to take up their positions was clearly audible.

Napoleon walked about in front of his tent, looked at the fires, and listened to these sounds, and as he was passing a tall guardsman in a shaggy cap, who was standing sentinel before his tent and had drawn himself up like a black pillar at sight of the Emperor, Napoleon stopped in front of him.

'What year did you enter the service?' he asked with that affectation of military bluntness and geniality with which he always addressed the soldiers.

The man answered the question.

'Ah! One of the old ones! Has your regiment had its rice?'

'It has, your Majesty.'

Napoleon nodded and walked away.

At half-past five Napoleon rode to the village of Shevárdino.

It was growing light, the sky was clearing, only a single cloud lay in the east. The abandoned camp-fires were burning themselves out in the faint morning light.

On the right a single deep report of a cannon resounded and died away in the prevailing silence. Some minutes passed. A second and a third report shook the air, then a fourth and a fifth boomed solemnly near by on the right.

The first shots had not yet ceased to reverberate before others rang out and yet more were heard mingling with and overtaking one another.

Napoleon with his suite rode up to the Shevárdino Redoubt where he dismounted. The game had begun.

CHAPTER XXX

ON returning to Górki after having seen Prince Andrew, Pierre ordered his groom to get the horses ready and to call him early in the morning, and then immediately fell asleep behind a partition in a corner Borís had given up to him.

Before he was thoroughly awake next morning, everybody had already left the hut. The panes were rattling in the little windows and his groom was shaking him.

'Your Excellency! Your Excellency! Your Excellency!'
he kept repeating pertinaciously while he shook Pierre by
the shoulder without looking at him, having apparently
lost hope of getting him to wake up.

'What? Has it begun? Is it time?' Pierre asked,
waking up.

'Hear the firing,' said the groom, a discharged soldier.
'All the gentlemen have all gone out, and his Serene
Highness himself rode past long ago.'

Pierre dressed hastily and ran out to the porch. Outside all was bright, fresh, dewy, and cheerful. The sun,
just bursting forth from behind a cloud that had concealed it, was shining, with rays still half broken by the
clouds, over the roofs of the street opposite, on the dew-
besprinkled dust of the road, on the walls of the houses,
on the windows, the fence, and on Pierre's horses standing
before the hut. The roar of guns sounded more distinct
outside. An adjutant accompanied by a Cossack passed
by at a sharp trot.

'It's time, Count; it's time!' cried the adjutant.

Telling the groom to follow him with the horses, Pierre
went down the street to the knoll from which he had
looked at the field of battle the day before. A crowd of
military men was assembled there, members of the staff
could be heard conversing in French, and Kutúzov's
grey head in a white cap with a red band was visible, his
grey nape sunk between his shoulders. He was looking
through a field-glass down the high road before him.

Mounting the steps to the knoll, Pierre looked at the
scene before him, spellbound by its beauty. It was the
same panorama he had admired from that spot the day
before, but now the whole place was full of troops and
covered by smoke-clouds from the guns, and the slanting
rays of the bright sun, rising slightly to the left behind
Pierre, cast upon it through the clear morning air pene-
trating streaks of rosy, golden-tinted light and long dark
shadows. The forest at the farthest extremity of the
panorama seemed carved in some precious stone of a
yellowish-green colour, its undulating outline was sil-
houetted against the horizon and was pierced beyond
Valúevo by the Smolénsk high road, crowded with troops

Nearer at hand glittered golden cornfields interspersed with copses. There were troops to be seen everywhere, in front and to the right and left. All this was vivid, majestic, and unexpected; but what impressed Pierre most of all was the view of the battle-field itself, of Borodinó and the hollows on both sides of the Kolochá.

Above the Kolochá, in Borodinó and on both sides of it, especially to the left where the Vóyna flowing between its marshy banks falls into the Kolochá, a mist had spread which seemed to melt, to dissolve and to become translucent when the brilliant sun appeared and magically coloured and outlined everything. The smoke of the guns mingled with this mist, and over the whole expanse and through that mist the rays of the morning sun were reflected, flashing back like lightning from the water, from the dew, and from the bayonets of the troops crowded together by the river banks and in Borodinó. A white church could be seen through the mist, and here and there the roofs of huts in Borodinó, as well as dense masses of soldiers, or green ammunition-chests and ordnance. And all this moved, or seemed to move, as the smoke and mist spread out over the whole space. Just as in the mist-enveloped hollow near Borodinó, so along the entire line outside and above it and especially in the woods and fields to the left, in the valleys and on the summits of the high ground, clouds of powder-smoke seemed continually to spring up out of nothing, now singly now several at a time, some translucent others dense, which, swelling, growing, rolling, and blending, extended over the whole expanse.

These puffs of smoke and (strange to say) the sound of the firing, produced the chief beauty of the spectacle.

'*Puff!*'—suddenly a round compact cloud of smoke was seen merging from violet into grey and milky-white, and '*boom!*' came the report a second later.

'*Puff! puff!*'—and two clouds arose pushing one another and blending together; and '*boom, boom!*' came the sounds confirming what the eye had seen.

Pierre glanced round at the first cloud, which he had seen as a round compact ball, and in its place already were balloons of smoke floating to one side, and—'*puff*' (with a pause)—'*puff, puff!*' three and then four more appeared and then from each, with the same interval— '*boom—boom, boom!*' came the fine, firm, precise sounds in reply. It seemed as if those smoke-clouds sometimes ran, and sometimes stood still while woods, fields, and glittering bayonets ran past them. From the left, over fields and bushes, those large balls of smoke were continually appearing followed by their solemn reports, while nearer still, in the hollows and woods, there burst from the muskets small cloudlets that had no time to become balls, but had their little echoes in just the same way. '*Trakh-ta-ta-takh!*' came the frequent crackle of musketry, but it was irregular and feeble in comparison with the reports of the cannon.

Pierre wished to be there with that smoke, those shining bayonets, that movement, and those sounds. He turned to look at Kutúzov and his suite, to compare his impressions with those of others. They were all looking at the field of battle as he was, and, as it seemed to him, with the same feelings. All their faces were now shining with that latent warmth of feeling Pierre had noticed the day before, and had fully understood after his talk with Prince Andrew.

'Go, my dear fellow, go . . . and Christ be with you!' Kutúzov was saying to a general who stood beside him, not taking his eye from the battle-field.

Having received this order the general passed by Pierre on his way down the knoll.

'To the crossing!' said the general coldly and sternly in reply to one of the staff who asked where he was going.

'I'll go there too, I too!' thought Pierre, and followed the general.

The general mounted a horse a Cossack had brought him. Pierre went to his groom who was holding his horses, and asking which was the quietest, clambered onto it, seized it by the mane, and turning out his toes, pressed his heels against its sides and, feeling that his spectacles were slipping off but unable to let go of the mane and reins, he galloped after the general, causing the staff officers to smile as they watched him from the knoll.

CHAPTER XXXI

HAVING descended the hill the general after whom Pierre was galloping turned sharply to the left, and Pierre, losing sight of him, galloped in among some ranks of infantry marching ahead of him. He tried to pass either in front of them or to the right or left, but there were soldiers everywhere, all with the same preoccupied expression and busy with some unseen but evidently important task. They all gazed with the same dissatisfied and inquiring expression at this stout man in a white hat, who for some unknown reason threatened to trample them under his horse's hoofs.

'Why ride into the middle of the battalion?' one of them shouted at him.

Another prodded his horse with the butt-end of a musket, and Pierre, bending over his saddle-bow and hardly able to control his shying horse, galloped ahead of the soldiers where there was a free space.

There was a bridge ahead of him, where other soldiers stood firing. Pierre rode up to them. Without being aware of it he had come to the bridge across the Kolochá between Górki and Borodinó, which the French (having occupied Borodinó) were attacking in the first phase of the battle. Pierre saw that there was a bridge in front of him and that soldiers were doing something on both sides of it and in the meadow, among the rows of new-mown hay which he had taken no notice of amid the smoke of the camp-fires the day before; but despite the incessant firing going on there, he had no idea that this was the field of battle. He did not notice the sound of the bullets whistling from every side, or the projectiles that flew over him, did not see the enemy on the other side of the river, and for a long time did not notice the killed and wounded, though many fell near him. He looked about him with a smile which did not leave his face.

'Why's that fellow in front of the line?' shouted somebody at him again.

'To the left! . . . Keep to the right!' the men shouted to him.

Pierre went to the right, and unexpectedly encountered

one of Raévski's adjutants whom he knew. The adjutant looked angrily at him, evidently also intending to shout at him, but on recognizing him he nodded.

'How have you got here?' he said, and galloped on.

Pierre feeling out of place there, having nothing to do, and afraid of getting in some one's way again, galloped after the adjutant.

'What's happening here? May I come with you?' he asked.

'One moment, one moment!' replied the adjutant, and riding up to a stout colonel who was standing in the meadow, he gave him some message and then addressed Pierre.

'Why have you come here, Count?' he asked with a smile. 'Still inquisitive?'

'Yes, yes,' assented Pierre.

But the adjutant turned his horse about and rode on.

'Here it's tolerable,' said he, 'but with Bagratión on the left flank they're getting it frightfully hot.'

'Really?' said Pierre. 'Where is that?'

'Come along with me to our knoll. We can get a view from there and in our battery it is still bearable,' said the adjutant. 'Will you come?'

'Yes, I'll come with you,' replied Pierre, looking round for his groom.

It was only now that he noticed wounded men, staggering along or being carried on stretchers. On that very meadow he had ridden over the day before, a soldier was lying athwart the rows of scented hay, with his head thrown awkwardly back and his shako off.

'Why haven't they carried him away?' Pierre was about to ask, but seeing the stern expression of the adjutant who was also looking that way, he checked himself.

Pierre did not find his groom, and rode along the hollow with the adjutant to Ravéski's Redoubt. His horse lagged behind the adjutant's and jolted him at every step.

'You don't seem to be used to riding, Count?' remarked the adjutant.

'No, it's not that, but her action seems so jerky,' said Pierre in a puzzled tone.

'Why . . . she's wounded!' said the adjutant. 'In the

off foreleg above the knee. A bullet, no doubt. I congratulate you, Count, on your baptism of fire!'

Having ridden in the smoke past the Sixth Corps, behind the artillery which had been moved forward and was in action, deafening them with the noise of firing, they came to a small wood. There it was cool and quiet, with a scent of autumn. Pierre and the adjutant dismounted and walked up the hill on foot.

'Is the general here?' asked the adjutant on reaching the knoll.

'He was here a minute ago but has just gone that way,' some one told him, pointing to the right.

The adjutant looked at Pierre as if puzzled what to do with him now.

'Don't trouble about me,' said Pierre. 'I'll go up onto the knoll if I may?'

'Yes, do. You'll see everything from there and it's less dangerous, and I'll come for you.'

Pierre went to the battery and the adjutant rode on. They did not meet again, and only much later did Pierre learn that he lost an arm that day.

The knoll to which Pierre ascended was that famous one afterwards known to the Russians as the Knoll Battery or Raévski's Redoubt, and to the French as *la grande redoute, la fatale redoute, la redoute du centre*, around which tens of thousands fell, and which the French regarded as the key to the whole position.

This redoubt consisted of a knoll, on three sides of which trenches had been dug. Within the entrenchment stood ten guns, that were being fired through openings in the earthwork.

In line with the knoll on both sides stood other guns which also fired incessantly. A little behind the guns stood infantry. When ascending that knoll Pierre had no notion that this spot, on which small trenches had been dug and from which a few guns were firing, was the most important point of the battle.

On the contrary, just because he happened to be there he thought it one of the least significant parts of the field.

Having reached the knoll, Pierre sat down at one end

of a trench surrounding the battery, and gazed at what
was going on around him with an unconsciously happy
smile. Occasionally he rose and walked about the
battery, still with that same smile, trying not to obstruct
the soldiers who were loading, hauling the guns, and continually running past him with bags and charges. The
guns of that battery were being fired continually one
after another with a deafening roar, enveloping the
whole neighbourhood in powder-smoke.

In contrast with the dread felt by the infantrymen
placed in support, here in the battery where a small
number of men busy at their work were separated from
the rest by a trench, every one experienced a common
and as it were family feeling of animation.

The intrusion of Pierre's non-military figure in a white
hat made an unpleasant impression at first. The soldiers
looked askance at him with surprise and even alarm as
they went past him. The senior artillery officer, a tall,
long-legged, pock-marked man, moved over to Pierre as
if to see the action of the farthest gun, and looked at him
with curiosity.

A young round-faced officer, quite a boy still and
evidently only just out of the Cadet College, who was
zealously commanding the two guns entrusted to him,
addressed Pierre sternly.

'Sir,' he said, 'permit me to ask you to stand aside.
You must not be here.'

The soldiers shook their heads disapprovingly as they
looked at Pierre. But when they had convinced themselves that this man in the white hat was doing no harm,
but either sat quietly on the slope of the trench with a shy
smile, or, politely making way for the soldiers, paced up
and down the battery under fire as calmly as if he were
on a boulevard, their feeling of hostile distrust gradually
began to change into a kindly and bantering sympathy,
such as soldiers feel for their dogs, cocks, goats, and in
general for the animals that live with the regiment. The
men soon accepted Pierre into their family, adopted him,
gave him a nickname ('our gentleman'), and made kindly
fun of him among themselves.

A shell tore up the earth two paces from Pierre and he

looked around with a smile as he brushed from his clothes some earth it had thrown up.

'And how's it you're not afraid, sir, really now?' a red-faced, broad-shouldered soldier asked Pierre, with a grin that disclosed a set of sound, white teeth.

'Are you afraid, then?' said Pierre.

'What else do you expect?' answered the soldier. 'She has no mercy, you know! When she comes spluttering down, out go your innards. One can't help being afraid,' he said laughing.

Several of the men, with bright kindly faces, stopped beside Pierre. They seemed not to have expected him to talk like anybody else, and the discovery that he did so delighted them.

'It's the business of us soldiers. But in a gentleman it's wonderful! There's a gentleman for you!'

'To your places!' cried the young officer to the men gathered round Pierre.

The young officer was evidently exercising his duties for the first or second time, and therefore treated both his superiors and the men with great precision and formality.

The booming cannonade and the fusillade of musketry was growing more intense over the whole field, especially to the left where Bagratión's flèches were, but where Pierre was the smoke of the firing made it almost impossible to distinguish anything. Moreover his whole attention was engrossed by watching the family circle—separated from all else—formed by the men in the battery. His first unconscious feeling of joyful animation produced by the sights and sounds of the battle-field was now replaced by another, especially since he had seen that soldier lying alone in the hayfield. Now, seated on the slope of the trench, he observed the faces of those around him.

By ten o'clock some twenty men had already been carried away from the battery; two guns were smashed and cannon-balls fell more and more frequently on the battery, and spent bullets buzzed and whistled around. But the men in the battery seemed not to notice this, and merry voices and jokes were heard on all sides.

'A live one!' shouted a man as a whistling shell approached.

'Not this way! To the infantry!' added another with loud laughter, seeing the shell fly past and fall into the ranks of the supports.

'Are you bowing to a friend, eh?' remarked another, chaffing a peasant who ducked low as a cannon-ball flew over.

Several soldiers gathered by the wall of the trench, looking out to see what was happening in front.

'They've withdrawn the front line, it has retired,' said they, pointing over the earthwork.

'Mind your own business,' an old sergeant shouted at them. 'If they've retired it's because there's work for them to do farther back.'

And the sergeant, taking one of the men by the shoulders, gave him a shove with his knee. This was followed by a burst of laughter.

'To the fifth gun, wheel it up!' came shouts from one side.

'Now then, all together, like bargees!' rose the merry voices of those who were moving the gun.

'Oh, she nearly knocked our gentleman's hat off!' cried the red-faced humorist, showing his teeth and chaffing Pierre. 'Awkward baggage!' he added reproachfully to a cannon-ball that struck a cannon-wheel and a man's leg.

'Now then, you foxes!' another said, laughing at some militiamen who, stooping low, entered the battery to carry away the wounded man.

'So this gruel isn't to your taste? Oh, you crows! You're scared!' they shouted at the militiamen who stood hesitating before the man whose leg had been torn off.

'There lads . . . oh, oh!' they mimicked the peasants, 'they don't like it at all!'

Pierre noticed that after every ball that hit the redoubt, and after every loss, the liveliness increased more and more.

As the flames of the fire hidden within come more and more vividly and rapidly from an approaching thunder-cloud, so, as if in opposition to what was taking place, the lightning of hidden fire growing more and more intense glowed in the faces of these men.

Pierre did not look out at the battle-field and was not concerned to know what was happening there, he was entirely absorbed in watching this fire which burnt ever more brightly and which he felt was flaming up in the same way in his own soul.

At ten o'clock the infantry that had been among the bushes in front of the battery and along the Kámenka streamlet retreated. From the battery they could be seen running back past it carrying their wounded on their muskets. A general with his suite came to the battery, and after speaking to the colonel gave Pierre an angry look and went away again having ordered the infantry supports behind the battery to lie down, so as to be less exposed to fire. After this from amid the ranks of infantry to the right of the battery came the sound of a drum and shouts of command, and from the battery one saw how those ranks of infantry moved forward.

Pierre looked over the wall of the trench, and was particularly struck by a pale young officer who, letting his sword hang down, was walking backwards and kept glancing uneasily round.

The ranks of the infantry disappeared amid the smoke but their long-drawn shout and rapid musketry firing could still be heard. A few minutes later crowds of wounded men and stretcher-bearers came back from that direction. Projectiles began to fall still more frequently in the battery. Several men were lying about who had not been removed. Around the cannon the men moved still more briskly and busily. No one any longer took notice of Pierre. Once or twice he was shouted at for being in the way. The senior officer moved with big, rapid strides from one gun to another with a frowning face. The young officer, with his face still more flushed, commanded the men more scrupulously than ever. The soldiers handed up the charges, turned, loaded, and did their business with strained smartness. They gave little jumps as they walked, as though they were on springs.

The storm-cloud had come upon them, and in every face the fire which Pierre had watched kindle burnt up

brightly. Pierre was standing beside the commanding
officer. The young officer, his hand to his shako, ran up
to his superior.

'I have the honour to report, sir, that only eight rounds
are left. Are we to continue firing?' he asked.

'Grape-shot!' the senior shouted, without answering
the question, looking over the wall of the trench.

Suddenly something happened; the young officer gave
a gasp, and bending double sat down on the ground like
a bird shot on the wing. Everything became strange,
confused, and misty in Pierre's eyes.

One cannon-ball after another whistled by and struck
the earthwork, a soldier, or a gun. Pierre, who had not
noticed these sounds before, now heard nothing else. On
the right of the battery soldiers shouting 'Hurrah!' were
running not forwards but backwards it seemed to Pierre.

A cannon-ball struck the very end of the earthwork by
which he was standing, crumbling down the earth; a
black ball flashed before his eyes and at the same instant
plumped into something. Some militiamen who were
entering the battery ran back.

'All with grape-shot!' shouted the officer.

The sergeant ran up to the officer and in a frightened
whisper informed him (as a butler at dinner informs his
master that there is no more of some wine asked for) that
there were no more charges.

'The scoundrels! What are they doing?' shouted the
officer, turning to Pierre.

The officer's face was red and perspiring and his eyes
glittered under his frowning brow.

'Run to the reserves and bring up the ammunition-
boxes!' he yelled, angrily avoiding Pierre with his eyes
and speaking to his men.

'I'll go,' said Pierre.

The officer, without answering him, strode across to
the opposite side.

'Don't fire . . . Wait!' he shouted.

The man who had been ordered to go for ammunition
stumbled against Pierre.

'Eh, sir, this is no place for you,' said he, and ran down
the slope.

Pierre ran after him, avoiding the spot where the young officer was sitting.

One cannon-ball, another, and a third, flew over him, falling in front, beside, and behind him. Pierre ran down the slope. 'Where am I going?' he suddenly asked himself when he was already near the green ammunition-wagons. He halted irresolutely, not knowing whether to return or go on. Suddenly a terrible concussion threw him backwards to the ground. At the same instant he was dazzled by a great flash of flame, and immediately a deafening roar, crackling and whistling, made his ears tingle.

When he came to himself he was sitting on the ground leaning on his hands; the ammunition-wagons he had been approaching no longer existed, only charred green boards and rags littered the scorched grass, and a horse, dangling fragments of its shafts behind it, galloped past, while another horse lay, like Pierre, on the ground, uttering prolonged and piercing cries.

CHAPTER XXXII

BESIDE himself with terror Pierre jumped up and ran back to the battery, as to the only refuge from the horrors that surrounded him.

On entering the earthwork he noticed that there were men doing something there but that no shots were being fired from the battery. He had no time to realize who these men were. He saw the senior officer lying on the earth wall with his back turned as if he were examining something down below, and that one of the soldiers he had noticed before was struggling forward shouting 'Brothers!' and trying to free himself from some men who were holding him by the arm. He also saw something else that was strange.

But he had not time to realize that the colonel had been killed, that the soldier shouting 'Brothers!' was a prisoner, and that another man had been bayoneted in the back before his eyes, for hardly had he run into the redoubt before a thin, sallow-faced, perspiring man in a blue uniform rushed on him sword in hand, shouting something. Instinctively guarding against the shock—for they had been running together at full speed before they saw one another—Pierre put out his hands and seized the man (a French officer) by the shoulder with one hand and by the throat with the other. The officer, dropping his sword, seized Pierre by his collar.

For some seconds they gazed with frightened eyes at one another's unfamiliar faces, and both were perplexed at what they had done and what they were to do next. 'Am I taken prisoner or have I taken him prisoner?' each was thinking. But the French officer was evidently more inclined to think he had been taken prisoner, because Pierre's strong hand, impelled by instinctive fear, squeezed his throat ever tighter and tighter. The Frenchman was about to say something, when just above their heads, terrible and low, a cannon-ball whistled, and it seemed to Pierre that the French officer's head had been torn off, so swiftly had he ducked it.

Pierre too bent his head and let his hands fall. Without further thought as to who had taken whom prisoner, the Frenchman ran back to the battery and Pierre ran down the slope stumbling over the dead and wounded who, it seemed to him, caught at his feet. But before he reached the foot of the knoll he was met by a dense crowd of Russian soldiers who, stumbling, tripping up, and shouting, ran merrily and wildly towards the battery. (This was the attack for which Ermólov claimed the credit, declaring that only his courage and good luck made such a feat possible: it was the attack in which he was said to have thrown some St. George's Crosses he had in his pocket into the battery, for the first soldiers to take who got there.)

The French who had occupied the battery fled, and our troops, shouting 'Hurrah!' pursued them so far beyond the battery that it was difficult to call them back.

The prisoners were brought down from the battery and among them was a wounded French general, whom the officers surrounded. Crowds of wounded—some known to Pierre and some unknown—Russians and

French, with faces distorted by suffering, walked, crawled, and were carried on stretchers, from the battery. Pierre again went up onto the knoll where he had spent over an hour, and of that family circle which had received him as a member he did not find a single one. There were many dead whom he did not know, but some he recognized. The young officer still sat in the same way bent double, in a pool of blood at the edge of the earth wall. The red-faced man was still twitching, but they did not carry him away.

Pierre ran down the slope once more.

'Now they will stop it, now they will be horrified at what they have done!' he thought, aimlessly going towards a crowd of stretcher-bearers moving from the battle-field.

But behind the veil of smoke the sun was still high, and in front and especially to the left, near Semënovsk, something seemed to be seething in the smoke, and the roar of cannon and musketry did not diminish, but even increased to desperation like a man who, straining himself, shrieks with all his remaining strength.

CHAPTER XXXIII

THE chief action of the battle of Borodinó was fought within the seven thousand feet between Borodinó and Bagratión's flèches. Beyond that space there was, on the one side a demonstration made by the Russians with Uvárov's cavalry at midday, and on the other side, beyond Utítsa, Poniatowski's collision with Tuchkóv; but these two were detached and feeble actions in comparison with what took place in the centre of the battle-field. On the field between Borodinó and the flèches, beside the wood, the chief action of the day took place on an open space visible from both sides, and was fought in the simplest and most artless way.

The battle began on both sides with a cannonade from several hundred guns.

Then when the whole field was covered with smoke, two divisions, Campan's and Dessaix's, advanced from the French right, while Murat's troops advanced on Borodinó from their left.

From the Shevárdino Redoubt where Napoleon was standing the flèches were a verst away, and it was more than two versts as the crow flies to Borodinó, so that Napoleon could not see what was happening there, especially as the smoke mingling with the mist hid the whole locality. The soldiers of Dessaix's division advancing against the flèches could only be seen till they had entered the hollow that lay between them and the flèches. As soon as they had descended into that hollow the smoke of the guns and musketry on the flèches grew so dense that it covered the whole approach on that side of it. Through the smoke glimpses could be caught of something black—probably men—and at times the glint of bayonets. But whether they were moving or stationary, whether they were French or Russian, could not be discovered from the Shevárdino Redoubt.

The sun had risen brightly, and its slanting rays struck straight into Napoleon's face as, shading his eyes with his hand, he looked at the flèches. The smoke spread out before them, and at times it looked as if the smoke were moving, at times as if the troops moved. Sometimes shouts were heard through the firing, but it was impossible to tell what was being done there.

Napoleon, standing on the knoll, looked through a field-glass, and in its small circlet saw smoke and men, sometimes his own and sometimes Russians, but when he looked again with the naked eye, he could not tell where what he had seen was.

He descended the knoll and began walking up and down before it.

Occasionally he stopped, listened to the firing, and gazed intently at the battle-field.

But not only was it impossible to make out what was happening from where he was standing down below, or from the knoll above on which some of his generals had taken their stand, but even from the flèches themselves—in which by this time there were now Russian and now French soldiers, alternately or together, dead, wounded, alive, frightened, or maddened—even at those flèches themselves it was impossible to make out what was taking place. There for several hours amid incessant cannon and musketry fire, now Russians were seen alone, now Frenchmen alone, now infantry and now cavalry; they appeared, fired, fell, collided not knowing what to do with one another, screamed and ran back again.

From the battle-field adjutants he had sent out, and orderlies from his marshals, kept galloping up to Napoleon with reports of the progress of the action, but all these reports were false, both because it was impossible in the heat of battle to say what was happening at any given moment, and because many of the adjutants did not go to the actual place of conflict, but reported what they had heard from others; and also because while an adjutant was riding the couple of versts to Napoleon circumstances changed and the news he brought was already becoming false. Thus an adjutant galloped up from Murat with tidings that Borodinó had been occupied and the bridge over the Kolochá was in the hands of the French. The adjutant asked whether Napoleon wished the troops to cross it? Napoleon gave orders that the troops should form up on the farther side and wait. But before that order was given—almost as soon in fact as the adjutant had left Borodinó—the bridge had been retaken by the Russians and burnt, in the very skirmish at which Pierre had been present at the beginning of the battle.

An adjutant galloped up from the flèches with a pale and frightened face and reported to Napoleon that their attack had been repulsed, Campan wounded, and Davoût killed; yet at the very time the adjutant had been told that the French had been repulsed, the flèches had in fact been recaptured by other French troops, and Davoût was alive and only slightly bruised. On the basis of these necessarily untrustworthy reports Napoleon gave his orders, which had either been executed before he gave them, or could not be and were not executed.

The marshals and generals, who were nearer to the field of battle but, like Napoleon, did not take part in the actual fighting and only occasionally went within musket range, made their own arrangements without asking Napoleon and issued orders where and in what directior to fire, and where cavalry should gallop and infantry should run. But even their orders, like Napoleon's, were seldom carried out, and then but partially. For the most part things happened contrary to their orders. Soldiers ordered to advance ran back on meeting grape-shot; soldiers ordered to remain where they were, suddenly, seeing Russians unexpectedly before them, sometimes rushed back and sometimes forward, and the cavalry dashed without orders in pursuit of the flying Russians. In this way two cavalry regiments galloped through the Semënovsk hollow and as soon as they reached the top of the incline turned round and galloped full speed back again. The infantry moved in the same way, sometimes running to quite other places than those they were ordered to go to. All orders as to where and when to move the guns, when to send infantry to shoot or horsemen to ride down the Russian infantry—all such orders were given by the officers on the spot nearest to the units concerned, without asking either Ney, Davoût, or Murat, much less Napoleon. They did not fear getting into trouble for not fulfilling orders or for acting on their own initiative, for in battle what is at stake is what is dearest to man—his own life, and it sometimes seems that safety lies in running back, sometimes in running forward; and these men who were right in the heat of the battle, acted according to the mood of the moment. In reality however all these movements forward and backward did not improve or alter the position of the troops. All their rushing and galloping at one another did little harm, the harm of disablement and death was caused by the balls and bullets that flew over the fields on which these men were floundering about. As soon as they left the place where the balls and bullets were flying about, their superiors, located in the background, re-formed them and brought them under discipline, and under the influence of that discipline led them back to the zone of fire, where under the influence of fear of death they lost their discipline and rushed about according to the chance promptings of the throng.

CHAPTER XXXIV

NAPOLEON'S generals—Davoût, Ney, and Murat, who were near that region of fire and sometimes even entered it—repeatedly led into it huge masses of well-ordered troops. But contrary to what had always happened in their former battles, instead of the news they expected of the enemy's flight, these orderly masses returned thence as disorganized and terrified mobs. The generals re-formed them, but their numbers constantly decreased. In the middle of the day Murat sent his adjutant to Napoleon to demand reinforcements.

Napoleon sat at the foot of the knoll, drinking punch, when Murat's adjutant galloped up with an assurance that the Russians would be routed if his Majesty would let him have another division.

'Reinforcements?' said Napoleon in a tone of stern surprise, looking at the adjutant—a handsome lad with long black curls arranged like Murat's own—as though he did not understand his words.

'Reinforcements!' thought Napoleon to himself. 'How can they need reinforcements when they already have half the army directed against a weak, unentrenched Russian wing?'

'Tell the King of Naples,' said he sternly, 'that it is not noon yet, and I don't yet see my chess-board clearly. Go! . . .'

The handsome boy-adjutant with the long hair sighed deeply without removing his hand from his hat, and galloped back to where his men were being slaughtered.

Napoleon rose, and having summoned Caulaincourt and Berthier began talking to them about matters unconnected with the battle.

In the midst of this conversation, which was beginning to interest Napoleon, Berthier's eyes turned to look at a general with a suite who was galloping towards the knoll on a lathering horse. It was Belliard. Having dismounted he went up to the Emperor with rapid strides, and in a loud voice began boldly demonstrating the necessity of sending reinforcements. He swore on his honour that the Russians were lost if the Emperor would give another division.

Napoleon shrugged his shoulders and continued to pace up and down without replying. Belliard began talking loudly and eagerly to the generals of the suite around him.

'You are very fiery, Belliard,' said Napoleon when he again came up to the general. 'In the heat of a battle it is easy to make a mistake. Go and have another look and then come back to me.'

Before Belliard was out of sight a messenger from another part of the battle-field galloped up.

'Now then, what do you want?' asked Napoleon in the tone of a man irritated at being continually disturbed.

'Sire, the Prince . . .' began the adjutant.

'Asks for reinforcements?' said Napoleon with an angry gesture.

The adjutant bent his head affirmatively and began to report, but the Emperor turned from him, took a couple of steps, stopped, came back, and called Berthier.

'We must give reserves,' he said, moving his arms slightly apart. 'Who do you think should be sent there?' he asked of Berthier (whom he subsequently termed 'that gosling I have made an eagle').

'Send Claparède's division, Sire,' replied Berthier who knew all the divisions, regiments, and battalions, by heart.

Napoleon nodded assent.

The adjutant galloped to Claparède's division and a few minutes later the Young Guards stationed behind the knoll moved forward. Napoleon gazed silently in that direction.

'No!' he suddenly said to Berthier. 'I can't send Claparède. Send Friant's division.'

Though there was no advantage in sending Friant's division instead of Claparède's, and even an obvious inconvenience and delay in stopping Claparède and sending Friant now, the order was carried out exactly. Napoleon did not notice that in regard to his army he was playing the part of a doctor who hinders by his medicines—a role he so justly understood and condemned.

Friant's division disappeared, as the others had done, into the smoke of the battle-field. From all sides adjutants continued to arrive at a gallop, and as if by agreement all said the same thing. They all asked for reinforcements, and all said that the Russians were holding their positions and maintaining a hellish fire under which the French army was melting away.

Napoleon sat on a camp-stool wrapped in thought.

M. de Beausset, the man so fond of travel, having fasted since morning came up to the Emperor and ventured respectfully to suggest lunch to his Majesty.

'I hope I may now congratulate your Majesty on a victory?' said he.

Napoleon silently shook his head in negation. Assuming the negation to refer only to the victory and not to the lunch, M. de Beausset ventured with respectful jocularity to remark that there is no reason for not having lunch when one can get it.

'Go away . . .' exclaimed Napoleon suddenly and morosely, and turned aside.

A beatific smile of regret, repentance, and ecstasy, beamed on M. de Beausset's face and he glided away to the other generals.

Napoleon was experiencing a feeling of depression like that of an ever-lucky gambler who after recklessly flinging money about and always winning, suddenly, just when he has calculated all the chances of the game, finds that the more he considers his play the more surely he loses.

His troops were the same, his generals the same, the same preparations had been made, the same dispositions, and the same proclamation *courte et énergique*, he himself was still the same, he knew that and knew that he was now even more experienced and skilful than before. Even the enemy was the same as at Austerlitz and Friedland—yet the terrible stroke of his arm had supernaturally become impotent.

All the old methods that had been unfailingly crowned with success: the concentration of batteries on one point, an attack by reserves to break the enemy's line and a cavalry attack by 'the men of iron', all these methods had already been employed, yet not only was there no victory, but from all sides came the same news of generals killed and wounded, of reinforcements needed, of the impossibility of driving back the Russians, and of disorganization among his own troops.

Formerly, after he had given two or three orders and uttered a few phrases, marshals and adjutants had come galloping up with congratulations and happy faces, announcing the trophies taken, the corps of prisoners, bundles of enemy eagles and standards, cannon and stores, and Murat had only begged leave to loose the cavalry to gather in the baggage-wagons. So it had been at Lodi, Marengo, Arcola, Jena, Austerlitz, Wagram, and so on. But now something strange was happening to his troops.

Despite news of the capture of the flèches, Napoleon saw that this was not the same, not at all the same, as what had happened in his former battles. He saw that what he was feeling was felt by all the men about him experienced in the art of war. All their faces looked dejected, and they all shunned one another's eyes—only a de Beausset could fail to grasp the meaning of what was happening.

But Napoleon with his long experience of war well knew the meaning of a battle not gained by the attacking side in eight hours, after all efforts had been expended. He knew that it was a lost battle and that the least accident might now—with the fight balanced on such a strained centre—destroy him and his army.

When he ran his mind over the whole of this strange Russian campaign, in which not one battle had been won, and in which not a flag, or cannon, or army corps, had been captured in two months, when he looked at the concealed depression on the faces around him and heard reports of the Russians still holding their ground—a terrible feeling like a nightmare took possession of him, and all the unlucky accidents that might destroy him occurred to his mind. The Russians might fall on his left wing, might break through his centre, he himself might be killed by a stray cannon-ball. All this was possible. In former battles he had only considered the possibilities of success, but now innumerable unlucky chances presented themselves, and he expected them all. Yes, it was like a dream in which a man fancies that a ruffian is coming to

attack him, and raises his arm to strike that ruffian a
terrible blow which he knows should annihilate him, but
then feels that his arm drops powerless and limp like a
rag, and the horror of unavoidable destruction seizes him
in his helplessness.

The news that the Russians were attacking the left flank
of the French army aroused that horror in Napoleon.
He sat silently on a camp-stool below the knoll, with head
bowed and elbows on his knees. Berthier approached and
suggested that they should ride along the line to ascertain
the position of affairs.

'What? What do you say?' asked Napoleon. 'Yes, tell
them to bring me my horse.'

He mounted and rode towards Semënovsk.

Amid the powder-smoke slowly dispersing over the
whole space through which Napoleon rode, horses and
men were lying in pools of blood, singly or in heaps.
Neither Napoleon nor any of his generals had ever before
seen such horrors or so many slain in such a small area.
The roar of guns, that had not ceased for ten hours,
wearied the ear and gave a peculiar significance to the
spectacle, as music does to *tableaux vivants*. Napoleon
rode up the high ground at Semënovsk, and through the
smoke saw ranks of men in uniforms of a colour unfamiliar to him. They were Russians.

The Russians stood in serried ranks behind Semënovsk
village and its knoll, and their guns boomed incessantly
along their line and sent forth clouds of smoke. It was
no longer a battle: it was a continuous slaughter which
could be of no avail either to the French or the Russians.
Napoleon stopped his horse and again fell into the reverie
from which Berthier had roused him. He could not stop
what was going on before him and around him and was
supposed to be directed by him and to depend on him,
and from its lack of success this affair, for the first time,
seemed to him unnecessary and horrible.

One of the generals rode up to Napoleon and ventured
to offer to lead the Old Guard into action. Ney and
Berthier, standing near Napoleon, exchanged looks
and smiled contemptuously at this general's senseless
offer.

Napoleon bowed his head and remained silent a long time.

'At eight hundred leagues[1] from France I will not have my Guard destroyed!' he said, and turning his horse rode back to Shevárdino.

CHAPTER XXXV

ON the rug-covered bench where Pierre had seen him in the morning sat Kutúzov, his grey head hanging, his heavy body relaxed. He gave no orders, but only assented to or dissented from what others suggested.

'Yes, yes, do that,' he replied to various proposals. 'Yes, yes: go, dear boy, and have a look,' he would say to one or another of those about him; or, 'No, don't, we'd better wait!' He listened to the reports that were brought him, and gave directions when his subordinates demanded that of him; but when listening to the reports it seemed as if he were not interested in the import of the words spoken, but rather in something else—in the expression of face and the tone of voice of those who were reporting. By long years of military experience he knew, and with the wisdom of age understood, that it is impossible for one man to direct hundreds of thousands of others struggling with death, and he knew that the result of a battle is decided not by the orders of a commander-in-chief, nor the place where the troops are stationed, not by the number of cannon or of slaughtered men, but by that intangible force called the spirit of the army, and he watched this force and guided it in as far as that was in his power.

Kutúzov's general expression was one of concentrated quiet attention, and his face wore a strained look as if he found it difficult to master the fatigue of his old and feeble body.

At eleven o'clock they brought him news that the flèches captured by the French had been retaken, but that

---

[1] The French *lieue*, or league, is about two and a half miles, so Napoleon's calculation was that he was two thousand miles march from home.

Prince Bagratión was wounded. Kutúzov groaned and swayed his head.

'Ride over to Prince Peter Ivánovich[1] and find out about it exactly,' he said to one of his adjutants, and then turned to the Duke of Würtemburg who was standing behind him.

'Will your Highness, please, take command of the First Army?'

Soon after the Duke's departure—before he could possibly have reached Semënovsk—his adjutant came back from him and told Kutúzov that the Duke asked for more troops.

Kutúzov made a grimace and sent an order to Dokh-túrov to take over the command of the First Army, and a request to the Duke—whom he said he could not spare at such an important moment—to return to him. When they brought him news that Murat had been taken prisoner, and the staff-officers congratulated him, Kutúzov smiled.

'Wait a little, gentlemen,' said he. 'The battle is won, and there is nothing extraordinary in the capture of Murat. Still, it is better to wait before we rejoice.'

But he sent an adjutant to take the news round the army.

When Scherbínin came galloping from the left flank with news that the French had captured the flèches and the village of Semënovsk, Kutúzov, guessing by the sounds of the battle and by Scherbínin's looks that the news was bad, rose as if to stretch his legs, and taking Scherbínin's arm led him aside.

'Go, my dear fellow,' he said to Ermólov, 'and see whether something can't be done.'

Kutúzov was in Górki, near the centre of the Russian position. The attack directed by Napoleon against our left flank had been several times repulsed. In the centre the French had not got beyond Borodinó, and on their left flank Uvárov's cavalry had put the French to flight.

Towards three o'clock the French attacks ceased. On the faces of all who came from the field of battle, and of those who stood around him, Kutúzov noticed an

---

[1] Bagratión.

expression of extreme tension. He was satisfied with the day's success—a success exceeding his expectation, but the old man's strength was failing him. Several times his head dropped low as if it were falling, and he dozed off. Dinner was brought him.

Adjutant-General Wolzogen, the man who when riding past Prince Andrew had said, 'the war should be extended widely,' and whom Bagratión so detested, rode up while Kutúzov was at dinner. Wolzogen had come from Barclay de Tolly to report on the progress of affairs on the left flank. The sagacious Barclay de Tolly, seeing crowds of wounded men running back and the disordered rear of the army, weighed all the circumstances, concluded that the battle was lost, and sent his favourite officer to the commander-in-chief with that news.

Kutúzov was chewing a piece of roast chicken with difficulty, and glanced at Wolzogen with eyes that brightened under their puckering lids.

Wolzogen nonchalantly stretching his legs, approached Kutúzov with a half-contemptuous smile on his lips, scarcely touching the peak of his cap.

He treated his Serene Highness with a somewhat affected nonchalance intended to show that, as a highly trained military man, he left it to Russians to make an idol of this useless old man, but that he knew whom he was dealing with. '*Der alte Herr*' (as in their own set the Germans called Kutúzov) 'is making himself very comfortable,' thought Wolzogen, and looking severely at the dishes in front of Kutúzov he began to report to 'the old gentleman' the position of affairs on the left flank as Barclay had ordered him to and as he had himself seen and understood it.

'All the points of our position are in the enemy's hands and we cannot dislodge them for lack of troops, the men are running away and it is impossible to stop them,' he reported.

Kutúzov ceased chewing and fixed an astonished gaze on Wolzogen, as if not understanding what was said to him. Wolzogen, noticing 'the old gentleman's' agitation, said with a smile:

'I have not considered it right to conceal from your

Serene Highness what I have seen. The troops are in complete disorder . . .'

'You have seen? You have seen? . . .' Kutúzov shouted frowning, and rising quickly he went up to Wolzogen.

'How . . . how dare you! . . .' he shouted, choking and making a threatening gesture with his trembling arms: 'How dare you, sir, say that to *me*? You know nothing about it. Tell General Barclay from me that his information is incorrect and that the real course of the battle is better known to me, the commander-in-chief, than to him.'

Wolzogen was about to make a rejoinder, but Kutúzov interrupted him.

'The enemy has been repulsed on the left and defeated on the right flank. If you have seen amiss, sir, do not allow yourself to say what you don't know! Be so good as to ride to General Barclay and inform him of my firm intention to attack the enemy to-morrow,' said Kutúzov sternly.

All were silent, and the only sound audible was the heavy breathing of the panting old general.

'They are repulsed everywhere, for which I thank God and our brave army! The enemy is beaten, and to-morrow we shall drive him from the sacred soil of Russia,' said Kutúzov crossing himself, and he suddenly sobbed as his eyes filled with tears.

Wolzogen, shrugging his shoulders and curling his lips, stepped silently aside, marvelling at 'the old gentleman's' conceited stupidity.

'Ah, here he is, my hero!' said Kutúzov to a portly, handsome, dark-haired general, who was just ascending the knoll.

This was Raévski, who had spent the whole day at the most important part of the field of Borodinó.

Raévski reported that the troops were firmly holding their ground and that the French no longer ventured to attack.

After hearing him, Kutúzov said in French:

'Then you do not think *like some others* that we must retreat?'

'On the contrary, your Highness, in indecisive actions it is always the most stubborn who remain victors,' replied Raévski, 'and in my opinion . . .'

'Kaysárov!' Kutúzov called to his adjutant. 'Sit down and write out the order of the day for to-morrow. And you,' he continued, addressing another, 'ride along the line and announce that to-morrow we attack.'

While Kutúzov was talking to Raévski and dictating the order of the day, Wolzogen returned from Barclay, and said that General Barclay de Tolly wished to have written confirmation of the order the field-marshal had given.

Kutúzov, without looking at Wolzogen, gave directions for the order to be written out which the former commander-in-chief, to avoid personal responsibility, very judiciously wished to receive.

And by means of that mysterious indefinable bond which maintains throughout an army one and the same temper, known as 'the spirit of the army', and which constitutes the chief sinew of war, Kutúzov's words, his order for a battle next day, immediately became known from one end of the army to the other.

It was far from being the same words or the same order that reached the farthest links of that chain. The tales passing from mouth to mouth at different ends of the army did not even resemble what Kutúzov had said, but the sense of his words spread everywhere because what he said was not the outcome of cunning calculations, but of a feeling that lay in the commander-in-chief's soul as in that of every Russian.

And on learning that to-morrow they were to attack the enemy, and hearing from the highest quarters a confirmation of what they wanted to believe, the exhausted wavering men felt comforted and inspirited.

CHAPTER XXXVI

PRINCE ANDREW'S regiment was among the reserves which till after one o'clock were stationed inactive behind Semënovsk under heavy artillery fire. Towards two o'clock the regiment, having already lost more than two hundred men, was moved forward into a trampled oatfield in the gap between Semënovsk and the Knoll Battery where thousands of men perished that day and on which an intense, concentrated fire from several hundred enemy guns was directed between one and two o'clock.

Without moving from that spot or firing a single shot the regiment here lost another third of its men. From in front and especially from the right, in the unlifting smoke the guns boomed, and out of the mysterious domain of smoke that overlay the whole space in front, quick hissing cannon-balls and slow whistling shells flew unceasingly. At times, as if to allow them a respite, a quarter of an hour passed during which the cannon-balls and shells all flew overhead, but sometimes several men were torn from the regiment in a minute, and the slain were continually being dragged away and the wounded carried off.

With each fresh blow less and less chance of life remained for those not yet killed. The regiment stood in columns of battalion three hundred paces apart, but nevertheless the men were always in one and the same mood. All alike were taciturn and morose. Talk was rarely heard in the ranks, and it ceased altogether every time the thud of a successful shot and the cry of 'stretchers!' was heard. Most of the time, by their officers' order, the men sat on the ground. One, having taken off his shako carefully loosened the gathers of its lining and drew them tight again; another, rubbing some dry clay between his palms, polished his bayonet; another fingered the strap and pulled the buckle of his bandolier, while another smoothed and refolded his leg-bands and put his boots on again. Some built little houses of the tufts in the ploughed ground, or plaited baskets from the straw in the cornfield. All seemed fully absorbed in these pursuits. When men were killed or wounded, when rows of stretchers went past, when some troops retreated, and when great masses of the enemy came into view through the smoke, no one paid any attention to these things. But when our artillery or cavalry advanced or some of our infantry were seen to move forward, words of approval were heard on all sides. But the liveliest attention was attracted by occurrences quite apart from, and unconnected with, the battle. It was as if the minds of these morally exhausted men found relief in everyday, commonplace occurrences. A battery of artillery was passing in front of the regiment. The horse of an ammunition cart put its leg over a trace. 'Hey, look at the trace horse! ... Get her leg out! She'll fall ... Ah, they don't see it!' came identical shouts from the ranks all along the regiment. Another time general attention was attracted by a small brown dog, coming heaven knows whence, which trotted in a preoccupied manner in front of the ranks with tail stiffly erect till suddenly a shell fell close by, when it yelped, tucked its tail between its legs, and darted aside. Yells and shrieks of laughter rose from the whole regiment. But such distractions lasted only a moment, and for eight hours the men had been inactive, without food, in constant fear of death, and their pale and gloomy faces grew ever paler and gloomier.

Prince Andrew, pale and gloomy like every one in the regiment, paced up and down from the border of one patch to another, at the edge of a meadow beside an oatfield, with head bowed and arms behind his back. There was nothing for him to do and no orders to be given. Everything went on of itself. The killed were dragged from the front, the wounded carried away, and the ranks closed up. If any soldiers ran to the rear they returned immediately and hastily. At first Prince Andrew, considering it his duty to rouse the courage of the men and to set them an example, walked about among the ranks, but he soon became convinced that this was unnecessary and that there was nothing he could teach them. All the powers of his soul, as of every soldier there, were unconsciously bent on avoiding the contemplation of the horrors of their situation. He walked along the meadow, dragging his feet, rustling the grass, and gazing at the dust that covered his boots; now he took big strides trying to keep to the footprints left on the meadow by mowers, then he counted his steps, calculating how often he must walk from one strip to another to walk a mile, then he stripped the flowers from the wormwood that grew along a boundary rut, rubbed them in his palms, and smelt their pungent sweetly bitter scent. Nothing remained of the previous day's thoughts. He thought of nothing. He listened with weary ears to the ever-recurring sounds, distinguishing the whistle of flying projectiles from the booming of the reports, glanced at the tiresomely familiar faces of the men of the first battalion, and waited. 'Here it comes . . . this one is coming our way again!' he thought, listening to the approaching whistle in the hidden region of smoke. 'One, another! Again! It has hit . . .' He stopped and looked at the ranks. 'No, it has gone over. But this one has hit!' And again he started trying to reach the boundary strip in sixteen paces. A whizz and a thud! Five paces from him a cannon-ball tore up the dry earth and disappeared. A chill ran down his back. Again he glanced at the ranks. Probably many had been hit—a large crowd had gathered near the second battalion.

'Adjutant!' he shouted. 'Order them not to crowd together.'

The adjutant, having obeyed this instruction, approached Prince Andrew. From the other side a battalion commander rode up.

'Look out!' came a frightened cry from a soldier and, like a bird whirring in rapid flight and alighting on the ground, a shell dropped with little noise within two steps of Prince Andrew and close to the battalion commander's horse. The horse first, regardless of whether it was right or wrong to show fear, snorted, reared almost throwing the major, and galloped aside. The horse's terror infected the men.

'Lie down!' cried the adjutant, throwing himself flat on the ground.

Prince Andrew hesitated. The smoking shell spun like a top between him and the prostrate adjutant near a wormwood plant between the field and the meadow.

'Can this be death?' thought Prince Andrew, looking with a quite new, envious glance at the grass, the wormwood, and the streamlet of smoke that curled up from the rotating black ball. 'I cannot, I do not wish to die. I love life—I love this grass, this earth, this air . . .' He thought this, and at the same time remembered that people were looking at him.

'It's shameful, sir!' he said to the adjutant. 'What . . .'

He did not finish speaking. At one and the same moment came the sound of an explosion, a whistle of splinters as from a breaking window frame, a suffocating smell of powder, and Prince Andrew started to one side, raising his arm, and fell on his chest. Several officers ran up to him. From the right side of his abdomen blood was welling out making a large stain on the grass.

The militiamen with stretchers, who were called up, stood behind the officers. Prince Andrew lay on his chest with his face in the grass, breathing heavily and noisily.

'What are you waiting for? Come along!'

The peasants went up and took him by his shoulders and legs, but he moaned piteously and, exchanging looks, they set him down again.

'Pick him up, lift him, it's all the same!' cried some one.

They again took him by the shoulders and laid him on the stretcher.

'Ah God! My God! What is it? The stomach? That means death! My God!'—voices among the officers were heard saying.

'It flew a hair's breadth past my ear,' said the adjutant.

The peasants, adjusting the stretcher to their shoulders, started hurriedly along the path they had trodden down, to the dressing-station.

'Keep in step! Ah . . . those peasants!' shouted an officer, seizing by their shoulders and checking the peasants, who were walking unevenly and jolting the stretcher.

'Get into step, Fëdor . . . I say, Fëdor!' said the foremost peasant.

'Now that's right!' said the one behind joyfully, when he had got into step.

'Your Excellency! Eh, Prince!' said the trembling voice of Timókhin, who had run up and was looking down on the stretcher.

Prince Andrew opened his eyes and looked up at the speaker from the stretcher into which his head had sunk deep, and again his eyelids drooped.

The militiamen carried Prince Andrew to the dressing-station by the wood, where wagons were stationed. The dressing-station consisted of three tents with flaps turned back, pitched at the edge of a birch wood. In the wood, wagons and horses were standing. The horses were eating oats from their movable troughs and sparrows flew down and pecked the grains that fell. Some crows, scenting blood, flew among the birch trees cawing impatiently. Around the tents, over more than five acres, blood-stained men in various garbs stood, sat, or lay. Around the wounded stood crowds of soldier stretcher-bearers with dismal and attentive faces, whom the officers keeping order tried in vain to drive from the spot. Disregarding the officers' orders the soldiers stood leaning against their stretchers and gazing intently, as if trying to comprehend the difficult problem of what was taking place before them. From the tents came now loud angry cries, and now plaintive groans. Occasionally dressers ran out to fetch water, or to point out those who were to be brought in next. The wounded men awaiting their turn outside the tents groaned, sighed, wept, screamed, swore, or asked for vodka. Some were delirious. Prince Andrew's bearers stepping over the wounded who had not yet been bandaged, took him, as a regimental commander, close up to one of the tents and there stopped, awaiting instructions. Prince Andrew opened his eyes and for a long time could not make out what was going on around him. He remembered the meadow, the wormwood, the field, the whirling black ball, and his sudden rush of passionate love of life. Two steps from him, leaning against a branch and talking loudly and attracting general attention, stood a tall, handsome, black-haired non-commissioned officer with a bandaged head. He had been wounded in the head and leg by bullets. Around him, eagerly listening to his talk, a crowd of wounded and stretcher-bearers was gathered.

'We kicked *him* out from there so that he chucked everything, we grabbed the King himself!' cried he, looking around him with eyes that glittered with fever. 'If only reserves had come up just then, lads, there wouldn't have been nothing left of him! I tell you surely . . .'

Like all the others near the speaker, Prince Andrew looked at him with shining eyes and experienced a sense of comfort. 'But isn't it all the same now?' thought he. 'And what will be there, and what has there been here? Why was I so reluctant to part with life? There was something in this life I did not and do not understand ...'

CHAPTER XXXVII

ONE of the doctors came out of the tent in a blood-stained apron, holding a cigar between the thumb and little finger of one of his small bloodstained hands, so as not to smear it. He raised his head and looked about him, but above the level of the wounded men. He evidently wanted a little respite. After turning his head from right to left for some time he sighed and looked down.

'All right, immediately,' he replied to a dresser who pointed Prince Andrew out to him, and he told them to carry him into the tent.

Murmurs arose among the wounded who were waiting.

'It seems that even in the next world only the gentry are to have a chance!' remarked one.

Prince Andrew was carried in and laid on a table that had only just been cleared, and which a dresser was washing down. Prince Andrew could not make out distinctly what was in that tent. The pitiful groans from all sides, and the torturing pain in his thigh, stomach, and back, distracted him. All he saw about him merged into a general impression of naked bleeding human bodies that seemed to fill the whole of the low tent, as a few weeks previously, on that hot August day, such bodies had filled the dirty pond beside the Smolénsk road. Yes, it was the same flesh, the same *chair à canon*, the sight of which had even then filled him with horror, as by a presentiment.

There were three operating tables in the tent. Two were occupied, and on the third they placed Prince Andrew. For a little while he was left alone and in-voluntarily witnessed what was taking place on the other two tables. On the nearest one sat a Tartar, probably a Cossack judging by the uniform thrown down beside him. Four soldiers were holding him, and a spectacled doctor was cutting into his muscular brown back.

'Ooh, ooh, ooh!' grunted the Tartar, and suddenly lifting up his swarthy snub-nosed face with its high cheek-bones, and baring his white teeth, he began to wriggle and twitch his body and utter piercing, ringing, and pro-longed yells. On the other table, round which many people were crowding, a tall well-fed man lay on his back with his head thrown back. His curly hair, its colour and the shape of his head, seemed strangely familiar to Prince Andrew. Several dressers were pressing on his chest to hold him down. One large white plump leg twitched rapidly all the time with a feverish tremor. The man was sobbing and choking convulsively. Two doctors—one of whom was pale and trembling—were silently doing something to this man's other, gory leg. When he had finished with the Tartar, whom they covered with an overcoat, the spectacled doctor came up to Prince Andrew wiping his hands.

He glanced at Prince Andrew's face and quickly turned away.

'Undress him! What are you waiting for?' he cried angrily to the dressers.

His very first remotest recollections of childhood came back to Prince Andrew's mind when the dresser with sleeves rolled up began hastily to undo the buttons of his clothes and undressed him. The doctor bent down over the wound, felt it, and sighed deeply. Then he made a sign to some one, and the torturing pain in his abdomen caused Prince Andrew to lose consciousness. When he came to himself the splintered portions of his thigh-bone had been extracted, the torn flesh cut away, and the wound bandaged. Water was being sprinkled on his face. As soon as Prince Andrew opened his eyes, the doctor bent over, kissed him silently on the lips, and hurried away.

After the sufferings he had been enduring Prince Andrew enjoyed a blissful feeling such as he had not experienced for a long time. All the best and happiest

moments of his life—especially his earliest childhood,
when he used to be undressed and put to bed, and when
leaning over him his nurse sang him to sleep and he,
burying his head in the pillow, felt happy in the mere
consciousness of life—returned to his memory, not merely
as something past but as something present.

The doctors were busily engaged with the wounded
man the shape of whose head seemed familiar to Prince
Andrew: they were lifting him up and trying to quiet him.

'Show it me . . . Oh, ooh . . . oh! Oh, ooh!' his
frightened moans could be heard, subdued by suffering
and broken by sobs.

Hearing those moans Prince Andrew wanted to weep.
Whether because he was dying without glory, or because
he was sorry to part with life, or because of those memories
of a childhood that could not return, or because he was
suffering and others were suffering and that man near
him was groaning so piteously—he felt like weeping
childlike, kindly, and almost happy, tears.

The wounded man was shown his amputated leg
stained with clotted blood and with the boot still on.

'Oh! Oh, ooh!' he sobbed, like a woman.

The doctor who had been standing beside him, pre-
venting Prince Andrew from seeing his face, moved away.

'My God! What is this? Why is he here?' said Prince
Andrew to himself.

In the miserable, sobbing, enfeebled man whose leg had
just been amputated, he recognized Anatole Kurágin.
Men were supporting him in their arms and offering him
a glass of water, but his trembling, swollen lips could not
grasp its rim. Anatole was sobbing painfully. 'Yes, it is
he! Yes, that man is somehow closely and painfully connected with me,' thought Prince Andrew, not yet clearly
grasping what he saw before him. 'What is the connexion
of that man with my childhood and my life?' he asked
himself, without finding an answer. And suddenly a new
unexpected memory from that realm of pure and loving
childhood presented itself to him. He remembered
Natásha as he had seen her for the first time at the ball
in 1810, with her slender neck and arms, and with a
frightened happy face ready for rapture, and love and

tenderness for her, stronger and more vivid than ever, awoke in his soul. He now remembered the connexion that existed between himself and this man who was dimly gazing at him through tears that filled his swollen eyes. He remembered everything, and ecstatic pity and love for that man overflowed his happy heart.

Prince Andrew could no longer restrain himself, and wept tender loving tears for his fellow men, for himself, and for his own and their errors.

'Compassion, love of our brothers, for those who love us and for those who hate us, love of our enemies; yes, that love which God preached on earth and which Princess Mary taught me and I did not understand—that is what made me sorry to part with life, that is what remained for me had I lived. But now it is too late. I know it!'

CHAPTER XXXVIII

THE terrible spectacle of the battle-field covered with dead and wounded, together with the heaviness of his head and the news that some twenty generals he knew personally had been killed or wounded, and the consciousness of the impotence of his once mighty arm, produced an unexpected impression on Napoleon who usually liked to look at the killed and wounded, thereby he considered testing his strength of mind. This day the horrible appearance of the battle-field overcame that strength of mind which he thought constituted his merit and his greatness. He rode hurriedly from the battle-field and returned to the Shevárdino knoll, where he sat on his camp stool, his sallow face swollen and heavy, his eyes dim, his nose red, and his voice hoarse, involuntarily listening, with downcast eyes, to the sounds of firing. With painful dejection he awaited the end of this action, in which he regarded himself as a participant and which he was unable to arrest. A personal, human feeling for a brief moment got the better of the artificial phantasm of life he had served so long. He felt in his own person the sufferings and death he had witnessed on the battle-field. The heaviness of his head and chest reminded him of the possibility of suffering and death for himself. At that moment he did not desire Moscow, or victory, or glory (what need had he of more glory?). The one thing he wished for was rest, tranquillity, and freedom. But when he had been on the Semënovsk heights the artillery commander had proposed to him to bring several batteries of artillery up to those heights to strengthen the fire on the Russian troops crowded in front of Knyazkóvo. Napoleon had assented and had given orders that news should be brought him of the effect those batteries produced.

An adjutant came now to inform him that the fire of two hundred guns had been concentrated on the Russians, as he had ordered, but that they still held their ground.

'Our fire is mowing them down by rows, but still they hold on,' said the adjutant.

'They want more!...' said Napoleon in a hoarse voice.

'Sire?' asked the adjutant, who had not heard the remark.

'They want more!' croaked Napoleon frowning. 'Let them have it!'

Even before he gave that order the thing he did not desire, and for which he only gave the order because he thought it was expected of him, was being done. And he fell back into that artificial realm of imaginary greatness, and again—as a horse walking a treadmill thinks it is doing something for itself—he submissively fulfilled the cruel, sad, gloomy, and inhuman role predestined for him.

And not for that day and hour alone were the mind and conscience of this man darkened on whom the responsibility for what was happening lay more than on all the others who took part in it. Never to the end of his life could he understand goodness, beauty, or truth, or the significance of his actions, which were too contrary to goodness and truth, too remote from everything human, for him ever to be able to grasp their meaning. He could not disavow his actions, belauded as they were by half the world, and so he had to repudiate truth, goodness, and all humanity.

Not only on that day, as he rode over the battle-field strewn with men killed and maimed (by his will as he believed) did he reckon as he looked at them how many Russians there were for each Frenchman and, deceiving himself, find reason for rejoicing in the calculation that there were five Russians for every Frenchman. Not on that day alone did he write in a letter to Paris, that 'the battle-field was superb', because fifty thousand corpses lay there, but even on the island of St. Helena, in the peaceful solitude where he said he intended to devote his leisure to an account of the great deeds he had done, he wrote:

'The Russian war should have been the most popular war of modern times: it was a war of good sense, for real interests, for the tranquillity and security of all; it was purely pacific and conservative.

'It was a war for a great cause, the end of uncertainties and the beginning of security. A new horizon and new labours were opening out, full of well-being and prosperity for all. The European system was already founded; all that remained was to organize it.

'Satisfied on these great points, and with tranquillity everywhere, I too should have had my *Congress* and my *Holy Alliance*. Those ideas were stolen from me. In that reunion of great sovereigns we should have discussed our interests like one family, and have rendered account to the peoples as clerk to master.

'Europe would in this way soon have been, in fact, but one people, and any one who travelled anywhere would have found himself always in the common fatherland. I should have demanded the freedom of all the navigable rivers for everybody, that the seas should be common to all, and that the great standing armies should be reduced henceforth to mere guards for the Sovereigns.

'On returning to France, to the bosom of the great, strong, magnificent, peaceful, and glorious fatherland, I should have proclaimed her frontiers immutable; all future wars purely *defensive*, all aggrandizement *antinational*. I should have associated my son in the Empire; my *dictatorship* would have been finished, and his constitutional reign would have begun.

'Paris would have been the capital of the world, and the French the envy of the nations!

'My leisure then, and my old age, would have been devoted, in company with the Empress and during the royal apprenticeship of my son, to leisurely visiting, with our own horses and like a true country couple, every corner of the Empire, receiving complaints, redressing wrongs, and scattering public buildings and benefactions on all sides and everywhere.'

Napoleon, predestined by Providence for the gloomy role of executioner of the peoples, assured himself that the aim of his actions had been the peoples' welfare, and that he could control the fate of millions and by the employment of power confer benefactions.

'Of four hundred thousand men who crossed the Vistula,' he wrote further of the Russian war, 'half were Austrians, Prussians, Saxons, Poles, Bavarians, Würtembergers, Mecklenburgers, Spaniards, Italians, and Neapolitans. The Imperial army, strictly speaking, was one-third composed of Dutch, Belgians, men from the borders of the Rhine, Piedmontese, Swiss, Genevese, Tuscans, Romans, inhabitants of the Thirty-Second Military Division, of Bremen, of Hamburg, and so on: it included scarcely a hundred and forty thousand who spoke French. The Russian expedition actually cost France less than fifty thousand men; the Russian army in the retreat from Vílna to Moscow lost in the various battles four times more men than the French army; the burning of Moscow cost the lives of a hundred thousand Russians who died of cold and want in the woods; finally, in its march from Moscow to the Oder the Russian army also suffered from the severity of the season; so that by the time it reached Vílna it numbered only fifty thousand and at Kálisch less than eighteen thousand.'

He imagined that the war with Russia came about by his will, and the horrors that occurred did not stagger his soul. He boldly took the whole responsibility for what happened, and his darkened mind found justification in the belief that among the hundreds of thousands who perished there were fewer Frenchmen than Hessians and Bavarians.

CHAPTER XXXIX

SEVERAL tens of thousands of the slain lay in diverse postures and various uniforms on the fields and meadows belonging to the Davýdov family and to the Crown serfs—those fields and meadows where for hundreds of years the peasants of Borodinó, Górki, Shevárdino, and Semënovsk had reaped their harvests and pastured their cattle. At the dressing-stations the grass and earth were soaked with blood for a space of some three acres around. Crowds of men of various arms, wounded and unwounded, with frightened faces, dragged themselves back to Mozháysk from the one army, and back to Valúevo from the other. Other crowds, exhausted and hungry, went forward led by their officers. Others held their ground and continued to fire.

Over the whole field, previously so gaily beautiful with the glitter of bayonets and cloudlets of smoke in the morning sun, there now spread a mist of damp and smoke and a strange acid smell of saltpetre and blood. Clouds gathered, and drops of rain began to fall on the dead and wounded, on the frightened, exhausted, and hesitating men, as if to say: 'Enough, men! Enough! Cease . . . bethink yourselves! What are you doing?'

To the men of both sides alike, worn out by want of food and rest, it began equally to appear doubtful whether they should continue to slaughter one another; all the faces expressed hesitation, and the question arose in every soul: 'For what, for whom, must I kill and be killed? . . . You may go and kill whom you please, but I don't want to do so any more!' By evening this thought had ripened in every soul. At any moment these men might have been seized with horror at what they were doing, and might have thrown up everything and run away anywhere.

But though towards the end of the battle the men felt all the horror of what they were doing, though they would have been glad to leave off, some incomprehensible, mysterious power continued to control them, and they still brought up the charges, loaded, aimed, and applied the match, though only one artilleryman survived out of every three, and though they stumbled and panted with fatigue, perspiring and stained with blood and powder. The cannon-balls flew just as swiftly and cruelly from both sides, crushing human bodies, and that terrible work, which was not done by the will of a man, but at the will of Him who governs men and worlds, continued.

Any one looking at the disorganized rear of the Russian army would have said that, if only the French made one more slight effort, it would disappear; and any one looking at the rear of the French army would have said that the Russians need only make one more slight effort and the French would be destroyed. But neither the French nor the Russians made that effort, and the flame of battle burnt slowly out.

The Russians did not make that effort because they were not attacking the French. At the beginning of the battle they stood blocking the way to Moscow and they still did so at the end of the battle as at the beginning. But even had the aim of the Russians been to drive the French from their positions, they could not have made this last effort, for all the Russian troops had been broken up, there was no part of the Russian army that had not suffered in the battle, and though still holding their positions they had lost one-half of their army.

The French, with the memory of all their former victories during fifteen years, with the assurance of Napoleon's invincibility, with the consciousness that they had captured part of the battle-field and had lost only a quarter of their men and still had their Guards intact, twenty thousand strong, might easily have made that effort. The French who had attacked the Russian army in order to drive it from its position ought to have made that effort, for as long as the Russians continued to block the road to Moscow as before, the aim of the French had not been attained and all their efforts and losses were in vain. But the French did not make that effort. Some historians say that Napoleon need only have used his Old Guards, who were intact, and the battle would have been won. To speak of what would have happened had Napoleon sent his Guards is like talking of what would happen if autumn became spring. It could not be.

Napoleon did not give his Guards, not because he did not want to, but because it could not be done. All the generals, officers, and soldiers of the French army knew it could not be done, because the flagging spirit of the troops would not permit it.

It was not Napoleon alone who had experienced that nightmare feeling of the mighty arm being stricken powerless, but all the generals and soldiers of his army, whether they had taken part in the battle or not, after all their experience of previous battles—when after one-tenth of such efforts the enemy had fled—experienced a similar feeling of terror before an enemy who, after losing HALF his men, stood as threateningly at the end as at the beginning of the battle. The moral force of the attacking French army was exhausted. Not that sort of victory which is defined by the capture of pieces of material fastened to sticks, called standards, and of the ground on which the troops had stood and were standing, but a moral victory that convinces the enemy of the moral superiority of his opponent and of his own impotence, was gained by the Russians at Borodinó. The French invaders, like an infuriated animal that has in its on-slaught received a mortal wound, felt that they were perishing, but could not stop, any more than the Russian army, weaker by one-half, could help swerving. By the impetus gained, the French army was still able to roll forward to Moscow, but there, without further effort on the part of the Russians, it had to perish, bleeding from the mortal wound it had received at Borodinó. The direct consequence of the battle of Borodinó was Napoleon's senseless flight from Moscow, his retreat along the old Smolénsk road, the destruction of the invading army of five hundred thousand men, and the downfall of Napoleonic France, on which at Borodinó for the first time the hand of an opponent of stronger spirit had been laid.

END OF BOOK X

NOTES

BOOK VI

CHAPTER II

P. 8. '...flying away! Like this...' Natásha's fancy tallies with one Tolstóy himself had at the age of seven or eight. Under its influence he actually threw himself out of a window some eighteen feet from the ground. He was picked up unconscious. This resulted in a slight concussion of the brain, but after sleeping eighteen hours on end he recovered and experienced no further ill effect.

CHAPTER IV

P. 11. '...the two famous decrees ... that so agitated society.' Nothing came of these two famous decrees beyond some purely formal changes at court, and a certain amount of bribery to secure diplomas.

P. 11. 'Arakchéev.' Count Alexéy Arakchéev (1769–1834) was Inspector-General of Artillery from 1803 onwards, and his reorganization of that arm largely contributed to Russia's success in the war of 1812. He became Minister of War in 1808, but took no active part in the campaign of 1812, during which and subsequently, he was the Emperor's constant companion and intimate adviser.

He was much hated for his harsh cruelty, and his whole influence was reactionary. The Military Colonies he established to render the army partially self-supporting involved extreme hardships on the colonists and their families. They were precursors of the State Farms now compulsorily established in the U.S.S.R., though Arakchéev had no Ford tractors to rely on. After greatly embittering the people, the Colonies proved a complete failure.

Tolstóy's dislike of Arakchéev, who has been previously alluded to at Austerlitz, is plainly indicated both there and in this chapter. He is referred to again in Chapter III of Book IX.

CHAPTERS V AND VI

Pp. 15–23. Prince Andrew's impression of Speránski indicates the respect and admiration an energetic and clever man felt for the still stronger and more active mind of a very capable statesman; but two unfavourable, half-suppressed, impressions are also indicated: the slight dislike of a nobleman for the parvenu son of a village priest, and a dim consciousness of Speránski's chief weaknesses—his contemptuous treatment of other people and his calm assurance that logic and theoretical reasoning can solve everything.

CHAPTER VII

P. 24. 'the three primordial elements—sulphur, mercury, and salt.' Some Freemasons were interested in discovering the laws of nature, but approached the subject mystically and relied on alchemistic theories for achieving the transmutation of elements, and so on. The Rosicrucian Masons, to whom the prominent Moscow Masons, Nóvikov, Schwartz, and Pozdéev, belonged, concerned themselves with such matters.

P. 27. 'dangerous designs of Illuminism.' The reference is to a German group founded in 1776 by Adam Weishaupt. It had a conspiratorial organization, with strict subordination of members to leaders and a secret aim known only to those at the head of the Order, viz. to substitute republican for monarchical institutions. The Illuminati were officially suppressed by the Bavarian Government in 1785, but their tendency continued to exert influence among other Masonic orders. In Moscow Professor Schwartz headed a group of Martinists who were called Illuminati and like the Bavarian group were Cabalists. The regular programme of Freemasonry included submission to the Government and non-interference with political affairs, but the contrary tendency had some influence in the Russian branches, and their connexion with the 'Decembrist' conspiracy in 1825 led to their suppression by Nicholas I.

CHAPTER VIII

P. 28. 'For three days after the delivery of his speech at the Lodge.' This incident recalls Tolstóy's own experience on the few occasions when he ventured to make a public speech—to him always a trying ordeal and one in which he had little success.

P. 29. 'Scottish Lodges.' These 'Scottish' Masonic Lodges were not in Scotland. Certain German Lodges were so called at that time.

CHAPTER IX

P. 31. 'the circle of Count Rumyántsev and Caulaincourt.' A. A. Louis, Marquis de Caulaincourt, a French general and diplomatist (1772–1827), was sent to Petersburg in 1801 to negotiate an understanding between Russia and France. In 1807 he became ambassador at Petersburg. In

1808 he was created Duc de Vicenza, and in 1812, after failing to dissuade Napoleon from the enterprise, accompanied him on the invasion of Russia. After the Restoration in France, Caulaincourt's name was placed on the proscription list, but was struck off on Alexander's personal intervention.

P. 31. 'Hélène had been at Erfurt.' At Erfurt in Prussia, in the autumn of 1808, a meeting which had been arranged at Tilsit, took place between Alexander, Napoleon, and the King of Prussia; the Emperor of Austria was excluded as a punishment for his military preparations. The agreement made at Tilsit was confirmed, and Prussia's lot was mitigated. In exchange for a promise of non-intervention in Europe, Russia received permission to annex Finland and take the Danubian provinces of Turkey if she could. The gathering at Erfurt was numerous and sumptuous, and the festivities included a series of triumphs and fêtes.

P. 31. 'Prince de Ligne.' Charles Joseph Prince de Ligne (1735–1814), soldier, writer, and diplomatist, whose works were published in thirty-four volumes, was born at Brussels. He took part in the Seven Years' War, became a lieutenant field-marshal, and a friend of the Emperor Joseph II. He spent some years in Russia, accompanied Catherine the Great on her journey to the Crimea, and was made by her a Russian field-marshal. He subsequently visited Russia repeatedly, not officially but as a man of culture and distinction belonging to the best society.

CHAPTER XI

P. 40. '[Berg] ... received two decorations for the Finnish war also.' By the war with Sweden in 1808 Russia acquired Finland. The treaty of Fredrikshavn, which ended that war, was confirmed by Napoleon at the Erfurt interview.

P. 40. 'I have arranged that rent for them in the Baltic Provinces.' Throughout the nineteenth century the Russian Government, as a reward for service, or simply by favouritism, used to make grants of 'rents' (*arenda*), that is to say, the usufruct of land.

CHAPTER XIII

P. 47. 'Natásha ... began kissing first one knuckle, then the space between the knuckles, then the next knuckle.' Natásha evidently remembered the way she had been taught the months that have thirty-one days. The method in question is to double up the fists, and, disregarding the thumbs, to take the knuckles as representing the thirty-one-day months, the spaces between representing the shorter months. The first fist represents the months from January to July, the first knuckle of the second fist representing August.

Natásha, however, makes a mistake, for a little farther on she says 'June' instead of 'July' for the knuckle of the little finger, which would bring August to a space and make the arrangement go wrong.

P. 48. 'Bezúkhov, now, is blue, dark-blue and red.' Physiologists are aware that to some people, especially young ones, certain sounds suggest colours or forms. To such people Natásha's remark will be quite understandable even if to them the names 'Borís' and 'Pierre' suggest other colours; but perhaps her perception of these colours may have arisen from their personal attributes, as in the theosophical theory of 'auras' coloured according to personality and mood.

CHAPTERS XV AND XVI

Pp. 54 and 56. 'Márya Antónovna Naryshkina' was a greatly admired court beauty, and Alexander I's mistress. She was by birth a Princess Chetvertínskaya.

CHAPTER XVII

P. 62. Readers acquainted with Tolstóy's life will note the similarity of Natásha's feeling with that which inspired his brother's story of the 'Green Stick'.

CHAPTER XVIII

P. 63. 'the interest Prince Andrew had felt in the impending reforms.' Alexander I's inconstancy wrecked Speránski's remarkable attempt to remodel the form of Russian government.

It is not difficult to see that Tolstóy has attributed to Prince Andrew his own relation to such attempts as Speránski's. The last words of this chapter indicate that while the peasant masses remained serfs they presented a formidable obstacle to the introduction of any enlightened system of jurisprudence or government, but it was an idiosyncrasy of Tolstóy's to regard such attempts at political reform as fundamentally futile, because 'how can all that possibly make men happier or better?' Concerned as Tolstóy was, in his own way, with the welfare of mankind, his outlook was intensely individualistic and he profoundly distrusted political movements.

P. 63. 'Magnítski.' M. L. Magnítski was a coadjutor of Speránski's and an ardent partisan of his projected reforms. After Speránski's fall he sided with the reactionary Arakchéev, and was an equally ardent opponent of all progress. Later on he was accused of making away with an enormous sum of money and was dismissed the service.

P. 65. 'Napoleon's Spanish affairs.' At that time, in 1810, Napoleon was already deeply involved in Spain. In 1808 he had made his brother Joseph King of Spain, but the Spaniards resisted this, and Napoleon for the first time encountered the opposition of guerrilla bands which proved formidable, such as he again encountered with disastrous results when he invaded Russia. England was helping Spain, and the Peninsular war continued till in 1813 Wellington drove the French armies out of the country.

CHAPTER XX

P. 72. 'the table for boston.' Boston was a card game invented by French officers at Boston, Massachusetts, during the Revolutionary war. It has a distant resemblance to auction bridge.

CHAPTER XXII

P. 77. 'everything seemed to him insignificant in comparison with eternity; again the question: For what? presented itself.' Note the similarity of Pierre's feeling here expressed, with what Tolstóy, some twelve years after writing this chapter, described himself as feeling. (Ch. iii, p. 18 of his *Confession*.)

BOOK VII

CHAPTERS III–VI

Pp. 105–26. The hunt. Readers should bear in mind that the hounds engaged in hunting of the kind here described were keen-scented but not very swift dogs. They had to find the game by scent and chase it in the desired direction, but the swift and strong borzois caught and killed the game. A borzoi has very poor scent and only chases the game when he sees it. It must be pointed out to him, and even when following it he sometimes loses sight of it. If the game shams dead, a borzoi is often balked and hesitates what to do, as in the case mentioned when the hare suddenly squatted and the borzoi did not seize it.

CHAPTER IV

P. 112. 'the buffoon ... Nastásya Ivánovna.' The practice of keeping a buffoon in country houses lasted till after the abolition of serfdom. 'Alësha the Pot', from whom Tolstóy later made so tragic a story, was a sort of buffoon Tolstóy's wife found at Yásnaya Polyána when she arrived there after her marriage in 1862.

CHAPTER VIII

P. 135. 'Dimmler the musician.' Tolstóy made himself so well acquainted with the times he was writing about that even to this character, only mentioned a couple of times, he has given the name of a real person who was a music-master then living in Moscow.

CHAPTER X

P. 145. John Field, born in Dublin, was a composer of nocturnes, &c. He settled in Russia in 1804, and was known as 'Russian Field'.

BOOK VIII

CHAPTER I

P. 168. 'Astræa Lodge against the Manna Seekers.' These were two Masonic Lodges in Petersburg.

P. 168. 'an authentic Scotch carpet.' A carpet with symbolic signs on it was considered important for the equipment of each Lodge. The Lodges competed with one another in obtaining such carpets from the most ancient and highly esteemed Masonic organizations, as well as copies of the ceremonies and 'acts'—that is, the rules of the Order.

CHAPTER III

P. 175. 'the famous Count Rostopchín.' F. V. Rostopchín (1763–1828) had been a favourite of the Emperor Paul, and was Governor-General and Commander-in-Chief of Moscow in 1812. He was an extreme reactionary, the author of many volumes, and a most eccentric and unreliable man.

P. 177. 'Napoleon's seizure of the Duke of Oldenburg's territory.' Considering the Duchy of Oldenburg to be an obstacle in his path, Napoleon, in 1810, dealt roughly and harshly with it. Commissaries were sent to announce the annexation of Oldenburg to France, and to seize it and all its funds. The Duke (who was Alexander I's uncle) was to be allowed a place of residence at Erfurt.

Alexander protested against this seizure. He had been given to understand at the Erfurt Congress, the year before, that Napoleon would like to marry his sister, Elizabeth. Nothing was definitely settled at the time however, and a little later Elizabeth married one of the Oldenburg princes. The following year Napoleon made a suggestion that he should marry Alexander's youngest sister, Anne. This proposal found favour in Petersburg, but Alexander delayed a decision as Napoleon was delaying the signature of an arrangement agreed on concerning Poland, and he feared that Napoleon might create an independent Poland or 'Grand Duchy of Warsaw' as it was then called. Alexander's delay irritated Napoleon and stung his vanity, and when the Emperor of Austria showed himself inclined to arrange an alliance with the conqueror who had just humiliated Austria afresh by the Peace of Schönbrunn, and to let him marry his daughter, the Princess Marie-Louise, Napoleon seized the opportunity to unite himself with one of the Imperial families, and prepared to break off his alliance with Russia. These things prompted his arbitrary treatment of the Duke of Oldenburg. Apart from that, the Treaty of Tilsit was falling to pieces, as the Continental system, aimed by Napoleon at England's commerce, was harmful to Russia's trade and was not observed by Russia as strictly as Napoleon demanded. From 1810 onwards both France and Russia were practically preparing for war, and it was only the ill success of the French army in Spain on the one hand, and the backwardness of Russia's military preparations on the other, that caused the year 1811 to pass without war being declared.

CHAPTER V

P. 184. 'bouts-rimés.' This was an amusement in which rhymes were given to the players, to which they had to fit lines making up a verse. It was much in fashion, and not among young people only.

P. 185. 'Poor Liza.' A very popular and sentimental story by Karamzín, which had appeared some years before this. It described the misfortunes of a peasant girl who fell in love with a nobleman, was abandoned by him, and drowned herself in a pond.

CHAPTER VIII

P. 198. 'They say Semënova acts marvellously.' Nymphodora Semënova had appeared on the stage in 1809, a couple of years before this, and though she was an opera singer it was her acting that was most highly appreciated, as Rostóv's remark suggests. Here as elsewhere Tolstóy keeps closely to the chronicles of the time of which he writes.

CHAPTER IX

P. 199. 'painted cardboard representing trees.' About the time Tolstóy was writing this novel, he wrote in a letter to his wife from Moscow about a visit to the theatre: 'I got there at the end of the second act. Fresh from the country it always seems to me all barbarous, forced, and false; but when one gets accustomed to it, it again pleases one.'

CHAPTER XXI

P. 247. 'Speránski—the news of whose sudden exile and alleged treachery had just reached Moscow.' Speránski's sudden fall from power and exile to Nízhni-Nóvgorod occurred on March 17th 1812 o.s. The causes of this event were certainly connected with the change in Alexander's outlook and plans from the liberal tendency of his early years to a more reactionary attitude. The constantly increasing dangers and difficulties in foreign policy also made it convenient to sacrifice Speránski, against whom—at a time when the conservative spirit of Russia was pitting itself against the more progressive watchwords of the new France—numerous inimical rumours reached the Emperor from reactionaries and from Speránski's numerous enemies at Court, who regarded him as an upstart intervening between Alexander and his former devoted servants and advisers.

Speránski wrote several letters to Alexander defending himself, but it was not till 1816 that an ukaz appeared which indirectly admitted that the accusations against him were unfounded. He was then made Governor of Pénza, and three years later Governor-General of Siberia. In 1821 he returned to Petersburg and entered the Council of State, but he no longer had any of his former influence with the Emperor.

In the next reign, Nicholas I, after testing his loyalty by appointing him to be one of the judges of the 'Decembrist' conspirators, placed him in charge of the compilation of the Code of Laws, and Speránski succeeded in publishing forty-two volumes of *The Complete Collection of Russian Laws*, which formed the basis of the systematic *Code of Laws of the Russian Empire* compiled in 1832.

BOOK IX

CHAPTER I

P. 255. 'the Continental System.' In 1806 Napoleon issued a decree forbidding all trade with England and closing all European ports to her ships. He compelled his allies to accede to this policy, which was disadvantageous to many countries. It led to great injury to trade and to much smuggling: the system was often infringed, and even Napoleon himself could not dispense with English goods and at times admitted them to France. It was particularly irksome to Russia, and her evasion of it was treated by Napoleon as a

violation of the treaty. In conjunction with other causes it
led to his invasion of Russia in 1812. One result of the
Continental System was the issue of the English Orders in
Council in reply to it. These Orders occasioned much
inconvenience to neutral nations and, together with the
intrigues conducted by Napoleon, led to the war between
England and the United States of America in 1812–14.

P. 256. 'Napoleon's refusal to withdraw his troops beyond
the Vistula.' The demand that Napoleon should withdraw
beyond that river was Alexander's last effort to avoid war,
and Napoleon's refusal led directly to the commencement of
hostilities in 1812.

P. 259. 'the intoxicating honours he received in Dresden.'
In May 1812, immediately before the war, Napoleon spent
about a month in Dresden with his new allies: the Emperor of
Austria, the King of Prussia, the King of Saxony, &c.—
attending a series of magnificent banquets and fêtes and
receiving flattery and honours from all sides.

CHAPTER II

P. 259. 'On the 29th of May Napoleon left Dresden.' Here,
probably by inadvertence, Tolstóy gives the date according
to the Gregorian or 'new style' calendar, not adopted in
Russia till after the Revolution of 1917. In the next sentence
he reverts to the Old Style, which he elsewhere employs
throughout the novel. The text makes it appear as if Napoleon
spent only twelve days (29th May to 10th June) on his way
from Dresden via Posen, Thorn, Danzig, and Königsberg to
the Russian frontier. He actually took twice as long, having
many arrangements to make in those towns.

P. 260. Napoleon's changing into a Polish uniform, and the
episode of the Uhlans swimming the river, briefly but vividly
indicate his relations with Poland. The Poles hoped to obtain
independence as a result of the war and Napoleon encouraged
their hopes by petty indications of his favour. The incident
of the uniform is given in Danílevski's history, and that of the
Uhlans swimming the river in Thiers'.

CHAPTER III

P. 264. 'Each of the three armies had its own commander-
in-chief.' The three armies were: (1) The Western army under
Barclay de Tolly, (2) one farther south under Bagratión, and
(3) an army of reserve in process of formation under Tormásov
near the Austrian frontier. A fourth army under Chichagóv
was still on the Turkish frontier, where war had just ended,

but this only became available against Napoleon towards the end of his retreat from Russia.

Barclay de Tolly (1761–1818) was born in Latvia and was descended from a Scottish family that settled in Russia in the seventeenth century. He was Minister of War in 1810–13, but resigned from the command of the army in 1812 after the abandonment of Smolénsk, when he was replaced by Kutúzov. He was present at the battle of Borodinó. He again became commander-in-chief in 1813, and was made field-marshal in 1814.

Prince P. I. Bagratión (1765–1812) was one of the most successful of the Russian generals. He had greatly distinguished himself at Schön Grabern, at Austerlitz, and in many other battles. He died of wounds received at Borodinó.

P. 267. 'his secretary, Shishkóv.' Admiral A. S. Shishkóv (1754–1841) succeeded Speránski as Secretary of State when the latter was dismissed.

P. 267. 'Field-Marshal Prince Saltykóv.' N. I. Saltykóv (1736–1816) had been Alexander's tutor, and in 1812, besides being a field-marshal was President of the Cabinet of Ministers.

P. 267. 'Count Lauriston.' A. J. B. Law (1768–1828), a great-nephew of John Law of Lauriston, of Mississippi Scheme fame. He was a fellow pupil of Napoleon's at the Artillery School. He greatly distinguished himself at the battle of Wagram (1809), was Napoleon's ambassador in Petersburg (1811–12) and accompanied him through the greater part of the Russian campaign, but did not side with Napoleon after his return from Elba in 1815. He was subsequently made a marquis and a Marshal of France by Louis XVIII.

P. 267. 'the Duc de Bassano.' H. B. Maret (1763–1839), Napoleon's Minister of Foreign Affairs in 1811–12.

CHAPTER V

P. 274. 'his Mameluke, Rustan.' The Mamelukes were Turko-Egyptian cavalry. Napoleon defeated them utterly at the battle of the Pyramids in 1798. From Egypt he brought Rustan (a Georgian by birth) back with him as a body-guard. From that time on Rustan never left his master, and he did not long survive Napoleon's death.

CHAPTER VI

P. 275. Napoleon's speeches to Baláshev are taken from Thiers and Danílevski.

P. 279. 'With Steins, Armfelts, Bennigsens, and Wintzin-gerodes.' Baron H. F. K. von Stein (1757–1831) was a

German statesman who entered the Prussian service in 1780.
In 1807 he succeeded Hardenburg—whom Napoleon had
refused to deal with—as Minister with very wide powers, and
he proposed the abolition of serfdom, later accomplished by
Hardenburg in 1811. Stein promoted the military reorganization of the country, and Napoleon demanded his dismissal and
expulsion from Germany. He fled to Bohemia, but in May
1812 was invited by Alexander to visit Petersburg. Subsequently in Russia Stein promoted the coalition against
Napoleon and played an important part in accomplishing
his downfall.

Count G. M. Armfelt (1757–1814) was a distinguished
general and a faithful supporter of Gustavus III of Sweden
and of his son Gustavus IV. When the latter lost power,
Armfelt was expelled from Sweden and found refuge in
Russia, where he obtained much influence with Alexander,
who entrusted him with the management of the affairs of
Finland, which had then recently been annexed. He secured
for the Finns the retention of their ancient constitution.

Count L. A. von Bennigsen (1745–1826) passed from the
Hanoverian service in 1773 to enter the Russian. He was
active in the conspiracy which involved the assassination of
the Emperor Paul. He claimed a victory over the French at
Pultúsk (1806) (see Bilíbin's letter, vol. i, p. 497); and was commander-in-chief at the indecisive battle of Prussisch-Eylau
(1807), but was defeated with heavy loss at Friedland (1807),
which reverse led to the alliance concluded at Tilsit. He
fought at Borodinó and defeated Murat at Tarútino, but
quarrelled with Kutúzov and had to retire from the service.
After Kutúzov's death he again obtained a command, and
led one of the columns which decided the victory at Leipzig
(1813), for which service he was made a count.

Baron F. T. Wintzingerode (1770–1818) was an Austrian
who in the course of his career passed more than once from
the Austrian service to the Russian. In 1812 he was employed
by Alexander to defend the road from the frontier to Petersburg. He was captured by the French but rescued again by
the Russians. At Leipzig in 1813 he was in command of the
whole Allied cavalry, and he served against Napoleon in the
campaign of 1814.

P. 279. 'Pfuel proposes.' Baron Carl Ludwig August Pfuel
(1751–1826), a Prussian general who entered the Russian
service after the battle of Jena (1806) and formulated the
first Russian plan for the campaign of 1812.

P. 280. 'You are cut in two.' The Russian forces were in
fact separated. Bagratión's army and Barclay's only succeeded

with great difficulty in uniting after falling back as far as Smolénsk.

P. 280. 'Bernadotte, who promptly went mad.' J. B. J. Bernadotte (1764–1844) was a lawyer's son born at Pau. He entered the French army as a private, became a marshal, and in 1810 was elected heir to the throne of Sweden. He guided its policy, and, after Napoleon had seized Swedish Pomerania, he fought against him. In 1818 he became King of Sweden, as Charles XIV, and founded a dynasty.

CHAPTER VII

P. 282. 'Bessières, Caulaincourt, and Berthier were present.' J. B. Bessières (1768–1813) was a Marshal of France. He served under Napoleon from the time of the Italian campaign of 1796, and in 1799 was made Duke of Istria. It was he, with his Guard cavalry, who routed the famous charge of the Russian Chevalier Guards at Austerlitz (mentioned in the description of that battle). He took an active part in the Peninsular war, and in 1812 commanded the Guard cavalry at Borodinó and in the retreat from Moscow. In 1813 he was appointed to the command of the whole of Napoleon's cavalry but was killed three days after the campaign began.

A. Berthier (1753–1815), Prince of Neuchâtel and Wagram, was a Marshal of France. He acted for many years as Napoleon's chief of staff. In 1815, unable to endure the sight of a Russian division marching towards the French frontier, he threw himself from a window into the street in Bamberg, and was picked up dying.

P. 283. 'the recent defeats of the French in Spain.' In the previous year (1811) Wellington had won the battles of Fuentes de Oñoro and Beresford that of Albuera; the Spanish had defeated the French at Ximena, and in 1812 both Ciudad Rodrigo and Badajoz had been captured from the French.

P. 284. 'all roads lead to Moscow ... among them the road through *Poltáva*, which Charles XII chose.' The reference of course is to the invasion of Russia, a hundred years previously (1709), by Charles XII of Sweden, whom Peter the Great defeated at Poltáva so thoroughly that Charles himself and Mazepa, the Cossack hetman who had joined him, barely succeeded in escaping to Turkey.

CHAPTER IX

P. 294. 'Tsarévich.' The correct title in Russian for the Heir-Apparent was Tsesarévich (the shorter form Tsarévich applying to any son of the Tsar). The incorrect use of Tsaré-

vich for Heir-Apparent has however become so common in
English that it is followed here, with apologies to Russian
readers who may notice it.

P. 294. 'Paulucci.' Marquis F. O. Paulucci passed in 1809
from the French to the Russian service. In 1812 he was for a
time head of the staff of the First Army, but owing to disagree-
ments with Barclay de Tolly was transferred to the post of
Governor-General of Livonia and Courland.

P. 295. 'Wolzogen.' Baron Ludwig Julius Wolzogen (1774–
1845), a Prussian general, who was from 1807 to 1815 on the
Russian General Staff. In 1812 he served with Barclay de
Tolly and subsequently with Kutúzov. His *Memoirs* were
published in 1851, and were among the historical material
at Tolstóy's disposal when writing *War and Peace*. He is
mentioned in Book IX, Chap. xi as acting as spokesman for
Pfuel at the military council, and later on, in a letter to
Arakchéev, Bagratión refers to him as almost a traitor.

P. 297. 'he will show what he can do, as he did in Finland.' In 1809 Barclay de Tolly, commanding the army in
the Finnish war, effected a daring two-days' march on the
ice across the Gulf of Bothnia, surprised and seized Umea and
secured peace with Sweden.

P. 297. 'Bennigsen showed his incapacity already in 1807.'
. . . 'Bennigsen, who made his mark in 1807 and to whom
Napoleon himself did justice.'

Both these conflicting opinions refer to the campaign in
Prussia mentioned in Bilíbin's letter given in Vol. I,
pp. 493–8.

CHAPTER X

P. 301. 'Toll.' K. F. Toll (1778–1842). A Russian general
of German origin, subsequently created count. He was
quartermaster-general of the main army in the war of 1812
in which he took a very active part after Napoleon's retreat
from Moscow.

CHAPTER XIX

P. 337. Apocalyptic calculations such as Pierre here indulged
in were not unusual among the Freemasons, and efforts to
foretell Napoleon's fate by consulting that book were made in
Russia even before his invasion.

CHAPTER XXII

P. 353. 'thoughts of the *Contrat Social* and the French
Revolution.' Here, and later on at the end of the novel,
Tolstóy indicates the influence France was exercising on

the minds of some of the more liberally minded Russians—influences that prepared the way for the 'Decembrist' conspiracy of 1825, and for much that has happened since.

P. 357. 'Glínka, the editor of the *Russian Messenger*.' S. N. Glínka (1776–1864), a prolific and patriotic writer, who in 1808 founded the *Russian Messenger* to counteract the French influence then prevalent. In 1812 he was resident and active in Moscow.

BOOK X

CHAPTER II

P. 369. Julie's letter. In this letter Tolstóy indicates the artificiality of the patriotic enthusiasm of the Frenchified circles of Russian nobility, who could not even express aversion for the French language except in phrases obviously modelled on a French construction to which they were habituated.

CHAPTER IV

P. 378. 'he put up in the Gáchina suburb . . . at the inn kept by Ferapóntov.' Ferapóntov's hostel catered for travellers, which explains the fact, mentioned four pages farther on, that a vehicle (not otherwise accounted for) drove out of the yard.

P. 379. 'Alpátych swayed his head.' Russians have a habit of bending their heads from side to side to express dismay, surprise, or disapproval. An Englishman's nod is an affirmative and his shake of the head a negative sign, but we have no word for *pokachál golovói*, which signifies a motion of the head to left and right. That is what 'swayed his head' stands for in this and similar passages.

P. 382. 'Matthew Iványch Plátov.' Plátov, hetman of the Cossack army, was one of the most popular Russian heroes of the war of 1812. On one occasion he nearly captured Napoleon.

CHAPTER VI

P. 395. 'Rumyántsev.' Count N. P. Rumyántsev had been Minister of Foreign Affairs in 1807, and in 1809 became Chancellor. The famous Rumyántsev Museum in Moscow was formed of collections presented by him.

CHAPTER VIII

P. 404. 'For three weeks the old prince lay stricken by paralysis.' This is a rare instance of Tolstóy making a mistake in the time-arrangement of his novel. On the 5th of August, the day Smolénsk was bombarded, the old prince was still well. He died on the 15th, and could not therefore have lain stricken by paralysis for three weeks.

CHAPTER IX

Pp. 412–13. 'in the lives of the peasantry of those parts the mysterious undercurrents in the life of the Russian people, the causes and meaning of which are so baffling to contemporaries, were more clearly and strongly noticeable than among others.'

One of the dangers of the Napoleonic invasion was that Napoleon might cause a great commotion among the Russian peasantry by proclaiming an emancipation of the serfs. Before the emancipation granted by Alexander II, Tolstóy convinced himself that there was grave danger of a peasant-rising to claim land and liberty. That danger was averted for a time by the Emancipation decree of 1861, but Tolstóy's later writings show that he still understood the unstable structure of Russian society, and foresaw the Revolution of 1917, clearly predicted in *What Then Must We Do?* published in 1886.

CHAPTER XV

P. 437. Tsárevo-Zaymíshche. After the abandonment of Smolénsk the Russian army, continuing its retreat, passed Vyázma on August 17th and stopped at the village of Tsárevo-Zaymíshche near Gzhatsk, where for a time it was intended to give battle. It was here that Kutúzov reached the army, having been appointed Commander-in-Chief. He had left Petersburg on August 11th, and reached Gzhatsk on the 17th.

P. 442. 'Denísov . . . began to expound his plan of cutting the enemy's lines of communication.' It was in reality D. Davýdov who proposed a guerrilla warfare and to cut Napoleon's lines of communication. Kutúzov consented to his making the attempt with a party of 130 Cossacks and hussars, but the battle of Borodinó was then impending and only after that battle was Davýdov able to begin his operations.

CHAPTER XVII

P. 449. 'Vasíli Lvóvich Púshkin's *bouts-rimés*.' V. L. Púshkin (1779–1830) was an uncle of the great poet A. S. Púshkin, and the author of unimportant lyric and didactic verses.

CHAPTER XVIII

P. 453. 'Count Wittgenstein had defeated the French.' Count L. P. Wittgenstein was a general in the Russian army.

He subsequently succeeded Kutúzov, and commanded the Russians at Lützen. A separate corps under Count Wittgenstein, which was guarding the road to Petersburg, fought some successful actions in July and early August 1812, and these had a cheering influence at a time when the country much needed encouragement.

P. 455. 'Although that patience did come out, Pierre did not join the army.' Tolstóy himself often laid out the cards for patience to decide questions he felt doubtful about, and like Pierre in this chapter he disregarded the decision given by the cards if it did not suit him.

When staying at Yásnaya Polyána in 1906, shortly before his daughter Mary died, she told me that being undecided about completing an article he had begun he had laid out a patience to decide whether that article would be of use to the world. The patience did not come out, but he rose from table with the remark: 'All the same I shall write it.'

P. 455. 'the great balloon Leppich was constructing.' This refers to an early and very unsuccessful attempt to utilize an air-force in warfare. A German, Leppich, made the proposal, but his balloon was not ready till November, when the scanty remains of the French army were with difficulty escaping from Russia. Even then the balloon would not rise owing to leakage of gas.

CHAPTER XIX

P. 462. This sketch-plan of Borodinó was made by Tolstóy in the summer of 1867, when he spent two days in the locality to study the ground before writing his description of the battle. He depended partly on Russian and French maps, plans, and historical accounts, partly on his own military experience, and partly on the *Memoirs* of Radozhítski, who viewed the position from some rising ground, and noticed its weak places, some time before the fight occurred and who like Pierre was present at the battle itself. The four decades that passed from Napoleon's time to the beginning of Tolstóy's army service had not much changed the muskets and smooth bore, muzzle-loading cannon used in the Russian army, nor had the general conditions of warfare much altered.

CHAPTER XXII

P. 475. 'those verses of Márin's . . . how do they go, eh? . . . Those he wrote about Gerákov.'

S. N. Márin was an aide-de-camp of Alexander I's, well known for his parodies and amusing verses. G. V. Gerákov was a captain in the army, a teacher in the military school, and the author of numerous patriotic works of very poor quality. He was the object of much ridicule. Márin's verse about him was in the form of a prophecy:

> You will always go on writing
> And to death your readers bore:
> Lectures for the corps inditing—
> Be a captain evermore.

CHAPTER XXV

P. 485. 'Prince Andrew recognized Wolzogen and Clausewitz.' Karl von Clausewitz (1780–1831), a Prussian general and celebrated writer on the theory and history of war. In 1812, like many other Prussian officers, he entered the Russian service though Prussia was officially in alliance with Napoleon. He first served as adjutant to Pfuel. His greatest work is *Vom Kriege*, an exposition of the philosophy of war. In his volumes on military history he treats of the war of 1812, as well as of Napoleon's other campaigns.

P. 487. 'The aim of war is murder.' Prince Andrew in this chapter expresses an opinion of the campaign of 1812 near to that held by Tolstóy when writing the novel, and in some places even expresses Tolstóy's *future* view of war as an absolutely evil social phenomenon. When writing *War and Peace* that view had not yet sunk deeply, or occupied a permanent place, in Tolstóy's outlook on life—that occurred considerably later—but it here flashes out in certain sentences like the lightning of a coming storm. Even before this, in *The Raid*, one of his very first stories (1853), describing a march through beautiful Caucasian scenery, he had written: 'Can it be that there is not room for all men on this beautiful earth under these immeasurable starry heavens? Can it be possible that in the midst of this entrancing Nature, feelings of hatred, vengeance, or the passion for exterminating their fellows, can endure in the souls of men? All that is unkind in the hearts of men ought, one would think, to vanish at the touch of Nature, that most direct expression of beauty and goodness.' And at the end of *Sevastopol in May* (1855) the same feeling was again expressed. We have here an instance of the way in which feelings Tolstóy experienced before thinking matters out, planted seed in his soul that many years later grew into great trees throwing their shade far around.

CHAPTER XXVI

P. 491. 'Salamanca . . . The result of that battle had been deplorable.' At the battle of Salamanca, on July 12th n.s.

1812, Wellington gained a brilliant victory over Marmont. In Spain Napoleon's attempt to hold a nation in subjection had been met by a strong and persistent popular resistance, and the drain on his resources during the Peninsular war was an important factor in the failure of his attempt to subdue Russia.

P. 492. 'A present to your Majesty from the Empress.' Material for this scene of Napoleon with the portrait of his son was supplied by the *Mémoires* of de Bausset himself, but Tolstóy has utilized it for his artistic purposes, quite changing the enthusiastically pathetic tone of that courtier's memoirs. For instance, when de Bausset, overflowing with amiabilities, told Napoleon that he expected to find him already under the walls of Moscow, Napoleon smiled, and replying: 'Yes, you will see Moscow,' absent-mindedly looked to the right, at which customary sign an aide-de-camp hastened to hand him his snuff-box. In Tolstóy's novel Napoleon always takes snuff when angry or encountering some obstacle, as for instance in the scenes with Baláshev where his mood rapidly alternates. On the present occasion, though hearing flattering remarks to which he smilingly replies, at the word 'Moscow' his instinctive gesture of looking round for a snuff-box betrays an uneasiness at having advanced so easily into the heart of the country. His recent conversation with his captive General Tuchkóv at Smolénsk, and the proposal for peace he had then made, showed that before Borodinó Napoleon felt seriously anxious at the course this strange war was taking—a war in which he had not once felt himself master of the situation, but had constantly had to reckon with conditions imposed upon him.

CHAPTER XXXIV

P. 521. 'a general with a suite . . . Belliard.' A. D. Belliard (1769-1832) was a French general who distinguished himself in the wars of the Republic and the Empire.

P. 524. 'Lodi, Marengo, Arcola, Jena, Austerlitz, Wagram, and so on.' These were some of Napoleon's most remarkable victories. Lodi and Marengo are places in northern Italy where Napoleon defeated the Austrians in 1800. Arcola is a village near Verona, where in 1796 he defeated an Austrian army numerically much superior to his own. At Jena in 1806 Napoleon heavily defeated the Prussians and Saxons. Wagram is a village near Vienna, where he gained a decisive victory over the Austrians in 1809, bringing that war to a successful conclusion.

CHAPTER XXXV

P. 527. 'the Duke of Würtemburg.' Duke Alexander Frederick of Würtemburg (1771–1833), brother of the Empress Márie Fëdorovna, wife of the Emperor Paul, had entered the Russian service in 1800.

P. 527. 'news that Murat had been taken prisoner.' This report turned out to be false. It was General Bonami who had been captured. Seeing a Russian grenadier's bayonet at his breast he cried out: 'I am the King!' and was taken alive to Kutúzov. The false rumour was spread by a major who spoke in a thick voice and rode along the line indistinctly shouting news of the capture.

CHAPTER XXXVIII

P. 542. 'the Thirty-Second Military Division' was Marshal Davoût's division, mainly recruited from the Hamburg-Bremen region.

PRINTED IN GREAT BRITAIN AT THE UNIVERSITY PRESS, OXFORD
BY JOHN JOHNSON, PRINTER TO THE UNIVERSITY